William Howard Russel

My Diary North and South

William Howard Russel

My Diary North and South

ISBN/EAN: 9783744660877

Printed in Europe, USA, Canada, Australia, Japan

Cover: Foto ©Andreas Hilbeck / pixelio.de

More available books at **www.hansebooks.com**

MY DIARY

NORTH AND SOUTH.

BY

WILLIAM HOWARD RUSSELL.

NEW YORK:
HARPER & BROTHERS, PUBLISHERS.
FRANKLIN SQUARE.
1863.

TO

RICHARD QUAIN, M.D.,

This Volume is Dedicated

IN TESTIMONY OF THE REGARD AND GRATITUDE OF

THE AUTHOR.

INTRODUCTORY.

A book which needs apologies ought never to have been written. This is a canon of criticism so universally accepted, that authors have abstained of late days from attempting to disarm hostility by confessions of weakness, and are almost afraid to say a prefatory word to the gentle reader.

It is not to plead in mitigation of punishment or make an appeal *ad misericordiam*, I break through the ordinary practice, but by way of introduction and explanation to those who may read this volume, I may remark that it consists for the most part of extracts from the diaries and note-books which I assiduously kept whilst I was in the United States, as records of the events and impressions of the hour. I have been obliged to omit many passages which might cause pain or injury to individuals still living in the midst of a civil war, but the spirit of the original is preserved as far as possible, and I would entreat my readers to attribute the frequent use of the personal pronoun and personal references to the nature of the sources from which the work is derived, rather than to the vanity of the author.

Had the pages been literally transcribed, without omitting a word, the fate of one whose task it was to sift the true from the false and to avoid error in statements of fact, in a country remarkable for the extraordinary fertility with which the unreal is produced, would have excited some commiseration; but though there is much extenuated in these pages, there is not, I believe, aught set down in malice. My aim has been to retain so much relating to events passing under my eyes, or to persons who have become famous in this great struggle, as may prove interesting at present, though they did not at the time always appear in their just proportions of littleness or magnitude.

During my sojourn in the States, many stars of the first order have risen out of space or fallen into the outer darkness. The watching, trustful millions have hailed with delight or witnessed with terror the advent of a shining planet or a splendid comet, which a little observation has resolved into watery nebulæ. In the Southern hemisphere, Bragg and Beauregard have given place to Lee and Jackson. In the North M'Dowell has faded away before M'Clellan, who having been put for a short season in eclipse by Pope, only to culminate with increased effulgence, has finally paled away before Burnside. The heroes of yesterday are the martyrs or outcasts of to-day, and no American general needs a slave behind him in the triumphal chariot to remind him that he is a mortal. Had I foreseen such rapid whirls in the wheel of fortune I might have taken more note of the men who were below, but my business was not to speculate but to describe.

The day I landed at Norfolk, a tall lean man, ill-dressed, in a slouching hat and wrinkled clothes, stood, with his arms folded and legs wide apart, against the wall of the hotel looking on the ground. One of the waiters told me it was "Professor Jackson," and I have been plagued by suspicions that in refusing an introduction which was offered to me, I missed an opportunity of making the acquaintance of the man of the stonewalls of Winchester. But, on the whole, I have been fortunate in meeting many of the soldiers and statesmen who have distinguished themselves in this unhappy war.

Although I have never for one moment seen reason to change the opinion I expressed in the first letter I wrote from the States, that the Union as it was could never be restored, I am satisfied the Free States of the North will retain and gain great advantages by the struggle, if they will only set themselves at work to accomplish their destiny, nor lose their time in sighing over vanished empire or indulging in abortive dreams of conquest and schemes of vengeance; but my readers need not expect from me any dissertations on the present or future of the great republics, which have been so loosely united by the Federal band, nor any description of the political system, social life, manners or customs of the people, beyond those which may be incidentally gathered from these pages.

It has been my fate to see Americans under their most unfavourable aspect; with all their national feelings, as well as the vices of our common humanity, exaggerated and developed by the terrible agonies of a civil war, and the throes of political revolution. Instead of the hum of industry, I heard the noise of cannon through the land. Society convulsed by cruel passions and apprehensions, and shattered by violence, presented its broken angles to the stranger, and I can readily conceive that the America I saw, was no more like the country of which her people boast so loudly, than the St. Lawrence when the ice breaks up, hurrying onwards the rugged drift and its snowy crust of crags, with hoarse roar, and crashing with irresistible force and fury to the sea, resembles the calm flow of the stately river on a summer's day.

The swarming communities and happy homes of the New England States —the most complete exhibition of the best results of the American system —it was denied me to witness; but if I was deprived of the gratification of worshipping the frigid intellectualism of Boston, I saw the effects in the field, among the men I met, of the teachings and theories of the political, moral, and religious professors, who are the chiefs of that universal Yankee nation, as they delight to call themselves, and there recognised the radical differences which must sever them for ever from a true union with the Southern States.

The contest, of which no man can predict the end or result, still rages, but notwithstanding the darkness and clouds which rest upon the scene, I place so much reliance on the innate good qualities of the great nations which are settled on the Continent of North America, as to believe they will be all the better for the sweet uses of adversity; learning to live in peace with their neighbours, adapting their institutions to their necessities, and working out, not in their old arrogance and insolence—mistaking material prosperity for good government—but in fear and trembling, the experiment on which they have cast so much discredit, and the glorious career which misfortune and folly can arrest but for a time.

W. H. RUSSELL.

London, December 8, 1862.

MY DIARY ~~NORTH~~ AND SOUTH.

CHAPTER I.

Departure from Cork—The Atlantic in March—Fellow passengers—American politics and parties—The Irish in New York—Approach to New York.

On the evening of 3rd March, 1861, I was transferred from the little steam-tender, which plies between Cork and the anchorage of the Cunard steamers at the entrance of the harbour, to the deck of the good steamship Arabia, Captain Stone; and at nightfall we were breasting the long rolling waves of the Atlantic.

The voyage across the Atlantic has been done by so many able hands, that it would be superfluous to describe mine, though it is certain no one passage ever resembled another, and no crew or set of passengers in one ship were ever identical with those in any other. For thirteen days the Atlantic followed its usual course in the month of March, and was true to the traditions which affix to it in that month the character of violence and moody changes, from bad to worse and back again. The wind was sometimes dead against us, and then the infelix Arabia with iron energy set to work, storming great Malakhofs of water, which rose above her like the side of some sward-coated hill crested with snow-drifts; and having gained the summit, and settled for an instant among the hissing sea-horses, ran plunging headlong down to the encounter of another wave, and thus went battling on with heart of fire and breath of flame—*igneus est ollis vigor*—hour after hour.

The traveller for pleasure had better avoid the Atlantic in the month of March. The wind was sometimes with us, and then the sensations of the passengers and the conduct of the ship were pretty much as they had been during the adverse breezes before, varied by the performance of a very violent "yawing" from side to side, and certain squashings of the paddle-boxes into the yeasty waters, which now ran a race with us and each other, as if bent on chasing us down, and rolling their boarding parties with foaming crests down on our decks. The boss, which we represented in the stormy shield around us, still moved on; day by day our microcosm shifted its position in the ever-advancing circle of which it was the centre, with all around and within it ever undergoing a sea change.

The Americans on board were, of course, the most interesting passengers to one like myself, who was going out to visit the great Republic under very peculiar circumstances. There was, first, Major Garnett, a Virginian, who was going back to his State to follow her fortunes. He was an officer of the regular army of the United States, who had served with distinction in Mexico; an accomplished, well-read man; reserved, and rather gloomy; full of the doctrine of States' Rights, and animated with a considerable feeling of contempt for the New Englanders, and with the strongest prejudices in favour of the institution of slavery. He laughed to scorn the doctrine that all men are born equal in the sense of all men having equal rights. Some were born to be slaves—some to be labourers in the lower strata above the slaves—others to follow useful mechanical arts—the rest were born to rule and to own their fellow-men. There was next a young Carolinian, who had left his post as attaché at St. Petersburgh to return to his State: thus, in all probability, avoiding the inevitable supercession which awaited him at the hands of the new Government at Washington. He represented, in an intensified form, all the Virginian's opinions, and held that Mr. Calhoun's interpretation of the Constitution was incontrovertibly right. There were difficulties in the way of State sovereignty, he confessed; but they were only in detail—the principle was unassailable.

To Mr. Mitchell, South Carolina represented a power quite sufficient to meet all the Northern States in arms. "The North will attempt to blockade our coast," said he; "and in that case, the South must march to the attack by land, and will probably act in Virginia." "But if the North attempts to do more than institute a blockade?—for instance, if their fleet attack your seaport towns, and land men to occupy them?" "Oh, in that case, we are quite certain of beating them." Mr. Julian Mitchell was indignant at the idea of submitting to the rule of a "rail-splitter," and of such men as Seward and Cameron. "No gentleman could tolerate such a Government."

An American family from Nashville, consisting of a lady and her son and daughter, were warm advocates of a "gentlemanly" government, and derided the Yankees with great bitterness. But they were by no means as ready to encounter the evils of war, or to break up the Union, as the South-Carolinian or the Virginian; and in that respect they represented, I was told, the negative feelings of the Border States, which are disposed to a temporising, moderate course of action, most distasteful to the passionate seceders.

There were also two Louisiana sugar-planters on board—one owning 500 slaves, the other rich in some thousands of acres; they seemed to care very little for the political aspects of the question of Secession, and regarded it merely in reference to its bearing on the sugar crop, and the security of slave property. Secession was regarded by them as a very extreme and violent measure, to which the State had resorted with reluctance; but it was obvious, at the same time, that, in event of a general secession of the Slave States from the North, Louisiana could neither have maintained her connection with the North, nor have stood in isolation from her sister States.

All these, and some others who were fellow passengers, might be termed Americans—*pur sang*. Garnett belonged to a very old family in Virginia. Mitchell came from a stock of several generations' residence in South Carolina. The Tennessee family were, in speech and thought, types of what Europeans consider true Americans to be. Now take the other side. First there was an exceedingly intelligent, well-informed young merchant of New York—nephew of an English county Member, known for his wealth, liberality, and munificence. Educated at a university in the Northern States, he had lived a good deal in England, and was returning to his father from a course of book-keeping in the house of his uncle's firm in Liverpool. His father and uncle were born near Coleraine, and he had just been to see the humble dwelling, close to the Giant's Causeway, which sheltered their youth, and where their race was cradled. In the war of 1812, the brothers were about sailing in a privateer fitted out to prey against the British, when accident fixed one of them in Liverpool, where he founded the house which has grown so greatly with the development of trade between New York and Lancashire, whilst the other settled in the States. Without being violent in tone, the young Northerner was very resolute in temper, and determined to do all which lay in his power to prevent the "glorious Union" being broken up.

The "Union" has thus founded on two continents a family of princely wealth, whose originals had probably fought with bitterness in their early youth against the union of Great Britain and Ireland. But did Mr. Brown, or the other Americans who shared his views, unreservedly approve of American institutions, and consider them faultless? By no means. The New Yorkers especially were eloquent on the evils of the suffrage, and of the licence of the Press in their own city; and displayed much irritation on the subject of naturalisation. The Irish were useful, in their way, making roads and working hard, for there were few Americans who condescended to manual labour, or who could not make far more money in higher kinds of work; but it was absurd to give the Irish votes which they used to destroy the influence of native-born citizens, and to sustain a corporation and local bodies of unsurpassable turpitude, corruption, and inefficiency.

Another young merchant, a college friend of the former, was just returning from a tour in Europe with his amiable sister. His father was the son of an Irish immigrant, but he did not at all differ from the other gentlemen of his city in the estimate in which he held the Irish element; and though he had no strong bias one way or other, he was quite resolved to support the abstraction called the Union, and its representative fact—the Federal Government. Thus the agriculturist and the trader—the grower of raw produce and the merchant who dealt in it—were at opposite sides of the question—wide apart as the Northern and Southern Poles. They sat apart, ate apart, talked apart—two distinct nations, with intense antipathies on the part of the South, which was active and aggressive in all its demonstrations.

The Southerners have got a strange charge de plus against the Irish. It appears that the regular army of the United States is mainly composed of Irish and Germans; very few Americans indeed being low enough, or martially disposed enough, to "take the shilling." In case of a conflict, which these gentlemen think inevitable, "low Irish mercenaries would," they say, "be pitted against the gentlemen of the South, and the best blood in the States would be spilled by fellows whose lives are worth nothing whatever." Poor Paddy is regarded as a mere working machine, fit, at best, to serve against Choctaws and Seminoles. His facility of reproduction has to compensate for the waste which is caused by the development in his unhappy head of the organs of combativeness and destructiveness. Certainly, if the war is to be carried on by the United States' regulars, the Southern States will soon dispose of them, for they do not number 20,000 men, and their officers are not much in love with the new Government. But can it come to War? Mr. Mitchell assures me I shall see some "pretty tall fighting."

The most vehement Northerners in the steamer are Germans, who are going to the States for the first time, or returning there. They have become satisfied, no doubt, by long process of reasoning, that there is some anomaly in the condition of a country which calls itself the land of liberty, and is at the same time the potent palladium of serfdom and human chattelry. When they are not sea-sick, which is seldom, the Teutons rise up in all the might of their misery and dirt, and, making spasmodic efforts to smoke, blurt out between the puffs, or in moody intervals, sundry remarks on American politics. "These are the swine," quoth Garnett, "who are swept out of German gutters as too foul for them, and who come over to the States and presume to control the fate and the wishes of our people. In their own country they proved they were incapable of either earning a living, or exercising the duties of citizenship; and they seek in our country a licence denied them in their own, and the means of living which they could not acquire anywhere else."

And for myself I may truly say this, that no man ever set foot on the soil of the United States with a stronger and sincerer desire to ascertain and to tell the truth, as it appeared to him. I had no theories to uphold, no prejudices to subserve, no interests to advance, no instructions to fulfil; I was a free agent, bound to communicate to the powerful organ of public opinion I represented, my own daily impressions of the men, scenes, and actions around me, without fear, favour, or affection of or for anything but that which seemed to me to be the truth. As to the questions which were distracting the States, my mind was a *tabula rasa*, or, rather, *tabula non scripta*. I felt indisposed to view with favour a rebellion against one of the established and recognized governments of the world, which, though not friendly to Great Britain, nor opposed to slavery, was without, so far as I could see, any legitimate cause of revolt, or any injury or grievance, perpetrated or imminent, assailed by States still less friendly to us, which the slave States, pure and simple, certainly were and probably are. At the same time, I knew that these were grounds which I could justly take, whilst they would not be tenable by an American, who is by the theory on which he revolted from us and created his own system of government, bound to recognise the principle that the discontent of the popular majority with its rulers, is ample ground and justification for revolution.

It was on the morning of the fourteenth day

that the shores of New York loomed through the drift of a cold wintry sea, leaden-grey and comfortless, and in a little time more the coast, covered with snow, rose in sight. Towards the afternoon the sun came out and brightened the waters and the sails of the pretty trim schooners and coasters which were dancing around us. How different the graceful, tautly-rigged, clean, white-sailed vessels from the round-sterned, lumpish billyboys and nondescripts of the eastern coast of our isle! Presently there came bowling down towards us a lively little schooner-yacht, very like the once famed "America," brightly painted in green, sails dazzling white, lofty ponderous masts, no tops. As she came nearer, we saw she was crowded with men in chimney-pot black hats, and coats, and the like—perhaps a party of citizens on pleasure, cold as the day was. Nothing of the kind. The craft was our pilot-boat, and the hats and coats belonged to the hardy mariners who act as guides to the port of New York. Their boat was lowered, and was soon under our mainchains; and a chimney-pot hat having duly come over the side, delivered a mass of newspapers to the captain, which were distributed among the eager passengers, when each at once became the centre of a spell-bound circle.

CHAPTER II.

Arrival at New York—Custom house—General impressions as to North and South—Street in New York—Hotel—Breakfast—American women and men—Visit to Mr. Bancroft—Street railways.

THE entrance to New York, as it was seen by us on 16th March, is not remarkable for beauty or picturesque scenery, and I incurred the ire of several passengers, because I could not consistently say it was very pretty. It was difficult to distinguish through the snow the villas and country houses, which are said to be so charming in summer. But beyond these rose a forest of masts close by a low shore of brick houses and blue roofs, above the level of which again spires of churches and domes and cupolas announced a great city. On our left, at the narrowest part of the entrance, there was a very powerful casemated work of fine close stone, in three tiers, something like Fort Paul at Sebastopol, built close to the water's edge, and armed on all the faces—apparently a tetragon with bastions. Extensive works were going on at the ground above it, which rises rapidly from the water to a height of more than a hundred feet, and the rudiments of an extensive work and heavily armed earthen parapets could be seen from the channel. On the right hand, crossing its fire with that of the batteries and works on our left, there was another regular stone fort with fortified enceinte, and higher up the channel, as it widens to the city on the same side, I could make out a smaller fort on the water's edge. The situation of the city renders it susceptible of powerful defence from the sea-side, and even now it would be hazardous to run the gauntlet of the batteries unless in powerful iron-clad ships favoured by wind and tide, which could hold the place at their mercy. Against a wooden fleet New York is now all but secure, save under exceptional circumstances in favour of the assailants.

It was dark as the steamer hauled up alongside the wharf on the New Jersey side of the river; but ere the sun set I could form some idea of the activity and industry of the people from the enormous ferry-boats moving backwards and forwards like arks on the water, impelled by the great walking-beam engines, the crowded stream full of merchantmen, steamers, and small craft, the smoke of the factories, the tall chimneys—the net-work of boats and rafts—all the evidences of commercial life in full development. What a swarming, eager crowd on the quay-wall! what a wonderful ragged regiment of labourers and porters, hailing us in broken or Hibernianized English! "These are all Irish and Germans," anxiously explained a New Yorker. "I'll bet fifty dollars there's not a native-born American among them."

With Anglo-Saxon disregard of official insignia, American Custom House officers dress very much like their British brethren, without any sign of authority as faint as even the brass button and crown, so that the stranger is somewhat uneasy when he sees unauthorised-looking people taking liberties with his plunder, especially after the admonition he has received on board ship to look sharp about his things as soon as he lands. I was provided with an introduction to one of the principal officers, and he facilitated my egress, and at last I was bundled out through a gate into a dark alley, ankle deep in melted snow and mud, where I was at once engaged in a brisk encounter with my Irish porterhood, and, after a long struggle, succeeded in stowing my effects in and about a remarkable specimen of the hackney-coach of the last century, very high in the axle, and weak in the springs, which plashed down towards the river through a crowd of men shouting out, "You haven't paid me yet, yer honour. You haven't given anything to your own man that's been waiting here the last six months for your honour!" "*I'm* the man that put the lugidge up, sir," &c., &c. The coach darted on board a great steam ferry-boat, which had on board a number of similar vehicles, and omnibuses, and the gliding, shifting lights, and the deep, strong breathing of the engine, told me I was moving and afloat before I was otherwise aware of it. A few minutes brought us over to the lights on the New York side—a jerk or two up a steep incline—and we were rattling over a most abominable pavement, plunging into mud-holes, squashing through snow-heaps in ill-lighted, narrow streets of low, mean-looking, wooden houses, of which an unusual proportion appeared to be lager-bier saloons, whisky-shops, oyster-houses, and billiard and smoking establishments.

The crowd on the pavement were very much what a stranger would be likely to see in a very bad part of London, Antwerp, or Hamburg, with a dash of the noisy exuberance which proceeds from the high animal spirits that defy police regulations and are superior to police force, called "rowdyism." The drive was long and tortuous; but by degrees the character of the thoroughfares and streets improved. At last we turned into a wide street with very tall houses, alternating with far humbler erections, blazing with lights, gay with shop-windows, thronged in spite of the mud with well-dressed people, and pervaded by strings of omnibuses—Oxford Street was nothing to it for length. At intervals there towered up a block of brickwork and stucco with long rows of windows lighted up tier above tier, and a swarming crowd passing in and out of the portals, which were recognised as the barrack-like glory of American civilisation—a Broadway monster hotel. More oyster-shops, lager-bier saloons, concert-rooms of astounding denominations, with external decorations very much in the style of the booths at Bartholomew Fair—churches, restaurants, confectioners, private-houses! again another series—they cannot go on expanding for ever. The coach at last drives into a large square, and lands me at the Clarendon Hotel.

Whilst I was crossing the sea, the President's Inaugural Message, the composition of which is generally attributed to Mr. Seward, had been delivered, and had reached Europe, and the causes which were at work in destroying the cohesion of the Union, had acquired greater strength and violence.

Whatever force "the declaration of causes which induced the Secession of South Carolina" might have for Carolinians, it could not influence a foreigner who knew nothing at all of the rights, sovereignty, and individual independence of a state, which, however, had no right to make war or peace, to coin money, or enter into treaty obligations with any other country. The South Carolinian was nothing to us, *quoad* South Carolina—he was merely a citizen of the United States, and we knew no more of him in any other capacity than a French authority would know of a British subject as a Yorkshireman or a Munsterman.

But the moving force of revolution is neither reason nor justice—it is most frequently passion—it is often interest. The American, when he seeks to prove that the Southern States have no right to revolt from a confederacy of states created by revolt, has by the principles on which he justifies his own revolution, placed between himself and the European a great gulf in the level of argument. According to the deeds and words, of Americans, it is difficult to see why South Carolina should not use the rights claimed for each of the thirteen colonies, "to alter and abolish a form of government when it becomes destructive of the ends for which it is established, and to institute a new one." And the people must be left to decide the question as regards their own government for themselves, or the principle is worthless. The arguments, however, which are now going on are fast tending towards the *ultima ratio regum*. At present I find public attention is concentrated on the two Federal forts, Pickens and Sumter, called after two officers of the revolutionary armies in the old war. As Alabama and South Carolina have gone out, they now demand the possession of these forts, as of the soil of their several states and attached to their sovereignty. On the other hand, the Government of Mr. Lincoln considers it has no right to give up any thing belonging to the Federal Government, but evidently desires to temporize and evade any decision which might precipitate an attack on the forts by the batteries and forces prepared to act against them. There is not sufficient garrison in either for an adequate defence, and the difficulty of procuring supplies is very great. Under the circumstances every one is asking what the Government is going to do? The Southern people have declared they will resist any attempt to supply or reinforce the garrisons, and in Charleston, at least, have shown they mean to keep their word. It is a strange situation. The Federal Government, afraid to speak, and unable to act, is leaving the soldiers to do as they please. In some instances, officers of rank, such as General Twiggs, have surrendered everything to the State authorities, and the treachery and secession of many officers in the army and navy no doubt paralyze and intimidate the civilians at the head of affairs.

Sunday, 17*th March*.—The first thing I saw this morning, after a vision of a waiter pretending to brush my clothes with a feeble twitch composed of fine fibre had vanished, was a procession of men, forty or fifty perhaps, preceded by a small band (by no excess of compliment can I say, of music), trudging through the cold and slush two and two: they wore shamrocks, or the best resemblance thereto which the American soil can produce, in their hats, and green silk sashes emblazoned with crownless harp upon their coats, but it needed not these insignia to tell they were Irishmen, and their solemn mien indicated that they were going to mass. It was agreeable to see them so well clad and respectable looking, though occasional hats seemed as if they had just recovered from severe contusions, and others had the picturesque irregularity of outline now and then observable in the old country. The aspect of the street was irregular, and its abnormal look was increased by the air of the passers-by, who at that hour were domestics—very finely dressed negroes, Irish, or German. The coloured ladies made most elaborate toilettes, and as they held up their broad crinolines over the mud looked not unlike double-stemmed mushrooms. "They're concayted poor craythures them niggers, male and faymale," was the remark of the waiter as he saw me watching them. "There seem to be no sparrows in the streets," said I. "Sparras!" he exclaimed; "and then how did you think a little baste of a sparra could fly across the ochean?" I felt rather ashamed of myself.

And so down-stairs where there was a *table d'hôte* room, with great long tables covered with cloths, plates, and breakfast apparatus, and a smaller room inside, to which I was directed by one of the white-jacketted waiters. Breakfast over, visitors began to drop in. At the "office" of the hotel, as it is styled, there is a tray of blank cards and a big pencil, whereby the cardless man who is visiting is enabled to send you his name and title. There is a comfortable "reception room," in which he can remain and read the papers, if you are engaged, so that there is little chance of your ultimately escaping him. And, indeed, not one of those who came had any but most hospitable intents.

Out of doors the weather was not tempting. The snow lay in irregular layers and discoloured mounds along the streets, and the gutters gorged with "snow-bree" flooded the broken pavement. But after a time the crowds began to issue from the churches, and it was announced as the necessity of the day, that we were to walk up and down the Fifth Avenue and look at each other. This is the west-end of London—its Belgravia and Grosvenoria represented in one long street, with offshoots of inferior dignity at right angles to it. Some of the houses are handsome, but the greater number have a compressed, squeezed-up aspect, which arises from the compulsory narrowness of frontage in proportion to the height of the building, and all of them are bright and new, as if they were just finished to order,—a most astonishing proof of the rapid development of the city. As the hall door is made an important feature in the residence, the front parlour is generally a narrow, lanky apartment, struggling for existence between the hall and the partition of the next house. The outer door, which is always provided with fine carved panels and mouldings, is of some rich varnished wood, and looks much better than our painted doors. It is generously thrown open so as to show an inner door with curtains and plate glass. The windows, which are double on account of the climate, are frequently of plate glass also. Some of the doors are on the same level as the street, with a basement story beneath; others are approached by flights of steps, the basement for servants having the entrance below the steps, and this, I believe, is the old Dutch fashion, and the name of "stoop" is still retained for it.

No liveried servants are to be seen about the streets, the doorways, or the area-steps. Black faces in gaudy caps, or an unmistakeable "Biddy" in crinoline are their substitutes. The chief charm of the street was the living ornature which moved up and down the *trottoirs.* The costumes of Paris, adapted to the severity of this wintry weather, were draped round pretty, graceful figures which, if wanting somewhat in that rounded fulness of the Medician Venus, or in height, were *svelte* and well poised. The French boot has been driven off the field by the Balmoral, better suited to the snow; and one must at once admit—all prejudices notwithstanding—that the American woman is not only well shod and well gloved, but that she has no reason to fear comparisons in foot or hand with any daughter of Eve, except, perhaps, the Hindoo.

The great and most frequent fault of the stranger in any land is that of generalising from a few facts. Every one must feel there are "pretty days" and "ugly days" in the world, and that his experience on the one would lead him to conclusions very different from that to which he would arrive on the other. To-day I am quite satisfied that if the American women are deficient in stature and in that which makes us say, "There is a fine woman," they are easy, well formed, and full of grace and prettiness. Admitting a certain pallor—which the Russians, by the bye, were wont to admire so much that they took vinegar to produce it—the face is not only pretty, but sometimes of extraordinary beauty, the features fine, delicate, well-defined. Ruby lips, indeed, are seldom to be seen, but now and then the flashing of snowy-white evenly-set ivory teeth dispels the delusion that the Americans are —though the excellence of their dentists be granted—naturally ill provided with what they take so much pains, by eating bon-bons and confectionery, to deprive of their purity and colour.

My friend R——, with whom I was walking, knew every one in the Fifth Avenue, and we worked our way through a succession of small talk nearly as far as the end of the street, which runs out among divers places in the State of New York, through a *débris* of unfinished conceptions in masonry. The abrupt transition of the city into the country is not unfavourable to an idea that the Fifth Avenue might have been transported from some great workshop, where it had been built to order by a despot, and dropped among the Red men: indeed, the immense growth of New York in this direction, although far inferior to that of many parts of London, is remarkable as the work of eighteen or twenty years, and is rendered more conspicuous by being developed in this elongated street, and its contingents. I was introduced to many persons to-day, and was only once or twice asked how I liked New-York; perhaps I anticipated the question by expressing my high opinion of the Fifth Avenue. Those to whom I spoke had generally something to say in reference to the troubled condition of the country, but it was principally of a self-complacent nature. "I suppose, sir, you are rather surprised, coming from Europe, to find us so quiet here in New York: we are a peculiar people, and you don't understand us in Europe."

In the afternoon I called on Mr. Bancroft, formerly minister to England, whose work on America must be rather rudely interrupted by this crisis. Any thing with an "ex" to it in America is of little weight—ex-presidents are nobodies, though they have had the advantage, during their four years' tenure of office, of being prayed for as long as they live. So it is of ex-ministers, whom nobody prays for at all. Mr. Bancroft conversed for some time on the aspect of affairs, but he appeared to be unable to arrive at any settled conclusion, except that the republic, though in danger, was the most stable and beneficial form of government in the world, and that as a Government it had no power to coerce the people of the South or to save itself from the danger. I was indeed astonished to hear from him and others so much philosophical abstract reasoning as to the right of seceding, or, what is next to it, the want of any power in the Government to prevent it.

Returning home in order to dress for dinner, I got into a street-railway-car, a long low omnibus drawn by horses over a *strada ferrata* in the middle of the street. It was filled with people of all classes, and at every crossing some one or other rang the bell, and the driver stopped to let out or take in passengers, whereby the unoffending traveler became possessed of much snow-droppings and mud on boots and clothing. I found that by far a greater inconvenience caused by these street-railways was the destruction of all comfort or rapidity in ordinary carriages.

I dined with a New York banker, who gave such a dinner as bankers generally give all over the world. He is a man still young, very kindly, hospitable, well-informed, with a most charming household—an American by theory, an Englishman in instincts and tastes—educated in Europe, and sprung from British stock. Considering the enormous interests he has at stake, I was astonished to perceive how calmly he spoke of the impending troubles. His friends, all men of position in New York society, had the same dilettante tone, and were as little anxious for the future, or excited by the present, as a party of *savans* chronicling the movements of a "magnetic storm."

On going back to the hotel, I heard that Judge Daly and some gentlemen had called to request that I would dine with the Friendly Society of St. Patrick to-morrow at Astor House. In what is called "the bar," I met several gentlemen, one of whom said, "the majority of the people of New York, and all the respectable people, were disgusted at the election of such a fellow as Lincoln to be President, and would back the Southern States, if it came to a split."

CHAPTER III.

"St. Patrick's day" in New York—Public dinner—American Constitution—General topics of conversation—Public estimate of the Government—Evening party at Mons. B——'s.

Monday, 18*th*. — "St. Patrick's day in the morning" being on the 17th, was kept by the Irish to-day. In the early morning the sounds of drumming, fifing, and bugling came with the hot water and my Irish attendant into the room. He told me: "We'll have a pretty nice day for it. The weather's often agin us on St. Patrick's day." At the angle of the square outside I saw a company of volunteers assembling. They wore bear-skin caps, some turned brown, and rusty green coatees, with white facings and crossbelts, a good deal of gold-lace and heavy worsted epaulettes, and were armed with ordinary muskets, some of them with flint-locks. Over their heads floated a green and gold flag with mystic emblems, and a harp and sunbeams. A gentleman, with an imperfect seat on horseback, which justified a suspicion that he was not to the manner born of Squire or Squireen, with much difficulty was getting them into line, and endangering his personal safety by a large infantry-sword, the hilt of which was complicated with the bridle of his charger in some inexplicable manner. This gentleman was the officer in command of the martial body, who were gathering to do honour to the festival of the old country, and the din and clamour in the streets, the strains of music, and the tramp of feet outside announced that similar associations were on their way to the rendezvous. The waiters in the hotel, all of whom were Irish, had on their best, and wore an air of pleased importance. Many of their countrymen outside on the pavement exhibited very large decorations, plates of metal, and badges attached to broad ribands over their left breasts.

After breakfast I struggled with a friend through the crowd which thronged Union Square. Bless them! They were all Irish, judging from speech, and gesture, and look; for the most part decently dressed, and comfortable, evidently bent on enjoying the day in spite of the cold, and proud of the privilege of interrupting all the trade of the principal streets, in which the Yankees most do congregate, for the day. They were on the door-steps, and on the pavement men, women, and children, admiring the big policemen—many of them compatriots—and they swarmed at the corners, cheering popular town-councillors or local celebrities. Broadway was equally full. Flags were flying from the windows and steeples—and on the cold breeze came the hammering of drums, and the blasts of many wind instruments. The display, such as it was, partook of a military character, though not much more formidable in that sense than the march of the Trades Unions, or of Temperance Societies. Imagine Broadway lined for the long miles of its course by specta[illegible] mostly Hibernian, and the great gaudy stars and stripes, or as one of the Secession journals I see styles it, the "Sanguinary United States Gridiron"—waving in all directions, whilst up its centre in the mud march the children of Erin.

First came the acting Brigadier-General and his staff, escorted by 40 lancers, very ill-dressed, and worse mounted; horses dirty, accoutrements in the same condition, bits, bridles, and buttons rusty and tarnished; uniforms ill-fitting, and badly put on. But the red flags and the show pleased the crowd, and they cheered "bould Nugent" right loudly. A band followed, some members of which had been evidently "smiling" with each other; and next marched a body of drummers in military uniform, rattling away in the French fashion. Here comes the 69th N. Y. State Militia Regiment — the battalion which would not turn out when the Prince of Wales was in New York, and whose Colonel, Corcoran, is still under court-martial for his refusal. Well, the Prince had no loss, and the Colonel may have had other besides political reasons for his dislike to parade his men.

The regiment turned out, I should think, only 200 or 220 men, fine fellows enough, but not in the least like soldiers or militia. The United States uniform which most of the military bodies wore, consists of a blue tunic and trousers, and a kepi-like cap, with "U. S." in front for undress. In full dress the officers wear large gold epaulettes, and officers and men a bandit-sort of felt hat looped up at one side, and decorated with a plume of black-ostrich feathers and silk cords. The absence of facings, and the want of something to finish off the collar and cuffs, render the tunic very bald and unsightly. Another band closed the rear of the 69th, and to eke out the military show, which in all was less than 1,200 men, some companies were borrowed from another regiment of State Militia, and a troop of very poor cavalry cleared the way for the Napper-Tandy Artillery, which actually had three whole guns with them! It was strange to dwell on some of the names of the societies which followed. For instance, there were the "Dungannon Volunteers of '82," prepared of course to vindicate the famous declaration that none should make laws for Ireland, but the Queen, Lords, and Commons of Ireland! Every honest Catholic among them ignorant of the fact that the Volunteers of '82 were all Protestants. Then there was the "Sarsfield Guard!" One cannot conceive anything more hateful to the fiery high-spirited cavalier, than the republican form of Government, which these poor Irishmen are, they think, so fond of. A good deal of what passes for national sentiment, is in reality dislike to England and religious animosity.

It was much more interesting to see the long string of Benevolent, Friendly and Provident Societies, with bands, numbering many thousands, all decently clad, and marching in order with banners, insignia, badges and ribands, and the Irish flag flying alongside the "stars and stripes." I cannot congratulate them on the taste or good effect of their accessories—on their symbolical standards, and ridiculous old harpers, carried on stages in "bardic costume," very like artificial white wigs and white cotton dressing-gowns, but the actual good done by these societies, is, I am told, very great, and their charity would cover far greater sins than incorrectness of dress, and a proneness to "piper's playing on the national bagpipes." The various societies mustered upwards of 10,000 men, some of them uniformed and armed, others dressed in quaint garments, and all as noisy as music and talking could make them. The Americans appeared to regard the whole thing very much as an ancient Roman might have looked on the Saturnalia; but Paddy was in the ascendant, and could not be openly trifled with.

The crowds remained in the streets long after the procession had passed, and I saw various pickpockets captured by the big policemen, and conveyed to appropriate receptacles. "Was there any man of eminence in that procession?" I asked. "No; a few small local politicians, some wealthy store-keepers, and beer-saloon owners perhaps; but the mass were of the small bourgeoisie. Such a man as Mr. O'Conor, who may be considered at the head of the New York bar for instance, would not take part in it."

In the evening I went, according to invitation, to the Astor House—a large hotel, with a front like a railway terminus, in the Americo-Classical style, with great Doric columns and portico, and found, to my surprise, that the friendly party was to be a great public dinner. The halls were filled with the company, few or none in evening dress; and in a few minutes I was presented to at least twenty-four gentlemen, whose names I did not even hear. The use of badges, medals, and ribands, might, at first, lead a stranger to believe he was in very distinguished military society; but he would soon learn that these insignia were the decorations of benevolent or convivial associations. There is a latent taste for these things in spite of pure republicanism. At the dinner there were Americans of Dutch and English descent, some "Yankees," one or two Englishmen, Scotchmen, and Welchmen. The chairman, Judge Daly, was indeed a true son of the soil, and his speeches were full of good humour, fluency, and wit; but his greatest effect was produced by the exhibition of a tuft of shamrocks in a flower pot, which had been sent from Ireland for the occasion. This is done annually, but, like the miracle of St. Januarius, it never loses its effect, and always touches the heart.

I confess it was to some extent curiosity to observe the sentiment of the meeting, and a desire to see how Irishmen were affected by the change in their climate, which led me to the room. I came away regretting deeply that so many natives of the British Isles should be animated with a hostile feeling towards England, and that no statesman has yet arisen who can devise a panacea for the evils of these passionate and unmeaning differences between races and religions. Their strong antipathy is not diminished by the impossibility of gratifying it. They live in hope, and certainly the existence of these feelings is not only troublesome to American statesmen, but mischievous to the Irish themselves, inasmuch as they are rendered with unusual readiness the victims of agitators or political intriguers. The Irish element, as it is called, is much regarded in voting times, by suffraging bishops and others; at other times, it is left to its work and its toil — Mr. Seward and Bishop Hughes are supposed to be its present masters. Undoubtedly the mass of those I saw to-day were better clad than they would have been if they remained at home. As I said in the speech which I was forced to make much against my will, by the gentle violence of my companions, never had I seen so many good hats and coats in an assemblage of Irishmen in any other part of the world.

March 19. The morning newspapers contain reports of last night's speeches which are amusing in one respect, at all events, as affording specimens of the different versions which may be given of the same matter. A "citizen" who was kind enough to come in to shave me, paid me some easy compliments, in the manner of the "Barber of Seville," on what he termed the "oration" of the night before, and then proceeded to give his notions of the merits and defects of the American Constitution. "He did not care much about the Franchise—it was given to too many he thought. A man must be five years resident in New York before he is admitted to the privileges of voting. When an emigrant arrived, a paper was delivered to him to certify the fact, which he produced after a lapse of five years, when he might be registered as a voter; if he omitted the process of registration, he could however vote if identified by two householders, and a low lot," observed the barber, "they are—Irish and such like. I don't want any of their votes."

In the afternoon a number of gentlemen called, and made the kindest offers of service; letters of introduction to all parts of the States; facilities of every description—all tendered with frankness.

I was astonished to find little sympathy and no respect for the newly installed Government. They were regarded as obscure or undistinguished men. I alluded to the circumstance that one of the journals continued to speak of "The President" in the most contemptuous manner, and to designate him as the great "Rail-Splitter." "Oh yes," said the gentleman with whom I was conversing, "that must strike you as a strange way of mentioning the Chief Magistrate of our great Republic, but the fact is, no one minds what the man writes of any one, his game is to abuse every respectable man in the country in order to take his revenge on them for his social exclusion, and at the same time to please the ignorant masses who delight in vituperation and scandal."

In the evening, dining again with my friend the banker, I had a favorable opportunity of hearing more of the special pleading which is brought to bear on the solution of the gravest political questions. It would seem as if a council of physicians were wrangling with each other over abstract dogmas respecting life and health, whilst their patient was struggling in the agonies of death before them! In the comfortable and well-appointed house wherein I met several men of position, acquirements, and natural sagacity, there was not the smallest evidence of uneasiness on account of circumstances which, to the eye of a stranger, betokened an awful crisis, if not the impending dissolution of society itself. Stranger still, the acts which are bringing about such a calamity are not regarded with disfavour, or, at least, are not considered unjustifiable.

Among the guests were the Hon. Horatio Seymour, a former Governor of the State of New York; Mr. Tylden, an acute lawyer; and Mr.

Bancroft; the result left on my mind by their conversations and arguments was that, according to the Constitution, the Government could not employ force to prevent secession, or to compel States which had seceded by the will of the people to acknowledge the Federal power. In fact, according to them, the Federal Government was the mere machine put forward by a Society of Sovereign States, as a common instrument for certain ministerial acts, more particularly those which affected the external relations of the Confederation. I do not think that any of the guests sought to turn the channel of talk upon politics, but the occasion offered itself to Mr. Horatio Seymour to give me his views of the Constitution of the United States, and by degrees the theme spread over the table. I had bought the "Constitution" for three cents in Broadway in the forenoon, and had read it carefully, but I could not find that it was self-expounding; it referred itself to the Supreme Court, but what was to support the Supreme Court in a contest with armed power, either of Government or people? There was not a man who maintained the Government had any power to coerce the people of a State, or to force a State to remain in the Union, or under the action of the Federal Government; in other words, the symbol of power at Washington is not at all analogous to that which represents an established Government in other countries. *Quid prosunt legis sine armis?* Although they admitted the Southern leaders had meditated "the treason against the Union" years ago, they could not bring themselves to allow their old opponents, the Republicans now in power, to dispose of the armed force of the Union against their brother democrats in the Southern States.

Mr. Seymour is a man of compromise, but his views go farther than those which were entertained by his party ten years ago. Although secession would produce revolution, it was, nevertheless, "a right," founded on abstract principles, which could scarcely be abrogated consistently with due regard to the original compact. One of the company made a remark which was true enough, I dare say. We were talking of the difficulty of relieving Fort Sumter—an infallible topic just now. "If the British or any foreign power were threatening the fort," said he, "our Government would find means of relieving it fast enough." In fact, the Federal Government is groping in the dark; and whilst its friends are telling it to advance boldly, there are myriad voices shrieking out in its ears, "If you put out a foot you are lost." There is neither army nor navy available, and the ministers have no machinery of rewards, and means of intrigue, or modes of gaining adherents known to European administrations. The democrats behold with silent satisfaction the troubles into which the republican triumph has plunged the country, and are not at all disposed to extricate them. The most notable way of impeding their efforts is to knock them down with the "Constitution" every time they rise to the surface and begin to swim out.

New York society, however, is easy in its mind just now, and the upper world of millionaire merchants, bankers, contractors, and great traders are glad that the vulgar republicans are suffering for their success. Not a man there but resented the influence given by universal suffrage to the mob of the city, and complained of the intolerable effects of their ascendency—of the corruption of the municipal bodies, the venality of electors and elected, and the abuse, waste, and profligate outlay of the public funds. Of these there were many illustrations given to me, garnished with historiettes of some of the civic dignitaries, and of their coadjutors in the press; but it did not require proof that universal suffrage in a city of which perhaps three-fourths of the voters were born abroad or of foreign parents, and of whom many were the scum swept off the seethings of European populations, must work most injuriously on property and capital. I confess it is to be much wondered at that the consequences are not more evil; but no doubt the time is coming when the mischief can no longer be borne, and a social reform and revolution must be inevitable.

Within only a very few hundreds of yards from the house and picture-gallery of Mons. B——, the representative of European millions, are the hovels and lodgings of his equals in political power. This evening I visited the house of Mons. B——, where his wife had a reception, to which nearly the whole of the party went. When a man looks at a suit of armour made to order by the first blacksmith in Europe, he observes that the finish of the joints and hinges is much higher than in the old iron clothes of the former time. Possibly the metal is better, and the chasings and garniture as good as the work of Milan, but the observer is not for a moment led to imagine that the fabric has stood proof of blows, or that it smacks of ancient watch-fire. If he were asked why it is so, he could not tell; any more perhaps than he could define exactly the difference between the lustrous, highly-jewelled, well-greaved Achaian of New York and the very less effective and showy creature who will in every society over the world pass muster as a gentleman. Here was an elegant house—I use the word in its real meaning—with pretty statues, rich carpets, handsome furniture, and a gallery of charming Meissoniers and genre pieces; the saloons admirably lighted—a fair fine large suite, filled with the prettiest women in the most delightful toilettes, with a proper fringe of young men, orderly, neat, and well turned-out, fretting against the usual advanced posts of turbaned and jewelled dowagers, and provided with every accessory to make the whole good society; for there was wit, sense, intelligence, vivacity; and yet there was something wanting—not in host or hostess, or company, or house—where was it?—which was conspicuous by its absence. Mr. Bancroft was kind enough to introduce me to the most lovely faces and figures, and so far enabled me to judge that nothing could be more beautiful, easy, or natural than the womanhood or girlhood of New York. It is prettiness rather than fineness; regular, intelligent, wax-like faces, graceful little figures; none of the grandiose Roman type which Von Raumer recognised in London, as in the Holy City, a quarter of a century ago. Natheless, the young men of New York ought to be thankful and grateful, and try to be worthy of it. Late in the evening I saw these same young men, Novi Eboracenses, at their club, dicing for drinks and oathing for nothing, and all very friendly and hospitable.

The club-house is remarkable as the mansion of a happy man who invented or patented a waterproof hat-lining, whereby he built a sort of Sallustian villa, with a central court-yard, à l'Alhambra, with fountains and flowers, now passed away to the New York Club. Here was Pratt's, or the defunct Fielding, or the old C. C. C.'s in disregard of time and regard of drinks—and nothing more.

CHAPTER IV.

Streets and shops in New York—Literature—A funeral—Dinner at Mr. H——'s—Dinner at Mr. Bancroft's—Political and social features—Literary breakfast; Heenan and Sayers.

March 20th.—The papers are still full of Sumter and Pickens. The reports that they are or are not to be relieved are stated and contradicted in each paper without any regard to individual consistency. The "Tribune" has an article on my speech at the St. Patrick's dinner, to which it is pleased to assign reasons and motives which the speaker, at all events, never had in making it.

Received several begging letters, some of them apparently with only too much of the stamp of reality about their tales of disappointment, distress, and suffering. In the afternoon went down Broadway, which was crowded, notwithstanding the piles of blackened snow by the kerbstones, and the sloughs of mud, and half frozen pools at the crossings. Visited several large stores or shops—some rival the best establishments in Paris or London in richness and in value, and far exceed them in size and splendour of exterior. Some on Broadway, built of marble, or of fine cut stone, cost from 6000*l.* to 8000*l.* a year in mere rent. Here, from the base to the fourth or fifth story, are piled collections of all the world can produce, often in excess of all possible requirements of the country; indeed I was told that the United States have always imported more goods than they could pay for. Jewellers' shops are not numerous, but there are two in Broadway which have splendid collections of jewels, and of workmanship in gold and silver, displayed to the greatest advantage in fine apartments decorated with black marble, statuary, and plate-glass.

New York has certainly all the air of a "nouveau riche." There is about it an utter absence of any appearance of a grandfather—one does not see even such evidences of eccentric taste as are afforded in Paris and London, by the existence of shops where the old families of a country cast off their "exuviæ" which are sought by the new, that they may persuade the world they are old; there is no curiosity shop, not to speak of a Wardour Street, and such efforts as are made to supply the deficiency reveal an enormous amount of ignorance or of bad taste. The new arts, however, flourish; the plague of photography has spread through all the corners of the city, and the shop-windows glare with flagrant displays of the most tawdry art. In some of the large booksellers' shops—Appleton's for example—are striking proofs of the activity of the American press, if not of the vigour and originality of the American intellect. I passed down long rows of shelves laden with the works of European authors, for the most part, oh shame! stolen and translated into American type without the smallest compunction or scruple, and without the least intention of ever yielding the most pitiful deodand to the authors. Mr. Appleton sells no less than one million and a half of Webster's spelling books a year; his tables are covered with a flood of pamphlets, some for, others against coercion; some for, others opposed to slavery,—but when I asked for a single solid, substantial work on the present difficulty, I was told there was not one published worth a cent. With such men as Audubon and Wilson in natural history, Prescott and Motley in history, Washington Irving and Cooper in fiction, Longfellow and Edgar Poe in poetry, even Bryant and the respectabilities in rhyme, and Emerson as essayist, there is no reason why New York should be a paltry imitation of Leipzig, without the good faith of Tauchnitz.

I dined with a litterateur well known in England to many people a year or two ago—sprightly, loquacious, and well informed, if neither witty nor profound—now a Southern man with Southern proclivities, as Americans say; once a Southern man with such strong anti-slavery convictions, that his expression of them in an English quarterly had secured him the hostility of his own people—one of the emanations of American literary life for which their own country finds no fitting receiver. As the best proof of his sincerity, he has just now abandoned his connection with one of the New York papers on the republican side, because he believed that the course of the journal was dictated by anti-Southern fanaticism. He is, in fact, persuaded that there will be a civil war, and that the South will have much of the right on its side in the contest. At his rooms were Mons. B——, Dr. Gwin, a Californian ex-senator, Mr. Barlow, and several of the leading men of a certain clique in New York. The Americans complain, or assert, that we do not understand them, and I confess the reproach, or statement, was felt to be well founded by myself at all events, when I heard it declared and admitted that "if Mons. Belmont had not gone to the Charleston Convention, the present crisis would never have occurred."

March 22nd.—A snow-storm worthy of Moscow or Riga flew through New York all day, depositing more food for the mud. I paid a visit to Mr. Horace Greeley, and had a long conversation with him. He expressed great pleasure at the intelligence that I was going to visit the Southern States. "Be sure you examine the slave-pens. *They* will be afraid to refuse you, and you can tell the truth." As the capital and the South form the chief attractions at present, I am preparing to escape from "the divine calm" and snows of New York. I was recommended to visit many places before I left New York, principally hospitals and prisons. Sing-Sing, the state penitentiary, is "claimed," as the Americans say, to be the first "institution" of its kind in the world. Time presses, however, and Sing-Sing is a long way off. I am told a system of torture prevails there for hardened or obdurate offenders—torture by dropping cold water on them, torture by thumb-screws, and the like—rather opposed to the views of prison philanthropists in modern days.

March 23rd.—It is announced positively that

the authorities in Pensacola and Charleston have refused to allow any further supplies to be sent to Fort Pickens, the United States fleet in the Gulf, and to Fort Sumter. Everywhere the Southern leaders are forcing on a solution with decision and energy, whilst the Government appears to be helplessly drifting with the current of events, having neither bow nor stern, neither keel nor deck, neither rudder, compass, sails, or steam. Mr. Seward has declined to receive or hold any intercourse with the three gentlemen called Southern Commissioners, who repaired to Washington accredited by the Government and Congress of the Seceding States now sitting at Montgomery, so that there is no channel of mediation or means of adjustment left open. I hear, indeed, that Government is secretly preparing what force it can to strengthen the garrison at Pickens, and to reinforce Sumter at any hazard; but that its want of men, ships, and money compels it to temporise, lest the Southern authorities should forestall their designs by a vigorous attack on the enfeebled forts.

There is, in reality, very little done by New York to support or encourage the Government in any decided policy, and the journals are more engaged now in abusing each other, and in small party aggressive warfare, than in the performance of the duties of a patriotic press, whose mission at such a time is beyond all question the resignation of little differences for the sake of the whole country, and an entire devotion to its safety, honour, and integrity. But the New York people must have their intellectual drams every morning, and it matters little what the course of Government may be, so long as the aristocratic democrat can be amused by ridicule of the Great Rail-Splitter, or a vivid portraiture of Mr. Horace Greeley's old coat, hat, breeches, and umbrella. The coarsest personalities are read with gusto, and attacks of a kind which would not have been admitted into the "Age" or "Satirist" in their worst days, form the staple leading articles of one or two of the most largely circulated journals in the city. "Slang" in its worst Americanised form is freely used in sensation headings and leaders, and a class of advertisements which are not allowed to appear in respectable English papers, have possession of columns of the principal newspapers, few, indeed, excluding them. It is strange, too, to see in journals which profess to represent the civilisation and intelligence of the most enlightened and highly educated people on the face of the earth, advertisements of sorcerers, wizards, and fortune-tellers by the score—"wonderful clairvoyants," "the seventh child of a seventh child," "mesmeristic necromancers," and the like, who can tell your thoughts as soon as you enter the room, can secure the affections you prize, give lucky numbers in lotteries, and make everybody's fortunes but their own. Then there are the most impudent quack programmes—very doubtful "personals" addressed to "the young lady with black hair and blue eyes, who got out of the omnibus at the corner of 7th Street"—appeals by "a lady about to be confined" to any respectable person who is desirous of adopting a child: all rather curious reading for a stranger, or for a family.

It is not to be expected, of course, that New York is a very pure city, for more than London or Paris it is the sewer of nations. It is a city of luxury also—French and Italian cooks and milliners, German and Italian musicians, high prices, extravagant tastes and dressing, money readily made, a life in hotels, bar-rooms, heavy gambling, sporting, and prize-fighting flourish here, and combine to lower the standard of the *bourgeoisie* at all events. Where wealth is the sole aristocracy, there is great danger of mistaking excess and profusion for elegance and good taste. To-day as I was going down Broadway, some dozen or more of the most over-dressed men I ever saw were pointed out to me as "sports;" that is, men who lived by gambling-houses and betting on races; and the class is so numerous that it has its own influence, particularly at elections, when the power of a hard-hitting prize-fighter with a following makes itself unmistakeably felt. Young America essays to look like martial France in mufti, but the hat and the coat suited to the Colonel of Carabiniers *en retraite* do not at all become the thin, tall, rather long-faced gentlemen one sees lounging about Broadway. It is true, indeed, the type, though not French, is not English. The characteristics of the American are straight hair, keen, bright, penetrating eyes, and want of colour in the cheeks.

March 25th.—I had an invitation to meet several members of the New York press association at breakfast. Among the company were—Mr. Bayard Taylor, with whose extensive notes of travel his countrymen are familiar—a kind of enlarged Inglis, full of the genial spirit which makes travelling in company so agreeable, but he has come back as travellers generally do, satisfied there is no country like his own—Prince Leeboo loved his own isle the best after all—Mr. Raymond, of the "New York Times" (formerly Lieutenant-Governor of the State); Mr. Olmsted, the indefatigable, able, and earnest writer, whom to describe simply as an Abolitionist would be to confound with ignorant if zealous, unphilosophical, and impracticable men; Mr. Dana, of the "Tribune;" Mr. Hurlbert, of the "Times;" the Editor of the "Courier des Etats Unis;" Mr. Young, of the "Albion," which is the only English journal published in the States; and others. There was a good deal of pleasant conversation, though every one differed with his neighbour, as a matter of course, as soon as he touched on politics. There was talk *de omnibus rebut et quibusdam aliis*, such as Heenan and Sayers, Secession and Sumter, the press, politicians, New York life, and so on. The first topic occupied a larger place than it was entitled to, because in all likelihood the sporting editor of one of the papers who was present expressed, perhaps, some justifiable feeling in reference to the refusal of the belt to the American. All admitted the courage and great endurance of his antagonist, but seemed convinced that Heenan, if not the better man, was at least the victor in that particular contest. It would be strange to see the great tendency of Americans to institute comparisons with ancient and recognised standards, if it were not that they are adopting the natural mode of judging of their own capabilities. The nation is like a growing lad who is constantly testing his powers in competition with his elders. He is in his youth and nonage, and he is calling down the lanes and alleys to all comers to look at his muscle, to run against or to fight him. It is a sign of youth, not a proof of weakness, though it does offend the old hands and vex the veterans.

Then one finds that Great Britain is often treated very much as an old Peninsula man may be by a set of young soldiers at a club. He is no doubt a very gallant fellow, and has done very fine things in his day, and he is listened to with respectful endurance, but there is a secret belief that he will never do anything very great again.

One of the gentlemen present said that England might dispute the right of the United States Government to blockade the ports of her own States, to which she was entitled to access under treaty, and might urge that such a blockade was not justifiable; but then, it was argued, that the President could open and shut ports as he pleased; and that he might close the Southern ports by a proclamation in the nature of an Order of Council. It was taken for granted that Great Britain would only act on sordid motives, but that the well known affection of France for the United States is to check the selfishness of her rival, and prevent a speedy recognition.

CHAPTER V.

Off to the railway station—Railway carriages—Philadelphia—Washington—Willard's Hotel—Mr. Seward—North and South—The "State Department" at Washington—President Lincoln—Dinner at Mr. Seward's.

After our pleasant breakfast came that necessity for activity which makes such meals disguised as mere light morning repasts take their revenge. I had to pack up, and I am bound to say the moral aid afforded me by the waiter, who stood with a sympathising expression of face, and looked on as I wrestled with boots, books, and great coats, was of a most comprehensive character. At last I conquered, and at six o'clock P.M. I left the Clarendon, and was conveyed over the roughest and most execrable pavements through several miles of unsympathetic, gloomy, dirty streets, and crowded thoroughfares, over jaw-wrenching street-railway tracks, to a large wooden shed covered with inscriptions respecting routes and destinations on the bank of the river, which as far as the eye could see, was bordered by similar establishments, where my baggage was deposited in the mud. There were no porters, none of the recognised and established aides to locomotion to which we are accustomed in Europe, but a number of amateurs divided the spoil, and carried it into the offices, whilst I was directed to struggle for my ticket in another little wooden box, from which I presently received the necessary document, full of the dreadful warnings and conditions, which railway companies inflict on the public in all free countries.

The whole of my luggage, except a large bag, was taken charge of by a man at the New York side of the ferry, who "checked it through" to the capital—giving me a slip of brass with a number corresponding with a brass ticket for each piece. When the boat arrived at the stage at the other side of the Hudson, in my innocence I called for a porter to take my bag. The passengers were moving out of the capacious ferry-boat in a steady stream, and the steam throat and bell of the engine were going whilst I was looking for my porter; but at last a gentleman passing said, "I guess y'ill remain here a considerable time before y'ill get any one to come for that bag of yours," and taking the hint, I just got off in time to stumble into a long box on wheels, with a double row of most uncomfortable seats, and a passage down the middle, where I found a place beside Mr. Sanford, the newly-appointed United States Minister to Belgium, who was kind enough to take me under his charge to Washington.

The night was closing in very fast as the train started, but such glimpses as I had of the continuous line of pretty-looking villages of wooden houses, two stories high, painted white, each with its Corinthian portico, gave a most favourable impression of the comfort and prosperity of the people. The rail passed through the main street of most of these hamlets and villages, and the bell of the engine was tolled to warn the inhabitants, who drew up on the side walks and let us go by. Soon the white houses faded away into faint blurred marks on the black ground of the landscape, or twinkled with starlike lights, and there was nothing more to see. The passengers were crowded as close as they could pack, and as there was an immense iron stove in the centre of the car, the heat and stuffiness became most trying, although I had been undergoing the ordeal of the stove-heated New York houses for nearly a week. Once a minute, at least, the door at either end of the carriage was opened, and then closed with a sharp crashing noise, that jarred the nerves, and effectually prevented sleep. It generally was done by a man whose sole object seemed to be to walk up the centre of the carriage in order to go out of the opposite door—occasionally it was the work of the newspaper boy, with a sheaf of journals and trashy illustrated papers under his arm. Now and then it was the conductor; but the periodical visitor was a young gentleman with a chain and rings, who bore a tray before him, and solicited orders for "gum drops," and "lemon drops," which, with tobacco, apples, and cakes, were consumed in great quantities by the passengers.

At 10 o'clock, P.M., we crossed the river by a ferry boat to Philadelphia, and drove through the streets, stopping for supper a few moments at the La Pierre Hotel. To judge from the vast extent of the streets, of small, low, yet snug-looking houses, through which we passed, Philadelphia must contain in comfort the largest number of small householders of any city in the world. At the other terminus of the rail, to which we drove in a carriage, we procured for a small sum, a dollar I think, berths in a sleeping car, an American institution of considerable merit. Unfortunately a party of prize-fighters had a mind to make themselves comfortable, and the result was anything but conducive to sleep. They had plenty of whiskey, and were full of song and fight, nor was it possible to escape their urgent solicitations "to take a drink," by feigning the soundest sleep. One of these, a big man, with a broken nose, a mellow eye, and a very large display of rings, jewels, chains and pins, was in very high spirits, and informed us he was "Going to Washington to get a foreign mission from Bill Seward. He wouldn't take Paris, as he didn't care much about French or Frenchmen; but he'd just like to show John Bull how to do it; or he'd take Japan if they were very pressing." Another told us he was "Going to the bosom of Uncle Abe" (meaning the President)—"that he knew him well in Kentucky years ago, and a high toned gentleman he was." Any attempts to persuade them to retire to rest made by the conductors were treated with sovereign contempt, but at last whiskey asserted its supremacy, and having established the point that they "would not sleep unless they —— pleased," they slept and snored.

At six, A.M., we were roused up by the arrival of the train at Washington, having crossed great rivers and traversed cities without knowing it during the night. I looked out and saw a vast mass of white marble towering above us on the left, stretching out in colonnaded porticoes, and long flanks of windowed masonry, and surmounted by an unfinished cupola, from which scaffold and cranes raised their black arms. This was the Capitol. To the right was a cleared space of mud, sand, and fields studded with wooden sheds and huts, beyond which, again, could be seen rudimentary streets of small red brick houses, and some church-spires above them.

Emerging from the station, we found a vociferous crowd of blacks, who were the hackney-coachmen of the place; but Mr. Sanford had his carriage in waiting, and drove me straight to Willard's Hotel, where he consigned me to the landlord at the bar. Our route lay through Pennsylvania avenue—a street of much breadth and length, lined with ælanthus trees, each in a white-washen wooded sentry box, and by most irregularly-built houses in all kinds of material, from deal plank to marble—of all heights, and every sort of trade. Few shop-windows were open, and the principal population consisted of blacks, who were moving about on domestic affairs. At one end of the long vista there is the Capitol; and at the other, the Treasury buildings—a fine block in marble, with the usual American classical colonnades.

Close to these rises the great pile of Willard's Hotel, now occupied by applicants for office, and by the members of the newly-assembled Congress. It is a quadrangular mass of rooms, six stories high, and some hundred yards square; and it probably contains at this moment more scheming, plotting, planning heads, more aching and joyful hearts, than any building of the same size ever held in the world. I was ushered into a bed-room which had just been vacated by some candidate—whether he succeeded or not I cannot tell, but if his testimonials spoke truth, he ought to have been selected at once for the highest office. The room was littered with printed copies of letters testifying that J. Smith, of Hartford, Conn., was about the ablest, honestest, cleverest, and best man the writers ever knew. Up and down the long passages doors were opening and shutting for men with papers bulging out of their pockets, who hurried as if for their life in and out, and the building almost shook with the tread of the candidature, which did not always in its present aspect justify the correctness of the original appellation.

It was a remarkable sight, and difficult to understand unless seen. From California, Texas, from the Indian Reserves, and the Mormon territory, from Nebraska, as from the remotest borders of Minniesota, from every portion of the vast territories of the Union, except from the Seceded States, the triumphant republicans had winged their way to the prey.

There were crowds in the hall through which one could scarce make his way—the writing-room was crowded, and the rustle of pens rose to a little breeze—the smoking-room, the bar, the barbers, the reception-room, the ladies' drawing-room—all were crowded. At present not less than 2,500 people dine in the public room every day. On the kitchen floor there is a vast apartment, a hall without carpets or any furniture but plain chairs and tables, which are ranged in close rows, at which flocks of people are feeding, or discoursing, or from which they are flying away. The servants never cease shoving the chairs to and fro with a harsh screeching noise over the floor, so that one can scarce hear his neighbour speak. If he did, he would probably hear as I did, at this very hotel, a man order breakfast, "Black tea and toast, scrambled eggs, fresh spring shad, wild pigeon, pigs' feet, two robins on toast, oysters," and a quantity of breads and cakes of various denominations. The waste consequent on such orders is enormous—and the ability required to conduct these enormous establishments successfully is expressed by the common phrase in the States, "Brown is a clever man, but he can't manage an hotel." The tumult, the miscellaneous nature of the company —my friends the prize-fighters are already in possession of the doorway—the heated, muggy rooms, not to speak of the great abominableness of the passages and halls, despite a most liberal provision of spittoons, conduce to render these institutions by no means agreeable to a European. Late in the day I succeeded in obtaining a sitting-room with a small bed-room attached, which made me somewhat more independent and comfortable—but you must pay highly for any departure from the routine life of the natives. Ladies enjoy a handsome drawing-room, with piano, sofas, and easy-chairs, all to themselves.

I dined at Mr. Sanford's, where I was introduced to Mr. Seward, Secretary of State; Mr. Truman Smith, an ex-senator, much respected among the Republican party; Mr. Antony, a senator of the United States, a journalist, a very intelligent-looking man, with an Israelitish cast of face; Colonel Foster of the Illinois railway, of reputation in the States as a geologist; and one or two more gentlemen. Mr. Seward is a slight, middle-sized man, of feeble build, with the stoop contracted from sedentary habits and application to the desk, and has a peculiar attitude when seated, which immediately attracts attention. A well-formed and large head is placed on a long, slender neck, and projects over the chest in an argumentative kind of way, as if the keen eyes were seeking for an adversary; the mouth is remarkably flexible, large but well-formed, the nose prominent and aquiline, the eyes secret, but penetrating, and lively with humour of some kind twinkling about them; the brow bold and broad, but not remarkably elevated; the white hair silvery and fine—a subtle, quick man, rejoicing in power, given to perorate and to oracular utterances, fond of badinage, bursting with the importance of state mysteries, and with the dignity of directing the foreign policy of the greatest country—as all Americans think—in the world. After dinner he told some stories of the pressure on the President for place, which very much amused the guests who knew the men, and talked freely and pleasantly of many things—stating, however, few facts positively. In reference to an assertion in a New York paper, that orders had been given to evacuate Sumter, "That," he said, "is a plain lie—no such orders have been given. We will give up nothing we have—abandon nothing that has been entrusted to us. If people would only read these statements by the light of the President's inaugural, they would not be deceived." He wanted no extra session of Congress. "History tells us that kings who call extra parliaments lose their heads," and he informed the company he had impressed the President with his historical parallels.

All through this conversation his tone was that of a man very sanguine, and with a supreme contempt for those who thought there was anything serious in secession. "Why," said he, "I myself, my brothers, and sisters, have been all secessionists—we seceded from home when we were young, but we all went back to it sooner or later. These States will all come back in the same way." I doubt if he was ever in the South; but he affirmed that the state of living and of society there was something like that in the State of New York sixty or seventy years ago. In the North all was life, enterprise, industry, mechanical skill. In the South there was dependence on black labour, and an idle extravagance which was mistaken for elegant luxury—tumble-down old hackney-coaches, such as had not been seen north of the Potomac for half a century, harness never cleaned, ungroomed horses, worked at the mill one day and sent to town the next, badly furnished houses, bad cookery, imperfect education. No parallel could be drawn between them and the Northern States at all. "You are all very angry," he said, "about the Morrill tariff. You must, however, let us be best judges of our own affairs. If we judge rightly, you have no right to complain; if we judge wrongly, we shall soon be taught by the results, and shall correct our error. It is evident that if the Morrill tariff fulfils expectations, and raises a revenue, British manufacturers suffer nothing, and we suffer nothing, for the revenue is raised here, and trade is not injured. If the tariff fails to create a revenue, we shall be driven to modify or repeal it."

The company addressed him as "Governor," which led to Mr. Seward's mentioning that when he was in England he was induced to put his name down with that prefix in a hotel book, and caused a discussion among the waiters as to whether he was the "Governor" of a prison or of a public company. I hope the great people of England treated Mr. Seward with the attention due to his position, as he would assuredly feel and resent very much any slight on the part of those in high places. From what he said, however, I infer that he was satisfied with the reception he had met in London. Like most Americans who can afford it, he has been up the Nile. The weird old stream has great fascinations for the people of the Mississippi—as far at least as the first cataract.

March 27th.—This morning, after breakfast, Mr. Sanford called, according to promise, and took me to the State department. It is a very humble — in fact, dingy — mansion, two stories high, and situated at the end of the magnificent line of colonnade in white marble, called the Treasury, which is hereafter to do duty as the head-quarters of nearly all the public departments. People familiar with Downing Street, however, cannot object to the dinginess of the bureaux in which the foreign and state affairs of the American Republic are transacted. A flight of steps leads to the hall-door, on which an announcement in writing is affixed, to indicate the days of reception for the various classes of persons who have business with the Secretary of State; in the hall, on the right and left, are small rooms, with the names of the different officers on the doors—most of them persons of importance; half-way in the hall a flight of stairs conducts us to a similar corridor, rather dark, with doors on each side opening into the bureaux of the chief clerks. All the appointments were very quiet, and one would see much more bustle in the passage of a Poor Law Board or a parish vestry.

In a moderately sized, but very comfortable, apartment, surrounded with book-shelves, and ornamented with a few engravings, we found the Secretary of State seated at his table, and enjoying a cigar; he received me with great courtesy and kindness, and after a time said he would take occasion to present me to the President, who was to give audience that day to the minister of the new kingdom of Italy, who had hitherto only represented the kingdom of Sardinia.

I have already described Mr. Seward's personal appearance; his son, to whom he introduced me, is the Assistant-Secretary of State, and is editor or proprietor of a journal in the State of New York, which has a reputation for ability and fairness. Mr. Frederick Seward is a slight delicate-looking man, with a high forehead, thoughtful brow, dark eyes, and amiable expression; his manner is very placid and modest, and, if not reserved, he is by no means loquacious. As we were speaking, a carriage drove up to the door, and Mr. Seward exclaimed to his father, with something like dismay in his voice, "Here comes the Chevalier in full uniform!"—and in a few seconds in effect the Chevalier Bertinatti made his appearance, in cocked hat, white gloves, diplomatic suit of blue and silver lace, sword, sash, and riband of the cross of Savoy. I thought there was a quiet smile on Mr. Seward's face as he saw his brilliant companion, who contrasted so strongly with the more than republican simplicity of his own attire. "Fred, do you take Mr. Russell round to the President's, whilst I go with the Chevalier. We will meet at the White House." We accordingly set out through a private door leading to the grounds, and within a few seconds entered the hall of the moderate mansion, White House, which has very much the air of a portion of a bank or public office, being provided with glass doors and plain heavy chairs and forms. The domestic who was in attendance was dressed like any ordinary citizen, and seemed perfectly indifferent to the high position of the great personage with whom he conversed, when Mr. Seward asked him, "Where is the President?" Passing through one of the doors on the left, we entered a handsome spacious room, richly and rather gorgeously furnished, and rejoicing in a kind of "*demi-jour*," which gave increased effect to the gilt chairs and ormolu ornaments. Mr. Seward and the Chevalier stood in the centre of the room, whils his son and I remained a little on one side: "For," said Mr. Seward, "you are not to be supposed to be here."

Soon afterwards there entered, with a shambling, loose, irregular, almost unsteady gait, a tall, lank, lean man, considerably over six feet in height, with stooping shoulders, long pendulous arms, terminating in hands of extraordinary dimensions, which, however, were far exceeded in proportion by his feet. He was dressed in an ill-fitting, wrinkled suit of black, which put one in mind of an undertaker's uniform at a funeral; round his neck a rope of black silk was knotted in a large bulb, with flying ends projecting beyond the collar of his coat; his turned-down shirt-collar disclosed a sinewy muscular yellow neck, and above that, nestling in a great black mass of hair, bristling and compact like a ruff of mourning pins, rose the strange quaint face and head, covered with its thatch of wild republican hair, of President Lincoln. The impression produced by the size of his extremities, and by his flapping and wide projecting ears, may be removed by the appearance of kindliness, sagacity, and the awkward bonhommie of his face; the mouth is absolutely prodigious; the lips, straggling and extending almost from one line of black beard to the other, are only kept in order by two deep furrows from the nostril to the chin; the nose itself—a prominent organ—stands out from the face with an inquiring, anxious air, as though it were sniffing for some good thing in the wind; the eyes dark, full, and deeply set, are penetrating, but full of an expression which almost amounts to tenderness; and above them projects the shaggy brow, running into the small hard frontal space, the development of which can scarcely be estimated accurately, owing to the irregular flocks of thick hair carelessly brushed across it. One would say that, although the mouth was made to enjoy a joke, it could also utter the severest sentence which the head could dictate, but that Mr. Lincoln would be ever more willing to temper justice with mercy, and to enjoy what he considers the amenities of life, than to take a harsh view of men's nature and of the world, and to estimate things in an ascetic or puritan spirit. A person who met Mr. Lincoln in the street would not take him to be what—according to the usages of European society—is called a "gentleman;" and, indeed, since I came to the United States, I have heard more disparaging allusions made by Americans to him on that account than I could have expected among simple republicans, where all should be equals; but, at the same time, it would not be possible for the most indifferent observer to pass him in the street without notice.

As he advanced through the room, he evidently controlled a desire to shake hands all round with everybody, and smiled good-humouredly till he was suddenly brought up by the staid deportment of Mr. Seward, and by the profound diplomatic bows of the Chevalier Bertinatti. Then, indeed, he suddenly jerked himself back, and stood in front of the two ministers, with his body slightly drooped forward, and his hands behind his back, his knees touching, and his feet apart. Mr. Seward formally presented the minister, whereupon the President made a prodigiously violent demonstration of his body in a bow which had almost the effect of a smack in its rapidity and abruptness, and, recovering himself, proceeded to give his utmost attention, whilst the Chevalier, with another bow, read from a paper a long address in presenting the royal letter accrediting him as "minister resident;" and when he said that "the king desired to give, under your enlightened administration, all possible strength and extent to those sentiments of frank sympathy which do not cease to be exhibited every moment between the two peoples, and whose origin dates back as far as the exertions which have presided over their common destiny as self-governing and free nations," the President gave another bow still more violent, as much as to accept the allusion.

The minister forthwith handed his letter to the President, who gave it into the custody of Mr. Seward, and then, dipping his hand into his coat-pocket, Mr. Lincoln drew out a sheet of paper, from which he read his reply, the most remarkable part of which was his doctrine "that the United States were bound by duty not to interfere with the differences of foreign governments and countries." After some words of compliment, the President shook hands with the minister, who soon afterwards retired. Mr. Seward then took me by the hand and said—"Mr. President, allow me to present to you Mr. Russell, of the London 'Times.'" On which Mr. Lincoln put out his hand in a very friendly manner, and said, "Mr. Russell, I am very glad to make your acquaintance, and to see you in this country. The London 'Times' is one of the greatest powers in the world,—in fact, I don't know anything which has much more power,—except perhaps the Mississippi. I am glad to know you as its minister." Conversation ensued for some minutes, which the President enlivened by two or three peculiar little sallies, and I left agreeably impressed with his shrewdness, humour, and natural sagacity.

In the evening I dined with Mr. Seward, in company with his son, Mr. Seward, junior, Mr. Sanford, and a quaint, natural specimen of an American rustic lawyer, who was going to Brussels as Secretary of Legation. His chief, Mr. Sanford, did not appear altogether happy when introduced to his secretary, for he found that he had a very limited knowledge (if any) of French, and of other things which it is generally considered desirable that secretaries should know.

Very naturally, conversation turned on politics. Although no man can foresee the nature of the crisis which is coming, nor the mode in which it is to be encountered, the faith of men like Mr. Sanford and Mr. Seward in the ultimate success of their principles, and in the integrity of the Republic, is very remarkable; and the boldness of their language in reference to foreign powers almost amounts to arrogance and menace, if not to temerity. Mr. Seward asserted that the Ministers of England or of France had no right to make any allusion to the civil war which appeared imminent; and that the Southern Commissioners who had been sent abroad could not be received by the Government of any foreign power, officially or otherwise, even to hand in a document or to make a representation, without incurring the risk of breaking off relations with the Government of the United States. As regards the great object of public curiosity, the relief of Fort Sumter, Mr. Seward maintains a profound silence, beyond the mere declaration, made with a pleasant twinkle of the eye, that "the whole policy of the Government, on that and other questions, is put forth in the President's inaugural, from which there will be no deviation." Turning to the inaugural message, however, there is no such very certain indication, as Mr. Seward pretends to discover, of the course to be pursued by Mr. Lincoln and the cabinet. To an outside observer, like myself, it seems as if they were waiting for events to develop themselves, and rested their policy rather upon acts that had occurred, than upon any definite principle designed to control or direct the future.

I should here add that Mr. Seward spoke in high terms of the ability, dexterity, and personal qualities of Mr. Jefferson Davis, and declared his belief that but for him the Secession movement never could have succeeded as far as it has gone, and would, in all probability, indeed, have never taken place at all. After dinner cigars were introduced, and a quiet little rubber of whist followed. The Secretary is given to expatiate at large, and told us many anecdotes of foreign travel;—if I am not doing him injustice, I would say further, that he remembers his visit to England, and the attention he received there, with peculiar satisfaction. He cannot be found fault with because he has formed a most exalted notion of the superior intelligence, virtue, happiness, and prosperity of his own people. He said that it would not be proper for him to hold any communication with the Southern Commissioners then in Washington; which rather surprised me, after what I had heard from their friend, Mr. Banks. On returning to my hotel, I found a card from the President, inviting me to dinner the following day.

CHAPTER VI.

A state dinner at the White House—Mrs. Lincoln—The Cabinet Ministers—A newspaper correspondent—Good Friday at Washington.

March 28th.—I was honoured to-day by visits from a great number of Members of Congress, journalists, and others. Judging from the expressions of most of the Washington people, they would gladly see a Southern Cabinet installed in their city. The cold shoulder is given to Mr. Lincoln, and all kinds of stories and jokes are circulated at his expense. People take particular pleasure in telling how he came towards the seat of his Government disguised in a Scotch cap and cloak, whatever that may mean.

In the evening I repaired to the White House. The servant who took my hat and coat was particularly inquisitive as to my name and condition in life; and when he heard I was not a minister, he seemed inclined to question my right to be there at all: "for," said he, "there are none but members of the cabinet, and their wives and daughters, dining here to-day." Eventually he relaxed—instructed me how to place my hat so that it would be exposed to no indignity, and informed me that I was about to participate in a prandial enjoyment of no ordinary character. There was no parade or display, no announcement—no gilded staircase, with its liveried heralds, transmitting and translating one's name from landing to landing. From the unpretending ante-chamber, a walk across the lofty hall led us to the reception-room, which was the same as that in which the President held his interview yesterday.

Mrs. Lincoln was already seated to receive her guests. She is of the middle age and height, of a plumpness degenerating to the *embonpoint* natural to her years; her features are plain, her nose and mouth of an ordinary type, and her manners and appearance homely, stiffened, however, by the consciousness that her position requires her to be something more than plain Mrs. Lincoln, the wife of the Illinois lawyer; she is profuse in the introduction of the word "sir" in every sentence, which is now almost an Americanism confined to certain classes, although it was once as common in England. Her dress I shall not attempt to describe, though it was very gorgeous and highly coloured. She handled a fan with much energy, displaying a round, well-proportioned arm, and was adorned with some simple jewellery. Mrs. Lincoln struck me as being desirous of making herself agreeable; and I own I was agreeably disappointed, as the Secessionist ladies at Washington had been amusing themselves by anecdotes which could scarcely have been founded on fact.

Several of the Ministers had already arrived; by-and-by all had come, and the party only waited for General Scott, who seemed to be the representative man in Washington of the monarchical idea, and to absorb some of the feeling which is lavished on the pictures and memory, if not on the monument, of Washington. Whilst we were waiting, Mr. Seward took me round, and introduced me to the Ministers, and to their wives and daughters, among the latter, Miss Chase, who is very attractive, agreeable, and sprightly. Her father, the Finance Minister, struck me as one of the most intelligent and distinguished persons in the whole assemblage; tall, of a good presence, with a well-formed head, fine forehead, and a face indicating energy and power. There is a peculiar droop and motion of the lid of one eye, which seems to have suffered from some injury, that detracts from the agreeable effect of his face; but, on the whole, he is one who would not pass quite unnoticed in a European crowd of the same description.

In the whole assemblage there was not a scrap of lace or a piece of ribbon, except the gorgeous epaulettes of an old naval officer who had served against us in the last war, and who represented some branch of the naval department. Nor were the Ministers by any means remarkable for their personal appearance.

Mr. Cameron, the Secretary for War, a slight man, above the middle height, with grey hair, deep-set keen grey eyes, and a thin mouth, gave me the idea of a person of ability and adroitness. His colleague, the Secretary of the Navy, a small man, with a great long grey beard and spectacles, did not look like one of much originality or ability; but people who know Mr. Welles declare that he is possessed of administrative power, although they admit that he does not know the stem from the stern of a ship, and are in doubt whether he ever saw the sea in his life.

Mr. Smith, the Minister of the Interior, is a bright-eyed, smart (I use the word in the English sense) gentleman, with the reputation of being one of the most conservative members of the cabinet. Mr. Blair, the Postmaster-General, is a person of much greater influence than his position would indicate. He has the reputation of being one of the most determined republicans in the Ministry; but he held peculiar notions with reference to the black and the white races, which, if carried out, would not by any means conduce to the comfort or happiness of free negroes in the United States. He is a tall, lean man, with a hard, Scotch, practical-looking head —an anvil for ideas to be hammered on. His eyes are small and deeply set, and have a rat-like expression; and he speaks with caution, as though he weighed every word before he uttered it. The last of the Ministers is Mr. Bates, a stout, thick-set, common-looking man, with a large beard, who fills the office of Attorney-General. Some of the gentlemen were in evening dress; others wore black frock coats, which it seems, as in Turkey, are considered to be *en regle* at a Republican Ministerial dinner.

In the conversation which occurred before dinner, I was amused to observe the manner in which Mr. Lincoln used the anecdotes for which he is famous. Where men bred in courts, accustomed to the world, or versed in diplomacy, would use some subterfuge, or would make a polite speech, or give a shrug of the shoulders as the means of getting out of an embarrassing position, Mr. Lincoln raises a laugh by some bold west-country anecdote, and moves off in the cloud of merriment produced by his joke. Thus, when Mr. Bates was remonstrating apparently against the appointment of some indifferent lawyer to a place of judicial importance, the President interposed with, "Come now, Bates, he's not half as bad as you think. Besides that, I must tell you, he did me a good turn long ago. When I took to the law, I was going to court one morning, with some ten or twelve miles of bad road before me, and I had no horse. The judge overtook me in his wagon. 'Hollo, Lincoln! Are you not going to the court-house? Come in and I'll give you a seat.' Well, I got in, and the judge went on reading his papers. Presently the waggon struck a stump on one side of the road; then it hopped off to the other. I looked out, and I saw the driver was jerking from side to side in his seat; so says I, 'Judge, I think your coachman has been taking a little drop too much this morning.' 'Well I declare, Lincoln,' said he, 'I should not much wonder if you are right, for he has nearly upset me half-a-dozen of times since starting.' So, putting his head out of the window, he shouted, 'Why, you infernal scoundrel, you are drunk!' Upon which, pulling up his horses, and turning round with great gravity, the coachman said, 'By gorra! that's the first rightful decision you have given for the last twelvemonth.'" Whilst the company were laughing, the President beat a quiet retreat from the neighborhood of the Attorney-General.

It was at last announced that General Scott was unable to be present, and that, although actually in the house, he had been compelled to retire from indisposition, and we moved in to the banquetting-hall. The first "state dinner," as it is called, of the President was not remarkable for ostentation. No liveried servants, no Persic splendour of ancient plate, or *chefs d' œuvre* of art glittered round the board. Vases of flowers decorated the table, combined with dishes in what may be called the "Gallo-American" style, with wines which owed their parentage to France, and their rearing and education to the United States, which abound in cunning nurses for such productions. The conversation was suited to the state dinner of a cabinet at which women and strangers were present. I was seated next Mr. Bates and the very agreeable and lively Secretary of the President, Mr. Hay, and except when there was an attentive silence caused by one of the President's stories, there was a Babel of small talk round the table, in which I was surprised to find a diversity of accent almost as great as if a number of foreigners had been speaking English. I omitted the name of Mr. Hamlin, the Vice-President, as well as those of less remarkable people who were present; but it would not be becoming to pass over a man distinguished for nothing so much as his persistent and unvarying adhesion to one political doctrine, which has made him, in combination with the belief in his honesty, the occupant of a post which leads to the Presidency, in event of any occurrence which may remove Mr. Lincoln.

After dinner the ladies and gentlemen retired to the drawing-room, and the circle was increased by the addition of several politicians. I had an opportunity of conversing with some of the Ministers, if not with all, from time to time, and I was struck by the uniform tendency of their remarks in reference to the policy of Great Britain. They seemed to think that England was bound by her anti-slavery antecedents to discourage to the utmost any attempts of the South to establish its independence on a basis of slavery, and to assume that they were the representatives of an active war of emancipation. As the veteran Commodore Stewart passed the chair of the young lady to whom I was speaking, she said, "I suppose, Mr. Russell, you do not admire that officer?" "On the contrary," I said, "I think he is a very fine-looking old man." "I don't mean that," she replied; "but you know he can't be very much liked by you, because he fought so gallantly against you in the last war, as you must know." I had not the courage to confess ignorance of the Captain's antecedents. There is a delusion among more than the fair American who spoke to me, that we entertain in England the sort of feeling, morbid or wholesome as it may be, in reference to our reverses at New Orleans and elsewhere, that is attributed to Frenchmen respecting Waterloo.

On returning to Willard's Hotel, I was accosted by a gentleman who came out from the crowd in front of the office. "Sir," he said, "you have been dining with our President to-night." I bowed. "Was it an agreeable party?" said he. "What do you think of Mr. Lincoln?" "May I ask to whom I have the pleasure of speaking?" "My name is Mr. ——, and I am the correspondent of the New York ——." "Then, sir," I replied, "it gives me satisfaction to tell you that I think a great deal of Mr. Lincoln, and that I am equally pleased with my dinner. I have the honour to bid you good evening." The same gentleman informed me afterwards that he had created the office of Washington Correspondent to the New York papers. "At first," said he, "I merely wrote news, and no one cared much; then I spiced it up, squibbed a little, and let off stories of my own. Congress men contradicted me — issued cards — said they were not facts. The public attention was attracted, and I was told to go on; and so the Washington correspondence became a feature in all the New York papers by degrees." The hum and bustle in the hotel to-night were wonderful. All the office seekers were in the passages, hungering after senators and representatives, and the ladies in any way related to influential people, had an *entourage* of courtiers sedulously paying their respects. Miss Chase, indeed, laughingly told me that she was pestered by applicants for her father's good offices, and by persons seeking introduction to her as a means of making demands on "Uncle Sam."

As I was visiting a book-shop to-day, a pert, smiling young fellow, of slight figure and boyish appearance, came up and introduced himself to me as an artist who had contributed to an illustrated London paper during the Prince of Wales's tour, and who had become acquainted with some of my friends; and he requested permission to call on me, which I gave without difficulty or hesitation. He visited me this evening, poor lad! and told me a sad story of his struggles, and of the dependence of his family on his efforts, as a prelude to a request that I would allow him to go South when I was making the tour there, of which he had heard. He was under an engagement with the London paper, and had no doubt that if he was with me his sketches would all be received as illustrations of the places to which my letters were attracting public interest in England at the time. There was no reason why I should be averse to his travelling with me in the same train. He could certainly go if he pleased. At the same time I intimated that I was in no way to be connected with or responsible for him.

March 29th, Good Friday.—The religious observance of the day was not quite as strict as it would be in England. The Puritan aversion to ceremonials and formulary observances has apparently affected the American world, even as far south as this. The people of colour were in the streets dressed in their best. The first impression produced by fine bonnets, gay shawls, brightly-coloured dresses, and silk brodequins, on black faces, flat figures, and feet to match, is singular; but, in justice to the backs of many of the gaudily-dressed women, who, in little groups, were going to church or chapel, it must be admitted that this surprise only came upon one when he got a front view. The men generally affected black coats, silk or satin waistcoats, and parti-coloured pantaloons. They carried Missal or Prayer-book, pocket-handkerchief, cane or parasol, with infinite affectation of correctness.

As I was looking out of the window, a very fine, tall young negro, dressed irreproachably, save as to hat and boots, passed by. "I wonder what he is?" I exclaimed inquiringly to a gentleman who stood beside me. "Well," he said, "that fellow is not a free nigger; he looks too respectable. I daresay you could get him for 1500 dollars, without his clothes. You know," continued he, "what our Minister said when he saw a nigger at some Court in Europe, and was asked what he thought of him: 'Well, I guess,' said he, 'if you take off his fixings, he may be worth 1000 dollars down.' In the course of the day, Mr. Banks, a corpulent, energetic young Virginian, of strong Southern views, again called on me. As the friend of the Southern Commissioners, he complained vehemently of the refusal of Mr. Seward to hold intercourse with him. "These fellows mean treachery, but we will baulk them." In answer to a remark of mine, that the English Minister would certainly refuse to receive Commissioners from any part of the Queen's dominions which had seized upon the forts and arsenals of the empire and menaced war, he replied: "The case is quite different. The Crown claims a right to govern the whole of your empire; but the Austrian Government could not refuse to receive a deputation from Hungary for an adjustment of grievances; nor could any State belonging to the German Diet attempt to claim sovereignty over another, because they were members of the same Confederation." I remarked "that his views of the obligations of each State of the Union were perfectly new to me, as a stranger ignorant of the controversies which distracted them. An Englishman had nothing to do with a Virginian and New Yorkist, or a South Carolinian — he scarcely knew anything of a Texan, or of an Arkansasian; we only were conversant with the United States as an entity; and all our dealings were with citizens of the United States of North America." This, however, only provoked logically diffuse dissertations on the Articles of the Constitution, and on the spirit of the Federal Compact.

Later in the day, I had the advantage of a conversation with Mr. Truman Smith, an old and respected representative in former days, who gave me a very different account of the matter; and who maintained that by the Federal Compact each State had delegated irrevocably the essence of its sovereignty to a Government to be established in perpetuity for the benefit of the whole body. The Slave States, seeing that the progress of free ideas, and the material power of the North, were obtaining an influence which must be subversive of the supremacy they had so long exercised in the Federal Government for their own advantage, had developed this doctrine of States' Rights as a cloak to treason, preferring the material advantages to be gained by the extension of their system to the grand moral position which they would occupy as a portion of the United States in the face of all the world.

It is on such radical differences of ideas as these, that the whole of the quarrel, which is widening every day, is founded. The Federal Compact, at the very outset, was written on a torn sheet of paper, and time has worn away the artificial cement by which it was kept together. The corner stone of the Constitution had a crack in it, which the heat and fury of faction have widened into a fissure from top to bottom, never to be closed again.

In the evening I had the pleasure of dining with an American-gentleman who has seen much of the world, travelled far and wide, who has read much and beheld more, a scholar, a politician, after his way, a poet, and an ologist—one of those modern Græculi, who is unlike his prototype in Juvenal only in this, that he is not hungry, and that he will not go to heaven if you order him.

Such men never do or can succeed in the United States; they are far too refined, philosophical, and cosmopolitan. From what I see, success here may be obtained by refined men, if they are dishonest, never by philosophical men, unless they be corrupt—not by cosmopolitan men under any circumstances whatever; for to have sympathies with any people, or with any nation in the world, except his own, is to doom a statesman with the American public, unless it be in the form of an affectation of pity or good will, intended really as an offence to some allied people. At dinner there was the very largest naval officer I have seen in company, although I must own that our own service is not destitute of some good specimens, and I have seen an Austrian admiral at Pola, and the superintendent of the Arsenal at Tophaneh, who were not unfit to be marshals of France. This Lieutenant, named Nelson, was certainly greater in one sense than his British namesake, for he weighed 260 pounds.

It may be here remarked, *passim* and *obiter*, that the Americans are much more precise than ourselves in the enumeration of weights and matters of this kind. They speak of pieces of artillery, for example, as being of so many pounds weight, and of so many inches long, where we would use cwts. and feet. With a people addicted to vertical rather than lateral extension in every thing but politics and morals, precision is a matter of importance. I was amused by a description of some popular personage I saw in one of the papers the other day, which after an enumeration of many high mental and physical attributes, ended thus: "In fact, he is a remarkably fine, high-toned gentleman, and weighs 210 pounds."

The Lieutenant was a strong Union man, and he inveighed fiercely, and even coarsely, against the members of his profession who had thrown up their commissions. The superintendent of the Washington Navy Yard is supposed to be very little disposed in favour of this present Government; in fact, Capt. Buchanan may be called a Secessionist, nevertheless, I am invited to the wedding of his daughter, in order to see the President give away the bride. Mr. Nelson says, Sumter and Pickens are to be reinforced. Charleston is to be reduced to order, and all traitors hanged, or he will know the reason why; and, says he, "I have some weight in the country." In the evening, as we were going home, notwithstanding the cold, we saw a number of ladies sitting out on the door-steps, in white dresses. The streets were remarkably quiet and deserted; all the coloured population had been sent to bed long ago. The fire-bell, as usual, made an alarm or two about midnight.

CHAPTER VII.

Barbers' shops—Place-hunting—The Navy Yard—Dinner at Lord Lyons'—Estimate of Washington among his countrymen—Washington's house and tomb—The Southern Commissioners—Dinner with the Southern Commissioners—Feeling towards England among the Southerners—Animosity between North and South.

March 30th.—Descended into the barber's shop off the hall of the hotel; all the operators, men of colour, mostly mulattoes, or yellow lads, good-looking, dressed in clean white jackets and aprons, were smart, quick, and attentive. Some seven or eight shaving chairs were occupied by gentlemen intent on early morning calls. Shaving is carried in all its accessories to a high degree of publicity, if not of perfection, in America; and as the poorest, or as I may call them without offence, the lowest orders in England have their easy shaving for a penny, so the highest, if there be any in America, submit themselves in public to the inexpensive operations of the negro barber. It must be admitted that the chairs are easy and well-arranged, the fingers nimble, sure, and light; but the affectation of French names, and the corruption of foreign languages, in which the hairdressers and barbers delight, are exceedingly amusing. On my way down a small street near the Capitol, I observed in a shop window, "Rowland's make easier paste," which I attribute to an imperfect view of the etymology of the great "Macassar;" on another occasion, I was asked to try Somebody's "Curious Elison," which I am afraid was an attempt to adapt to a shaving paste, an address not at all suited to profane uses. It appears that the trade of barber is almost the birthright of the free negro or coloured man in the United States. There is a striking exemplification of natural equality in the use of brushes, and the senator flops down in the seat, and has his noble nose seized by the same fingers which the moment before were occupied by the person and chin of an unmistakeable rowdy.

In the midst of the divine calm produced by hard hand rubbing of my head, I was aroused by a stout gentleman who sat in a chair directly opposite. Through the door which opened into the hall of the hotel, one could see the great crowd passing to and fro, thronging the passage as though it had been the entrance to the Forum, or the "Salle de pas perdus." I had observed my friend's eye gazing fixedly through the opening on the outer world. Suddenly, with his face half-covered with lather, and a bib tucked under his chin, he got up from his seat exclaiming, "Senator! Senator! hallo!" and made a dive into the passage—whether he received a stern rebuke, or became aware of his impropriety, I know not, but in an instant he came back again, and submitted quietly, till the work of the barber was completed.

The great employment of four-fifths of the people at Willard's at present seems to be to hunt senators and congress men through the lobbies. Every man is heavy with documents—those which he cannot carry in his pockets and hat, occupy his hands, or are thrust under his arms. In the hall are advertisements announcing that certificates, and letters of testimonial, and such documents, are printed with expedition and neatness. From paper collars, and cards of address to carriages, and new suites of clothes, and long hotel bills, nothing is left untried or uninvigorated. The whole city is placarded with announcements of facilities for assaulting the powers that be, among which must not be forgotten the claims of the "excelsior card-writer," at Willard's, who prepares names, addresses, styles, and titles in superior penmanship. The men who have got places, having been elected by the people, must submit to the people, who think they have established a claim on them by their favours. The majority confer power, but they seem to forget that it is only the minority who can enjoy the first fruits of success. It is as if the whole constituency of Marylebone insisted on getting some office under the Crown the moment a member was returned to Parliament. There are men at Willard's who have come literally thousands of miles to seek for places which can only be theirs for four years, and who with true American facility have abandoned the calling and pursuits of a lifetime for this doubtful canvas; and I was told of one gentleman, who having been informed that he could not get a judgeship, condescended to seek a place in the Post Office, and finally applied to Mr. Chase to be appointed keeper of a "lighthouse," he was not particular where. In the forenoon I drove to the Washington Navy Yard, in company with Lieutenant Nelson and two friends. It is about two miles outside the city, situated on a fork of land projecting between a creek and the Potomac river, which is here three-quarters of a mile broad. If the French had a Navy Yard at Paris it could scarcely be contended that English, Russians, or Austrians would not have been justified in destroying it in case they got possession of the city by force of arms, after a pitched battle fought outside its gates. I confess I would not give much for Deptford or Woolwich if an American fleet succeeded in forcing its way up the Thames; but our American cousins,—a little more than kin and less than kind, who speak with pride of Paul Jones and of their exploits on the Lakes,—affect to regard the burning of the Washington Navy Yard by us, in the last war, as an unpardonable outrage on the law of nations, and an atrocious exercise of power. For all the good it did, for my own part, I think it were as well had it never happened, but no jurisconsult will for a moment deny that it was a legitimate, even if extreme, exercise of a belligerent right in the case of an enemy who did not seek terms from the conqueror; and who, after battle lost, fled and abandoned the property of their state, which might be useful to them in war, to the power of the victor. Notwithstanding all the unreasonableness of the American people in reference to their relations with foreign powers, it is deplorable such scenes should ever have been enacted between members of the human family so closely allied by all that shall make them of the same household.

The Navy Yard is surrounded by high brick walls; in the gateway stood two sentries in dark blue tunics, yellow facings, with eagle buttons, brightly polished arms, and white Berlin gloves, wearing a cap something like a French kepi, all very clean and creditable. Inside are some few trophies of guns taken from us at York Town, and from the Mexicans in the land of Cortez. The interior inclosure is surrounded by red brick houses and stores and magazines, picked out with white stone; and two or three green grass-plots, fenced in by pillars and chains and bordered by trees, give an air of agreeable freshness to the place. Close to the river are the workshops: of course there is smoke and noise of steam and machinery. In a modest office, surrounded by books, papers, drawings, and models, as well as by shell and shot and racks of arms of different descriptions, we found Capt. Dahlgren, the acting superintendent of the yard, and the inventor of the famous gun which bears his name, and is the favourite armament of the American navy. By our own sailors they are irreverently termed "soda-water bottles," owing to their shape. Capt. Dahlgren contends that guns capable of throwing the heaviest shot may be constructed of cast-iron, carefully prepared and moulded so that the greatest thickness of metal may be placed at the points of resistance, at the base of the gun, the muzzle and forward portions being of very moderate thickness.

All inventors, or even adapters of systems, must be earnest self-reliant persons, full of confidence, and, above all, impressive, or they will make little way in the conservative, *status-quo*-loving world. Captain Dahlgren has certainly most of these characteristics, but he has to fight with his navy department, with the army, with boards and with commissioners,—in fact, with all sorts of obstructors. When I was going over the yard, he deplored the parsimony of the department, which refused to yield to his urgent entreaties for additional furnaces to cast guns.

No large guns are cast at Washington. The foundries are only capable of turning out brass field-pieces and boat-guns. Capt. Dahlgren obligingly got one of the latter out to practice for us—a 12-pounder howitzer, which can be carried in a boat, run on land on its carriage, which is provided with wheels, and is so light that the gun can be drawn readily about by the crew. He made some good practice with shrapnel at a target 1200 yards distant, firing so rapidly as to keep three shells in the air at the same time. Compared with our establishments, this dockyard is a mere toy, and but few hands are employed in it. One steam sloop, the "Pawnee," was under the shears, nearly ready for sea: the frame of another was under the building-shed. There are no facilities for making iron ships, or putting on plate-armour here. Everything was shown to us with the utmost frankness. The fuse of the Dahlgren shell is constructed on the *vis inertiæ* principle, and is not unlike that of the Armstrong.

On returning to the hotel, I found a magnificent bouquet of flowers, with a card attached to them, with Mrs. Lincoln's compliments, and another card announcing that she had a "reception" at 3 o'clock. It was rather late before I could get to the White House, and there were only two or three ladies in the drawing-room when I arrived. I was informed afterwards that the attendance was very scanty. The Washington ladies have not yet made up their minds that Mrs. Lincoln is the fashion. They miss their Southern friends, and constantly draw comparisons between them and the vulgar Yankee women and men who are now in power. I do not know enough to say whether the affectation of superiority be justified; but assuredly if New York be Yankee, there is nothing in which it does not far surpass this preposterous capital. The impression of homeliness produced by Mrs. Lincoln on first sight, is not diminished by closer acquaintance. Few women not to the manner born there are, whose heads would not be disordered, and circulation disturbed, by a rapid transition, almost instantaneous, from a condition of obscurity in a country town to be mistress of the White House. Her smiles and her frowns become a matter of consequence to the whole

American world. As the wife of the country lawyer, or even of the congress man, her movements were of no consequence. The journals of Springfield would not have wasted a line upon them. Now, if she but drive down Pennsylvania Avenue, the electric wire thrills the news to every hamlet in the Union which has a newspaper; and fortunate is the correspondent who, in a special despatch, can give authentic particulars of her destination and of her dress. The lady is surrounded by flatterers and intriguers, seeking for influence or such places as she can give. As Selden says, "Those who wish to set a house on fire begin with the thatch."

March 31st, Easter Sunday.—I dined with Lord Lyons and the members of the Legation; the only stranger present being Senator Sumner. Politics were of course eschewed, for Mr. Sumner is Chairman of the Committee on Foreign Relations of the Senate, and Lord Lyons is a very discreet Minister; but still there crept in a word of Pickens and Sumter, and that was all. Mr. Fox, formerly of the United States' Navy, and since that a master of a steamer in the commercial marine, who is related to Mr. Blair, has been sent on some mission to Fort Sumter, and has been allowed to visit Major Anderson by the authorities at Charleston; but it is not known what was the object of his mission. Everywhere there is Secession resignation, in a military sense of the word. The Southern Commissioners declare they will soon retire to Montgomery, and that any attempt to reinforce or supply the forts will be a *casus belli*. There is the utmost anxiety to know what Virginia will do. General Scott belongs to the State, and it is feared he may be shaken if the State goes out. Already the authorities of Richmond have intimated they will not allow the foundry to furnish guns to the seaboard forts, such as Monroe and Norfolk in Virginia. This concession of an autonomy is really a recognition of States' Rights. For if a State can vote itself in or out of the Union, why can it not make war or peace, and accept or refuse the Federal Government? In fact, the Federal system is radically defective against internal convulsion, however excellent it is or may be for purposes of external polity. I walked home with Mr. Sumner to his rooms, and heard some of his views, which were not so sanguine as those of Mr. Seward, and I thought I detected a desire to let the Southern States go out with their slavery if they so desired it. Mr. Chase, by the way, expressed sentiments of the same kind more decidedly the other day.

April 1st.—On Easter Monday, after breakfast with Mr. Olmsted, I drove over to visit Senator Douglas. Originally engaged in some mechanical avocation, by his ability and eloquence he has raised himself to the highest position in the State short of the Presidency, which might have been his but for the extraordinary success of his opponent in a fortuitous suffrage scramble. He is called the Little Giant, being *modo bipedali staturâ*, but his head entitles him to some recognition of intellectual height. His sketch of the causes which have led to the present disruption of parties, and the hazard of civil war, was most vivid and able; and for more than an hour he spoke with a vigour of thought and terseness of phrase which, even on such dreary and uninviting themes as squatter sovereignty and the Kansas-Nebraska question, interested a foreigner in the man and the subject. Although his sympathies seemed to go with the South on the question of slavery and territorial extension, he condemned altogether the attempt to destroy the Union.

April 2nd.—The following day I started early, and performed my pilgrimage to "the shrine of St. Washington," at Mount Vernon, as a foreigner on board called the place. Mr. Bancroft has in his possession a letter of the General's mother, in which she expresses her gratification at his leaving the British army in a manner which implies that he had been either extravagant in his expenses or wild in his manner of living. But if he had any human frailties in after life, they neither offended the morality of his age, or shocked the susceptibility of his countrymen; and from the time that the much maligned and unfortunate Braddock gave scope to his ability, down to his retirement into private life, after a career of singular trials and extraordinary successes, his character acquired each day greater altitude, strength, and lustre. Had his work failed, had the Republic broken up into small anarchical states, we should hear now little of Washington. But the principles of liberty founded in the original Constitution of the colonies themselves, and in no degree derived from or dependent on the revolution, combined with the sufferings of the Old and the bounty of nature in the New World to carry to an unprecedented degree the material prosperity, which Americans have mistaken for good government, and the physical comforts which have made some States in the Union the nearest approach to Utopia. The Federal Government hitherto "let the people alone," and they went on their way singing and praising their Washington as the author of so much greatness and happiness. To doubt his superiority to any man of woman born, is to insult the American people. They are not content with his being great—or even greater than the great: he must be greatest of all;—"first in peace, and first in war." The rest of the world cannot find fault with the assertion, that he is "first in the hearts of his countrymen." But he was not possessed of the highest military qualities, if we are to judge from most of the regular actions, in which the British had the best of it; and the final blow, when Cornwallis surrendered at York Town, was struck by the arm of France, by Rochambeau and the French fleet, rather than by Washington and his Americans. He had all the qualities for the work for which he was designed, and is fairly entitled to the position his countrymen have given him as the immortal czar of the United States. His pictures are visible everywhere—in the humblest inn, in the Minister's bureau, in the millionaire's gallery. There are far more engravings of Washington in America than there are of Napoleon in France, and that is saying a good deal.

What have we here? The steamer, which has been paddling down the gentle current of the Potomac, here a mile or more in breadth, banked in by forest, through which can be seen homesteads and white farm-houses, in the midst of large clearings and corn-fields—has moved in towards a high bluff, covered with trees, on the summit of which is visible the trace of some sort of building—a ruined summer-house, rustic temple—whatever it may be; and the bell on deck begins to toll solemnly, and some of the pilgrims uncover their heads for a moment. The boat stops at a rotten, tumble-down little pier, which leads to a waste of mud, and a path rudely cut through the wilderness of briars on the hill-side. The pilgrims, of whom there are some thirty or forty, of both sexes, mostly belonging to the lower classes of citizens, and comprising a few foreigners like myself, proceed to climb this steep, which seemed in a state of nature covered with primeval forest, and tangled weeds and briars, till the plateau, on which stands the house of Washington and the domestic offices around it, is reached. It is an oblong wooden house, of two stories in height, with a colonnade towards the river face, and a small balcony on the top and on the level of the roof, over which rises a little paltry gazebo. There are two windows, a glass door at one end of the oblong, and a wooden alcove extending towards the slave quarters, which are very small sentry-box huts, that have been recently painted, and stand at right angles to the end of the house, with dog-houses and poultry-hutches attached to them. There is no attempt at neatness or order about the place; though the exterior of the house is undergoing repair, the grass is unkempt, the shrubs untrimmed, —neglect, squalor, and chicken feathers have marked the lawn for their own. The house is in keeping, and threatens to fall to ruin. I entered the door, and found myself in a small hall, stained with tobacco juice. An iron railing ran across the entrance to the stairs. Here stood a man at a gate, who presented a book to the visitors, and pointed out the notice therein, that "no person is permitted to inscribe his name in this book who does not contribute to the Washington Fund, and that any name put down without money would be erased." Notwithstanding the warning, some patriots succeeded in recording their names without any pecuniary mulct, and others did so at a most reasonable rate. When I had contributed in a manner which must have represented an immense amount of Washingtoniolatry, estimated by the standard of the day, I was informed I could not go upstairs, as the rooms above were closed to the public, and thus the most interesting portion of the house was shut from the strangers. The lower rooms presented nothing worthy of notice—some lumbering, dusty, decayed furniture; a broken harpsichord, dust, cobwebs—no remnant of the man himself. But over the door of one room hung the key of the Bastille.* The gardens, too, were tabooed; but through the gate I could see a wilderness of neglected trees and shrubs, not unmingled with a suspicion of a present kitchen-ground. Let us pass to the Tomb, which is some distance from the house, beneath the shade of some fine trees. It is a plain brick mausoleum, with a pointed arch, barred by an iron grating, through which the light penetrates a chamber or small room containing two sarcophagi of stone. Over the arch, on a slab let into the brick, are the words: "Within this enclosure rest the remains of Gen. George Washington." The fallen leaves which had drifted into the chamber rested thickly on the floor, and were piled up on the sarcophagi, and it was difficult to determine which was the hero's grave without the aid of an expert, but there was neither guide nor guardian on the spot. Some four or five gravestones, of various members of the family, stand in the ground outside the little mausoleum. The place was most depressing. One felt angry with a people whose lip service was accompanied by so little of actual respect. The owner of this property, inherited from the "Pater Patriæ," has been abused in good set terms because he asked its value from the country which has been so very mindful of the services of his ancestor, and which is now erecting by slow stages the overgrown Cleopatra's needle that is to be a Washington monument when it is finished. Mr. Everett has been lecturing, the Ladies' Mount Vernon Association has been working, and every one has been adjuring everybody else to give liberally; but the result so lately achieved is by no means worthy of the object. Perhaps the Americans think it is enough to say—"*Si monumentum quæris, circumspice.*" But, at all events, there is a St. Paul's round those words.

On the return of the steamer I visited Fort Washington, which is situated on the left bank of the Potomac. I found everything in a state of neglect—gun-carriages rotten, shot-piles rusty, furnaces tumbling to pieces. The place might be made strong enough on the river front, but the rear is weak, though there is low marshy land at the back. A company of regulars were on duty. The sentries took no precautions against surprise. Twenty determined men, armed with revolvers, could have taken the whole work; and, for all the authorities knew, we might have had that number of Virginians and the famous Ben McCullough himself on board. Afterwards, when I ventured to make a remark to General Scott as to the carelessness of the garrison, he said: "A few weeks ago it might have been taken with a bottle of whiskey. The whole garrison consisted of an old Irish pensioner." Now at this very moment Washington is full of rumours of desperate descents on the capital, and an attack on the President and his Cabinet. The long bridge across the Potomac into Virginia is guarded, and the militia and volunteers of the District of Columbia are to be called out to resist McCullough and his Richmond desperadoes.

April 3rd.—I had an interview with the Southern Commissioners to-day, at their hotel. For more than an hour I heard, from men of position and of different sections in the South, expressions which satisfied me the Union could never be restored, if they truly represented the feelings and opinions of their fellow-citizens. They have the idea they are ministers of a foreign power treating with Yankeedom, and their indignation is moved by the refusal of Government to negotiate with them, armed as they are with full authority to arrange all questions arising out of an amicable separation—such as the adjustment of Federal claims for property, forts, stores, public works, debt, land purchases, and the like. One of the Judges of the Supreme Court of the United States, Mr. Campbell, is their intermediary, and of course it is not known what hopes Mr. Seward has held out to him; but there is some

* Since borrowed, it is supposed, by Mr. Seward, and handed over by him to Mr. Stanton. Lafayette gave it to Washington, he also gave his name to the Fort which has played so conspicuous a part in the war for liberty—"La liberté des deux mondes," might well sigh if he could see his work, and what it has led to.

imputation of Punic faith against the Government on account of recent acts, and there is no doubt the Commissioners hear, as I do, that there are preparations at the Navy Yard and at New York to relieve Sumter, at any rate, with provisions, and that Pickens has actually been reinforced by sea. In the evening I dined at the British Legation, and went over to the house of the Russian minister, M. de Stoeckl, in the evening. The diplomatic body in Washington constitute a small and very agreeable society of their own, in which few Americans mingle except at the receptions and large evening assemblies. As the people now in power are *novi homines*, the wives and daughters of ministers and attachés are deprived of their friends who belonged to the old society in Washington, and who have either gone off to Secession, or sympathise so deeply with the Southern States that it is scarcely becoming to hold very intimate relations with them in the face of Government. From the house of M. de Stoeckl I went to a party at the residence of M. Tassara, the Spanish Minister, where there was a crowd of diplomats, young and old. Diplomatists seldom or never talk politics, and so Pickens and Sumter were unheard of; but it is stated nevertheless that Virginia is on the eve of secession, and will certainly go if the President attempts to use force in relieving and strengthening the Federal forts.

April 4th.—I had a long interview with Mr. Seward to-day at the State Department. He set forth at great length the helpless condition in which the President and the cabinet found themselves when they began the conduct of public affairs at Washington. The last cabinet had tampered with treason, and had contained traitors; a miserable imbecility had encouraged the leaders of the South to mature their plans, and had furnished them with the means of carrying out their design. One Minister had purposely sent away the navy of the United States to distant and scattered stations; another had purposely placed the arms, ordnance, and munitions of war in undue proportions in the Southern States, and had weakened the Federal Government so that they might easily fall into the hands of the traitors and enable them to secure the war *materiel* of the Union; a Minister had stolen the public funds for traitorous purposes—in every port, in every department of the State, at home and abroad, on sea and by land, men were placed who were engaged in this deep conspiracy—and when the voice of the people declared Mr. Lincoln President of the United States, they set to work as one man to destroy the Union under the most flimsy pretexts. The President's duty was clearly defined by the Constitution. He had to guard what he had, and to regain, if possible, what he had lost. He would not consent to any dismemberment of the Union nor to the abandonment of one iota of Federal property—nor could he do so if he desired.

These and many more topics were presented to me to show that the Cabinet were not accountable for the temporising policy of inaction, which was forced upon them by circumstances, and that they would deal vigorously with the Secession movement—as vigorously as Jackson did with nullification in South Carolina, if they had the means. But what could they do when such men as Twiggs surrendered his trust and sacrificed the troops to a crowd of Texans; or when naval and military officers resigned *en masse*, that they might accept service in the rebel forces? All this excitement would come right in a very short time—it was a brief madness, which would pass away when the people had opportunity for reflection. Meantime the danger was that foreign powers would be led to imagine the Federal Government was too weak to defend its rights, and that the attempt to destroy the Union and to set up a Southern Confederacy was successful. In other words, again, Mr. Seward fears that, in this transition state between their forced inaction and the *coup* by which they intend to strike down Secession, Great Britain may recognise the Government established at Montgomery, and is ready, if needs be, to threaten Great Britain with war as the consequence of such recognition. But he certainly assumed the existence of strong Union sentiments in many of the seceded States, as a basis for his remarks, and admitted that it would not become the spirit of the American Government, or of the Federal system, to use armed force in subjugating the Southern States against the will of the majority of the people. Therefore if the majority desire Secession, Mr. Seward would let them have it—but he cannot believe in anything so monstrous, for to him the Federal Government and Constitution, as interpreted by his party, are divine, heaven-born. He is fond of repeating that the Federal Government never yet sacrificed any man's life on account of his political opinions, but if this struggle goes on it will sacrifice thousands — tens of thousands, to the idea of a Federal Union. "Any attempt against us," he said, "would revolt the good men of the South, and arm all men in the North to defend their Government."

But I had seen that day an assemblage of men doing a goose-step march forth dressed in blue tunics and grey trowsers, shakoes and cross-belts, armed with musket and bayonet, cheering and hurrahing in the square before the War Department, who were, I am told, the District of Columbia volunteers and militia. They had indeed been visible in various forms parading, marching, and trumpeting about the town with a poor imitation of French *pas* and *élan*, but they did not, to the eye of a soldier, give any appearance of military efficiency, or to the eye of the anxious statesman any indication of the *animus pugnandi*. Starved, washed-out creatures most of them, interpolated with Irish and flat-footed, stumpy Germans. It was matter for wonderment that the Foreign Minister of a nation which was in such imminent danger in its very capital, and which, with its chief and his cabinet, was almost at the mercy of the enemy, should hold the language I was aware he had transmitted to the most powerful nations of Europe. Was it consciousness of the strength of a great people, who would be united by the first apprehension of foreign interference, or was it the peculiar emptiness of a bombast which is called Buncombe? In all sincerity I think Mr. Seward meant it as it was written.

When I arrived at the hotel, I found our young artist waiting for me, to entreat I would permit him to accompany me to the South. I had been annoyed by a paragraph which had appeared in several papers, to the effect that "The talented young artist, our gifted countryman, Mr. Deodore F. Moses, was about to accompany Mr. &c. &c., in his tour through the South." I had informed the young gentleman that I could not sanction such an announcement, whereupon he assured me he had not in any way authorised it; but having mentioned incidentally to a person connected with the press that he was going to travel southwards with me, the injudicious zeal of his friend had led him to think he would do a service to the youth by making the most of the very trifling circumstance.

I dined with Senator Douglas, where there was a large party, among whom were Mr. Chase, Secretary of the Treasury; Mr. Smith, Secretary of the Interior; Mr. Forsyth, Southern Commissioner; and several members of the Senate and Congress. Mrs. Douglas did the honours of her house with grace and charming goodnature. I observe a great tendency to abstract speculation and theorising among Americans, and their after-dinner conversation is apt to become didactic and sententious. Few men speak better than Senator Douglas: his words are well chosen, the flow of his ideas even and constant, his intellect vigorous, and thoughts well cut, precise, and vigorous—he seems a man of great ambition, and he told me he is engaged in preparing a sort of Zollverein scheme for the North American continent, including Canada, which will fix public attention everywhere, and may lead to a settlement of the Northern and Southern controversies. For his mind, as for that of many Americans, the aristocratic idea embodied in Russia is very seductive; and he dwelt with pleasure on the courtesies he had received at the court of the Czar, implying that he had been treated differently in England, and perhaps France. And yet, had Mr. Douglas become President of the United States, his goodwill towards Great Britain might have been invaluable, and surely it had been cheaply purchased by a little civility and attention to a distinguished citizen and statesman of the Republic. Our Galleos very often care for none of these things.

April 5th.—Dined with the Southern Commissioners and a small party at Gautier's, a French restaurateur in Pennsylvania Avenue. The gentlemen present were, I need not say, all of one way of thinking; but as these leaves will see the light before the civil war is at an end, it is advisable not to give their names, for it would expose persons resident in Washington, who may not be suspected by the Government, to those marks of attention which they have not yet ceased to pay to their political enemies. Although I confess that in my judgment too much stress has been laid in England on the severity with which the Federal authorities have acted towards their political enemies, who were seeking their destruction, it may be candidly admitted, that they have forfeited all claim to the lofty position they once occupied as a Government existing by moral force, and by the consent of the governed, to which Bastilles and *lettrès de cachêt*, arbitrary arrests, and doubtful, illegal, if not altogether unconstitutional, suspension of *habeas corpus* and of trial by jury were unknown.

As Col. Pickett and Mr. Banks are notorious Secessionists, and Mr. Phillips has since gone South, after the arrest of his wife on account of her anti-federal tendencies, it may be permitted to mention that they were among the guests. I had pleasure in making the acquaintance of Governor Roman. Mr. Crawford, his brother commissioner, is a much younger man, of considerably greater energy and determination, but probably of less judgment. The third commissioner, Mr. Forsyth, is fanatical in his opposition to any suggestions of compromise or reconstruction; but, indeed, upon that point, there is little difference of opinion amongst any of the real adherents of the South. Mr. Lincoln they spoke of with contempt; Mr. Seward they evidently regarded as the ablest and most unscrupulous of their enemies; but the tone in which they alluded to the whole of the Northern people indicated the clear conviction that trade, commerce, the pursuit of gain, manufacture, and the base mechanical arts, had so degraded the whole race, they would never attempt to strike a blow in fair fight for what they prized so highly in theory and in words. Whether it be in consequence of some secret influence which slavery has upon the minds of men, or that the aggression of the North upon their institutions has been of a nature to excite the deepest animosity and most vindictive hate, certain it is there is a degree of something like ferocity in the Southern mind towards New England which exceeds belief. I am persuaded that these feelings of contempt are extended towards England. They believe that we, too, have had the canker of peace upon us. One evidence of this, according to Southern men, is the abolition of duelling. This practice, according to them, is highly wholesome and meritorious; and, indeed, it may be admitted that in the state of society which is reported to exist in the Southern States, it is a useful check on such men as it restrained in our own islands in the last century. In the course of conversation, one gentleman remarked, that he considered it disgraceful for any man to take money for the dishonour of his wife or his daughter. "With us," he said, "there is but one mode of dealing known. The man who dares tamper with the honour of a white woman, knows what he has to expect. We shoot him down like a dog, and no jury in the South will ever find any man guilty of murder for punishing such a scoundrel." An argument which can scarcely be alluded to was used by them, to show that these offences in slave States had not the excuse which might be adduced to diminish their gravity when they occurred in States where all the population were white. Indeed, in this, as in some other matters of a similar character, slavery is their *summum bonum* of morality, physical excellence, and social purity. I was inclined to question the correctness of the standard which they had set up, and to inquire whether the virtue which needed this murderous use of the pistol and the dagger to defend it, was not open to some doubt; but I found there was very little sympathy with my views among the company.

The gentlemen at table asserted that the white men in the slave States are physically superior to the men of the free States; and indulged in curious theories in morals and physics to which I was a stranger. Disbelief of anything a Northern man—that is, a Republican—can say, is a fixed principle in their minds. I could not help remarking, when the conversation turned on the duplicity of Mr. Seward, and the wickedness of the Federal Government in refusing to give the assurance Sumter would not be relieved by force of arms, that it must be of very little consequence what promises Mr. Seward made, as, according to them, not the least reliance was to be placed on his word. The notion that the Northern men are cowards is justified by instances in which Congress-men have been insulted by Southern men without calling them out, and Mr. Sumner's case was quoted as the type of the affairs of the kind between the two sides.

I happened to say that I always understood Mr. Sumner had been attacked suddenly and unexpectedly, and struck down before he could rise from his desk to defend himself; whereupon a warm refutation of that version of the story was given, and I was assured that Mr. Brooks, who was a very slight man, and much inferior in height to Mr. Sumner, struck him a slight blow at first, and only inflicted the heavier strokes when irritated by the Senator's cowardly demeanor. In reference to some remark made about the cavaliers and their connection with the South, I reminded the gentlemen that, after all, the descendants of the Puritans were not to be despised in battle; and that the best gentry in England were worsted at last by the train-bands of London, and the "rabbledom" of Cromwell's Independents.

Mr., or Colonel Pickett, is a tall, good-looking man, of pleasant manners, and well educated. But this gentleman was a professed buccaneer, a friend of Walker, the grey-eyed man of destiny —his comrade in his most dangerous razzie. He was a newspaper writer, a soldier, a filibuster; and he now threw himself into the cause of the South with vehemence; it was not difficult to imagine he saw in that cause the realisation of the dreams of empire in the south of the Gulf, and of conquest in the islands of the sea, which have such a fascinating influence over the imagination of a large portion of the American people. He referred to Walker's fate with much bitterness, and insinuated he was betrayed by the British officer who ought to have protected him.

The acts of Mr. Floyd and Mr. Howell Cobb, which must be esteemed of doubtful morality, are here justified by the States' Rights doctrine. If the States had a right to go out, they were quite right in obtaining their quota of the national property which would not have been given to them by the Lincolnites. Therefore, their friends were not to be censured because they had sent arms and money to the South.

Altogether the evening, notwithstanding the occasional warmth of the controversy, was exceedingly instructive; one could understand from the vehemence and force of the speakers the full meaning of the phrase of "firing the Southern heart," so often quoted as an illustration of the peculiar force of political passion to be brought to bear against the Republicans in the Secession contest. Mr. Forsyth struck me as being the most astute, and perhaps most capable, of the gentlemen whose mission to Washington seems likely to be so abortive. His name is historical in America—his father filled high office, and his son has also exercised diplomatic function. Despotisms and Republics of the American model approach each other closely. In Turkey the Pasha unemployed sinks into insignificance, and the son of the Pasha deceased is literally nobody. Mr. Forsyth was not selected as Southern Commissioner on account of the political status acquired by his father; but the position gained by his own ability, as editor of "The Mobile Register," induced the Confederate authorities to select him for the post. It is quite possible to have made a mistake in such matters, but I am almost certain that the coloured waiters who attended us at table looked as sour and discontented as could be, and seemed to give their service with a sort of protest. I am told that the tradespeople of Washington are strongly inclined to favour the Southern side.

April 6th.—To-day I paid a second visit to General Scott, who received me very kindly, and made many inquiries respecting the events in the Crimea and the Indian mutiny and rebellion. He professed to have no apprehension for the safety of the capital; but in reality there are only some 700 or 800 regulars to protect it and the Navy Yard, and two field-batteries, commanded by an officer of very doubtful attachment to the Union. The head of the Navy Yard is openly accused of treasonable sympathies.

Mr. Seward has definitely refused to hold any intercourse whatever with the Southern Commissioners, and they will retire almost immediately from the capital. As matters look very threatening, I must go South and see with my own eyes how affairs stand there, before the two sections come to open rupture. Mr. Seward, the other day, in talking of the South, described them as being in every respect behind the age, with fashions, habits, level of thought, and modes of life, belonging to the worst part of the last century. But still he never has been there himself! The Southern men come up to the Northern cities and springs, but the Northerner rarely travels southwards. Indeed, I am informed, that if he were a well-known Abolitionist, it would not be safe for him to appear in a Southern city. I quite agree with my thoughtful and earnest friend, Olmsted, that the United States can never be considered as a free country till a man can speak as freely in Charleston as he can in New York or Boston.

I dined with Mr. Riggs, the banker, who had an agreeable party to meet me. Mr. Corcoran, his former partner, who was present, erected at his own cost, and presented to the city, a fine building, to be used as an art gallery and museum; but as yet the arts which are to be found in Washington are political and feminine only. Mr. Corcoran has a private gallery of pictures, and a collection, in which is the much-praised Greek Slave of Hiram Powers. The gentry of Columbia are thoroughly Virginian in sentiment, and look rather south than north of the Potomac for political results. The President, I hear this evening, is alarmed lest Virginia should become hostile, and his policy, if he has any, is temporising and timid. It is perfectly wonderful to hear people using the word "Government" at all, as applied to the President and his cabinet—a body which has no power "according to the Constitution" to save the country governed or itself from destruction. In fact, from the circumstances under which the Constitution was framed, it was natural that the principal point kept in view should be the exhibition of a strong front to foreign powers, combined with the least possible amount of constriction on the internal relations of the different States.

In the hotel the roar of office-seekers is unabated. Train after train adds to their numbers. They cumber the passages. The hall is crowded to such a degree that suffocation might describe the degree to which the pressure reaches, were it not that tobacco-smoke invigorates and sustains the constitution. As to the condition of the floor it is beyond description.

CHAPTER VIII.

New York Press—Rumours as to the Southerners—Visit to the Smithsonian Institute—Pythons—Evening at Mr. Seward's—Rough draft of official dispatch to Lord J. Russell—Estimate of its effect in Europe—The attitude of Virginia.

April 7th.—Raining all day, cold and wet. I am tired and weary of this perpetual jabber about Fort Sumter. Men here who know nothing at all of what is passing send letters to the New York papers, which are eagerly read by the people in Washington as soon as the journals reach the city, and then all these vague surmises are taken as gospel, and argued upon as if they were facts. The "Herald" keeps up the courage and spirit of its Southern friends by giving the most florid accounts of their prospects, and making continual attacks on Mr. Lincoln and his Government; but the majority of the New York papers are inclined to resist Secession and aid the Government. I dined with Lord Lyons in the evening, and met Mr. Sumner, Mr. Blackwell, the manager of the Grand Trunk Railway of Canada, his wife, and the members of the Legation. After dinner I visited M. de Stoeckl, the Russian Minister, and M. Tassara, the Minister of Spain, who had small receptions. There were few Americans present. As a rule, the diplomatic circle, which has, by-the-by, no particular centre, radii, or circumference, keeps its members pretty much within itself. The great people here are mostly the representatives of the South American powers, who are on more intimate relations with the native families in Washington than are the transatlantic ministers.

April 8th.—How it does rain! Last night there were torrents of water in the streets literally a foot deep. It still runs in muddy whirling streams through the channels, and the rain is falling incessantly from a dull leaden sky. The air is warm and clammy. There are all kind of rumours abroad, and the barbers' shops shook with "shaves" this morning. Sumter, of course, was the main topic. Some reported that the President had promised the Southern Commissioners, through their friend Mr. Campbell, Judge of the Supreme Court, not to use force in respect to Pickens or Sumter. I wrote to Mr. Seward, to ask him if he could enable me to make any definite statement on these important matters. The Southerners are alarmed at the accounts they have received of great activity and preparations in the Brooklyn and Boston navy yards, and declare that "treachery" is meant. I find myself quite incapable of comprehending their position. How can the United States Government be guilty of "treachery" towards subjects of States which are preparing to assert their independence, unless that Government has been guilty of falsehood or admitted the justice of the decision to which the States had arrived?

As soon as I had finished my letters, I drove over to the Smithsonian Institute, and was most kindly received by Professor Henry, who took me through the library and museum, and introduced me to Professor Baird, who is great in natural history, and more particularly in ornithology. I promised the professors some skins of Himalayan pheasants, as an addition to the collection. In the library we were presented to two very fine and lively rock snakes, or pythons, I believe, some six feet long or more, which moved about with much grace and agility, putting out their forked tongues and hissing sharply when seized by the hand or menaced with a stick. I was told that some persons doubted if serpents hissed; I can answer for it that rock snakes do most audibly. They are not venomous, but their teeth are sharp and needle like. The eye is bright and glistening; the red forked tongue, when protruded, has a rapid vibratory motion, as if it were moved by the muscles which produce the quivering hissing noise. I was much interested by Professor Henry's remarks on the large map of the continent of North America in his study: he pointed out the climatic conditions which determined the use, profits, and necessity of slave labour, and argued that the vast increase of population anticipated in the valley of the Mississippi, and the prophecies of imperial greatness attached to it, were fallacious. He seems to be of opinion that most of the good land of America is already cultivated, and that the crops which it produces tend to exhaust it, so as to compel the cultivators eventually to let it go to fallow or to use manure. The fact is, that the influence of the great mountain-chain in the west, which intercepts all the rain on the Pacific side, causes an immense extent of country between the eastern slope of the chain and the Mississippi, as well as the district west of Minnesota, to be perfectly dry and uninhabitable; and, as far as we know, it is as worthless as a moor, except for the pasturage of wild cattle and the like.

On returning to my hotel, I found a note from Mr. Seward, asking me to visit him at nine o'clock. On going to his house, I was shown to the drawing-room, and found there only the Secretary of State, his son, and Mrs. Seward. I made a *parti carré* for a friendly rubber of whist, and Mr. Seward, who was my partner, talked as he played, so that the score of the game was not favourable. But his talk was very interesting. "All the preparations of which you hear mean this only. The Government, finding the property of the State and Federal forts neglected and left without protection, are determined to take steps to relieve them from that neglect, and to protect them. But we are determined in doing so to make no aggression. The President's inaugural clearly shadows out our policy. We will not go beyond it—we have no intention of doing so—nor will we withdraw from it." After a time Mr. Seward put down his cards, and told his son to go for a portfolio which he would find in a drawer of his table. Mrs. Seward lighted the drop light of the gas, and on her husband's return with the paper left the room. The Secretary then lit his cigar, gave one to me, and proceeded to read slowly and with marked emphasis, a very long, strong, and able dispatch, which he told me was to be read by Mr. Adams, the American minister in London, to Lord John Russell. It struck me that the tone of the paper was hostile, that there was an undercurrent of menace through it, and that it contained insinuations that Great Britain would interfere to split up the Republic, if she could, and was pleased at the prospect of the dangers which threatened it.

At all the stronger passages Mr. Seward raised his voice, and made a pause at their conclusion as if to challenge remark or approval. At length I could not help saying, that the dispatch would, no doubt, have an excellent effect when it came to light in Congress, and that the Americans would think highly of the writer; but I ventured to express an opinion that it would not be quite so acceptable to the Government and people of Great Britain. This Mr. Seward, as an American statesman, had a right to make but a secondary consideration. By affecting to regard Secession as a mere political heresy which can be easily confuted, and by forbidding foreign countries alluding to it, Mr. Seward thinks he can establish the supremacy of his own Government, and at the same time gratify the vanity of the people. Even war with us may not be out of the list of those means which would be available for re-fusing the broken union into a mass once more. However, the Secretary is quite confident in what he calls "re-action." "When the Southern States," he says, "see that we mean them no wrong—that we intend no violence to persons, rights, or things—that the Federal Government seeks only to fulfil obligations imposed on it in respect to the national property, they will see their mistake, and one after another they will come back into the union." Mr. Seward anticipates this process will at once begin, and that Secession will all be done and over in three months—at least, so he says. It was after midnight ere our conversation was over, much of which of course I cannot mention in these pages.

April 9th. — A storm of rain, thunder, and lightning. The streets are converted into water-courses. From the country we hear of bridges washed away by inundations, and roads rendered impassable. Accounts from the South are gloomy, but the *turba Remi* in Willard's are as happy as ever, at least as noisy and as greedy of place. By-the-by, I observe that my prize-fighting friend of the battered nose has been rewarded for his exertions at last. He has been standing drinks all round till he is not able to stand himself, and he has expressed his determination never to forget all the people in the passage. I dined at the Legation in the evening, where there was a small party, and returned to the hotel in torrents of rain.

CHAPTER IX.

Dinner at General Scott's—Anecdotes of General Scott's early life—The startling dispatch—Insecurity of the Capital.

April 10th.—To-day I devoted to packing up such things as I did not require, and sending them to New York. I received a characteristic note from General Scott, asking me to dine with him to-morrow, and apologising for the shortness of his invitation, which arose from his only having just heard that I was about to leave so soon for the South. The General is much admired by his countrymen, though they do not spare some "amiable weaknesses;" but, in my mind, he can only be accused of a little vanity, which is often found in characters of the highest standard. He likes to display his reading, and is troubled with a desire to indulge in fine writing. Some time ago he wrote a long letter to the "National Intelligencer," in which he quoted Shakspeare and Paley to prove that President Buchanan ought to have garrisoned the forts at Charleston and Pensacola, as he advised him to do; and he has been the victim of poetic aspirations. The General's dinner hour was early; and when I arrived at his modest lodgings, which, however, were in the house of a famous French cook, I found a troop of mounted volunteers of the district parading up and down the street. They were not bad of their class, and the horses, though light, were active, hardy, and spirited; but the men put on their uniforms badly, wore long hair, their coats and buttons and boots were unbrushed, and the horses' coats and accoutrements bore evidence of neglect. The General, who wore an undress blue frock-coat, with eagle-covered brass buttons, and velvet collar and cuffs, was with Mr. Seward and Mr. Bates, the Attorney-General, and received me very courteously. He was interrupted by cheering from the soldiers in the street, and by clamours for "General Scott." He moves with difficulty, owing to a fall from his horse, and from the pressure of increasing years; and he evidently would not have gone out if he could have avoided it. But there is no privacy for public men in America.

Out the General went to them, and addressed a few words to his audience in the usual style about "rallying round," and "dying gloriously," and "old flag of our country," and all that kind of thing; after which, the band struck up "Yankee Doodle." Mr. Seward called out "General, make them play the 'Star-Spangled Banner,' and 'Hail Columbia.'" And so I was treated to the strains of the old bacchanalian chant, "When Bibo," &c., which the Americans have impressed to do duty as a national air. Then came an attempt to play "God save the Queen," which I duly appreciated as a compliment; and then followed dinner, which did credit to the cook, and wine, which was most excellent, from France, Spain, and Madeira. The only addition to our party was Major Cullum, aide-de-camp to General Scott, an United States' engineer, educated at West Point. The General underwent a little badinage about the phrase "a hasty plate of soup," which he used in one of his despatches during the Mexican War, and he appealed to me to decide whether it was so erroneous or ridiculous as Mr. Seward insisted. I said I was not a judge, but certainly similar liberal usage of a well-known figure of prosody might be found to justify the phrase. The only attendants at table were the General's English valet and a coloured servant; and the table apparatus which bore such good things was simple and unpretending. Of course the conversation was of a general character, and the General, evidently picking out his words with great precision, took the lead in it, telling anecdotes of great length, graced now and then with episodes, and fortified by such episodes as—"Bear with me, dear sir, for a while, that I may here diverge from the main current of my story, and proceed to mention a curious—" &c., and so on.

To me his conversation was very interesting, particularly that portion which referred to his part in the last war, where he was wounded and taken prisoner. He gave an account of the Battle of Chippewa, which was, he said, fought on true scientific principles; and in the ignorance common to most Englishmen of reverses to their arms, I was injudicious enough, when the battle was at its height, and whole masses of men were moving in battalions and columns over the table, to ask how many men were engaged. The General made the most of his side: "We had, sir, twenty-one hundred and seventy-five men in the field." He told us how, when the British men-of-war provoked general indignation in Virginia by searching American vessels for deserters in the Chesapeake, the State of Virginia organised a volunteer force to guard the shores, and, above all things, to prevent the country people sending down supplies to the vessels, in pursuance of the orders of the Legislature and Governor. Young Scott, then reading for the bar, became corporal of a troop of these patrols. One night, as they were on duty by the banks of the Potomac, they heard a boat with muffled oars coming rapidly down the river, and soon saw her approaching quite close to the shore under cover of the trees. When she was abreast of the troopers, Scott challenged "What boat is that?" "It's His Majesty's ship 'Leopard,' and what the d—— is that to you? Give way, my lads!" "I at once called on him to surrender," said the General, "and giving the word to charge, we dashed into the water. Fortunately, it was not deep, and the midshipman in charge, taken by surprise by a superior force, did not attempt to resist us. We found the boat manned by four sailors, and filled with vegetables and other supplies, and took possession of it; and I believe it is the first instance of a man-of-war's boat being captured by cavalry. The Legislature of Virginia, however, did not approve of the capture, and the officer was given up accordingly.

"Many years afterwards, when I visited Europe, I happened to be dining at the hospitable mansion of Lord Holland, and observed during the banquet that a gentleman at table was scrutinising my countenance in a manner indicative of some special curiosity. Several times, as my eye wandered in his direction, I perceived that he had been continuing his investigations, and at length I rebuked him by a continuous glance. After dinner, this gentleman came round to me and said, 'General Scott, I hope you will pardon my rudeness in staring at you, but the fact is that you bear a most remarkable resemblance to a great overgrown, clumsy, country fellow of the same name, who took me prisoner in my boat when I was a midshipman in the "Chesapeake," at the head of a body of mounted men. He was, I remember quite well, Corporal Scot.' 'That Corporal Scott, sir, and the individual who addresses you, are identical one with the other.' The officer whose acquaintance I thus so auspiciously renewed, was Captain Fox, a relation of Lord Holland, and a post-captain in the British navy."

Whilst he was speaking, a telegraphic dispatch was brought in, which the General perused with evident uneasiness. He apologised to me for reading it by saying the dispatch was from the President on Cabinet business, and then handed it across the table to Mr. Seward. The Secretary read it, and became a little agitated, and raised his eyes inquiringly to the General's face, who only shook his head. Then the paper was given to Mr. Bates, who read it, and gave a grunt, as it were, of surprise. The General took back the paper, read it twice over, and then folded it up and put it in his pocket. "You had better not put it there, General," interposed Mr. Seward; "it will be getting lost, or into some other hands." And so the General seemed to think, for he immediately threw it into the fire, before which certain bottles of claret were gently mellowing.

The communication was evidently of a very unpleasant character. In order to give the Ministers opportunity for a conference, I asked Major Cullum to accompany me into the garden, and lighted a cigar. As I was walking about in the twilight, I observed two figures at the end of the little enclosure, standing as if in concealment close to the wall. Major Cullum said "The men you see are sentries I have thought it expedient to place there for the protection of the General. The villains might assassinate him, and would do it in a moment if they could. He would not hear of a guard, nor anything of the sort, so, without his knowing it, I have sentries posted all round the house all night." This was a curious state of things for the commander of the American army, in the midst of a crowded city, the capital of the free and enlightened Republic, to be placed in! On our return to the sitting-room, the conversation was continued some hour or so longer. I retired with Mr. Seward in his carriage. As we were going up Pennsylvania Avenue—almost lifeless at that time—I asked Mr. Seward whether he felt quite secure against any irruption from Virginia, as it was reported that one Ben McCullough, the famous Texan desperado, had assembled 500 men at Richmond for some daring enterprise: some said to carry off the President, cabinet, and all. He replied that, although the capital was almost defenceless, it must be remembered that the bold bad men who were their enemies were equally unprepared for active measures of aggression.

CHAPTER X.

Preparations for war at Charleston—My own departure for the Southern States—Arrival at Baltimore—Commencement of hostilities at Fort Sumter—Bombardment of the Fort—General feeling as to North and South—Slavery—First impressions of the City of Baltimore—Departure by steamer.

April 12th.—This morning I received an intimation that the Government had resolved on taking decisive steps which would lead to a development of events in the South and test the sincerity of Secession. The Confederate general at Charleston, Beauregard, has sent to the Federal officer in command at Sumter, Major Anderson, to say, that all communication between his garrison and the city must cease; and, at the same time, or probably before it, the Government at Washington informed the Confederate authorities that they intended to forward supplies to Major Anderson, peaceably if permitted, but at all hazards to send them. The Charleston people are manning the batteries they have erected against Sumter, have fired on a vessel under the United

States flag, endeavoring to communicate with the fort, and have called out and organized a large force in the islands opposite the place and in the city of Charleston.

I resolved therefore to start for the Southern States to-day, proceeding by Baltimore to Norfolk instead of going by Richmond, which was cut off by the floods. Before leaving, I visited Lord Lyons, Mr. Seward, the French and Russian Ministers; left cards on the President, Mrs. Lincoln, General Scott, Mr. Douglas, Mr. Sumner, and others. There was no appearance of any excitement in Washington, but Lord Lyons mentioned, as an unusual circumstance, that he had received no telegraphic communication from Mr. Bunch, the British Consul at Charleston. Some ladies said to me that when I came back I would find some nice people at Washington, and that the rail-splitter, his wife, the Sewards, and all the rest of them, would be driven to the place where they ought to be: "Varina Davis is a lady, at all events, not like the other. We can't put up with such people as these!" A naval officer whom I met, told me, "if the Government are really going to try force at Charleston, you'll see they'll be beaten, and we'll have a war between the gentlemen and the Yankee rowdies; if they attempt violence, you know how that will end." The Government are so uneasy that they have put soldiers into the Capitol, and are preparing it for defence.

At 6 P.M. I drove to the Baltimore station in a storm of rain, accompanied by Mr. Warre, of the British Legation. In the train there was a crowd of people, many of them disappointed place-hunters, and much discussion took place respecting the propriety of giving supplies to Sumter by force, the weight of opinion being against the propriety of such a step. The tone in which the President and his cabinet were spoken of was very disrespectful. One big man, in a fur coat, who was sitting near me, said, "Well, darn me if I wouldn't draw a bead on Old Abe, Seward—aye, or General Scott himself, though I've got a perty good thing out of them, if they due try to use their soldiers and sailors to beat down States' Rights. If they want to go they've a right to go." To which many said, "That's so! That's true!"

When we arrived at Baltimore, at 8 P.M., the streets were deep in water. A coachman, seeing I was a stranger, asked me two dollars, or 8*s.* 4*d.*, to drive to the Eutaw House, a quarter of a mile distant; but I was not surprised, as I had paid three-and-a-half and four dollars to go to dinner and return to the hotel in Washington. On my arrival, the landlord, no less a person than a major or colonel, took me aside, and asked me if I had heard the news. "No, what is it?" "The President of the Telegraph Company tells me he has received a message from his clerk at Charleston that the batteries have opened fire on Sumter because the Government has sent down a fleet to force in supplies." The news had, however, spread. The hall and bar of the hotel were full, and I was asked by many people whom I had never seen in my life, what my opinions were as to the authenticity of the rumour. There was nothing surprising in the fact that the Charleston people had resented any attempt to reinforce the forts, as I was aware, from the language of the Southern Commissioners, that they would resist any such attempt to the last, and make it a *casus* and *causa belli*.

April 14.—The Eutaw House is not a very good specimen of an American hotel, but the landlord does his best to make his guests comfortable, when he likes them. The American landlord is a despot who regulates his dominions by ukases affixed to the walls, by certain state departments called "offices" and "bars," and who generally is represented, whilst he is away on some military, political, or commercial undertaking, by a lieutenant; the deputy being, if possible, a greater man than the chief. It requires so much capital to establish a large hotel, that there is little fear of external competition in the towns. And Americans are so gregarious that they will not patronise small establishments.

I was the more complimented by the landlord's attention this morning when he came to the room, and in much excitement informed me the news of Fort Sumter being bombarded by the Charleston batteries was confirmed; "And now," said he, "there's no saying where it will all end."

After breakfast I was visited by some gentlemen of Baltimore, who were highly delighted with the news, and I learned from them there was a probability of their State joining those which had seceded. The whole feeling of the landed and respectable classes is with the South. The dislike to the Federal Government at Washington is largely spiced with personal ridicule and contempt of Mr. Lincoln. Your Marylander is very tenacious about being a gentleman, and what he does not consider gentlemanly is simply unfit for anything, far less for place and authority.

The young draughtsman, of whom I spoke, turned up this morning, having pursued me from Washington. He asked me whether I would still let him accompany me. I observed that I had no objection, but that I could not permit such paragraphs in the papers again, and suggested there would be no difficulty in his travelling by himself, if he pleased. He replied that his former connection with a Black Republican paper might lead to his detention or molestation in the South, but that if he was allowed to come with me, no one would doubt that he was employed by an Illustrated London paper. The young gentleman will certainly never lose anything for the want of asking.

At the black barber's I was meekly interrogated by my attendant as to my belief in the story of the bombardment. He was astonished to find a stranger could think the event was probable. "De gen'lmen of Baltimore will be quite glad ov it. But maybe it'l come bad after all." I discovered my barber had strong ideas that the days of slavery were drawing to an end. "And what will take place then, do you think?" "Wall, sare, 'spose coloured men will be good as white men." That is it. They do not understand what a vast gulf flows between them and the equality of position with the white race which most of those who have aspirations imagine to be meant by emancipation. He said the town slave-owners were very severe and harsh in demanding larger sums than the slaves could earn. The slaves are sent out to do jobs, to stand for hire, to work on the quays and docks. Their earnings go to the master, who punishes them if they do not bring home enough. Sometimes the master is content with a fixed sum, and all over that amount which the slave can get may be retained for his private purposes.

Baltimore looks more ancient and respectable than the towns I have passed through, and the site on which it stands is undulating, so that the houses have not that flatness and uniformity of height which make the streets of New York and Philadelphia resemble those of a toy city magnified. Why Baltimore should be called the "Monumental City" could not be divined by a stranger. He would never think that a great town of 250,000 inhabitants could derive its name from an obelisk cased in white marble to George Washington, even though it be more than 200 feet high, nor from the grotesque column called "Battle Monument," erected to the memory of those who fell in the skirmish outside the city in which the British were repulsed in 1814. I could not procure any guide to the city worth reading, and strolled about at discretion, after a visit to the Maryland Club, of which I was made an honorary member. At dark I started for Norfolk, in the steamer "Georgianna."

CHAPTER XI.

Scenes on board an American steamer—The "Merrimac"—Irish sailors in America—Norfolk—A telegram on Sunday; news from the seat of war—American "chaff" and our Jack Tars.

Sunday, April 14.—A night of disturbed sleep, owing to the ponderous thumping of the walking beam close to my head, the whizzing of steam, and the roaring of the steam-trumpet to warn vessels out of the way—musquitoes, too, had a good deal to say to me in spite of my dirty gauze curtains. Soon after dawn the vessel ran alongside the jetty at Fortress Monroe, and I saw indistinctly the waterface of the work which is in some danger of being attacked, it is said, by the Virginians. There was no flag on the staff above the walls, and the place looked dreary and desolate. It has a fine bastioned profile, with moat and armed lunettes—the casemates were bricked up or occupied by glass windows, and all the guns I could make out were on the parapets. A few soldiers were lounging on the jetty, and after we had discharged a tipsy old officer, a few negroes, and some parcels, the steam-pipe brayed—it does not whistle—again, and we proceeded across the mouth of the channel and James' River towards Elizabeth River, on which stand Portsmouth and Gosport.

Just as I was dressing, the door opened, and a tall, neatly dressed negress came in and asked me for my ticket. She told me she was ticket-collector for the boat, and that she was a slave. The latter intelligence was given without any reluctance or hesitation. On my way to the upper deck I observed the bar was crowded by gentlemen engaged in consuming, or waiting for, cocktails or mint-juleps. The latter, however, could not be had just now in such perfection as usual, owing to the inferior condition of the mint. In the matter of drinks, how hospitable the Americans are! I was asked to take as many as would have rendered me incapable of drinking again; my excuse on the plea of inability to grapple with cocktails and the like before breakfast, was heard with surprise, and I was urgently entreated to abandon so bad a habit.

A clear, fine sun rose from the waters of the bay up into the purest of pure blue skies. On our right lay a low coast fringed with trees, and wooded densely with stunted forest, through which creeks could be seen glinting far through the foliage. Anxious-looking little wooden lighthouses, hard set to preserve their equilibrium in the muddy waters, and bent at various angles, marked the narrow channels to the towns and hamlets on the banks, the principal trade and occupation of which are oyster selling and oyster eating. We are sailing over wondrous deposits and submarine crops of the much-loved bivalve. Wooden houses painted white appear on the shores, and one large building with wings and a central portico surmounted by a belvedere, destined for the reception of the United States' sailors in sickness, is a striking object in the landscape.

The steamer in a few minutes came alongside a dirty, broken down, wooden quay, lined with open booths, on which a small crowd, mostly of negroes, had gathered. Behind the shed there rose tiled and shingled roofs of mean dingy houses, and we could catch glimpses of the line of poor streets, narrow, crooked, ill-paved, surmounted by a few church-steeples, and the large sprawling advertisement-boards of the tobacco-stores and oyster-sellers, which was all we could see of Portsmouth or Gosport. Our vessel was in a narrow creek; at one side was the town—in the centre of the stream the old "Pennsylvania," intended to be of 120 guns, but never commissioned, and used as receiving ship, was anchored—alongside the wall of the Navy Yard below us, lay the "Merrimac," apparently in ordinary. The only man-of-war fit for sea was a curiosity—a stumpy bluff-bowed, Dutch-built-looking sloop, called the "Cumberland." Two or three smaller vessels, dismasted, were below the "Merrimac," and we could just see the building-sheds in which were one or two others, I believe, on the stocks. A fleet of oyster-boats anchored, or in sailless observance of the Sunday, dotted the waters. There was an ancient and fishlike smell about the town worthy of its appearance and of its functions as a seaport. As the vessel came close alongside, there was the usual greeting between friends, and many a cry, "Well, you've heard the news? The Yankees out of Sumter! Isn't it fine?" There were few who did not participate in that sentiment, but there were some who looked black as night and said nothing.

Whilst we were waiting for the steam ferry-boat, which plies to Norfolk at the other side of the creek, to take us over, a man-of-war-boat pulled alongside, and the coxswain, a handsome, fine-looking sailor, came on deck, and, as I happened to be next him, asked me if Captain Blank had come down with us? I replied that I did not know, but that the captain could tell him no doubt. "He?" said the sailor, pointing with great disgust to the skipper of the steamer, "Why he knows nothin' of his passengers, except how many dollars they come to," and started off to prosecute his inquiries among the other passengers. The boat alongside was clean, and was manned by six as stout fellows as ever handled an oar. Two I made sure of were Englishmen, and when the coxswain was retiring from his fruitless search, I asked him where he hailed from. "The Cove of Cork. I was in the navy nine years, but when I got on the West Ingy Station, I heerd how Uncle Sam treated his fellows, and so I joined him." "Cut and run, I suppose?" "Well, not exactly. I got away, sir. Emigrated, you know!" "Are there any other Irishmen or Englishmen on board?" "I should think there was. That man in the bow there is a mate of mine, from the sweet Cove of Cork, Driscoll by name; and there's a Belfast man pulls number two; and the stroke, and the chap that pulls next to him is Englishmen, and fine sailors they are, Bates and Rookey. They were in men-of-war too." "What! five out of seven, British subjects!" "Oh, aye, that is—we onst was—most of us now are 'Mericans, I think. There's plenty more of us aboard the ship."

The steam ferry was a ricketty affair, and combined with the tumble-down sheds and quays to give a poor idea of Norfolk. The infliction of tobacco-juice on board was remarkable. Although it was but seven o'clock every one had his quid in working order, and the air was filled with yellowish-brown rainbows and liquid parabolas, which tumbled in spray or in little flocks of the weed on the foul decks. As it was Sunday, some of the numerous flagstaffs which adorn the houses in both cities displayed the United States' bunting; but nothing could relieve the decayed air of Norfolk. The omnibus which was waiting to receive us must have been the earliest specimen of carriage building in that style on the Continent; and as it lunged and flopped over the prodigious bad pavement, the severe nature of which was aggravated by a street railway, it opened the seams as if it were going to fall into firewood. The shops were all closed, of course; but the houses, wooden and brick, were covered with signs and placards indicative of large trade in tobacco and oysters.

Poor G. P. R. James, who spent many years here, could have scarce caught a novel from such a place, spite of great oysters, famous wild fowl, and the lauded poultry and vegetables which are produced in the surrounding districts. There is not a hill for the traveller to ascend towards the close of a summer's day, nor a moated castle for a thousand miles around. An execrable, tooth-cracking drive ended at last in front of the Atlantic Hotel, where I was doomed to take up my quarters. It is a dilapidated, uncleanly place, with tobacco-stained floor, full of flies and strong odours. The waiters were all slaves: untidy, slip-shod, and careless creatures. I was shut up in a small room, with the usual notice on the door, that the proprietor would not be responsible for anything, and that you were to lock your doors for fear of robbers, and that you must take your meals at certain hours, and other matters of the kind. My *umbra* went over to Gosport to take some sketches, he said; and after a poor meal, in a long room filled with "citizens," all of them discussing Sumter, I went out into the street.

The people, I observe, are of a new and marked type,—very tall, loosely yet powerfully made, with dark complexions, strongly-marked features, prominent noses, large angular mouths in square jaws, deep-seated bright eyes, low, narrow foreheads,—and are all of them much given to ruminate tobacco. The bells of the churches were tolling, and I turned into one; but the heat, great enough outside, soon became nearly intolerable; nor was it rendered more bearable by my proximity to some blacks, who were, I presume, servants or slaves of the great people in the forward pews. The clergyman or minister had got to the Psalms, when a bustle arose near the door which attracted his attention, and caused all to turn round. Several persons were standing up and whispering, whilst others were stealing on tiptoe out of the church. The influence extended itself gradually, and all the men near the doors were leaving rapidly. The minister, obviously interested, continued to read, raising his eyes towards the door. At last the persons near him rose up and walked boldly forth, and I at length followed the example, and getting into the street, saw men running towards the hotel. "What is it?" exclaimed I to one. "Come along, the telegraph's in at the Day Book. The Yankees are whipped!" and so continued. I came at last to a crowd of men, struggling, with their faces toward the wall of a shabby house, increased by fresh arrivals, and diminished by those who, having satisfied their curiosity, came elbowing forth in a state of much excitement, exultation, and perspiration. "It's all right enough!" "Didn't I tell you so?" "Bully for Beauregard and the Palmetto State?" I shoved on, and read at last the programme of the cannonade and bombardment, and of the effects upon the fort, on a dirty piece of yellowish paper on the wall. It was a terrible writing. At all the street corners men were discussing the news with every symptom of joy and gratification. Now I confess I could not share in the excitement at all. The act seemed to me the prelude to certain war.

I walked up the main street, and turned up some of the alleys to have a look at the town, coming out on patches of water and bridges over the creeks, or sandy lanes shaded by trees, and lined here and there by pretty wooden villas, painted in bright colours. Everywhere negroes, male and female, gaudily dressed or in rags; the door-steps of the narrow lanes swarming with infant niggerdom—big-stomached, curve-legged, rugged-headed, and happy—tumbling about dim-eyed toothless hags, or thick-lipped mothers. Not a word were they talking about Sumter. "Any news to-day?" said I to a respectable-looking negro in a blue coat and brass buttons, wonderful hat, and vest of amber silk, check trowsers, and very broken-down shoes. "Well, sare, I tink nothin' much occur. Der hem a fire at Squire Nichol's house last night; leastway so I hear, sare." Squire, let me say parenthetically, is used to designate justices of the peace. Was it a very stupid *poco-curante*, or a very cunning, subtle Sambo?

In my walk I arrived at a small pier, covered with oyster-shells, which projected into the sea. Around it, on both sides, were hosts of schooners and pungys, smaller half-decked boats, waiting for their load of the much-loved fish for Washington, Baltimore, and Richmond. Some brigs and large vessels lay alongside the wharves and large warehouses higher up the creek. Observing a small group at the end of the pier I walked on, and found that they consisted of fifteen or twenty well-dressed mechanical kind of men, busily engaged in "chaffing," as Cockneys would call it, the crew of the man-of-war boat I had seen in the morning. The sailors were stretched on the thwarts, some rather amused, others sullen at the ordeal. "You better just pull down that cussed old rag of yours, and bring your old ship over to the Southern Confederacy. I guess we can take your 'Cumberland' whenever we like! Why don't you go, and touch off your guns at Charleston?" Presently the coxswain came down with a parcel under his arm, and stepped into the boat. "Give way, my lads;" and the oars dipped in the water. When the boat had gone a few yards from the shore, the crowd cried out: "Down with the Yankees! Hurrah for the Southern Confederacy!" and some among them threw oyster-shells at the boat, one of which struck the coxswain on the head. "Back water! Back water all. Hard!" he shouted; and as the boat's stern neared the land, he stood up and made a leap in among the crowd like a tiger. "You cowardly d——d set. Who threw the shells?" No one answered at first, but a little wizened man at last squeaked out: "I guess you'll have shells of another kind if you remain here much longer." The sailor howled with rage: "Why, you poor devils, I'd whip any half dozen of you,—teeth, knives, and all—in five minutes; and my boys there in the boat would clear your whole town. What do you mean by barking at the Stars and Stripes? Do you see that ship?" he shouted, pointing towards the "Cumberland." "Why the lads aboard of her would knock every darned seceder in your State into a cocked hat in a brace of shakes! And now who's coming on?" The invitation was not accepted, and the sailor withdrew, with his angry eyes fixed on the people, who gave him a kind of groan; but there were no oyster shells this time. "In spite of his blowing, I tell yer," said one of them, "there's some good men from old Virginny abo'rd o' that ship that will never fire a shot agin us." "Oh, we'll fix her right enough," remarked another, "when the time comes." I returned to my room, sat down, and wrote for some hours. The dinner in the Atlantic Hotel was of a description to make one wish the desire for food had never been invented. My neighbour said he was not "quite content about this Sumter business. There's nary one killed nor wounded."

Sunday is a very dull day in Norfolk—no mails, no post, no steamers; and, at the best, Norfolk must be dull exceedingly. The superintendent of the Seaboard and Roanoke Railway, having heard that I was about proceeding to Charleston, called upon me to offer every facility in his power. Sent Moses with letters to post-office. At night the musquitoes were very aggressive and successful. This is the first place in which the bedrooms are unprovided with gas. A mutton dip almost made me regret the fact.

CHAPTER XII.

Portsmouth—Railway journey through the forest—The great Dismal Swamp—American newspapers—Cattle on the line—Negro labour—On through the Pine Forest—The Confederate flag—Goldsborough; popular excitement—Weldon—Wilmington—The Vigilance Committee.

Monday, April 15.—Up at dawn. Crossed by ferry to Portsmouth, and arrived at railway station, which was at no place in particular, in a street down which the rails were laid. Mr. Robinson, the superintendent, gave me permission to take a seat in the engine car, to which I mounted accordingly, was duly introduced to, and shook hands with the engineer and the stoker, and took my seat next the boiler. Can any solid reason be given why we should not have those engine sheds or cars in England? They consist of a light frame, placed on the connection of the engine with the tender, and projecting so as to include the end of the boiler and the stoke-hole. They protect the engineer from rain, storm, sun, or dust. Windows at each side afford a clear view in all directions, and the engineer can step out on the engine itself by the doors on the front part of the shed. There is just room for four persons to sit uncomfortably, the persons next the boiler being continually in dread of roasting their legs at the furnace, and those next the tender being in danger of getting logs of wood from it shaken down on their feet. Nevertheless I rarely enjoyed anything more than that trip. It is true one's enjoyment was marred by want of breakfast, for I could not manage the cake of dough and the cup of bitter, sour, greasy nastiness, called coffee, which were presented to me in lieu of that meal this morning.

But the novelty of the scene through which I passed atoned for the small privation. I do not speak of the ragged streets and lines of sheds through which the train passed, with the great bell of the engine tolling as if it were threatening death to the early pigs, cocks, hens, and negroes and dogs which walked between the rails—the latter, by-the-bye, were always the first to leave—the negroes generally divided with the pigs the honour of making the nearest stand to the train—nor do I speak of the miserable suburbs of wooden shanties, nor of the expanse of inundated lands outside the town. Passing all these, we settled down at last to our work: the stoker fired up, the engine rattled along over the rugged lane between the trees which now began to sweep around us from the horizon, where they rose like the bank of a river or the shores of a sea, and presently we plunged into the gloom of the primeval forest, struggling as it were, with the last wave of the deluge.

The railroad, leaving the land, boldly leaped into the air, and was carried on frailest cobweb-seeming tracery of wood far above black waters, from which rose a thick growth and upshooting of black stems of dead trees, mingled with the trunks and branches of others still living, throwing out a most luxuriant vegetation. The trestle-work over which the train was hung, judged by the eye, was of the slightest possible construction. Sometimes one series of trestles was placed above another, so that the cars ran on a level with the tops of the trees; and, looking down, we could see before the train passed the inky surface of the waters, broken into rings and agitated, round the beams of wood. The trees were draped with long creepers and shrouds of Spanish moss, which fell from branch to branch, smothering the leaves in their clammy embrace, or waving in pendulous folds in the air. Cypress, live oak, the dogwood, and pine struggled for life with the water, and about their stems floated balks of timber, waifs and strays carried from the rafts by flood or the forgotten spoils of the lumberer. On these lay tortoises, turtles, and enormous frogs, which lifted their heads with a lazy curiosity when the train rushed by, or flopped into the water as if the sight and noise were too much for their nerves. Once a dark body of greater size plashed into the current which marked the course of a river. "There's many allygaitors come up here at times," said the engineer, in reply to my question; "but I don't take much account of them."

When the trestle-work ceased, the line was continued through the same description of scenery, generally in the midst of water, on high embankments which were continually cut by black rapid streams, crossed by bridges on trestles of great span. The strange tract we are passing through is the "Dismal Swamp," a name which must have but imperfectly expressed its horrors before the railway had traversed its outskirts, and the canal, which is constructed in its midst, left traces of the presence of man in that remnant of the world's exit from the flood. In the centre of this vast desolation there is a large loch, called "Lake Drummond," in the jungle and brakes around which the runaway slaves of the plantations long harboured, and once or twice assembled bands of depredators, which were hunted down, broken up, and destroyed like wild beasts.

Mr. Robinson, a young man some twenty-seven years of age, was an excellent representative of the young American—full of intelligence, well-read, a little romantic in spite of his practical habits and dealings with matters of fact, much attached to the literature, if not to the people, of the old country; and so far satisfied that English engineers knew something of their business, as to be anxious to show that American engineers were not behind them. He asked me about Washington politics with as much interest as if he had never read a newspaper. I made a remark to that effect. "Oh, sir, we can't believe," exclaimed he, "a word we read in our papers. They tell a story one day, to contradict it the next. We never know when to trust them, and that's one reason, I believe, you find us all so anxious to ask questions and get information from gentlemen we meet travelling." Of the future he spoke with apprehension; "but," said he, "I am here representing the interests of a large number of Northern shareholders, and I will do my best for them. If it comes to blows after this, they will lose all, and I must stand by my own friends down South, though I don't belong to it."

So we rattle on, till the scene, at first so attractive, becomes dreary and monotonous, and I tire of looking out for larger turtles or more alligators. The silence of these woods is oppressive. There is no sign of life where the train passes through the water, except among the amphibious creatures. After a time, however, when we draw out of the swamp and get into a dry patch, wild, ragged-looking cattle may be seen staring at us through the trees, or tearing across the rail, and herds of porkers, nearly in the wild-boar stage, scuttle over the open. Then the engineer opens the valve; the sonorous roar of the engine echoes through the woods, and now and then there is a little excitement caused by a race between a pig and the engine, and a piggy is occasionally whipped off his legs by the cow-lifter, and hoisted volatile into the ditch at one side. When a herd of cattle, however, get on the line and show fight, the matter is serious. The steam horn is sounded, the bell rung, and steam is eased off, and every means used to escape collision; for the railway company is obliged to pay the owner for whatever animals the trains kill, and a cow's body on one of these poor rails is an impediment sufficient to throw the engine off, and "send us to immortal smash."

It was long before we saw any workmen or guards on the line; but at one place I got out to look at a shanty of one of the road watchmen. It was a building of logs, some 20ft. long by 12ft. broad, made in the rudest manner, with an earthen roof, and mud stuffed and plastered between the logs to keep out the rain. Although the day was exceedingly hot, there were two logs blazing on the hearth, over which was suspended a pot of potatoes. The air inside was stifling, and the black beams of the roof glistened with a clammy sweat from smoke and unwholesome vapours. There was not an article of furniture, except a big deal chest and a small stool, in the place; a mug and a teacup stood on a rude shelf nailed to the wall. The owner of this establishment, a stout negro, was busily engaged with others in "wooding up" the engine from the pile of cut timber by the roadside. The necessity of stopping caused by the rapid consumption is one of the *désagrémens* of wood fuel. The wood is cut down and stacked on platforms, at certain intervals along the line; and the quantity used is checked off against the company at the rate of so much per cord. The negro was one of many slaves let out to the company. White men would not do the work, or were too expensive; but the overseers and gangsmen were whites. "How can they bear that fire in the hut?" "Well. If you went into it in the very hottest day in summer, you would find the niggers sitting close up to blazing pine logs, and they sleep at night, or by day when they've fed to the full, in the same way." My friend, nevertheless, did not seem to understand that any country could get on without negro labourers.

By degrees we got beyond the swamps, and came upon patches of cleared land—that is, the forest had been cut down, and the only traces left of it were the stumps, some four or five feet high, "snagging" up above the ground; or the trees had been girdled round, so as to kill them, and the black trunks and stiff arms gave an air of meagre melancholy and desertion to the place, which was quite opposite to their real condition. Here it was that the normal forest and swamp had been subjugated by man. Presently we came in sight of a flag fluttering from a lofty pine, which had been stripped of its branches, throwing broad bars of red and white to the air, with a blue square in the upper quarter containing seven stars. "That's our flag," said the engineer, who was a quiet man, much given to turning steam cocks, examining gauges, wiping his hands in fluffy impromptu handkerchiefs, and smoking tobacco—"That's our flag! And long may it wave—o'er the land of the free and the home of the ber-rave!" As we passed, a small crowd of men, women, and children, of all colours, in front of a group of poor broken-down shanties or log huts, cheered—to speak more correctly—whooped and yelled vehemently. The cry was returned by the passengers in the train. "We're all right sort hereabouts," said the engineer. "Hurrah for Jeff Davis!" The right sort were not particularly flourishing in outward aspect, at all events. The women, pale-faced, were tawdry and ragged; the men, yellow, seedy looking. For the first time in the States, I noticed bare-footed people.

Now began another phase of scenery—an interminable pine forest, far as the eye could reach, shutting out the light on each side by a wooden wall. From this forest came the strongest odour of turpentine; presently black streaks of smoke floated out of the wood, and here and there we passed clearer spaces, where in rude-looking furnaces and factories people more squalid and miserable looking than before were preparing pitch, tar, turpentine, resin, and other naval stores, for which this part of North Carolina is famous. The stems of the trees around are marked by white scars, where the tappings for the turpentine take place, and many dead trunks testified how the process ended.

Again, over another log village, a Confederate flag floated in the air; and the people ran out, negroes and all, and cheered as before. The new flag is not so glaring and gaudy as the Stars and Stripes; but, at a distance, when the folds hang together, there is a considerable resemblance in the general effect of the two. If ever there is a real *sentiment du drapeau* got up in the South, it will be difficult indeed for the North to restore the Union. These pieces of coloured bunting seem to twine themselves through heart and brain.

The stations along the roadside now gradually grew in proportion, and instead of a small sentry-box beside a wood-pile, there were three or four wooden houses, a platform, a booking office, an "exchange" or drinking room, and general stores, like the shops of assorted articles in an Irish town. Around these still grew the eternal forest, or patches of cleared land dotted with black stumps. These stations have very grand names, and the stores are dignified by high-sounding titles; nor are "billiard saloons" and "restaurants" wanting. We generally found a group of people waiting at each; and it really was most astonishing to see well-dressed, respectable-looking men and women emerge out of the "dismal swamp," and out of the depths of the forest, with silk parasols and crinoline, bandboxes and portmanteaux, in the most civilised style. There were always some negroes, male and female, in attendance on the voyagers, handling the baggage or the babies, and looking comfortable enough, but not happy. The only evidence of the good spirits and happiness of these people which I saw was on the part of a number of men who were going off from the plantation for the fishing on the coast. They and their wives and sisters, arrayed in their best—which means their brightest, colours—were grinning from ear to ear as they bade good-bye. The negro likes the mild excitement of sea fishing, and in pursuit of it he feels for the moment free.

At Goldsborough, which is the first place of importance on the line, the wave of the secession tide struck us in full career. The station, the hotels, the street through which the rail ran was filled with an excited mob, all carrying arms, with signs here and there of a desire to get up some kind of uniform—flushed faces, wild eyes, screaming mouths, hurrahing for "Jeff Davis" and "the Southern Confederacy," so that the yells overpowered the discordant bands which were busy with "Dixie's Land." Here was the true revolutionary furor in full sway. The men hectored, swore, cheered, and slapped each other on the backs; the women, in their best, waved handkerchiefs and flung down garlands from the windows. All was noise, dust, and patriotism.

It was a strange sight and a wonderful event at which we were assisting. These men were a levy of the people of North Carolina called out by the Governor of the State for the purpose of seizing upon forts Caswell and Macon, belonging to the Federal Government, and left unprotected and undefended. The enthusiasm of the "citizens" was unbounded, nor was it quite free from a taint of alcohol. Many of the Volunteers had flint firelocks, only a few had rifles. All kinds of head-dress were visible, and caps, belts and pouches of infinite variety. A man in a large wide-awake, with a cock's feather in it, a blue frockcoat, with a red sash and a pair of cotton trowsers thrust into his boots, came out of Griswold's hotel with a sword under his arm, and an article, which might have been a napkin of long service, in one hand. He waved the article enthusiastically, swaying to and fro on his legs, and ejaculating "H'ra for Jeff Dav's—H'ra for S'thern E'r'rights!" and tottered over to the carriage through the crowd amid the violent vibration of all the ladies' handkerchiefs in the balcony. Just as he got into the train, a man in uniform dashed after him, and caught him by the elbow, exclaiming, "Them's not the cars, General! The cars this way, General!" The military dignitary, however, felt that if he permitted such liberties in the hour of victory he was degraded for ever, so, screwing up his lips and looking grave and grand, he proceeded as follows: "Sergeant, you go be ——. I say these are my cars! They're *all* my cars! I'll send them where I please—to —— if I like, sir. They shall go where I please—to New York, sir, or New Orleans, sir! And —— sir, I'll arrest you." This famous idea distracted the General's attention from his project of entering the train, and muttering, "I'll arrest you," he tacked backwards and forwards to the hotel again.

As the train started on its journey, there was renewed yelling, which split the car—a savage cry many notes higher than the most ringing cheer. At the wayside inn, where we dined—*pièce de résistance* being pig—the attendants, comely, well-dressed, clean negresses, were slaves—"worth a thousand dollars each." I am not favourably impressed by either the food or the mode of living, or the manners of the company. One man made very coarse jokes about "Abe Lincoln" and "negro wenches," which nothing but extreme party passion and bad taste could tolerate. Several of the passengers had been clerks in Government offices at Washington, and had been dismissed because they would not take the oath of allegiance. They were hurrying off full of zeal and patriotism to tender their services to the Montgomery Government.

* * * * *

I had been the object of many attentions and civilities from gentlemen in the train during my journey. One of them, who told me he was a municipal dignitary of Weldon, having exhausted all the inducements that he could think of to induce me to spend some time there, at last, in desperation, said he would be happy to show me "the antiquities of the place." Weldon is a recent uprising in wood and log houses from the swamps, and it would puzzle the archæologists of the world to find anything antique about it.

At nightfall the train stopped at Wilmington, and I was shot out on a platform under a shed, to do the best I could. In a long, lofty, and comfortless room, like a barn, which abutted on the platform, there was a table covered with a dirty cloth, on which lay little dishes of pickles, fish, meat, and potatoes, at which were seated some of our fellow-passengers. The equality of all men is painfully illustrated when your neighbour at table eats with his knife, dips the end of it into the salt, and disregards the object and end of napkins. But it is carried to a more disagreeable extent when it is held to mean that any man who comes to an inn has a right to share your bed. I asked for a room, but I was told that there were so many people moving about just now that it was not possible to give me one to myself; but at last I made a bargain for exclusive possession. When the next train came in, however, the woman very coolly inquired whether I had any objection to allow a passenger to divide my bed, and seemed very much displeased at my refusal; and I perceived three big-bearded men snoring asleep in one bed in the next room to me as I passed through the passage to the dining-room.

The "artist" Moses, who had gone with my letter to the post, returned, after a long absence, pale and agitated. He said he had been pounced upon by the Vigilance Committee, who were rather drunk, and very inquisitive. They were haunting the precincts of the Post-office and the railway station, to detect Lincolnites and Abolitionists, and were obliged to keep themselves wide awake by frequent visits to the adjacent bars, and he had with difficulty dissuaded them from paying me a visit. They cross-examined him respecting my opinion of secession, and desired to have an audience with me in order to give me any information which might be required. I cannot say what reply was given to their questioning; but I certainly refused to have any interview with the Vigilance Committee of Wilmington, and was glad they did not disturb me. Rest, however, there was little or none. I might have as well slept on the platform of the railway station outside. Trains coming in and going out shook the room and the bed on which I lay, and engines snorted, puffed, roared, whistled, and rang bells close to my keyhole.

CHAPTER XIII.

Sketches round Wilmington—Public opinion—Approach to Charleston and Fort Sumter—Introduction to General Beauregard—Ex-Governor Manning—Conversation on the chances of the war—"King Cotton" and England—Visit to Fort Sumter—Market-place at Charleston.

Early next morning, soon after dawn, I crossed the Cape Fear River, on which Wilmington is situated, by a steam ferry-boat. On the quay lay quantities of shot and shell. "How came these here?" I inquired. "They're anti-abolition pills," said my neighbour; "they've been waiting here for two months back, but now that Sumter's taken, I guess they won't be wanted." To my mind, the conclusion was by no means legitimate. From the small glance I had of Wilmington, with its fleet of schooners and brigs crowding the broad and rapid river, I should think it was a thriving place. Confederate flags waved over the public buildings, and I was informed that the Forts had been seized without opposition or difficulty. I can see no sign here of the "affection to the Union," which, according to Mr. Seward, underlies all "secession proclivities."

As we traversed the flat and uninteresting country, through which the rail passes, Confederate flags and sentiments greeted us everywhere; men and women repeated the national cry; at every station militia men and volunteers were waiting for the train, and the everlasting word "Sumter" ran through all the conversation in the cars.

The Carolinians are capable of turning out a fair force of cavalry. At each stopping-place I observed saddle-horses tethered under the trees, and light driving vehicles, drawn by wiry muscular animals, not remarkable for size, but strong-looking and active. Some farmers in blue jackets, and yellow braid and facings, handed round their swords to be admired by the company. A few blades had flashed in obscure Mexican skirmishes—one, however, had been borne against "the Britishers." I inquired of a fine, tall, fair-haired young fellow whom they expected to fight. "That's more than I can tell," quoth he. "The Yankees ain't such cussed fools as to think they can come here and whip us, let alone the British." "Why, what have the British got to do with it?" "They are bound to take our part: if they don't, we'll just give them a hint about cotton, and that will set matters right." This was said very much with the air of a man who knows what he is talking about, and who was quite satisfied "he had you there." I found it was still displeasing to most people, particularly one or two of the fair sex, that more Yankees were not killed at Sumter. All the people who addressed me prefixed my name, which they soon found out, by "Major" or "Colonel"—"Captain" is very low, almost indicative of contempt. The conductor who took our tickets was called "Captain."

At the Peedee river the rail is carried over marsh and stream on trestle work for two miles. "This is the kind of country we'll catch the Yankees in, if they come to invade us. They'll have some pretty tall swimming, and get knocked on the head, if ever they gets to land. I wish there was ten thousand of the cusses in it this minute." At Nichol's station on the frontiers of South Carolina, our baggage was regularly examined at the Custom House, but I did not see any one pay duties. As the train approached the level and marshy land near Charleston, the square block of Fort Sumter was seen rising above the water with the "stars and bars" flying over it, and the spectacle created great enthusiasm among the passengers. The smoke was still rising from an angle of the walls. Outside the village-like suburbs of the city a regiment was marching for old Virginny amid the cheers of the people—cavalry were picketed in the fields and gardens—tents and men were visible in the byways.

It was nearly dark when we reached the station. I was recommended to go to the Mills House, and on arriving there found Mr. Ward, whom I. had already met in New York and Washington, and who gave me an account of the bombardment and surrender of the fort. The hotel was full of notabilities. I was introduced to ex-Governor Manning, Senator Chesnut, Hon. Porcher Miles, on the staff of General Beauregard, and to Colonel Lucas, aide-de-camp to Governor Pickens. I was taken after dinner and introduced to General Beauregard, who was engaged, late as it was, in his room at the Head Quarters writing despatches. The General is a small, compact man, about thirty-six years of age, with a quick and intelligent eye and action, and a good deal of the Frenchman in his manner and look. He received me in the most cordial manner, and introduced me to his engineer officer, Major Whiting, whom he assigned to lead me over the works next day.

After some general conversation I took my leave; but before I went, the General said, "You shall go everywhere and see everything; we rely on your discretion, and knowledge of what is fair in dealing with what you see. Of course you don't expect to find regular soldiers in our camps or very scientific works." I answered the General, that he might rely on my making no improper use of what I saw in this country, but, "unless you tell me to the contrary, I shall write an account of all I see to the other side of the water, and if, when it comes back, there are things you would rather not have known, you must not blame me." He smiled, and said, "I dare say we'll have great changes by that time."

That night I sat in the Charleston club with John Manning. Who that has ever met him can be indifferent to the charms of manner and of personal appearance, which render the ex-Governor of the State so attractive? There were others present, senators or congressmen, like Mr. Chesnut, and Mr. Porcher Miles. We talked long, and at last angrily, as might be between friends, of political affairs.

I own it was a little irritating to me to hear men indulge in extravagant broad menace and rhodomontade, such as came from their lips. "They would welcome the world in arms with hospitable hands to bloody graves." "They never could be conquered." "Creation could not do it," and so on. I was obliged to handle the question quietly at first—to ask them "if they admitted the French were a brave and warlike people?" "Yes, certainly." "Do you think you could better defend yourselves against invasion than the people of France?" "Well, no; but we'd make it a pretty hard business for the Yankees." "Suppose the Yankees, as you call them, come with such preponderance of men and matériel, that they are three to your one, will you not be forced to submit?" "Never." "Then either you are braver, better disciplined, more warlike than the people and soldiers of France, or you alone, of all the nations in the world, possess the means of resisting physical laws which prevail in war, as in other affairs of life." "No. The Yankees are cowardly rascals. We have proved it by kicking and cuffing them till we are tired of it; besides, we know John Bull very well. He will make a great fuss about non-interference at first, but when he begins to want cotton he'll come off his perch." I found this was the fixed idea everywhere. The doctrine of "cotton is king,"—to us who have not much considered the question a grievous delusion or an unmeaning babble—to them is a lively all-powerful faith without distracting heresies or schisms. They have in it enunciated their full belief, and indeed there is some truth in it, in so far as we year after year, by the stimulants of coal, capital, and machinery, have been working up a manufacture on which four or five millions of our population depend for bread and life, which cannot be carried on without the assistance of a nation, that may at any time refuse us an adequate supply, or be cut off from giving it by war.

Political economy, we are well aware, is a fine science, but its followers are capable of tremendous absurdities in practice. The dependence of such a large proportion of the English people on this sole article of American cotton is fraught with the utmost danger to our honour and to our prosperity. Here were these Southern gentlemen exulting in their power to control the policy of Great Britain, and it was small consolation to me to assure them they were mistaken; in case we did not act as they anticipated, it could not be denied Great Britain would plunge an immense proportion of her people—a nation of manufacturers—into pauperism, which must leave them dependent on the national funds, or more properly on the property and accumulated capital of the district.

About 8.30 P.M., a deep bell began to toll. "What is that?" "It's for all the coloured people to clear out of the streets and go home. The guards will arrest any who are found out without passes in half an hour." There was much noise in the streets, drums beating, men cheering, and marching, and the hotel is crammed full with soldiers.

April 17th.—The streets of Charleston present some such aspect as those of Paris in the last revolution. Crowds of armed men singing and promenading the streets. The battle-blood running through their veins—that hot oxygen which is called "the flush of victory" on the cheek; restaurants full, revelling in bar-rooms, club-rooms crowded, orgies and carousings in tavern or private house, in tap-room, from cabaret—down narrow alleys, in the broad highway. Sumter has set them distraught; never was such a victory; never such brave lads; never such a fight. There are pamphlets already full of the incident. It is a bloodless Waterloo or Solferino.

After breakfast I went down to the quay, with a party of the General's staff, to visit Fort Sumter. The senators and governors turned soldiers wore blue military caps, with "palmetto" trees embroidered thereon; blue frockcoats, with upright collars, and shoulder-straps edged with lace, and marked with two silver bars, to designate their rank of captain; gilt buttons, with the palmetto in relief; blue trowsers, with a gold-lace cord, and brass spurs—no straps. The day was sweltering, but a strong breeze blew in the harbour, and puffed the dust of Charleston, coating our clothes, and filling our eyes with powder. The streets were crowded with lanky lads, clanking spurs, and sabres, with awkward squads marching to and fro, with drummers beating calls, and ruffles, and points of war; around them groups of grinning negroes delighted with the glare and glitter, a holiday, and a new idea for them—secession flags waving out of all the windows—little Irish boys shouting out, "Battle of Fort Sumter! New edishun!"—As we walked towards the quay, where the steamer was lying, numerous traces of the unsettled state of men's minds broke out in the hurried conversations of the various friends who stopped to speak for a few moments. "Well, governor, the old Union is gone at last!" "Have you heard what Abe is going to do?" "I don't think Beauregard will have much more fighting for it. What do you think?" And so on. Our little Creole friend, by the bye, is popular beyond description. There are all kinds of doggerel rhymes in his honour—one with a refrain—

"With cannon and musket, with shell and petard,
We salute the North with our Beau-regard"—

is much in favour.

We passed through the market, where the stalls are kept by fat negresses and old "unkeys." There is a sort of vulture or buzzard here, much encouraged as scavengers, and—but all the world has heard of the Charleston vultures—so we will leave them to their garbage. Near the quay, where the steamer was lying, there is a very fine building in white marble, which attracted our notice. It was unfinished, and immense blocks of the glistening stone destined for its completion lay on the ground. "What is that?" I inquired. "Why, it's a custom-house Uncle Sam was building for our benefit, but I don't think he'll ever raise a cent for his treasury out of it." "Will you complete it?" "I should think not. We'll lay on few duties; and what we want is free-trade, and no duties at all, except for public purposes. The Yankees have plundered us with their custom-houses and duties long enough." An old gentleman here stopped us. "You will do me the greatest favour," he said to one of our party who knew him, "if you will get me something to do for our glorious cause. Old as I am, I can carry a musket—not far, to be sure, but I can kill a Yankee if he comes near." When he had gone, my friend told me the speaker was a man of fortune, two of whose sons were in camp at Morris' Island, but that he was suspected of Union sentiments, as he had a Northern wife, and hence his extreme vehemence and devotion.

CHAPTER XIV.

Southern volunteers—Unpopularity of the press—Charleston—Fort Sumter—Morris' Island—Anti-union enthusiasm—Anecdote of Colonel Wigfall—Interior view of the fort—North versus South.

THERE was a large crowd around the pier staring at the men in uniform on the boat, which was filled with bales of goods, commissariat stores, trusses of hay, and hampers, supplies for the volunteer army on Morris' Island. I was amused by the names of the various corps, "Tigers," "Lions," "Scorpions," "Palmetto Eagles," "Guards," of Pickens, Sumter, Marion, and of various other denominations, painted on the boxes. The original formation of these volunteers is in companies, and they know nothing of battalions or regiments. The tendency in volunteer outbursts is sometimes to gratify the greatest vanity of the greatest number. These companies do not muster more than fifty or sixty strong. Some were "dandies," and "swells," and affected to look down on their neighbours and comrades. Major Whiting told me there was difficulty in getting them to obey orders at first, as each man had an idea that he was as good an engineer as any body else, "and a good deal better, if it came to that." It was easy to perceive it was the old story of volunteer and regular in this little army.

As we got on deck, the major saw a number of rough, long-haired-looking fellows in coarse gray tunics, with pewter buttons and worsted braid lying on the hay-bales smoking their cigars. "Gentlemen," quoth he, very courteously, "you'll oblige me by not smoking over the hay. There's powder below." "I don't believe we're going to burn the hay this time, kernel," was the reply, "and anyway, we'll put it out afore it reaches the 'bustibles," and they went on smoking. The major grumbled, and worse, and drew off.

Among the passengers were some brethren of mine belonging to the New York and local papers. I saw a short time afterward a description of the trip by one of these gentlemen, in which he described it as an affair got up specially for himself, probably in order to avenge himself on his military persecutors, for he had complained to me the evening before that the chief of General Beauregard's staff told him to go to ——, when he applied to head-quarters for some information. I found, from the tone and looks of my friends, that these literary gentlemen were received with great disfavour, and Major Whiting, who is a bibliomaniac, and has a very great liking for the best English writers, could not conceal his repugnance and antipathy to my unfortunate confrères. "If I had my way, I would fling them into the water; but the General has given them orders to come on board. It is these fellows who have brought all this trouble on our country."

The traces of dislike of the freedom of the press, which I, to my astonishment, discovered in the North, are broader and deeper in the South, and they are not accompanied by the signs of dread of its power which exist in New York, where men speak of the chiefs of the most notorious journals very much as people in Italian cities of past time might have talked of the most infamous bravo or the chief of some band of assassins. Whiting comforted himself by the reflection that they would soon have their fingers in a vice, and then pulling out a ragged little sheet, turned suddenly on the representative thereof, and proceeded to give the most unqualified contradiction to most of the statements contained in "the full and accurate particulars of the Bombardment and Fall of Fort Sumter," in the said journal, which the person in question listened to with becoming meekness and contrition. "If I knew who wrote it," said the major, "I'd make him eat it."

I was presented to many judges, colonels, and others of the mass of society on board, and, "after compliments," as the Orientals say, I was generally asked, in the first place, what I thought of the capture of Sumter, and in the second, what England would do when the news reached the other side. Already the Carolinians regard the Northern States as an alien and detested enemy, and entertain, or profess, an immense affection for Great Britain.

When we had shipped all our passengers, nine-tenths of them in uniform, and a larger proportion engaged in chewing, the whistle blew, and the steamer sidled off from the quay into the yellowish muddy water of the Ashley River, which is a creek from the sea, with a streamlet running into the head waters some distance up.

The shore opposite Charleston is more than a mile distant, and is low and sandy, covered here and there with brilliant patches of vegetation, and long lines of trees. It is cut up with creeks, which divide it into islands, so that passages out to sea exist between some of them for light craft, though the navigation is perplexed and difficult. The city lies on a spur or promontory between the Ashley and the Cooper rivers, and the land behind it is divided in the same manner by similar creeks, and is sandy and light, bearing, nevertheless, very fine crops, and trees of magnificent vegetation. The steeples, the domes of public buildings, the rows of massive warehouses and cotton stores on the wharfs, and the bright colours of the houses, render the appearance of Charleston, as seen from the river front, rather imposing. From the mastheads of the few large vessels in harbour floated the Confederate flag. Looking to our right, the same standard was visible, waving on the low, white parapets of the earth-works which had been engaged in reducing Sumter.

That much-talked-of fortress lay some two miles ahead of us now, rising up out of the water near the middle of the passage out to sea between James' Island and Sullivan's Island. It struck me at first as being like one of the smaller forts off Cronstadt, but a closer inspection very much diminished its importance; the material is brick, not stone, and the size of the place is exaggerated by the low back ground, and by contrast with the sea-line. The land contracts on both sides opposite the fort, a projection of Morris' Island, called "Cumming's Point," running out on the left. There is a similar promontory from Sullivan's Island, on which is erected Fort Moultrie, on the right from the sea entrance. Castle Pinckney, which stands on a small island at the exit of the Cooper River, is a place of no importance, and it was too far from Sumter to take any share in the bombardment: the same remarks apply to Fort Johnson on James' Island, on the right bank of the Ashley River below Charleston. The works which did the mischief were the batteries of sand on Morris' Island, at Cumming's Point, and Fort Moultrie. The floating battery, covered with railroad-iron, lay a long way off, and could not have contributed much to the result.

As we approached Morris' Island, which is an accumulation of sand covered with mounds of the same material, on which there is a scanty vegetation alternating with salt-water marshes, we could perceive a few tents in the distance among the sand-hills. The sand-bag batteries, and an ugly black parapet, with guns peering through port-holes as if from a ship's side, lay before us. Around them men were swarming like ants, and a crowd in uniform were gathered on the beach to receive us as we landed from the boat of the steamer, all eager for news, and provisions, and newspapers, of which an immense flight immediately fell upon them. A guard with bayonets crossed in a very odd sort of manner, prevented any unauthorised persons from landing. They wore the universal coarse gray jacket and trousers, with worsted braid and yellow facings, uncouth caps, lead buttons stamped with the palmetto-tree. Their unbronzed firelocks were covered with rust. The soldiers lounging about were mostly tall, well-grown men, young and old, some with the air of gentlemen; others coarse, long-haired fellows, without any semblance of military bearing, but full of fight, and burning with enthusiasm, not unaided, in some instances, by coarser stimulus.

The day was exceedingly warm and unpleasant, the hot wind blew the fine white sand into our faces, and wafted it in minute clouds inside eyelids, nostrils, and clothing; but it was necessary to visit the batteries, so on we trudged into one and out of another, walked up parapets, examined profiles, looked along guns, and did everything that could be required of us. The result of the examination was to establish in my mind the conviction, that if the commander of Sumter had been allowed to open his guns on the island, the first time he saw an indication of throwing up a battery against him, he could have saved his fort. Moultrie, in its original state, on the opposite side, could have been readily demolished by Sumter. The design of the works was better than their execution—the sand-bags were rotten, the sand not properly rivetted or banked up, and the traverses imperfectly constructed. The barbette guns of the fort looked into many of the embrasures, and commanded them.

The whole of the island was full of life and excitement. Officers were galloping about as if on a field-day or in action. Commissariat carts were toiling to and fro between the beach and the camps, and sounds of laughter and revelling came from the tents. These were pitched without order, and were of all shapes, hues, and sizes, many being disfigured by rude charcoal drawings outside, and inscriptions such as "The Live Tigers," "Rattlesnake's-hole," "Yankee Smashers," &c. The vicinity of the camps was in an intolerable state, and on calling the attention of the medical officer who was with me, to the danger arising from such a condition of things, he said with a sigh, "I know it all. But we can do nothing. Remember they're all volunteers, and do just as they please."

In every tent was hospitality, and a hearty welcome to all comers. Cases of champagne and claret, French pâtés, and the like, were piled outside the canvas walls, when there was no room for them inside. In the middle of these excited gatherings I felt like a man in the full possession of his senses coming in late to a wine party. "Won't you drink with me, sir, to the—(something awful)—of Lincoln and all Yankees?" "No! if you'll be good enough to excuse me." "Well, I think you're the only Englishman who won't." Our Carolinians are very fine fellows, but a little given to the Bobadil style—hectoring after a cavalier fashion, which they fondly believe to be theirs by hereditary right. They assume that the British crown rests on a cotton bale, as the Lord Chancellor sits on a pack of wool.

In one long tent there was a party of roystering young men, opening claret, and mixing "cup" in large buckets; whilst others were helping the servants to set out a table for a banquet to one of their generals. Such heat, tobacco-smoke, clamour, toasts, drinking, hand-shaking, vows of friendship! Many were the excuses made for the more demonstrative of the Edonian youths by their friends. "Tom is a little cut, sir; but he's a splendid fellow—he's worth half a million of dollars." This reference to a money standard of value was not unusual or perhaps unnatural, but it was made repeatedly; and I was told wonderful tales of the riches of men who were lounging round, dressed as privates, some of whom at that season, in years gone by, were looked for at the watering-places as the great lions of American fashion. But Secession is the fashion here. Young ladies sing for it; old ladies pray for it; young men are dying to fight for it; old men are ready to demonstrate it. The founder of the school was St. Calhoun. Here his pupils carry out their teaching in thunder and fire. States' Rights are displayed after its legitimate teaching, and the Palmetto flag and the red bars of the Confederacy are its exposition. The utter contempt and loathing for the venerated Stars and Stripes, the abhorrence of the very words United States, the intense hatred of the Yankee on the part of these people, cannot be conceived by any one who has not seen them. I am more satisfied than ever that the Union can never be restored as it was, and that it has gone to pieces, never to be put together again, in the old shape, at all events by any power on earth.

After a long and tiresome promenade in the dust, heat, and fine sand, through the tents, our party returned to the beach, where we took boat, and pushed off for Fort Sumter. The Confederate flag rose above the walls. On near approach the marks of the shot against the *pain coupé*, and the embrasures near the salient were visible enough; but the damage done to the hard brickwork was trifling, except at the angles: the edges of the parapets were ragged and pockmarked, and the quay wall was rifted here and there by shot; but no injury of a kind to render the work untenable could be made out. The greatest damage inflicted was, no doubt, the burning of the barracks, which were culpably erected inside the fort, close to the flank wall facing Cumming's Point.

As the boat touched the quay of the fort, a tall, powerful-looking man came through the shattered gateway, and with uneven steps strode over the rubbish towards a skiff which was waiting to receive him, and into which he jumped and rowed off. Recognising one of my companions as he passed our boat, he suddenly stood up, and with a leap and a scramble tumbled in among us, to the imminent danger of upsetting the party. Our new friend was dressed in the blue frockcoat of a civilian, round which he had tied a red silk sash—his waistbelt supported a straight sword, something like those worn with Court dress. His muscular neck was surrounded with a loosely-fastened silk handkerchief; and wild masses of black hair, tinged with grey, fell from under a civilian's hat over his collar; his unstrapped trousers were gathered up high on his legs, displaying ample boots, garnished with formidable brass spurs. But his face was not one to be forgotten—a straight, broad brow, from which the hair rose up like the vegetation on a river bank, beetling black eyebrows—a mouth coarse and grim, yet full of power, a square jaw—a thick argumentative nose—a new growth of scrubby beard and moustache—these were relieved by eyes of wonderful depth and light, such as I never saw before but in the head of a wild beast. If you look some day when the sun is not too bright into the eye of the Bengal tiger, in the Regent's Park, as the keeper is coming round, you will form some notion of the expression I mean. It was flashing, fierce, yet calm—with a well of fire burning behind and spouting through it, an eye pitiless in anger, which now and then sought to conceal its expression beneath half-closed lids, and then burst out with an angry glare, as if disdaining concealment.

This was none other than Louis T. Wigfall, Colonel (then of his own creation) in the Confederate army, and Senator from Texas in the United States—a good type of the men whom the institutions of the country produce or throw off—a remarkable man, noted for his ready, natural eloquence; his exceeding ability as a quick, bitter debater; the acerbity of his taunts; and his readiness for personal encounter. To the last he stood in his place in the Senate at Washington, when nearly every other Southern man had seceded, lashing with a venomous and instant tongue, and covering with insults, ridicule, and abuse, such men as Mr. Chandler, of Michigan, and other Republicans: never missing a sitting of the House, and seeking out adversaries in the bar rooms or the gambling tables. The other day, when the fire against Sumter was at its height, and the fort, in flames, was reduced almost to silence, a small boat put off from the shore, and steered through the shot and the splashing waters right for the walls. It bore the colonel and a negro oarsman. Holding up a white handkerchief on the end of his sword, Wigfall landed on the quay, clambered through an embrasure, and presented himself before the astonished Federals with a proposal to surrender, quite unauthorized, and "on his own hook," which led to the final capitulation of Major Anderson.

I am sorry to say, our distinguished friend had just been paying his respects *sans bornes* to Bacchus or Bourbon, for he was decidedly unsteady in his gait and thick in speech; but his head was quite clear, and he was determined I should know all about his exploit. Major Whiting desired to show me round the work, but he had no chance. "Here is where I got in," quoth Colonel Wigfall. "I found a Yankee standing here by the traverse, out of the way of our shot. He was pretty well scared when he saw me, but I told him not to be alarmed, but to take me to the officers. There they were, huddled up in that corner behind the brickwork, for our shells were tumbling into the yard, and bursting like—" &c. (The Colonel used strong illustrations and strange expletives in narrative.) Major Whiting shook his military head, and said something uncivil to me, in private, in reference to volunteer colonels and the like, which gave him relief; whilst the martial Senator—I forgot to say that he has the name, particularly in the North, of having killed more than half a dozen men in duels—(I had an escape of being another)—conducted me through the casemates with uneven steps, stopping at every traverse to expatiate on some phase of his personal experiences, with his sword dangling between his legs, and spurs involved in rubbish and soldiers' blankets.

In my letter I described the real extent of the damage inflicted, and the state of the fort as I found it. At first the batteries thrown up by the Carolinians were so poor, that the United States' officers in the fort were mightily amused at them, and anticipated easy work in enfilading, ricocheting, and battering them to pieces, if they ever dared to open fire. One morning, however, Captain Foster, to whom really belongs the credit of putting Sumter into a tolerable condition of defence with the most limited means, was unpleasantly surprised by seeing through his glass a new work in the best possible situation for attacking the place, growing up under the strenuous labours of a band of negroes. "I knew at once," he said, "the rascals had got an engineer at last." In fact, the Carolinians were actually talking of an escalade when the officers of the regular army, who had "seceded," came down and took the direction of affairs, which otherwise might have had very different results.

There was a working party of Volunteers clearing away the rubbish in the place. It was evident they were not accustomed to labour. And on my asking why negroes were not employed, I was informed: "The niggers would blow us all up, they're so stupid; and the State would have to pay the owners for any of them who were killed and injured." "In one respect, then, white men are not so valuable as negroes?" "Yes, sir,—that's a fact."

Very few shell craters were visible in the terre-plein; the military mischief, such as it was, showed most conspicuously on the parapet platform, over which shells had been burst as heavily as could be, to prevent the manning of the barbette guns. A very small affair, indeed, that shelling of Fort Sumter. And yet who can tell what may arise from it? "Well, sir," exclaimed one of my companions, "I thank God for it, if it's only because we are beginning to have a history for Europe. The universal Yankee nation swallowed us up."

Never did men plunge into unknown depth of peril and trouble more recklessly than these Carolinians. They fling themselves against the grim, black future, as the cavaliers under Rupert may have rushed against the grim, black Ironsides. Will they carry the image farther? Well! The exploration of Sumter was finished at last, not till we had visited the officers of the garrison, who lived in a windowless, shattered room, reached by a crumbling staircase, and who produced whiskey and crackers, many pleasant stories and boundless welcome. One young fellow grumbled about pay. He said: "I have not received a cent since I came to Charleston for this business." But Major Whiting, some days afterwards, told me he had not got a dollar on account of his pay, though on leaving the United States' army he had abandoned nearly all his means of subsistence. These gentlemen were quite satisfied it would all be right eventually; and no one questioned the power or inclination of the Government, which had just been inaugurated under such strange auspices, to perpetuate its principles and reward its servants.

After a time our party went down to the boats, in which we were rowed to the steamer that lay waiting for us at Morris' Island. The original intention of the officers was to carry us over to Fort Moultrie, on the opposite side of the Channel, and to examine it and the floating iron battery; but it was too late to do so when we got off, and the steamer only ran across and swept around homewards by the other shore. Below, in the cabin, there was spread a lunch or quasi dinner; and the party of Senators, past and present, aides-de-camp, journalists, and flaneurs, were not indisposed to join it. For me there was only one circumstance which marred the pleasure of that agreeable reunion. Colonel and Senator Wigfall, who had not sobered himself by drinking deeply, in the plenitude of his exultation alluded to the assault on Senator Sumner as a type of the manner in which the Southerners would deal with the Northerners generally, and cited it as a good exemplification of the fashion in which they would bear their "whipping." Thence, by a natural digression, he adverted to the inevitable consequences of the magnificent outburst of Southern indignation against the Yankees on all the nations of the world, and to the immediate action of England in the matter as soon as the news came. Suddenly reverting to Mr. Sumner, whose name he loaded with obloquy, he spoke of Lord Lyons in terms so coarse, that, forgetting the condition of the speaker, I resented the language applied to the English Minister in a very unmistakeable manner; and then rose and left the cabin. In a moment I was followed on deck by Senator Wigfall: his manner much calmer, his hair brushed back, his eye sparkling. There was nothing left to be desired in his apologies, which were repeated and energetic. We were joined by Mr. Manning, Major Whiting, and Senator Chesnut, and others, to whom I expressed my complete contentment with Mr. Wigfall's explanations. And so we returned to Charleston. The Colonel and Senator, however, did not desist from his attentions to the good—or bad—things below. It was a strange scene—these men, hot and red-handed in rebellion, with their lives on the cast, trifling and jesting, and carousing as if they had no care on earth — all excepting the gentlemen of the local press, who were assiduous in note and food taking. It was near nightfall before we set foot on the quay of Charleston. The city was indicated by the blaze of lights, and by the continual roll of drums, and the noisy music, and the yelling cheers which rose above its streets. As I walked towards the hotel, the evening drove of negroes, male and female, shuffling through the streets in all haste, in order to escape the patrol and the last peal of the curfew bell, swept by me; and as I passed the guard-house of the police, one of my friends pointed out the armed sentries pacing up and down before the porch, and the gleam of arms in the room inside. Further on, a squad of mounted horsemen, heavily armed, turned up a bye-street, and with jingling spurs and sabres disappeared in the dust and darkness. That is the horse patrol. They scour the country around the city, and meet at certain places during the night to see if the niggers are all right. Ah, Fuscus! these are signs of trouble.

> "Integer vitæ, scelerisque purus
> Non eget Mauri jaculis neque arcu,
> Nec venenatis gravidâ sagittis,
> Fusce, pharetrâ."

But Fuscus is going to his club; a kindly, pleasant, chatty, card-playing, cocktail-consuming place. He nods proudly to an old white-wooled negro steward or head-waiter—a slave—as a proof which I cannot accept, with the curfew tolling in my ears, of the excellencies of the domestic institution. The club was filled with officers, one of them, Mr. Ransome Calhoun,* asked me what was the object which most struck me at Morris' Island; I tell him—as was indeed the case—that it was a letter-copying machine, a case of official stationery, and a box of Red Tape, lying on the beach, just landed and ready to grow with the strength of the young independence.

But listen! There is a great tumult, as of many voices coming up the street, heralded by blasts of music. It is a speech-making from the front of the hotel. Such an agitated, lively multitude! How they cheer the pale, frantic man, limber and dark-haired, with uplifted arms and clenched fists, who is perorating on the balcony! "What did he say?" "Who is he?" "Why it's he again!" "That's Roger Pryor—he says that if them Yankee trash don't listen to reason, and stand from under, we'll march to the North and dictate the terms of peace in Faneuil Hall! Yes, sir—and so we will, certa-i-n su-re!" "No matter, for all that; we have shown we can whip the Yankees whenever we meet them—at Washington or down here." How much I heard of all this to-day—how much more this evening! The hotel as noisy as ever—more men in uniform arriving every few minutes, and the hall and passages crowded with tall, good-looking Carolinians.

CHAPTER XV.

Slaves, their masters and mistresses—Hotels—Attempted boat-journey to Fort Moultrie—Excitement at Charleston against New York—Preparations for War—General Beauregard—Southern opinion as to the policy of the North, and estimate of the effect of the war on England, through the cotton market—Aristocratic feeling in the South.

April 18th.—It is as though we woke up in a barrack. No! There is the distinction, that in the passages slaves are moving up and down with cups of iced milk or water for their mistresses in the early morning, cleanly dressed, neatly clad, with the conceptions of Parisian millinery adumbrated to their condition, and transmitted by the white race, hovering round their heads and bodies. They sit outside the doors, and chatter in the passages; and as the Irish waiter brings in my hot water for shaving, there is that odd, round, oily, half-strangled, chuckling, gobble of a laugh peculiar to the female Ethiop, coming in through the doorway.

Later in the day, their mistresses sail out from the inner harbours, and launch all their sails along the passages, down the stairs, and into the long, hot, fluffy salle-à-manger, where, blackened with flies which dispute the viands, they take their tremendous meals. They are pale, pretty, svelte—just as I was about to say they were rather small, there rises before me the recollection of one Titanic dame—a Carolinian Juno, with two lovely peacock daughters—and I refrain from generalising. Exceedingly proud these ladies are said to be—for a generation or two of family suffice in this new country, if properly supported by the possession of negroes and acres, to give pride of birth, and all the grandeur which is derived from raising raw produce, cereals, and cotton—suâ terrâ. Their enemies say that the grandfathers of some of these noble people were mere pirates and smugglers, who dealt in a cavalier fashion with the laws and with the flotsam and jetsam of fortune on the seas and reefs hereabouts. Cotton suddenly—almost unnaturally, as far as the ordinary laws of commerce are concerned, grew up whilst land was cheap, and slaves were of moderate price—the pirates, and piratesses had control of both, and in a night the gourd swelled and grew to a prodigious size. These are Northern stories. What the Southerners say of their countrymen and women in the upper part of this "blessed Union" I have written for the edification of people at home.

The tables in the eating-room are disposed in long rows, or detached so as to suit private parties. When I was coming down to Charleston, one of my fellow-passengers told me he was quite shocked the first time he saw white people acting as servants; but no such scruples existed in the Mills House, for the waiters were all Irish, except one or two Germans. The carte is much the same at all American hotels, the variations depending on local luxuries or tastes. Marvellous exceedingly is it to see the quantities of butter, treacle, and farinaceous matters prepared in the heaviest form—of fish, of many meats, of eggs scrambled or scarred or otherwise prepared, of iced milk and water, which an American will consume in a few minutes in the mornings. There is, positively, no rest at these meals—no repose. The guests are ever passing in and out of the room, chairs are for ever pushed to and fro with a harsh grating noise that sets the teeth on edge, and there is a continual clatter of plates and metal. Every man is reading his paper, or discussing the news with his neighbour. I was introduced to a vast number of people and was asked many questions respecting my views of Sumter, or what I thought "old Abe and Seward would do?" The proclamation calling out 75,000 men issued by said old Abe, they treat with the most profound contempt or unsparing ridicule, as the case may be. Five out of six of the men at table wore uniforms this morning.

Having made the acquaintance of several warriors, as well as that of a Russian gentleman, Baron Sternberg, who was engaged in looking about him in Charleston, and was, like most foreigners, impressed with the conviction that *actum este de Republicâ*, I went out with Major Whiting* and Mr. Ward, the former of whom was anxious to show to me Fort Moultrie and the left side of the Channel, in continuation of my trip yesterday. It was arranged that we should go off as quietly as possible, "so as to prevent the newspapers knowing anything about it." The major has a great dislike to the gentlemen of the press, and General Beauregard had sent

* Since killed in a duel by Mr. Rhett.

* Now Confederate General.

orders for the staff-boat to be prepared, so as to be quiet and private, but the fates were against us. On going down to the quay, we learned that a gentleman had come down with an officer and gone off in our skiff, the boat-keepers believing they were the persons for whom it was intended. In fact, our Russian friend, Baron Sternberg, had stolen a march upon us.

After a time, the major succeeded in securing the services of the very smallest, most untrustworthy, and ridiculous-looking craft ever seen by mortal eyes. If Charon had put a two-horse power engine into his skiff, it might have borne some resemblance to this egregious cymbalus, which had once been a flat-bottomed, open decked cutter or galley, into the midst of which the owner had forced a small engine and paddle-wheels, and at the stern had erected a roofed caboose, or oblong pantry, sacred to oil-cans and cockroaches. The crew consisted of the first captain and the second captain, a lad of tender years, and that was all. Into the pantry we scrambled, and sat down knee to knee, whilst the engine was getting up its steam: a very obstinate and anti-caloric little engine it was—puffing and squeaking, leaking, and distilling drops of water, and driving out blasts of steam in unexpected places.

As long as we lay at the quay all was right. The major was supremely happy, for he could talk about Thackeray and his writings—a theme of which he never tired—nay, on which his enthusiasm reached the height of devotional fervour. Did I ever know any one like Major Pendennis? Was it known who Becky Sharp was? Who was the O'Mulligan? These questions were mere hooks on which to hang rhapsodies and delighted dissertation. He might have got down as far as Pendennis himself, when a lively swash of water flying over the preposterous little gunwales, and dashing over our boots into the cabin, announced that our bark was under weigh. There is, we were told, for several months in the year, a brisk breeze from the southward and eastward in and off Charleston Harbour, and there was to-day a small joggle in the water which would not have affected anything floating except our steamer; but as we proceeded down the narrow channel by Castle Pinckney, the little boat rolled as if she would capsize every moment, and made no pretence at doing more than a mile an hour at her best; and it became evident that our voyage would be neither pleasant, prosperous, nor speedy. Still the major went on between the lurches, and drew his feet up out of the water, in order to have "a quiet chat," as he said, "about my favourite author." My companion and myself could not condense ourselves or foreshorten our nether limbs quite so deftly.

Standing out from the shelter towards Sumter, the sea came rolling on our beam, making the miserable craft oscillate as if some great hand had caught her by the funnel—Yankeeicé, smoke-stack—and was rolling her backwards and forwards, as a preliminary to a final keel over. The water came in plentifully, and the cabin was flooded with a small sea: the latter partook of the lively character of the external fluid, and made violent efforts to get overboard to join it, which generally were counteracted by the better sustained and directed attempts of the external to get inside. The captain seemed very unhappy; the rest of the crew—our steerer—had discovered that the steamer would not steer at all, and that we were rolling like a log on the water. Certainly neither Pinckney, nor Sumter, nor Moultrie altered their relative bearings and distances towards us for half an hour or so, though they bobbed up and down continuously. "But it is," said the major, "in the character of Colonel Newcome that Thackeray has, in my opinion, exhibited the greatest amount of power; the tenderness, simplicity, love, manliness, and——" Here a walloping muddy green wave came "all aboard," and the cymbalus gave decided indications of turning turtle. We were wet and miserable, and two hours or more had now passed in making a couple of miles. The tide was setting more strongly against us, and just off Moultrie, in the tideway between its walls and Sumter, could be seen the heads of the sea-horses unpleasantly crested. I know not what of eloquent disquisition I lost, for the major was evidently in his finest moment and on his best subject, but I ventured to suggest that we should bout ship and return—and thus aroused him to a sense of his situation. And so we wore round—a very delicate operation, which, by judicious management in getting side bumps of the sea at favourable moments, we were enabled to effect in some fifteen or twenty minutes; and then we became so parboiled by the heat from the engine, that conversation was impossible.

How glad we were to land once more I need not say. As I gave the captain a small votive tablet of metal, he said, "I'm thinkin' it's very well yes turned back. Av we'd gone any further, devil aback ever we'd have come." "Why didn't you say so before?" "Sure I didn't like to spoil the trip." My gifted countryman and I parted to meet no more.

* * * * * *

Second and third editions and extras! News of Secession meetings and of Union meetings! Every one is filled with indignation against the city of New York, on account of the way in which the news of the reduction of Fort Sumter has been received there. New England has acted just as was expected, but better things were anticipated on the part of the Empire city. There is no sign of shrinking from a contest: on the contrary, the Carolinians are full of eagerness to test their force in the field. "Let them come!" is their boastful *mot d'ordre*.

The anger which is reported to exist in the North only adds to the fury and animosity of the Carolinians. They are determined now to act on their sovereign rights as a state, cost what it may, and uphold the ordinance of secession. The answers of several State Governors to President Lincoln's demand for troops have delighted our friends. Beriah Magoffin, of Kentucky, declares he won't give any men for such a wicked purpose; and another gubernatorial dignitary laconically replied to the demand for so many thousand soldiers, "Nary one." Letcher, Governor of Virginia, has also sent a refusal. From the North comes news of mass-meetings, of hauling down Secession colours, mobbing Secession papers, of military bodies turning out, banks subscribing and lending.

Jefferson Davis has met President Lincoln's proclamation by a counter manifesto, issuing letters of marque and reprisal—on all sides preparations for war. The Southern agents are buying steamers, but they fear the Northern states will use their navy to enforce a blockade, which is much dreaded, as it will cut off supplies and injure the commerce, on which they so much depend. Assuredly Mr. Seward cannot know anything of the feeling of the South, or he would not be so confident as he was that all would blow over, and that the states, deprived of the care and fostering influences of the general Government, would get tired of their Secession ordinances, and of their experiment to maintain a national life, so that the United States will be re-established before long.

I went over and saw General Beauregard at his quarters. He was busy with papers, orderlies, and despatches, and the outer room was crowded with officers. His present task, he told me, was to put Sumter in a state of defence, and to disarm the works bearing on it, so as to get their fire directed on the harbour approaches, as "the North in its madness" might attempt a naval attack on Charleston. His manner of transacting business is clear and rapid. Two vases filled with flowers on his table, flanking his maps and plans; and a little hand bouquet of roses, geraniums, and scented flowers lay on a letter which he was writing as I came in, by way of paper weight. He offered me every assistance and facility, relying, of course, on my strict observance of a neutral's duty. I reminded him once more, that as the representative of an English journal, it would be my duty to write freely to England respecting what I saw; and that I must not be held accountable if, on the return of my letters to America, a month after they were written, it was found they contained information to which circumstances might attach an objectionable character. The General said, "I quite understand you. We must take our chance of that, and leave you to exercise your discretion."

In the evening I dined with our excellent Consul, Mr. Bunch, who had a small and very agreeable party to meet me. One very venerable old gentleman, named Huger (pronounced as Hugeē), was particularly interesting in appearance and conversation. He formerly held some official appointment under the Federal Government, but had gone out with his state, and had been confirmed in his appointment by the Confederate Government. Still he was not happy at the prospect before him or his country. "I have lived too long," he exclaimed; "I should have died 'ere these evil days arrived." What thoughts, indeed, must have troubled his mind when he reflected that his country was but little older than himself; for, he was one who had shaken hands with the framers of the Declaration of Independence. But though the tears rolled down his cheeks when he spoke of the prospect of civil war, there was no symptom of apprehension for the result, or indeed of any regret for the contest, which he regarded as the natural consequence of the insults, injustice, and aggression of the North against Southern rights.

Only one of the company, a most lively, quaint, witty old lawyer named Petigru, dissented from the doctrines of Secession; but he seems to be treated as an amiable, harmless person, who has a weakness of intellect or a "bee in his bonnet" on this particular matter.

It was scarcely very agreeable to my host or myself to find that no considerations were believed to be of consequence in reference to England except her material interests, and that these worthy gentlemen regarded her as a sort of appanage of their cotton kingdom. "Why, sir, we have only to shut off your supply of cotton for a few weeks, and we can create a revolution in Great Britain. There are four millions of your people depending on us for their bread, not to speak of the many millions of dollars. No, sir, we know that England must recognise us," &c.

Liverpool and Manchester have obscured all Great Britain to the Southern eye. I confess the tone of my friends irritated me. I said so to Mr. Bunch, who laughed, and remarked, "You'll not mind it when you get as much accustomed to this sort of thing as I am." I could not help saying, that if Great Britain were such a sham as they supposed, the sooner a hole was drilled in her, and the whole empire sunk under water, the better for the world, the cause of truth, and of liberty.

These tall, thin, fine-faced Carolinians are great materialists. Slavery perhaps has aggravated the tendency to look at all the world through parapets of cotton bales and rice bags, and though more stately and less vulgar, the worshippers here are not less prostrate before the "almighty dollar" than the Northerners. Again cropping out of the dead level of hate to the Yankee, grows its climax in the profession from nearly every one of the guests, that he would prefer a return to the British rule to any reunion with New England. "The names in South Carolina show our origin—Charleston, and Ashley, and Cooper, &c. Our Gadsden, Sumter, and Pinckney were true cavaliers," &c. They did not say anything about Pedee, or Tombigbee, or Sullivan's Island, or the like. We all have our little or big weaknesses.

I see no trace of cavalier descent in the names of Huger, Rose, Manning, Chesnut, Pickens; but there is a profession of faith in the cavaliers and their cause among them because it is fashionable in Carolina. They affect the agricultural faith and the belief of a landed gentry. It is not only over the wine-glass—why call it cup?—that they ask for a Prince to reign over them; I have heard the wish repeatedly expressed within the last two days that we could spare them one of our young Princes, but never in jest or in any frivolous manner.

On my way home again I saw the sentries on their march, the mounted patrols starting on their ride, and other evidences that though the slaves are "the happiest and most contented race in the world," they require to be taken care of like less favoured mortals. The city watch-house is filled every night with slaves, who are confined there until reclaimed by their owners, whenever they are found out after nine o'clock, P.M., without special passes or permits. Guns are firing for the Ordinance of Secession in Virginia.

CHAPTER XVI.

Charleston; the Market-place—Irishmen at Charleston—Governor Pickens: his political economy and theories—Newspaper offices and counting-houses—Rumours as to the war policy of the South.

April 19th.—An exceeding hot day. The sun

pours on the broad sandy street of Charleston with immense power, and when the wind blows down the thoroughfare it sends before it vast masses of hot dust. The houses are generally detached, surrounded by small gardens, well provided with verandahs to protect the windows from the glare, and are sheltered with creepers and shrubs and flowering plants, through which flit humming-birds and fly-catchers. In some places the streets and roadways are covered with planking, and as long as the wood is sound they are pleasant to walk or drive upon.

I paid a visit to the markets; the stalls are presided over by negroes, male and female; the coloured people engaged in selling and buying are well clad; the butchers' meat by no means tempting to the eye, but the fruit and vegetable stalls well filled. Fish is scarce at present, as the boats are not permitted to proceed to sea lest they should be whipped up by the expected Yankee cruisers, or carry malcontents to communicate with the enemy. Around the flesh-market there is a skirling crowd of a kind of turkey-buzzard; these are useful as scavengers and are protected by law. They do their nasty work very zealously, descending on the offal thrown out to them with the peculiar crawling, puffy, soft sort of flight which is the badge of all their tribe, and contending with wing and beak against the dogs which dispute the viands with the harpies. It is curious to watch the expression of their eyes as with outstretched necks they peer down from the ledge of the market roof on the stalls and scrutinise the operations of the butchers below. They do not prevent a disagreeable odour in the vicinity of the markets, nor are they deadly to a fine and active breed of rats.

Much drumming and marching through the streets to-day. One very ragged regiment which had been some time at Morris' Island halted in the shade near me, and I was soon made aware they consisted, for the great majority, of Irishmen. The Emerald Isle, indeed, has contributed largely to the population of Charleston. In the principal street there is a large and fine red sandstone building with the usual Greek-Yankee-composite portico, over which is emblazoned the crownless harp and the shamrock wreath proper to a St. Patrick's Hall, and several Roman Catholic churches also attest the Hibernian presence.

I again called on General Beauregard, and had a few moments' conversation with him. He told me that an immense deal depended on Virginia, and that as yet the action of the people in that State had not been as prompt as might have been hoped, for the President's proclamation was a declaration of war against the South, in which all would be ultimately involved. He is going to Montgomery to confer with Mr. Jefferson Davis. I have no doubt there is to be some movement made in Virginia. Whiting is under orders to repair there, and he hinted that he had a task of no common nicety and difficulty to perform. He is to visit the forts which had been seized on the coast of North Carolina, and probably will have a look at Portsmouth. It is incredible that the Federal authorities should have neglected to secure this place.

Later I visited the Governor of the State, Mr. Pickens, to whom I was conducted by Colonel Lucas, his aide-de-camp. His palace was a very humble shed-like edifice with large rooms, on the doors of which were pasted pieces of paper with sundry high-reading inscriptions, such as "Adjutant General's Dept., Quartermaster-General's Dept., Attorney General of State," &c., and through the doorways could be seen men in uniform, and grave, earnest people busy at their desks with pen, ink, paper, tobacco, and spittoons. The governor, a stout man, of a big head, and a large important looking face, with watery eyes and flabby features, was seated in a barrack-like room, furnished in the plainest way and decorated by the inevitable portrait of George Washington, close to which was the "Ordinance of Secession of the State of South Carolina" of last year.

Governor Pickens is considerably laughed at by his subjects, and I was amused by a little middy, who described with much unction the governor's alarm on his visit to Fort Pickens, when he was told that there were a number of live shells and a quantity of powder still in the place. He is said to have commenced one of his speeches with "Born insensible to fear," &c. To me the governor was very courteous, but I confess the heat of the day did not dispose me to listen with due attention to a lecture on political economy with which he favoured me. I was told, however, that he had practised with success on the late Czar when he was United States Minister to St. Petersburg, and that he does not suffer his immediate staff to escape from having their minds improved on the relations of capital to labour, and on the vicious condition of capital and labour in the North.

"In the North, then, you will perceive, Mr. Russell, they have maximised the hostile condition of opposed interests in the accumulation of capital and in the employment of labour, whilst we in the South, by the peculiar excellence of our domestic institution, have minimised their opposition and maximised the identity of interest by the investment of capital in the labourer himself," and so on, or something like it. I could not help remarking it struck me there was "another difference betwixt the North and South which he had overlooked — the capital of the North is represented by gold, silver, notes, and other exponents, which are good all the world over and are recognised as such; your capital has power of locomotion, and ceases to exist the moment it crosses a geographical line." "That remark, sir," said the Governor, "requires that I should call your attention to the fundamental principles on which the abstract idea of capital should be formed. In order to clear the ground, let us first inquire into the soundness of the ideas put forward by your Adam Smith"—I had to look at my watch and to promise I would come back to be illuminated on some other occasion, and hurried off to keep an engagement with myself to write letters by the next mail.

The Governor writes very good proclamations, nevertheless, and his confidence in South Carolina is unbounded. "If we stand alone, sir, we must win. They can't whip us." A gentleman named Pringle, for whom I had letters of introduction, has come to Charleston to ask me to his plantation, but there will be no boat from the port till Monday, and it is uncertain then whether the blockading vessels, of which we hear so much, may not be down by that time.

April 20th.—I visited the editors of the *Charleston Mercury* and the *Charleston Courier* to-day at their offices. The Rhett family have been active agitators for secession, and it is said they are not over well pleased with Jefferson Davis for neglecting their claims to office. The elder, a pompous, hard, ambitious man, possesses ability. He is fond of alluding to his English connections and predilections, and is intolerant of New England to the last degree. I received from him, ere I left, a pamphlet on his life, career, and services. In the newspaper offices there was nothing worthy of remark; they were possessed of that obscurity which is such a characteristic of the haunts of journalism—the clouds in which the lightning is hiding. Thence to haunts more dingy still where Plutus lives—to the counting houses of the cotton brokers, up many pairs of stairs into large rooms furnished with hard seats, engravings of celebrated clippers, advertisements of emigrant agencies and of lines of steamers, little flocks of cotton, specimens of rice, grain, and seed in wooden bowls, and clerks living inside railings, with secluded spittoons, and ledgers, and tumblers of water.

I called on several of the leading merchants and bankers, such as Mr. Rose, Mr. Muir, Mr. Trenholm, and others. With all it was the same story. Their young men were off to the wars—no business doing. In one office I saw an announcement of a company for a direct communication by steamers between a southern port and Europe. "When do you expect that line to be opened?" I asked. "The United States' cruisers will surely interfere with it." "Why, I expect, sir," replied the merchant, "that if those miserable Yankees try to blockade us, and keep you from our cotton, you'll just send their ships to the bottom and acknowledge us. That will be before autumn, I think." It was in vain I assured him he would be disappointed. "Look out there," he said, pointing to the wharf, on which were piled some cotton bales; "there's the key will open all our ports, and put us into John Bull's strong box as well."

I dined to-day at the hotel, notwithstanding many hospitable invitations, with Messrs. Manning, Porcher Miles, Reed, and Pringle. Mr. Trescot, who was Under-Secretary-of-State in Mr. Buchanan's Cabinet, joined us, and I promised to visit his plantation as soon as I have returned from Mr. Pringle's. We heard much the same conversation as usual, relieved by Mr. Trescot's sound sense and philosophy. He sees clearly the evils of slavery, but is, like all of us, unable to discover the solution and means of averting them.

The Secessionists are in great delight with Governor Letcher's proclamation, calling out troops and volunteers, and it is hinted that Washington will be attacked, and the nest of Black Republican vermin which haunt the capital driven out. Agents are to be at once despatched to get up a navy, and every effort made to carry out the policy indicated in Jeff Davis's issue of letters of marque and reprisal. Norfolk harbour is blocked up to prevent the United States ships getting away; and at the same time we hear that the United States officer commanding at the arsenal of Harper's Ferry has retired into Pennsylvania, after destroying the place by fire. How "old John Brown" would have wondered and rejoiced had he lived a few months longer!

CHAPTER XVII.

Visit to a plantation; hospitable reception—By steamer to Georgetown—Description of the town—A country mansion—Masters and slaves—Slave diet—Humming-birds—Land irrigation—Negro quarters—Back to Georgetown.

April 21st.—In the afternoon I went with Mr. Porcher Miles to visit a small farm and plantation, some miles from the city, belonging to Mr. Crafts. Our arrival was unexpected, but the planter's welcome was warm. Mrs. Crafts showed us round the place, of which the beauties were due to nature rather than to art, and so far the lady was the fitting mistress of the farm.

We wandered through tangled brakes and thick Indian-like jungle, filled with disagreeable insects, down to the edge of a small lagoon. The beech was perforated with small holes, in which Mrs. Crafts said little crabs, called "fiddlers" from their resemblance *in petto* to a performer on the fiddle, make their abode; but neither them nor "spotted snakes" did we see. And so to dinner, for which our hostess made needless excuses. "I am afraid I shall have to ask you to eke out your dinner with potted meats, but I can answer for Mr. Crafts giving you a bottle of good old wine." "And what better, madam," quoth Mr. Miles, "what better can you offer a soldier? What do we expect but grape and canister?"

Mr. Miles, who was formerly member of the United States Congress, and who has now migrated to the Confederate States of America, rendered himself conspicuous a few years ago when a dreadful visitation of yellow fever came upon Norfolk and destroyed one-half of the inhabitants. At that terrible time, when all who could move were flying from the plague-stricken spot, Mr. Porcher Miles flew to it, visited the hospitals, tended the sick; and although a weakly, delicate man, gave an example of such energy and courage as materially tended to save those who were left. I never heard him say a word to indicate that he had been at Norfolk at all.

At the rear of the cottage-like residence (to the best of my belief built of wood), in which the planter's family lived, was a small enclosure, surrounded by a palisade, containing a number of wooden sheds, which were the negro quarters; and after dinner, as we sat on the steps, the children were sent for to sing for us. They came very shyly, and by degrees; first peeping round the corners and from behind trees, oftentimes running away in spite of the orders of their haggard mammies, till they were chased, captured, and brought back by their elder brethren. They were ragged, dirty, shoeless urchins of both sexes; the younger ones abdominous as infant Hindoos, and wild as if just caught. With much difficulty the elder children were dressed into line; then they began to shuffle their flat feet, to clap their hands, and to drawl out in a monotonous sort of chant something about the "River Jawdam," after which Mrs. Crafts rewarded them with lumps of sugar, which were as fruitful of disputes as the apple of discord. A few fathers and mothers gazed at the scene from a distance.

As we sat listening to the wonderful song of

the mocking-birds, when these young Sybarites had retired, a great, big, burly red-faced gentleman, as like a Yorkshire farmer in high perfection as any man I ever saw in the old country, rode up to the door, and, after the usual ceremony of introduction and the collating of news, and the customary assurance "They can't whip us, sir!" invited me then and there to attend a fête champêtre at his residence, where there is a lawn famous for trees dating from the first settlement of the colony, and planted by this gentleman's ancestor.

Trees are objects of great veneration in America if they are of any size. There are perhaps two reasons for this. In the first place, the indigenous forest trees are rarely of any great magnitude. In the second place, it is natural to Americans to admire dimension and antiquity; and a big tree gratifies both organs—size and veneration.

I must record an astonishing feat of this noble Carolinian. The heat of the evening was indubitably thirst-compelling, and we went in to "have a drink." Among other things on the table were a decanter of cognac and a flask of white curaçoa. The planter filled a tumbler half full of brandy. "What's in that flat bottle, Crafts?" "That's white curaçoa." The planter tasted a little, and having smacked his lips and exclaimed "first-rate stuff," proceeded to *water* his brandy with it, and tossed off a full brimmer of the mixture without any remarkable ulterior results. They are a hard-headed race. I doubt if cavalier or puritan ever drank a more potent bumper than our friend the big planter.

April 22nd.—To-day was fixed for the visit to Mr. Pringle's plantation, which lies above Georgetown near the Peedee River. Our party, which consisted of Mr. Mitchell, an eminent lawyer of Charleston, Colonel Reed, a neighbouring planter, Mr. Ward of New York, our host, and myself, were on board the Georgetown steamer at seven o'clock, A.M., and started with a quantity of commissariat stores, ammunition, and the like, for the use of the troops quartered along the coast. There was, of course, a large supply of newspapers also. At that early hour invitations to the "bar" were not uncommon, where the news was discussed by long-legged, grave, sallow men. There was a good deal of joking about "old Abe Lincoln's paper blockade," and the report that the Government had ordered their cruisers to treat the crew of Confederate privateers as "pirates" provoked derisive and menacing comments. The full impulses of national life are breathing through the whole of this people. There is their flag flying over Sumter, and the Confederate banner is waving on all the sand-forts and headlands which guard the approaches to Charleston.

A civil war and persecution have already commenced. "Suspected Abolitionists" are ill-treated in the South, and "Suspected Secessionists" are mobbed and beaten in the North. The news of the attack on the 6th Massachusetts, and the Pennsylvania regiment, by the mob in Baltimore, has been received with great delight; but some long-headed people say that it will only expose Baltimore and Maryland to the full force of the Northern States. The riot took place on the anniversary of Lexington.

The "Nina" was soon in open sea, steering northwards and keeping four miles from shore in order to clear the shoals and banks which fringe the low sandy coasts, and effectually prevent even light gunboats covering a descent by their ordnance. This was one of the reasons why the Federal fleet did not make any attempt to relieve Fort Sumter during the engagement. On our way out we could see the holes made in the large hotel and other buildings on Sullivan's Island behind Fort Moultrie, by the shot from the fort, which caused terror among the negroes "miles away." There was no sign of any blockading vessel, but look-out parties were posted along the beach, and as the skipper said we might have to make our return-journey by land, every sail on the horizon was anxiously scanned through our glasses.

Having passed the broad mouth of the Santee, the steamer in three hours and a half ran up an estuary, into which the Maccamaw River and the Peedee River pour their united waters.

Our vessel proceeded along shore to a small jetty, at the end of which was a group of armed men, some of them being part of a military post, to defend the coast and river, established under cover of an earthwork and palisades constructed with trunks of trees, and mounting three 32-pounders. Several posts of a similar character lay on the river banks, and from some of these we were boarded by men in boats hungry for news and newspapers. Most of the men at the pier were cavalry troopers, belonging to a volunteer association of the gentry for coast defence, and they had been out night and day patrolling the shores, and doing the work of common soldiers—very precious material for such work. They wore grey tunics, slashed and faced with yellow, buff belts, slouched felt hats, ornamented with drooping cocks' plumes, and long jack-boots, which well became their fine persons and bold bearing, and were evidently due to "Cavalier" associations. They were all equals. Our friends on board the boat hailed them by their Christian names, and gave and heard the news. Among the cases landed at the pier were certain of champagne and pâtés, on which Captain Blank was wont to regale his company daily at his own expense, or that of his cotton broker. Their horses picketed in the shade of trees close to the beach, the parties of women riding up and down the sands, or driving in light tax-carts, suggested images of a large pic-nic, and a state of society quite indifferent to Uncle Abe's cruisers and "Hessians." After a short delay here, the steamer proceeded on her way to Georgetown, an ancient and once important settlement and port, which was marked in the distance by the little forest of masts rising above the level land, and the tops of the trees beyond, and by a solitary church-spire.

As the "Nina" approaches the tumble-down wharf of the old town, two or three citizens advance from the shade of shaky sheds to welcome us, and a few country vehicles and light phaetons are drawn forth from the same shelter to receive the passengers, while the negro boys and girls who have been playing upon the bales of cotton and barrels of rice, which represent the trade of the place on the wharf, take up commanding positions for the better observation of our proceedings.

There is about Georgetown an air of quaint

simplicity and old-fashioned quiet, which contrasts refreshingly with the bustle and tumult of American cities. While waiting for our vehicle we enjoyed the hospitality of Colonel Reed, who took us into an old-fashioned, angular, wooden mansion, more than a century old, still sound in every timber, and testifying, in its quaint wainscotings, and the rigid framework of door and window, to the durability of its cypress timbers and the preservative character of the atmosphere. In early days it was the grand house of the old settlement, and the residence of the founder of the female branch of the family of our host, who now only makes it his halting-place when passing to and fro between Charleston and his plantation, leaving it the year round in charge of an old servant and her grandchild. Rose-trees and flowering shrubs clustered before the porch and filled the garden in front, and the establishment gave one a good idea of a London merchant's retreat about Chelsea a hundred and fifty years ago.

At length we were ready for our journey, and, in two light covered gigs, proceeded along the sandy track which, after a while, led us to a road cut deep in the bosom of the woods, where silence was only broken by the cry of a woodpecker, the screams of a crane, or the sharp challenge of the jay. For miles we passed through the shades of this forest, meeting only two or three vehicles containing female planterdom on little excursions of pleasure or business, who smiled their welcome as we passed. Arrived at a deep chocolate-coloured stream, called Black River, full of fish and alligators, we find a flat large enough to accommodate vehicles and passengers, and propelled by two negroes pulling upon a stretched rope, in the manner usual in the ferry-boats of Switzerland.

Another drive through a more open country, and we reach a fine grove of pine and live-oak, which melts away into a shrubbery guarded by a rustic gateway: passing through this, we are brought by a sudden turn to the planter's house, buried in trees, which dispute with the green sward and with wild flower-beds the space between the hall-door and the waters of the Peedee; and in a few minutes, as we gaze over the expanse of fields marked by the deep water-cuts, and bounded by a fringe of unceasing forest, just tinged with green by the first life of the early rice crops, the chimneys of the steamer we had left at Georgetown, gliding as it were through the fields, indicate the existence of another navigable river still beyond.

Leaving the verandah which commanded this agreeable foreground, we enter the mansion, and are reminded by its low-browed, old-fashioned rooms, of the country houses yet to be found in parts of Ireland or on the Scottish border, with additions, made by the luxury and love of foreign travel, of more than one generation of educated Southern planters. Paintings from Italy illustrate the walls, in juxta-position with interesting portraits of early colonial governors and their womankind, limned with no uncertain hand, and full of the vigour of touch and naturalness of drapery, of which Copley has left us too few exemplars; and one portrait of Benjamin West claims for itself such honour as his own pencil can give. An excellent library—filled with collections of French and English classics, and with those ponderous editions of Voltaire, Rousseau, the "Mémoires pour Servir," books of travel and history which delighted our forefathers in the last century, and many works of American and general history—affords ample occupation for a rainy day.

It was five o'clock before we reached our planter's house—White House Plantation. My small luggage was carried into my room by an old negro in livery, who took great pains to assure me of my perfect welcome, and who turned out to be a most excellent valet. A low room hung with coloured mezzotints, windows covered with creepers, and an old-fashioned bedstead and quaint chairs, lodged me sumptuously; and after such toilette as was considered necessary by our host for a bachelor's party, we sat down to an excellent dinner, cooked by negroes and served by negroes, and aided by claret mellowed in Carolinian suns, and by Madeira brought down stairs cautiously, as in the days of Horace and Mæcenas, from the cellar between the attic and the thatched roof.

Our party was increased by a neighboring planter, and after dinner the conversation returned to the old channel—all the frogs praying for a king—anyhow a prince—to rule over them. Our good host is anxious to get away to Europe, where his wife and children are, and all he fears is being mobbed at New York, where Southerners are exposed to insult, though they may get off better in that respect than Black Republicans would down South. Some of our guests talked of the duello, and of famous hands with the pistol in these parts. The conversation had altogether very much the tone which would have probably characterized the talk of a group of Tory Irish gentlemen over their wine some sixty years ago, and very pleasant it was. Not a man—no, not one—will ever join the Union again! "Thank God!" they say, "we are freed from that tyranny at last." And yet Mr. Seward calls it the most beneficent government in the world, which never hurt a human being yet!

But alas! all the good things which the house affords, can be enjoyed but for a brief season. Just as nature has expanded every charm, developed every grace, and clothed the scene with all the beauty of opened flower, of ripening grain, and of mature vegetation, on the wings of the wind the poisoned breath comes borne to the home of the white man, and he must fly before it or perish. The books lie unopened on the shelves, the flower blooms and dies unheeded, and, pity 'tis, 'tis true, the old Madeira garnered 'neath the roof, settles down for a fresh lease of life, and sets about its solitary task of acquiring a finer flavour for the infrequent lips of its banished master and his welcome visitors. This is the story, at least, that we hear on all sides, and such is the tale repeated to us beneath the porch, when the moon, while softening, enhances the loveliness of the scene, and the rich melody of mocking-birds fills the grove.

Within these hospitable doors Horace might banquet better than he did with Nasidienus, and drink such wine as can be only found among the descendants of the ancestry who, improvident enough in all else, learnt the wisdom of bottling up choice old Bual and Sercial, ere the demon of oidium had dried up their generous sources for ever. To these must be added excellent bread, ingenious varieties of the *galette*, compounded now of rice and now of Indian meal, delicious butter and fruits, all good of their kind. And is there anything better rising up from the bottom of the social bowl? My black friends who attend on me are grave as Mussulman Khitmutgars. They are attired in liveries and wear white cravats and Berlin gloves. At night when we retire, off they go to their outer darkness in the small settlement of negro-hood, which is separated from our house by a wooden palisade. Their fidelity is undoubted. The house breathes an air of security. The doors and windows are unlocked. There is but one gun, a fowling-piece, on the premises. No planter hereabouts has any dread of his slaves. But I have seen, within the short time I have been in this part of the world, several dreadful accounts of murder and violence, in which masters suffered at the hands of their slaves. There is something suspicious in the constant never-ending statement that "we are not afraid of our slaves." The curfew and the night patrol in the streets, the prisons and watch-houses, and the police regulations, prove that strict supervision, at all events, is needed and necessary. My host is a kind man and a good master. If slaves are happy anywhere, they should be so with him.

These people are fed by their master. They have half a pound per diem of fat pork, and corn in abundance. They rear poultry and sell their chickens and eggs to the house. They are clothed by their master. He keeps them in sickness as in health. Now and then there are gifts of tobacco and molasses for the deserving. There was little labour going on in the fields, for the rice has been just exerting itself to get its head above water. These fields yield plentifully; the waters of the river are fat, and they are let in whenever the planter requires it by means of floodgates and small canals through which the flats can carry their loads of grain to the river for loading the steamers.

April 23rd.—A lovely morning grew into a hot day. After breakfast, I sat in the shade watching the vagaries of some little tortoises, or terrapins, in a vessel of water close at hand, or trying to follow the bee-like flight of the humming-birds. Ah me! one wee brownie, with a purple head and red facings, managed to dash into a small grape or flower conservatory close at hand, and, innocent of the ways of the glassy wall, he or she—I am much puzzled as to the genders of humming-birds, and Mr. Gould, with his wonderful mastery of Greek prefixes and Latin terminations, has not aided me much—dashed up and down from pane to pane, seeking to perforate each with its bill, and carrying death and destruction among the big spiders and their cobweb castles which for the time barred the way.

The humming-bird had, as the Yankees say, a bad time of it, for its efforts to escape were incessant, and our host said tenderly, through his moustaches, "Pooty little thing, don't frighten it!" as if he was quite sure of getting off to Saxony by the next steamer. Encumbered by cobwebs and exhausted, now and then our little friend toppled down among the green shrubs, and lay panting like a living nugget of ore. Again he, she, or it took wing and resumed that mad career; but at last on some happy turn the bright head saw an opening through the door, and out wings, body, and legs dashed, and sought shelter in a creeper, where the little flutterer lay, all but dead, so inanimate indeed, that I could have taken the lovely thing and put it in the hollow of my hand. What would poets of Greece and Rome have said of the humming-bird? What would Hafiz, or Waller, or Spenser have sung, had they but seen that offspring of the sun and flowers?

Later in the day, when the sun was a little less fierce, we walked out from the belt of trees round the house on the plantation itself. At this time of the year there is nothing to recommend to the eye the great breadth of flat fields, surrounded by small canals, which look like the bottoms of dried-up ponds, for the green rice has barely succeeded in forcing its way above the level of the rich dark earth. The river bounds the estate, and when it rises after the rains, its waters, loaded with loam and fertilising mud, are let in upon the lands through the small canals, which are provided with sluices and banks and floodgates to control and regulate the supply.

The negroes had but little to occupy them now. The children of both sexes, scantily clad, were fishing in the canals and stagnant waters, pulling out horrible-looking little catfish. They were so shy that they generally fled at our approach. The men and women were apathetic, neither seeking nor shunning us, and I found that their master knew nothing about them. It is only the servants engaged in household duties who are at all on familiar terms with their masters.

The bailiff or steward was not to be seen. One big slouching negro, who seemed to be a gangsman or something of the kind, followed us in our walk, and answered any questions we put to him very readily. It was a picture to see his face when one of our party, on returning to the house, gave him a larger sum of money than he had ever probably possessed before in a lump. "What will he do with it?" Buy sweet things,—sugar, tobacco, a penknife, and such things. "They have few luxuries, and all their wants are provided for." Took a cursory glance at the negro quarters, which are not very enticing or cleanly. They are surrounded by high palings, and the *entourage* is alive with their poultry.

Very much I doubt whether Mr. Mitchell is satisfied the Southerners are right in their present course, but he and Mr. Petigru are lawyers, and do not take a popular view of the question. After dinner the conversation again turned on the resources and power of the South, and on the determination of the people never to go back into the Union. Then cropped out again the expression of regret for the rebellion of 1776, and the desire that if it came to the worst, England would receive back her erring children, or give them a prince under whom they could secure a monarchical form of government. There is no doubt about the earnestness with which these things are said.

As the "Nina" starts down the river on her return voyage from Georgetown to-night, and Charleston Harbour may be blockaded at any time, thus compelling us to make a long *détour* by land, I resolve to leave by her, in spite of many invitations and pressure from neighbouring planters. At midnight our carriage came round, and we started in a lovely moonlight to

Georgetown, crossing the ferry after some delay, in consequence of the profound sleep of the boatmen in their cabins. One of them said to me, "Musn't go too near de edge ob de boat, massa." "Why not?" "Becas if massa fall ober, he not come up agin likely,—a bad ribber for drowned, massa." He informed me it was full of alligators, which are always on the look-out for the planters' and negroes' dogs, and are hated and hunted accordingly.

The "Nina" was blowing the signal for departure, the only sound we heard all through the night, as we drove through the deserted streets of Georgetown, and soon after three o'clock, A.M., we were on board and in our berths.

CHAPTER XVIII.

Climate of the Southern States—General Beauregard—Risks of the post-office—Hatred of New England—By railway to Sea Island plantation—Sporting in South Carolina—An hour on board a canoe in the dark.

April 24th.—In the morning we found ourselves in chopping little sea-way for which the "Nina" was particularly unsuited, laden as she was with provisions and produce. Eyes and glasses anxiously straining seawards for any trace of the blockading vessels. Every sail scrutinised, but no 'stars and stripes' visible.

Our captain—a good specimen of one of the inland-water navigators, shrewd, intelligent, and active—told me a good deal about the country. He laughed at the fears of the whites as regards the climate. "Why, here am I," said he, "going up the river, and down the river all times of the year, and at times of day and night when they reckon the air is most deadly, and I've done so for years without any bad effects. The planters whose houses I pass all run away in May, and go off to Europe, or to the piney wood, or to the springs, or they'd all die. There's Captain Buck, who lives above here,—he comes from the State of Maine. He had only a thousand dollars to begin with, but he sets to work and gets land on the Maccamaw River at twenty cents an acre. It was death to go nigh it, but it was first-rate rice land, and Captain Buck is now worth a million of dollars. He lives on his estate all the year round, and is as healthy a man as ever you seen."

To such historiettes my planting friends turn a deaf ear. "I tell you what," said Pringle, "just to show you what kind our climate is. I had an excellent overseer once, who would insist on staying near the river, and wouldn't go away. He fought against it for more than five-and-twenty years, but he went down with fever at last." As the overseer was more than thirty years of age when he came to the estate, he had not been cut off so very suddenly. I thought of the quack's advertisement of the "bad leg of sixty years standing." The captain says the negroes on the river plantations are very well off. He can buy enough of pork from the slaves on one plantation to last his ship's crew for the whole winter. The money goes to them, as the hogs are their own. One of the stewards on board had bought himself and his family out of bondage with his earnings. The State in general, however, does not approve of such practices.

At three o'clock, P.M., ran into Charleston harbour, and landed soon afterwards.

I saw General Beauregard in the evening; he was very lively and in good spirits, though he admitted he was rather surprised by the spirit displayed in the North. "A good deal of it is got up, however," he said, "and belongs to that washy sort of enthusiasm which is promoted by their lecturing and spouting." Beauregard is very proud of his personal strength, which for his slight frame is said to be very extraordinary, and he seemed to insist on it that the Southern men had more physical strength, owing to their mode of life and their education, than their Northern "brethren." In the evening held a sort of *tabaks consilium* in the hotel, where a number of officers—Manning, Lucas, Chesnut, Calhoun, &c.—discoursed of the affairs of the nation. All my friends, except Trescot, I think were elated at the prospect of hostilities with the North, and overjoyed that a South Carolina regiment had already set out for the frontiers of Virginia.

April 25th.—Sent off my letters by an English gentleman, who was taking despatches from Mr. Bunch to Lord Lyons, as the post-office is becoming a dangerous institution. We hear of letters being tampered with on both sides. Adams's Express Company, which acts as a sort of express post under certain conditions, is more trustworthy; but it is doubtful how long communications will be permitted to exist between the two hostile nations, as they may now be considered.

Dined with Mr. Petigru, who had most kindly postponed his dinner party till my return from the plantations, and met there General Beauregard, Judge King, and others, among whom, distinguished for their *esprit* and accomplishments, were Mrs. King and Mrs. Carson, daughters of my host. The dislike, which seems innate, to New England is universal, and varies only in the form of its expression. It is quite true Mr. Petigru is a decided Unionist, but he is the sole specimen of the genus in Charleston, and he is tolerated on account of his rarity. As the witty, pleasant old man trots down the street, utterly unconscious of the world around him, he is pointed out proudly by the Carolinians as an instance of forbearance on their part, and as a proof at the same time of popular unanimity of sentiment.

There are also people who regret the dissolution of the Union—such as Mr. Huger, who shed tears in talking of it the other night; but they regard the fact very much as they would the demolition of some article which can never be restored and reunited, which was valued for the uses it rendered and its antiquity.

General Beauregard is apprehensive of an attack by the Northern "fanatics" before the South is prepared, and he considers they will carry out coercive measures most rigorously. He dreads the cutting of the levées, or high artificial works, raised along the whole course of the Mississippi, for many hundreds of miles above New Orleans, which the Federals may resort to in order to drown the plantations and ruin the planters.

We had a good-humoured argument in the evening about the ethics of burning the Norfolk navy yard. The Southerners consider the appropriation of the arms, moneys, and stores of the United States as rightful acts, inasmuch as they represent, according to them, their contribution, or a portion of it, to the national stock in trade. When a State goes out of the Union she should be permitted to carry her forts, armaments, arsenals, &c., along with her, and it was a burning shame for the Yankees to destroy the property of Virginia at Norfolk. These ideas, and many like them, have the merit of novelty to English people, who were accustomed to think there were such things as the Union and the people of the United States.

April 26th.—Bade good-by to Charleston at 9.45 a.m. this day, and proceeded by railway, in company with Mr. Ward, to visit Mr. Trescot's Sea Island Plantation. Crossed the river to the terminus in a ferry steamer. No blockading vessels in sight yet. The water alive with small silvery fish, like mullet, which sprang up and leaped along the surface incessantly. An old gentleman, who was fishing on the pier, combined the pursuit of sport with instruction very ingeniously by means of a fork of bamboo in his rod, just above the reel, into which he stuck his inevitable newspaper, and read gravely in his cane-bottomed chair till he had a bite, when the fork was unhitched and the fish was landed. The negroes are very much addicted to the contemplative man's recreation, and they were fishing in all directions.

On the move again. Took our places in the Charleston and Savannah Railway for Pocotaligo, which is the station for Barnwell Island. Our fellow-passengers were all full of politics—the pretty women being the fiercest of all—no! the least good-looking were the most bitterly patriotic, as if they hoped to talk themselves into husbands by the most unfeminine expressions towards the Yankees.

The country is a dead flat, perforated by rivers and watercourses, over which the rail is carried on long and lofty trestle-work. But for the fine trees, the magnolias and live oak, the landscape would be unbearably hideous, for there are none of the quaint, cleanly, delightful villages of Holland to relieve the monotonous level of rice swamps and wastes of land and water and mud. At the humble little stations there were invariably groups of horsemen waiting under the trees, and ladies with their black nurses and servants who had driven over in the odd-looking old-fashioned vehicles which were drawn up in the shade. Those who were going on a long journey, aware of the utter barrenness of the land, took with them a viaticum and bottles of milk. The nurses and slaves squatted down by their side in the train, on perfectly well-understood terms. No one objected to their presence—on the contrary, the passengers treated them with a certain sort of special consideration, and they were on the happiest terms with their charges, some of which were in the absorbent condition of life, and dived their little white faces against the tawny bosom of their nurses with anything but reluctance.

The train stopped, at 12.20, at Pocotaligo; and there we found Mr. Trescot and a couple of neighbouring planters, famous as fishers for "drum," of which more by-and-bye. I had met old Mr. Elliot in Charleston, and his account of this sport, and of the pursuit of an enormous sea monster called the devil-fish, which he was one of the first to kill in these waters, excited my curiosity very much. Mr. Elliot has written a most agreeable account of the sports of South Carolina, and I had hoped he would have been well enough to have been my guide, philosopher, and friend in drum fishing in Port Royal; but he sent over his son to say that he was too unwell to come, and had therefore dispatched most excellent representatives in two members of his family. It was arranged that they should row down from their place and meet us to-morrow morning at Trescot's Island, which lies above Beaufort, in Port Royal Sound and river.

Got into Trescot's gig, and plunged into a shady lane with wood on each side, through which we drove for some distance. The country, on each side and beyond, perfectly flat—all rice lands—few houses visible—scarcely a human being on the road—drove six or seven miles without meeting a soul. After a couple of hours or so, I should think, the gig turned up by an open gateway on a path or road made through a waste of rich black mud, "glorious for rice," and landed us at the door of a planter, Mr Heyward, who came out and gave us a most hearty welcome, in the true Southern style. His house is charming, surrounded with trees, and covered with roses and creepers, through which birds and butterflies are flying. Mr. Hayward took it as a matter of course that we stopped to dinner, which we were by no means disinclined to do, as the day was hot, the road was dusty, and his reception frank and kindly. A fine specimen of the planter man; and, minus his broad-brimmed straw hat and loose clothing, not a bad representative of an English squire at home.

Whilst we were sitting in the porch, a strange sort of booming noise attracted my attention in one of the trees. "It is a rain-crow," said Mr. Heyward; "a bird which we believe to foretell rain. I'll shoot it for you." And, going into the hall, he took down a double-barreled fowling-piece, walked out, and fired into the tree; whence the rain-crow, poor creature, fell fluttering to the ground and died. It seemed to me a kind of cuckoo—the same size, but of darker plumage. I could gather no facts to account for the impression that it's call is a token of rain.

My attention was also called to a curious kind of snake-killing hawk, or falcon, which makes an extraordinary noise by putting its wings point upwards, close together, above its back, so as to offer no resistance to the air, and then, beginning to descend from a great height, with fast-increasing rapidity, makes, by its rushing through the air, a strange loud hum, till it is near the ground, when the bird stops its downward swoop and flies in a curve over the meadow. This I saw two of these birds doing repeatedly to-night.

After dinner, at which Mr. Heyward expressed some alarm lest Secession would deprive the Southern States of "ice," we continued our journey towards the river. There is still a remarkable absence of population or life along the road, and even the houses are either hidden or lie too far off to be seen. The trees are much admired by the people, though they would not be thought much of in England.

At length, towards sundown, having taken to a track by a forest, part of which was burning, we came to a broad muddy river, with steep clay banks. A canoe was lying in a little harbour formed by a slope in the bank, and four stout negroes, who were seated round a burning log, engaged in smoking and eating oysters, rose as we approached, and helped the party into the "dug-out," or canoe, a narrow, long, and heavy boat, with wall sides and a flat floor. A row of one hour, the latter part of it in darkness, took us to the verge of Mr. Trescot's estate, Barnwell Island; and the oarsmen, as they bent to their task, beguiled the way by singing in unison a real negro melody, which was as unlike the works of the Ethiopian Serenaders as anything in song could be unlike another. It was a barbaric sort of madrigal, in which one singer beginning was followed by the others in unison, repeating the refrain in chorus, and full of quaint expression and melancholy:—

> "Oh, your soul! oh, my soul! I'm going to the church-yard to lay this body down;
> Oh, my soul! oh, your soul! we're going to the church-yard to lay this nigger down."

And then some appeal to the difficulty of passing "the Jawdam," constituted the whole of the song, which continued with unabated energy during the whole of the little voyage. To me it was a strange scene. The stream, dark as Lethe, flowing between the silent, houseless, rugged banks, lighted up near the landing by the fire in the woods, which reddened the sky—the wild strain, and the unearthly adjurations to the singers' souls, as though they were palpable, put me in mind of the fancied voyage across the Styx.

"Here we are at last." All I could see was a dark shadow of trees and the tops of rushes by the river side. "Mind where you step, and follow me close." And so, groping along through a thick shrubbery for a short space, I came out on a garden and enclosure, in the midst of which the white outlines of a house were visible. Lights in the drawing-room—a lady to receive and welcome us—a snug library—tea, and to bed: but not without more talk about the Southern Confederacy, in which Mrs. Trescot explained how easily she could feed an army, from her experience in feeding her negroes.

CHAPTER XIX.

Domestic negroes—Negro oarsmen—Off to the fishing-grounds—The devil-fish—Bad sport—The drum-fish—Negro-quarters—Want of drainage—Thievish propensities of the blacks—A Southern estimate of Southerners.

April 27th.—Mrs. Trescot, it seems, spent part of her night in attendance on a young gentleman of colour, who was introduced into the world in a state of servitude by his poor chattel of a mother. Such kindly acts as these are more common than we may suppose; and it would be unfair to put a strict or unfair construction on the motives of slave owners in paying such attention to their property. Indeed, as Mrs. Trescot says, "When people talk of my having so many slaves, I always tell them it is the slaves who own me. Morning, noon, and night, I'm obliged to look after them, to doctor them, and attend to them in every way." Property has its duties, you see, madam, as well as its rights.

The planter's house is quite new, and was built by himself; the principal material being wood, and most of the work being done by his own negroes. Such work as window-sashes and panelings, however, was executed in Charleston. A pretty garden runs at the back, and from the windows there are wide stretches of cotton-fields visible, and glimpses of the river to be seen.

After breakfast our little party repaired to the river-side, and sat under the shade of some noble trees waiting for the boat which was to bear us to the fishing-grounds. The wind blew up stream, running with the tide, and we strained our eyes in vain for the boat. The river is here nearly a mile across,—a noble estuary rather,—with low banks lined with forests, into which the axe has made deep forays and clearings for cotton-fields.

It would have astonished a stray English traveller, if, penetrating the shade, he heard in such an out-of-the-way place familiar names and things spoken of by the three lazy persons who were stretched out—cigar in mouth—on the ant-haunted trunks which lay prostrate by the sea-shore. Mr. Trescot spent some time in London as *attaché* to the United States Legation, was a club man, and had a large circle of acquaintance among the young men about town, of whom he remembered many anecdotes and peculiarities, and little adventures. Since that time he was Under-Secretary of State in Mr. Buchanan's administration, and went out with Secession. He is the author of a very agreeable book on a dry subject, "The History of American Diplomacy," which is curious enough as an unconscious exposition of the anti-British jealousies, and even antipathies, which have animated American statesmen since they were created. In fact, much of American diplomacy means hostility to England, and the skilful employment of the anti-British sentiment at their disposal in their own country and elsewhere. Now he was talking pleasantly of people he had met—many of them mutual friends.

"Here is the boat at last!" I had been sweeping the broad river with my glass occasionally, and at length detected a speck on its broad surface moving down towards us, with a white dot marking the foam at its bows. Spite of wind and tideway, it came rapidly, and soon approached us, pulled by six powerful negroes, attired in red flannel jackets and white straw hats with broad ribands. The craft itself—a kind of monster canoe, some forty-five feet long, narrow, wall-sided, with high bow and raised stern—lay deep in the water, for there were extra negroes for the fishing, servants, baskets of provisions, water buckets, stone jars of less innocent drinking, and abaft there was a knot of great strong planters—Elliots all—cousins, uncles, and brothers. A friendly hail as they swept up alongside,—an exchange of salutations.

"Well, Trescot, have you got plenty of crabs?"

A groan burst forth at his *insouciant* reply. He had been charged to find bait, and he had told the negroes to do so, and the negroes had not done so. The fishermen looked grievously at each other, and fiercely at Trescot, who assumed an air of recklessness, and threw doubts on the existence of fish in the river, and resorted to similar miserable subterfuges; indeed, it was subsequently discovered that he was an utter infidel in regard to the delights of piscicapture.

"Now, all aboard! Over, you fellows, and take these gentlemen in!" The negroes were over in a moment, waist deep, and, each taking one on his back, deposited us dry in the boat. I only mention this to record the fact, that I was much impressed by a practical demonstration from my bearer respecting the strong odour of the skin of a heated African. I have been wedged up in a column of infantry on a hot day, and have marched to leeward of Ghoorkhas in India, but the overpowering pungent smell of the negro exceeds everything of the kind I have been unfortunate enough to experience.

The vessel was soon moving again, against a ripple, caused by the wind, which blew dead against us; and notwithstanding the praises bestowed on the boat, it was easy to perceive that the labour of pulling such a dead-log-like thing through the water told severely on the rowers, who had already come some twelve miles, I think. Nevertheless, they were told to sing, and they began accordingly one of those wild Baptist chants about the Jordan in which they delight,—not destitute of music, but utterly unlike what is called an Ethiopian melody.

The banks of the river on both sides are low; on the left covered with wood, through which, here and there, at intervals, one could see a planter's or overseer's cottage. The course of this great combination of salt and fresh water sometimes changes, so that houses are swept away and plantations submerged; but the land is much valued nevertheless, on account of the fineness of the cotton grown among the islands. "Cotton at 12 cents a pound, and we don't fear the world."

As the boat was going to the fishing-ground, which lay towards the mouth of the river at Hilton Head, our friends talked politics and sporting combined,—the first of the usual character, the second quite new.

I heard much of the mighty devil-fish which frequents these waters. One of our party, Mr. Elliot, sen., a tall, knotty, gnarled sort of man, with a mellow eye and a hearty voice, was a famous hand at the sport, and had had some hair-breadth escapes in pursuit of it. The fish is described as of enormous size and strength, a monster ray, which possesses formidable antennæ-like horns, and a pair of huge fins, or flappers, one of which rises above the water as the creature moves below the surface. The hunters, as they may be called, go out in parties—three or four boats, or more, with good store of sharp harpoons and tow-lines, and lances. When they perceive the creature, one boat takes the lead, and moves down towards it, the others following, each with a harpooner standing in the bow. The devil-fish sometimes is wary, and dives, when it sees a boat, taking such a long spell below that it is never seen again. At other times, however, it backs, and lets the boat come so near as to allow of the harpooner striking it, or it dives for a short way and comes up near the boats again. The moment the harpoon is fixed, the line is paid out by the rush of the creature, which is made with tremendous force, and all the boats at once hurry up, so that one after another they are made fast to that in which the lucky sportsman is seated. At length, when the line is run out, checked from time to time as much as can be done with safety, the crew take their oars and follow the course of the ray, which swims so fast, however, that it keeps the line taught, and drags the whole flotilla seawards. It depends on its size and strength to determine how soon it rises to the surface; by degrees the line is warped in and hove short till the boats are brought near, and when the ray comes up it is attacked with a shower of lances and harpoons, and dragged off into shoal water to die.

On one occasion, our Nimrod told us, he was standing in the bows of the boat, harpoon in hand, when a devil-fish came up close to him; he threw the harpoon, struck it, but at the same time the boat ran against the creature with a shock which threw him right forward on its back, and in an instant it caught him in its horrid arms and plunged down with him to the depths. Imagine the horror of the moment! Imagine the joy of the terrified drowning, dying man, when, for some inscrutable reason, the devil-fish relaxed its grip, and enabled him to strike for the surface, where he was dragged into the boat more dead than alive by his terror-smitten companions,—the only man who ever got out of the embraces of the thing alive. "Tom is so tough that even the devil-fish could make nothing out of him."

At last we came to our fishing-ground. There was a substitute found for the favourite crab, and it was fondly hoped our toils might be rewarded with success. And these were toils, for the water is deep and the lines heavy. But to alleviate them, some hampers were produced from the stern, and wonderful pies from Mrs. Trescot's hands, and from those of fair ladies up the river whom we shall never see, were spread out, and bottles which represented distant cellars in friendly nooks far away. "No drum here! Up anchor, and pull away a few miles lower down." Trescot shook his head, and again asserted his disbelief in fishing, or rather in catching, and indeed made a sort of pretence at arguing that it was wiser to remain quiet and talk philosophical politics; but, as judge of appeal, I gave it against him, and the negroes bent to their oars, and we went thumping through the spray, till, rounding a point of land, we saw pitched on the sandy shore ahead of us, on the right bank, a tent, and close by two boats. "There is a party at it!" A fire was burning on the beach, and as we came near, Tom and Jack and Harry were successively identified. "There's no take on, or they would not be on shore. This is very unfortunate."

All the regret of my friends was on my account, so to ease their minds I assured them I did not mind the disappointment much. "Hallo, Dick! Caught any drum?" "A few this morning; bad sport now, and will be till tide turns again." I was introduced to all the party from a distance, and presently I saw one of them raising from a boat something in look and shape and colour like a sack of flour, which he gave to a negro, who proceeded to carry it towards us in a little skiff. "Thank you, Charley. I just want to let Mr. Russell see a drum-fish." And a very odd fish it was,—a thick lumpish form, about 4½ feet long, with enormous head and scales, and teeth like the grinders of a ruminant animal, acting on a great pad of bone in the roof of the mouth,—a very unlovely thing, swollen with roe, which is the great delicacy.

"No chance till the tide turned,"—but that would be too late for our return, and so unwillingly we were compelled to steer towards home, hearing now and then the singular noise like the tap on a large unbraced drum, from which the fish takes its name. At first, when I heard it, I was inclined to think it was made by some one in the boat, so near and close did it sound; but soon it came from all sides of us, and evidently from the depths of the water beneath us,—not a sharp rat-tat-tap, but a full muffled blow with a heavy thud on the sheepskin. Mr. Trescot told me that on a still evening by the river-side the effect sometimes is most curious,—the rolling and puttering is audible at a great distance. Our friends were in excellent humour with everything and everybody, except the Yankees, though they had caught no fish, and kept the negroes at singing and rowing till at nightfall we landed at the island, and so to bed after supper and a little conversation, in which Mrs. Trescot again explained how easily she could maintain a battalion on the island by her simple commissariat, already adapted to the niggers, and that it would therefore be very easy for the South to feed an army if the people were friendly.

April 28th.—The church is a long way off, only available by a boat and then a drive in a carriage. In the morning a child brings in my water and boots—an intelligent, curly-headed creature, dressed in a sort of sack, without any particular waist, barefooted. I imagined it was a boy till it told me it was a girl. I asked if she was going to church, which seemed to puzzle her exceedingly; but she told me finally she would hear prayers from "uncle" in one of the cottages. The use of the words "uncle" and "aunt" for old people is very general. Is it because they have no fathers and mothers? In the course of the day, the child, who was fourteen or fifteen years of age, asked me "whether I would not buy her. She could wash and sew very well, and she thought missus wouldn't want much for her." The object she had in view leaked out at last. It was a desire to see the glories of Beaufort, of which she had heard from the fishermen; and she seemed quite wonder-struck when she was informed I did not live there, and had never seen it. She had never been outside the plantation in her life.

After breakfast we loitered about the grounds, strolling through the cotton-fields, which had as yet put forth no bloom or flower, and coming down others to the thick fringes of wood and sedge bordering the marshy banks of the island. The silence was profound, broken only by the husky mid-day crowing of the cocks in the negro quarters.

In the afternoon I took a short drive "to see a tree," which was not very remarkable, and looked in at the negro quarters and the cotton mill. The old negroes were mostly indoors, and came shambling out to the doors of their wooden cottages, making clumsy bows at our approach, but not expressing any interest or pleasure at the sight of their master and the strangers. They were shabbily clad; in tattered clothes, bad straw hats and felt bonnets, and broken shoes. The latter are expensive articles, and negroes cannot dig without them. Trescot sighed as he spoke of the increase of price since the troubles broke out.

The huts stand in a row, like a street, each detached, with a poultry-house of rude planks behind it. The mutilations which the poultry undergo for the sake of distinction are striking. Some are deprived of a claw, others have the wattles cut, and tails and wings suffer in all ways. No attempt at any drainage or any convenience existed near them, and the same remark applies to very good houses of white people in the south. Heaps of oyster-shells, broken crockery, old shoes, rags, and feathers were found near each hut. The huts were all alike windowless, and the apertures, intended to be glazed some fine day, were generally filled up with a deal board. The roofs were shingle, and the whitewash which had once given the settlement an air of cleanliness, was now only to be traced by patches which had escaped the action of the rain. I observed that many of the doors were fastened by a padlock and chain outside. "Why is that?" "The owners have gone out, and honesty is not a virtue they have towards each other. They would find their things stolen if they did not lock their doors." Mrs. Trescot, however, insisted on it that nothing could exceed the probity of the slaves in the house, except in regard to sweet things, sugar and the like; but money and jewels were quite safe. It is obvious that some reason must exist for this regard to the distinctions twixt meum and tuum in the case of masters and mistresses, when it does not guide their conduct towards each other, and I think it might easily be found in the fact that the negroes could scarcely take money without detection. Jewels and jewellery would be of little value to them; they could not wear them, could not part with them. The system has made the white population a police against the black race, and the punishment is not only sure but grievous. Such things as they can steal from each other are not to be so readily traced.

One particularly dirty-looking little hut was described to me as "the church." It was about fifteen feet square, begrimed with dirt and smoke, and windowless. A few benches were placed across it, and "the preacher," a slave from another plantation, was expected next week. These preachings are not encouraged in many plantations. They "do the niggers no good"—"they talk about things that are going on elsewhere, and get their minds unsettled," and so on.

On our return to the house, I found that Mr. Edmund Rhett, one of the active and influential political family of that name, had called—a very intelligent and agreeable gentleman, but one of the most ultra and violent speakers against the Yankees I have yet heard. He declared there were few persons in South Carolina who would not sooner ask great Britain to take back the State than submit to the triumph of the Yankees. "We are an agricultural people, pursuing our own system, and working out our own destiny, breeding up women and men with some other purpose than to make them vulgar, fanatical, cheating Yankees—hypocritical, if as women they pretend to real virtue; and lying, if as men they pretend to be honest. We have gentlemen and gentlewomen in your sense of it. We have a system which enables us to reap the fruits of the earth by a race which we save from barbarism in restoring them to their real place in the world as laborers, whilst we are enabled to cultivate the arts, the graces, and accomplishments of life, to develop science, to apply ourselves to the duties of government, and to understand the affairs of the country."

This is a very common line of remark here. The Southerners also take pride to themselves, and not unjustly, for their wisdom in keeping in

Congress those men who have proved themselves useful and capable. "We do not," they say, "cast able men aside at the caprices of a mob, or in obedience to some low party intrigue, and hence we are sure of the best men, and are served by gentlemen conversant with public affairs, far superior in every way to the ignorant clowns who are sent to Congress by the North. Look at the fellows who are sent out by Lincoln to insult foreign courts by their presence." I said that I understood Mr. Adams and Mr. Drayton were very respectable gentlemen, but I did not receive any sympathy; in fact, a neutral who attempts to moderate the violence of either side, is very like an ice between two hot plates. Mr. Rhett is also persuaded that the Lord Chancellor sits on a cotton-bale. "You must recognise us, sir, before the end of October." In the evening a distant thunder-storm attracted me to the garden, and I remained out watching the broad flashes and sheets of fire worthy of the tropics till it was bed-time.

CHAPTER XX.

By railway to Savannah—Description of the city—Rumours of the last few days—State of affairs at Washington—Preparations for war—Cemetery of Bonaventure—Road made of oyster-shells—Appropriate features of the Cemetery—The Tatnall family—Dinner-party at Mr. Green's—Feeling in Georgia against the North.

April 20th.—This morning up at 6 A.M., bade farewell to our hostess and Barnwell Island, and proceeded with Trescot back to the Pocotaligo station, which we reached at 12.20. On our way Mr. Heyward and his son rode out of a field, looking very like a couple of English country squires in all but hats and saddles. The young gentleman was good enough to bring over a snake hawk he had shot for me. At the station, to which the Heywards accompanied us, were the Elliots and others, who had come over with invitations and adieux; and I beguiled the time to Savannah reading the very interesting book by Mr. Elliot, senior, on the Wild Sports of Carolina, which was taken up by some one when I left the car-carriage for a moment and not returned to me. The country through which we passed was flat and flooded as usual, and the rail passed over dark deep rivers on lofty trestle-work, by pine wood and dogwood tree, by the green plantation clearing, with mud bank, dyke, and tiny canal mile by mile, the train stopping for the usual freight of ladies, and negro nurses, and young planters, all very much of the same class, till at 3 o'clock P.M., the cars rattled up alongside a large shed, and we were told we had arrived at Savannah.

Here was waiting for me Mr. Charles Green, who had already claimed me and my friend as his guests, and I found in his carriage the young American designer, who had preceded me from Charleston, and had informed Mr. Green of my coming.

The drive through such portion of Savannah as lay between the terminus and Mr. Green's house, soon satisfied my eyes that it had two peculiarities. In the first-place, it had the deepest sand in the streets I have ever seen; and next, the streets were composed of the most odd, quaint, green-windowed, many-coloured little houses I ever beheld, with an odd population of lean, sallow, ill-dressed unwholesome-looking whites, lounging about the exchanges and corners, and a busy, well-clad, gaily-attired race of negroes, working their way through piles of children, under the shade of the trees which bordered all the streets. The fringe of green, and the height attained by the live oak, Pride of India, and magnolia, give a delicious freshness and novelty to the streets of Savannah, which is increased by the great number of squares and openings covered with something like sward, fenced round by white rail, and embellished with noble trees to be seen at every few hundred yards. It is difficult to believe you are in the midst of a city, and I was repeatedly reminded of the environs of a large Indian cantonment—the same kind of churches and detached houses, with their plantations and gardens not unlike. The wealthier classes, however, have houses of the New York Fifth Avenue character: one of the best of these, a handsome mansion of rich red sandstone, belonged to my host, who coming out from England many years ago, raised himself by industry and intelligence to the position of one of the first merchants in Savannah. Italian statuary graced the hall; finely carved tables and furniture, stained glass, and pictures from Europe set forth the sitting-rooms; and the luxury of bath-rooms and a supply of cold fresh water, rendered it an exception to the general run of Southern edifices. Mr. Green drove me through the town, which impressed me more than ever with its peculiar character. We visited Brigadier-General Lawton, who is charged with the defences of the place against the expected Yankees, and found him just setting out to inspect a band of volunteers, whose drums we heard in the distance, and whose bayonets were gleaming through the clouds of Savannah dust, close to the statue erected to the memory of one Pulaski, a Pole, who was mortally wounded in the unsuccessful defence of the city against the British in the war of Independence. He turned back and led us into his house. The hall was filled with little round rolls of flannel. "These," said he, "are cartridges for cannon of various calibres, made by the ladies of Mrs. Lawton's 'cartridge class.'" There were more cartridges in the back parlour, so that the house was not quite a safe place to smoke a cigar in. The General has been in the United States' army, and has now come forward to head the people of this State in their resistance to the Yankees.

We took a stroll in the park, and I learned the news of the last few days. The people of the South, I find, are delighted at a snubbing which Mr. Seward has given to Governor Hicks of Maryland, for recommending the arbitration of Lord Lyons, and he is stated to have informed Governor Hicks that "our troubles could not be referred to foreign arbitration, least of all to that of the representatives of a European monarchy." The most terrible accounts are given of the state of things in Washington. Mr. Lincoln consoles himself for his miseries by drinking. Mr. Seward follows suit. The White House and capital are full of drunken border ruffians, headed by one Jim Lane of Kansas. But, on the other hand, the Yankees, under one Butler, a Massachusetts lawyer, have arrived at Annapolis, in Maryland, secured the "Constitution" man-of-war, and are raising masses of men for the invasion of the South all over the States. The most important thing, as it strikes me, is the proclamation of the Governor of Georgia, forbidding citizens to pay any money on account of debts due to Northerners, till the end of the war. General Robert E. Lee has been named Commander-in-Chief of the Forces of the Commonwealth of Virginia, and troops are flocking to that State from Alabama and other States. Governor Ellis has called out 30,000 volunteers in North Carolina, and Governor Rector of Arkansas has seized the United States' military stores at Napoleon. There is a rumour that Fort Pickens has been taken also, but it is very probably untrue. In Texas and Arkansas the United States regulars have not made an attempt to defend any of the forts.

In the midst of all this warlike work, volunteers drilling, bands playing, it was pleasant to walk in the shady park, with its cool fountains, and to see the children playing about—many of them, alas! "playing at soldiers"—in charge of their nurses. Returning, sat in the verandah and smoked a cigar; but the musquitoes were very keen and numerous. My host did not mind them, but my cuticle will never be sting-proof.

April 30th.—At 1.30 P.M., a small party started from Mr. Green's to visit the cemetery of Bonaventure, to which every visitor to Savannah must pay his pilgrimage; *difficiles aditus primos habet*—a deep sandy road which strains the horses and the carriages; but at last "the shell road" is reached—a highway several miles long, consisting of oyster-shells—the pride of Savannah, which eats as many oysters as it can to add to the length of this wonderful road. There is no stone in the whole of the vast alluvial ranges of South Carolina and Maritime Georgia, and the only substance available for making a road is the oyster-shell. There is a toll-gate at each end to aid the oyster-shells. Remember they are three times the size of any European crustacean of the sort.

A pleasant drive through the shady hedgerows and bordering trees lead to a dilapidated porter's lodge and gateway, within which rose in a towering mass of green one of the finest pictures of forest architecture possible; nothing to be sure like Burnham Beeches, or some of the forest glades of Windsor, but possessed, nevertheless, of a character quite its own. What we gazed upon was, in fact, the ruin of grand avenues of live oak, so well-disposed that their peculiar mode of growth afforded an unusual development of the "Gothic idea," worked out and elaborated by a superabundant fall from the overlacing arms and intertwined branches of the tillandsia, or Spanish moss, a weeping, drooping, plumaceous parasite, which does to the tree what its animal type, the yellow fever—*vomito prieto*—does to man—clings to it everlastingly, drying up sap, poisoning blood, killing the principle of life till it dies. The only differ, as they say in Ireland, is, that the tillandsia all the time looks very pretty, and that the process lasts very long. Some there are who praise this tillandsia, hanging like the tresses of a witch's hair over an invisible face, but to me it is a paltry parasite, destroying the grace and beauty of that it preys upon, and letting fall its dull tendrils over the fresh lovely green, as clouds drop over the face of some beautiful landscape. Despite all this, Bonaventure is a scene of remarkable interest; it seems to have been intended for a place of tombs. The Turks would have filled it with turbaned white pillars, and with warm ghosts at night. The French would have decorated it with interlaced hands of stone, with tears of red and black on white ground, with wreaths of immortelles. I am not sure that we would have done much more than have got up a cemetery company, interested Shillibeer, hired a beadle, and erected an iron paling. The Savannah people not following any of these fashions, all of which are adopted in Northern cities, have left everything to nature and the gatekeeper, and to the owner of one of the hotels, who has got up a grave-yard in the ground. And there, scattered up and down under the grand old trees, which drop tears of Spanish moss, and weave wreaths of Spanish moss, and shake plumes of Spanish moss over them, are a few monumental stones to certain citizens of Savannah. There is a melancholy air about the place independently of these emblems of our mortality, which might recommend it specially for picnics. There never was before a cemetery where nature seemed to aid the effect intended by man so thoroughly. Every one knows a weeping willow will cry over a wedding party if they sit under it, as well as over a grave. But here the Spanish moss looks like weepers wreathed by some fantastic hand out of the crape of Dreamland. Lucian's Ghostlander, the son of Skeleton of the Tribe of the Juiceless, could tell us something of such weird trappings. They are known indeed as the best bunting for yellow fever to fight under. Wherever their flickering horsehair tresses wave in the breeze, taper ends downwards, Squire Black Jack is bearing lance and sword. One great green oak says to the other, "This fellow is killing me. Take his deadly robes off my limbs!" "Alas! See how he is ruining me! I have no life to help you." It is, indeed, a strange and very ghastly place. Here are so many *querci virentes*, old enough to be strong, and big, and great, sapfull, lusty, wide-armed, green-honoured—all dying out slowly beneath tillandsia, as if they were so many monarchies perishing of decay—or so many youthful republics dying of buncombe brag, richness of blood, and other diseases fatal to overgrown bodies politic.

The void left in the midst of all these designed walks and stately avenues, by the absence of any suitable centre, increases the seclusion and solitude. A house ought to be there somewhere you feel—in fact there was once the mansion of the Tatnalls, a good old English family, whose ancestors came from the old country, ere the rights of man were talked of, and lived among the Oglethorpes, and such men of the pigtail school, who would have been greatly astonished at finding themselves in company with Benjamin Franklin or his kind. I don't know anything of old Tatnall. Indeed who does? But he had a fine idea of planting trees, which he never got in America, where he would have received scant praise for anything but his power to plant cotton or sugar-cane just now. In his kneebreeches and top boots, I can fancy the old gentleman reproducing some home scene, and boasting to himself, "I will make it as fine as Lord Nihilo's park." Could he see it now?—A decaying army of the dead. The mansion was burned down during a Christmas merrymaking, and was never built again, and the young trees have grown up despite the Spanish moss, and now they stand, as it were in cathedral aisles, around the ruins of the departed house, shading the ground, and enshrining its memories in an antiquity which seems of the remotest, although it is not as ancient as that of the youngest oak in the Squire's park at home.

I have before oftentimes in my short voyages here, wondered greatly at the reverence bestowed on a tree. In fact, it is because a tree of any decent growth is sure to be older than anything else around it; and although young America revels in her future, she is becoming old enough to think about her past.

In the evening Mr. Green gave a dinner to some very agreeable people, Mr. Ward, the Chinese Minister—(who tried, by-the-bye, to make it appear that his wooden box was the Pekin State carriage for distinguished foreigners)—Mr. Locke, the clever and intelligent editor of the principal journal in Savannah, Brigadier Lawton, one of the Judges, a Britisher, owner of the once renowned America which, under the name of Camilla, was now lying in the river (not perhaps without reference to a little speculation in running the blockade, hourly expected), Mr. Ward, and Commodore Tatnall, so well known to us in England for his gallant conduct in the Peiho affair, when he offered and gave our vessels aid, though a neutral, and uttered the exclamation in doing so,—in his despatch at all events,—"that blood was thicker than water." Of our party was also Mr. Hodgson, well known to most of our Mediterranean travellers some years back, when he was United States' Consul in the East. He amuses his leisure still by inditing and reading monographs on the languages of divers barbarous tribes in Numidia and Mauritania.

The Georgians are not quite so vehement as the South Carolinians in their hate of the Northerners; but they are scarcely less determined to fight President Lincoln and all his men. And that is the test of this rebellion's strength. I did not hear any profession of a desire to become subject to England, or to borrow a prince of us; but I have nowhere seen stronger determination to resist any reunion with the New England States. "They can't conquer us, Sir?" "If they try it, we'll whip them."

CHAPTER XXI.

The river at Savannah—Commodore Tatnall—Fort Pulaski—Want of a fleet to the Southerners—Strong feeling of the women—Slavery considered in its results—Cotton and Georgia—Off for Montgomery—The Bishop of Georgia—The Bible and Slavery—Macon—Dislike of United States' gold.

May Day.—Not unworthy of the best effort of English fine weather before the change in the kalendar robbed the poets of twelve days, but still a little warm for choice. The young American artist Moses, who was to have called our party to meet the officers who were going to Fort Pulaski, for some reason known to himself remained on board the Camilla, and when at last we got down to the river-side I found Commodore Tatnall and Brigadier Lawton in full uniform waiting for me.

The river is about the width of the Thames below Gravesend, very muddy, with a strong current, and rather fetid. That effect might have been produced from the rice-swamps at the other side of it, where the land is quite low, and stretches away as far as the sea in one level green, smooth as a billiard-cloth. The bank at the city side is higher, so that the houses stand on a little eminence over the stream, affording convenient wharfage and slips for merchant vessels.

Of these there were few indeed visible—nearly all had cleared out for fear of the blockade; some coasting vessels were lying idle at the quay side, and in the middle of the stream near a floating dock the Camilla was moored, with her club ensign flying. These are the times for bold ventures, and if Uncle Sam is not very quick with his blockades, there will be plenty of privateers and the like under C. S. A. colours looking out for his fat merchantmen all over the world.

I have been trying to persuade my friends here they will find very few Englishmen willing to take letters of marque and reprisal.

The steamer which was waiting to receive us had the Confederate flag flying, and Commodore Tatnall, pointing to a young officer in a naval uniform, told me he had just "come over from the other side," and that he had pressed hard to be allowed to hoist a Commodore or flag-officer's ensign in honour of the visit and of the occasion. I was much interested in the fine white-headed, blue-eyed, ruddy-cheeked old man — who suddenly found himself blown into the air by a great political explosion, and in doubt and wonderment was floating to shore, under a strange flag in unknown waters. He was full of anecdote too, as to strange flags in distant waters and well-known names. The gentry of Savannah had a sort of Celtic feeling towards him in regard of his old name, and seemed determined to support him.

He has served the Stars and Stripes for three fourths of a long life — his friends are in the North, his wife's kindred are there, and so are all his best associations—but his State has gone out. How could he fight against the country that gave him birth! The United States is no country, in the sense we understand the words. It is a corporation or a body corporate for certain purposes, and a man might as well call himself a native of the common council of the city of London, or a native of the Swiss Diet, in the estimation of our Americans, as say he is a citizen of the United States; though it answers very well to say so when he is abroad, or for purposes of a legal character.

Of Fort Pulaski itself I wrote on my return a long account to the "Times."

When I was venturing to point out to General Lawton the weakness of Fort Pulaski, placed as it is in low land, accessible to boats, and quite open enough for approaches from the city side, he said, "Oh, that is true enough. All our sea-coast works are liable to that remark, but the Commodore will take care of the Yankees at sea, and we shall manage them on land." These people all make a mistake in referring to the events of the old war. "We beat off the British fleet at Charleston by the militia—ergo, we'll sink the Yankees now." They do not understand the nature of the new shell and heavy vertical fire, or the effect of projectiles from great distances falling into open works. The Commodore afterwards, smiling, remarked, "I have no fleet. Long before the Southern Confederacy has a fleet that can cope with the Stars and Stripes, my bones will be white in the grave."

We got back by eight o'clock P.M., after a pleasant day. What I saw did not satisfy me that Pulaski was strong, or Savannah very safe. At Bonaventure yesterday I saw a poor fort called "Thunderbolt," on an inlet from which the city was quite accessible. It could be easily menaced from that point, while attempts at landing were made elsewhere as soon as Pulaski was reduced. At dinner met a very strong and very well informed Southerner—there are some who are neither—or either—whose name was spelled Gourdin and pronounced Go-dine—just as Huger is called Hugee—and Tagliaferro, Telfer in these parts.

May 2nd.—Breakfasted with Mr. Hodgson, where I met Mr. Locke, Mr. Ward, Mr. Green, and Mrs. Hodgson and her sister. There were in attendance some good-looking little negro boys and men dressed in liveries, which smacked of our host's Orientalism, and they must have heard our discussion, or rather allusion, to the question which would decide whether we thought they are human beings or black two-legged cattle, with some interest, unless indeed the boast of their masters, that slavery elevates the character and civilises the mind of a negro, is another of the false pretences on which the institution is rested by its advocates. The native African, poor wretch, avoids being carried into slavery *totis viribus*, and it would argue ill for the effect on his mind of becoming a slave if he prefers a piece of gaudy calico even to his loin-cloth and feather head-dress. This question of civilising the African in slavery is answered in the assertion of the slave-owners themselves, that if the negroes were left to their own devices by emancipation, they would become the worst sort of barbarians—a veritable Quasheedom, the like of which was never thought of by Mr. Thomas Carlyle. I doubt if the aboriginal is not as civilised, in the true sense of the word, as any negro, after three degrees of descent in servitude, whom I have seen on any of the plantations—even though the latter have leather shoes and fustian or cloth raiment, and felt hat, and sings about the Jordan. He is exempted from any bloody raid indeed, but he is liable to be carried from his village and borne from one captivity to another, and his family are exposed to the same exile in America as in Africa. The extreme anger with which any unfavourable comment is met publicly, shows the sensitiveness of the slave-owners. Privately, they affect philosophy; and the blue books, and reports of Education Commissions and Mining Committees, furnish them with an inexhaustible source of argument if you once admit that the *summum bonum* lies in a certain rotundity of person and a regular supply of coarse food. A long conversation on the old topics—old to me, but of only a few weeks' birth. People are swimming with the tide. Here are many men who would willingly stand aside if they could, and see the battle between the Yankees, whom they hate, and the Secessionists. But there are no women in this party. Wo betide the Northern Pyrrhus whose head is within reach of a Southern tile and a Southern woman's arm!

I re-visited some of the big houses afterwards, and found the merchants not cheerful, but fierce and resolute. There is a considerable population of Irish and Germans in Savannah, who to a man are in favour of the Confederacy, and will fight to support it. Indeed, it is expected they will do so, and there is a pressure brought to bear on them by their employers which they cannot well resist. The negroes will be forced into the place the whites hitherto occupied as labourers—only a few useful mechanics will be kept, and the white population will be obliged by a moral force draughting to go to the wars. The kingdom of cotton is most essentially of this world, and it will be fought for vigorously. On the quays of Savannah, and in the warehouses, there is not a man who doubts that he ought to strike his hardest for it, or apprehends failure. And then, what a career is before them! All the world asking for cotton, and England dependent on it. What a change since Whitney first set his cotton gin to work in this state close by us! Georgia, as a vast country only partially reclaimed, yet looks to a magnificent future. In her past history the Florida wars, and the treatment of the unfortunate Cherokee Indians, who were expelled from their lands as late as 1838, show the people who descended from old Oglethorpe's band were fierce and tyrannical, and apt at aggression, nor will slavery improve them. I do not speak of the cultivated and hospitable citizens of the large towns, but of the bulk of the slaveless whites.

May 3rd.—I bade good-by to Mr. Green, who with several of his friends came down to see me off, at the terminus or "depôt" of the Central Railway, on my way to Montgomery—and looked my last on Savannah, its squares and leafy streets, its churches, and institutes with a feeling of regret that I could not see more of them, and that I was forced to be content with the outer aspect of the public buildings. I had been serenaded and invited out in all directions, asked to visit plantations and big trees, to make excursions to famous or beautiful spots, and specially warned not to leave the State without visiting the mountain district in the northern and western portion; but the march of events called me to Montgomery.

From Savannah to Macon, 191 miles, the road passes through level country only partially cleared. That is, there are patches of forest still intruding on the green fields, where the jagged black teeth of the destroyed trees rise from above the maize and cotton. There were but few negroes visible at work, nor did the land appear rich, but I was told the rail was laid along the most barren part of the country. The Indians had roamed in these woods little more than twenty years ago—now the wooden huts of the planters' slaves and the larger edifice with its verandah and timber colonnade stood in the place of their wigwam.

Among the passengers to whom I was introduced was the Bishop of Georgia, the Rev. Mr. Elliott, a man of exceeding fine presence, of great stature, and handsome face, with a manner easy and graceful, but we got on the unfortunate subject of slavery, and I rather revolted at hearing a Christian prelate advocating the institution on scriptural grounds.

This application of biblical sanction and ordinance as the basis of slavery was not new to me, though it is not much known at the other side of the Atlantic. I had read in a work on slavery, that it was permitted by both the Scriptures and the Constitution of the United States, and that it must, therefore, be doubly right. A nation that could approve of such interpretations of the Scriptures and at the same time read the "New York Herald," seemed ripe for destruction as a corporate existence. The *malum prohibitum* was the only evil its crass senses could detect, and the *malum per se* was its good, if it only came covered with cotton or gold. The miserable sophists who expose themselves to the contempt of the world by their paltry thesicles on the divine origin and uses of slavery, are infinitely more contemptible than the wretched bigots who published themes long ago on the propriety of burning witches, or on the necessity for the offices of the Inquisition.

Whenever the Southern Confederacy shall achieve its independence—no matter what its resources, its allies, or its aims—it will have to stand face to face with civilized Europe on this question of slavery, and the strength which it derived from the ægis of the Constitution—"the league with the devil and covenant with Hell"—will be withered and gone.

I am well aware of the danger of drawing summary conclusions off-hand from the windows of a railway, but there is also a right of sight which exists under all circumstances, and so one can determine if a man's face be dirty as well from a glance as if he inspected it for half an hour. For instance, no one can doubt the evidence of his senses, when he sees from the windows of the carriages that the children are barefooted, shoeless, stockingless — that the people who congregate at the wooden huts and grog-shops of the stations are rude, unkempt, but great fighting material too—that the villages are miserable places, compared with the trim, snug settlements one saw in New Jersey from the carriage-windows. Slaves in the fields looked happy enough — but their masters certainly were rough-looking and uncivilised—and the land was but badly cleared. But then we were traversing the least fertile portions of the State—a recent acquirement—gained only one generation since.

The train halted at a snug little wood-embowered restaurant, surrounded by trellis and lattice-work, and in the midst of a pretty garden, which presented a marked contrast to the "surroundings" we had seen. The dinner, served by slaves, was good of its kind, and the charge not high. On tendering the landlord a piece of gold for payment, he looked at it with disgust, and asked, "Have you no Charleston money? No Confederate notes?" "Well, no! Why do you object to gold?" "Well, do you see, I'd rather have our own paper! I don't care to take any of the United States' gold. I don't want their stars and their eagles; I hate the sight of them." The man was quite sincere—my companion gave him notes of some South Carolina bank.

It was dark when the train reached Macon, one of the principal cities of the State. We drove to the best hotel, but the regular time for dinner-hour was over, and that for supper not yet come. The landlord directed us to a subterranean restaurant, in which were a series of crypts closed in by dirty curtains, where we made a very extraordinary repast, served by a half-clad little negress, who watched us at the meal with great interest through the curtains—the service was of the coarsest description; thick French earthenware, the spoons of pewter, the knives and forks steel or iron, with scarce a pretext of being cleaned. On the doors were the usual warnings against pickpockets, and the customary internal police regulations and ukases. Pickpockets and gamblers abound in American cities, and thrive greatly at the large hotels and the lines of railways.

CHAPTER XXII.

Slave-pens; Negroes on sale or hire—Popular feeling as to Secession—Beauregard and speech-making—Arrival at Montgomery—Bad hotel accommodation—Knights of the Golden Circle—Reflections on Slavery — Slave auction—The Legislative Assembly—A "live chattel" knocked down — Rumours from the North (true and false) and prospects of war.

May 4th.—In the morning I took a drive about the city, which is loosely built in detached houses over a pretty undulating country covered with wood and fruit-trees. Many good houses of dazzling white, with bright green blinds, verandahs, and doors, stand in their own grounds or gardens. In the course of the drive I saw two or three signboards and placards announcing that "Smith & Co. advanced money on slaves, and had constant supplies of Virginian negroes on sale or hire." These establishments were surrounded by high walls enclosing the slave-pens or large rooms, in which the slaves are kept for inspection. The train for Montgomery started at 9.45 A.M., but I had no time to stop and visit them.

It is evident we are approaching the Confederate capital, for the candidates for office begin to show, and I detected a printed testimonial in my room in the hotel. The country, from Macon in Georgia to Montgomery in Alabama, offers no features to interest the traveller which are not common to the districts already described. It is, indeed, more undulating, and somewhat more picturesque, or less unattractive, but, on the whole, there is little to recommend it, except the natural fertility of the soil. The people are rawer, ruder, bigger—there is the same amount of tobacco-chewing and its consequences—and as much swearing or use of expletives. The men are tall, lean, uncouth, but they are not peasants. There are, so far as I have seen, no rustics, no peasantry in America; men dress after the same type, differing only in finer or coarser material; every man would wear, if he could, a black satin waistcoat and a large diamond pin stuck in the front of his shirt, as he certainly has a watch and a gilt or gold chain of some sort or other. The Irish labourer, or the German husbandman is the nearest approach to our Giles Jolter or the Jacques Bonhomme to be found in the States. The mean white affects the style of the large proprietor of slaves or capital as closely as he can; he reads his papers—and, by-the-by, they are becoming smaller and more whitey-brown as we proceed—and takes his drink with the same air—takes up as much room, and speaks a good deal in the same fashion.

The people are all hearty Secessionists here—the Bars and Stars are flying at the road-stations and from the pine-tops, and there are lusty cheers for Jeff Davis and the Southern Confederacy. Troops are flocking towards Virginia from the Southern States in reply to the march of Volunteers from Northern States to Washington; but it is felt that the steps taken by the Federal Government to secure Baltimore have obviated any chance of successfully opposing the "Lincolnites" going through that city. There is a strong disposition on the part of the Southerners to believe they have many friends in the North, and they endeavour to attach a factious character to the actions of the Government by calling the Volunteers and the war party in the North "Lincolnites," "Lincoln's Mercenaries," "Black Republicans," "Abolitionists," and the like. The report of an armistice, now denied by Mr. Seward officially, was for some time current, but it is plain that the South must make good its words, and justify its acts by the sword. General Scott would, it was fondly believed, retire from the United States' army, and either remain neutral or take command under the Confederate flag, but now that it is certain he will not follow any of these courses, he is assailed in the foulest manner by the press and in private conversation. Heaven help the idol of a democracy!

At one of the junctions General Beauregard, attended by Mr. Manning, and others of his staff, got into the car, and tried to elude observation, but the conductors take great pleasure in unearthing distinguished passengers for the public, and the General was called on for a speech by the crowd of idlers. The General hates speech-making, he told me, and he had besides been bored to death at every station by similar demands. But a man must be popular or he is nothing. So, as next best thing, Governor Manning made a speech in the General's name, in which he dwelt on Southern Rights, Sumter, victory, and abolitiondom, and was carried off from the cheers of his auditors by the train in the midst of an unfinished sentence. There were a number of blacks listening to the Governor, who were appreciative.

Towards evening, having thrown out some slight outworks against accidental sallies of my fellow-passengers' saliva, I went to sleep, and woke up at 11 P.M. to hear we were in Montgomery. A very ricketty omnibus took the party to the hotel, which was crowded to excess. The General and his friends had one room to themselves. Three gentlemen and myself were crammed into a filthy room which already contained two strangers, and as there were only three beds in the apartment it was apparent that we were intended to "double up considerably;" but after strenuous efforts, a little bribery and cajoling, we succeeded in procuring mattresses to put on the floor, which was regarded by our neighbours as a proof of miserable aristocratic fastidiousness. Had it not been for the flies, the fleas would have been intolerable, but one nuisance neutralised the other. Then, as to food—nothing could be had in the hotel—but one of the waiters led us to a restaurant, where we selected from a choice bill of fare, which contained, I think, as many odd dishes as ever I saw, some unknown fishes, oyster-plants, 'possums, racoons, frogs, and other delicacies, and, eschewing toads and the like, really made a good meal off dirty plates on a vile table-cloth, our appetites being sharpened by the best of condiments.

Colonel Pickett has turned up here, having made his escape from Washington just in time to escape arrest—travelling in disguise on foot through out-of-the-way places till he got among friends.

I was glad, when bed-time approached, that I was not among the mattress men. One of the gentlemen in the bed next the door was a tremendous projector in the tobacco-juice line: his final rumination ere he sank to repose was a masterpiece of art—a perfect liquid pyrotechny, Roman candles and falling stars. A horrid thought occurred as I gazed and wondered. In case he should in a supreme moment turn his attention my way!—I was only seven or eight yards off, and that might be nothing to him!—I hauled down my musquito curtain at once, and watched him till, completely satiated, he slept.

May 5th.—Very warm, and no cold water, unless one went to the river. The hotel baths were not promising. This hotel is worse than Mill's House or Willard's. The feeding and the flies are intolerable. One of our party comes in to say that he could scarce get down to the hall on account of the crowd, and that all the people who passed him had very hard, sharp bones. He remarks thereupon to the clerk at the bar, who tells him that the particular projections he alludes to are implements of defence or offence, as the case may be, and adds, "I suppose you and your friends are the only people in the house who haven't a bowie-knife, or a six-shooter, or Derringer about them." The house is full of Confederate Congress men, politicians, colonels, and placemen with or without places, and a vast number of speculators, contractors, and the like, attracted by the embryo government. Among the visitors are many fillibusters, such as Henningsen, Pickett, Tochman, Wheat.* I hear a good deal about the association called the Knights of the Golden Circle, a Protestant association for securing the Gulf provinces and states, including—which has been largely developed by recent events—them in the Southern Confederacy, and creating them into an independent government.

Montgomery has little claims to be called a capital. The streets are very hot, unpleasant, and uninteresting. I have rarely seen a more dull, lifeless place; it looks like a small Russian town in the interior. The names of the shopkeepers indicate German and French origin. I looked in at one or two of the slave magazines, which are not unlike similar establishments in Cairo and Smyrna. A certain degree of freedom is enjoyed by some of the men, who lounge about the doors, and are careless of escape or liberty, knowing too well the difficulties of either.

It is not in its external aspects generally that slavery is so painful. The observer must go with Sterne, and gaze in on the captives' dungeons through the bars. The condition of a pig in a stye is not, in an animal sense, anything but good. Well fed, over fed, covered from the winds and storms of heaven, with clothing, food, medicine provided, children taken care of, aged relatives and old age itself succoured and guarded—is not this ——? Get thee behind us, slave philosopher! The hour comes when the butch-

* Since killed in action.

er steals to the stye, and the knife leaps from the sheath.

Now there is this one thing in being a ἄναξ ἀνδρων, that be the race of men bad as it may, a kind of grandiose character is given to their leader. The stag which sweeps his rivals from his course is the largest of the herd; but a man who drives the largest drove of sheep is no better than he who drives the smallest. The flock he compels must consist of human beings to develop the property of which I speak, and so the very superiority of the slave master in the ways and habits of command proves that the negro is a man. But, at the same time, the law which regulates all these relations between man and his fellows, asserts itself here. The dominant race becomes dependent on some other body of men, less martial, arrogant, and wealthy, for its elegances, luxuries, and necessaries. The poor villeins round the Norman castle forge the armour, make the furniture, and exercise the mechanical arts which the baron and his followers are too ignorant and too proud to pursue; if there is no population to serve this purpose, some energetic race comes in their place, and the Yankee does the part of the little hungry Greek to the Roman patrician.

The South has at present little or no manufactures, takes everything from the Yankee outside or the mean white within her gates, and despises both. Both are reconciled by interest. The one gets a good price for his manufacture and the fruit of his ingenuity from a careless, spendthrift proprietor; the other hopes to be as good as his master some day, and sees the beginning of his fortune in the possession of a negro. It is fortunate for our great British Catherine-wheel, which is continually throwing off light and heat to the remotest parts of the world —I hope not burning down to a dull red cinder in the centre at last—that it had not to send its emigrants to the Southern States, as assuredly the emigration would soon have been checked. The United States has been represented to the British and Irish emigrants by the free States—the Northern States and the great West—and the British and German emigrant who finds himself in the South, has drifted there through the Northern States, and either is a migratory labourer, or hopes to return with a little money to the North and West, if he does not see his way to the possession of land and negroes.

After dinner at the hotel table, which was crowded with officers, and where I met Mr. Howell Cobb and several senators of the new Congress, I spent the evening with Colonel Deas, Quartermaster-General, and a number of his staff, in their quarters. As I was walking over to the house, one of the detached villa-like residences so common in Southern cities, I perceived a crowd of very well-dressed negroes, men and women, in front of a plain brick building which I was informed was their Baptist meeting-house, into which white people rarely or never intrude. These were domestic servants, or persons employed in stores, and their general appearance indicated much comfort and even luxury. I doubted if they all were slaves. One of my companions went up to a young woman in a straw-hat, with bright red-and-green riband trimmings and artificial flowers, a gaudy Paisley shawl, and a rainbow-like gown, blown out over her yellow boots by a prodigious crinoline, and asked her "Whom do you belong to?" She replied, "I b'long to Massa Smith, sar." Well, we have men who "belong" to horses in England. I am not sure if Americans, North and South, do not consider their superiority to all Englishmen so thoroughly established, that they can speak of them as if they were talking of inferior animals. To-night, for example, a gallant young South Carolinian, one Ransome Calhoun,* was good enough to say that "Great Britain was in mortal fear of France, and was abjectly subdued by her great rival." Hence came controversy, short and acrimonious.

May 6th.—I forgot to say that yesterday before dinner I drove out with some gentlemen and the ladies of the family of Mr. George N. Sanders, once United States' consul at Liverpool, now a doubtful man here, seeking some office from the Government, and accused by a portion of the press of being a Confederate spy—*Porcus de grege epicuri*—but a learned pig withal, and weather-wise, and mindful of the signs of the times, catching straws and whisking them upwards to detect the currents. Well, in this great moment I am bound to say there was much talk of ice. The North owns the frozen climates; but it was hoped that Great Britain, to whom belongs the North Pole, might force the blockade and send aid.

The environs of Montgomery are agreeable—well-wooded, undulating, villas abounding, public gardens, and a large negro and mulatto suburb. It is not usual, as far as I can judge, to see women riding on horseback in the South, but on the road here we encountered several.

After breakfast I walked down with Senator Wigfall to the capitol of Montgomery—one of the true Athenian Yankeeized structures of this novo-classic land, erected on a site worthy of a better fate and edifice. By an open cistern, on our way, I came on a gentleman engaged in disposing of some living ebony carvings to a small circle, who had more curiosity than cash, for they did not at all respond to the energetic appeals of the auctioneer.

The sight was a bad preparation for an introduction to the legislative assembly of a Confederacy which rests on the Institution as the cornerstone of the social and political arch which maintains it. But there they were, the legislators or conspirators, in a large room provided with benches and seats, and listening to such a sermon as a Balfour of Burley might have preached to his Covenanters—resolute and massive heads, and large frames—such men as must have a faith to inspire them. And that is so. Assaulted by reason, by logic, argument, philanthropy, progress directed against his peculiar institutions, the Southerner at last is driven to a fanaticism—a sacred faith which is above all reason or logical attack in the propriety, righteousness, and divinity of slavery.

The chaplain, a venerable old man, loudly invoked curses on the heads of the enemy, and blessings on the arms and councils of the New State. When he was done, Mr. Howell Cobb, a fat, double-chinned, mellow-eyed man, rapped with his hammer on the desk before the chair on which he sat as speaker of the assembly, and the house proceeded to business. I could fancy that,

* Since killed.

in all but garments, they were like the men who first conceived the great rebellion which led to the independence of this wonderful country—so earnest, so grave, so sober, and so vindictive—at least, so embittered against the power which they consider tyrannical and insulting.

The word "liberty" was used repeatedly in the short time allotted to the public transaction of business and the reading of documents; the Congress was anxious to get to its work, and Mr. Howell Cobb again thumped his desk and announced that the house was going into "secret session," which intimated that all persons who were not members should leave. I was introduced to what is called the floor of the house, and had a delegate's chair, and of course I moved away with the others, and with the disappointed ladies and men from the galleries, but one of the members, Mr. Rhett, I believe, said jokingly: "I think you ought to retain your seat. If the "Times" will support the South, we'll accept you as a delegate." I replied that I was afraid I could not act as a delegate to a Congress of Slave States. And, indeed, I had been much affected at the slave auction held just outside the hotel, on the steps of the public fountain, which I had witnessed on my way to the capitol. The auctioneer, who was an ill-favoured, dissipated-looking rascal, had his "article" beside him on, not in, a deal packing-case—a stout young negro badly dressed and ill-shod, who stood with all his goods fastened in a small bundle in his hand, looking out at the small and listless gathering of men, who, whittling and chewing, had moved out from the shady side of the street as they saw the man put up. The chattel character of slavery in the States renders it most repulsive. What a pity the nigger is not polypoid—so that he could be cut up in junks, and each junk should reproduce itself!

A man in a cart, some volunteers in coarse uniform, a few Irish labourers in a long van, and four or five men in the usual black coat, satin waistcoat, and black hat, constituted the audience, whom the auctioneer addressed volubly: "A prime field-hand! Just look at him—good-natered, well-tempered; no marks, nary sign of bad about him! En-i-ne hunthered—only nine hun-ther-ed and fifty dol'rs for 'em! Why, it's quite rad-aklous! Nine hundred and fifty dol'rs! I can't raly——That's good. Thank you, sir. Twenty-five bid—nine hun-therd and seventy-five dol'rs for this most useful hand." The price rose to one thousand dollars, at which the useful hand was knocked down to one of the black hats near me. The auctioneer and the negro and his buyer all walked off together to settle the transaction, and the crowd moved away.

"That nigger went cheap," said one of them to a companion, as he walked towards the shade. "Yes, *Sirr!* Niggers is cheap now—that's a fact." I must admit that I felt myself indulging in a sort of reflection whether it would not be nice to own a man as absolutely as one might possess a horse—to hold him subject to my will and pleasure, as if he were a brute beast without the power of kicking or biting—to make him work for me—to hold his fate in my hands: but the thought was for a moment. It was followed by disgust.

I have seen slave markets in the East, where the traditions of the race, the condition of family and social relations divest slavery of the most odious characteristics which pertain to it in the States; but the use of the English tongue in such transactions, and the idea of its taking place among a civilized Christian people, produced in me a feeling of inexpressible loathing and indignation. Yesterday I was much struck by the intelligence, activity, and desire to please of a good-looking coloured waiter, who seemed so light-hearted and light-coloured I could not imagine he was a slave. So one of our party, who was an American, asked him: "What are you, boy—a free nigger?" Of course he knew that in Alabama it was most unlikely he could reply in the affirmative. The young man's smile died away from his lips, a flush of blood embrowned the face for a moment, and he answered in a sad, low tone: "No, sir! I b'long to Massa Jackson," and left the room at once. As I stood at an upper window of the capitol, and looked on the wide expanse of richly-wooded, well-cultivated land which sweeps round the hill side away to the horizon, I could not help thinking of the misery and cruelty which must have been borne in tilling the land and raising the houses and streets of the dominant race before whom one nationality of coloured people have perished within the memory of man. The misery and cruelty of the system are established by the advertisements for runaway negroes, and by the description of the stigmata on their persons—whippings and brandings, scars and cuts—though these, indeed, are less frequent here than in the border States.

On my return, the Hon. W. M. Browne, Assistant Secretary of State, came to visit me—a cadet of an Irish family, who came to America some years ago, and having lost his money in land speculations, turned his pen to good account as a journalist, and gained Mr. Buchanan's patronage and support as a newspaper editor in Washington. There he became intimate with the Southern gentlemen, with whom he naturally associated in preference to the Northern members; and when they went out, he walked over along with them. He told me the Government had already received numerous—I think he said 400—letters from shipowners applying for letters of marque and reprisal. Many of these applications were from merchants in Boston, and other maritime cities in the New England States. He further stated that the President was determined to take the whole control of the army, and the appointments to command in all ranks of officers into his own hands.

There is now no possible chance of preserving the peace or of averting the horrors of war from these great and prosperous communities. The Southern people, right or wrong, are bent on independence and on separation, and they will fight to the last for their object.

The press is fanning the flame on both sides: it would be difficult to say whether it or the telegraphs circulate lies most largely; but that as the papers print the telegrams they must have the palm. The Southerners are told there is a reign of terror in New York—that the 7th New York Regiment has been captured by the Baltimore people—that Abe Lincoln is always drunk—that General Lee has seized Arlington heights, and is bombarding Washington. The New York people are regaled with similar stories from the

South. The coincidence between the date of the skirmish at Lexington and of the attack on the 6th Massachusetts Regiment at Baltimore is not so remarkable as the fact, that the first man who was killed at the latter place, 86 years ago, was a direct descendant of the first of the colonists who was killed by the royal soldiery. Baltimore may do the same for the South which Lexington did for all the Colonies. Head-shaving, forcible deportations, tarring and feathering are recommended and adopted as specifics to produce conversion from erroneous opinions. The President of the United States has called into service of the Federal Government 42,000 volunteers, and increased the regular army by 22,000 men, and the navy by 18,000 men. If the South secede, they ought certainly to take over with them some Yankee hotel keepers. This "Exchange" is in a frightful state—nothing but noise, dirt, drinking, wrangling.

CHAPTER XXIII.

Proclamation of war—Jefferson Davis—Interview with the President of the Confederacy—Passport and safe-conduct—Messrs. Wigfall, Walker, and Benjamin—Privateering and letters of marque—A reception at Jefferson Davis's—Dinner at Mr. Benjamin's.

May 9th.—To-day the papers contain a proclamation by the President of the Confederate States of America, declaring a state of war between the Confederacy and the United States, and notifying the issue of letters of marque and reprisal. I went out with Mr. Wigfall in the forenoon to pay my respects to Mr. Jefferson Davis at the State Department. Mr. Seward told me that but for Jefferson Davis the Secession plot could never have been carried out. No other man of the party had the brain, or the courage and dexterity, to bring it to a successful issue. All the persons in the Southern States spoke of him with admiration, though their forms of speech and thought generally forbid them to be respectful to any one.

There before me was "Jeff Davis's State Department"—a large brick building, at the corner of a street, with a Confederate flag floating above it. The door stood open, and "gave" on a large hall white-washed, with doors plainly painted belonging to small rooms, in which was transacted most important business, judging by the names written on sheets of paper and applied outside, denoting bureaux of the highest functions. A few clerks were passing in and out, and one or two gentlemen were on the stairs, but there was no appearance of any bustle in the building.

We walked straight up-stairs to the first-floor, which was surrounded by doors opening from a quadrangular platform. On one of these was written simply, "The President." Mr. Wigfall went in, and after a moment returned and said, "The President will be glad to see you; walk in, sir." When I entered, the President was engaged with four gentlemen, who were making some offer of aid to him. He was thanking them "in the name of the Government." Shaking hands with each, he saw them to the door, bowed them and Mr. Wigfall out, and turning to me said, "Mr. Russell, I am glad to welcome you here, though I fear your appearance is a symptom that our affairs are not quite prosperous," or words to that effect. He then requested me to sit down close to his own chair at his office-table, and proceeded to speak on general matters, adverting to the Crimean War and the Indian Mutiny, and asking questions about Sebastopol, the Redan, and the Siege of Lucknow.

I had an opportunity of observing the President very closely: he did not impress me as favourably as I had expected, though he is certainly a very different looking man from Mr. Lincoln. He is like a gentleman—has a slight, light figure, little exceeding middle height, and holds himself erect and straight. He was dressed in a rustic suit of slate-coloured stuff, with a black silk handkerchief round his neck; his manner is plain, and rather reserved and drastic; his head is well formed, with a fine full forehead, square and high, covered with innumerable fine lines and wrinkles, features regular, though the cheek-bones are too high, and the jaws too hollow to be handsome; the lips are thin, flexible, and curved, the chin square, well-defined; the nose very regular, with wide nostrils; and the eyes deep set, large and full—one seems nearly blind, and is partly covered with a film, owing to excruciating attacks of neuralgia and tic. Wonderful to relate, he does not chew, and is neat and clean-looking, with hair trimmed and boots brushed. The expression of his face is anxious, he has a very haggard, care-worn, and pain-drawn look, though no trace of anything but the utmost confidence and the greatest decision could be detected in his conversation. He asked me some questions respecting the route I had taken in the States.

I mentioned that I had seen great military preparations through the South, and was astonished at the alacrity with which the people sprang to arms. "Yes, sir," he remarked, and his tone of voice and manner of speech are rather remarkable for what are considered Yankee peculiarities, "in Eu-rope" (Mr. Seward also indulges in that pronunciation) "they laugh at us because of our fondness for military titles and displays. All your travellers in this country have commented on the number of generals, and colonels, and majors all over the States. But the fact is, we are a military people, and these signs of the fact were ignored. We are not less military because we have had no great standing armies. But perhaps we are the only people in the world where gentlemen go to a military academy, who do not intend to follow the profession of arms."

In the course of our conversation, I asked him to have the goodness to direct that a sort of passport or protection should be given to me, as I might possibly fall in with some guerilla leader on my way northwards, in whose eyes I might not be entitled to safe conduct. Mr. Davis said, "I shall give such instructions to the Secretary of War as shall be necessary. But, sir, you are among civilised, intelligent people who understand your position, and appreciate your character. We do not seek the sympathy of England by unworthy means, for we respect ourselves, and we are glad to invite the scrutiny of men into our acts; as for our motives, we meet the eye of Heaven." I thought I could judge from his words that he had the highest idea of the French as soldiers, but that his feelings and associations were more identified with England, although he was quite aware of the difficulty of conquering the repugnance which exists to slavery.

Mr. Davis made no allusion to the authorities at Washington, but he asked me if I thought it was supposed in England there would be war between the two States? I answered, that I was under the impression the public thought there would be no actual hostilities. "And yet you see we are driven to take up arms for the defence of our rights and liberties."

As I saw an immense mass of papers on his table, I rose and made my bow, and Mr. Davis, seeing me to the door, gave me his hand and said, "As long as you may stay among us you shall receive every facility it is in our power to afford to you, and I shall always be glad to see you." Colonel Wigfall was outside, and took me to the room of the Secretary of War, Mr. Walker, whom we found closeted with General Beauregard and two other officers in a room full of maps and plans. He is the kind of man generally represented in our types of a "Yankee"—tall, lean, straight-haired, angular, with fiery, impulsive eyes and manner—a ruminator of tobacco and a profuse spitter—a lawyer, I believe, certainly not a soldier; ardent, devoted to the cause, and confident to the last degree of its speedy success.

The news that two more States had joined the Confederacy, making ten in all, was enough to put them in good humour. "Is it not too bad these Yankees will not let us go our own way, and keep their cursed Union to themselves? If they force us to it, we may be obliged to drive them beyond the Susquehanna." Beauregard was in excellent spirits, busy measuring off miles of country with his compass, as if he were dividing empires.

From this room I proceeded to the office of Mr. Benjamin, the Attorney-General of the Confederate States, the most brilliant perhaps of the whole of the famous Southern orators. He is a short, stout man, with a full face, olive-coloured, and most decidedly Jewish features, with the brightest large black eyes, one of which is somewhat diverse from the other, and a brisk, lively, agreeable manner, combined with much vivacity of speech and quickness of utterance. He is one of the first lawyers or advocates in the United States, and had a large practice at Washington, where his annual receipts from his profession were not less than £8000 to £10,000 a year. But his love of the card-table rendered him a prey to older and cooler hands, who waited till the sponge was full at the end of the session, and then squeezed it to the last drop.

Mr. Benjamin is the most open, frank, and cordial of the Confederates whom I have yet met. In a few seconds he was telling me all about the course of Government with respect to privateers and letters of marque and reprisal, in order probably to ascertain what were our views in England on the subject. I observed it was likely the North would not respect their flag, and would treat their privateers as pirates. "We have an easy remedy for that. For any man under our flag whom the authorities of the United States dare to execute, we shall hang two of their people." "Suppose, Mr. Attorney-General, England, or any of the great powers which decreed the abolition of privateering, refuses to recognise your flag?" "We intend to claim, and do claim, the exercise of all the rights and privileges of an independent sovereign State, and any attempt to refuse us the full measure of those rights would be an act of hostility to our country." "But if England, for example, declared your privateers were pirates?" "As the United States never admitted the principle laid down at the Congress of Paris, neither have the Confederate States. If England thinks fit to declare privateers under our flag pirates, it would be nothing more or less than a declaration of war against us, and we must meet it as best we can." In fact, Mr. Benjamin did not appear afraid of anything; but his confidence respecting Great Britain was based a good deal, no doubt, on his firm faith in cotton, and in England's utter subjection to her cotton interest and manufactures. "All this coyness about acknowledging a slave power will come right at last. We hear our commissioners have gone on to Paris, which looks as if they had met with no encouragement at London; but we are quite easy in our minds on this point at present."

So Great Britain is in a pleasant condition, Mr. Seward is threatening us with war if we recognise the South, and the South declares that if we don't recognise their flag, they will take it as an act of hostility. Lord Lyons is pressed to give an assurance to the Government at Washington, that under no circumstances will Great Britain recognise the Southern rebels; but, at the same time, Mr. Seward refuses to give any assurance whatever that the right of neutrals will be respected in the impending struggle.

As I was going down stairs, Mr. Browne called me into his room. He said that the Attorney-General and himself were in a state of perplexity as to the form in which letters of marque and reprisal should be made out. They had consulted all the books they could get, but found no examples to suit their case, and he wished to know, as I was a barrister, whether I could aid him. I told him it was not so much my regard to my own position as a neutral, as the *vafri inscitia juris* which prevented me throwing any light on the subject. There are not only Yankee shipowners but English firms ready with sailors and steamers for the Confederate Government, and the owner of the Camilla might be tempted to part with his yacht by the offers made to him.

Being invited to attend a levée or reception held by Mrs. Davis, the President's wife, I returned to the hotel to prepare for the occasion. On my way I passed a company of volunteers, one hundred and twenty artillerymen, and three field-pieces, on their way to the station for Virginia, followed by a crowd of "citizens" and negroes of both sexes, cheering vociferously. The band was playing that excellent quick-step "Dixie." The men were stout, fine fellows, dressed in coarse grey tunics with yellow facings, and French caps. They were armed with smooth-bore muskets, and their knapsacks were unfit for marching, being water-proof bags slung from the shoulders. The guns had no caissons, and the shoeing of the troops was certainly deficient in soleing. The Zouave mania is quite as rampant here as it is in New York, and the smallest children are thrust into baggy red breeches, which the learned Lipsius might have appreciated, and are sent out with flags and tin swords to impede the highways.

The modest villa in which the President lives is painted white—another "White House"—and stands in a small garden. The door was open. A coloured servant took in our names, and Mr. Browne presented me to Mrs. Davis, whom I could just make out in the *demi-jour* of a moderately-sized parlour, surrounded by a few ladies and gentlemen, the former in bonnets, the latter in morning dress *à la midi*. There was no affectation of state or ceremony in the reception. Mrs. Davis, whom some of her friends call "Queen Varina," is a comely, sprightly woman, verging on matronhood, of good figure and manners, well-dressed, lady-like, and clever, and she seemed a great favourite with those around her, though I did hear one of them say "It must be very nice to be the President's wife, and be the first lady in the Confederate States." Mrs. Davis, whom the President C. S. married *en secondes noces*, exercised considerable social influence in Washington, where I met many of her friends. She was just now inclined to be angry, because the papers contained a report that a reward was offered in the North for the head of the arch rebel Jeff Davis. "They are quite capable, I believe," she said, "of such acts." There were not more than eighteen or twenty persons present, as each party came in and staid only for a few moments, and, after a time, I made my bow and retired, receiving from Mrs. Davis an invitation to come in the evening, when I would find the President at home.

At sundown, amid great cheering, the guns in front of the State Department fired ten rounds, to announce that Tennessee and Arkansas had joined the Confederacy.

In the evening I dined with Mr. Benjamin and his brother-in-law, a gentleman of New Orleans, Colonel Wigfall coming in at the end of dinner. The New Orleans people of French descent, or "Creoles," as they call themselves, speak French in preference to English, and Mr. Benjamin's brother-in-law laboured considerably in trying to make himself understood in our vernacular. The conversation, Franco-English, very pleasant, for Mr. Benjamin is agreeable and lively. He is certain that the English law authorities must advise the Government that the blockade of the Southern ports is illegal so long as the President claims them to be ports of the United States. "At present," he said, "their paper blockade does no harm; the season for shipping cotton is over; but in October next, when the Mississippi is floating cotton by the thousands of bales, and all our wharves are full, it is inevitable that the Yankees must come to trouble with this attempt to coerce us." Mr. Benjamin walked back to the hotel with me, and we found our room full of tobacco-smoke, filibusters, and conversation, in which, as sleep was impossible, we were obliged to join. I resisted a vigorous attempt of Mr. G. N. Sanders and a friend of his to take me to visit a planter who had a beaver-dam some miles outside Montgomery. They succeeded in capturing Mr. Deasy.

CHAPTER XXIV.

Mr. Wigfall on the Confederacy—Intended departure from the South—Northern apathy and Southern activity—Future prospects of the Union—South Carolina and cotton—The theory of slavery—Indifference at New York—Departure from Montgomery.

May 8th.—I tried to write, as I have taken my place in the steamer to Mobile to-morrow, and I was obliged to do my best in a room full of people, constantly disturbed by visitors. Early this morning, as usual, my faithful Wigfall comes in and sits by my bedside, and passing his hands through his locks, pours out his ideas with wonderful lucidity and odd affectation of logic all his own. "We are a peculiar people, sir! You don't understand us, and you can't understand us, because we are known to you only by Northern writers and Northern papers, who know nothing of us themselves, or misrepresent what they do know. We are an agricultural people; we are a primitive but a civilised people. We have no cities—we don't want them. We have no literature—we don't need any yet. We have no press—we are glad of it. We do not require a press, because we go out and discuss all public questions from the stump with our people. We have no commercial marine—no navy—we don't want them. We are better without them. Your ships carry our produce, and you can protect your own vessels. We want no manufactures: we desire no trading, no mechanical or manufacturing classes. As long as we have our rice, our sugar, our tobacco, and our cotton, we can command wealth to purchase all we want from those nations with which we are in amity, and to lay up money besides. But with the Yankees we will never trade—never. Not one pound of cotton shall ever go from the South to their accursed cities; not one ounce of their steel or their manufactures shall ever cross our border." And so on. What the Senator who is preparing a bill for drafting the people into the army fears is, that the North will begin active operations before the South is ready for resistance. "Give us till November to drill our men, and we shall be irresistible." He deprecates any offensive movement, and is opposed to an attack on Washington, which many journals here advocate.

Mr. Walker sent me over a letter recommending me to all officers of the Confederate States, and I received an invitation from the President to dine with him to-morrow, which I was much chagrined to be obliged to refuse. In fact, it is most important to complete my Southern tour speedily, as all mail communication will soon be suspended from the South, and the blockade effectually cuts off any communication by sea. Rails torn up, bridges broken, telegraphs down—trains searched—the war is begun. The North is pouring its hosts to the battle, and it has met the pæans of the conquering Charlestonians with a universal yell of indignation and an oath of vengeance.

I expressed a belief in a letter, written a few days after my arrival (March 27th), that the South would never go back into the Union. The North think that they can coerce the South, and I am not prepared to say they are right or wrong; but I am convinced that the South can only be forced back by such a conquest as that which laid Poland prostrate at the feet of Russia. It may be that such a conquest can be made by the North, but success must destroy the Union as it has been constituted in times past. A strong Government must be the logical consequence of victory, and the triumph of the South will be attended by a similar result, for which, indeed, many Southerners are very well disposed. To the people of the Confederate States there would be no terror in such an issue, for it appears to me they are pining for a strong Government exceedingly. The North must accept it, whether they like it or not.

Neither party—if such a term can be applied to the rest of the United States, and to those States which disclaim the authority of the Federal Government—was prepared for the aggressive or resisting power of the other. Already the Confederate States perceive that they cannot carry all before them with a rush, while the North have learnt that they must put forth all their strength to make good a tithe of their lately uttered threats. But the Montgomery Government are anxious to gain time, and to prepare a regular army. The North, distracted by apprehensions of vast disturbance in their complicated relations, are clamouring for instant action and speedy consummation. The counsels of moderate men, as they were called, have been utterly overruled.

The whole foundation on which South Carolina rests is cotton and a certain amount of rice; or rather she bases her whole fabric on the necessity which exists in Europe for those products of her soil, believing and asserting, as she does, that England and France cannot and will not do without them. Cotton, without a market, is so much flocculent matter encumbering the ground. Rice, without demand for it, is unsaleable grain in store and on the field. Cotton at ten cents a pound is boundless prosperity, empire and superiority, and rice or grain need no longer be regarded.

In the matter of slave-labour, South Carolina argues pretty much in the following manner: England and France (she says) require our products. In order to meet their wants, we must cultivate our soil. There is only one way of doing so. The white man cannot live on our land at certain seasons of the year; he cannot work in the manner required by the crops. He must, therefore, employ a race suited to the labour, and that is a race which will only work when it is obliged to do so. That race was imported from Africa, under the sanction of the law, by our ancestors, when we were a British colony, and it has been fostered by us, so that its increase here has been as great as that of the most flourishing people in the world. In other places, where its labour was not productive or imperatively essential, that race has been made free, sometimes with disastrous consequences to itself and to industry. But we will not make it free. We cannot do so. We hold that slavery is essential to our existence as producers of what Europe requires; nay more, we maintain it is in the abstract right in principle; and some of us go so far as to maintain that the only proper form of society, according to the law of God and the exigencies of man, is that which has slavery as its basis. As to the slave, he is happier far in his state of servitude, more civilised and religious, than he is or could be if free or in his native Africa. For this system we will fight to the end.

In the evening I paid farewell visits, and spent an hour with Mr. Toombs, who is unquestionably one of the most original, quaint, and earnest of the Southern leaders, and whose eloquence and power as a debater are greatly esteemed by his countrymen. He is something of an Anglomaniac, and an Anglo-phobist—a combination not unusual in America—that is, he is proud of being connected with and descended from respectable English families, and admires our mixed constitution, whilst he is an enemy to what is called English policy, and is a strong pro-slavery champion. Wigfall and he are very uneasy about the scant supply of gunpowder in the Southern States, and the difficulty of obtaining it.

In the evening had a little reunion in the bedroom as before—Mr. Wigfall, Mr. Keitt, an eminent Southern politician, Colonel Pickett, Mr. Browne, Mr. Benjamin, Mr. George Sanders, and others. The last-named gentleman was dismissed or recalled from his post at Liverpool, because he fraternised with Mazzini and other Red Republicans *à ce qu' on dit*. Here he is a slavery man, and a friend of an oligarchy. Your "Rights of Man" man is often most inconsistent with himself, and is generally found associated with the men of force and violence.

May the 9th.—My faithful Wigfall was good enough to come in early, in order to show me some comments on my letters in the "New York Times." It appears the papers are angry because I said that New York was apathetic when I landed, and they try to prove I was wrong by showing there was a "glorious outburst of Union feeling," after the news of the fall of Sumter. But I now know that the very apathy of which I spoke was felt by the Government of Washington, and was most weakening and embarrassing to them. What would not the value of "the glorious outburst" have been, had it taken place *before* the Charleston batteries had opened on Sumter — when the Federal flag, for example, was fired on, flying from the 'Star of the West,' or when Beauregard cut off supplies, or Bragg threatened Pickens, or the first shovel of earth was thrown up in hostile battery? But no! New York was then engaged in discussing State rights, and in reading articles to prove the new Government would be traitors if they endeavoured to reinforce the Federal forts, or were perusing leaders in favor of the Southern Government. Haply, they may remember one, not so many weeks old, in which the "New York Herald" compared Jeff Davis and his Cabinet to the "Great Rail Splitter," and Seward, and Chase, and came to the conclusion that the former "were gentlemen"—(a matter of which it is quite incompetent to judge)—"and would, and ought to succeed." The glorious outburst of "Union feeling" which threatened to demolish the "Herald" office, has created a most wonderful change in the views of the proprietor, whose diverse-eyed vision is now directed solely to the beauties of the Union, and whose faith is expressed in "a hearty adhesion to the Government of our country." New York must pay the penalty of its indifference, and bear the consequences of listening to such counsellors.

Mr. Deasy, much dilapidated, returned about twelve o'clock from his planter, who was drunk when he went over, and would not let him go to the beaver-dam. To console him, the planter stayed up all night drinking, and waking him up at intervals, that he might refresh him with a glass of whisky. This man was well off, owned land, and a good stock of slaves, but he must have been a "mean white," who had raised himself in the world. He lived in a three-roomed wooden cabin, and in one of the rooms he kept his wife shut up from the strangers' gaze. One of his negroes was unwell, and he took Deasy to see him. The result of his examination was, "Nigger! I guess you won't live more than an hour." His diagnosis was quite correct.

Before my departure I had a little farewell levée—Mr. Toombs, Mr. Browne, Mr. Benjamin, Mr. Walker, Major Deas, Colonel Pickett, Major Calhoun, Captain Ripley, and others—who were exceedingly kind with letters of introduction and offers of service. Dined as usual on a composite dinner — Southern meat and poultry bad — at three o'clock, and at four P.M. drove down to the steep banks of the Alabama River, where the castle-like hulk of the "Southern Republic" was waiting to receive us. I bade good-by to Montgomery without regret. The native people were not very attractive, and the city has nothing to make up for their deficiency, but of my friends there I must always retain pleasant memories, and, indeed, I hope some day I shall be able to keep my promise to return and see more of the Confederate ministers and their chief.

CHAPTER XXV.

The River Alabama — Voyage by steamer—Selma—Our captain and his slaves — "Running" slaves — Negro views of happiness — Mobile — Hotel — The city—Mr. Forsyth.

The vessel was nothing more than a vast wooden house, of three separate storeys, floating on a pontoon which upheld the engine, with a dining-hall or saloon on the second storey surrounded by sleeping-berths, and a nest of smaller rooms up-stairs; on the metal roof was a "musical" instrument called a "calliope," played like a piano by keys, which acted on levers and valves, admitting steam into metal cups, where it produced the requisite notes—high, resonant, and not unpleasing at a moderate distance. It is 417 miles to Mobile, but at this season the steamer can maintain a good rate of speed, as there is very little cotton or cargo to be taken on board at the landings, and the stream is full.

The river is about 200 yards broad, and of the colour of chocolate and milk, with high, steep, wooded banks, rising so much above the surface of the stream, that a person on the upper deck of the towering Southern Republic, cannot get a glimpse of the fields and country beyond. High banks and bluffs spring up to the height of 150 or even 200 feet above the river, the breadth of which is so uniform as to give the Alabama the appearance of a canal, only relieved by sudden bends and rapid curves. The surface is covered with masses of drift wood, whole trees, and small islands of branches. Now and then a sharp, black, fang-like projection standing stiffly in the current gives warning of a snag, but the helmsman, who commands the whole course of the river, from an elevated house amidships on the upper deck, can see these in time; and at night pine boughs are lighted in iron cressets at the bows to illuminate the water.

The captain, who was not particular whether his name was spelt Maher, or Meaher, or Meagher (*les trois se disent*), was evidently a character—perhaps a good one. One with a grey eye full of cunning and of some humour, strongly-marked features, and a very Celtic mouth of the Kerry type. He soon attached himself to me, and favoured me with some wonderful yarns, which I hope he was not foolish enough to think I believed. One relating to a wholesale destruction and massacre of Indians he narrated with evident gusto. Pointing to one of the bluffs, he said that some thirty years ago the whole of the Indians in the district being surrounded by the whites, betook themselves to that spot, and remained there without any means of escape, till they were quite starved out. So they sent down to know if the whites would let them go, and it was agreed that they should be permitted to move down the river in boats. When the day came, and they were all afloat, the whites anticipated the boat-massacre of Nana Sahib at Cawnpore, and destroyed the helpless red skins. Many hundreds thus perished, and the whole affair was very much approved of.

The value of land on the sides of this river is great, as it yields nine to eleven bales of cotton to the acre—worth 10*l*. a bale at present prices. The only evidences of this wealth to be seen by us consisted of the cotton sheds on the top of the banks, and slides of timber, with steps at each side down to the landings, so constructed that the cotton bales could be shot down on board the vessel. These shoots and staircases are generally protected by a roof of planks, and lead to unknown regions inhabited by niggers and their masters, the latter all talking politics. They never will, never can be conquered—nothing on earth could induce them to go back into the Union. They will burn every bale of cotton, and fire every house, and lay waste every field and homestead before they will yield to the Yankees. And so they talk through the glimmering of bad cigars for hours.

The management of the boat is dexterous,—as she approaches a landing-place, the helm is put hard over, to the screaming of the steam-pipe and the wild strains of "Dixie" floating out of the throats of the calliope, and as the engines are detached, one wheel is worked forward, and the other backs water, so she soon turns head up stream, and is then gently paddled up to the river bank, to which she is just kept up by steam—the plank is run ashore, and the few passengers who are coming in or out are lighted on their way by the flames of pine in an iron basket, swinging above the bow by a long pole. Then we see them vanishing into black darkness up the steps, or coming down clearer and clearer till they stand in the full blaze of the beacon which casts dark shadows on the yellow water. The air is glistening with fire-flies, which dot the darkness with specks and points of flame, just as sparks fly through the embers of tinder or half-burnt paper.

Some of the landings were by far more important than others. There were some, for example, where an iron rail-road was worked down the bank by windlasses for hoisting up goods; others where the negroes half-naked leaped ashore, and rushing at piles of firewood, tossed them on board to feed the engine, which, all uncovered and open to the lower deck, lighted up the darkness by the glare from the stoke-holes, which cried for ever "Give, give!" as the negroes ceaselessly thrust the pine-beams into their hungry maws. I could understand how easily a steamer can "burn up," and how hopeless escape would be under such circumstances. The whole framework of the vessel is of the lightest resinous pine, so raw that the turpentine oozes out through the paint; the hull is a mere shell. If the vessel once caught fire, all that could be done would be to turn her round, and run her to the bank, in the hope of holding there long enough to enable the people to escape into the trees; but if she were not near a landing, many must be lost; as the bank is steep down, the vessel cannot be run aground; and in some places the trees are in 8 and 10 feet of water. A few minutes would suffice to set the vessel in a blaze from stem to stern; and if there were cotton on board, the bales would burn almost like powder. The scene at each landing was repeated, with few variations, ten times till we reached Selma, 110 miles distance, at 11.30 at night.

Selma, which is connected with the Tennessee and Mississippi rivers by railroad, is built upon a steep, lofty bluff, and the lights in the windows, and the lofty hotels above us, put me in mind of the old town of Edinburgh, seen from Princes Street. Beside us there was a huge storied wharf, so that our passengers could step on shore from any deck they pleased. Here Mr. Deasy, being attacked by illness, became alarmed at the idea of continuing his journey without any opportunity of medical assistance, and went on shore.

May 10*th*.—The cabin of one of these steamers, in the month of May, is not favourable to sleep. The wooden beams of the engines creak and scream "consumedly," and the great engines themselves throb as if they would break through their thin, pulse covers of pine,—and the whistle sounds, and the calliope shrieks out "Dixie" incessantly. So, when I was up and dressed, breakfast was over, and I had an opportunity of seeing the slaves on board, male and female, acting as stewards and stewardesses, at their morning meal, which they took with much good spirits and decorum. They were nicely dressed—clean and neat. I was forced to admit to myself that their Ashantee grandsires and grandmothers, or their Kroo and Dahomey progenitors were certainly less comfortable and well clad, and that these slaves had other social advantages, though I could not recognise the force of the Bishop of Georgia's assertion, that from slavery must come the sole hope of, and machinery for, the evangelisation of Africa. I confess I would not give much for the influence of the stewards and stewardesses in Christianising the blacks.

The river, the scenery, and the scenes were just the same as yesterday's—high banks, cotton-slides, wooding stations, cane-brakes—and a very miserable negro population, if the specimens of women and children at the landings fairly represented the mass of the slaves. They were in strong contrast to the comfortable, well-dressed domestic slaves on board, and it can well be imagined there is a wide difference between the classes, and that those condemned to work in the open fields must suffer exceedingly.

A passenger told us the captain's story. A number of planters, the narrator among them, subscribed a thousand dollars each to get up a vessel for the purpose of running a cargo of slaves, with the understanding they were to pay so much for the vessel, and so much per head if she succeeded, and so much if she was taken or lost. The vessel made her voyage to the coast, was laden with native Africans, and in due time made her appearance off Mobile. The collector heard of her, but, oddly enough, the sheriff was not about at the time, the United States' Marshal was away, and as the vessel could not be seen next morning, it was fair to suppose she had gone up the river, or somewhere or another. But it so happened that Captain Maher, then commanding a river steamer called the Czar (a name once very appropriate for the work, but since the serf emancipation rather out of place), found himself in the neighbourhood of the brig about nightfall; next morning, indeed, the Czar was at her moorings in the river; but Captain Maher began to grow rich, he had fine negroes fresh run on his land, and bought fresh acres, and finally built the "Southern Republic." The planters asked him for their share of the slaves. Captain Maher laughed pleasantly; he did not understand what they meant. If he had done anything wrong they had their legal remedy. They were completely beaten; for they could not have recourse to the tribunals in a case which rendered them liable to capital punishment. And so Captain Maher, as an act of grace, gave them a few old niggers, and kept the rest of the cargo.

It was worth while to see the leer with which he listened to this story about himself, "Wall now! You think them niggers I've abord came from Africa! I'll show you. Just come up here, Bully!" A boy of some twelve years of age, stout, fat, nearly naked, came up to us; his colour was jet black, his wool close as felt, his cheeks were marked with regular parallel scars, and his teeth very white, looked as if they had been filed to a point, his belly was slightly protuberant, and his chest was marked with tracings of tattoo marks.

"What's your name, sir?"

"My name—Bully."

"Where were you born?"

"Me born Sout Karliner, sar!"

"There, you see he wasn't taken from Africa," exclaimed the Captain, knowingly. "I've a lot of these black South Caroliny niggers abord, haven't I, Bully?"

"Yas, sar."

"Are you happy, Bully?"

"Yas, sar."

"Show how you're happy."

Here the boy rubbed his stomach, and grinning with delight, said, "Yummy! yummy! plenty belly full."

"That's what I call a real happy feelosophical chap," quoth the Captain. "I guess you've got a lot in your country can't pat *their* stomachs and say, 'yummy, yummy, plenty belly full?'"

"Where did he get those marks on his face?"

"Oh, them? Wall, it's a way them nigger women has of marking their children to know them; isn't it, Bully?"

"Yas, sar! me 'spose so!"

"And on his chest!"

"Wall, r'ally I do b'l'eve them's marks agin the smallpox."

"Why are his teeth filed?"

"Ah, there now! You'd never have guessed

it; Bully done that himself, for the greater ease of biting his vittels."

In fact, the lad, and a good many of the hands, were the results of Captain Maher's little sail in the Czar.

"We're obleeged to let 'em in some times to keep up the balance agin the niggers you run into Canaydy."

From 1848 to 1852 there were no slaves run; but since the migrations to Canada and the personal liberty laws, it has been found profitable to run them. There is a bucolic ferocity about these Southern people which will stand them good stead in the shock of battle. How the Spartans would have fought against any barbarians who came to emancipate their slaves, or the Romans have smitten those who would manumit slave and creditor together!

To-night, on the lower deck, amid wood faggots and barrels, a dance of negroes was arranged by an enthusiast, who desired to show how "happy they were." That is the favourite theme of the Southerners; the gallant Captain Maher becomes quite eloquent when he points to Bully's prominent "yummy," and descants on the misery of his condition if he had been left to the precarious chances of obtaining such developments in his native land; then turns a quid, and, as if uttering some sacred refrain to the universal hymn of the South, says, "Yes, sir, they're the happiest people on the face of the airth!"

There was a fiddler, and also a banjo-player, who played uncouth music to the clumsiest of dances, which it would be insulting to compare to the worst Irish jig, and the men with immense gravity and great effusion of *sudor*, shuffled, and cut, and heeled and buckled to each other with an overwhelming solemnity, till the rum-bottle warmed them up to the lighter graces of the dance, when they became quite overpowering. "Yes, sir, jist look at them how they're enjoying it; they're the happiest people on the face of the airth." When "wooding" and firing up they don't seem to be in the possession of the same exquisite felicity.

May 11*th*.—At early dawn the steamer went its way through a broad bay of snags bordered with drift-wood, and with steam-trumpet and calliope announced its arrival at the quay of Mobile, which presented a fringe of tall warehouses, and shops alongside, over which were names indicating Scotch, Irish, English, many Spanish, German, Italian, and French owners, Captain Maher at once set off to his plantation, and we descended the stories of the walled castle to the beach, and walked on towards the "Battle House," so called from the name of its proprietor, for Mobile has not yet had its fight like New Orleans. The quays which usually, as we were told, are lined with stately hulls and a forest of masts, were deserted; although the port was not actually blockaded, there were squadrons of the United States ships at Pensacola on the east, and at New Orleans on the west.

The hotel, a fine building of the American stamp, was the seat of a Vigilance Committee, and as we put down our names in the book they were minutely inspected by some gentlemen who came out of the parlour. It was fortunate they did not find traces of Lincolnism about us, as it appeared by the papers they were busy deporting "Abolitionists" after certain preliminary processes supposed to

"Give them a rise, and open their eyes
To a sense of their situation."

The citizens were busy in drilling, marching, and drum-beating, and the Confederate flag flew from every spire and steeple. The day was so hot that it was little more inviting to go out in the sun than it would be in the dog-days at Malaga, to which, by-the-bye, Mobile bears some "kinder sorter" resemblance, but, nevertheless, I sallied forth, and had a drive on a shell road by the head of the bay, where there were pretty villarettes in charming groves of magnolia, orange-trees, and lime oaks. Wide streets of similar houses spring out to meet the country through sandy roads; some worthy of Streatham or Balham, and all surrounded in such vegetation as Kew might envy.

Many Mobilians called, and among them the mayor, Mr. Forsyth, in whom I recognized the most remarkable of the Southern Commissioners I had met at Washington. Mr. Magee, the acting British Consul, was also good enough to wait upon me, with offers of any assistance in his power. I hear he has most difficult questions to deal with, arising out of the claims of distressed British subjects, and disputed nationality. In the evening the Consul and Dr. Nott, a savant and physician of Mobile, well known to ethnologists for his work on the "Types of Mankind," written conjointly with the late Mr. Gliddon, dined with me, and I learned from them that, notwithstanding the intimate commercial relations between Mobile and the Great Northern cities, the people here are of the most ultra-secessionist doctrines. The wealth and manhood of the city will be devoted to repel the "Lincolnite mercenaries" to the last.

After dinner we walked through the city, which abounds in oyster saloons, drinking-houses, lager-bier and wine-shops, and gambling and dancing places. The market was well worthy of a visit —something like St. John's at Liverpool on a Saturday night, crowded with negroes, mulattoes, quadroons, and mestizos of all sorts, Spanish, Italian, and French, speaking their own tongues, or a quaint lingua franca, and dressed in very striking and pretty costumes. The fruit and vegetable stalls displayed very fine produce, and some staples, remarkable for novelty, ugliness, and goodness. After our stroll we went into one of the great oyster saloons, and in a room up-stairs had opportunity of tasting those great bivalvians in the form of natural fish puddings, fried in batter, roasted, stewed, devilled, broiled, and in many other ways, *plus* raw. I am bound to observe that the Mobile people ate them as if there was no blockade, as though oysters were a specific for political indigestions and civil wars; a fierce Marseillais are they—living in the most foreign-looking city I have yet seen in the States. My private room in the hotel was large, well-lighted with gas, and exceedingly well furnished in the German fashion, with French pendule and mirrors. The charge for a private room varies from 1*l.* to 1*l.* 5*s.* a day; the bed-room and board are charged separately, from 10*s.* 6*d.* to 12*s.* 6*d.* a day, but meals served in the private room are charged extra, and heavily too. Exclusiveness is an aristocratic taste which must be paid for.

CHAPTER XXVI.

Visit to Forts Gaines and Morgan—War to the knife the cry of the South—The "State" and the "States"—Bay of Mobile—The forts and their inmates—Opinions as to an attack on Washington—Rumours of actual war.

May 12th.—Mr. Forsyth had been good enough to invite me to an excursion down the Bay of Mobile, to the forts built by Uncle Sam and his French engineers to sink his Britishers—now turned by "C. S. A." against the hated Stars and Stripes. The mayor and the principal merchants and many politicians—and are not all men politicians in America?—formed the party. If any judgment of men's acts can be formed from their words, the Mobilites, who are the representatives of the third greatest port of the United States, will perish ere they submit to the Yankees and people of New York. I have now been in North Carolina, South Carolina, Georgia, Alabama, and in none of these great States have I found the least indication of the Union sentiment, or of the attachment for the Union which Mr. Seward always assumes to exist in the South. If there were any considerable amount of it, I was in a position as a neutral to have been aware of its existence.

Those who might have at one time opposed secession, have now bowed their heads to the majesty of the majority; and with the cowardice, which is the result of the irresponsible and cruel tyranny of the multitude, hasten to swell the cry of revolution. But the multitude are the law in the United States. "There's a divinity doth hedge" the mob here, which is omnipotent and all good. The majority in each State determines its political status according to Southern views. The Northerners are endeavouring to maintain that the majority of the people in the mass of the States generally shall regulate that point for each State individually and collectively. If there be any party in the Southern States which thinks such an attempt justifiable, it sits silent, and fearful, and hopeless, in darkness and sorrow, hid from the light of day. General Scott, who was a short time ago written of in the usual inflated style, to which respectable military mediocrity and success are entitled in the States, is now reviled by the Southern papers as an infamous hoary traitor and the like. If an officer prefers his allegiance to the United States' flag, and remains in the Federal service after his State has gone out, his property is liable to confiscation by the State authorities, and his family and kindred are exposed to the gravest suspicion, and must prove their loyalty by extra zeal in the cause of secession.

Our merry company comprised naval and military officers in the service of the Confederate States, journalists, politicians, professional men, merchants, and not one of them had a word but of hate and execration for the North. The British and German settlers are quite as vehement as the natives in upholding States' rights, and among the most ardent upholders of slavery are the Irish proprietors and mercantile classes.

The Bay of Mobile, which is about thirty miles long, with a breadth varying from three to seven miles, is formed by the outfall of the Alabama and of the Tombigbee river, and is shallow and dangerous, full of banks and trees, embedded in the sands; but all large vessels lie at the entrance between Fort Morgan and Fort Gaines, to the satisfaction of the masters, who are thus spared the trouble with their crews which occurs in the low haunts of a maritime town. The cotton is sent down in lighters, which employ many hands at high wages. The shores are low wooded, and are dotted here and there with pretty villas, but present no attractive scenery.

The sea-breeze somewhat alleviated the fierceness of the sun, which was however too hot to be quite agreeable. Our steamer, crowded to the sponsons, made little way against the tide; but at length, after nearly four hours' sail, we hauled up alongside a jetty at Fort Gaines, which is on the right hand or western exit of the harbour, and would command, were it finished, the light draft channel; it is now merely a shell of masonry, but Colonel Hardee, who has charge of the defences of Mobile, told me that they would finish it speedily.

The Colonel is an agreeable, delicate-looking man, scarcely of middle age, and is well-known in the States as the author of "The Tactics," which is, however, merely a translation of the French manual of arms. He does not appear to be possessed of any great energy or capacity, but is, no doubt, a respectable officer.

Upon landing we found a small body of men on guard in the fort. A few cannon of moderate calibre were mounted on the sandhills and on the beach. We entered the unfinished work, and were received with a salute. The men felt difficulty in combining discipline with citizenship. They were "bored" with their sandhill, and one of them asked me when I "thought them damned Yankees were coming. He wanted to touch off a few pills he knew would be good for their complaint." I must say I could sympathise with the feelings of the young officer who said he would sooner have a day with the Lincolnites, than a week with the musquitoes, for which this locality is famous.

From Fort Gaines the steamer ran across to Fort Morgan, about three miles distant, passing in its way seven vessels, mostly British, at anchor, where hundreds may be seen, I am told, during the cotton season. This work has a formidable sea face, and may give great trouble to Uncle Sam, when he wants to visit his loving subjects in Mobile in his gunboats. It is the work of Bernard, I presume, and like most of his designs has a weak long base towards the land; but it is provided with a wet ditch and drawbridge, with demi lunes covering the curtains, and has a regular bastioned trace. It has one row of casemates, armed with 32 and 42-pounders. The barbette guns are 8-inch and 10-inch guns; the external works at the salients are armed with howitzers and field-pieces, and as we crossed the drawbridge, a salute was fired from a field battery, on a flanking bastion, in our honour.

Inside the work was crammed with men, some of whom slept in the casemates—others in tents in the parade grounds and enceinte of the fort. They were Alabama Volunteers, and as sturdy a lot of fellows as ever shouldered musket; dressed in homespun coarse grey suits, with blue and yellow worsted facings and stripes—to European eyes not very respectful to their officers, but very obedient, I am told, and very peremptorily ordered about, as I heard.

There were 700 or 800 men in the work, and an undue proportion of officers, all of whom were introduced to the strangers in turn. The officers were a very gentlemanly, nice-looking set of young fellows, and some of them had just come over from Europe to take up arms for their State. I forget the name of the officer in command, though I cannot forget his courtesy, nor an excellent lunch he gave us in his casemate after a hot walk round the parapets, and some practice with solid shot from the barbette guns, which did not tend to make me think much of the greatly-be-praised Columbiads.

One of the officers named Maury, a relative of "deep-sea Maury," struck me as an ingenious and clever officer; the utmost harmony, kindliness, and devotion to the cause prevailed among the garrison, from the chief down to the youngest ensign. In its present state the Fort would suffer exceedingly from a heavy bombardment—the magazines would be in danger, and the traverses are inadequate. All the barracks and wooden buildings should be destroyed if they wish to avoid the fate of Sumter.

On our cruise homewards, in the enjoyment of a cold dinner, we had the inevitable discussion of the Northern and Southern contest. Mr. Forsyth, the editor and proprietor of the "Mobile Register," is impassioned for the cause, though he was not at one time considered a pure Southerner. There is difference of opinion relative to an attack on Washington. General St. George Cooke, commanding the army of Virginia on the Potomac, declares there is no intention of attacking it, or any place outside the limits of that free and sovereign State. But then the conduct of the Federal Government in Maryland is considered by the more fiery Southerners to justify the expulsion of "Lincoln and his Myrmidons," "the Border Ruffians and Cassius M. Clay," from the capital. Butler has seized on the Relay House, on the junction of the Baltimore and Ohio Railroad, with the rail from Washington, and has displayed a good deal of vigour since his arrival at Annapolis. He is a democrat, and a celebrated criminal lawyer in Massachusetts. Troops are pouring into New York, and are preparing to attack Alexandria, on the Virginia side, below Washington and the Navy Yard, where a large Confederate flag is flying, which can be seen from the President's windows in the White House.

There is a secret soreness even here at the small effect produced in England compared with what they anticipated by the attack on Sumter; but hopes are excited that Mr. Gregory, who was travelling through the States some time ago, will have a strong party to support his forthcoming motion for a recognition of the South. The next conflict which takes place will be more bloody than that at Sumter. The gladiators are approaching—Washington, Annapolis, Pennsylvania are military departments, each with a chief and Staff, to which is now added that of Ohio, under Major G. B. M'Clellan, Major General of Ohio Volunteers at Cincinnati. The authorities on each side are busy administering oaths of allegiance.

The harbour of Charleston is reported to be under blockade by the Niagara steam frigate, and a force of United States' troops at St. Louis, Missouri, under Captain Lyon, has attacked and dispersed a body of State Militia under one Brigadier General Frost, to the intense indignation of all Mobile. The argument is, that Missouri gave up the St. Louis Arsenal to the United States' Government, and could take it back if she pleased, and was certainly competent to prevent the United States' troops stirring beyond the Arsenal.

CHAPTER XXVII.

Pensacola and Fort Pickens—Neutrals and their friends—Coasting—Sharks—The blockading fleet—The stars and stripes, and stars and bars—Domestic feuds caused by the war—Captain Adams and General Bragg—Interior of Fort Pickens.

May 13th.—I was busy making arrangements to get to Pensacola, and Fort Pickens, all day. The land journey was represented as being most tedious and exceedingly comfortless in all respects, through a waste of sand, in which we ran the chance of being smothered or lost. And then I had set my mind on seeing Fort Pickens as well as Pensacola, and it would be difficult, to say the least of it, to get across from an enemy's camp to the Federal fortress, and then return again. The United States' squadron blockaded the port of Pensacola, but I thought it likely they would permit me to run in to visit Fort Pickens, and that the Federals would allow me to sail thence across to General Bragg, as they might be assured I would not communicate any information of what I had seen in my character as neutral to any but the journal in Europe, which I represented, and in the interests of which I was bound to see and report all that I could as to the state of both parties. It was, at all events, worth while to make the attempt, and after a long search I heard of a schooner which was ready for the voyage at a reasonable rate, all things considered.

Mr. Forsyth asked if I had any objection to take with me three gentlemen of Mobile, who were anxious to be of the party, as they wanted to see their friends at Pensacola, where it was believed a "fight" was to come off immediately. Since I came South I have seen the daily announcement that "Braxton Bragg is ready," and his present state of preparation must be beyond all conception. But here was a difficulty. I told Mr. Forsyth that I could not possibly assent to any persons coming with me who were not neutrals, or prepared to adhere to the obligations of neutrals. There was a suggestion that I should say these gentlemen were my friends, but as I had only seen two of them on board the steamer yesterday, I could not accede to that idea. "Then if you are asked if Mr. Ravesies is your friend, you will say he is not." "Certainly." "But surely you don't wish to have Mr. Ravesies hanged?" "No, I do not, and I shall do nothing to cause him to be hanged; but if he meets that fate by his own act, I can't help it. I will not allow him to accompany me under false pretences."

At last it was agreed that Mr. Ravesies and his friends Mr. Bartré and Mr. Lynes, being in no way employed by or connected with the Confederate Government, should have a place in the little schooner which we had picked out at the quayside and hired for the occasion, and go on the voyage with the plain understanding that they were to accept all the consequences of being citizens of Mobile.

Mr. Forsyth, Mr. Ravesies, and a couple of gentlemen dined with me in the evening. After dinner, Mr. Forsyth, who, as mayor of the town, is the Executive of the Vigilance Committee, took a copy of *Harper's Illustrated Paper*, which is a very poor imitation of the *Illustrated London News*, and called my attention to the announcement that Mr. Moses, their special artist, was travelling with me in the South, as well as to an engraving, which purported to be by Moses aforesaid. I could only say that I knew nothing of the young designer, except what he told me, and that he led me to believe he was furnishing sketches to the *London News*. As he was in the hotel, though he did not live with me, I sent for him, and the young gentleman, who was very pale and agitated on being shown the advertisement and sketch, declared that he had renounced all connection with Harper, that he was sketching for the *Illustrated London News*, and that the advertisement was contrary to fact, and utterly unknown to him; and so he was let go forth, and retired uneasily. After dinner I went to the Bienville Club. "Rule No. 1" is, "No gentleman shall be admitted in a state of intoxication." The club very social, very small, and very hospitable.

Later paid my respects to Mrs. Forsyth, whom I found anxiously waiting for news of her young son, who had gone off to join the Confederate army. She told me that nearly all the ladies in Mobile are engaged in making cartridges, and in preparing lint or clothing for the army. Not the smallest fear is entertained of the swarming black population.

May 14th.—Down to our yacht, the Diana, which is to be ready this afternoon, and saw her cleared out a little—a broad-beamed, flat-floored schooner, some fifty tons burthen, with a centreboard, badly caulked, and dirty enough—unfamiliar with paint. The skipper was a long-legged, ungainly young fellow, with long hair and an inexpressive face, just relieved by the twinkle of a very "Yankee" eye; but that was all of the hated creature about him, for a more earnest seceder I never heard.

His crew consisted of three rough, mechanical sort of men and a negro cook. Having freighted the vessel with a small stock of stores, a British flag, kindly lent by the acting Consul, Mr. Magee, and a tablecloth to serve as a flag of truce, our party, consisting of the gentlemen previously named, Mr. Ward, and the young artist, weighed from the quay of Mobile at five o'clock in the evening, with the manifest approbation of the small crowd who had assembled to see us off, the rumour having spread through the town that we were bound to see the great fight. The breeze was favourable and steady; at nine o'clock P.M., the lights of Fort Morgan were on our port beam, and for some time we were expecting to see the flash of a gun, as the skipper confidently declared they would never allow us to pass unchallenged.

The darkness of the night might possibly have favoured us, or the sentries were remiss; at all events, we were soon creeping through the "Swash," which is a narrow channel over the bar, through which our skipper worked us by means of a sounding-pole. The air was delightful, and blew directly off the low shore, in a line parallel to which we were moving. When the evening vapours passed away, the stars shone out brilliantly, and though the wind was strong, and sent us at a good eight knots through the water, there was scarcely a ripple on the sea. Our course lay within a quarter of a mile of the shore, which looked like a white ribbon fringed with fire, from the ceaseless play of the phosphorescent surf. Above this belt of sand rose the black, jagged outlines of a pine forest, through which steal immense lagoons and marshy creeks.

Driftwood and trees strew the beach, and from Fort Morgan, for forty miles, to the entrance of Pensacola, not a human habitation disturbs the domain sacred to alligators, serpents, pelicans, and wild-fowl. Some of the lagoons, like the Perdida, swell into inland seas, deep buried in pine woods, and known only to the wild creatures swarming along its brink and in its waters; once, if report says true, frequented, however, by the filibusters and by the pirates of the Spanish Main.

If the musquitoes were as numerous and as persecuting in those days as they are at present, the most adventurous youth would have soon repented the infatuation which led him to join the brethren of the Main. The musquito is a great enemy to romance, and our skipper tells us that there is no such place known in the world for them as this coast.

As the Diana flew along the grim shore, we lay listlessly on the deck admiring the excessive brightness of the stars, or watching the trailing fire of her wake. Now and then great fish flew off from the shallows, cleaving their path in flame; and one shining gleam came up from leeward like a watery comet, till its horrible outline was revealed close to us—a monster shark—which accompanied us with an easy play of the fin, distinctly visible in the wonderful phosphorescence, now shooting on ahead, now dropping astern, till suddenly it dashed off seaward with tremendous rapidity and strength on some errand of destruction, and vanished in the waste of waters. Despite the multitudes of fish on the coast, the Spaniards who colonize this ill-named Florida must have had a trying life of it between the Indians, now hunted to death or exiled by rigorous Uncle Sam, the musquitoes, and the numberless plagues which abound along these shores.

Hour after hour passed watching the play of large fish and the surf on the beach; one by one the cigar-lights died out; and muffling ourselves up on deck, or creeping into the little cabin, the party slumbered. I was awoke by the Captain talking to one of his hands close to me, and on looking up saw that he was staring through a wonderful black tube, which he denominated his "tallowscope," at the shore.

Looking in the direction, I observed the glare of a fire in the wood, which on examination through an opera glass resolved itself into a steady central light, with some smaller specks around it. "Wa'll," said the Captain, "I guess it is just some of them d——d Yankees as is landed from their tarnation boats, and is 'connoitering' for a road to Mobile." There was an old iron cannonade on board, and it struck me as a curious exemplification of the recklessness of our American cousins, when the skipper said, "Let us put a bag of bullets in the ould gun, and touch it off at them;" which he no doubt would have done, seconded by one of our party, who drew his revolver to contribute to the broadside, but that I represented to them it was just as likely to be a party out from the camp at Pensacola, and that, anyhow, I strongly objected to any belligerent act whilst I was on board. It was very probably, indeed, the watchfire of a Confederate patrol, for the gentry of the country have formed themselves into a body of regular cavalry for such service; but the skipper declared that our chaps knew better than to be showing their lights in that way, when we were within ten miles of the entrance to Pensacola.

The skipper lay-to, as he, very wisely, did not like to run into the centre of the United States squadron at night; but just at the first glimpse of dawn the Diana resumed her course, and bowled along merrily till, with the first rays of the sun, Fort M'Rae, Fort Pickens, and the masts of the squadron were visible ahead, rising above the blended horizon of land and sea. We drew upon them rapidly, and soon could make out the rival flags—the Stars and Bars and Stars and Stripes—flouting defiance at each other.

On the land side on our left is Fort M'Rae, and on the end of the sand-bank, called Santa Rosa Island, directly opposite, rises the outline of the much-talked-of Fort Pickens, which is not unlike Fort Paul on a small scale. Through the glass the blockading squadron is seen to consist of a sailing frigate, a sloop, and three steamers; and as we are scrutinising them, a small schooner glides from under the shelter of the guardship, and makes towards us like a hawk on a sparrow. Hand over hand she comes, a great swaggering ensign at her peak, and a gun all ready at her bow; and rounding up alongside us, a boat, manned by four men, is lowered, an officer jumps in, and is soon under our counter. The officer, a bluff, sailor-like looking fellow, in a uniform a little the worse for wear, and wearing his beard as officers of the United States navy generally do, fixed his eye upon the skipper—who did not seem quite at his ease, and had, indeed, confessed to us that he had been warned off by the Oriental, as the tender was named, only a short time before—and said, "Hallo, sir, I think I have seen you before: what schooner is this?" "The Diana of Mobile." "I thought so." Stepping on deck, he said, "Gentlemen, I am Mr. Brown, Master in the United States navy, in charge of the boarding schooner Oriental." We each gave our names; whereupon Mr. Brown says, "I have no doubt it will be all right; be good enough to let me have your papers. And now, sir, make sail, and lie-to under the quarter of that steamer there, the Powhatan." The Captain did not look at all happy when the officer called his attention to the indorsement on his papers; nor did the Mobile party seem very comfortable when he remarked, "I suppose, gentlemen, you are quite well aware there is a strict blockade of this port?"

In half an hour the schooner lay under the guns of the Powhatan, which is a stumpy, thickset, powerful steamer of the old paddle-wheel kind, something like our Leopard. We proceeded alongside in the cutter's boat, and were ushered into the cabin, where the officer commanding, Lieutenant David Porter, received us, begged us to be seated, and then inquired into the object of our visit, which he communicated to the flag-ship by signal, in order to get instructions as to our disposal. Nothing could exceed his courtesy; and I was most favourably impressed by himself, his officers, and crew. He took me over the ship, which is armed with 10-inch Dahlgrens and an 11-inch pivot gun, with rifled field-pieces and howitzers on the sponsons. Her boarding nettings were triced up, bows and weak portions padded with dead wood and old sails, and everything ready for action.

Lieutenant Porter has been in and out of the harbour examining the enemy's works at all hours of the night, and he has marked off on the chart, as he showed me, the bearings of the various spots where he can sweep or enfilade their works. The crew, all things considered, were very clean, and their personnel exceedingly fine.

We were not the only prize that was made by the Oriental this morning. A ragged little schooner lay at the other side of the Powhatan, the master of which stood rubbing his knuckles into his eyes, and uttering dolorous expressions in broken English and Italian, for he was a noble Roman of Civita Vecchia. Lieutenant Porter let me into the secret. These small traders at Mobile, pretending great zeal for the Confederate cause, load their vessels with fruit, vegetables, and things of which they know the squadron is much in want, as well as the garrison of the Confederate forts. They set out with the most valiant intention of running the blockade, and are duly captured by the squadron, the officers of which are only too glad to pay fair prices for the cargoes. They return to Mobile, keep their money in their pockets, and declare they have been plundered by the Yankees. If they get in, they demand still higher prices from the Confederates, and lay claim to the most exalted patriotism.

By signal from the flag-ship Sabine, we were ordered to repair on board to see the senior officer, Captain Adams; and for the first time since I trod the deck of the old Leander in Balaklava harbour, I stood on board a 50-gun sailing frigate. Captain Adams, a grey-haired veteran of very gentle manners and great urbanity, received us in his cabin, and listened to my explanation of the cause of my visit with interest. About myself there was no difficulty; but he very justly observed he did not think it would be right to let the gentlemen from Mobile examine Fort Pickens, and then go among the Confederate camps. I am bound to say these gentlemen scarcely seemed to desire or anticipate such a favour.

Major Vogdes, an engineer officer from the fort, who happened to be on board, volunteered to take a letter from me to Colonel Harvey Browne, requesting permission to visit it; and I finally arranged with Captain Adams that the Diana was to be permitted to pass the blockade into Pensacola harbour, and thence to return to Mobile, my visit to Pickens depending on the pleasure of the Commandant of the place. "I fear, Mr. Russell," said Captain Adams, "in giving you this permission, I expose myself to misrepresentation and unfounded attacks. Gentlemen of the press in our country care little about private character, and are, I fear, rather unscrupulous in what they say; but I rely upon your character that no improper use shall be made of this permission. You must hoist a flag of truce, as General Bragg, who commands over there, has sent me word he considers our blockade a declaration of war, and will fire upon any vessel which approaches him from our fleet."

In the course of conversation, whilst treating me to such man-of-war luxuries as the friendly officer had at his disposal, he gave me an illustration of the miseries of this cruel conflict—of the unspeakable desolation of homes, of the bitterness of feeling engendered in families. A Pennsylvanian by birth, he married long ago a lady of Louisiana, where he resided on his plantation till his ship was commissioned. He was absent on foreign service when the feud first began, and received orders at sea, on the South American station, to repair direct to blockade Pensacola. He has just heard that one of his sons is enlisted in the Confederate army, and that two others have joined the forces in Virginia; and as he said sadly, "God knows, when I open my broadside, but that I may be killing my own children." But that was not all. One of the Mobile gentlemen brought him a letter from his daughter, in which she informs him that she has been elected vivandière to a New Orleans regiment, with which she intends to push on to Washington, and get a lock of old Abe Lincoln's hair; and the letter concluded with the charitable wish that her father might starve to death if he persisted in his wicked blockade. But not the less determined was the gallant old sailor to do his duty.

Mr. Ward, one of my companions, had sailed in the Sabine in the Paraguay expedition, and I availed myself of his acquaintance with his old comrades to take a glance round the ship. Wherever they came from, four hundred more sailor-like, strong, handy young fellows could not be seen than the crew; and the officers were as hospitable as their limited resources in whisky grog, cheese, and junk allowed them to be.

With thanks for his kindness and courtesy, I parted from Captain Adams, feeling more than ever the terrible and earnest nature of the impending conflict. May the kindly good old man be shielded on the day of battle!

A ten-oared barge conveyed us to the Oriental, which, with flowing sheet, ran down to the Powhatan. There I saw Captain Porter, and told him that Captain Adams had given me permission to visit the Confederate camp, and that I had written for leave to go on shore at Fort Pickens. An officer was in his cabin, to whom I was introduced as Captain Poore, of the Brooklyn. "You don't mean to say, Mr. Russell," said he, "that these editors of Southern newspapers who are with you have leave to go on shore?" This was rather a fishing question. "I assure you, Captain Poore, that there is no editor of a Southern newspaper in my company."

The boat which took us from the Powhatan to the Diana was in charge of a young officer related to Captain Porter, who amused me by the spirit with which he bandied remarks about the Mobile men, who had now recovered their equanimity, and were indulging in what is called chaff about the blockade. "Well," he said, "you were the first to begin it; let us see whether you won't be the first to leave it off. I guess our Northern ice will pretty soon put out your Southern fire."

When we came on board, the skipper heard our orders to up stick and away with an air of pity and incredulity; nor was it till I had repeated it, he kicked up his crew from their sleep on deck, and with a "Wa'll, really, I never did see sich a thing!" made sail towards the entrance to the harbour.

As we got abreast of Fort Pickens, I ordered table-cloth No. 1 to be hoisted to the peak; and through the glass I saw that our appearance attracted no ordinary attention from the garrison of Pickens close at hand on our right, and the more distant Confederates on Fort M'Rae and the sand-hills on our left. The latter work is weak and badly built, quite under the command of Pickens, but it is supported by the old Spanish fort of Barrancas upon high ground further inland, and by numerous batteries at the water-line, and partly concealed amid the woods which fringe the shore as far as the navy yard of Warrington, near Pensacola. The wind was light, but the tide bore us on towards the Confederate works. Arms glanced in the blazing sun where regiments were engaged at drill, clouds of dust rose from the sandy roads, horsemen riding along the beach, groups of men in uniform, gave a martial appearance to the place in unison with the black muzzles of the guns which peeped from the white sand batteries from the entrance of the harbour to the navy yard now close at hand. As at Sumter Major Anderson permitted the Carolinians to erect the batteries he might have so readily destroyed in the commencement, so the Federal officers here have allowed General Bragg to work away at his leisure, mounting cannon after cannon, throwing up earthworks, and strengthening his batteries, till he has assumed so formidable an attitude, that I doubt very much whether the fort and the fleet combined can silence his fire.

On the low shore close to us were numerous wooden houses and detached villas, surrounded by orange-groves. At last the captain let go his anchor off the end of a wooden jetty, which was crowded with ammunition, shot, shell, casks of provisions, and commissariat stores. A small steamer was engaged in adding to the collection, and numerous light craft gave evidence that all trade had not ceased. Indeed, inside Santa Rosa Island, which runs for forty-five miles from Pickens eastward parallel to the shore, there is a considerable coasting traffic carried on for the benefit of the Confederates.

The skipper went ashore with my letters to General Bragg, and speedily returned with an orderly, who brought permission for the Diana to come alongside the wharf. The Mobile gentlemen were soon on shore, eager to seek their friends; and in a few seconds the officer of the quartermaster-general's department on duty came on board to conduct me to the officers' quarters, whilst waiting for my reply from General Bragg.

The navy yard is surrounded by a high wall, the gates closely guarded by sentries; the houses, gardens, workshops, factories, forges, slips, and building-sheds are complete of their kind, and cover upwards of three hundred acres; and with the forts which protect the entrance, cost the United States Government not less than six millions sterling. Inside these was the greatest activity and life,—Zouave, Chasseurs, and all kind of military eccentricities—were drilling, parading, exercising, sitting in the shade, loading tumbrils, playing cards, or sleeping on the grass. Tents were pitched under the trees and on the little lawns and grass-covered quadrangles. The houses, each numbered and marked with the name of the functionary to whose use it was assigned, were models of neatness, with gardens in front, filled with glorious tropical flowers. They were painted green and white, provided with porticoes, Venetian blinds, verandahs, and colonnades, to protect the inmates as much as possible from the blazing sun, which in the dog-days is worthy of Calcutta. The old Fulton is the only ship on the stocks. From the naval arsenal quantities of shot and shell are constantly pouring to the batteries. Piles of cannon-balls dot the grounds, but the only ordnance I saw were two old mortars placed as ornaments in the main avenue, one dated 1776.

The quartermaster conducted me through shady walks into one of the houses, then into a long room, and presented me *en masse* to a body of officers, mostly belonging to a Zouave regiment from New Orleans, who were seated at a very comfortable dinner, with abundance of champagne, claret, beer, and ice. They were all young, full of life and spirits, except three or four graver and older men, who were Europeans. One, a Dane, had fought against the Prussians and Schleswig-Holsteiners at Idstedt and Friederichstadt; another, an Italian, seemed to have been indifferently engaged in fighting all over the South American continent; a third, a Pole, had been at Comorn, and had participated in the revolutionary guerilla of 1848. From these officers I learned that Mr. Jefferson Davis, his wife, Mr. Wigfall, and Mr. Mallory, Secretary to the Navy, had come down from Montgomery, and had been visiting the works all day.

Every one here believes the attack so long threatened is to come off at last and at once.

After dinner an aide-de-camp from General Bragg entered with a request that I would accompany him to the commanding officer's quarters. As the sand outside the navy yard was deep, and rendered walking very disagreeable, the young officer stopped a cart, into which we got, and were proceeding on our way, when a tall, elderly man, in a blue frock-coat with a gold star on the shoulder, trowsers with a gold stripe and gilt buttons, rode past, followed by an orderly, who looked more like a dragoon than anything I have yet seen in the States. "There's General Bragg," quoth the aide, and I was duly presented to the General, who reined up by the waggon. He sent his orderly off at once for a light cart drawn by a pair of mules, in which I completed my journey, and was safely decarted at the door of a substantial house surrounded by trees of lime, oak, and sycamore.

Led horses and orderlies thronged the front of the portico, and gave it the usual head-quarter-like aspect. General Bragg received me at the steps, and took me to his private room, where we remained for a long time in conversation. He had retired from the United States army after the Mexican war—in which, by the way, he played a distinguished part, his name being generally coupled with the phrase "a little more grape, Captain Bragg," used in one of the hottest encounters of that campaign—to his plantation in Louisiana; but suddenly the Northern States declared their intention of using force to free and sovereign states, which were exercising their constitutional rights to secede from the Federal Union.

Neither he nor his family were responsible for the system of slavery. His ancestors found it established by law and flourishing, and had left him property, consisting of slaves, which was granted to him by the laws and constitution of the United States. Slaves were necessary for the actual cultivation of the soil in the South; Europeans and Yankees who settled there speedily became convinced of that; and if a Northern population were settled in Louisiana to-morrow, they would discover that they must till the land by the labour of the black race, and that the only mode of making the black race work was to hold them in a condition of involuntary servitude. "Only the other day, Colonel Harvey Browne, at Pickens, over the way, carried off a number of negroes from Tortugas, and put them to work at Santa Rosa. Why? Because his white soldiers were not able for it. No. The North was bent on subjugating the South, and as long as he had a drop of blood in his body, he would resist such an infamous attempt."

Before supper General Bragg opened his maps, and pointed out to me in detail the position of all his works, the line of fire of each gun, and the particular object to be expected from its effects. "I know every inch of Pickens," he said, "for I happened to be stationed there as soon as I left West Point, and I don't think there is a stone in it that I am not as well acquainted with as Harvey Browne."

His staff, consisting of four intelligent young men, two of them lately belonging to the United States army, supped with us, and after a very agreeable evening, horses were ordered round to the door, and I returned to the navy yard attended by the General's orderly, and provided with a pass and countersign. As a mark of complete confidence, General Bragg told me, for my private ear, that he had no present intention whatever of opening fire, and that his batteries were far from being in a state, either as regards armament or ammunition, which would justify him in meeting the fire of the forts and the ships.

And so we bade good-by. "To-morrow," said the General, "I will send down one of my best horses and Mr. Ellis, my aide-de-camp, to take you over all the works and batteries." As I rode home with my honest orderly beside instead of behind me, for he was of a conversational turn, I was much perplexed in my mind, endeavouring to determine which was right and which was wrong in this quarrel, and at last, as at Montgomery, I was forced to ask myself if right and wrong were geographical expressions depending for extension or limitation on certain conditions of climate and lines of latitude and longitude. Here was the General's orderly beside me, an intelligent middle-aged man, who had come to do battle with as much sincerity—aye, and religious confidence—as ever actuated old John Brown or any New England puritan to make war against slavery. "I have left my old woman and the children to the care of the niggers; I have turned up all my cotton land and planted it with corn, and I don't intend to go back alive till I've seen the back of the last Yankee in our Southern States." "And are wife and children alone with the negroes?" "Yes, sir. There's only one white man on the plantation, an overseer sort of chap." "Are not you afraid of the slaves rising?" "They're ignorant poor creatures, to be sure, but as yet they're faithful. Any way, I put my trust in God, and I know He'll watch over the house while I'm away fighting for this good cause!" This man came from Mississippi, and had twenty-five slaves, which represented a money value of at least £5000. He was beyond the age of enthusiasm, and was actuated, no doubt, by strong principles, to him unquestionable and sacred.

My pass and countersign, which were only once demanded, took me through the sentries, and I got on board the schooner shortly before midnight, and found nearly all the party on deck, enchanted with their reception. More than once we were awoke by the vigilant sentries, who would not let what Americans call "the balance" of our friends on board till they had seen my authority to receive them.

CHAPTER XXVIII.

Bitters before breakfast—An old Crimean acquaintance—Earthworks and batteries—Estimate of cannons—Magazines—Hospitality—English and American introductions and leave-takings—Fort Pickens; its interior—Return towards Mobile—Pursued by a strange sail—Running the blockade—Landing at Mobile.

May 16th.—The réveillé of the Zouaves, note for note the same as that which, in the Crimea, so often woke up poor fellows who slept the long sleep ere nightfall, roused us this morning early, and then the clang of trumpets and the roll of drums beating French calls summoned the volunteers to early parade. As there was a heavy dew, and many winged things about last night, I turned in to my berth below, where four human beings were supposed to lie in layers, like mummies beneath a pyramid, and there, after contention with cockroaches, sank to rest. No wonder I was rather puzzled to know where I was now; for in addition to the music and the familiar sounds outside, I was somewhat perturbed in my mental calculations by bringing my head sharply in contact with a beam of the deck, which had the best of it; but, at last, facts accomplished themselves and got into place, much aided by the appearance of the negro cook with a cup of coffee in his hand, who asked, "Mosieu! Capitaine vant to ax vedder you take some bitter, sar! Lisbon bitter, sar." I saw the captain on deck busily engaged in the manufacture of a liquid which I was adjured by all the party on deck to take, if I wished to make a Redan or a Malakhoff of my stomach, and accordingly I swallowed a *petit verre* of a very strong, intensely bitter preparation of brandy and tonic roots, sweetened with sugar, for which Mobile is famous.

The noise of our arrival had gone abroad; haply the report of the good things with which the men of Mobile had laden the craft, for a few officers came aboard even at that early hour, and we asked two who were known to our friends to stay for breakfast. That meal, to which the negro cook applied his whole mind and all the galley, consisted of an ugly-looking but well-flavored fish from the waters outside us, fried ham and onions, biscuit, coffee, iced water and Bordeaux, served with charming simplicity, and no way calculated to move the ire of Horace by a display of Persic apparatus.

A more greasy, oniony meal was never better enjoyed. One of our guests was a jolly Yorkshire farmer-looking man, up to about 16 stone weight, with any hounds, dressed in a tunic of green baize or frieze, with scarlet worsted braid down the front, gold lace on the cuffs and collar, and a felt wide-awake, with a bunch of feathers in it. He wiped the sweat off his brow, and swore that he would never give in, and that the whole of the company of riflemen whom he commanded, if not as heavy, were quite as patriotic. He was evidently a kindly affectionate man, without a trace of malice in his composition, but his sentiments were quite ferocious when he came to speak of the Yankees. He was a large slave-owner, and therefore a man of fortune, and he spoke with all the fervour of a capitalist menaced by a set of Red Republicans.

His companion, who wore a plain blue uniform, spoke sensibly about a matter with which sense has rarely anything to do—namely uniform. Many of the United States volunteers adopt the same grey colours so much in vogue among the Confederates. The officers of both armies were similar distinguishing marks of rank, and he was quite right in supposing that in night marches, or in serious actions on a large scale, much confusion and loss would be caused by men of the same army firing on each other, or mistaking enemies for friends.

Whilst we were talking, large shoals of mullet and other fish were flying before the porpoises, red fish, and other enemies, in the tide-way astern of the schooner. Once, as a large white fish came leaping up to the surface, a gleam of something still whiter shot through the waves, and a boiling whirl, tinged with crimson, which gradually melted off in the tide, marked where the fish had been.

"There's a ground sheark as has got his breakfast," quoth the Skipper. "There's quite a many of them about here." Now and then a turtle showed his head, exciting *desiderium tam cari capitis*, above the envied flood which he honoured with his presence.

Far away, towards Pensacola, floated three British ensigns, from as many merchantmen, which as yet had fifteen days to clear out from the blockaded port. Fort Pickens had hoisted the stars and stripes to the wind, and Fort M'Rae, as if to irritate its neighbour, displayed a flag almost identical, but for the "lone star," which the glass detected instead of the ordinary galaxy—the star of Florida.

Lieutenant Ellis, General Bragg's aide-de-camp, came on board at an early hour, in order to take me round the works, and I was soon on the back of the General's charger, safely ensconced between the raised pummel and cantle of a great brass-bound saddle, with emblazoned saddle-cloth and mighty stirrups of brass, fit for the fattest marshal that ever led an army of France to victory; but General Bragg is longer in the leg than the Duke of Malakhoff or Marshal Canrobert, and all my efforts to touch with my toe the wonderful supports which, in consonance with the American idea, dangled far beneath, were ineffectual.

As our road lay by head-quarters, the aide-de-camp took me into the court and called out "Orderly;" and at the summons a smart soldier-like young fellow came to the front, took me three holes up, and as I was riding away touched his cap and said, "I beg your pardon, sir, but I often saw you in the Crimea." He had been in the 11th Hussars, and on the day of Balaklava he was following close to Lord Cardigan and Captain Nolan, when his horse was killed by a round shot. As he was endeavouring to escape on foot the Cossacks took him prisoner, and he remained for eleven months in captivity in Russia, till he was exchanged at Odessa, towards the close of the war; then, being one of two sergeants who were permitted to get their discharge, he left the service. "But here you are again," said I, "soldiering once more, and merely acting as an orderly!" "Well, that's true enough; but I came over here, thinking to better myself as some of our fellows did, and then the war broke out, and I entered one of what they called their cavalry regiments—Lord bless you, sir, it would just break your heart to see them—and here I am now, and the general has made me an orderly. He is a kind man, sir, and the pay is good, but they are not like the old lot; I do not know what my lord would think of them." The man's name was Montague, and he told me his father lived "at a place called Windsor," twenty-one miles from London. Lieutenant Ellis said he was a very clean, smart, well-conducted soldier.

From head-quarters we started on our little tour of inspection of the batteries. Certainly, anything more calculated to shake confidence in American journalism could not be seen; for I had been led to believe that the works were of the most formidable description, mounting hundreds of guns. Where hundreds was written, tens would have been nearer the truth.

I visited ten out of the thirteen batteries which General Bragg has erected against Fort Pickens. I saw but five heavy siege guns in the whole of the works among the fifty or fifty-five pieces with which they were armed. There may be about eighty altogether on the lines, which describe an arc of 135 degrees for about three miles round Pickens, at an average distance of a mile and one-third. I was rather interested with Fort Barrancas, built by the Spaniards long ago—an old work on the old plan, weakly armed, but possessing a tolerable command from the face of fire.

In all the batteries there were covered galleries in the rear, connected with the magazines, and called "rat-holes," intended by the constructors as a refuge for the men whenever a shell from Pickens dropped in. The rush to the rat-hole does not impress one as being very conducive to a sustained and heavy fire, or at all likely to improve the *morale* of the gunners. The working parties, as they were called—volunteers from Mississippi and Alabama, great long-bearded fellows in flannel shirts and slouched hats, uniformless in all save brightly burnished arms and resolute purpose—were lying about among the works, or contributing languidly to their completion.

Considerable improvements were in the course of execution; but the officers were not always agreed as to the work to be done. Captain A., at the wheelbarrows: "Now then, you men, wheel up these sandbags, and range them just at this corner." Major B.: "My good Captain A., what do you want the bags there for? Did I not tell you, these merlons were not to be finished till we had completed the parapet on the front?" Captain A.: "Well, Major, so you did, and your order made me think you knew darned little about your business; and so I am going to do a little engineering of my own."

Altogether, I was quite satisfied General Bragg was perfectly correct in refusing to open his fire on Fort Pickens and on the fleet, which ought certainly to have knocked his works about his ears, in spite of his advantages of position, and of some well-placed mortar batteries among the brushwood, at distances from Pickens of 2500 and 2800 yards. The magazines of the batteries I visited did not contain ammunition for more than one day's ordinary firing. The shot were badly cast, with projecting flanges from the mould, which would be very injurious to soft metal guns in firing. As to men, as in guns, the Southern papers had lied consumedly. I could not say how many were in Pensacola itself, for I did not visit the camp: at the outside guess of the numbers there was 2000. I saw, however, all the camps here, and I doubt exceedingly if General Bragg—who at this time is represented to have any number from 30,000 to 50,000 men under his command—has 8000 troops to support his batteries, or 10,000, including Pensacola, all told.

If hospitality consists in the most liberal participation of all the owner has with his visitors, here, indeed, Philemon has his type in every tent. As we rode along through every battery, by every officer's quarters, some great Mississippian or Alabamian came forward with "Captain Ellis, I am glad to see you." "Colonel," to me, "won't you get down and have a drink?" Mr. Ellis duly introduces me. The Colonel with effusion grasps my hand and says, as if he had just gained the particular object of his existence, "Sir, I am very glad to know you. I hope you have been pretty well since you have been in our country, sir. Here, Pompey, take the colonel's horse. Step in, sir, and have a drink." Then comes out the great big whisky bottle, and an immense amount of adhesion to the first law of nature is required to get you off with less than half a pint of "Bourbon;" but the most trying thing to a stranger is the fact that when he is going away, the officer, who has been so delighted to see him, does not seem to care a farthing for his guest or his health.

The truth is, these introductions are ceremonial observances, and compliances with the universal curiosity of Americans to know people they meet. The Englishman bows frigidly to his acquaintance on the first introduction, and if he likes him shakes hands with him on leaving—a much more sensible and justifiable proceeding. The American's warmth at the first interview must be artificial, and the indifference at parting is ill-bred and in bad taste. I had already observed this on many occasions, especially at Montgomery, where I noticed it to Colonel Wigfall, but the custom is not incompatible with the most profuse hospitality, nor with the desire to render service.

On my return to head-quarters I found General Bragg in his room, engaged writing an official letter in reply to my request to be permitted to visit Fort Pickens, in which he gave me full permission to do as I pleased. Not only this, but he had prepared a number of letters of introduction to the military authorities, and to his personal friends at New Orleans, requesting them to give me every facility and friendly assistance in their power. He asked me my opinion about the batteries and their armament, which I freely gave him *quantum valeat.* "Well," he said, "I think your conclusions are pretty just; but, nevertheless, some fine day I shall be forced to try the mettle of our friends on the opposite side." All I could say was, "May God defend the right." "A good saying, to which I say, Amen. And drink with you to it."

There was a room outside, full of generals and colonels, to whom I was duly introduced; but the time for departure had come, and I bade good-by to the general and rode down to the wharf. I had always heard, during my brief sojourn in the North, that the Southern people were exceedingly illiterate and ignorant. It may be so, but I am bound to say that I observed a large proportion of the soldiers, on their way to the navy yard, engaged in reading newspapers, though they did not neglect the various drinking bars and exchanges, which were only too numerous in the vicinity of the camps.

The schooner was all ready for sea, but the Mobile gentlemen had gone off to Pensacola, and as I did not desire to invite them to visit Fort Pickens—where, indeed, they would have most likely met with a refusal—I resolved to sail without them and to return to the navy yard in the evening, in order to take them back on our homeward voyage. "Now then, captain, cast loose; we are going to Fort Pickens." The worthy seaman had by this time become utterly at sea, and did not appear to know whether he belonged to the Confederate States, Abraham Lincoln, or the British navy. But this order roused him a little, and looking at me with all his eyes, he exclaimed, "Why, you don't mean to say you are going to make me bring the Diana alongside that darned Yankee Fort!" Our tablecloth, somewhat maculated with gravy, was hoisted once more to the peak, and, after some formalities between the guardians of the jetty and ourselves, the schooner canted round in the tideway, and with a fine light breeze ran down towards the stars and stripes.

What magical power there is in the colours of a piece of bunting! My companions, I dare say, felt as proud of their flag as if their ancestors had fought under it at Acre or Jerusalem. And yet how fictitious its influence! Death, and dishonor worse than death, to desert it one day! Patriotism and glory to leave it in the dust, and fight under its rival, the next! How indignant would George Washington have been, if the Frenchman at Fort Du Quesne had asked him to abandon the old rag which Braddock held aloft in the wilderness, and to serve under the very *fleur-de-lys* which the same great George hailed with so much joy but a few years afterwards, when it was advanced to the front at York Town, to win one of its few victories over the Lions and the Harp. And in this Confederate flag there is a meaning which cannot die—it marks the birthplace of a new nationality, and its place must know it for ever. Even the flag of a rebellion leaves indelible colours in the political atmosphere. The hopes that sustained it may vanish in the gloom of night, but the national faith still believes that its sun will rise on some glorious morrow. Hard must it be for this race, so arrogant, so great, to see stripe and star torn from the fair standard with which they would fain have shadowed all the kingdoms of the world; but their great continent is large enough for many nations.

"And now," said the skipper, "I think we'd best lie to—them cussed Yankees on the beach is shouting to us." And so they were. A sentry on the end of a wooden jetty sung out, "Hallo you there! Stand off or I'll fire," and "drew a bead-line on us." At the same time the skipper hailed, "Please to send a boat off to go ashore." "No, sir! Come in your own boat!" cried the officer of the guard. Our own boat! A very skiff of Charon! Leaky, rotten, lopsided. We were a hundred yards from the beach, and it was to be hoped that with all its burthen, it could not go down in such a short row. As I stepped in, however, followed by my two companions, the water flew in as if forced by a pump, and when the sailors came after us the skipper said, through a mouthful of juice, "Deevid! pull your hardest, for there an't a more terrible place for shearks along the whole coast." Deevid and his friend pulled like men, and our hopes rose with the water in the boat and the decreasing distance to shore. They worked like Doggett's badgers, and in five minutes we were out of "sheark" depth and alongside the jetty, where Major Vogdes, Mr. Brown, of the Oriental, and an officer, introduced as Captain Barry of the United States artillery, were waiting to receive us. Major Vogdes said that Colonel Brown would most gladly permit me to go over the fort, but that he could not receive any of the other gentlemen of the party; they were permitted to wander about at their discretion. Some friends whom they picked up amongst the officers took them on a ride along the island, which is merely a sand-bank covered with coarse vegetation, a few trees, and pools of brackish water.

If I were selecting a summer habitation I should certainly not choose Fort Pickens. It is, like all other American works I have seen, strong on the sea faces and weak towards the land. The outer gate was closed, but at a talismanic knock from Captain Barry, the wicket was thrown open by the guard, and we passed through a vaulted gallery into the parade-ground, which was full of men engaged in strengthening the place, and digging deep pits in the centre as shell traps. The men were United States regulars, not comparable in physique to the Southern volunteers, but infinitely superior in cleanliness and soldierly smartness. The officer on duty led me to one of the angles of the fort and turned in to a covered way, which had been ingeniously contrived by tilting up the gun platforms and beams of wood at an angle against the wall, and piling earth and sand banks against them for several feet in thickness. The casemates, which otherwise would have been exposed to a plunging fire in the rear, were thus effectually protected.

Emerging from this dark passage I entered

one of the bomb-proofs, fitted up as a bed-room, and thence proceeded to the casemate, in which Colonel Harvey Browne has his head-quarters. After some conversation, he took me out upon the parapet and went all over the defences.

Fort Pickens is an oblique, and somewhat narrow parallelogram, with one obtuse angle facing the sea and the other towards the land. The bastion at the acute angle towards Barrancas is the weakest part of the work, and men were engaged in throwing up an extempore glacis to cover the wall and the casemates from fire. The guns were of what is considered small calibre in these days, 32 and 42 pounders, with four or five heavy columbiads. An immense amount of work has been done within the last three weeks, but as yet the preparations are by no means complete. From the walls, which are made of a hard-baked brick, nine feet in thickness, there is a good view of the enemy's position. There is a broad ditch round the work, now dry, and probably not intended for water. The cuvette has lately been cleared out, and in proof of the agreeable nature of the locality, the officers told me that sixty very fine rattlesnakes were killed by the workmen during the operation.

As I was looking at the works from the wall, Captain Vogdes made a sly remark now and then, blinking his eyes and looking closely at my face to see if he could extract any information. "There are the quarters of your friend General Bragg; he pretends, we hear, that it is an hospital, but we will soon have him out when we open fire." "Oh, indeed." "That's their best battery beside the lighthouse; we can't well make out whether there are ten, eleven, or twelve guns in it." Then Captain Vogdes became quite meditative, and thought aloud, "Well, I'm sure, Colonel, they've got a strong entrenched camp in that wood behind their mortar batteries. I'm quite sure of it—we must look to that with our long-range guns." What the engineer saw, must have been certain absurd little furrows in the sand, which the Confederates have thrown up about three feet in front of their tents, but whether to carry off or to hold rain water, or as cover for rattlesnakes, the best judge cannot determine.

The Confederates have been greatly delighted with the idea that Pickens will be almost untenable during the summer for the United States troops, on account of the heat and musquitoes, not to speak of yellow fever; but in fact they are far better off than the troops on the shore—the casemates are exceedingly well ventilated, light and airy. Musquitoes, yellow fever, and dysentery will make no distinction between Trojan and Tyrian. On the whole, I should prefer being inside, to being outside of Pickens, in case of a bombardment; and there can be no doubt the entire destruction of the navy yard and station by the Federals can be accomplished whenever they please. Colonel Browne pointed out the tall chimney at Warrington smoking away, and said, "There, sir, is the whole reason of Bragg's forbearance, as it is called. Do you see?—they are casting shot and shell there as fast as they can. They know well if they opened a gun on us I could lay that yard and all their works there in ruin;" and Colonel Harvey Browne seems quite the man for the work—a resolute, energetic veteran, animated by the utmost dislike to secession and its leaders, and full of what are called "Union Principles," which are rapidly becóming the mere expression of a desire to destroy life, liberty, property, anything in fact which opposes itself to the consolidation of the Federal government.

Probably no person has ever been permitted to visit two hostile camps within sight of each other save myself. I was neither spy, herald, nor ambassador; and both sides trusted to me fully on the understanding that I would not make use of any information here, but that it might be communicated to the world at the other side of the Atlantic.

Apropos of this, Colonel Browne told me an amusing story, which shows that 'cuteness is not altogether confined to the Yankees. Some days ago a gentleman was found wandering about the island, who stated he was a correspondent of a New York paper. Colonel Browne was not satisfied with the account he gave of himself, and sent him on board one of the ships of the fleet, to be confined as a prisoner. Soon afterwards a flag of truce came over from the Confederates, carrying a letter from General Bragg, requesting Colonel Browne to give up the prisoner, as he had escaped to the island after committing a felony, and enclosing a warrant signed by a justice of the peace for his arrest. Colonel Browne laughed at the *ruse*, and keeps his prisoner.

As it was approaching evening and I had seen everything in the fort, the hospital, casemates, magazines, bakehouses, tasted the rations, and drank the whisky, I set out for the schooner, accompanied by Colonel Browne and Captain Barry and other officers, and picking up my friends at the bakehouse outside.

Having bidden our acquaintances good-by, we got on board the Diana, which steered towards the Warrington navy yard, to take the rest of the party on board. The sentries along the beach and on the batteries grounded arms, and stared with surprise as the Diana, with her tablecloth flying, crossed over from Fort Pickens, and ran slowly along the Confederate works. Whilst we were spying for the Mobile gentlemen, the mate took it into his head to take up the Confederate bunting, and wave it over the quarter. "Hollo, what's that you're doing?" "It's only a signal to the gentlemen on shore." "Wave some other flag, if you please, when we are in these waters, with a flag of truce flying."

After standing off and on for some time, the Mobilians at last boarded us in a boat. They were full of excitement, quite eager to stay and see the bombardment, which must come off in twenty-four hours. Before we had left Mobile harbour I had made a bet for a small sum that neither side would attack within the next few days; but now I could not even shake my head one way or the other, and it required the utmost self-possession and artifice of which I was master to evade the acute inquiries and suggestions of my good friends. I was determined to go—they were equally bent upon remaining; and so we parted after a short but very pleasant cruise together.

We had arranged with Mr. Brown that we would look out for him on leaving the harbour, and a bottle of wine was put in the remnants of our ice to drink farewell; but it was almost dark as the Diana shot out seawards between Pickens and M'Rae; and for some anxious minutes we were doubtful which would be the first to take a shot at us. Our tablecloth still fluttered; but the colour might be invisible. A lantern was hoisted astern by my order as soon as the schooner was clear of the forts; and with a cool sea-breeze we glided out into the night, the black form of the Powhatan being just visible, the rest of the squadron lost in the darkness. We strained our eyes for the Oriental, but in vain; and it occurred to us that it would scarcely be a very safe proceeding to stand from the Confederate forts down toward the guardship, unless under the convoy of the Oriental. It seemed quite certain she must be cruising some way to the westward, waiting for us.

The wind was from the north, on the best point for our return; and the Diana, heeling over in the smooth water, proceeded on her way towards Mobile, running so close to the shore that I could shy a biscuit on the sand. She seemed to breathe the wind through her sails, and flew with a crest of flame at her bow, and a bubbling wake of meteor-like streams flowing astern, as though liquid metal were flowing from a furnace.

The night was exceedingly lovely, but after the heat of the day the horizon was somewhat hazy. "No sign of the Oriental on our lee-bow?" "Nothing at all in sight, sir, ahead or astern." Sharks and large fish ran off from the shallows as we passed, and rushed out seawards in runs of brilliant light. The Perdida was left far astern.

On sped the Diana, but no Oriental came in view. I felt exceedingly tired, heated, and fagged; had been up early, ridden in a broiling sun, gone through batteries, examined forts, sailed backwards and forwards, so I was glad to turn in out of the night dew, and leaving injunctions to the captain to keep a bright look-out for the Federal boarding schooner, I went to sleep without the smallest notion that I had seen my last of Mr. Brown.

I had been two or three hours asleep when I was awoke by the negro cook, who was leaning over the berth, and, with teeth chattering, said, "Monsieur! nous sommes perdus! un bâtiment de guerre nous poursuit—il va tirer bientôt. Nous serons coulé! Oh, Mon Dieu! Oh, Mon Dieu!" I started up and popped my head through the hatchway. The skipper himself was at the helm, glancing from the compass to the quivering reef-points of the mainsail. "What's the matter, captain." "Waal, sir," said the captain, speaking very slowly, "there has been a something a running after us for nigh the last two hours, but he ain't a gaining on us. I don't think he'll kitch us up nohow this time; if the wind holds this pint a leetle, Diana will beat him."

The confidence of coasting captains in their own craft is an hallucination which no risk or danger will ever prevent them from cherishing most tenderly. There's not a skipper from Hartlepool to Whitstable who does not believe his Maryanne Smith or the Two Grandmothers is able, "on certain pints," to bump her fat bows, and drag her coal-scuttle-shaped stern faster through the sea than any clipper afloat. I was once told by the captain of a Margate Billy Boy he believed he could run to windward of any frigate in Her Majesty's service.

"But, good heavens, man, it may be the Oriental—no doubt it is Mr. Brown who is looking after us." "Ah! Waal, may be. Whoever it is, he creeped quite close up on me in the dark. It give me quite a sterk when I seen him. 'May be,' says I, 'he is a privateering—pirating—chap.' So I runs in shore as close as I could; gets my centre board in, and, says I, 'I'll see what you're made of, my boy.' And so we goes on. He ain't a gaining on us, I can tell you."

I looked through the glass, and could just make out, half or three-quarters of a mile astern, and to leeward, a vessel, looking quite black, which seemed to be standing on in pursuit of us. The shore was so close, we could almost have leaped into the surf, for when the centre board was up the Diana did not draw much more than four feet water. The skipper held grimly on. "You had better shake your wind, and see who it is; it may be Mr. Brown." "No, *sir*, Mr. Brown or no, I can't help carrying on now; there's a bank runs all along outside of us, and if I don't hold my course I'll be on it in one minute." I confess I was rather annoyed, but the captain was master of the situation. He said, that if it had been the Oriental she would have fired a blank gun to bring us to as soon as she saw us. To my inquiries why he did not awaken me when she was first made out, he innocently replied, "You was in such a beautiful sleep, I thought it would be regular cruelty to disturb you."

By creeping close inshore the Diana was enabled to keep to windward of the stranger, who was seen once or twice to bump or strike, for her sails shivered. "There, she's struck again." "She's off once more," and the chase is renewed. Every moment I expected to have my eyes blinded by the flash of her bow gun, but for some reason or another, possibly because she did not wish to check her way, the Oriental—privateer, or whatever it was—saved her powder.

A stern chase is a long chase. It is two o'clock in the morning—the skipper grinned with delight. "I'll lead him into a pretty mess if he follows me through the 'Swash,' whoever he is." We were but ten miles from Fort Morgan. Nearer and nearer to the shore creeps the Diana.

"Take a cast of the lead, John." "Nine feet." "Good. Again." "Seven feet." "Again." "Five feet." "Charlie, bring the lantern." We were now in the "Swash," with a boiling tideway.

Just at the moment that the negro uncovered the lantern, out it went, a fact which elicited the most remarkable amount of imprecations ear ever heard. The captain went dancing mad in intervals of deadly calmness, and gave his commands to the crew, and strange oaths to the cook alternately, as the mate sung out, "Five feet and a half." "About she goes!' Confound you, you black scoundrel, I'll teach you," &c., &c. "Six feet! Eight feet and a half!" "About she comes again." "Five feet! Four feet and a half." (Oh, Lord! Six inches under our keel!) And so we went, with a measurement between us and death of inches, not by any means agreeable, in which the captain showed remarkable coolness and skill in the management of his craft, combined with a most unseemly animosity towards his unfortunate cook.

It was very little short of a miracle that we got past the "Elbow," as the most narrow part of the channel is called, for it was just at the critical moment the binnacle light was extinguished, and went out with a splutter, and there we were left in darkness in a channel not one hundred yards wide and only six feet deep. The centre board also got jammed once or twice when it was most important to lie as close to the wind as possible; but at last the captain shouted out, "It's all right, we're in deep water," and calling the mate to the helm, proceeded to relieve his mind by chasing Charlie into a corner and belabouring him with a dead shark or dog-fish, about four feet long, which he picked up from the deck, as the handiest weapon he could find. For the whole morning, henceforth, the captain found great comfort in making constant charges on the hapless cook, who at last slyly threw the shark overboard at a favourable opportunity, and forced his master to resort to other varieties of Rhadamantine implements. But where was the Oriental all this time? No one could say; but Charlie, who seemed an authority as to her movements, averred she put her helm round as soon as we entered the "Swash," and disappeared in black night.

The Diana had thus distinguished herself by running the blockade of Pensacola, but a new triumph awaited her. As we approached Fort Morgan, a grey streak in the East just offered light enough to distinguish the outlines of the fort and of the Confederate flag which waved above it. A fair breeze carried us abreast of the signal station, one solitary light gleamed from the walls, but neither guard boat put off to board us, nor did sentry hail, nor was gun fired—still we stood on. "Captain, had you not better lie to? They'll be sending a round shot after us presently." "No, *sir*. They are all asleep in that fort," replied the indomitable skipper.

Down went his helm, and away ran the Diana into Mobile Bay, and was soon safe in the haze beyond shot or shell, running towards the opposite shore. This was glory enough for the Diana of Mobile. The wind blew straight from the North into our teeth, and at bright sunrise she was only a few miles inside the bay.

All the livelong day was spent in tacking from one low shore to another low shore, through water which looked like pea soup. We had to be sure the pleasure of seeing Mobile from every point of view, east and west, with all the varieties between northing and southing, and numerous changes in the position of steeples, sandhills, and villas, the sun roasting us all the time and boiling the pitch out of the seams.

The greatest excitement of the day was an encounter with a young alligator, making an involuntary voyage out to sea in the tide-way. The crew said he was drowning, having lost his way or being exhausted by struggling with the current. He was about ten feet long, and appeared to be so utterly done up that he would willingly have come aboard as he passed within two yards of us; but desponding as he was, it would have been positive cruelty to have added him to the number of our party.

The next event of the day was dinner, in which Charlie outrivalled himself by a tremendous fry of onions and sliced Bologna sausage, and a piece of pig, which had not decided whether it was to be pork or bacon.

Having been fourteen hours beating some twenty-seven miles, I was landed at last at a wharf in the suburbs of the town about five o'clock in the evening. On my way to the Battle House I met seven distinct companies marching through the streets to drill, and the air was filled with sounds of bugling and drumming. In the evening a number of gentlemen called upon me to inquire what I thought of Fort Pickens and Pensacola, and I had some difficulty in parrying their very home questions, but at last adopted a formula which appeared to please them—I assured my friends I thought it would be an exceedingly tough business whenever the bombardment took place.

One of the most important steps which I have yet heard of has excited little attention, namely, the refusal of the officer commanding Fort Mac Henry, at Baltimore, to obey the writ of *habeas corpus* issued by a judge of that city for the person of a soldier of his garrison. This military officer takes upon himself to aver there is a state of civil war in Baltimore, which he considers sufficient legal cause for the suspension of the writ.

CHAPTER XXIX.

Judge Campbell—Dr. Nott—Slavery—Departure for New Orleans—Down the river—Fear of Cruisers—Approach to New Orleans—Duelling—Streets of New Orleans—Unhealthiness of the city—Public opinion as to the war—Happy and contented negroes.

May 18th.—An exceedingly hot day, which gives bad promise of comfort for the Federal soldiers, who are coming, as the Washington Government asserts, to put down the rebellion in these quarters. The musquitoes are advancing in numbers and force. The day I first came I asked the waiter if they were numerous. "I wish they were a hundred times as many," said he. On inquiring if he had any possible reason for such an extraordinary aspiration, he said, "Because we would get rid of these darned black republicans out of Fort Pickens all the sooner." The man seemed to infer they would not bite the Confederate soldiers.

I dined at Dr Nott's, and met Judge Campbell, who has resigned his high post as one of the Judges of the Supreme Court of the United States, and explained his reasons for doing so in a letter, charging Mr. Seward with treachery, dissimulation, and falsehood. He seemed to me a great casuist rather than a profound lawyer, and to delight in subtle distinctions and technical abstractions; but I had the advantage of hearing from him at great length the whole history of the Dred Scot case, and a recapitulation of the arguments used on both sides, the force of which, in his opinion, was irresistibly in favor of the decision of the Court. Mr. Forsyth, Colonel Hardee, and others were of the company.

To me it was very painful to hear a sweet ringing silvery voice, issuing from a very pretty mouth, "I'm so delighted to hear that the Yankees in Fortress Monroe have got typhus fever. I hope it may kill them all." This was said by one of the most charming young persons possible, and uttered with unmistakeable sincerity, just as if she had said, "I hear all the snakes in Virginia are dying of poison." I fear the young lady did not think very highly of me for refusing to sympathise with her wishes in that particular form. But all the ladies in Mobile belong to "The Yankee Emancipation Society." They spend their days sewing cartridges, carding lint, preparing bandages, and I'm not quite sure that they don't fill shells and fuses as well. Their zeal and energy will go far to sustain the South in the forthcoming struggle, and nowhere is the influence of women greater than in America.

As to Dr. Nott, his studies have induced him to take a purely materialist view of the question of slavery, and, according to him, questions of morals and ethics, pertaining to its consideration, ought to be referred to the cubic capacity of the human cranium—the head that can take the largest charge of snipe-shot will eventually dominate in some form or other over the head of inferior capacity. Dr. Nott detests slavery, but he does not see what is to be done with the slaves, and how the four millions of negroes are to be prevented from becoming six, eight, or ten millions, if their growth is stimulated by high prices for Southern produce.

There is a good deal of force in the observation which I have heard more than once down here, that Great Britain could not have emancipated her negroes had they been dwelling within her border, say in Lancashire or Yorkshire. No inconvenience was experienced by the English people *per se* in consequence of the emancipation, which for the time destroyed industry and shook society to pieces in Jamaica. Whilst the States were colonies, Great Britain viewed the introduction of slaves to such remote dependencies with satisfaction, and when the United States had established their sovereignty they found the institution of slavery established within their own borders, and an important, if not essential, stratum in their social system. The work of emancipation would have then been comparatively easy, it now is a stupendous problem which no human being has offered to solve.

May 19th.—The heat out of doors was so great that I felt little tempted to stir out, but at two o'clock Mr. Magee drove me to a pretty place, called Spring Hill, where Mr. Stein, a German merchant of the city, has his country residence. The houses of Mobile merchants are scattered around the rising ground in that vicinity; they look like marble at a distance, but a nearer approach resolves them into painted wood. Stone is almost unknown on all this seaboard region. The worthy German was very hospitable, and I enjoyed a cool walk before dinner under the shade of his grapes, which formed pleasant walks in his garden. The Scuppernung grape, which grow in profusion—a native of North Carolina—has a remarkable appearance. The stalk, which is smooth, and covered with a close-grained grey bark, has not the character of a vine, but grows straight and stiff like the branch of a tree, and is crowded with delicious grapes. Cherokee plum and rose trees, and magnificent magnolias, clustered round his house, and beneath their shadow I listened to the worthy German comparing the Fatherland to his adopted country, and now and then letting out the secret love of his heart for the old place. He, like all the better classes in the South, has the utmost dread of universal suffrage, and would restrict the franchise largely to-morrow if he could.

May 20th.—I left Mobile in the steamer Florida for New Orleans this morning at eight o'clock. She was crowded with passengers in uniform. In my cabin was a notice of the rules and regulations of the steamer. No. 6 was as follows: "All slave servants must be cleared at the Custom House. Passengers having slaves will please report as soon as they come on board."

A few miles from Mobile the steamer, turning to the right, entered one of the narrow channels which perforate the whole of the coast, called "Grant's Pass." An ingenious person has rendered it navigable by an artificial cut; but as he was not an universal philanthropist, and possibly may have come from north of the Tweed, he further erected a series of barriers, which can only be cleared by means of a little pepper-castor iron lighthouse; and he charges toll on all passing vessels. A small island at the pass, just above water-level, about twenty yards broad and one hundred and fifty yards long, was being fortified. Some of our military friends landed here; and it required a good deal of patriotism to look cheerfully at the prospect of remaining cooped up among the musquitoes in a box, on this miserable sand-bank, which a shell would suffice to blow into atoms.

Having passed this channel, our steamer proceeded up a kind of internal sea, formed by the shore, on the right hand and on the left by a chain almost uninterrupted of reefs covered with sand, and exceedingly narrow, so that the surf of the ocean rollers at the other side could be seen through the foliage of the pine trees which line them. On our right the endless pines closed up the land view of the horizon; the beach was pierced by creeks without number, called bayous; and it was curious to watch the white sails of the little schooners gliding in and out among the trees, along the green meadows that seemed to stretch as an impassable barrier to their exit. Immense troops of pelicans flapped over the sea, dropping incessantly on the fish which abounded in the inner water; and long rows of the same birds stood digesting their plentiful meals on the white beach by the ocean foam.

There was some anxiety in the passengers' minds, as it was reported that the United States' cruisers had been seen inside, and that they had even burned the batteries on Ship Island. We saw nothing of a character more formidable than coasting craft and a return steamer from New Orleans till we approached the entrance to Pontchartrain, when a large schooner, which sailed like a witch and was crammed with men, attracted our attention. Through the glass I could make out two guns on her deck, and quite reason enough for any well-filled merchantman sailing under the Stars and Stripes to avoid her close companionship.

The approach to New Orleans is indicated by large hamlets and scattered towns along the seashore, hid in the piney woods, which offer a retreat to the merchants and their families from the fervid heat of the unwholesome city in summer time. As seen from the sea, these sanitary settlements have a picturesque effect, and an air of charming freshness and lightness. There are detached villas of every variety of architecture in which timber can be constructed, painted in the brightest hues—greens, and blues, and rose tints—each embowered in magnolias and rhododendrons. From every garden a very long and slender pier, terminated by a bathing-box, stretches into the shallow sea; and the general aspect of these houses, with the light domes and spires of churches rising above the lines of white railings set in the dark green of the pines, is light and novel. To each of these cities there is a jetty, at two of which we touched, and landed newspapers, received or discharged a few bales of goods, and were off again.

Of the little crowd assembled on each, the majority were blacks—the whites, almost without exception, in uniform, and armed. A nearer approach did not induce me to think that any agencies less powerful than epidemics and summer-heats could render Pascagoula, Passchristian, Mississippi City, and the rest of these settlements very eligible residences for people of an active turn of mind.

The live-long day my fellow-passengers never ceased talking politics, except when they were eating and drinking, because the horrible chewing and spitting are not at all incompatible with the maintenance of active discussion. The fiercest of them all was a thin, fiery-eyed little woman, who at dinner expressed a fervid desire for bits of "Old Abe"—his ear, his hair; but whether for the purpose of eating or as curious reliques, she did not enlighten the company.

After dinner there was some slight difficulty among the military gentlemen, though whether of a political or personal character I could not determine; but it was much aggravated by the appearance of a six-shooter on the scene, which, to my no small perturbation, was presented in a right line with my berth, out of the window of which I was looking at the combatants. I am happy to say the immediate delivery of the fire was averted by an amicable arrangement that the disputants should meet at the St. Charles Hotel at 12 o'clock on the second day after their arrival, in order to fix time, place, and conditions of a more orthodox and regular encounter.

At night the steamer entered a dismal canal, through a swamp which is infamous as the most musquito haunted place along the infested shore; the mouths of the Mississippi themselves being quite innocent, compared to the entrance of Lake Pontchartrain. When I woke up at daylight, I found the vessel lying alongside a wharf with a railway train alongside, which is to take us to the city of New Orleans, six miles distant.

A village of restaurants or "restaurats" as they are called here, and of bathing-boxes, has grown up around the terminus; all the names of the owners, the notices and sign-boards, being French. Outside the settlement the railroad passes through a swamp, like an Indian jungle, through which the overflowings of the Mississippi creep in black currents. The spires of New Orleans rise above the underwood and semi-tropical vegetation of this swamp. Nearer to the city lies a marshy plain, in which flocks of cattle, up to the belly in the soft earth, are floundering among the clumps of vegetation. The nearer approach to New Orleans by rail lies through a suburb of exceedingly broad lanes, lined on each side by rows of miserable mean one-storied houses, inhabited, if I am to judge from the specimens I saw, by a miserable and sickly population.

A great number of the men and women had evident traces of negro blood in their veins, and of the purer blooded whites many had the peculiar look of the fishy-fleshy population of the Levantine towns, and all were pale and lean. The railway terminus is marked by a dirty, barrack-like shed in the city. Selecting one of the numerous tumble-down hackney carriages which crowded the street outside the station, I directed the man to drive me to the house of Mr. Mure, the British consul, who had been kind enough to invite me as his guest for the period of my stay in New Orleans.

The streets are badly paved, as those of most of the American cities, if not all that I have ever been in, but in other respects they are more worthy of a great city than are those of New York. There is an air thoroughly French about the people—cafés, restaurants, billiard-rooms abound, with oyster and lager-bier saloons interspersed. The shops are all *magazins;* the people in the streets are speaking French, particularly the negroes, who are going out shopping with their masters and mistresses, exceedingly well dressed, noisy, and not unhappy looking. The extent of the drive gave an imposing idea of the size of New Orleans—the richness of some of the shops, the vehicles in the streets, and the multitude of well-dressed people on the pavements, an impression of its wealth and the comfort of the inhabitants. The Confederate flag was flying from the public buildings and from many private houses. Military companies paraded through the streets, and a large proportion of the men were in uniform.

In the day I drove through the city, delivered letters of introduction, paid visits, and examined the shops and the public places; but there is such a whirl of secession and politics surrounding one it is impossible to discern much of the outer world.

Whatever may be the number of the unionists or of the non-secessionists, a pressure too potent to be resisted has been directed by the popular party against the friends of the Federal government. The agent of Brown Brothers, of Liverpool and New York, has closed their office, and is going away in consequence of the intimidation of the mob, or as the phrase is here, the "excitement of the citizens," on hearing of the subscription made by the firm to the New York fund, after Sumter had been fired upon. Their agent in Mobile has been compelled to adopt the same course. Other houses follow their example, but as most business transactions are over for the season, the mercantile community hope the contest will be ended before the next season, by the recognition of Southern independence.

The streets are full of Turcos, Zouaves, Chasseurs; walls are covered with placards of volunteer companies; there are Pickwick rifles, La Fayette, Beauregard, MacMahon guards, Irish, German, Italian, and Spanish, and native volunteers, among whom the Meagher rifles, indignant with the gentleman from whom they took their name, because of his adhesion to the North, are going to rebaptise themselves and to seek glory under one more auspicious. In fact, New Orleans looks like a suburb of the camp at Châlons. Tailors are busy night and day making uniforms. I went into a shop with the consul for some shirts—the mistress and all her seamstresses were busy preparing flags as hard as the sewing machine could stitch them, and could attend to no business for the present. The Irish population, finding themselves unable to migrate Northwards, and being without work, have rushed to arms with enthusiasm to support Southern institutions, and Mr. John Mitchell and Mr. Meagher stand opposed to each other in hostile camps.

May 22nd.—The thermometer to-day marked 95° in the shade. It is not to be wondered at that New Orleans suffers from terrible epidemics. At the side of each street a filthy open sewer flows to and fro with the tide in the blazing sun, and Mr. Mure tells me the city lies so low that he has been obliged to go to his office in a boat along the streets.

I sat for some time listening to the opinions of the various merchants who came to talk over the news and politics in general. They were all persuaded that Great Britain would speedily recognise the South, but I cannot find that any of them had examined into the effects of such a recognition. One gentleman seemed to think to-day that recognition meant forcing the blockade; whereas it must, as I endeavoured to show him, merely lead to the recognition of the rights of the United States to establish a blockade of ports belonging to an independent and hostile nation. There are some who maintain that there will be no war after all; that the North will not fight, and that the friends of the Southern cause will recover their courage when this tyranny is over. No one imagines the South will ever go back to the Union voluntarily, or that the North has power to thrust it back at the point of the bayonet.

The South has commenced preparations for the contest by sowing grain instead of planting cotton, to compensate for the loss of supplies from the North. The payment of debts to Northern creditors is declared to be illegal, and "stay laws" have been adopted in most of the seceding states, by which the ordinary laws for the recovery of debts in the States themselves are for the time suspended, which may lead one into the belief that the legislators themselves belong to the debtor instead of the creditor class.

May 23rd.—As the mail communication has been suspended between North and South, and the Express Companies are ordered not to carry letters, I sent off my packet of despatches to-day by Mr. Ewell, of the house of Dennistoun & Co.; and resumed my excursions through New Orleans.

The young artist who is stopping at the St. Charles Hotel, came to me in great agitation to say his life was in danger, in consequence of his former connexion with an abolition paper of New York, and that he had been threatened with death by a man with whom he had had a quarrel in Washington. Mr. Mure, to calm his apprehensions, offered to take him to the authorities of the town, who would, no doubt, protect him, as he was merely engaged in making sketches for an English periodical, but the young man declared he was in danger of assassination. He entreated Mr. Mure to give him despatches which would serve to protect him, on his way Northward; and the Consul, moved by his mental distress, promised that if he had any letters of an official character for Washington, he would send them by him, in default of other opportunities.

I dined with Major Ranney, the president of one of the railways, with whom Mr. Ward was stopping. Among the company were Mr. Eustis, son-in-law of Mr. Slidell; Mr. Morse, the attorney-general of the State; Mr. Moise, a Jew, supposed to have considerable influence with the governor, and a vehement politician; Messrs. Hunt, and others. The table was excellent, and the wines were worthy of the reputation which our host enjoys, in a city where Sallusts and Luculli are said to abound. One of the slave servants who waited at table, an intelligent yellow "boy," was pointed out to me as a son of General Andrew Jackson.

We had a full account of the attack of the British troops on the city, and their repulse. Mr. Morse denied emphatically that there was any cotton-bag fortification in front of the lines, where our troops were defeated; he asserted that there were only a few bales, I think seventy-five, used in the construction of one battery, and that they and some sugar hogsheads constituted the sole defences of the American trench. Only one citizen applied to the state for compensation on account of the cotton used by Jackson's troops, and he owned the whole of the bales so appropriated.

None of the Southern gentlemen have the smallest apprehension of a servile insurrection. They use the universal formula "our negroes are the happiest, most contented, and most comfortable people on the face of the earth." I admit I have been struck by well-clad and good-humoured negroes in the streets, but they are in the minority; many look morose, ill-clad, and discontented. The patrols I know have been strengthened, and I heard a young lady the other night say, "I shall not be a bit afraid to go back to the plantation, though mamma says the negroes are after mischief."

CHAPTER XXX.

The first blow struck—The St. Charles hotel—Invasion of Virginia by the Federals—Death of Colonel Ellsworth—Evening at Mr. Slidell's—Public comments on the war—Richmond the capital of the Confederacy—Military preparations—General society—Jewish element—Visit to a battle-field of 1815.

May 24th.—A great budget of news to-day, which with the events of the week may be briefly enumerated. The fighting has actually commenced between the United States steamers off Fortress Monroe, and the Confederate battery erected at Sewall's point — both sides claim a certain success. The Confederates declare they riddled the steamer, and that they killed and wounded a number of the sailors. The captain of the vessel says he desisted from want of ammunition, but believes he killed a number of the rebels, and knows he had no loss himself. Beriah Magoffin, governor of the sovereign state of Kentucky, has warned off both Federal and Confederate soldiers from his territory. The Confederate congress has passed an act authorizing persons indebted to the United States, except Delaware, Maryland, Kentucky, Missouri, and the district of Columbia, to pay the amount of their debts to the Confederate treasury. The State Convention of North Carolina has passed an ordinance of secession. Arkansas has sent its delegates to the Southern congress. Several Southern vessels have been made prizes by the blockading squadron; but the event which causes the greatest excitement and indignation here, was the seizure, on Monday, by the United States' marshals, in every large city thoughout the Union, of the telegraphic despatches of the last twelve months.

In the course of the day, I went to the St. Charles Hotel, which is an enormous establishment, of the American type, with a Southern character about it. A number of gentlemen were seated in the hall, and front of the office, with their legs up against the wall, and on the backs of chairs, smoking, spitting, and reading the papers. Officers crowded the bar. The bustle and noise of the place would make it anything but an agreeable residence for one fond of quiet; but this hotel is famous for its difficulties. Not the least disgraceful among them was the assault committed by some of Walker's filibusters upon Captain Aldham, of the R. Navy.

The young artist, who has been living in great seclusion, was fastened up in his room; and when I informed him that Mr. Mure had despatches, which he might take, if he liked, that night, he was overjoyed to excess. He started off north in the evening, and I saw him no more.

At half-past four, I went down by train to the terminus on the lake where I had landed, which is the New Orleans Richmond, or rather, Greenwich, and dined with Mr. Eustis, Mr. Johnson an English merchant, Mr. Josephs a New Orleans lawyer, and Mr. Hunt. The dinner was worthy of the reputation of the French cook. The terrapin soup excellent, though not comparable, as Americans assert, to the best turtle. The creature from which it derives its name, is a small tortoise, the flesh is boiled somewhat in the manner of turtle, but the soup abounds in small bones, and the black paws with the white nail-like stumps projecting from them, found amongst the *disjecta membra*, are not agreeable to look upon. The bouillabaisse was unexceptionable, the soft crab worthy of every commendation, but the best dish was, unquestionably, the pompinoe, an odd fish, something like an unusually ugly John Dory, but possessing admirable qualities in all that makes fish good. The pleasures of the evening were enhanced by a most glorious sunset, which cast its last rays through a wilderness of laurel roses in full bloom, which thronged the garden. At dusk, the air was perfectly alive with fire-flies and strange beetles. Flies and coleopters buzzed in through the open windows, and flopped among the glasses. At half-past nine we returned home in cars drawn by horses along the rail.

May 25th.—Virginia has indeed been invaded by the Federals. Alexandria has been seized. It is impossible to describe the excitement and rage of the people; they take, however, some consolation in the fact that Colonel Ellsworth, in command of a regiment of New York Zouaves, was shot by J. T. Jackson, the landlord of an inn in the city, called the Marshal House. Ellsworth, on the arrival of his regiment in Alexandria, proceeded to take down the secession flag, which had been long seen from the President's windows. He went out upon the roof, cut it from the staff, and was proceeding with it down stairs, when a man rushed out of a room, levelling a double-barrelled gun, shot Colonel Ellsworth dead, and fired the other barrel at one of his men, who had struck at the piece when the murderer presented it at the Colonel. Almost instantaneously, the Zouave shot Jackson in the head, and as he was falling dead thrust his sabre bayonet through his body. Strange to say, the people of New Orleans consider Jackson was completely right in shooting the Federal colonel, and maintain that the Zouave, who shot Jackson, was guilty of murder. Their theory is that Ellsworth had come over with a horde of ruffianly abolitionists, or, as the Richmond *Examiner* has it, "the band of thieves, robbers and assassins, in the pay of Abraham Lincoln, commonly known as the United States' Army," to violate the territory of a sovereign state, in order to execute their bloody and brutal purposes, and that he was in the act of committing a robbery, by taking a flag which did not belong to him, when he met his righteous fate.

It is curious to observe how passion blinds man's reason in this quarrel. More curious still to see, by the light of this event, how differently the same occurrence is viewed by Northerners and Southerners respectively. Jackson is depicted in the Northern papers as a fiend and an assassin; even his face in death is declared to have worn a revolting expression of rage and hate. The Confederate flag, which was the cause of the fatal affray, is described by one writer as having been purified of its baseness by contact with Ellsworth's blood. The invasion of Virginia is hailed on all sides of the North with the utmost enthusiasm. "Ellsworth is a martyr hero, whose name is to be held sacred forever."

On the other hand, the Southern papers declare that the invasion of Virginia is "an act of the Washington tyrants, which indicates their bloody and brutal purpose to exterminate the Southern people. The Virginians will give the world another proof, like that of Moscow, that a free people, fighting on a free soil, are invincible when contending for all that is dear to man." Again—"A band of execrable cutthroats and jail-birds, known as the Zouaves of New York, under that chief of all scoundrels, Ellsworth, broke open the door of a citizen, to tear down the flag of the house—the courageous owner met the favorite hero of the Yankees in his own hall, alone, against thousands, and shot him through the heart—he died a death which emperors might envy, and his memory will live through endless generations." Desperate, indeed, must have been the passion and anger of the man who, in the fullest certainty that immediate death must be its penalty, committed such a deed. As it seems to me, Colonel Ellsworth, however injudicious he may have been, was actually in the performance of his duty when taking down the flag of an enemy.

In the evening I visited Mr. Slidell, whom I found at home, with his family, Mrs. Slidell and her sister Madame Beauregard, wife of the general, two very charming young ladies, daughters of the house, and a parlour full of fair companions, engaged, as hard as they could, in carding lint with their fair hands. Among the company was Mr. Slidell's son, who had just travelled from school at the North, under a feigned name, in order to escape violence at the hands of the Union mobs which are said to be insulting and outraging every Southern man. The conversation, as is the case in most creole domestic circles, was carried on in French. I rarely met a man whose features have a greater *finesse* and firmness of purpose than Mr. Slidell's; his keen grey eye is full of life, his thin, firmly-set lips indicate resolution and passion. Mr. Slidell, though born in a Northern state, is perhaps one of the most determined disunionists in the Southern confederacy; he is not a speaker of note, nor a ready stump orator, nor an able writer; but he is an excellent judge of mankind, adroit, persevering, and subtle, full of device, and fond of intrigue; one of those men who, unknown almost to the outer world, organises and sustains a faction, and exalts it into the position of a party—what is called here a "wire-puller." Mr. Slidell is to the South something greater than Mr. Thurlow Weed has been to his party in the North. He, like every one else, is convinced that recognition must come soon; but, under any circumstances, he is quite satisfied the government and independence of the Southern confederacy are as completely established as those of any power in the world. Mr. Slidell and the members of his family possess *naïveté*, good sense, and agreeable manners; and the regrets I heard expressed in Washington society at their absence had every justification.

I supped at the club, which I visited every day since I was made an honorary member, as all the journals are there, and a great number of planters and merchants, well acquainted with the state of affairs in the South. There were two Englishmen present, Mr. Lingam and another, the most determined secessionists and the most devoted advocates of slavery I have yet met in the course of my travels.

May 26th.—The heat to-day was so great that I felt a return of my old Indian experiences, and was unable to go, as I intended, to hear a very eminent preacher discourse on the war at one of the principal chapels.

All disposable regiments are on the march to Virginia. It was bad policy for Mr. Jefferson Davis to menace Washington before he could seriously carry out his threats, because the North was excited by the speech of his Secretary at War to take extraordinary measures for the defence of their capital; and General Scott was enabled by their enthusiasm not only to provide for its defence, but to effect a lodgment at Alexandria, as a base of operations against the enemy.

When the Congress at Montgomery adjourned, the other day, they resolved to meet on the 20th of July at Richmond, which thus becomes the capital of the Confederacy. The city is not much more than one hundred miles south of Washington, with which it was in communication by rail and river; and the selection must cause a collision between the two armies in front of the rival capitals. The seizure of the Norfolk navy yard by the Confederates rendered it necessary to reinforce Fortress Monroe; and for the present the Potomac and the Chesapeake are out of danger.

The military precautions taken by General Scott, and the movements attributed to him to hold Baltimore and to maintain his communications between Washington and the North, afford evidence of judgment and military skill. The Northern papers are clamouring for an immediate advance of their raw levies to Richmond, which General Scott resists.

In one respect the South has shown greater sagacity than the North. Mr. Jefferson Davis having seen service in the field, and having been Secretary of War, perceived the dangers and inefficiency of irregular levies, and therefore induced the Montgomery Congress to pass a bill which binds volunteers to serve during the war, unless sooner discharged, and reserves to the President of the Southern Confederacy the appointment of staff and field officers, the right of veto to battalion officers elected by each company, and the power of organising companies of volunteers into squadrons, battalions, and regiments. Writing to the *Times* at this date, I observed: "Although immense levies of men may be got together for purposes of local defence or aggressive operations, it will be very difficult to move these masses like regular armies. There is an utter want of field-trains, equipage, and commissariat, which cannot be made good in a day, a week, or a month. The absence of cavalry, and the utter deficiency of artillery, may prevent either side obtaining any decisive result in one engagement; but there can be no doubt large losses will be incurred whenever these masses of men are fairly opposed to each other in the open field."

May 27th.—I visited several of the local companies, their drill-grounds and parades; but few of the men were present, as nearly all are under orders to proceed to the Camp at Tangipao or to march to Richmond. Privates and officers are busy in the sweltering streets purchasing necessaries for their journey. As one looks at the resolute, quick, angry faces around him, and hears but the single theme, he must feel the South will never yield to the North, unless as a nation which is beaten beneath the feet of a victorious enemy.

In every state there is only one voice audible. Hereafter, indeed, state jealousies may work their own way; but if words mean anything, all the Southern people are determined to resist Mr. Lincoln's invasion as long as they have a man or a dollar. Still, there are certain hard facts which militate against the truth of their own assertions, "that they are united to a man, and prepared to fight to a man." Only 15,000 are under arms out of the 50,000 men in the state of Louisiana liable to military service.

"Charges of abolitionism" appear in the reports of police cases in the papers every morning; and persons found guilty not of expressing opinions against slavery, but of stating their belief that the Northerners will be successful, are sent to prison for six months. The accused are generally foreigners, or belong to the lower orders, who have got no interest in the support of slavery. The moral suasion of the lasso, of tarring and feathering, head-shaving, ducking, and horse-ponds, deportation on rails, and similar ethical processes, are highly in favor. As yet the North have not arrived at such an elevated view of the necessities of their position.

The New Orleans papers are facetious over their new mode of securing unanimity, and highly laud what they call "the course of instruction in the humane institution for the amelioration of the condition of northern barbarians and abolition fanatics, presided over by Professor Henry Mitchell," who, in other words, is the jailer of the workhouse reformatory.

I dined at the Lake with Mr. Mure, General

Lewis, Major Ranney, Mr. Duncan Kenner a Mississippi planter, Mr. Claiborne, &c., and visited the club in the evening. Every night since I have been in New Orleans there have been one or two fires; to-night there were three—one a tremendous conflagration. When I inquired to what they were attributable, a gentleman who sat near, bent over, and looking me straight in the face, said, in a low voice, "The slaves." The flues, perhaps, and the system of stoves, may also bear some of the blame. There is great enthusiasm among the townspeople in consequence of the Washington artillery, a crack corps, furnished by the first people in New Orleans, being ordered off for Virginia.

May 28th.—On dropping in at the Consulate to-day, I found the skippers of several English vessels who are anxious to clear out, lest they be detained by the Federal cruisers. The United States steam frigates Brooklyn and Niagara have been for some days past blockading Pass à l'outre. One citizen made a remarkable proposition to Mr. Mure. He came in to borrow an ensign of the Royal Yacht Squadron for the purpose, he said, of hoisting it on board his yacht, and running down to have a look at the Yankee ships. Mr. Mure had no flag to lend; whereupon he asked for a description by which he could get one made. On being applied to, I asked "whether the gentleman was a member of the Squadron?" "Oh, no," said he, "but my yacht was built in England, and I wrote over some time ago to say I would join the squadron." I ventured to tell him that it by no means followed he was a member, and that if he went out with the flag and could not show by his papers he had a right to carry it, the yacht would be seized. However, he was quite satisfied that he had an English yacht, and a right to hoist an English flag, and went off to an outfitter's to order a *facsimile* of the Squadron ensign, and subsequently cruised among the blockading vessels.

We hear Mr. Ewell was attacked by an Union mob in Tennessee, his luggage was broken open and plundered, and he narrowly escaped personal injury. *Per contra*, "charges of abolitionism" continue to multiply here, and are almost as numerous as the coroner's inquests, not to speak of the difficulties which sometimes attain the magnitude of murder.

I dined with a large party at the Lake, who had invited me as their guest, among whom were Mr. Slidell, Governor Hebert, Mr. Hunt, Mr. Norton, Mr. Fellows, and others. I observed in New York that every man had his own solution of the cause of the present difficulty, and contradicted plumply his neighbor the moment he attempted to propound his own theory. Here I found every one agreed as to the righteousness of the quarrel, but all differed as to the best mode of action for the South to pursue. Nor was there any approach to unanimity as the evening waxed older. Incidentally we had wild tales of Southern life, some good songs, curiously intermingled with political discussions, and what the Northerns call hifalutin talk.

When I was in the Consulate to-day, a tall and well-dressed, but not very prepossessing-looking man, entered to speak to Mr. Mure on business, and was introduced to me at his own request. His name was mentioned incidentally to-night, and I heard a passage in his life not of an agreeable character, to say the least of it. A good many years ago there was a ball at New Orleans, at which this gentleman was present; he paid particular attention to a lady who, however, preferred the society of one of the company, and in the course of the evening an altercation occurred respecting an engagement to dance, in which violent language was exchanged, and a push or blow given by the favoured partner to his rival, who left the room, and, as it is stated, proceeded to a cutler's shop, where he procured a powerful dagger-knife. Armed with this, he returned, and sent in a message to the gentleman with whom he had quarrelled. Suspecting nothing, the latter came into the antechamber, the assassin rushed upon him, stabbed him to the heart, and left him weltering in his blood. Another version of the story was, that he waited for his victim till he came into the cloak-room, and struck him as he was in the act of putting on his overcoat. After a long delay, the criminal was tried. The defence put forward on his behalf was that he had seized a knife in the heat of the moment when the quarrel took place, and had slain his adversary in a moment of passion; but evidence, as I understand, went strongly to prove that a considerable interval elapsed between the time of the dispute and the commission of the murder. The prisoner had the assistance of able and ingenious counsel; he was acquitted. His acquittal was mainly due to the judicious disposition of a large sum of money; each juror, when he retired to dinner previous to consulting over the verdict, was enabled to find the sum of 1000 dollars under his plate; nor was it clear that the judge and sheriff had not participated in the bounty; in fact, I heard a dispute as to the exact amount which it is supposed the murderer had to pay. He now occupies, under the Confederate Government, the post at New Orleans which he lately held as representative of the Government of the United States.

After dinner I went in company of some of my hosts to the Boston Club, which has, I need not say, no connection with the city of that name. More fires, the tocsin sounding, and so to bed.

May 29th.—Dined in the evening with M. Aristide Milten-berger, where I met His Excellency Mr. Moore, the Governor of Louisiana, his military secretary, and a small party.

It is a strange country, indeed; one of the evils which afflicts the Louisianians, they say, is the preponderance and influence of South Carolinian Jews, and Jews generally, such as Moise, Mordecai, Josephs, and Judah Benjamin, and others. The subtlety and keenness of the Caucasian intellect give men a high place among a people who admire ability and dexterity, and are at the same time reckless of means and averse to labour. The Governor is supposed to be somewhat under the influence of the Hebrews, but he is a man quite competent to think and to act for himself—a plain, sincere ruler of a slave state, and an upholder of the patriarchal institute. After dinner we accompanied Madame Milten-berger (who affords in her own person a very complete refutation of the dogma that American women furnish no examples of the charms which surround their English sisters in the transit from the prime of life toward middle age), in a drive along the shell road to the lake and canal; the most remarkable object being a long wall lined with a glorious growth of orange trees: clouds of musquitoes effectually interfered with an enjoyment of the drive.

May 30th.—Wrote in the heat of the day, enlivened by my neighbour, a wonderful mocking-bird, whose songs and imitations would make his fortune in any society capable of appreciating native-born genius. His restlessness, courage, activity, and talent ought not to be confined to Mr. Mure's cage, but he seems contented and happy. I dined with Madame and M. Milten-berger, and drove out with them to visit the scene of our defeat in 1815, which lies at the distance of some miles down the river.

A dilapidated farmhouse surrounded by trees and negro huts marks the spot where Pakenham was buried, but his body was subsequently exhumed and sent home to England. Close to the point of the canal which constitutes a portion of the American defences, a negro guide came forth to conduct us round the place, but he knew as little as most guides of the incidents of the fight. The most remarkable testimony to the severity of the fire to which the British were exposed, is afforded by the trees in the neighbourhood of the tomb. In one live oak there are no less than eight round shot embedded, others contain two or three, and many are lopped, rent, and scarred by the flight of cannon ball. The American lines extended nearly three miles, and were covered in the front by swamps, marshes, and water-cuts; their batteries and the vessels in the river enfiladed the British as they advanced to the attack.

Among the prominent defenders of the cotton-bales was a notorious pirate and murderer named Lafitte, who with his band was released from prison on condition that he enlisted in the defence, and did substantial service to his friends and deliverers.

Without knowing all the circumstances of the case, it would be rash now to condemn the officers who directed the assault; but so far as one could judge from the present condition of the ground, the position must have been very formidable, and should not have been assaulted till the enfilading fire was subdued, and a very heavy covering fire directed to silence the guns in front. The Americans are naturally very proud of their victory, which was gained at a most trifling loss to themselves, which they erroneously conceive to be a proof of their gallantry in resisting the assault. It is one of the events which have created a fixed idea in their minds that they are able to "whip the world."

On returning from my visit I went to the club, where I had a long conversation with Dr. Rushton, who is strongly convinced of the impossibility of carrying on government, or conducting municipal affairs, until universal suffrage is put down. He gave many instances of the terrorism, violence, and assassinations which prevail during election-times in New Orleans. M. Milten-berger, on the contrary, thinks matters are very well as they are, and declares all these stories are fanciful: Incendiarism rife again. All the club windows crowded with men looking at a tremendous fire, which burned down three or four stores and houses.

CHAPTER XXXI.

Carrying arms—New Orleans jail—Desperate characters—Executions—Female maniacs and prisoners—The river and levee—Climate of New Orleans—Population—General distress—Pressure of the blockade—Money—Philosophy of abstract rights—The doctrine of state rights—Theoretical defect in the constitution.

May 31st.—I went with Mr. Mure to visit the jail. We met the sheriff, according to appointment, at the police court. Something like a sheriff—a great, big, burly, six-foot man, with revolvers stuck in his belt, and strength and arms quite sufficient to enable him to execute his office in its highest degree. Speaking of the numerous crimes committed in New Orleans, he declared it was a perfect hell upon earth, and that nothing would ever put an end to murders, manslaughters, and deadly assaults till it was made penal to carry arms; but by law every American citizen may walk with an armoury round his waist if he likes. Bar-rooms, cocktails, mint juleps, gambling-houses, political discussions, and imperfect civilization do the rest.

The jail is a square white-washed building, with cracked walls and barred windows. In front of the open door were seated four men on chairs, with their legs cocked against the wall, smoking and reading newspapers. "Well, what do you want?" said one of them, without rising. "To visit the prison." "Have you got friends inside, or do you carry an order?" The necessary document from our friend the sheriff was produced. We entered through the doorway, into a small hall, at the end of which was an iron grating and door. A slightly-built young man, who was lolling in his shirt sleeves on a chair, rose and examined the order, and, taking down a bunch of keys from a hook, and introducing himself to us as one of the warders, opened the iron door, and preceded us through a small passage into a square court-yard, formed on one side by a high wall, and on the other three by windowed walls and cells, with doors opening on the court. It was filled with a crowd of men and boys; some walking up and down, others sitting, and groups on the pavement; some moodily apart, smoking or chewing; one or two cleaning their clothes or washing at a small tank. We walked into the midst of them, and the warder, smoking his cigar and looking coolly about him, pointed out the most desperate criminals.

This crowded and most noisome place was filled with felons of every description, as well as with poor wretches merely guilty of larceny. Hardened murderers, thieves, and assassins were here associated with boys in their teens who were undergoing imprisonment for some trifling robbery. It was not pleasant to rub elbows with miscreants who lounged past, almost smiling defiance, whilst the slim warder, in his straw hat, shirt sleeves, and drawers, told you how such a fellow had murdered his mother, how another had killed a policeman, or a third had destroyed no less than three persons in a few moments. Here were seventy murderers, pirates, burglars, violaters, and thieves circulating among men who had been proved guilty of no offence, but were merely waiting for their trial.

A verandah ran along one side of the wall, above a row of small cells, containing truckle-beds for the inmates. "That's a desperate chap, I can tell you," said the warder, pointing to a man who, naked to his shirt, was sitting on the floor, with heavy irons on his legs, which they chafed notwithstanding the bloody rags around them, engaged in playing cards with a fellow-prisoner, and smoking with an air of supreme contentment. The prisoner turned at the words, and gave a kind of grunt and chuckle, and then played his next card. "That," said the warder, in the proud tone of a menagerie keeper exhibiting his fiercest wild beast, "is a real desperate character; his name is Gordon: I guess he comes from your country; he made a most miraculous attempt to escape, and all but succeeded; and you would never believe me if I told you that he hooked on to that little spout, climbed up the angle of that wall there, and managed to get across to the ledge of that window over the outside wall before he was discovered." And indeed it did require the corroborative twinkle in the fellow's eye, as he heard of his own exploit, to make me believe that the feat thus indicated could be performed by mortal man.

"There's where we hang them," continued he, pointing to a small black door, let into the wall, about 18 feet from the ground, with some iron hooks above it. "They walk out on the door, which is shot on a bolt, and when the rope is round their necks from the hook, the door's let flop, and they swing over the court-yard." The prisoners are shut up in their cells during the execution, but they can see what is passing, at least those who get good places at the windows. "Some of them," added the warder, "do die very brave indeed. Some of them abuse as you never heard. But most of them don't seem to like it."

Passing from the yard, we proceeded upstairs to the first floor, where were the debtors' rooms. These were tolerably comfortable, in comparison to the wretched cells we had seen; but the poorer debtors were crowded together, three or four in a room. As far as I could ascertain, there is no insolvency law, but the debtor is free, after ninety days' imprisonment, if his board and lodging be paid for. "And what if they are not?" "Oh, well, in that case we keep them till all is paid, adding of course for every day they are kept."

In one of these rooms, sitting on his bed, looking wicked and gloomy, and with a glare like that of a wild beast in his eyes, was a Doctor Withers, who a few days ago murdered his son-in-law and his wife, in a house close to Mr. Mure's. He was able to pay for this privilege, and "as he is a respectable man," said the warder, "perhaps he may escape the worst."

Turning from this department into another gallery, the warder went to an iron door, above which was painted a death's head and cross-bones, beneath were the words "condemned cell."

He opened the door, which led to a short, narrow covered gallery, one side of which looked into a court-yard, admitting light into two small chambers, in which were pallets of straw covered with clean counterpanes.

Six men were walking up and down in the passage. In the first room there was a table, on which were placed missals, neatly bound, and very clean religious books, a crucifix, and *Agnus Dei*. The whitewashed wall of this chamber was covered with most curious drawings in charcoal or black chalk, divided into compartments, and representing scenes in the life of the unhappy artist, a Frenchman, executed some years ago for murdering his mistress, depicting his temptations—his gradual fall from innocence—his society with abandoned men and women—intermingled with Scriptural subjects, Christ walking on the waters, and holding out his hand to the culprit—the murderer's corpse in the grave—angels visiting and lamenting over it;—finally, the resurrection, in which he is seen ascending to heaven!

My attention was attracted from this extraordinary room to an open gallery at the other side of the courtyard, in which were a number of women with dishevelled hair and torn clothes, some walking up and down restlessly, others screaming loudly, while some with indecent gestures were yelling to the wretched men opposite to them, as they were engaged in their miserable promenade.

Shame and horror to a Christian land! These women were maniacs! They are kept here until there is room for them at the State Lunatic Asylum. Night and day their terrible cries and ravings echo through the dreary, waking hours and the fitful slumbers of the wretched men so soon to die.

Two of those who walked in that gallery are to die to-morrow.

What a mockery—the crucifix!—the *Agnus Dei!*—the holy books! I turned with sickness and loathing from the dreadful place. "But," said the keeper, apologetically, "there's not one of them believes he'll be hanged."

* * * * * * *

We next visited the women's gallery, where female criminals of all classes are huddled together indiscriminately. On opening the door, the stench from the open verandah, in which the prisoners were sitting, was so vile that I could not proceed further; but I saw enough to convince me that the poor, erring woman who was put in there for some trifling offence, and placed in contact with the beings who were uttering such language as we heard, might indeed leave hope behind her.

The prisoners have no beds to sleep upon, not even a blanket, and are thrust in to lie as they please, five in each small cell. It may be imagined what the tropical heat produces under such conditions as these; but as the surgeon was out, I could obtain no information respecting the rates of sickness or mortality.

I next proceeded to a yard somewhat smaller than that appropriated to serious offenders, in which were confined prisoners condemned for short sentences, for such offences as drunkenness, assault, and the like. Among the prisoners were some English sailors, confined for assaults on their officers, or breach of articles; all of whom had complaints to make to the Consul, as to arbitrary arrests and unfounded charges. Mr. Mure told me that when the port is full he is constantly engaged inquiring into such cases; and I am sorry to learn that the men of our commercial marine occasion a good deal of trouble to the authorities.

I left the prison in no very charitable mood towards the people who sanctioned such a disgraceful institution, and proceeded to complete my tour of the city.

The "Levee," which is an enormous embankment to prevent the inundation of the river, is now nearly deserted except by the river steamers, and those which have been unable to run the blockade. As New Orleans is on an average three feet below the level of the river at high water, this work requires constant supervision; it is not less than fifteen feet broad, and rises five or six feet above the level of the adjacent street, and it is continued in an almost unbroken line for several hundreds of miles up the course of the Mississippi. When the bank gives way, or a "crevasse," as it is technically called, occurs, the damage done to the plantations has sometimes to be calculated by millions of dollars. When the river is very low there is a new form of danger, in what is called the "caving in" of the bank, which, left without the support of the water pressure, slides into the bed of the giant river.

New Orleans is called the "crescent city" in consequence of its being built on a curve of the river, which is here about the breadth of the Thames at Gravesend, and of great depth. Enormous cotton presses are erected near the banks, where the bales are compressed by machinery before stowage on shipboard, at a heavy cost to the planter.

The custom-house, the city hall, and the United States mint, are fine buildings, of rather pretentious architecture. The former is the largest building in the States, next the capitol. I was informed that on the levee, now almost deserted, there is during the cotton and sugar season a scene of activity, life, and noise, the like of which is not in the world. Even Canton does not show so many boats on the river, not to speak of steamers, tugs, flat-boats, and the like; and it may be easily imagined that such is the case, when we know that the value of the cotton sent in the year from this port alone exceeds twenty millions sterling, and that the other exports are of the value of at least fifteen millions sterling, whilst the imports amount to nearly four millions.

As the city of New Orleans is nearly 1700 miles south of New York, it is not surprising that it rejoices in a semi-tropical climate. The squares are surrounded with lemon-trees, orange-groves, myrtle, and magnificent magnolias. Palmettoes and peach-trees are found in all the gardens, and in the neighbourhood are enormous cypresses, hung round with the everlasting Spanish moss.

The streets of the extended city are different in character from the narrow chaussés of the old town, and the general rectangular arrangement common in the United States, Russia, and British Indian cantonments is followed as much as possible. The markets are excellent, each municipality, or grand division, being provided with its own. They swarm with specimens of the composite races which inhabit the city, from the thorough-bred, woolly-headed negro, who is suspiciously like a native-born African, to the Creole who boasts that every drop of blood in his veins is purely French.

I was struck by the absence of any whites of the labouring classes; and when I inquired what had become of the men who work on the levee and at the cotton presses in competition with the negroes, I was told that they had been enlisted for the war.

I forgot to mention that among the criminals in the prison there was one Mr. Bibb, a respectable citizen, who had a little affair of his own on Sunday morning.

Mr. Bibb was coming from market, and had secured an early copy of a morning paper. Three citizens, anxious for news, or, as Bibb avows, for his watch and purse, came up and insisted that he should read the paper for them. Bibb declined, whereupon the three citizens, in the full exercise of their rights as a majority, proceeded to coerce him; but Bibb had a casual revolver in his pocket, and in a moment he shot one of his literary assailants dead, and wounded the two others severely, if not mortally. The paper which narrates the circumstances, in stating that the successful combatant had been committed to prison, adds, "great sympathy is felt for Mr. Bibb." If the Southern minority is equally successful in its resistance to *force majeure* as this eminent citizen, the fate of the Confederacy cannot long be doubtful.

June 1st.—The respectable people of the city are menaced with two internal evils in consequence of the destitution caused by the stoppage of trade with the North and with Europe. The municipal authorities, for want of funds, threaten to close the city schools, and to disband the police; at the same time, employers refuse to pay their workmen on the ground of inability. The British Consulate was thronged to-day by Irish, English, and Scotch, entreating to be sent North or to Europe. The stories told by some of these poor fellows were most pitiable, and were vouched for by facts and papers; but Mr. Mure has no funds at his disposal to enable him to comply with their prayers. Nothing remains for them but to enlist. For the third or fourth time I heard cases of British subjects being forcibly carried off to fill the ranks of so-called volunteer companies and regiments. In some instances they have been knocked down, bound, and confined in barracks, till in despair they consented to serve. Those who have friends aware of their condition were relieved by the interference of the Consul; but there are many, no doubt, thus coerced and placed in involuntary servitude without his knowledge. Mr. Mure has acted with energy, judgment, and success on these occasions; but I much wish he could have, from national sources, assisted the many distressed English subjects who thronged his office.

The great commercial community of New Orleans, which now feels the pressure of the blockade, depends on the interference of the European Powers next October. They have among them men who refuse to pay their debts to Northern houses, but they deny that they intend to repudiate, and promise to pay all who are not black Republicans when the war is over. Repudiation is a word out of favour, as they feel the character of the Southern States and of Mr. Jefferson Davis himself has been much injured in Europe by the breach of honesty and honour of which they have been guilty; but I am assured on all sides that every State will eventually redeem all its obligations. Meantime, money here is fast vanishing. Bills on New York are worth nothing, and bills on England are at 18 per cent. discount from the par value of gold; but the people of this city will endure all this and much more to escape from the hated rule of the Yankees.

Through the present gloom come the rays of

a glorious future, which shall see a grand slave confederacy enclosing the Gulf in its arms, and swelling to the shores of the Potomac and Chesapeake, with the entire control of the Mississippi and a monopoly of the great staples on which so much of the manufactures and commerce of England and France depend. They believe themselves, in fact, to be masters of the destiny of the world. Cotton is king—not alone king, but czar; and coupled with the gratification and profit to be derived from this mighty agency, they look forward with intense satisfaction to the complete humiliation of their hated enemies in the New England States, to the destruction of their usurious rival New York, and to the impoverishment and ruin of the states which have excited their enmity by personal liberty bills, and have outraged and insulted them by harbouring abolitionists and an anti-slavery press.

The abolitionists have said, "We will never rest till every slave is free in the United States." Men of larger views than those have declared, "They will never rest from agitation until a man may as freely express his opinions, be they what they may, on slavery, or anything else, in the streets of Charleston or of New Orleans as in those of Boston or New York." "Our rights are guaranteed by the Constitution," exclaim the South. "The Constitution," retorts Wendell Phillips, "is a league with the devil—a covenant with hell."

The doctrine of State Rights has been consistently advocated not only by Southern statesmen, but by the great party who have ever maintained there was danger to liberty in the establishment of a strong central Government; but the contending interests and opinions on both sides had hitherto been kept from open collision by artful compromises and by ingenious contrivances, which ceased with the election of Mr. Lincoln.

There was in the very corner-stone of the republican edifice a small fissure, which has been widening as the grand structure increased in height and weight. The early statesmen and authors of the Republic knew of its existence, but left to posterity the duty of dealing with it and guarding against its consequences. Washington himself was perfectly aware of the danger; and he looked forward to a duration of some sixty or seventy years only for the great fabric he contributed to erect. He was satisfied a crisis must come, when the States whom in his farewell address he warned against rivalry and faction would be unable to overcome the animosities excited by different interests, and the passions arising out of adverse institutions; and now that the separation has come, there is not, in the Constitution, or out of it, power to cement the broken fragments together.

It is remarkable that in New Orleans, as in New York, the opinion of the most wealthy and intelligent men in the community, so far as I can judge, regards universal suffrage as organised confiscation, legalised violence and corruption, a mortal disease in the body politic. The other night, as I sat in the club-house, I heard a discussion in reference to the operations of the Thugs in this city, a band of native-born Americans, who at election-times were wont deliberately to shoot down Irish and German voters occupying positions as leaders of their mobs. These Thugs were only suppressed by an armed vigilance committee, of which a physician who sat at table was one of the members.

Having made some purchases, and paid all my visits, I returned to prepare for my voyage up the Mississippi and visits to several planters on its banks—my first being to Governor Roman.

CHAPTER XXXII.

Up the Mississippi — Free negroes and English policy — Monotony of the river scenery — Visit to M. Roman — Slave quarters—A slave dance—Slave children—Negro hospital — General opinion — Confidence in Jefferson Davis.

June 2nd.—My good friend the Consul was up early to see me off; and we drove together to the steamer J. L. Cotten. The people were going to mass as we passed through the streets; and it was pitiable to see the children dressed out as Zouaves, with tin swords and all sorts of pseudo-military tomfoolery; streets crowded with military companies; bands playing on all sides.

Before we left the door a poor black sailor came up to entreat Mr. Mure's interference. He had been sent by Mr. Magee, the Consul at Mobile, by land to New Orleans, in the hope that Mr. Mure would be able to procure him a free passage to some British port. He had served in the Royal Navy, and had received a wound in the Russian war. The moment he arrived in New Orleans he had been seized by the police. On his stating that he was a free-born British subject, the authorities ordered him to be taken to Mr. Mure; he could not be allowed to go at liberty on account of his colour; the laws of the State forbad such dangerous experiments on the feelings of the slave population; and if the Consul did not provide for him, he would be arrested and kept in prison, if no worse fate befell him. He was suffering from the effect of his wound, and was evidently in ill health. Mr. Mure gave him a letter to the Sailors' Hospital, and some relief out of his own pocket. The police came as far as the door with him, and remained outside to arrest him if the Consul did not afford him protection and provide for him, so that he should not be seen at large in the streets of the city. The other day a New Orleans privateer captured three northern brigs, on board which were ten free negroes. The captain handed them over to the Recorder, who applied to the Confederate States' Marshal to take charge of them. The Marshal refused to receive them, whereupon the Recorder, as a magistrate and a good citizen, decided on keeping them in jail, as it would be a bad and dangerous policy to let them loose upon the community.

I cannot help thinking that the position taken by England in reference to the question of her coloured subjects is humiliating and degrading. People who live in London may esteem this question a light matter; but it has not only been inconsistent with the national honour; it has so degraded us in the opinion of Americans themselves, that they are encouraged to indulge in an insolent tone and in violent acts towards us, which will some day leave Great Britain no alternative but an appeal to arms. Free coloured persons are liable to seizure by the police, and to imprisonment, and may be sold into servitude under certain circumstances.

On arriving at the steamer I found a considerable party of citizens assembled to see off their friends. Governor Roman's son apologised to me for his inability to accompany me up the river, as he was going to the drill of his company of volunteers. Several other gentlemen were in uniform; and when we had passed the houses of the city, I observed companies and troops of horse exercising on both sides of the banks. On board were Mr. Burnside, a very extensive proprietor, and Mr. Forstal, agent to Messrs. Baring, who claims descent from an Irish family near Rochestown, though he speaks our vernacular with difficulty, and is much more French than British. He is considered one of the ablest financiers and economists in the United States, and is certainly very ingenious, and well crammed with facts and figures.

The aspect of New Orleans from the river is marred by the very poor houses lining the quays on the levee. Wide streets open on long vistas bordered by the most paltry little domiciles; and the great conceptions of those who planned them, notwithstanding the prosperity of the city, have not been realised.

As we were now floating nine feet higher than the level of the streets, we could look down upon a sea of flat roofs and low wooden houses, painted white, pierced by the domes and spires of churches and public buildings. Grass was growing in many of these streets. At the other side of the river there is a smaller city of shingle-roofed houses, with a background of low timber.

The steamer stopped continually at various points along the levee, discharging commissariat stores, parcels, and passengers; and after a time glided up into the open country, which spread beneath us for several miles at each side of the banks, with a continuous background of forest. All this part of the river is called the Coast, and the country adjacent is remarkable for its fertility. The sugar plantations are bounded by lines drawn at right angles to the banks of the river, and extending through the forest. The villas of the proprietors are thickly planted in the midst of the green fields, with the usual porticoes, pillars, verandahs, and green blinds; and in the vicinity of each are rows of whitewashed huts, which are the slave quarters. These fields, level as a billiard-table, are of the brightest green with crops of maize and sugar.

But few persons were visible; not a boat was to be seen; and in the course of sixty-two miles we met only two steamers. No shelving banks, no pebbly shoals, no rocky margins mark the course or diversify the outline of the Mississippi. The dead, uniform line of the levee compresses it at each side, and the turbid waters flow without let in a current of uniform breadth between the monotonous banks. The gables and summit of one house resemble those of another; and but for the enormous scale of river and banks, and the black faces of the few negroes visible, a passenger might think he was on board a Dutch "treckshuyt." In fact, the Mississippi is a huge trench-like canal draining a continent.

At half-past three P.M. the steamer ran alongside the levee at the right bank, and discharged me at "Cahabanooze," in the Indian tongue, or "The ducks' sleeping-place," together with an English merchant of New Orleans, M. La Ville Beaufevre, son-in-law of Governor Roman, and his wife. The Governor was waiting to receive us in the levee, and led the way through a gate in the paling which separated his ground from the roadside, towards the house, a substantial, square, two-storied mansion, with a verandah all round it, embosomed amid venerable trees, and surrounded by magnolias. By way of explaining the proximity of his house to the river, M. Roman told me that a considerable portion of the garden in front had a short time ago been carried off by the Mississippi; nor is he at all sure the house itself will not share the same fate; I hope sincerely it may not. My quarters were in a detached house, complete in itself, containing four bedrooms, library, and sitting-room, close to the mansion, and surrounded, like it, by fine trees.

After we had sat for some time in the shade of the finest group, M. Roman, or, as he is called, the Governor—once a captain always a captain—asked me whether I would like to visit the slave quarters. I assented, and the Governor led the way to a high paling at the back of the house, inside which the scraping of the fiddles was audible. As we passed the back of the mansion some young women flitted past in snow-white dresses, crinolines, pink sashes, and gaudily coloured handkerchiefs on their heads, who were, the Governor told me, the domestic servants going off to a dance at the sugar-house; he lets his slaves dance every Sunday. The American planters who are not Catholics, although they do not make the slaves work on Sunday except there is something to do, rarely grant them the indulgence of a dance, but a few permit them some hours of relaxation on each Saturday afternoon.

We entered, by a wicket gate, a square enclosure, lined with negro huts, built of wood, something like those which came from Malta to the Crimea in the early part of the campaign. They are not furnished with windows—a wooden slide or grating admits all the air a negro desires. There is a partition dividing the hut into two departments, one of which is used as the sleeping-room, and contains a truckle bedstead and a mattress stuffed with cotton wool, or the hair-like fibres of dried Spanish moss. The wardrobes of the inmates hang from nails or pegs driven into the wall. The other room is furnished with a dresser, on which are arranged a few articles of crockery and kitchen utensils. Sometimes there is a table in addition to the plain wooden chairs, more or less dilapidated, constituting the furniture—a hearth, in connection with a brick chimney outside the cottage, in which, hot as the day may be, some embers are sure to be found burning. The ground round the huts was covered with litter and dust, heaps of old shoes, fragments of clothing and feathers, amidst which pigs and poultry were recreating. Curs of low degree scampered in and out of the shade, or around two huge dogs, *chiens de garde*, which are let loose at night to guard the precincts; belly deep, in a pool of stagnant water, thirty or forty mules were swinking in the sun and enjoying their day of rest.

The huts of the negroes engaged in the house are separated from those of the slaves devoted to field-labour out of doors by a wooden paling. I looked into several of the houses, but somehow or other I felt a repugnance, I dare say unjustifiable, to examine the penetralia, although invited—indeed, urged to do so by the Governor. It was not that I expected to come upon anything dreadful, but I could not divest myself of some regard for the feelings of the poor creatures, slaves though they were, who stood by, shy, curtseying, and silent, as I broke in upon their family circle, felt their beds, and turned over their clothing. What right had I to do so?

Swarms of flies, tin cooking utensils attracting them by remnants of molasses, crockery, broken and old, on the dressers, more or less old clothes on the wall, these varied over and over again, were found in all the huts; not a sign of ornament or decoration was visible; not the most tawdry print, image of Virgin or Saviour; not a prayerbook or printed volume. The slaves are not encouraged, or indeed permitted to read, and some communities of slave-owners punish heavily those attempting to instruct them.

All the slaves seemed respectful to their master; dressed in their best, they curtseyed, and came up to shake hands with him and with me. Among them were some very old men and women, the canker-worms of the estate, who were dozing away into eternity, mindful only of hominy, and pig, and molasses. Two negro fiddlers were working their bows with energy in front of one of the huts, and a crowd of little children were listening to the music, together with a few grown-up persons of colour, some of them from the adjoining plantations. The children are generally dressed in a little sack of coarse calico, which answers all reasonable purposes, even if it be not very clean.

It might be an interesting subject of inquiry to the natural philosophers who follow crinology to determine why it is that the hair of the infant negro, or child, up to six or seven years of age, is generally a fine red russet, or even gamboge colour, and gradually darkens into dull ebon. These little bodies were mostly large-stomached, well fed, and not less happy than freeborn children, although much more valuable—for if once they get over juvenile dangers, and advance toward nine or ten years of age, they rise in value to £100 or more, even in times when the market is low and money is scarce.

The women were not very well-favoured; one yellow girl, with fair hair and light eyes, whose child was quite white, excepted; the men were disguised in such strangely-cut clothes, their hats, and shoes, and coats so wonderfully made, that one could not tell what their figures were like. On all faces there was a gravity which must be the index to serene contentment and perfect comfort, for those who ought to know best declare they are the happiest race in the world.

It struck me more and more, however, as I examined the expression of the faces of the slaves, that deep dejection is the prevailing, if not universal, characteristic of the race. Here there were abundant evidences that they were all well treated; they had good clothing of its kind, food, and a master who wittingly could do them no injustice, as he is, I am sure, incapable of it. Still, they all looked sad, and even the old woman who boasted that she had held her old owner in her arms when he was an infant, did not smile cheerfully, as the nurse at home would have done at the sight of her ancient charge.

The negroes rear domestic birds of all kinds, and sell eggs and poultry to their masters. The money is spent in purchasing tobacco, molasses, clothes, and flour; whisky, their great delight, they must not have. Some seventy or eighty hands were quartered in this part of the estate.

Before leaving the enclosure I was taken to the hospital, which was in charge of an old negress. The naked rooms contained several flock beds on rough stands, and five patients, three of whom were women. They sat listlessly on the beds, looking out into space; no books to amuse them, no conversation—nothing but their own dull thoughts, if they had any. They were suffering from pneumonia and swelling of the glands of the neck: one man had fever. Their medical attendant visits them regularly, and each plantation has a practitioner, who is engaged by the term for his services. If the growth of sugar-cane, cotton, and corn be the great end of man's mission on earth, and if all masters were like Governor Roman, slavery might be defended as a natural and innocuous institution. Sugar and cotton are, assuredly, two great agencies in this latter world. The older one got on well enough without them.

The scraping of the fiddles attracted us to the sugar-house, where the juice of the cane is expressed, boiled, granulated, and prepared for the refinery, a large brick building, with a factory-looking chimney. In a space of the floor unoccupied by machinery some fifteen women and as many men were assembled, and four couples were dancing a kind of Irish jig to the music of the negro musicians—a double shuffle in a thumping ecstasy, with loose elbows, pendulous paws, angulated knees, heads thrown back, and backs arched inwards—a glazed eye, intense solemnity of mien.

At this time of year there is no work done in the sugar-house, but when the crushing and boiling are going on the labour is intensely trying, and the hands work in gangs night and day; and, if the heat of the fires be superadded to the temperature in September, it may be conceded that nothing but "involuntary servitude" could go through the toil and suffering required to produce sugar.

In the afternoon the Governor's son came in from the company which he commands: his men are of the best families in the country—planters and the like. We sauntered about the gardens, diminished, as I have said, by a freak of the river. The French creoles love gardens; the Anglo-Saxons hereabout do not much affect them, and cultivate their crops up to the very doorway.

It was curious to observe so far away from France so many traces of the life of the old seigneur—the early meals, in which supper took the place of dinner—frugal simplicity—and yet a refinement of manner, kindliness, and courtesy not to be exceeded.

In the evening several officers of M. Alfred Roman's company and neighbouring planters dropped in, and we sat out in the twilight, under the trees in the verandah, illuminated by the flashing fireflies, and talking politics. I was struck by the profound silence which reigned all around us, except a low rushing sound, like that made by the wind blowing over cornfields, which came from the mighty river before us. Nothing else was audible but the sound of our own voices and the distant bark of a dog. After the steamer which bore us had passed on, I do not believe a single boat floated up or down the stream, and but one solitary planter, in his gig or buggy, traversed the road, which lay between the garden palings and the bank of the great river.

Our friends were all creoles—that is, natives of Louisiana—of French or Spanish descent. They are kinder and better masters, according to universal repute, than native Americans or Scotch; but the New England Yankee is reputed to be the severest of all slave-owners. All these gentlemen to a man are resolute that England must get their cotton or perish. She will take it, therefore, by force; but as the South is determined never to let a Yankee vessel carry any of its produce, a question has been raised by Monsieur Baroche, who is at present looking around him in New Orleans, which causes some difficulty to the astute and statistical Mr. Forstall. The French economist has calculated that if the Yankee vessels be excluded from the carrying trade, the commercial marine of France and England together will be quite inadequate to carry Southern produce to Europe.

But Southern faith is indomitable. With their faithful negroes to raise their corn, sugar, and cotton, whilst their young men are at the wars; with France and England to pour gold into their lap with which to purchase all they need in the contest, they believe they can beat all the powers of the Northern world in arms. Illimitable fields, tilled by multitudinous negroes, open on their sight, and they behold the empires of Europe, with their manufactures, their industry, and their wealth, prostrate at the base of their throne, crying out, "Cotton! More cotton! That is all we ask!"

Mr. Forstall maintains the South can raise an enormous revenue by a small direct taxation; whilst the North, deprived of Southern resources, will refuse to pay taxes at all, and will accumulate enormous debts, inevitably leading to its financial ruin. He, like every Southern man I have as yet met, expresses unbounded confidence in Mr. Jefferson Davis. I am asked invariably, as the second question from a stranger, "Have you seen our President, sir? don't you think him a very able man?" This unanimity in the estimate of his character, and universal confidence in the head of the State, will prove of incalculable value in a civil war.

CHAPTER XXXIII.

Ride through the maize-fields—Sugar plantation; negroes at work—Use of the lash—Feeling towards France—Silence of the country—Negroes and dogs—Theory of slavery—Physical formation of the negro—The defence of slavery—The masses for negro souls—Convent of the Sacré Cœur—Ferry house—A large landowner.

June 3rd.—At five o'clock this morning, having been awakened an hour earlier by a wonderful chorus of riotous mocking-birds, my old negro attendant brought in my bath of Mississippi water, which, Nile like, casts down a strong deposit, and becomes as clear, if not so sweet, after standing. "Le seigneur vous attend;" and already I saw, outside my window, the Governor mounted on a stout cob, and a nice chestnut horse waiting, led by a slave. Early as it was, the sun felt excessively hot, and I envied the Governor his slouched hat as we rode through the fields, crisp with dew. In a few minutes our horses were traversing narrow alleys between the tall fields of maize, which rose far above our heads. This corn, as it is called, is the principal food of the negroes; and every planter lays down a sufficient quantity to afford him, on an average, a supply all the year round. Outside this spread vast fields, hedgeless, wall-less, and unfenced, where the green cane was just learning to wave its long shoots in the wind—a lake of bright green sugar-sprouts, along the margin of which, in the distance, rose an unbroken boundary of forest, two miles in depth, up to the swampy morass, all to be cleared and turned into arable land in process of time. From the river front to this forest, the fields of rich loam, unfathomable, and yielding from one to one and a half hogsheads of sugar per acre under cultivation, extend for a mile and a half in depth. In the midst of this expanse white dots were visible like Sowars seen on the early march, in Indian fields, many a time and oft. Those are the gangs of hands at work—we will see what they are at presently. This little reminiscence of Indian life was further heightened by the negroes who ran beside us to whisk flies from the horses, and to open the gates in the plantation boundary. When the Indian corn is not good, peas are sowed, alternately, between the stalks, and are considered to be of much benefit; and when the cane is bad, corn is sowed with it, for the same object. Before we came up to the gangs we passed a cart on the road containing a large cask, a bucket full of molasses, a pail of hominy, or boiled Indian corn, and a quantity of tin pannikins. The cask contained water for the negroes, and the other vessels held the materials for their breakfast; in addition to which, they generally have each a dried fish. The food was ample, and looked wholesome; such as any labouring man would be well content with. Passing along through maize on one side, and cane at another, we arrived at last at a patch of ground where thirty-six men and women were hoeing.

Three gangs of negroes were at work: one gang of men, with twenty mules and ploughs, was engaged in running through the furrows between the canes, cutting up the weeds and clearing away the grass, which is the enemy of the growing shoot. The mules are of a fine, large, good-tempered kind, and understand their work almost as well as the drivers, who are usually the more intelligent hands on the plantation. The overseer, a sharp-looking creole, on a lanky pony, whip in hand, superintended their labours, and, after a salutation to the Governor, to whom he made some remarks on the condition of the crops, rode off to another part of the farm. With the exception of crying to their mules, the negroes kept silence at their work.

Another gang consisted of forty men, who were hoeing out the grass in Indian corn. The third gang, of thirty-six women, were engaged in hoeing out cane. Their clothing seemed heavy for the climate; their shoes, ponderous and ill-made, had worn away the feet of their thick stockings, which hung in fringes over the upper leathers. Coarse straw hats and bright cotton handkerchiefs protected their heads from the sun. The silence which I have already alluded to prevailed among these gangs also—not a sound could be heard but the blows of the hoe on the heavy clods. In the rear of each gang stood a black overseer, with a heavy-thonged whip over his shoulder. If "Alcibíade" or "Pompée" were called out, he came with outstretched hand to ask "How do you do," and then returned to his labour; but the ladies were coy, and scarcely looked up from under their flapping *chapeaux de paille* at their visitors.

Those who are mothers leave their children in the charge of certain old women, unfit for anything else, and "suckers," as they are called, are permitted to go home, at appointed periods in the day, to give the infants the breast. The overseers have power to give ten lashes; but heavier punishment ought to be reported to the Governor; however, it is not likely a good overseer would be checked, in any way, by his master. The anxieties attending the cultivation of sugar are great, and so much depends upon the judicious employment of labour, it is scarcely possible to exaggerate the importance of experience in directing it, and of power to insist on its application. When the frost comes, the cane is rendered worthless—one touch destroys the sugar. But if frost is the enemy of the white planter, the sun is scarcely the friend of the black man. The sun condemns him to slavery, because it is the heat which is the barrier to the white man's labour. The Governor told me that, in August, when the crops are close, thick set, and high, and the vertical sun beats down on the labourers, nothing but a black skin and head covered with wool can enable a man to walk out in the open and live.

We returned to the house in time for breakfast, for which our early cup of coffee and biscuit and the ride had been good preparation. Here was old France again. One might imagine a lord of the seventeenth century in his hall, but for the black faces of the servitors and the strange dishes of tropical origin. There was the old French abundance, the numerous dishes and efflorescence of napkins, and the long-necked bottles of Bordeaux, with a steady current of pleasant small talk. I saw some numbers of a paper called *La Misachibée*, which was the primitive Indian name of the grand river, not improved by the addition of sibilant Anglo-Saxon syllables.

The Americans, not unmindful of the aid to which, at the end of the War of Independence, their efforts were merely auxiliary, delight, even in the North, to exalt France above her ancient rival; but, as if to show the innate dissimilarity of the two races, the French creoles exhibit towards the New Englanders and the North an animosity, mingled with contempt, which argues badly for a future amalgamation or reunion. As the South Carolinians declare, they would rather return to their allegiance under the English monarchy, so the Louisianians, although they have no sentiment in common with the people of republican and imperial France, assert they would far sooner seek a connection with the old country than submit to the yoke of the Yankees.

After breakfast, the Governor drove out by the ever-silent levée for some miles, passing estate after estate, where grove nodded to grove, each alley saw its brother. One could form no idea, from the small limited frontage of these plantations, that the proprietors were men of many thousands a year, because the estates extend on an average for three or four miles back to the forest. The absence of human beings on the road was a feature which impressed one more and more. But for the tall chimneys of the factories and the sugar-houses, one might believe that these villas had been erected by some pleasure-loving people who had all fled from the river banks for fear of pestilence. The gangs of negroes at work were hidden in the deep corn, and their quarters were silent and deserted. We met but one planter, in his gig, until we arrived at the estate of Monsieur Potier, the Governor's brother-in-law. The proprietor was at home, and received us very kindly, though suffering from the effects of a recent domestic calamity. He is a grave, earnest man, with a face like Jerome Bonaparte, and a most devout Catholic; and any man more unfit to live in any sort of community with New England Puritans one cannot well conceive; for equal intensity of purpose and sincerity of conviction on their part could only lead them to mortal strife. His house was like a French château erected under tropical influences, and he led us through a handsome garden laid out with hothouses, conservatories, orange-trees, and date-palms, and ponds full of the magnificent Victoria Regia in flower. We visited his refining factories and mills, but the heat from the boilers, which seemed too much even for the all-but-naked negroes who were at work, did not tempt us to make a very long sojourn inside. The ebony faces and polished black backs of the slaves were streaming with perspiration as they toiled over boilers, vat, and centrifugal driers. The good refiner was not gaining much money at present, for sugar has been rapidly falling in New Orleans, and the 300,000 barrels produced annually in the South will fall short in the yield of profits, which on an average may be taken at £11 a hogshead, without counting the molasses for the planter. With a most perfect faith in States Rights, he seemed to combine either indifference or ignorance in respect to the power and determination of the North to resist secession to the last. All the planters hereabouts have sown an unusual quantity of Indian corn, to have food for the negroes if the war lasts, without any distress from inland or sea blockade. The absurdity of supposing that a blockade can injure them in the way of supply is a favourite theme to descant upon. They may find out, however, that it is no contemptible means of warfare.

At night, there are regular patrols and watchmen, who look after the levée and the negroes. A number of dogs are also loosed, but I am assured that the creatures do not tear the negroes; they are taught "merely" to catch and mumble them, to treat them as a well-broken retriever uses a wounded wild duck.

At six A.M., Moïse came to ask me if I should like a glass of absinthe, or anything stomachic. At breakfast was Doctor Laporte, formerly a member of the Legislative Assembly of France, who was exiled by Louis Napoleon; in other words, he was ordered to give in his adhesion to the new *régime*, or to take a passport for abroad. He preferred the latter course, and now, true Frenchman, finding the Emperor has aggrandised France and added to her military reputation, he admires the man on whom but a few years ago he lavished the bitterest hate.

The carriage is ready, and the word farewell is spoken at last. M. Alfred Roman, my companion, has travelled in Europe, and learned philosophy; is not so orthodox as many of the gentlemen I have met who indulge in ingenious hypotheses to comfort the consciences of the anthropoproprietors. The negro skull won't hold as many ounces of shot as the white man's. Potent proof that the white man has a right to sell and to own the creature! He is plantigrade, and curved as to the tibia! Cogent demonstration that he was made expressly to work for the arch-footed, straight-tibiaed Caucasian. He has a *rete mucosum* and a coloured pigment! Surely he cannot have a soul of the same colour as that of an Italian or a Spaniard, far less of a flaxen-haired Saxon! See these peculiarities in the frontal sinus—in sinciput or occiput! Can you doubt that the being with a head of that shape was made only to till, hoe, and dig for another race? Besides, the Bible says that he is a son of Ham, and prophecy must be carried out in the rice-swamps, sugar-canes, and maize-fields of the Southern Confederation. It is flat blasphemy to set yourself against it. Our Saviour sanctions slavery because he does not say a word against it, and it is very likely that St. Paul was a slave-owner. Had cotton and sugar been known, the apostle might have been a planter! Furthermore, the negro is civilised by being carried away from Africa and set to work, instead of idling in native inutility. What hope is there of Christianising the African races, except by the agency of the apostles from New Orleans, Mobile, or Charleston, who sing the sweet songs of Zion with such vehemence, and clamour so fervently for baptism in the waters of the "Jawdam?"

If these high physical, metaphysical, moral and religious reasonings do not satisfy you, and you are bold enough to venture still to be unconvinced and to say so, then I advise you not to come within reach of a mass meeting of our citizens, who may be able to find a rope and a tree in the neighbourhood.

As we jog along in an easy rolling carriage drawn by a pair of stout horses, a number of white people meet us coming from the Catholic chapel of the parish, where they had been attending the service for the repose of the soul of a lady much beloved in the neighbourhood. The black people must be supposed to have very happy souls, or to be as utterly lost as Mr. Shandy's homunculus was under certain circumstances, for I have failed to find that any such services are ever considered necessary in their case, although they may have been very good — or, where the services would be most desirable—very bad Catholics. The dead, leaden uniformity of the scenery forced one to converse, in order to escape profound melancholy: the levée on the right hand, above which nothing was visible but the sky; on the left, plantations with cypress fences, whitewashed and pointed wooden gates leading to the planters' houses, and rugged gardens surrounded with shrubs, through which could be seen the slave quarters. Men making eighty or ninety hogsheads of sugar in a year lived in most wretched tumble-down wooden houses not much larger than ox-sheds.

As we drove on the storm gathered overhead, and the rain fell in torrents — the Mississippi flowed lifelessly by—not a boat on its broad surface.

At last we reached Governor Manning's place, and went to the house of the overseer, a large, heavy-eyed old man.

"This rain will do good to the corn," said the overseer. "The niggers has had sceerce nothin' to do leetly, as they 'eve clearied out the fields pretty well."

At the ferry-house I was attended by one stout young slave, who was to row me over. Two flat-bottomed skiffs lay on the bank. The negro groped under the shed, and pulled out a piece of wood like a large spatula, some four feet long, and a small round pole a little longer. "What are those?" quoth I. "Dem's oars, Massa," was my sable ferryman's brisk reply. "I'm very sure they are not; if they were spliced they might make an oar between them." "Golly, and dat's the trute, Massa." "Then go and get oars, will you?" While he was hunting about we entered the shed at the ferry for shelter from the rain. We found "a solitary woman sitting" smoking a pipe by the ashes on the hearth, blear-eyed, low-browed and morose—young as she was. She never said a word nor moved as we came in, sat and smoked, and looked through her gummy eyes at chickens about the size of sparrows, and at a cat not larger than a rat which ran about on the dirty floor. A little girl, some four years of age, not overdressed — indeed, half naked, "not to put too fine a point upon it"—crawled out from under the bed, where she had hid on our approach. As she seemed incapable of appreciating the use of a small piece of silver presented to her — having no precise ideas in coinage or toffy — her parent took the obolus in charge, with unmistakeable decision; but still the lady would not stir a step to aid our guide, who now insisted on the "key ov de oar-house." The little thing sidled off and hunted it out from the top of the bedstead, and when it was found, and the boat was ready, I was not sorry to quit the company of the silent woman in black. The boatman pushed his skiff, in shape a snuffer-dish, some ten feet long and a foot deep, into the water—there was a good deal of rain in it. I got in too, and the conscious waters immediately began vigorously spurting through the cotton wadding wherewith the craft was caulked. Had we gone out into the stream we should have had a swim for it, and they do say that the Mississippi is the most dangerous river in the known world for that healthful exercise. "Why! deuce take you" (I said at least that, in my wrath), "don't you see the boat is leaky?" "See it now for true, Massa. Nobody able to tell dat till Massa get in, though." Another skiff proved to be more staunch. I bade good-bye to my friend Roman, and sat down in my boat, which was forced by the negro against the stream close to the bank, in order to get a good start across to the other side. The view from my lonely position was curious, but not at all picturesque. The world was bounded on both sides by a high bank, which constricted the broad river, just as if one were sailing down an open sewer of enormous length and breadth. Above the bank rose the tops of tall trees and the chimneys of sugar-houses, and that was all to be seen save the sky.

A quarter of an hour brought us to the levée on the other side. I ascended the bank, and across the road, directly in front, appeared a carriage gateway and wickets of wood, painted white, in a line of park palings of the same material, which extended up and down the road far as the eye could see, and guarded wide-spread fields of maize and sugar-cane. An avenue lined with trees, with branches close set, drooping and overarching a walk paved with red brick, led to the house, the porch of which was visible at the extremity of the lawn, with clustering flowers, rose, jessamine, and creepers clinging to the pillars supporting the verandah. The view from the belvedere on the roof was one of the most striking of its kind in the world.

If an English agriculturist could see six thousand acres of the finest land in one field, unbroken by hedge or boundary, and covered with the most magnificent crops of tasseling Indian corn and sprouting sugar-cane, as level as a billiard-table, he would surely doubt his senses. But here is literally such a sight—six thousand acres, better tilled than the finest patch in all the Lothians, green as Meath pastures, which can be turned up for a hundred years to come without requiring manure, of depth practically unlimited, and yielding an average profit on what is sold off it of at least 20*l.* an acre, at the old prices and usual yield of sugar. Rising up in the midst of the verdure are the white lines of the negro cottages and the plantation offices and sugar-houses, which look like large public edifices in the distance. My host was not ostentatiously proud in telling me that, in the year 1857, he had purchased this estate for 300,000*l.*, and an adjacent property, of 8000 acres, for 150,000*l.*, and that he had left Belfast in early youth, poor and unfriended, to seek his fortune, and indeed scarcely knowing what fortune meant, in the New World. In fact, he had invested in these purchases the greater part, but not all, of the profits arising from the business in New Orleans, which he inherited from his master; of which there still remained a solid nucleus in the shape of a great woollen magazine and country house. He is not yet fifty years of age, and his confidence in the great future of sugar induced him to embark this enormous fortune in an estate which the blockade has stricken with paralysis. I cannot doubt, however, that he regrets he did not invest his money in a certain great estate in the North of Ireland, which he had nearly decided on buying; and, had he done so, he would now be in the position to which his unaffected good sense, modesty, kindliness, and benevolence, always adding the rental, entitle him. Six thousand acres on this one estate all covered with sugar-cane, and 16,000 acres more of Indian corn, to feed the slaves;—these were great possessions, but not less than 18,000 acres still remained, covered with brake and forest, and swampy, to be reclaimed and turned into gold. As easy to persuade the owner of such wealth that slavery is indefensible as to have convinced the Norman baron that the Saxon churl who tilled his lands ought to be his equal.

I found Mr. Ward and a few merchants from New Orleans in possession of the bachelor's house. The service was performed by slaves, and the order and regularity of the attendants were worthy of a well-regulated English mansion. In Southern houses along the coast, as the Mississippi above New Orleans is termed, beef and mutton are rarely met with, and the more seldom the better. Fish, also, is scarce, but turkeys, geese, poultry, and preparations of pig, excellent vegetables, and wine of the best quality, render the absence of the accustomed dishes little to be regretted.

The silence which struck me at Governor Roman's is not broken at Mr. Burnside's; and when the last thrill of the mocking-bird's song has died out through the grove, a stillness of Avernian profundity settles on hut, field, and river.

CHAPTER XXXIV.

Negroes—Sugar-cane plantations—The negro and cheap labour—Mortality of blacks and whites—Irish labour in Louisiana—A sugar-house—Negro children—Want of education—Negro diet—Negro hospital—Spirits in the morning—Breakfast—More slaves—Creole planters.

June 5th.—The smart negro who waited on me this morning spoke English. I asked him if he knew how to read and write.—"We must not do that, sir." "Where were you born?"—"I were raised on the plantation, Massa, but I have been to New Orleens;" and then he added, with an air of pride, "I s'pose, sir, Massa Burnside not take less than 1500 dollars for me." Downstairs to breakfast, the luxuries of which are fish, prawns, and red meat which has been sent for to Donaldsonville by boat rowed by an old negro. Breakfast over, I walked down to the yard, where the horses were waiting, and proceeded to visit the saccharine principality. Mr. Seal, the overseer of this portion of the estate, was my guide, if not philosopher and friend. Our road lay through a lane formed by a cart-track, between fields of Indian corn just beginning to flower—as it is called technically, to "tassel"—and sugar-cane. There were stalks of the former twelve or fifteen feet in height, with three or four ears each, round which the pea twined in leafy masses. The maize affords food to the negro, and the husks are eaten by the horses and mules, which also fatten on the peas in rolling time.

The wealth of the land is inexhaustible: all the soil requires is an alternation of maize and cane; and the latter, when cut in the stalk, called "rattoons," at the end of the year, produces a fresh crop, yielding excellent sugar. The cane is grown from stalks which are laid in pits during the winter till the ground has been ploughed, when each piece of cane is laid longitudinally on the ridge and covered with earth, and from each joint of the stalk springs forth a separate sprout when the crop begins to grow. At present the sugar-cane is waiting for its full development, but the negro labour around its stem has ceased. It is planted in long continuous furrows; and although the palm-like tops have not yet united in a uniform arch over the six feet which separates row from row, the stalks are higher than a man. The plantation is pierced with wagon roads, for the purpose of conveying the cane to the sugar-mills, and these again are intersected by and run parallel with drains and ditches, portions of the great system of irrigation and drainage, in connection with a canal to carry off the surplus water to a bayou. The extent of these works may be estimated by the fact that there are thirty miles of road and twenty miles of open deep drainage through the estate, and that the main canal is fifteen feet wide, and at present four feet deep; but in the midst of this waste of plenty and wealth, where are the human beings who produce both? One must go far to discover them; they are buried in sugar and in maize, or hidden in negro quarters. In truth, there is no trace of them, over all this expanse of land, unless one knows where to seek; no "ploughboy whistles over the lea;" no rustic stands to do his own work, but the gang is moved off in silence from point to point, like a corps d'armée of some despotic emperor manœuvring in the battle-field.

Admitting everything that can be said, I am the more persuaded, from what I see, that the real foundation of slavery in the Southern States lies in the power of obtaining labour at will at a rate which cannot be controlled by any combination of the labourers. Granting the heat and the malaria, it is not for a moment to be argued that planters could not find white men to do their work if they would pay them for the risk. A negro, it is true, bears heat well, and can toil under the blazing sun of Louisiana, in the stifling air between the thick-set sugar-canes, but the Irishman who is employed in the stoke-hole of a steamer is exposed to a higher temperature and physical exertion even more arduous. The Irish labourer can, however, set a value on his work; the African slave can only determine the amount of work to be got from him by the exhaustion of his powers. Again, the indigo planter in India, out from morn till night amidst his ryots, or the sportsman toiling under the midday sun through swamp and jungle, proves that the white man can endure the utmost power of the hottest sun in the world as well as the native. More than that, the white man seems to be exempt from the inflammatory disease, pneumonia, and attacks of the mucous membrane and respiratory organs to which the blacks are subject; and if the statistics of negro mortality were rigidly examined, I doubt that they would exhibit as large a proportion of mortality and sickness as would be found amongst gangs of white men under similar circumstances. But the slave is subjected to rigid control; he is deprived of stimulating drinks in which the free white labourer would indulge; and he is obliged to support life upon an antiphlogistic diet, which gives him, however, sufficient strength to execute his daily task.

It is in the supposed cheapness of slave labour and its profitable adaptation in the production of Southern crops, that the whole gist and essence of the question really lie. The planter can get from the labour of a slave for whom he has paid 200*l.*, a sum of money which will enable him to use up that slave in comparatively a few years of his life, whilst he would have to pay to the white labourer a sum that would be a great apparent diminution of his profits, for the same amount of work. It is calculated that each field-hand, as an able-bodied negro is called, yields seven hogsheads of sugar a year, which, at the rate of fourpence a pound, at an average of a hogshead an acre, would produce to the planter 140*l.* for every slave. This is wonderful interest on the planter's money; but he sometimes gets two hogsheads an acre, and even as many as three hogsheads have been produced in good years on the best lands; in other words, two and a quarter tons of sugar and refuse stuff, called "bagasse," have been obtained from an acre of cane. Not one planter of the many I have asked has ever given an estimate of the annual cost of a slave's maintenance; the idea of calculating it never comes into their heads.

Much depends upon the period at which frost sets in; and if the planters can escape till January without any cold to nip the juices and the cane, their crop is increased in value each day; but it is not till October they can begin to send cane to the mill, in average seasons; and if the frost does not come till December, they may count upon the fair average of a hogshead of 1200 pounds of sugar to every acre.

The labour of ditching, trenching, cleaning the waste lands, and hewing down the forests is generally done by Irish labourers, who travel about the country under contractors, or are engaged by resident gangsmen for the task. Mr. Seal lamented the high prices of this work; but then, as he said, "It was much better to have Irish to do it, who cost nothing to the planter if they died, than to use up good field-hands in such severe employment." There is a wonderful mine of truth in this observation. Heaven knows how many poor Hibernians have been consumed and buried in these Louisianian swamps, leaving their earnings to the dramshop keeper and the contractor, and the results of their toil to the planter. This estate derives its name from an Indian tribe called Houmas; and when Mr. Burnside purchased it for 300,000*l.* he received in the first year 63,000*l.* as the clear value of the crops on his investment.

The first place I visited with the overseer was a new sugar-house, which negro carpenters and masons were engaged in erecting. It would have been amusing had not the subject been so grave, to hear the overseer's praises of the intelligence and skill of these workmen, and his boast that they did all the work of skilled labourers on the estate, and then to listen to him, in a few minutes, expatiating on the utter helplessness and ignorance of the black race, their incapacity to do any good, or even to take care of themselves.

There are four sugar-houses on this portion of Mr. Burnside's estate, consisting of grinding-mills, boiling-houses, and crystallising sheds.

The sugar-house is the capital of the negro quarters, and to each of them is attached an enclosure, in which there is a double row of single-storied wooden cottages, divided into two or four rooms. An avenue of trees runs down the centre of the negro street, and behind each hut are rude poultry-hutches, which, with geese and turkeys and a few pigs, form the perquisites of the slaves, and the sole source from which they derive their acquaintance with currency. Their terms are strictly cash. An old negro brought up some ducks to Mr. Burnside last night, and offered the lot of six for three dollars. "Very well, Louis; if you come to-morrow, I'll pay you." "No, massa; me want de money now." "But won't you give me credit, Louis? Don't you think I'll pay the three dollars?" "Oh, pay some day, massa, sure enough. Massa good to pay de tree dollar; but this nigger want money now to buy food and things for him leetle famly. They will trust massa at Donaldsville, but they won't trust this nigger." I was told that a thrifty negro will sometimes make ten or twelve pounds a year from his corn and poultry; but he can have no inducement to hoard; for whatever is his, as well as himself, belongs to his master.

Mr. Seal conducted me to a kind of forcing-house, where the young negroes are kept in charge of certain old crones too old for work, whilst their parents are away in the cane and Indian corn. A host of children of both sexes were seated in the verandah of a large wooden shed, or playing around it, very happily and noisily. I was glad to see the boys and girls of nine, ten, and eleven years of age were at this season, at all events, exempted from the cruel fate which befalls poor children of their age in the mining and manufacturing districts of England. At the sight of the overseer the little ones came forward in tumultuous glee, babbling out, "Massa Seal," and evidently pleased to see him.

As a jolly agriculturist looks at his yearlings or young beeves, the kindly overseer, lolling in his saddle, pointed with his whip to the glistening fat ribs and corpulent paunches of his woolly-headed flock. "There's not a plantation in the State," quoth he, "can show such a lot of young niggers. The way to get them right is not to work the mothers too hard when they are near their time; to give them plenty to eat, and not to send them to the fields too soon." He told me the increase was about five per cent. per annum. The children were quite sufficiently clad, ran about round us, patted the horses, felt our legs, tried to climb up on the stirrup, and twinkled their black and ochrey eyes at Massa Seal. Some were exceedingly fair; and Mr. Seal, observing that my eye followed these, murmured something about the overseers before Mr. Burnside's time being rather a bad lot. He talked about their colour and complexion quite openly; nor did it seem to strike him that there was any particular turpitude in the white man who had left his offspring as slaves on the plantation.

A tall, well-built lad of some nine or ten years stood by me, looking curiously into my face. "What is your name?" said I. "George," he replied. "Do you know how to read or write?" He evidently did not understand the question. "Do you go to church or chapel?" A dubious shake of the head. "Did you ever hear of our Saviour?" At this point Mr. Seal interposed, and said, "I think we had better go on, as the sun is getting hot," and so we rode gently through the little ones; and when we had got some distance he said, rather apologetically, "We don't think it right to put these things into their heads so young; it only disturbs their minds and leads them astray.

Now, in this one quarter there were no less than eighty children, some twelve and some even fourteen years of age. No education—no God—their whole life—food and play, to strengthen their muscles and fit them for the work of a slave. "And when they die?" "Well," said Mr. Seal, "they are buried in that field there by their own people, and some of them have a sort of prayers over them, I believe." The overseer, it is certain, had no fastidious notions about slavery; it was to him the right thing in the right place, and his *summum bonum* was a high price for sugar, a good crop, and a heathy plantation. Nay, I am sure I would not wrong him if I said he could see no impropriety in running a good cargo of regular black slaves, who might clear the great backwood and swampy undergrowth, which was now exhausting the energies of his field-hands, in the absence of Irish navvies.

Each negro gets 5 lbs. of pork a week, and as much Indian corn bread as he can eat, with a portion of molasses, and occasionally they have fish for breakfast. All the carpenters and smiths' work, the erection of sheds, repairing of carts and ploughs, and the baking of bricks for the farm buildings, are done on the estate by the slaves. The machinery comes from the manufacturing cities of the North; but great efforts are made to procure it from New Orleans, where factories have been already established. On the borders of the forest the negroes are allowed to plant corn for their own use, and sometimes they have an overplus, which they sell to their masters. Except when there is any harvest pressure on their hands, they have from noon on Saturday till dawn on Monday morning to do as they please, but they must not stir off the plantation on the road, unless with special permit, which is rarely granted.

There is an hospital on the estate, and even shrewd Mr. Seal did not perceive the conclusion that was to be drawn from his testimony to its excellent arrangements. "Once a nigger gets in there, he'd like to live there for the rest of his life." But are they not the happiest, most contented people in the world—at any rate, when they are in hospital? I declare that to me the more orderly, methodical, and perfect the arrangements for economising slave labour—regulating slaves—are, the more hateful and odious does slavery become. I would much rather be the animated human chattel of a Turk, Egyptian, Spaniard, or French creole, than the labouring beast of a Yankee or of a New England capitalist.

When I returned back to the house I found my friends enjoying a quiet *siesta*, and the rest of the afternoon was devoted to idleness, not at all disagreeable with a thermometer worthy of Agra. Even the mocking-birds were roasted into silence, and the bird which answers to our rook or crow sat on the under branches of the trees, gaping for air with his bill wide open. It must be hot indeed when the mocking-bird loses his activity. There is one, with its nest in a rose-bush trailed along the verandah under my window, which now sits over its young ones with outspread wings, as if to protect them from being baked; and it is so courageous and affectionate, that when I approach quite close, it merely turns round its head, dilates its beautiful dark eye, and opens its beak, within which the tiny sharp tongue is saying, "Don't for goodness sake disturb me, for if you force me to leave, the children will be burned to death."

June 6th.—My chattel Joe, "adscriptus mihi domino," awoke me to a bath of Mississippi water with huge lumps of ice in it, to which he recommended a mint-julep as an adjunct. It was not here that I was first exposed to an ordeal of mint-julep, for in the early morning a stranger in a Southern planter's house may expect the offer of a glassful of brandy, sugar, and peppermint beneath an island of ice—an obligatory panacea for all the evils of climate. After it has been disposed of, Pompey may come up again with glass number two: "Massa say fever very bad this morning—much dew." It is possible that the degenerate Anglo-Saxon stomach has not the fine tone and temper of that of an Hibernian friend of mine, who considered the finest thing to counteract the effects of a little excess was a tumbler of hot whisky and water the moment the sufferer opened his eyes in the morning. Therefore, the kindly offering may be rejected. But on one occasion before breakfast the negro brought up mint-julep number three, the acceptance of which he enforced by the emphatic declaration, "Massa says, sir, you had better take this, because it'll be the last he make before breakfast."

Breakfast is served: there is on the table a profusion of dishes—grilled fowl, prawns, eggs and ham, fish from New Orleans, potted salmon from England, preserved meats from France, claret, iced water, coffee and tea, varieties of hominy, mush, and African vegetable preparations. Then come the newspapers, which are perused eagerly with ejaculations, "Do you hear what they are doing now—infernal villains! that Lincoln must be mad!" and the like. At one o'clock, in spite of the sun, I rode out with Mr. Lee, along the road by the Mississippi, to Mr. Burnside's plantation, called Orange Grove, from a few trees which still remain in front of the overseer's house. We visited an old negro, called "Boatswain," who lives with his old wife in a wooden hut close by the margin of the Mississippi. His business is to go to Donaldsonville for letters, or meat, or ice for the house—a tough row for the withered old man. He is an African born, and he just remembers being carried on board ship and taken to some big city before he came upon the plantation.

"Do you remember nothing of the country you came from, Boatswain?" "Yes, sir. Jist remember trees and sweet things my mother gave me, and much hot sand I put my feet in, and big leaves that we play with—all us little children—and plenty to eat, and big birds and shells." "Would you like to go back, Boatswain?" "What for, sir? no one know old Boatswain there. My old missus Sally inside." "Are you quite happy, Boatswain?" "Im getting very old, massa. Massa Burnside very good to Boatswain, but who care for such dam old nigger? Golla Mighty gave me fourteen children, but he took them all away again from Sally and me. No body care much for dam old nigger like me."

Further on Mr. Seal salutes us from the verandah of his house, but we are bound for overseer Gibbs, who meets us, mounted, by the roadside—a man grim in beard and eye, and silent withal, with a big whip in his hand and a large knife stuck in his belt. He leads us through a magnificent area of cane and maize, the latter towering far above our heads; but I was most anxious to see the forest primæval which borders the clear land at the back of the estate, and spreads away over alligator-haunted swamps into distant bayous. It was not, however, possible to gratify one's curiosity very extensively beyond the borders of the cleared land, for rising round the roots of the cypress, swamp pine, and live oak there was a barrier of undergrowth and bush twined round the cane brake which stands some sixteen feet high, so stiff that the united force of man and horse could not make way against the rigid fibres, and indeed, as Mr. Gibbs told us, "When the niggers take to the cane brake they can beat man or dog, and nothing beats them but snakes and starvation."

He pointed out some sheds around which were broken bottles where the last Irish gang had been working, under one "John Loghlin," of Donaldsonville, a great contractor, who, he says, made plenty of money out of his countrymen, whose bones are lying up and down the Mississippi. "They due work like fire," he said. "Loghlin does not give them half the rations we give our negroes, but he can always manage them with whisky, and when he wants them to do a job he gives them plenty of 'forty rod,' and they have their fight out—reglar free fight, I can tell you, while it lasts. Next morning they will sign anything and go anywhere with him."

On the Orange Grove Plantation, although the crops were so fine, the negroes unquestionably seemed less comfortable than those in the quarters of Houmas, separated from them by a mere nominal division. Then, again, there were more children with fair complexions to be seen peeping out of the huts; some of these were attributed to the former overseer, one Johnson by name, but Mr. Gibbs, as if to vindicate his memory, told me confidentially he had paid a large sum of money to the former proprietor of the estate for one of his children, and had carried it away with him when he left. "You could not expect him, you know," said Gibbs, "to buy them all at the prices that were then going in '56. All the children on the estate," added he, "are healthy, and I can show my lot against Seal's over there, though I hear tell he had a great show of them out to you yesterday."

The bank of the river below the large plantation was occupied by a set of small Creole planters, whose poor houses were close together, indicating very limited farms, which had been subdivided from time to time, according to the French fashion; so that the owners have at last approached pauperism; but they are tenacious of their rights, and will not yield to the tempting price offered by the large planters. They cling to the soil without enterprise and without care. The Spanish settlers along the river are open to the same reproach, and prefer their own ease to the extension of their race in other lands, or to the aggrandisement of their posterity; and an Epicurean would aver, they were truer philosophers than the restless creatures who wear out their lives in toil and labour, to found empires for the future.

It is among these men that, at times, slavery assumes its harshest aspect, and that the negroes are exposed to the severest labour; but it is also true that the slaves have closer relations with the families of their owners, and live in more intimate connection with them than they do under the strict police of the large plantations. These people sometimes get forty bushels of corn to the acre, and a hogshead and a half of sugar. We saw their children going to school, whilst the heads of the houses sat in the verandah smoking, and their mothers were busy with household duties; and the signs of life, the voices of women and children, and the activity visible on the little farms, contrasted not unpleasantly with the desert-like stillness of the larger settlements. Rode back in a thunderstorm.

At dinner in the evening Mr. Burnside entertained a number of planters in the neighbourhood —M. Bringier, M. Coulon (French creoles), Mr. Duncan Kenner, a medical gentleman named Cotmann, and others—the last-named gentleman is an Unionist, and does not hesitate to defend his opinions; but he has, during a visit to Russia, formed high ideas of the necessity and virtues of an absolute and centralised government.

CHAPTER XXXV.

War-rumours and military movements—Governor Manning's slave plantations—Fortunes made by slave labour —Frogs for the table—Cotton and sugar—A thunderstorm.

June 7th.—The Confederate issue of ten millions sterling, in bonds payable in twenty years, is not sufficient to meet the demands of Government; and the four millions of small Treasury notes, without interest, issued by Congress, are being rapidly absorbed. Whilst the Richmond papers demand an immediate movement on Washington, the journals of New York are clamouring for an advance upon Richmond. The planters are called upon to accept the Confederate bonds in payment of the cotton to be contributed by the States.

Extraordinary delusions prevail on both sides. The North believe that battalions of scalping Indian savages are actually stationed at Harper's Ferry. One of the most important movements has been made by Major-General M'Clellan, who has marched a force into Western Virginia from Cincinnati, has occupied a portion of the line of the Baltimore and Ohio railway, which was threatened with destruction by the Secessionists; and has already advanced as far as Grafton. Gen. M'Dowell has been appointed to the command of the Federal forces in Virginia. Every day regiments are pouring down from the North to Washington. General Butler, who is in command at Fortress Monroe, has determined to employ negro fugitives, whom he has called "Contrabands," in the works about the fort, feeding them, and charging the cost of their keep against the worth of their services; and Mr. Cameron, the Secretary of War, has ordered him to refrain from surrendering such slaves to their masters, whilst he is to permit no interference by his soldiers with the relations of persons held to service under the laws of the States in which they are in.

Mr. Jefferson Davis has arrived at Richmond. At sea the Federal steamers have captured a number of Southern vessels; and some small retaliations have been made by the Confederate privateers. The largest mass of the Confederate troops have assembled at a place called Manassas Junction, on the railway from Western Virginia to Alexandria.

The Northern papers are filled with an account of a battle at Philippi, and a great victory, in which no less than two of their men were wounded and two were reported missing as the whole casualties; but Napoleon scarcely expended so much ink over Austerlitz as is absorbed on this glory in the sensation headings of the New York papers.

After breakfast I accompanied a party of Mr. Burnside's friends to visit the plantations of Governor Manning, close at hand. One plantation is as like another as two peas. We had the same paths through tasseling corn, high above our heads, or through wastes of rising sugar-cane; but the slave quarters on Governor Manning's were larger, better built, and more comfortable-looking than any I have seen.

Mr. Bateman, the overseer, a dour strong man, with spectacles on nose, and a quid in his cheek, led us over the ground. As he saw my eye resting on a large knife in a leather case stuck in his belt, he thought it necessary to say, "I keep this to cut my way through the cane brakes about; they are so plaguy thick."

All the surface water upon the estate is carried into a large open drain, with a reservoir in which the fans of a large wheel, driven by steam-power, are worked so as to throw the water over to a cut below the level of the plantation, which carries it into a bayou connected with the lower Mississippi.

In this drain one of my companions saw a prodigious frog, about the size of a tortoise, on which he pounced with alacrity; and on carrying his prize to land he was much congratulated by his friend. "What on earth will you do with the horrid reptile?" "Do with it! why, eat it, to be sure." And it is actually true, that on our return the monster 'crapaud' was handed over to the old cook, and presently appeared on the breakfast-table, looking very like an uncommonly fine spatchcock, and was partaken of with enthusiasm by all the company.

From the draining-wheel we proceeded to visit the forest, where the negroes were engaged in clearing the trees, turning up the soil between the stumps, which marked where the mighty sycamore, live oak, gum-trees, and pines had lately shaded the rich earth. In some places the Indian corn was already waving its head and tassels above the black gnarled roots; in other spots the trees, girdled by the axe, but not yet down, rose up from thick crops of maize; and still deeper in the wood negroes were guiding the ploughs, dragged with pain and difficulty by mules, three abreast, through the tangled roots and rigid earth, which will next year be fit for sowing. There were one hundred and twenty negroes at work; and these, with an adequate number of mules, will clear four hundred and fifty acres of land this year. "But it's death on niggers and mules," said Mr. Bateman. "We generally do it with Irish, as well as the hedging and ditching; but we can't get them now, as they are all off to the wars."

Although the profits of sugar are large, the cost of erecting the machinery, the consumption of wood in the boiler, and the scientific apparatus demand a far larger capital than is required by the cotton planter, who, when he has got land, may procure negroes on credit, and only requires food and clothing till he can realise the proceeds of their labour, and make a certain fortune. Cotton will keep where sugar spoils. The prices are far more variable in the latter, although it has a protective tariff of 20 per cent.

The whole of the half million of hogsheads of sugar grown in the South is consumed in the United States, whereas most of the cotton is sent abroad; but in the event of a blockade the South can use its sugar *ad nauseam*, whilst the cotton is all but useless in consequence of the want of manufacturers in the South.

When I got back, Mr. Burnside was seated in his verandah, gazing with anxiety, but not with apprehension, on the marching columns of black clouds, which were lighted up from time to time by heavy flashes, and shaken by rolls of thunder. Day after day the planters have been looking for rain, tapping glasses, scrutinising aneroids, consulting negro weather prophets, and now and then their expectations were excited by clouds moving down the river, only to be disappointed by their departure into space, or, worse than all, their favouring more distant plantations with a shower that brought gold to many a coffer. "Did you ever see such luck? Kenner has got it again! That's the third shower Bringier has had in the last two days."

But it was now the turn of all our friends to envy us a tremendous thunder-storm, with a heavy, even downfall of rain, which was sucked up by the thirsty earth almost as fast as it fell, and filled the lusty young corn with growing pains, imparting such vigour to the cane that we literally saw it sprouting up, and could mark the increase in height of the stems from hour to hour.

My good host is rather uneasy about his prospects this year, owing to the war; and no wonder. He reckoned on an income of £100,000 for his sugar alone; but if he cannot send it North it is impossible to estimate the diminution of his profits. I fancy, indeed, he more and more regrets that he embarked his capital in these great sugar-swamps, and that he would gladly now invest it at a loss in the old country, of which he is yet a subject; for he has never been naturalised in the United States. Nevertheless, he rejoices in the finest clarets, and in wines of fabulous price, which are tended by an old white-headed negro, who takes as much care of the fluid as if he was accustomed to drink it every day.

CHAPTER XXXVI.

Visit to Mr. M'Call's plantation — Irish and Spaniards — The planter—A Southern sporting man—The creoles—Leave Houmas—Donaldsonville—Description of the City—Baton Rouge—Steamer to Natchez—Southern feeling; faith in Jefferson Davis—Rise and progress of prosperity for the planters—Ultimate issue of the war to both North and South.

June 8th.—According to promise, the inmates of Mr. Burnside's house proceeded to pay a visit to-day to the plantation of Mr. M'Call, who lives at the other side of the river some ten or twelve miles away. Still the same noiseless plantations, the same oppressive stillness, broken only by the tolling of the bell which summons the slaves to labour, or marks the brief periods of its respite! Whilst waiting for the ferry-boat, we visited Dr. Cotmann, who lives in a snug house near the levée, for, hurried as we were, 'twould nevertheless have been a gross breach of etiquette to have passed his doors; and I was not sorry for the opportunity of making the acquaintance of a lady so amiable as his wife, and of seeing a face with tender, pensive eyes, serene brow, and lovely contour, such as Guido or Greuse would have immortalised, and which Miss Cotmann, in the seclusion of that little villa on the banks of the Mississippi, scarcely seemed to know, would have made her a beauty in any capital in Europe.

The Doctor is allowed to rave on about his Union propensities and political power, as Mr. Petigru is permitted to indulge in similar vagaries in Charleston, simply because he is supposed to be helpless. There is, however, at the bottom of the Doctor's opposition to the prevailing political opinion of the neighbourhood, a jealousy of acres and slaves, and a sentiment of animosity to the great seigneurs and slave-owners, which actuate him without his being aware of their influence. After a halt of an hour in his house, we crossed in the ferry to Donaldsonville, where, whilst we were waiting for the carriages, we heard a dialogue between some drunken Irishmen and some still more inebriated Spaniards in front of the public house at hand. The Irishmen were going off to the wars, and were endeavouring in vain to arouse the foreign gentlemen to similar enthusiasm; but, as the latter were resolutely sitting in the gutter, it became necessary to exert eloquence and force to get them on their legs to march to the head-quarters of the Donaldsonville Chasseurs. "For the love of the Virgin and your own sowl's sake, Fernandey, get up and cum along wid us to fight the Yankees." "Josey, are you going to let us be murdered by a set of damned Protestins and rascally niggers?" "Gomey, my darling, get up; it's eleven dollars a month, and food and everything found. The boys will mind the fishing for you, and we'll come back as rich as Jews."

What success attended their appeals I cannot tell, for the carriages came round, and, having crossed a great bayou which runs down into an arm of the Mississippi near the sea, we proceeded on our way to Mr. M'Call's plantation, which we reached just as the sun was sinking into the clouds of another thunder-storm.

The more one sees of a planter's life the greater is the conviction that its charms come from a particular turn of mind, which is separated by a wide interval from modern ideas in Europe. The planter is a denomadised Arab; — he has fixed himself with horses and slaves in a fertile spot, where he guards his women with Oriental care, exercises patriarchal sway, and is at once fierce, tender, and hospitable. The inner life of his household is exceedingly charming, because one is astonished to find the graces and accomplishments of womanhood displayed in a scene which has a certain sort of savage rudeness about it after all, and where all kinds of incongruous accidents are visible in the service of the table, in the furniture of the house, in its decorations, menials, and surrounding scenery.

It was late in the evening when the party returned to Donaldsonville; and when we arrived at the other side of the bayou there were no carriages, so that we had to walk on foot to the wharf where Mr. Burnside's boats were supposed to be waiting—the negro ferryman having long since retired to rest. Under any circumstances, a march on foot through an unknown track covered with blocks of timber and other impedimenta which represented the road to the ferry, could not be agreeable; but the recent rains had converted the ground into a sea of mud filled with holes, with islands of plank and beams of timber, lighted only by the stars—and then this in dress trowsers and light boots!

We plunged, struggled, and splashed till we reached the levée, where boats there were none; and so Mr. Burnside shouted up and down the river, so did Mr. Lee, and so did Mr. Ward and all the others, whilst I sat on a log affecting philosophy and indifference, in spite of tortures from musquitoes innumerable, and severe bites from insects unknown.

The city and river were buried in darkness; the rush of the stream, which is sixty feet deep near the banks, was all that struck upon the ear in the intervals of the cries, "Boat ahoy!" "Ho Batelier!" and sundry ejaculations of a less regular and decent form. At length a boat did glide out of the darkness, and the man who rowed it stated he had been waiting all the time up the bayou, till by mere accident he came down to the jetty, having given us up for the night. In about half an hour we were across the river, and had per force another interview with Dr. Cotmann, who regaled us with his best in story and in wine till the carriages were ready, and we drove back to Mr. Burnside's, only meeting on the way two mounted horsemen with jingling arms, who were, we were told, the night patrol; of their duties I could, however, obtain no very definite account.

June 9th.—A thunder-storm, which lasted all the morning and afternoon till three o'clock. When it cleared, I drove, in company with Mr. Burnside and his friends, to dinner with Mr. Duncan Kenner, who lives some ten or twelve miles above Houmas. He is one of the sporting men of the South, well known on the Charleston race-course, and keeps a large stable of race-horses and brood mares, under the management of an Englishman. The jocks were negro lads; and when we arrived, about half a dozen of them were giving the colts a run in the paddock. The calveless legs and hollow thighs of the negro adapts him admirably for the pigskin; and these little fellows sat their horses so well, one might have thought, till the turn in the course displayed their black faces and grinning mouths, he was looking at a set of John Scott's young gentlemen out training.

The Carolinians are true sportsmen, and in the South the Charleston races create almost as much sensation as our Derby at home. One of the guests at Mr. Kenner's knew all about the winners at Epsom Oaks and Ascot, and took delight in showing his knowledge of the "Racing Calendar."

It is observable, however, that the creoles do not exhibit any great enthusiasm for horse-racing, but that they apply themselves rather to cultivate their plantations and to domestic duties; and it is even remarkable that they do not stand prominently forward in the State Legislature, or aspire to high political influence and position, although their numbers and wealth would fairly entitle them to both. The population of small settlers, scarcely removed from pauperism, along the river banks, is courted by men who obtain larger political influence than the great landowners, as the latter consider it beneath them to have recourse to the arts of the demagogue.

June 10th.—At last *venit summa dies et ineluctabile tempus.* I had seen as much as might be of the best phase of the great institution—less than I could desire of a most exemplary, kind-hearted, clear-headed, honest man. In the calm of a glorious summer evening we crossed the Father of Waters, waving an adieu to the good friend who stood on the shore, and turning our backs to the home we had left behind us. It was dark when the boat reached Donaldsonville on the opposite "coast."

I should not be surprised to hear that the founder of this remarkable city, which once contained the archives of the State, now transferred to Baton Rouge, was a North Briton. There is a simplicity and economy in the plan of the place not unfavourable to that view, but the motive which induced Donaldson to found his Rome on the west of Bayou La Fourche from the Mississippi must be a secret to all time. Much must the worthy Scot have been perplexed by his neighbours, a long-reaching colony of Spanish creoles, who toil not and spin nothing but fishing-nets, and who live better than Solomon, and are probably as well dressed, *minus* the barbaric pearl and gold of the Hebrew potentate. Take the odd, little, retiring, modest houses which grow in the hollows of Scarborough, add to them the least imposing mansions in the town of Folkstone, cast these broadsown over the surface of the Essex marshes, plant a few trees in front of them, then open a few *cafés billard* of the camp sort along the main street, and you have done a very good Donaldsonville.

A policeman welcomes us on the landing, and does the honours of the market, which has a beggarly account of empty benches, a Texan bull done into beef, and a coffee-shop. The policeman is a tall, lean, west countryman; his story is simple, and he has it to tell. He was one of Dan Rice's company—a travelling Astley. He came to Donaldsonville, saw, and was conquered by one of the Spanish beauties, married her, became tavern-keeper, failed, learned French, and is now constable of the parish. There was, however, a weight on his mind. He had studied the matter profoundly, but he was not near the bottom. How did the friends, relatives, and tribe of his wife live? No one could say. They reared chickens, and they caught fish: when there was a pressure on the planters, they turned out to work for 6*s.* 6*d.* a day, but those were rare occasions. The policeman had become quite grey while excogitating on the matter, and he had "nary notion how they did it."

Donaldsonville has done one fine thing. It has furnished two companies of soldiers—all Irishmen—to the wars, and the third is in the course of formation. Not much hedging, ditching, or hard work these times for Paddy! The blacksmith, a huge tower of muscle, claims exemption on the ground that "the divil a bit of him comes from Oireland; he nivir hird af it, barrin' from the buks he rid," and is doing his best to remain behind, but popular opinion is against him.

As the steamer could not be up from New Orleans till dawn, it was a relief to saunter through Donaldsonville to see society, which consisted of several gentlemen and various Jews playing games unknown to Hoyle, in oaken bar-rooms flanked by billiard tables. Doctor Cotmann, who had crossed the river to see patients suffering from an attack of euchre, took us round to a little club, where I was introduced to a number of gentlemen, who expressed great pleasure at seeing me, shook hands violently, and walked away; and, finally, melted off into a cloud of musquitoes by the river bank, into a box prepared for them, which was called a bedroom.

These rooms were built of timber on the stage close by the river. "Why can't I have one of those rooms?" asked I, pointing to a larger musquito box. "It is engaged by ladies." "How do you know?" "*Parceque elles ont envoyé leur butin.*" It was delicious to meet the French "plunder" for baggage—the old phrase, so nicely rendered—in the mouth of the Mississippi boatman.

Having passed a night of discomfiture with the winged demons of my box, I was aroused by the booming of the steam drum of the boat, dipped my head in water among drowned musquitoes, and went forth upon the landing. The policeman had just arrived. His eagle eye lighted upon a large flat moored alongside, on the stern of which was inscribed in chalk, "Pork, corn, butter, beef," &c. Several "spry" citizens were also on the platform. After salutations and compliments, policeman speaks—"When did *she* come in?" (meaning flat.) First citizen—"In the night, I guess." Second citizen—"There's a lot of whisky aboord, too." Policeman (with pleased surprise)—"You never mean it?" First citizen—"Yes, sir; one hundred and twenty gallons!" Policeman (inspired by patriotism)—"It's a west-country boat; why *don't* the citizens seize it? And whisky rising from 17c. to 35c. a gallon!" Citizens murmur approval, and I feel the whisky part of the cargo is not safe. "Yes, sir," says citizen three, "they seize all our property at Cairey (Cairo), and I'm making an example of this cargo."

Further reasons for the seizure were adduced, and it is probable they were as strong as the whisky, which has, no doubt, been drunk long ago on the very purest principles. In course of conversation with the committee of taste which had assembled, it was revealed to me that there was a strict watch kept over those boats which are freighted with whisky forbidden to the slaves, and with principles, when they come from the west-country, equally objectionable. "Did you hear, sir, of the chap over at Duncan Kenner's, as was caught the other day!" "No, sir; what was it?" "Well, sir, he was a man that came here and went over among the niggers at Kenner's to buy their chickens from them. He was took up, and they found he'd a lot of money about him." "Well, of course, he had money to buy the chickens." "Yes, sir, but it looked suspece-ious. He was a west-country fellow, tew, and he might have been tamperin' with 'em. Lucky for him he was not taken in the arternoon." "Why so?" "Because, if the citizens had been drunk, they'd have hung him on the spot."

The Acadia was now alongside, and in the early morning Donaldsonville receded rapidly into trees and clouds. To bed, and make amends for musquito visits, and after a long sleep look out again on the scene. It is difficult to believe that we have been going eleven miles an hour against the turbid river, which is of the same appearance as it was below—the same banks, bends, driftwood, and trees. Large timber rafts, navigated by a couple of men, who stood in the shade of a few upright boards, were encountered at long intervals. White egrets and blue herons rose from the marshes. At every landing the whites who came down were in some sort of uniform. There were two blacks placed on board at one of the landings in irons—captured runaways—and very miserable they looked at the thought of being restored to the bosom of the patriarchal family from which they had, no doubt, so prodigally eloped. I fear the fatted calf-skin would be applied to their backs.

June 11th.—Before noon the steamer hauled alongside a stationary hulk at Baton Rouge, which once "walked the waters" by the aid of machinery, but which was now used as a floating hotel, depôt, and storehouse—315 feet long, and fully thirty feet on the upper deck above the level of the river. The Acadia stopped, and I disembarked. Here were my quarters till the boat for Natchez should arrive. The proprietor of the floating hotel was somewhat excited because one of his servants was away. The man presently came in sight. "Where have you been, you ——?" "Away to buy de newspaper, Massa." "For who, you ——?" "Me buy 'em for no one, Massa; me sell 'um agin, Massa." "See, now, you ——, if ever you goes aboard them steamers to meddle with newspapers, I'm —— but I'll kill you, mind that!"

Baton Rouge is the capital of the State of Louisiana, and the State House thereof is a very quaint and very new example of bad taste. The Deaf and Dumb Asylum near it is in a much better style. It was my intention to have visited the State Prison and Penitentiary, but the day was too hot, and the distance too great, and so I dined at the oddest little creole restaurant, with the funniest old hostess, and the strangest company in the world.

On returning to the boat hotel, Mr. Conrad, one of the citizens of the place, and Mr. W. Avery, a judge of the district court, were good enough to call and to invite me to remain some time, but I was obliged to decline. These gentlemen were members of the home guard, and drilled assiduously every evening. Of the 1300 voters at Baton Rouge, more than 750 are already off to the wars, and another company is being formed to follow them. Mr. Conrad has three sons in the field, and another is anxious to follow, and he and his friend, Mr. Avery, are quite ready to die for the disunion. The waiter who served out drinks in the bar wore a uniform, and his musket lay in the corner among the brandy bottles. At night a patriotic meeting of citizen soldiery took place in the bow, with which song and whisky had much to do, so that sleep was difficult.

Precisely at seven o'clock on Wednesday morning the Mary T. came alongside, and soon afterward bore me on to Natchez, through scenery which became wilder and less cultivated as she got upwards. Of the 1500 steamers on the river, not a tithe are now in employment, and the owners of these profitless flotillas are "in a bad way." It was late at night when the steamer arrived at Natchez, and next morning early I took shelter in another engineless steamer beside the bank of the river at Natchez-under-the hill, which was thought to be a hotel by its owners.

In the morning I asked for breakfast. "There is nothing for breakfast; go to Curry's on shore." Walk up hill to Curry's—a bar-room occupied by a waiter and flies. "Can I have any breakfast?" "No, sir-ree; it's over half an hour ago." "Nothing to eat at all?" "No, sir." "Can I get some anywhere else?" "I guess not." It had been my belief that a man with money in his pocket could not starve in any country *soi-disant* civilized. I chewed the cud of fancy *faute de mieux*, and became the centre of attraction to citizens, from whose conversation I learned that this was "Jeff. Davis's fast day." Observed one, "It quite puts me in mind of Sunday; all the stores closed." Said another, "We'll soon have Sunday every day, then, for I 'spect it won't be worth while for most shops to keep open any longer." Natchez, a place of much trade and cotton export in the season, is now as dull—let us say, as Harwich without a regatta. But it is ultra-secessionist, *nil obstante*.

My hunger was assuaged by Mr. Marshall, who drove me to his comfortable mansion through a country like the wooded parts of Sussex, abounding in fine trees, and in the only lawns and park-like fields I have yet seen in America.

After dinner, my host took me out to visit a wealthy planter, who has raised and armed a cavalry corps at his own expense. We were obliged to get out of the carriage at a narrow lane and walk toward the encampment on foot in the dark; a sentry stopped us, and we observed that there was a semblance of military method in the camp. The captain was walking up and down in the verandah of the poor hut, for which he had abandoned his home. A book of tactics—Hardee's—lay on the table of his little room. Our friend was full of fight, and said he would give all he had in the world to the cause. But the day before, and a party of horse, composed of sixty gentlemen in the district, worth from £20,000 to £50,000 each, had started for the war in Virginia. Everything to be seen or heard testifies to the great zeal and resolution with which the South have entered upon the quarrel. But they hold the power of the United States and the loyalty of the North to the Union at far too cheap a rate.

Next day was passed in a delightful drive through cotton-fields, Indian corn, and undulating woodlands, amid which were some charming residences. I crossed the river at Natchez, and saw one fine plantation, in which the corn, however, was by no means so good as the crops I have seen on the coast. The cotton looks well, and some had already burst into flower—bloom, as it is called—which has turned to a flagrant pink, and seems saucily conscious that its boll will play an important part in the world.

The inhabitants of the tracts on the banks of the Mississippi, and on the island regions hereabout, ought to be, in the natural order of things, a people almost nomadic, living by the chase, and by a sparse agriculture, in the freedom which tempted their ancestors to leave Europe. But the Old World has been working for them. All its trials have been theirs; the fruits of its experience, its labours, its research, its discoveries, are theirs. Steam has enabled them to turn their rivers into highways, to open primeval forests to the light of day and to man. All these, however, would have availed them little had not the demands of manufacture abroad, and the increasing luxury and population of the North and West at home, enabled them to find in these swamps and uplands sources of wealth richer and more certain than all the gold mines of the world.

There must be gnomes to work these mines. Slavery was an institution ready to their hands. In its development there lay every material means for securing the prosperity which Manchester opened to them, and in supplying their own countrymen with sugar. The small, struggling, deeply-mortgaged proprietors of swamp and forest set their negroes to work to raise levées, to cut down trees, to plant and sow. Cotton at ten cents a pound gave a nugget in every boll. Land could be had for a few dollars an acre. Negroes were cheap in proportion. Men who made a few thousand dollars invested them in more negroes, and more land, and borrowed as much again for the same purpose. They waxed fat and rich—there seemed no bounds to their fortune.

But threatening voices came from the North—the echoes of the sentiments of the civilised world repenting of its evil pierced their ears, and they found their feet were of clay, and that they were nodding to their fall in the midst of their power. Ruin inevitable awaited them if they did not shut out these sounds and stop the fatal utterances.

The issue is to them one of life and death. Whoever raises it hereafter, if it be not decided now, must expect to meet the deadly animosity which is now displayed towards the North. The success of the South—if they can succeed—must lead to complications and results in other parts of the world, for which neither they nor Europe are prepared. Of one thing there can be no doubt—a slave state cannot long exist without a slave trade. The poor whites who have won the fight will demand their share of the spoils. The land for tilth is abundant, and all that is wanted to give them fortunes is a supply of slaves. They will have that in spite of their masters, unless a stronger power than the Slave States prevents the accomplishment of their wishes.

The gentleman in whose house I was stopping was not insensible to the dangers of the future, and would, I think, like many others, not at all regret to find himself and property safe in England. His father, the very day of our arrival, had proceeded to Canada with his daughters, but the Confederate authorities are now determined to confiscate all property belonging to persons who endeavour to evade the responsibilities of patriotism. In such matters the pressure of the majority is irresistible, and a sort of mob law supplants any remissness on the part of the authorities. In the South, where the deeds of the land of cypress and myrtle are exaggerated by passion, this power will be exercised very rigorously. The very language of the people is full of the excesses generally accepted as types of Americanism. Turning over a newspaper this morning, I came upon a "card," as it is called, signed by one "Mr. Bonner," relating to a dispute between himself and an Assistant-Quarter-Master-General, about the carriage of some wood at Mobile, which concludes with the sentence that I transcribe, as an evidence of the style which is tolerated, if not admired, down South:—

"If such a Shylock-hearted, caitiff scoundrel does exist, give me the evidence, and I will drag him before the bar of public opinion, and consign him to an infamy so deep and damnable that the hand of the Resurrection will never reach him."

CHAPTER XXXVII.

Down the Mississippi—Hotel at Vicksburg—Dinner—Public meeting—News of the progress of the war—Slavery and England—Jackson—Governor Pettus—Insecurity of life—Strong Southern enthusiasm—Troops bound for the North—Approach to Memphis—Slaves for sale—Memphis—General Pillow.

Friday, June 14th.—Last night with my good host from his plantation to the great two-storied steamer General Quitman, at Natchez. She was crowded with planters, soldiers and their families, and as the lights shone out of her windows, looked like a walled castle blazing from double lines of embrasures.

The Mississippi is assuredly the most uninteresting river in the world, and I can only describe it hereabout by referring to the account of its appearance which I have already given—not a particle of romance in spite of oratorical patriots and prophets, can ever shine from its depths, sacred to cat and buffalo fish, or vivify its turbid waters.

Before noon we were in sight of Vicksburg, which is situated on a high bank or bluff on the left bank of the river, about 400 miles above New Orleans and some 120 miles from Natchez.

Mr. MacMeekan, the proprietor of the "Washington," declares himself to have been the pioneer of hotels in the far west: but he has now built himself this huge caravanserai, and rests from his wanderings. We entered the dining saloon, and found the tables closely packed with a numerous company of every condition in life, from generals and planters down to soldiers in the uniform of privates. At the end of the room there was a long table on which the joints and dishes were brought hot from the kitchen to be carved by the negro waiters, male and female, and as each was brought in the proprietor, standing in the centre of the room, shouted out with a loud voice, "Now, then, here is a splendid goose! ladies and gentlemen, don't neglect the goose and apple-sauce! Here's a piece of beef that *I* can recommend! upon my honour you will never regret taking a slice of the beef. Oyster-pie! oyster-pie! never was better oyster-pie seen in Vicksburg. Run about, boys, and take orders. Ladies and gentlemen, just look at that turkey! who's for turkey?"—and so on, wiping the perspiration from his forehead and combating with the flies.

Altogether it was a semi-barbarous scene, but the host was active and attentive; and after all, his recommendations were very much like those which it was the habit of the taverners in old London to call out in the streets to the passers-by when the joints were ready. The little negroes who ran about to take orders were smart, but now and then came into violent collision, and were cuffed incontinently. One mild-looking little fellow stood by my chair and appeared so sad that I asked him "Are you happy, my boy?" He looked quite frightened. "Why don't you answer me?" "I'se afeered, sir; I can't tell that to Massa." "Is not your master kind to you?" "Massa very kind man, sir; very good man when he is not angry with me," and his eyes filled with tears to the brim.

The war fever is rife in Vicksburg, and the Irish and German labourers, to the extent of several hundreds, have all gone off to the war.

When dinner was over, the mayor and several gentlemen of the city were good enough to request that I would attend a meeting, at a room in the railway-station, where some of the inhabitants of the town had assembled. Accordingly I went to the terminus and found a room filled with gentlemen. Large china bowls, blocks of ice, bottles of wine and spirits, and boxes of cigars were on the table, and all the materials for a symposium.

The company discussed recent events, some of which I learned for the first time. Dislike was expressed to the course of the authorities in demanding negro labour for the fortifications along the river, and uneasiness was expressed respecting a negro plot in Arkansas; but the most interesting matter was Judge Taney's protest against the legality of the President's course in suspending the writ of *habeas corpus* in the case of Merriman. The lawyers who were present at this meeting were delighted with his argument, which insists that Congress alone can suspend the writ, and that the President cannot legally do so.

The news of the defeat of an expedition from Fortress Monroe against a Confederate post at Great Bethel, has caused great rejoicing. The accounts show that there was the grossest mismanagement on the part of the Federal officers. The Northern papers particularly regret the loss of Major Winthrop, aide-de-camp to General Butler, a writer of promise. At four o'clock p. m. I bade the company farewell, and the train started for Jackson. The line runs through a poor clay country, cut up with gullies and water-courses made by violent rain.

There were a number of volunteer soldiers in the train; and their presence no doubt attracted the girls and women, who waved flags and cheered for Jeff. Davis and States' Rights. Well, as I travel on through such scenes, with a fine critical nose in the air, I ask myself "Is any Englishman better than these publicans and sinners in regard to this question of slavery?" It was not on moral or religious grounds that our ancestors abolished serfdom. And if to-morrow our good farmers, deprived of mowers, reapers, ploughmen, hedgers and ditchers, were to find substitutes in certain people of a dark skin assigned to their use by Act of Parliament, I fear they would be almost as ingenious as the Rev. Dr. Seabury in discovering arguments physiological, ethnological, and biblical for the retention of their property. And an evil day would it be for them if they were so tempted; for assuredly, without any derogation to the intellect of the Southern men, it may be said that a large proportion of the population is in a state of very great moral degradation compared with civilised Anglo-Saxon communities.

The man is more natural, and more reckless; he has more of the qualities of the Arab than are to be reconciled with civilisation; and it is only among the upper classes that the influences of the aristocratic condition which is generated by the subjection of masses of men to their fellow-man are to be found.

At six o'clock the train stopped in the country at a railway crossing by the side of a large platform. On the right was a common, bounded by a few detached wooden houses, separated by palings from each other, and surrounded by rows of trees. In front of the station were two long wooden sheds, which, as the signboard indicates, were exchanges or drinking saloons; and beyond these again were visible some rudimentary streets of straggling houses, above which rose three pretentious spires and domes, resolved into insignificance by nearer approach. This was Jackson.

Our host was at the station in his carriage, and drove us to his residence, which consisted of some detached houses shaded by trees in a small inclosure, and bounded by a kitchen garden. He was one of the men who had been filled with the afflatus of 1848, and joined the Young Ireland party before it had seriously committed itself to an unfortunate outbreak; and when all hope of success had vanished, he sought, like many others of his countrymen, a shelter under the stars and stripes, which, like most of the Irish settled in Southern States, he was now bent on tearing asunder. He has the honour of being mayor of Jackson, and of enjoying a competitive examination with his medical rivals for the honour of attending the citizens.

In the evening I walked out with him to the adjacent city, which has no title to the name, except as being the State capital. The mushroom growth of these States, using that phrase merely as to their rapid development, raises hamlets in a small space to the dignity of cities. It is in such outlying expansion of the great republic that the influence of the foreign emigration is most forcibly displayed. It would be curious to inquire, for example, how many men there are in the city of Jackson exercising mechanical arts or engaged in small commerce, in skilled or manual labour, who are really Americans in the proper sense of the word. I was struck by the names over the doors of the shops, which were German, Italian, French, and by foreign tongues and accents in the streets; but, on the other hand, it is the native-born American who obtains the highest political stations and arrogates to himself the largest share of governmental emoluments.

Jackson proper consists of strings of wooden houses, with white porticoes and pillars a world too wide for their shrunk rooms, and various religious and other public edifices, of the hydrocephalic order of architecture, where vulgar cupola and exaggerated steeple tower above little bodies far too feeble to support them. There are of course a monster hotel and blazing bar-rooms—the former celebrated as the scene of many a serious difficulty, out of some of which the participators never escaped alive. The streets consist of rows of houses such as I have seen at Macon, Montgomery, and Bâton Rouge; and as we walked towards the capital or State-house there were many more invitations "to take a drink" addressed to my friend and me than we were able to comply with. Our steps were bent to the State-house, which is a pile of stone, with open colonnades, and an air of importance at a distance which a nearer examination of its dilapidated condition does not confirm. Mr. Pettus, the Governor of the State of Mississippi, was in the Capital; and on sending in our cards, we were introduced to his room, which certainly was of more than republican simplicity. The apartment was surrounded with some common glass cases, containing papers and odd volumes of books; the furniture, a table or desk, and a few chairs and a ragged carpet; the glass in the windows cracked and broken; the walls and ceiling discoloured by mildew.

The Governor is a silent man, of abrupt speech but easy of access; and, indeed, whilst we wer speaking, strangers and soldiers walked in an out of his room, looked around them, and acted in all respects as if they were in a public-house, except in ordering drinks. This grim, tall, angular man seemed to me such a development of public institutions in the South as Mr. Seward was in a higher phase in the North. For years he hunted deer and trapped in the forest of the far west, and lived in a Natty Bumpo or David Crocket state of life; and he was not ashamed of the fact when taunted with it during his election contest, but very rightly made the most of his independence and his hard work.

The pecuniary honours of his position are not very great as Governor of the enormous State of Mississippi. He has simply an income of £800 a year and a house provided for his use; he is not only quiet contented with what he has, but believes that the society in which he lives is the highest development of civilised life, notwithstanding the fact that there are more outrages on the person in his State, nay, more murders perpetrated in the very capital, than were known in the worst days of Mediæval Venice or Florence;—indeed, as a citizen said to me, "Well, I think our average in Jackson is a murder a month;" but he used a milder name for the crime.

The Governor conversed on the aspect of affairs, and evinced that wonderful confidence in his own people which, whether it arises from ignorance of the power of the North, or a conviction of greater resources, is to me so remarkable. "Well, sir," said he, dropping a portentous plug of tobacco just outside the spittoon, with the air of a man who wished to show he could have hit the centre if he liked, "England is no doubt a great country, and has got fleets and the like of that, and may have a good deal to do in Eu-*rope;* but the sovereign State of Mississippi can do a great deal better without England than England can do without her." Having some slight recollection of Mississippi repudiation, in which Mr. Jefferson Davis was so actively engaged, I thought it possible that the Governor might be right; and after a time his Excellency shook me by the hand, and I left, much wondering within myself what manner of men they must be in the State of Mississippi when Mr. Pettus is their chosen Governor; and yet, after all, he is honest and fierce; and perhaps he is so far qualified as well as any other man to be Governor of the State. There are newspapers, electric telegraphs, and railways; there are many educated families, even much good society, I am told, in the State; but the larger masses of the people struck me as being in a condition not much elevated from that of the original back woodsman. On my return to the Doctor's house I found some letters which had been forwarded to me from New Orleans had gone astray, and I was obliged, therefore, to make arrangements for my departure on the following evening.

June 16*th*.—I was compelled to send my excuses to Governor Pettus, and remained quietly within the house of my host, entreating him to protect me from visitors and especially from my own *confrères*, that I might secure a few hours even in that ardent heat to write letters to home. Now, there is some self-denial required, if one be at all solicitous of the *popularis aura*, to offend the susceptibilities of the irritable genus in America. It may make all the difference between millions of people hearing and believing you are a high-toned, whole-souled gentleman or a wretched ignorant and prejudiced John Bull; but, nevertheless, the solid pudding of self-content and the satisfaction of doing one's work are preferable to the praise even of a New York newspaper editor.

When my work was over I walked out and sat in the shade with a gentleman whose talk turned upon the practices of the Mississippi duello. Without the smallest animus, and in the most natural way in the world, he told us tale after tale of blood, and recounted terrible tragedies enacted outside of bars of hotels and in the public streets close beside us. The very air seemed to become purple as he spoke, the land around a veritable "Aceldama." There may, indeed, be security for property, but there is none for the life of its owner in difficulties, who may be shot by a stray bullet from a pistol as he walks up the street.

I learned many valuable facts. I was warned, for example, against the impolicy of trusting to small-bored pistols or to pocket six-shooters in case of a close fight, because suppose you hit your man mortally he may still run in upon you and rip you up with a bowie knife before he falls dead; whereas if you drive a good heavy bullet into him, or make a hole in him with a "Derringer" ball, he gets faintish and drops at once.

Many illustrations, too, were given of the value of practical lessons of this sort. One particularly struck me. If a gentleman with whom you are engaged in altercation moves his hand towards his breeches pocket, or behind his back, you must smash him or shoot him at once, for he is either going to draw his six-shooter, to pull out a bowie knife, or to shoot you through the lining of his pocket. The latter practice is considered rather ungentlemanly, but it has been somewhat more honoured lately in the observance than in the breach. In fact, the savage practice of walking about with pistols, knives, and poniards, in bar-rooms and gambling-saloons, with passions ungoverned, because there is no law to punish the deeds to which they lead, affords facilities for crime which an uncivilised condition of society leaves too often without punishment, but which must be put down or the country in which it is tolerated will become as barbarous as a jungle inhabited by wild beasts.

Our host gave me an early dinner, at which I met some of the citizens of Jackson, and at six o'clock I proceeded by the train for Memphis. The carriages were, of course, full of soldiers or volunteers, bound for a large camp at a place called Corinth, who made night hideous by their song and cries, stimulated by enormous draughts of whiskey and a proportionate consumption of tobacco, by teeth and by fire. The heat in the carriages added to the discomforts arising from these causes, and from great quantities of biting insects in the sleeping places. The people have all the air and manner of settlers. Altogether the impression produced on my mind was by no means agreeable, and I felt as if I was indeed in the land of Lynch law and bowie knives, where the passions of men have not yet been subordinated to the influence of the tribunals of justice. Much of this feeling has no doubt been produced by the tales to which I have been listening around me—most of which have a smack of manslaughter about them.

June 17*th*.—If it was any consolation to me that the very noisy and very turbulent warriors of last night were exceedingly sick, dejected, and crestfallen this morning, I had it to the full. Their cries for water were incessant to allay the internal fires caused by "40 rod" and "60 rod," as whiskey is called, which is supposed to kill people at those distances. Their officers had no control over them—and the only authority they seemed to respect was that of the "gentlemanly" conductor whom they were accustomed to fear individually, as he is a great man in America and has much authority and power to make himself disagreeable if he likes.

The victory at Big or Little Bethel has greatly elated these men, and they think they can walk all over the Northern States. It was a relief to get out of the train for a few minutes at a station called Holly Springs, where the passengers breakfasted at a dirty table on most execrable coffee, corn bread, rancid butter, and very dubious meats, and the wild soldiers outside made the most of their time, as they had recovered from their temporary depression by this time, and got out on the tops of the carriages, over which they performed tumultuous dances to the music of their band, and the great admiration of the surrounding negrodom. Their demeanour is very unlike that of the unexcitable staid people of the North.

There were in the train some Texans who were going to Richmond to offer their servcies to Mr. Davis. They denounced Sam Houston as a traitor, but admitted there were some Unionists, or as they termed them Lincolnite skunks, in the State. The real object of their journey was, in my mind, to get assistance from the Southern Confederacy to put down their enemies in Texas.

In order to conceal from the minds of the people that the government at Washington claims to be that of the United States, the press politicians and speakers divert their attention to the names of Lincoln, Seward, and other black republicans, and class the whole of the North together as the Abolitionists. They call the Federal levies "Lincoln's mercenaries" and "abolition hordes," though their own troops are paid at the same rate as those of the United States. This is a common mode of procedure in revolutions and rebellions, and is not unfrequent in wars.

The enthusiasm for the Southern cause among all the people is most remarkable,—the sight of the flag waving from the carriage windows drew all the population of the hamlets and the workers in the field, black and white, to the side of the carriages to cheer for Jeff. Davis and the Southern Confederacy, and to wave whatever they could lay hold of in the air. The country seems very poorly cultivated, the fields full of stumps of trees, and the plantation houses very indifferent. At every station more "soldiers," as they are called, got in, till the smell and heat were suffocating.

These men were as fanciful in their names and dress as could be. In the train which preceded us there was a band of volunteers armed with rifled pistols and enormous bowie knives, who called themselves "The Toothpick Company." They carried along with them a coffin, with a plate inscribed, "Abe Lincoln, died ——," and declared they were "bound" to bring his body back in it, and that they did not intend to use muskets or rifles, but just go in with knife and six-shooter, and whip the Yankees straight away. How astonished they will be when the first round shot flies into them, or a cap full of grape rattles about their bowie knives.

At the station of Grand Junction, north of Holly Springs, which latter is 210 miles north of Jackson, several hundreds of our warrior friends were turned out in order to take the train northwestward for Richmond, Virginia. The 1st Company, seventy rank and file, consisted of Irishmen armed with sporting rifles without bayonets. Five-sixths of the 2nd Company, who were armed with muskets, were of the same nationality. The 3rd Company were all Americans. The 4th Company were almost all Irish. Some were in green, others were in grey, the Americans who were in blue had not yet received their arms. When the word fix bayonets was given by the officer, a smart keen-looking man, there was an astonishing hurry and tumult in the ranks.

"Now then, Sweeny, where are yes dhriven me too? It is out of the redjmint amongst the officers yer shovin' me?"

"Sullivan, don't ye hear we're to fix beenits?"

"Sarjent, jewel, wud yes ayse the shtrap of me baynit?"

"If ye prod me wid that agin, I'll let dayloite into ye."

The officer, reading, "No. 23, James Phelan."

No reply.

Officer again, "No 23, James Phelan."

Voice from the rank, "Shure, captain, and faix Phelan's gone, he wint at the last depôt."

"No. 40, Miles Corrigan."

Voice further on, "He's the worse for dhrink in the cars, yer honour, and says he'll shoot us if we touch him;" and so on.

But these fellows were, nevertheless, the material for fighting and for marching after proper drill and with good officers, even though there was too large a proportion of old men and young lads in the ranks. To judge from their dress these recruits came from the labouring and poorest classes of whites. The officers affected a French cut and bearing with indifferent success, and in the luggage vans there were three foolish young women with slop-dress imitation clothes of the Vivandière type, who, with dishevelled hair, dirty faces, and dusty hats and jackets, looked sad, sorry, and absurd. Their notions of propriety did not justify them in adopting straps, boots, and trousers, and the rest of the tawdry ill-made costume looked very bad indeed.

The train which still bore a large number of soldiers for the camp of Corinth, proceeded through dreary swamps, stunted forests, and clearings of the rudest kind at very long intervals. We had got out of the cotton district and were entering poorer soil, or land which, when cleared, was devoted to wheat and corn, and I was told that the crops ran from forty to sixty bushels to the acre. A more uninteresting country than this portion of the State of Mississippi I have never witnessed. There was some variety of scenery about Holly Springs, where undulating ground covered with wood diversified the aspect of the flat, but since that we have been travelling through mile after mile of insignificantly grown timber and swamps.

On approaching Memphis the line ascends towards the bluff of the Mississippi, and farms of a better appearance come in sight on the side of the rail; but after all I do not envy the fate of the man who, surrounded by slaves and shut out from the world, has to pass his life in this dismal region, be the crops never so good.

At a station where a stone pillar marks the limit between the sovereign State of Mississippi and that of Tennessee, there was a house two stories high, from the windows of which a number of negro girls and young men were staring on the passengers. Some of them smiled, laughed, and chatted, but the majority of them looked gloomy and sad enough. They were packed as close as they could, and I observed that at the door a very ruffianly looking fellow in a straw hat, long straight hair, flannel shirt, and slippers, was standing with his legs across and a heavy whip in his hand. One of the passengers walked over and chatted to him. They looked in and up at the negroes and laughed, and when the man came near the carriage in which I sat, a friend called out, "Whose are they, Sam?" "He's a dealer at Jackson, Mr. Smith. They're as prime a lot of fine Virginny niggers as I've seen this long time, and he wants to realise, for the news looks so bad."

It was 1.40 p.m. when the train arrived at Memphis. I was speedily on my way to the Gayoso House, so called after an old Spanish ruler of the district, which is situated in the street on the bluff, which runs parallel with the course of the Mississippi. This resuscitated Egyptian city is a place of importance, and extends for several miles along the high bank of the river, though it does not run very far back The streets are at right angles to the principal thoroughfares, which are parallel to the stream; and I by no means expected to see the lofty stores, warehouses, rows of shops, and handsome buildings on the broad esplanade along the river, and the extent and size of the edifices public and private in this city, which is one of the developments of trade and commerce created by the Mississippi. Memphis contains nearly 30,000 inhabitants, but many of them are foreigners, and there is a nomad draft into and out of the place, which abounds in haunts for Bohemians, drinking and dancing-saloons, and gaming-rooms. And this strange kaleidoscope of negroes and whites of the extremes of civilisation in its American development, and of the semi-savage degraded by his contact with the white; of enormous steamers on the river, which bears equally the dug-out or canoe of the black fisherman; the rail, penetrating the inmost recesses of swamps, which on either side of it remain no doubt in the same state as they were centuries ago; the roll of heavily-laden waggons through the streets; the rattle of omnibuses and all the phenomena of active commercial life before our eyes, included in the same scope of vision which takes in at the other side of the Mississippi lands scarcely yet settled, though the march of empire has gone thousands of miles beyond them, amuses but perplexes the traveller in this new land.

The evening was so exceedingly warm that I was glad to remain within the walls of my darkened bed-room. All the six hundred and odd guests whom the Gayoso House is said to accommodate were apparently in the passage at one time. At present it is the headquarters of General Gideon J. Pillow, who is charged with the defences of the Tennessee side of the river, and commands a considerable body of troops around the city and in the works above. The house is consequently filled with men in uniform, belonging to the General's staff or the various regiments of Tennessee troops.

• The Governors and the Legislatures of the States, view with dislike every action on the part of Mr. Davis which tends to form the State troops into a national army. At first, indeed, the doctrine prevailed that troops could not be sent beyond the limits of the State in which they were raised—then it was argued that they ought not to be called upon to move outside their borders; and I have heard people in the South inveighing against the sloth and want of spirit of the Virginians, who allowed their State to be invaded without resisting the enemy. Such complaints were met by the remark that all the Northern States had combined to pour their troops into Virginia, and that her sister States ought in honour to protect her. Finally, the martial enthusiasm of the Southern regiments impelled them to press forward to the frontier, and by delicate management, and the perfect knowledge of his countrymen which Mr. Jefferson Davis possesses, he is now enabled to amalgamate in some sort the diverse individualities of his regiments into something like a national army.

On hearing of my arrival, General Pillow sent his aide-de-camp to inform me that he was about starting in a steamer up the river, to make an inspection of the works and garrison at Fort Randolph, and at other points where batteries had been erected to command the stream, supported by large levies of Tennesseans. The aide-de-camp conducted me to the General, whom I found in his bedroom, fitted up as an office, littered with plans and papers. Before the Mexican war General Pillow was a flourishing solicitor, connected in business with President Polk, and commanding so much influence that when the expedition was formed he received the nomination of brigadier-general of volunteers. He served with distinction, and was severely wounded at the battle of Chapultepec, and at the conclusion of the campaign he retired into civil life, and was engaged directing the work of his plantation till this great rebellion summoned him once more to the field.

Of course there is, and must be, always an inclination to deride these volunteer officers on the part of regular soldiers; and I was informed by one of the officers in attendance on the General, that he had made himself ludicrously celebrated in Mexico for having undertaken to throw up a battery which, when completed, was found to face the wrong way, so that the guns were exposed to the enemy. General Pillow is a small, compact, clear-complexioned man, with short grey whiskers, cut in the English fashion, a quick eye, and a pompous manner of speech; and I had not been long in his company before I heard of Chapultepec and his wound, which causes him to limp a little in his walk, and gives him inconvenience in the saddle. He wore a round black hat, plain blue frock coat, dark trousers, and brass spurs on his boots; but no signs of military rank. The General ordered carriages to the door, and we went to see the batteries on the bluff or front of the esplanade, which are intended to check any ship attempting to pass down the river from Cairo, where the Federals under General Prentiss have entrenched themselves, and are understood to meditate an expedition against the city. A parapet of cotton bales, covered with tarpaulin, has been erected close to the edge of the bank of earth, which rises to heights varying from 60 to 100 feet almost perpendicularly from the waters of the Mississippi, with zigzag roads running down through it to the landing-places. This parapet could offer no cover against vertical fire, and is so placed that well-directed shell into the bank below it would tumble it all into the water. The zigzag roads are barricaded with weak planks, which would be shivered to pieces by boat-guns; and the assaulting parties could easily mount through these covered ways to the rear of the parapet, and up to the very centre of the esplanade.

The blockade of the river at this point is complete; not a boat is permitted to pass either up or down. At the extremity of the esplanade, on an angle of the bank, an earthen battery, mounted with six heavy guns, has been thrown up, which has a fine command of the river; and the General informed me he intends to mount sixteen guns in addition, on a prolongation of the face of the same work.

The inspection over, we drove down a steep road to the water beneath, where the Ingomar, a large river steamer, now chartered for the service of the State of Tennessee, was lying to receive us. The vessel was crowded with troops—all volunteers, of course—about to join those in camp. Great as were their numbers, the proportion of the officers was inordinately large, and the rank of the greater number preposterously high. It seemed to me as if I was introduced to a battalion of colonels, and that I was not permitted to pierce to any lower strata of military rank. I counted seventeen colonels, and believe the number was not then exhausted.

General Clarke, of Mississippi, who had come over from the camp at Corinth, was on board, and I had the pleasure of making his acquaintance. He spoke with sense and firmness of the present troubles, and dealt with the political difficulties in a tone of moderation which bespoke a gentleman and a man of education and thought. He also had served in the Mexican war, and had the air and manner of a soldier. With all his quietness of tone, there was not the smallest disposition to be traced in his words to retire from the present contest, or to consent to a reunion with the United States under any circumstances whatever. Another general, of a very different type, was among our passengers—a dirty-faced, frightened-looking young man, of some twenty-three or twenty-four years of age, redolent of tobacco, his chin and shirt slavered by its foul juices, dressed in a green cutaway coat, white jean trousers, strapped under a pair of prunella slippers, in which he promenaded the deck in an Agag-like manner, which gave rise to a suspicion of bunions or corns. This strange figure was topped by a tremendous black felt sombrero, looped up at one side by a gilt eagle, in which was stuck a plume of ostrich feathers, and from the other side dangled a heavy gold tassel. This decrepit young warrior's name was Ruggles or Struggles, who came from Arkansas, where he passed, I was informed, for "quite a leading citizen."

Our voyage as we steamed up the river afforded no novelty, nor any physical difference worthy of remark, to contrast it with the lower portions of the stream, except that upon our right hand side, which is, in effect, the left bank, there are ranges of exceedingly high bluffs, some parallel with and others at right angles to the course of the stream. The river is of the same pea-soup colour with the same masses of leaves, decaying vegetation, stumps of trees, forming small floating islands, or giant cotton-trees, pines, and balks of timber whirling down the current. Our progress was slow; nor did I regret the captain's caution, as there must have been fully nine hundred persons on board; and although there is but little danger of being snagged in the present condition of the river, we encountered now and then a trunk of a tree, which struck against the bows with force enough to make the vessel quiver from stem to stern. I was furnished with a small berth, to which I retired at midnight, just as the Ingomar was brought to at the Chickasaw Bluffs, above which lies Camp Randolph.

CHAPTER XXXVIII.

Camp Randolph—Cannon practice—Volunteers—"Dixie"—Forced return from the South—Apathy of the North—General retrospect of politics—Energy and earnestness of the South—Fire-arms—Position of Great Britain towards the belligerents—Feeling towards the Old Country.

June 18th.—On looking out of my cabin window this morning I found the steamer fast alongside a small wharf, above which rose, to the height of 150 feet, at an angle of 45 degrees, the rugged bluff already mentioned. The wharf was covered with commissariat stores and ammunition. Three heavy guns, which some men were endeavouring to sling to rude bullock-carts, in a manner defiant of all the laws of gravitation, seemed likely to go slap into the water at every moment; but of the many great strapping fellows who were lounging about, not one gave a hand to the working party. A dusty track wound up the hill to the brow, and there disappeared; and at the height of fifty feet or so above the level of the river two earthworks had been rudely erected in an ineffective position. The volunteers who were lounging about the edge of the stream were dressed in different ways, and had no uniform.

Already the heat of the sun compelled me to seek the shade; and a number of the soldiers, labouring under the same infatuation as that which induces little boys to disport themselves in the Thames at Waterloo Bridge, under the notion that they are washing themselves, were swimming about in a back-water of the great river, regardless of cat-fish, mud, and fever.

General Pillow proceeded on shore after breakfast, and we mounted the coarse cart-horse chargers which were in waiting at the jetty to receive us. It is scarcely worth while to transcribe from my diary a description of the works, which I sent over at the time to England. Certainly, a more extraordinary maze could not be conceived, even in the dreams of a sick engineer—a number of mad beavers might possibly construct such dams. They were so ingeniously made as to prevent the troops engaged in their defence from resisting the enemy's attacks, or getting away from them when the assailants had got inside—most difficul and troublesome to defend, and still more diffi cult for the defenders to leave, the latter perhaps being their chief merit.

The General ordered some practice to be made with round shot down the river. An old forty-two pound carronade was loaded with some difficulty, and pointed at a tree about 1700 yards—which I was told, however, was not less than 2500 yards—distant. The General and his staff took their posts on the parapet to leeward, and I ventured to say, "I think, General, the smoke will prevent your seeing the shot." To which the General replied, "No, sir," in a tone which indicated, "I beg you to understand I have been wounded in Mexico, and know all about this kind of thing." "Fire," the string was pulled, and out of the touch-hole popped a piece of metal with a little chirrup. "Darn these friction tubes! I prefer the linstock and match," quoth one of the staff, *sotto voce*, "but General Pillow will have us use friction tubes made at Memphis, that ar'nt worth a cuss." Tube No. 2, however, did explode, but where the ball went no one could say, as the smoke drifted right into our eyes.

The General then moved to the other side of the gun, which was fired a third time, the shot falling short in good line, but without any ricochet. Gun No. 3 was next fired. Off went the ball down the river, but off went the gun, too, and with a frantic leap it jumped, carriage and all, clean off the platform. Nor was it at all wonderful, for the poor old-fashioned chamber cannonade had been loaded with a charge and a solid shot heavy enough to make it burst with indignation. Most of us felt relieved when the firing was over, and, for my own part, I would much rather have been close to the target than to the battery.

Slowly winding for some distance up the steep road in a blazing sun, we proceeded through the tents, which are scattered in small groups, for health's sake, fifteen and twenty together, on the wooded plateau above the river. The tents are of the small ridge-pole pattern, six men to each, many of whom, from their exposure to the sun, whilst working in these trenches, and from the badness of the water, had already been laid up with illness. As a proof of General Pillow's energy, it is only fair to say he is constructing, on the very summit of the plateau, large cisterns, which will be filled with water from the river by steam power.

The volunteers were mostly engaged at drill in distinct companies, but by order of the General some 700 or 800 of them were formed into line for inspection. Many of these men were in their shirt sleeves, and the awkwardness with which they handled their arms showed that, however good they might be as shots, they were bad hands at manual platoon exercise; but such great strapping fellows, that, as I walked down the ranks, there were few whose shoulders were not above the level of my head, excepting here and there a weedy old man or a growing lad. They were armed with old pattern percussion muskets, no two clad alike, many very badly shod, few with knapsacks, but all provided with a tin water-flask and a blanket. These men have been only five weeks enrolled and were called out by the State of Tennessee, in anticipation of the vote of secession.

I could get no exact details as to the supply of food, but from the Quartermaster-General I heard that each man had from ¾ lb. to 1½ lb. of meat, and a sufficiency of bread, sugar, coffee, and rice, daily; however, these military Olivers "asked for more." Neither whisky nor tobacco was served out to them, which to such heavy consumers of both, must prove one source of dissatisfaction. The officers were plain, farmerly planters, merchants, lawyers, and the like—energetic, determined men, but utterly ignorant of the most rudimentary parts of military science. It is this want of knowledge on the part of the officer which renders it so difficult to arrive at a tolerable condition of discipline among volunteers, as the privates are quite well aware they know as much of soldiering as the great majority of their officers.

Having gone down the lines of these motley companies, the General addressed them in a harangue in which he expatiated on their patriotism, on their courage, and the atrocity of the enemy, in an odd farrago of military and political subjects. But the only matter which appeared to interest them much was the announcement that they would be released from work in another day or so, and that negroes would be sent to perform all that was required. This announcement was received with the words, "Bully for us!" and "That's good." And when General Pillow wound up a florid peroration by assuring them, "When the hour of danger comes I will be with you," the effect was by no means equal to his expectations. The men did not seem to care much whether General Pillow was with them or not at that eventful moment; and, indeed, all dusty as he was in his plain clothes he did not look very imposing, or give one an idea that he would contribute much to the means of resistance. However, one of the officers called out, "Boys, three cheers for General Pillow."

What they may do in the North I know not, but certainly the Southern soldiers cannot cheer, and what passes muster for that jubilant sound is a shrill ringing scream with a touch of the Indian war-whoop in it. As these cries ended, a stentorian voice shouted out, "Who cares for General Pillow?" No one answered; whence I inferred the General would not be very popular until the niggers were actually at work in the trenches

We returned to the steamer, headed up stream and proceeded onwards for more than an hour, to another landing, protected by a battery, where we disembarked, the General being received by a guard dressed in uniform, who turned out with some appearance of soldierly smartness. On my remarking the difference to the General, he told me the corps encamped at this point was composed of gentlemen planters, and farmers. They had all clad themselves, and consisted of some of the best families in the State of Tennessee.

As we walked down the gangway to the shore, the band on the upper deck struck up, out of compliment to the English element in the party, the unaccustomed strains of "God save the Queen;" and I am not quite sure that the loyalty which induced me to stand in the sun, with uncovered head, till the musicians were good enough to desist, was appreciated. Certainly a gentleman, who asked me why I did so, looked very incredulous, and said "That he could understand it if it had been in a church; but that he would not broil his skull in the sun, not if General Washington was standing just before him." The General gave orders to exercise the battery at this point, and a working party was told off to firing drill. 'Twas fully six minutes between the giving of the orders and the first gun being ready.

On the word "fire" being given, the gunner pulled the lanyard, but the tube did not explode; a second tube was inserted, but a strong jerk pulled it out without exploding; a third time one of the General's fuses was applied, which gave way to the pull, and was broken in two; a fourth time was more successful—the gun exploded, and the shot fell short and under the mark—in fact, nothing could be worse than the artillery practice which I saw here, and a fleet of vessels coming down the river might, in the present state of the garrisons, escape unhurt.

There are no disparts, tangents, or elevating screws to the guns, which are laid by eye and wooden chocks. I could see no shells in the battery, but was told there were some in the magazine.

Altogether, though Randolph's Point and Fort Pillow afford strong positions, in the present state of the service, and equipment of guns and works, gunboats could run past them without serious loss, and, as the river falls, the fire of the batteries will be even less effective.

On returning to the boats the band struck up "The Marseillaise" and "Dixie's Land." There are two explanations of the word Dixie—one is that it is the general term for the Slave States, which are, of course, south of Mason and Dixon's line; another, that a planter named Dixie, died long ago, to the intense grief of his animated property. Whether they were ill-treated after he died, and thus had reason to regret his loss, or that they had merely a longing in the abstract after Heaven, no fact known to me can determine; but certain it is that they long much after Dixie, in the land to which his spirit was supposed by them to have departed, and console themselves in their sorrow by clamorous wishes to follow their master, where probably the revered spirit would be much surprised to find himself in their company. The song is the work of the negro melodists of New York.

In the afternoon we returned to Memphis. Here I was obliged to cut short my Southern tour, though I would willingly have stayed, to have seen the most remarkable social and political changes the world has probably ever witnessed. The necessity of my position obliged me to return northwards—unless I could write, there was no use in my being on the spot at all. By this time the Federal fleets have succeeded in closing the ports, if not effectually, so far as to render the carriage of letters precarious, and the route must be at best devious and uncertain.

Mr. Jefferson Davis was, I was assured, prepared to give me every facility at Richmond to enable me to know and to see all that was most interesting in the military and political action of the New Confederacy; but of what use could this knowledge be if I could not communicate it to the journal I served?

I had left the North when it was suffering from a political paralysis, and was in a state of coma in which it appeared conscious of the coming convulsion, but unable to avert it. The sole sign of life in the body corporate was some feeble twitching of the limbs at Washington, when the district militia were called out, whilst Mr. Seward descanted on the merits of the Inaugural, and believed that the anger of the South was a short madness, which would be cured by a mild application of philosophical essays.

The politicians, who were urging in the most forcible manner the complete vindication of the rights of the Union, were engaged, when I left them, arguing that the Union had no rights at all as opposed to those of the States. Men who had heard with nods of approval of the ordinance of secession passed by State after State were now shrieking out, "Slay the traitors!"

The printed rags which had been deriding the President as the great "rail splitter," and his Cabinet as a collection of ignoble fanatics, were now heading the popular rush, and calling out to the country to support Mr. Lincoln and his Ministry, and were menacing with war the foreign States which dared to stand neutral in the quarrel. The declaration of Lord John Russell that the Southern Confederacy should have limited belligerent rights had at first created a thrill of exultation in the South, because the politicians believed that in this concession was contained the principle of recognition; while it had stung to fury the people of the North, to whom it seemed the first warning of the coming disunion.

Much, therefore, as I desired to go to Richmond, where I was urged to repair by many considerations, and by the earnest appeals of those around me, I felt it would be impossible, notwithstanding the interest attached to the proceedings there, to perform my duties in a place cut off from all communication with the outer world; and so I decided to proceed to Chicago, and thence to Washington, where the Federals had assembled a large army, with the purpose of marching upon Richmond, in obedience to the cry of nearly every journal of influence in the Northern cities.

My resolution was mainly formed in consequence of the intelligence which was communicated to me at Memphis, and I told General Pillow that I would continue my journey to Cairo, in order to get within the Federal lines. As the river was blockaded, the only means of doing so was to proceed by rail to Columbus, and thence to take a steamer to the Federal position; and so, whilst the General was continuing his inspection, I rode to the telegraph office, in one of the camps, to order my luggage to be prepared for departure as soon as I arrived, and thence went on board the steamer, where I sat down in the cabin to write my last despatch from Dixie.

So far I had certainly no reason to agree with Mr. Seward in thinking this rebellion was the result of a localised energetic action on the part of a fierce minority in the seceding States, and that there was in each a large, if inert, mass opposed to secession, which would rally round the Stars and Stripes the instant they were displayed in their sight. On the contrary, I met everywhere with but one feeling, with exceptions which prove its unanimity and its force. To a man the people went with their States, and had but one battle-cry, "States' rights, and death to those who make war against them!"

Day after day I had seen this feeling intensified by the accounts which came from the North of a fixed determination to maintain the war and day after day, I am bound to add, the impression on my mind was strengthened tha "States' rights" meant protection to slavery, extension of slave territory, and free-trade in slave produce with the outer world; nor was it any argument against the conclusion that the popular passion gave vent to the most vehement outcries against Yankees, abolitionists, German mercenaries, and modern invasion. I was fully satisfied in my mind also that the population of the South, who had taken up arms, were so convinced of the righteousness of their cause, and so competent to vindicate it, that they would fight with the utmost energy and valour in its defence and successful establishment.

The saloon in which I was sitting afforded abundant evidence of the vigour with which the South are entering upon the contest. Men of every variety and condition of life had taken up arms against the cursed Yankee and the black Republican—there was not a man there who would not have given his life for the rare pleasure of striking Mr. Lincoln's head off his shoulders and yet to a cold European the scene was almost ludicrous.

Along the covered deck lay tall Tennesseans, asleep, whose plumed felt hats were generally the only indications of their martial calling, for few indeed had any other signs of uniform, except th rare volunteers, who wore stripes of red and yellow cloth on their trousers, or leaden buttons, and discoloured worsted braid and facings on their jackets. The afterpart of the saloon deck was appropriated to General Pillow, his staff, and officers. The approach to it was guarded by a sentry, a tall, good-looking young fellow, in a grey flannel shirt, grey trousers, fastened with a belt and a brass buckle, inscribed U.S., which came from some plundered Federal arsenal, and a black wide-awake hat, decorated with a green plume. His Enfield rifle lay beside him on the deck, and, with great interest expressed on his face, he leant forward in his rocking-chair to watch the varying features of a party squatted on the floor, who were employed in the national game of "Euchre." As he raised his eyes to examine the condition of the cigar he was smoking, he caught sight of me, and by the simple expedient of holding his leg across my chest, and calling out, "Hallo! where are you going to?" brought me to a standstill—whilst his captain, who was one of the happy euchreists, exclaimed, "Now, Sam, you let nobody go in there."

I was obliged to explain who I was, whereupon the sentry started to his feet, and said, "Oh! indeed, you are Russell that's been in that war with the Rooshians. Well, I'm very much pleased to know you. I shall be off sentry in a few minutes; I'll just ask you to tell me something about that fighting." He held out his hand, and shook mine warmly as he spoke. There was not the smallest intention to offend in his manner; but, sitting down again, he nodded to the captain, and said, "It's all right; it's Pillow's friend—that's Russell of the London *Times*."

The game of euchre was continued—and indeed it had been perhaps all night—for my last recollection on looking out of my cabin was a number of people playing cards on the floor and on the tables all down the saloon, and of shouts of "Eukerr!" "Ten dollars, you don't!" "I'll lay twenty on this!" and so on; and with breakfast the sport seemed to be fully revived.

There would have been much more animation in the game, no doubt, had the bar on board the Ingomar been opened; but the intelligent gentleman who presided inside had been restricted by General Pillow in his avocations; and when numerous thirsty souls from the camps came on board, with dry tongues and husky voices, and asked for "mint juleps," "brandy smashes," or "whisky cocktails," he seemed to take a saturnine pleasure by saying, "The General won't allow no spirit on board, but I can give you a nice drink of Pillow's own iced Missisippi water," an announcement which generally caused infinite disgust and some unhandsome wishes respecting the General's future happiness.

By and bye, a number of sick men were brought down on litters, and placed here and there along the deck. As there was a considerable misunderstanding between the civilian and military doctors, it appeared to be understood that the best way of arranging it was not to attend to the sick at all, and unfortunate men suffering from fever and dysentery were left to roll and groan, and lie on their stretchers, without a soul to help them. I had a medicine chest on board, and I ventured to use the lessons of my experience in such matters, administered my quinine, James's Powder, calomel, and opium, *secundum meam artem*, and nothing could be more grateful than the poor fellows were for the smallest mark of attention. "Stranger, remember, if I die," gasped one great fellow, attenuated to a skeleton by dysentery, "that I am Robert Tallon, of Tishimingo county, and that I died for States' rights; see, now, they put that in the papers, won't you? Robert Tallon died for States' rights," and so he turned round on his blanket.

Presently the General came on board, and the Ingomar proceeded on her way back to Memphis. General Clarke, to whom I mentioned the great neglect from which the soldiers were suffering, told me he was afraid the men had no medical attendance in camp. All the doctors, in fact, wanted to fight, and as they were educated men, and generally connected with respectable families, or had political influence in the State, they aspired to be colonels at the very least, and to wield the sword instead of the scalpel.

Next to the medical department, the commissariat and transport were most deficient; but by constant courts-martial, stoppages of pay, and severe sentences, he hoped these evils would be eventually somewhat mitigated. As one who had received a regular military education, General Clarke was probably shocked by volunteer irregularities; and in such matters as guard-mounting, reliefs, patrols, and picket-duties, he declared that they were enough to break one's heart; but I was astonished to hear from him that the Germans were by far the worst of the five thousand troops under his command, of whom they formed more than a fifth.

While we were conversing, the captain of the steamer invited us to come up into his cabin on the upper deck; and as railway conductors, steamboat captains, bar-keepers, hotel-clerks, and telegraph officers are among the natural aristocracy of the land, we could not disobey the invitation, which led to the consumption of some of the captain's private stores, and many warm professions of political faith.

The captain told me it was rough work aboard sometimes with "sports" and chaps of that kind; but "God bless you," said he, "the river now is not what it used to be a few years ago, when we'd have three or four difficulties of an afternoon, and may-be now and then a regular free fight all up and down the decks, that would last a couple of hours, so that when we came to a town we would have to send for all the doctors twenty miles round, and may-be some of them would die in spite of that. It was the rowdies used to get these fights up; but we've put them pretty well down. The citizens have hunted them out, and they's gone away west." "Well, then, captain, one's life was not very safe on board sometimes." "Safe! Lord bless you!" said the captain; "if you did not meddle, just as safe as you are now, if the boiler don't collapse. You must, in course, know how to handle your weepins, and be pretty spry in taking your own part." "Ho, you Bill!" to his coloured servant, "open that clothes-press." "Now, here," he continued, "is how I travel; so that I am always easy in my mind in case of trouble on board." Putting his hand under the pillow of the bed close beside him, he pulled out a formidable-looking double-barrelled pistol at half-cock, with the caps upon it. "That's as purty a pistol as Derringer ever made. I've got the brace of them —here's the other;" and with that he whipped out pistol No. 2, in an equal state of forwardness, from a little shelf over his bed; and then going over to the clothes-press, he said, "Here's a real old Kentuck, one of the old sort, as light on the trigger as gossamer, and sure as death—Why, law bless me, a child would cut a turkey's head off with it at a hundred yards." This was a huge lump of iron, about five feet long, with a small hole bored down the centre, fitted in a coarse German-fashioned stock. "But," continued he, "this is my main dependence; here is a regular beauty, a first-rate, with ball or buck-shot, or whatever you like—made in London; I gave two hundred dollars for it; and it is so short and handy and straight shooting, I'd just as soon part with my life as let it go to anybody," and, with a glow of pride in his face, the captain handed round again a very short double-barrelled gun, of some eleven or twelve bore, with back action locks, and an audacious "Joseph Manton, London," stamped on the plate. The manner of the man was perfectly simple and *bonâ fide;* very much as if Inspector Podger were revealing to a simpleton the mode by which the London police managed refractory characters in the station-house.

From such matters as these I was diverted by the more serious subject of the attitude taken by England in this quarrel. The concession of belligerent rights was, I found, misunderstood, and was considered as an admission, that the Southern States had established their independence before they had done more than declare their intention to fight for it.

It is not within my power to determine whether the North is as unfair to Great Britain as the South; but I fear the history of the people, and the tendency of their institutions, are adverse to any hope of fair-play and justice to the old country. And yet it is the only power in Europe for the good opinion of which they really seem to care. Let any French, Austrian, or Russian journal write what it pleases of the United States, it is received with indifferent criticism or callous head-shaking. But let a London paper speak, and the whole American press is delighted or furious.

The political sentiment quite overrides all other feelings; and it is the only symptom statesmen should care about, as it guides the policy of the country. If a man can put faith in the influence for peace of common interests, of common origin, common intentions, with the spectacle of this incipient war before his eyes, he must be incapable of appreciating the consequences which follow from man being an animal. A war between England and the United States would be unnatural; but it would not be nearly so unnatural now as it was when it was actually waged in 1776 between people who were barely separated from each other by a single generation; or in 1812-14, when the foreign immigration had done comparatively little to dilute the Anglo-Saxon blood. The Norman of Hampshire and Sussex did not care much for the ties of consanguinity and race when he followed his lord in fee to ravage Guienne or Brittany.

The general result of my intercourse with Americans is to produce the notion that they consider Great Britain in a state of corruption and decay, and eagerly seek to exalt France at her expense. Their language is the sole link between England and the United States, and it only binds the England of 1770 to the America of 1860.

There is scarcely an American on either side of Mason and Dixon's line who does not religiously believe that the colonies, alone and single-handed, encountered the whole undivided force of Great Britain in the Revolution and defeated it. I mean, of course, the vast mass of the people; and I do not think there is an orator or a writer who would venture to tell them the truth on the subject. Again, they firmly believe that their petty frigate engagements established as complete a naval ascendancy over Great Britain as the latter obtained by her great encounters with the fleets of France and Spain. Their reverses, defeats, and headlong routs in the first war, their reverses in the second, are covered over by a huge Buncombe plaster, made up of Bunker's Hill, Plattsburg, Baltimore, and New Orleans.

Their delusions are increased and solidified by the extraordinary text-books of so-called history, and by the feasts, and festivals, and celebrations of their every-day political life, in all of which we pass through imaginary Caudine Forks; and they entertain towards the old country at best very much the feeling which a high-spirited young man would feel towards the guardian who, when he had come of age, and was free from all control, sought to restrain the passions of his early life.

Now I could not refuse to believe that in New Orleans, Montgomery, Mobile, Jackson, and Memphis, there is a reckless and violent condition of society, unfavourable to civilization, and but little hopeful for the future. The most absolute and despotic rule, under which a man's life and property are safe, is better than the largest measure of democratic freedom, which deprives the freeman of any security for either. The state of legal protection for the most serious interests of man, considered as a civilized and social creature, which prevails in America, could not be tolerated for an instant, and would generate a revolution in the worst governed country in Europe. I would much sooner, as the accidental victim of a generally disorganized police, be plundered by a chance diligence robber in Mexico, or have a fair fight with a Greek Klepht, suffer from Italian banditti, or be garotted by a London ticket-of-leave man, than be bowie-knifed or revolvered in consequence of a political or personal difference with a man, who is certain not in the least degree to suffer from an accidental success in his argument.

On our return to the hotel I dined with the General and his staff at the public table, where there was a large assemblage of military men, Southern ladies, their families, and contractors. This latter race has risen up as if by magic, to meet the wants of the new Confederacy; and it is significant to measure the amount of the dependence on Northern manufacturers by the advertisements in Southern journals indicating the creation of new branches of workmanship, mechanical science, and manufacturing skill. Hitherto they have been dependent on the North for the very necessaries of their industrial life. These States were so intent on gathering in money for their produce, expending it luxuriously, and paying it out for Northern labor, that they found themselves suddenly in the condition of a child brought up by hand, whose nurse and mother have left it on the steps of the poor-house. But they have certainly essayed to remedy the evil and are endeavoring to make steam-engines, gunpowder, lamps, clothes, boots, railway carriages, steel springs, glass, and all the smaller articles for which even Southern households find a necessity.

The peculiar character of this contest develops itself in a manner almost incomprehensible to a stranger who has been accustomed to regard the United States as a nation. Here is General Pillow, for example, in the State of Tennessee, commanding the forces of the State, which, in effect, belongs to the Southern Confederacy; but he tells me that he cannot venture to move across a certain geographical line, dividing Tennessee from Kentucky, because the State of Kentucky, in the exercise of its sovereign powers and rights, which the Southern States are bound specially to respect, in virtue of their championship of States' rights, has, like the United Kingdom of Great Britain and Ireland, declared it will be neutral in the struggle; and Beriah Magoffin, Governor of the aforesaid State, has warned off Federal and Confederate troops from his territory.

General Pillow is particularly indignant with the cowardice of the well-known Secessionists of Kentucky; but I think he is rather more annoyed by the accumulation of Federal troops at Cairo, and their recent expedition to Columbus on the Kentucky shore, a little below them, where they seized a Confederate flag.

CHAPTER XXXIX.

Heavy Bill—Railway travelling—Introductions—Assassinations—Tennessee—"Corinth"—"Troy"—"Humbolt"—"The Confederate Camp"—Return Northwards—Columbus—Cairo—The Slavery Question—Prospects of the War—Coarse Journalism.

June 19*th*.—It is probable the landlord of the Gayoso House was a strong Secessionist, and resolved, therefore, to make the most out of a neutral customer, like myself—certainly Herodotus would have been astonished if he were called upon to pay the little bill which was presented to me in the modern Memphis; and had the old Egyptian hostelries been conducted on the same principles as those of the Tennessean Memphis, the "Father of History" would have had to sell off a good many editions in order to pay his way. I had to rise at three o'clock A.M., to reach the train, which started before five. The omnibus which took us to the station was literally nave deep in dust; and of all the bad roads and dusty streets I have yet seen in the New World, where both prevail, North and South, those of Memphis are the worst. Indeed, as the citizen, of Hibernian birth, who presided over the luggage of the passengers on the roof, declared, "The streets are paved with waves of mud, only the mud is all dust when it's fine weather."

By the time I had arrived at the station my clothes were covered with a fine alluvial deposit in a state of powder; the platform was crowded with volunteers moving off for the wars, and I was obliged to take my place in a carriage full of Confederate officers and soldiers who had a large supply of whisky, which at that early hour they were consuming as a prophylactic against the influence of the morning dews, which hereabouts are of such a deadly character that, to be quite safe from their influence, it appears to be necessary, judging from the examples of my companions, to get as nearly drunk as possible. Whisky, by-the-by, is also a sovereign specific against the bites of rattlesnakes. All the dews of the Mississippi and the rattlesnakes of the prairie might have spent their force or venom in vain on my companions before we had got as far as Union City.

I was evidently regarded with considerable suspicion by my fellow passengers, when they heard I was going to Cairo, until the conductor obligingly informed them who I was, whereupon I was much entreated to fortify myself against the dews and rattlesnakes, and received many offers of service and kindness.

Whatever may be the normal comforts of American railway cars, they are certainly most unpleasant conveyances when the war spirit is abroad, and the heat of the day, which was excessive, did not contribute to diminish the annoyance of foul air—the odour of whisky, tobacco, and the like, combined with innumerable flies. At Humbolt, which is eighty-two miles away, there was a change of cars, and an opportunity of obtaining some refreshment,—the station was crowded by great numbers of men and women dressed in their best, who were making holiday in order to visit Union City, forty-six miles distant, where a force of Tennesseean and Mississippi regiments are encamped. The ladies boldly advanced into carriages which were quite full, and as they looked quite prepared to sit down on the occupants of the seats if they did not move, and to destroy them with all-absorbing articles of feminine warfare, either offensive or aggressive, and crush them with iron-bound crinolines, they soon drove us out into the broiling sun.

Whilst I was on the platform I underwent the usual process of American introduction, not, I fear, very good-humouredly. A gentleman whom you never saw before in your life, walks up to you and says, "I am happy to see you among us, sir," and if he finds a hand wandering about, he shakes it cordially. "My name is Jones, sir, Judge Jones of Pumpkin County. Any information about this place or State that I can give is quite at your service." This is all very civil and well meant of Jones, but before you have made up your mind what to say, or on what matter to test the worth of his proffered information, he darts off and seizes one of the group who have been watching Jones's advance, and comes forward with a tall man, like himself, busily engaged with a piece of tobacco. "Colonel, let me introduce you to my friend, Mr. Russell. This, sir, is one of our leading citizens, Colonel Knags." Whereupon the Colonel shakes hands, uses nearly the same formula as Judge Jones, immediately returns to his friends, and cuts in before Jones is back with other friends, whom he is hurrying up the platform, introduces General Cassius Mudd and Dr. Ordlando Bellows, who go through the same ceremony, and as each man has a circle of his own, my acquaintance becomes prodigiously extended, and my hand considerably tortured in the space of a few minutes; finally I am introduced to the driver of the engine and the stoker, but they proved to be acquaintances not at all to be despised, for they gave me a seat on the engine, which was really a boon considering that the train was crowded beyond endurance, and in a state of internal nastiness scarcely conceivable.

When I had got up on the engine a gentleman clambered after me in order to have a little conversation, and he turned out to be an intelligent and clever man well acquainted with the people and the country. I had been much impressed by the account in the Memphis papers of the lawlessness and crime which seemed to prevail in the State of Mississippi, and of the brutal shootings and stabbings which disgraced it and other Southern States. He admitted it was true, but could not see any remedy. "Why not?" "Well, sir, the rowdies have rushed in on us, and we can't master them; they are too strong for the respectable people." "Then you admit the law is nearly powerless?" "Well, you see, sir, these men have got hold of the people who ought to administer the law, and when they fail to do so they are so powerful by reason of their numbers, and so reckless, they have things their own way."

"In effect then, you are living under a reign of terror, and the rule of a ruffian mob?" "It's not quite so bad as that, perhaps, for the respectable people are not much affected by it, and most of the crimes of which you speak are committed by these bad classes in their own section; but it is disgraceful to have such a state of things, and when this war is over, and we have started the Confederacy all fair, we'll put the whole thing down. We are quite determined to take the law into our own hands, and the first remedy for the condition of affairs which we all lament, will be to confine the suffrage to native-born

Americans, and to get rid of the infamous scoundrelly foreigners, who now overrule us in our country." "But are not many regiments of Irish and Germans now fighting for you? And will these foreigners who have taken up arms in your cause be content to receive as the result of their success an inferior position, politically, to that which they now hold?" "Well, sir, they must; we are bound to go through with this thing if we would save society." I had so often heard a similar determination expressed by men belonging to the thinking classes in the South that I am bound to believe the project is entertained by many of those engaged in this great revolt—one principle of which, indeed, may be considered hostility to universal suffrage, combining with it, of course, the limitation of the immigrant vote.

The portion of Tennessee through which the rail runs is exceedingly uninteresting, and looks unhealthy, the clearings occur at long intervals in the forest, and the unwholesome population, who came out of their low shanties, situated amidst blackened stumps of trees or fields of Indian corn, did not seem prosperous or comfortable. The twists and curves of the rail, through canebrakes and swamps, exceeded in that respect any line I have ever travelled on; but the vertical irregularities of the rail were still greater, and the engine bounded as if it were at sea.

The names of the stations show that a savant has been rambling about the district. Here is Corinth, which consists of a wooden grog-shop and three log shanties; the acropolis is represented by a grocery store, of which the proprietors, no doubt, have gone to the wars, as their names were suspiciously Milesian, and the doors and windows were fastened; but occasionally the names of the stations on the railway boards represented towns and villages, hidden in the wood some distance away, and Mummius might have something to ruin if he marched off the track but not otherwise.

The city of Troy was still simpler in architecture than the Grecian capitol. The Dardanian towers were represented by a timber-house, in the verandah of which the American Helen was seated, in the shape of an old woman smoking a pipe, and she certainly could have set the Palace of Priam on fire much more readily than her prototype. Four sheds, three log huts, a saw-mill, about twenty negroes sitting on a wood-pile, and looking at the train, constituted the rest of the place, which was certainly too new for one to say, *Troja fuit*, whilst the general "fixings" would scarcely authorize us to say with any confidence, *Troja fuerit*.

The train from Troy passed through a cypress swamp, over which the engine rattled, and hopped at a perilous rate along high trestle work, till forty-six miles from Humbolt we came to Union City, which was apparently formed by aggregate meetings of discontented shavings that had travelled out of the forest hard by. But a little beyond it was the Confederate camp, which so many citizens and citizenesses had come out into the wilderness to see; and a general descent was made upon the place whilst the volunteers came swarming out of their tents to meet their friends. It was interesting to observe the affectionate greetings between the young soldiers, mothers, wives, and sweethearts, and as a display of the force and earnestness of the Southern people—the camp itself containing thousands of men, many of whom were members of the first families in the State—was specially significant.

There is no appearance of military order or discipline about the camps, though they were guarded by sentries and cannon, and implements of war and soldiers' accoutrements were abundant. Some of the sentinels carried their firelocks under their arms like umbrellas, others carried the butt over the shoulder and the muzzle downwards, and one for his greater ease had stuck the bayonet of his firelock into the ground, and was leaning his elbow on the stock with his chin on his hand, whilst Sybarites less ingenious, had simply deposited their muskets against the trees, and were lying down reading newspapers. Their arms and uniforms were of different descriptions —sporting rifles, fowling pieces, flint muskets, smooth bores, long and short barrels, new Enfields, and the like; but the men, nevertheless, were undoubtedly material for excellent soldiers. There were some few boys, too young to carry arms, although the zeal and ardour of such lads cannot but have a good effect, if they behave well in action.

The great attraction of this train lay in a vast supply of stores, with which several large vans were closely packed, and for fully two hours the train was delayed, whilst hampers of wine, spirits, vegetables, fruit, meat, groceries, and all the various articles acceptable to soldiers living under canvas were disgorged on the platform, and carried away by the expectant military.

I was pleased to observe the perfect confidence that was felt in the honesty of the men. The railway servants simply deposited each article as it came out on the platform—the men came up, read the address, and carried it away, or left it, as the case might be; and only in one instance did I see a scramble, which was certainly quite justifiable, for in handing out a large basket the bottom gave way, and out tumbled onions, apples, and potatoes among the soldiery, who stuffed their pockets and haversacks with the unexpected bounty. One young fellow, who was handed a large wicker-covered jar from the van, having shaken it, and gratified his ear by the pleasant jingle inside, retired to the roadside, drew the cork, and, raising it slowly to his mouth, proceeded to take a good pull at the contents, to the envy of his comrades; but the pleasant expression upon his face rapidly vanished, and spurting out the fluid with a hideous grimace, he exclaimed, "D——; why, if the old woman has not gone and sent me a gallon of syrup." The matter was evidently considered too serious to joke about, for not a soul in the crowd even smiled; but they walked away from the man, who, putting down the jar, seemed in doubt as to whether he would take it away or not.

Numerous were the invitations to stop, which I received from the officers. "Why not stay with us, sir; what can a gentleman want to go among black Republicans and Yankees for?" It is quite obvious that my return to the Northern States is regarded with some suspicion; but I am bound to say that my explanation of the necessity of the step was always well received, and satisfied my Southern friends that I had no alternative. A special correspondent, whose letters cannot get out of the country in which he is engaged, can scarcely fulfil the purpose of his mission; and I used to point out, good-humouredly, to these gentlemen that until they had either opened the communication with the North, or had broken the blockade, and established steam communication with Europe, I must seek my base of operations elsewhere.

At last we started from Union City; and there came into the car, among other soldiers who were going out to Columbus, a fine specimen of the wild filibustering population of the South, which furnish many recruits to the ranks of the Confederate army—a tall, brawny-shouldered, brown-faced, black-bearded, hairy-handed man, with a hunter's eye, and rather a Jewish face, full of life, energy, and daring. I easily got into conversation with him, as my companion happened to be a freemason, and he told us he had been a planter in Mississippi, and once owned 110 negroes, worth at least some 20,000*l.*; but, as he said himself, "I was always patrioting it about;" and so he went off, first with Lopez to Cuba, was wounded and taken prisoner by the Spaniards, but had the good fortune to be saved from the execution which was inflicted on the ringleaders of the expedition. When he came back he found his plantation all the worse, and a decrease amongst his negroes; but his love of adventure and filibustering was stronger than his prudence or desire of gain. He took up with Walker, "the grey-eyed man of destiny," and accompanied him in his strange career till his leader received the *coup de grace* in the final raid upon Nicaragua.

Again he was taken prisoner, and would have been put to death by the Nicaraguans, but for the intervention of Captain Aldham. "I don't bear any love to the Britishers," said he, "but I'm bound to say, as so many charges have been made against Captain Aldham, that he behaved like a gentleman, and if I had been at New Orleans when them cussed cowardly blackguards ill-used him, I'd have left my mark so deep on a few of them, that their clothes would not cover them long." He told us that at present he had only five negroes left, "but I'm not going to let the black republicans lay hold of them, and I'm just going to stand up for States' rights as long as I can draw a trigger—so snakes and Abolitionists look out." He was so reduced by starvation, ill-treatment, and sickness in Nicaragua, when Captain Aldham procured his release, that he weighed only 110 pounds, but at present he was over 200 pounds, a splendid *bête fauve*, and without wishing so fine a looking fellow any harm, I could not but help thinking that it must be a benefit to American society to get rid of a considerable number of the class of which he is a representative man. And there is every probability that they will have a full opportunity of doing so.

On the arrival of the train at Columbus, twenty-five miles from Union City, my friend got out, and a good number of men in uniform joined him, which led me to conclude that they had some more serious object than a mere pleasure trip to the very uninteresting looking city on the banks of the Mississippi, which is asserted to be neutral territory, as it belongs to the sovereign state of Kentucky. I heard, accidentally, as I came in the train, that a party of Federal soldiers from the camp at Cairo, up the river, had recently descended to Columbus and torn down a secession flag which had been hoisted on the river's bank, to the great indignation of many of the inhabitants.

In those border states the coming war promises to produce the greatest misery; they will be the scenes of hostile operations; the population is divided in sentiment; the greatest efforts will be made by each side to gain the ascendancy in the state, and to crush the opposite faction, and it is not possible to believe that Kentucky can maintain a neutral position, or that either Federal or Confederates will pay the smallest regard to the proclamation of Governor McGoffin, and to his empty menaces.

At Columbus the steamer was waiting to convey us up to Cairo, and I congratulated myself on the good fortune of arriving in time for the last opportunity that will be afforded of proceeding northward by this route. General Pillow on the one hand, and General Prentiss on the other, have resolved to blockade the Mississippi, and as the facilities for Confederates going up to Columbus and obtaining information of what is happening in the Federal camps cannot readily be checked, the general in command of the port to which I am bound has intimated that the steamers must cease running. It was late in the day when we entered once more on the father of waters, which is here just as broad, as muddy, as deep, and as wooded as it is at Bâton Rouge, or Vicksburg.

Columbus is situated on an elevated spur or elbow of land projecting into the river, and has, in commercial faith, one of those futures which have so many rallying points down the centre of the great river. The steamer which lay at the wharf, or rather the wooden piles in the bank which afforded a resting-place for the gangway, carried no flag, and on board presented traces of better days, a list of refreshments no longer attainable, and a bill of fare utterly fanciful. About twenty passengers came on board, most of whom had a distracted air, as if they were doubtful of their journey. The captain was surly, the office-keeper petulant, the crew morose, and, perhaps, only one man on board, a stout Englishman, who was purser or chief of the victualling department, seemed at all inclined to be communicative. At dinner he asked me whether I thought there would be a fight, but as I was oscillating between one extreme and the other, I considered it right to conceal my opinion even from the steward of the Mississippi boat; and, as it happened, the expression of it would not have been of much consequence one way or the other, for it turned out that our friend was of very stern stuff. "This war," he said, "is all about niggers; I've been sixteen years in the country, and I never met one of them yet was fit to be anything but a slave; I know the two sections well, and I tell you, sir, the North can't whip the South, let them do their best; they may ruin the country, but they'll do no good."

There were men on board who had expressed the strongest secession sentiments in the train, but who now sat and listened and acquiesced in the opinions of Northern men, and by the time Cairo was in sight, they, no doubt, would have taken the oath of allegiance which every doubtful person is required to utter before he is allowed to go beyond the military post.

In about two hours or so the captain pointed

out to me a tall building and some sheds, which seemed to arise out of a wide reach in the river, "that's Cairey," said he, "where the Unionists have their camp," and very soon the stars and stripes were visible, waving from a lofty staff, at the angle of low land formed by the junction of the Mississippi and Ohio.

For two months I had seen only the rival stars and bars, with the exception of the rival banner floating from the ships and the fort at Pickens. One of the passengers told me that the place was supposed to be described by Mr. Dickens, in "Martin Chuzzlewit," and as the steamer approached the desolate embankment, which seemed the only barrier between the low land on which the so-called city was built, and the waters of the great river rising above it, it certainly became impossible to believe that sane men, even as speculators, could have fixed upon such a spot as the possible site of a great city,—an emporium of trade and commerce. A more desolate woebegone looking place, now that all trade and commerce had ceased, cannot be conceived; but as the southern terminus of the central Illinois railway, it displayed a very different scene before the war broke out.

With the exception of the large hotel, which rises far above the levée of the river, the public edifices are represented by a church and spire, and the rest of the town by a line of shanties and small houses, the rooms and upper stories of which are just visible above the embankment. The general impression effected by the place was decidedly like that which the Isle of Dogs produces on a despondent foreigner as he approaches London by the river on a drizzly day in November. The stream, formed by the united efforts of the Mississippi and the Ohio, did not appear to gain much breadth, and each of the confluents looked as large as its product with the other. Three steamers lay alongside the wooden wharves projecting from the embankment, which was also lined by some flat-boats. Sentries paraded the gangways as the steamer made fast along the shore, but no inquiry was directed to any of the passengers, and I walked up the levee and proceeded straight to the hotel, which put me very much in mind of an effort made by speculating proprietors to create a watering-place on some lifeless beach. In the hall there were a number of officers in United States' uniforms, and the lower part of the hotel was, apparently, occupied as a military bureau; finally, I was shoved into a small dungeon, with a window opening out on the angle formed by the two rivers, which was lined with sheds and huts and terminated by a battery.

These camps are such novelties in the country, and there is such romance in the mere fact of a man living in a tent, that people come far and wide to see their friends under such extraordinary circumstances, and the hotel at Cairo was crowded by men and women who had come from all parts of Illinois to visit their acquaintances and relations belonging to the state troops encamped at this important point. The *salle à manger*, a long and lofty room on the ground floor, which I visited at supper time, was almost untenable by reason of heat and flies; nor did I find that the free negroes, who acted as attendants, possessed any advantages over their enslaved brethren a few miles lower down the river; though their freedom was obvious enough in their demeanour and manners.

I was introduced to General Prentiss, an agreeable person, without anything about him to indicate the soldier. He gave me a number of newspapers, the articles in which were principally occupied with a discussion of Lord John Russell's speech on American affairs. Much as the South found fault with the British minister for the views he had expressed, the North appears much more indignant, and denounces in the press what the journalists are pleased to call "the hostility of the Foreign Minister to the United States." It admitted, however, that the extreme irritation caused by admitting the Southern States to exercise limited belligerent rights was not quite justifiable. Soon after nightfall I retired to my room and battled with mosquitoes till I sank into sleep and exhaustion, and abandoned myself to their mercies; perhaps, after all, there were not more than a hundred or so, and their united efforts could not absorb as much blood as would be taken out by one leech, but then their horrible acrimony, which leaves a wreck behind in the place where they have banqueted, inspires the utmost indignation, and appears to be an indefensible prolongation of the outrage of the original bite.

June 20th.—When I awoke this morning, and, gazing out of my little window on the regiments parading on the level below me, after an arduous struggle to obtain cold water for a bath, sat down to consider what I had seen within the last two months, and to arrive at some general results from the retrospect, I own that after much thought my mind was reduced to a hazy analysis of the abstract principles of right and wrong, in which it failed to come to any very definite conclusion: the space of a very few miles has completely altered the phases of thought and the forms of language.

I am living among "abolitionists, cut-throats, Lincolnite mercenaries, foreign invaders, assassins, and plundering Dutchmen." Such, at least, the men of Columbus tell me the garrison at Cairo consists of. Down below me are "rebels, conspirators, robbers, slave breeders, wretches bent upon destroying the most perfect government on the face of the earth, in order to perpetuate an accursed system, by which human beings are held in bondage and immortal souls consigned to perdition."

On the whole, the impression left upon my mind by what I had seen in slave states is unfavourable to the institution of slavery, both as regards its effects on the slave and its influence on the master. But my examination was necessarily superficial and hasty. I have reason to believe that the more deeply the institution is probed, the more clearly will its unsoundness and its radical evils be discerned. The constant appeals made to the physical comforts of the slaves, and their supposed contentment, have little or no effect on any person who acts up to a higher standard of human happiness than that which is applied to swine or the beasts of the fields. "See how fat my pigs are."

The arguments founded on a comparison of the condition of the slave population with the pauperised inhabitants of European states are utterly fallacious, inasmuch as in one point, which is the most important by far, there can be no comparison at all. In effect, slavery can only be justified in the abstract on the grounds which slavery advocates decline to take boldly, though they insinuate it now and then, that is, the inferiority of the negro in respect to white men, which removes them from the upper class of human beings and places them in a condition which is as much below the Caucasian standard as the quadrumanous creatures are beneath the negro. Slavery is a curse, with its time of accomplishment not quite at hand—it is a cancer, the ravages of which are covered by fair outward show, and by the apparent health of the sufferer.

The slave states, of course, would not support the Northern for a year if cotton, sugar, and tobacco became suddenly worthless. But, nevertheless, the slave owners would have strong grounds to stand upon if they were content to point to the difficulties in the way of emancipation, and the circumstances under which they received their *damnosa hereditas* from England, which fostered, nay forced, slavery in the legislative hotbeds throughout the colonies. The Englishman may say, "We abolished slavery when we saw its evils." The slave owner replies, "Yes, with you it was possible to decree the extinction—not with us."

Never did a people enter on a war so utterly destitute of any reason for waging it, or of the means of bringing it to a successful termination against internal enemies. The thirteen colonies had a large population of sea-faring and soldiering men, constantly engaged in military expeditions. There was a large infusion, compared with the numbers of men capable of commanding in the field, and their great enemy was separated by a space far greater than the whole circumference of the globe would be in the present time from the scene of operations. Most American officers who took part in the war of 1812–14 are now too old for service, or retired into private life soon after the campaign. The same remark applies to the senior officers who served in Mexico, and the experiences of that campaign could not be of much use to those now in the service, of whom the majority were subalterns, or at most, officers in command of volunteers.

A love of military display is very different indeed from a true soldierly spirit, and at the base of the volunteer system there lies a radical difficulty, which must be overcome before real military efficiency can be expected. In the South the foreign element has contributed largely to swell the ranks with many docile and a few experienced soldiers, the number of the latter predominating in the German levies, and the same remark is, I hear, true of the Northern armies.

The most active member of the staff here is a young Englishman named Binmore, who was a stenographic writer in London, but has now sharpened his pencil into a sword, and when I went into the guard-room this morning I found that three-fourths of the officers, including all who had seen actual service, were foreigners. One, Milotzky, was an Hungarian; another, Waagner, was of the same nationality; a third, Schuttner, was a German; another, Mac something, was a Scotchman; another was an Englishman. One only (Colonel Morgan), who had served in Mexico, was an American. The foreigners, of course, serve in this war as mercenaries; that is, they enter into the conflict to gain something by it, either in pay, in position, or in securing a status for themselves.

The utter absence of any fixed principle determining the side which the foreign nationalities adopt is proved by their going North or South with the state in which they live. On the other hand, the effects of discipline and of the principles of military life on rank and file are shown by the fact that the soldiers of the regular regiments of the United States and the sailors in the navy have to a man adhered to their colours, notwithstanding the examples and inducements of their officers.

After breakfast I went down about the works, which fortify the bank of mud, in the shape of a V, formed by the two rivers—a flèche with a ditch, scarp, and counter-scarp. Some heavy pieces cover the end of the spit at the other side of the Mississippi, at Bird's Point. On the side of Missouri there is a field entrenchment, held by a regiment of Germans, Poles, and Hungarians, about 1000 strong, with two field batteries. The sacred soil of Kentucky, on the other side of the Ohio, is tabooed by Beriah Magoffin, but it is not possible for the belligerents to stand so close face to face without occupying either Columbus or Hickman. The thermometer was at 100° soon after breakfast, and it was not wonderful to find that the men in Camp Defiance, which is the name of the cantonment on the mud between the levees of the Ohio and Mississippi, were suffering from diarrhœa and fever.

In the evening there was a review of three regiments, forming a brigade of some 2800 men, who went through their drill, advancing in columns of company, moving *en echelon*, changing front, deploying into line on the centre company, very creditably. It was curious to see what a start ran through the men during the parade when a gun was fired from the battery close at hand, and how their heads turned towards the river; but the steamer which had appeared round the bend hoisted the private signs by which she was known as a friend, and tranquillity was restored.

I am not sure that most of these troops desire anything but a long residence at a tolerably comfortable station, with plenty of pay and no marching. Cairo, indeed, is not comfortable, the worst barrack that ever asphyxiated the British soldier would be better than the best shed here, and the flies and the mosquitoes are beyond all conception virulent and pestiferous. I would give much to see Cairo in its normal state, but it is my fate to witness the most interesting scenes in the world through a glaze of gunpowder. It would be unfair to say that any marked superiority in dwelling, clothing, or comfort, was visible between the mean white of Cairo or the black chattel a few miles down the river. Brawling, rioting, and a good deal of drunkenness prevailed in the miserable sheds which line the stream, although there was nothing to justify the libels on the garrison of the *Columbus Crescent*, edited by one Colonel L. G. Faxon, of the Tennessee Tigers, with whose writings I was made acquainted by General Prentiss, to whom they appeared to give more annoyance than he was quite wise in showing.

This is a style of journalism which may have its merits, and which certainly is peculiar; I give a few small pieces. "The Irish are for us, and they will knock Bologna sausages out of the Dutch, and we will knock wooden nutmegs out of the Yankees." "The mosquitoes of Cairo have been sucking the lager-bier out of the dirty soldiers there so long, they are bloated and swelled up as large as spring 'possums. An assortment of Columbus mosquitoes went up there the other day to suck some, but as they have not returned, the probability is they went off with *delirium tremens*; in fact, the blood of these Hessians would poison the most degraded tumble bug in creation."

Our editor is particularly angry about the recent seizure of a Confederate flag at Columbus by Colonel Oglesby and a party of Federals from Cairo. Speaking of a flag intended for himself, he says, "Would that its folds had contained 1000 asps to sting 1000 Dutchmen to eternity unshriven." Our friend is certainly a genius. His paper of June the 19th opens with an apology for the non-appearance of the journal for several weeks. "Before leaving," he says, "we engaged the services of a competent editor, and left a printer here to issue the paper regularly. We were detained several weeks beyond our time, the aforesaid printer promised faithfully to perform his duties, but he left the same day we did, and consequently there was no one to get out the paper. We have the charity to suppose that fear and bad whisky had nothing to do with his evacuation of Columbus." Another elegant extract about the flag commences, "When the bow-legged, wooden shoed, sour craut stinking, Bologna sausage eating, hen roost robbing Dutch sons of —— had accomplished the brilliant feat of taking down the Secession flag on the river bank, they were pointed to another flag of the same sort which their guns did not cover, flying gloriously and defiantly, and dared yea! double big black dog-dared, as we used to say at school, to take that flag down—the cowardly pups, the thieving sheep dogs, the sneaking skunks, dare not do so, because their twelve pieces of artillery were not bearing on it." As to the Federal commander at Cairo, Colonel Faxon's sentiments are unambiguous. "The qualifications of this man, Prentiss," he says, "for the command of such a squad of villains and cut-throats are, that he is a miserable hound, a dirty dog, a sociable fellow, a treacherous villain, a notorious thief, a lying blackguard, who has served his regular five years in the Penitentiary and keeps his hide continually full of Cincinnati whisky, which he buys by the barrel in order to save his money—in him are embodied the leprous rascalities of the world, and in this living score, the gallows is cheated of its own. Prentiss wants our scalp; we propose a plan by which he may get that valuable article. Let him select 150 of his best fighting men, or 250 of his lager-bier Dutchmen, we will select 100, then let both parties meet where there will be no interruption at the scalping business, and the longest pole will knock the persimmon. If he does not accept this proposal, he is a coward. We think this a gentlemanly proposition and quite fair and equal to both parties."

CHAPTER XL.

Camp at Cairo—The North and the South in respect to Europe—Political reflections—Mr. Colonel Oglesby—My speech—Northern and Southern soldiers compared—American country-walks—Recklessness of life—Want of cavalry—Emeute in the camp—Defects of army medical department—Horrors of war—Bad discipline.

June 21st.—Verily I would be sooner in the Coptic Cairo, narrow streeted, dark bazaared, many flied, much vexed by donkeys and by overland route passengers, than the horrid tongue of land which licks the muddy margin of the Ohio and the Mississippi. The thermometer at 100° in the shade before noon indicates nowhere else such an amount of heat and suffering, and yet prostrate as I was, it was my fate to argue that England was justified in conceding belligerent rights to the South, and that the attitude of neutrality we had assumed in this terrible quarrel is not in effect an aggression on the United States; and here is a difference to be perceived between the North and the South.

The people of the seceding States, aware in their consciences that they have been most active in their hostility to Great Britain, and whilst they were in power were mainly responsible for the defiant, irritating, and insulting tone commonly used to us by American statesmen, are anxious at the present moment, when so much depends on the action of foreign countries, to remove all unfavourable impressions from our minds by declarations of good will respect, and admiration, not quite compatible with the language of their leaders in times not long gone by. The North, as yet unconscious of the loss of power, and reared in a school of menace and violent assertion of their rights, regarding themselves as the whole of the United States, and animated by their own feeling of commercial and political opposition to Great Britain, maintain the high tone of a people who have never known let or hindrance in their passions, and consider it an outrage that the whole world does not join in active sympathy for a government which in its brief career has contrived to affront every nation in Europe with which it had any dealings.

If the United States have astonished France by their ingratitude, they have certainly accustomed England to their petulance, and one can fancy the satisfaction with which the Austrian Statesmen who remember Mr. Webster's despatch to Mr. Hulsemann, contemplate the present condition of the United States in the face of an insurrection of these sovereign and independent States which the Cabinet at Washington stigmatises as an outbreak of rebels and traitors to the royalty of the Union.

During my short sojourn in this country I have never yet met any person who could show me where the sovereignty of the Union resides. General Prentiss, however, and his Illinois volunteers, are quite ready to fight for it.

In the afternoon the General drove me round the camps in company with Mr. Washburne, Member of Congress, from Illinois, his staff and a party of officers, among whom was Mr. Oglesby, colonel of a regiment of State Volunteers, who struck me by his shrewdness, simple honesty, and zeal.* He told me that he had begun life in the utmost obscurity, but that somehow or other he got into a lawyer's office, and there, by hard drudgery, by

* Since died of wounds received in action.

mother wit and industry, notwithstanding a defective education, he had raised himself not only to independence, but to such a position that 1000 men had gathered at his call and selected one who had never led a company in his life to be their colonel; in fact, he is an excellent orator of the western school, and made good homely, telling speeches to his men.

"I'm not as good as your Frenchmen of the schools of Paris, nor am I equal to the Russian colonels I met at St. Petersburg, who sketched me out how they had beaten you Britishers at Sebastopol," said he; "but I know I can do good straight fighting with my boys when I get a chance. There is a good deal in training, to be sure, but nature tells too. Why I believe I would make a good artillery officer if I was put to it. General, you heard how I laid one of them guns the other day and touched her off with my own hand and sent the ball right into a tree half-a-mile away." The colonel evidently thought he had by that feat proved his fitness for the command of a field battery. One of the German officers who was listening to the lively old man's talk, whispered to me, "Dere is a good many of tese colonels in dis camp."

At each station the officers came out of their tents, shook hands all round, and gave an unfailing invitation to get down and take a drink, and the guns on the General's approach fired salutes, as though it was a time of profoundest peace. Powder was certainly more plentiful than in the Confederate camps, where salutes are not permitted unless by special order on great occasions.

The General remained for some time in the camp of the Chicago light artillery, which was commanded by a fine young Scotchman of the Saxon genus Smith, who told me that the privates of his company represented a million and a half of dollars in property. Their guns, horses, carriages, and accoutrements were all in the most creditable order, and there was an air about the men and about their camp which showed they did not belong to the same class as the better disciplined Hungarians of Milotzky close at hand.

Whilst we were seated in Captain Smith's tent, a number of the privates came forward, and sang the "Star-spangled banner" and a patriotic song, to the air of "God save the Queen," and the rest of the artillerymen, and a number of stragglers from the other camps, assembled and then formed line behind the singers. When the chorus was over there arose a great shout for Washburne, and the honourable Congressman was fain to come forward and make a speech, in which he assured his hearers of a very speedy victory and the advent of liberty all over the land. Then "General Prentiss" was called for; and as citizen soldiers command their Generals on such occasions, he too was obliged to speak, and to tell his audience "the world had never seen any men more devoted, gallant, or patriotic than themselves." "Oglesby" was next summoned, and the tall, portly, good-humoured old man stepped to the front, and with excellent tact and good sense, dished up in the Buncombe style, told them the time for making speeches had passed, indeed it had lasted too long; and although it was said there was very little fighting when there was much talking, he believed too much talking was likely to lead to a great deal more fighting than any one desired to see between citizens of the United States of America, except their enemies, who, no doubt, were much better pleased to see Americans fighting each other than to find them engaged in any other employment. Great as the mischief of too much talking had been, too much writing had far more of the mischief to answer for. The pen was keener than the tongue, hit harder, and left a more incurable wound; but the pen was better than the tongue, because it was able to cure the mischief it had inflicted." And so by a series of sentences the Colonel got round to me, and to my consternation, remembering how I had fared with my speech at the little private dinner on St. Patrick's Day in New York, I was called upon by stentorian lungs, and hustled to the stump by a friendly circle, till I escaped by uttering a few sentences as to "mighty struggle," "Europe gazing," "the world anxious," "the virtues of discipline," "the admirable lessons of a soldier's life," and the "aspiration that in a quarrel wherein a British subject was ordered, by an authority he was bound to respect, to remain neutral, God might preserve the right."

Colonel, General, and all addressed the soldiers as "gentlemen," and their auditory did not on their part refrain from expressing their sentiments in the most unmistakeable manner. "Bully for you, General!" "Bravo, Washburne!" "That's so, Colonel!" and the like, interrupted the harangues, and when the oratorical exercises were over the men crowded round the staff, cheered and hurrahed, and tossed up their caps in the greatest delight.

With the exception of the foreign officers, and some of the Staff, there are very few of the colonels, majors, captains, or lieutenants who know anything of their business. The men do not care for them, and never think of saluting them. A regiment of Germans was sent across from Bird's Point this evening for plundering and robbing the houses in the district in which they were quartered.

It may be readily imagined that the scoundrels who had to fly from every city in Europe before the face of the police will not stay their hands when they find themselves masters of the situation in the so-called country of an enemy. In such matters the officers have little or no control, and discipline is exceedingly lax, and punishments but sparingly inflicted, the use of the lash being forbidden altogether. Fine as the men are, incomparably better armed, clad—and doubtless better fed—than the Southern troops, they will scarcely meet them man to man in the field with any chance of success. Among the officers are bar-room keepers, persons little above the position of potmen in England, grocers' apprentices, and such like—often inferior socially, and in every other respect, to the men whom they are supposed to command. General Prentiss has seen service, I believe, in Mexico; but he appears to me to be rather an ardent politician, embittered against slaveholders and the South, than a judicious or skilful military leader.

The principles on which these isolated commanders carry on the war are eminently defective. They apply their whole minds to petty expeditions, which go out from the camps, attack some Secessionist gathering, and then return, plundering as they go and come, exasperating enemies, converting neutrals into opponents, disgusting friends, and leaving it to the Secessionists to boast that they have repulsed them. Instead of encouraging the men and improving their discipline these ill-conducted expeditions have an opposite result.

June 22nd.—An active man would soon go mad if he were confined in Cairo. A mudbank stretching along the course of a muddy river is not attractive to a pedestrian; and, as is the case in most of the Southern cities, there is no place round Cairo where a man can stretch his legs or take an honest walk in the country. A walk in the country! The Americans have not an idea of what the thing means. I speak now only of the inhabitants of the towns of the States through which I have passed, as far as I have seen of them. The roads are either impassable in mud or knee-deep in dust. There are no green shady lanes, no sheltering groves, no quiet paths through green meadows beneath umbrageous trees. Off the rail there is a morass—or, at best, a clearing—full of stumps. No temptations to take a stroll. Down away South the planters ride or drive; indeed in many places the saunterer by the way-side would probably encounter an alligator, or disturb a society of rattle-snakes.

To-day I managed to struggle along the levee in a kind of sirocco, and visited the works at the extremity, which were constructed by an Hungarian named Waagner, one of the *emigrés* who came with Kossuth to the United States. I found him in a hut full of flies, suffering from camp diarrhœa, and waited on by Mr. O'Leary, who was formerly petty officer in our navy, served in the Furious in the Black Sea, and in the Shannon Brigade in India, now a lieutenant in the United States' army, where I should say he feels himself very much out of place. The Hungarian and the Milesian were, however, quite agreed about the utter incompetence of their military friends around them, and the great merits of heavy artillery. "When I tell them here the way poor Sir William made us rattle about them 68-pounder guns, the poor ignorant creatures laugh at me—not one of them believes it." "It is most astonishing," says the colonel, "how ignorant they are: there is not one of these men who can trace a regular work. Of Westpoint men I speak not, but of the people about here, and they will not learn of me—from me who knows." However, the works were well enough, strongly covered, commanded both rivers, and not to be reduced without trouble.

The heat drove me in among the flies of the crowded hotel, where Brigadier Prentiss is planning one of those absurd expeditions against a Secessionist camp at Commerce, in the State of Missouri, about two hours' steaming up the river, and some twelve or fourteen miles inland. Cairo abounds in Secessionists and spies, and it is needful to take great precautions lest the expedition be known; but, after all, stores must be got ready, and put on board the steamers, and preparations must be made which cannot be concealed from the world. At dusk 700 men, supported by a six pounder field-piece, were put on board the "City of Alton," on which they clustered like bees in a swarm, and as the huge engine laboured up and down against the stream, and the boat swayed from side to side, I felt a considerable desire to see General Prentiss chucked into the stream for his utter recklessness in cramming on board one huge tinder-box, all fire and touch-wood, so many human beings, who, in event of an explosion, or a shot in the boiler, or of a heavy musketry fire on the banks, would have been converted into a great slaughter-house. One small boat hung from her stern, and although there were plenty of river flats and numerous steamers, even the horses belonging to the field-piece were crammed in among the men along the deck.

In my letter to Europe I made, at the time, some remarks by which the belligerents might have profited, and which at the time these pages are reproduced may strike them as possessing some value, illustrated as they have been by many events in the war. "A handful of horsemen would have been admirable to move in advance, feel the covers, and make prisoners for political or other purposes in case of flight; but the Americans persist in ignoring the use of horsemen, or at least in depreciating it, though they will at last find that they may shed much blood, and lose much more, before they can gain a victory without the aid of artillery and charges after the retreating enemy. From the want of cavalry, I suppose it is, the unmilitary practice of 'scouting,' as it is called here, has arisen. It is all very well in the days of Indian wars for footmen to creep about in the bushes, and shoot or be shot by sentries and pickets; but no civilised war recognises such means of annoyance as firing upon sentinels, unless in case of an actual advance or feigned attack on the line. No camp can be safe without cavalry videttes and pickets; for the enemy can pour in impetuously after the alarm has been given, as fast as the outlying footmen can run in. In feeling the way for a column, cavalry are invaluable, and there can be little chance of ambuscades or surprises where they are judiciously employed; but 'scouting' on foot, or adventurous private expeditions on horseback, to have a look at the enemy, can do, and will do, nothing but harm. Every day the papers contain accounts of 'scouts' being killed, and sentries being picked off. The latter is a very barbarous and savage practice; and the Russian, in his most angry moments, abstained from it. If any officer wishes to obtain information as to his enemy, he has two ways of doing it. He can employ spies, who carry their lives in their hands, or he can beat up their quarters by a proper reconnoissance on his own responsibility, in which, however, it would be advisable not to trust his force to a railway train."

At night there was a kind of *émeute* in camp. The day, as I have said, was excessively hot, and on returning to their tents and huts from evening parade the men found the contractor who supplies them with water had not filled the barrels; so they forced the sentries, broke barracks after hours, mobbed their officers, and streamed up to the hotel, which they surrounded, calling out, "Water, water," in chorus. The General came out, and got up on a rail: "Gentlemen," said he, "it is not my fault you are without water. It's your officers who are to blame, not me." ("Groans for the Quartermaster," from the men.) "If it is the fault of the contractor, I'll see that he is punished. I'll take steps at once to see that the matter is remedied. And now, gentlemen, I hope you'll go back to your quarters;" and the gentlemen took it into their heads very good-humouredly to obey the suggestion, fell in, and marched back two deep to their huts.

As the General was smoking his cigar before going to bed, I asked him why the officers had not more control over the men. "Well," said he, "the officers are to blame for all this. The truth is, the term for which these volunteers enlisted is drawing to a close; and they have not as yet enrolled themselves in the United States' Army. They are merely volunteer regiments of the State of Illinois. If they were displeased with anything, therefore, they might refuse to enter the service or to take fresh engagements; and the officers would find themselves suddenly left without any men; they therefore curry favour with the privates, many of them, too, having an eye to the votes of the men when the elections of officers in the new regiments are to take place."

The contractors have commenced plunder on a gigantic scale; and their influence with the authorities of the State is so powerful, there is little chance of punishing them. Besides, it is not considered expedient to deter contractors, by too scrupulous an exactitude, in coming forward at such a trying period; and the Quartermaster's department, which ought to be the most perfect, considering the number of persons connected with transport and carriage, is in a most disgraceful and inefficient condition. I told the General that one of the Southern leaders proposed to hang any contractor who was found out in cheating the men, and that the press cordially approved of the suggestion. "I am afraid," said he, "if any such proposal was carried out here, there would scarcely be a contractor left throughout the States." Equal ignorance is shown by the medical authorities of the requirements of an army. There is not an ambulance or cacolet of any kind attached to this camp; and, as far as I could see, not even a litter was sent on board the steamer which has started with the expedition.

Although there has scarcely been a fought field or anything more serious than the miserable skirmishes of Shenck and Butler, the pressure of war has already told upon the people. The Cairo paper makes an urgent appeal to the authorities to relieve the distress and pauperism which the sudden interruption of trade has brought upon so many respectable citizens. And when I was at Memphis the other day, I observed a public notice in the journals, that the magistrates of the city would issue orders for money to families left in distress by the enrolment of the male members for military service. When General Scott, sorely against his will, was urged to make preparations for an armed invasion of the seceded states in case it became necessary, he said it would need some hundreds of thousands of men and many millions of money to effect that object. Mr. Seward, Mr. Chase, and Mr. Lincoln laughed pleasantly at this exaggeration, but they have begun to find by this time the old general was not quite so much in the wrong.

In reference to the discipline maintained in the camp, I must admit that proper precautions are used to prevent spies entering the lines. The sentries are posted closely, and permit no one to go in without a pass in the day and a countersign at night. A conversation with General Prentiss in the front of the hotel was interrupted this evening by an Irishman, who ran past us towards the camp, hotly pursued by two policemen. The sentry on duty at the point of the lines close to us brought him up by the point of the bayonet. "Who goes tere?" "A friend, shure, your honour; I'm a friend." "Advance three paces and give the countersign." "I don't know it, I tell you. Let me in, let me in." But the German was resolute, and the policemen now coming up in hot pursuit, seized the culprit, who resisted violently, till General Prentiss rose from his chair and ordered the guard, who had turned out, to make a prisoner of the soldier, and hand him over to the civil power, for which the man seemed to be most deeply grateful. As the policemen were walking off, he exclaimed, "Be quiet wid ye, till I spake a word to the Gineral," and then bowing and chuckling with drunken gravity he said, "an' indeed, Gineral, I'm much obleeged to ye altogither for this kindness. Long life to ye. We've got the better of that dirty German. Hoora for Gineral Prentiss." He preferred a chance of more whisky in the police office and a light punishment to the work in camp and a heavy drill in the morning. An officer who was challenged by a sentry the other evening, asked him, "do you know the countersign yourself?" "No, sir, it's not nine o'clock, and they have not given it out yet." Another sentry who stopped a man because he did not know the countersign. The fellow said, "I dare say you don't know it yourself." "That's a lie," he exclaimed, "it's Plattsburgh." "Plattsburgh it is, sure enough," said the other, and walked on without further parley.

The Americans, Irish, and Germans, do not always coincide in the phonetic value of each letter in the passwords, and several difficulties have occurred in consequence. An incautious approach towards the posts at night is attended with risk; for the raw sentries are very quick on the trigger. More fatal and serious injuries have been inflicted on the Federals by themselves than by the enemy. "I declare to you, sir, the way the boys touched off their irons at me going home to my camp last night, was just like a running fight with the Ingins. I was a little 'tight,' and didn't mind it a cuss."

CHAPTER XLI.

Impending battle—By railway to Chicago—Northern enlightenment—Mound City—"Cotton is King"—Land in the States—Dead level of American society—Return into the Union—American homes—Across the prairie—White labourers—New pillager—Lake Michigan.

June 23rd.—The latest information which I received to-day is of a nature to hasten my departure for Washington; it can no longer be doubted that a battle between the two armies assembled in the neighbourhood of the capital is imminent. The vague hope which from time to time I have entertained of being able to visit Richmond before I finally take up my quarters with the only army from which I can communicate regularly with Europe has now vanished.

At four o'clock in the evening I started by the train on the famous Central Illinois line from Cairo to Chicago.

The carriages were tolerably well filled with soldiers, and in addition to them there were a few unfortunate women, undergoing deportation to some less moral neighbourhood. Neither the look, language, nor manners of my fellow passengers inspired me with an exalted notion of the intelligence, comfort and respectability of the people which are so much vaunted by Mr. Seward and American journals, and which, though truly attributed, no doubt, to the people of the New England states, cannot be affirmed with equal justice to belong to all the other components of the Union.

As the Southerners say, their negroes are the happiest people on the earth, so the Northerners boast "We are the most enlightened nation in the world." The soldiers in the train were intelligent enough to think they ought not to be kept without pay, and free enough to say so. The soldiers abused Cairo roundly, and indeed it is wonderful if the people can live on any food but quinine. However, speculators, looking to its natural advantages as the point where the two great rivers join, bespeak for Cairo a magnificent and prosperous future. The present is not promising.

Leaving the shanties, which face the levees, and some poor wooden houses with a short vista of cross streets partially flooded at right angles to them, the rail suddenly plunges into an unmistakeable swamp, where a forest of dead trees wave their ghastly, leafless arms over their buried trunks, like plumes over a hearse—a cheerless, miserable place, sacred to the ague and fever. This occurs close to the cleared space on which the city is to stand,—when it is finished—and the rail, which runs on the top of the embankment or levee, here takes to the trestle, and is borne over the water on the usual timber framework.

"Mound City," which is the first station, is composed of a mere heap of earth, like a ruined brick-kiln, which rises to some height and is covered with fine white oaks, beneath which are a few log huts and hovels, giving the place its proud name. Tents were pitched on the mound side, from which wild-looking banditti sort of men, with arms, emerged as the train stopped. "I've been pretty well over Europe," said a meditative voice beside me, "and I've seen the despotic armies of the old world, but I don't think they equal that set of boys." The question was not worth arguing—the boys were in fact "very weedy," "splinter-shinned chaps," as another critic insisted.

There were some settlers in the woods around Mound City, and a jolly-looking, corpulent man, who introduced himself as one of the officers of the land department of the Central Illinois railroad, described them as awful warnings to the emigrants not to stick in the south part of Illinois. It was suggestive to find that a very genuine John Bull, "located," as they say in the States, for many years, had as much aversion to the principles of the abolitionists as if he had been born a Southern planter. Another countryman of his and mine, steward on board the steamer to Cairo, eagerly asked me what I thought of the quarrel, and which side I would back. I declined to say more than I thought the North possessed very great superiority of means if the conflict were to be fought on the same terms. Whereupon my Saxon friend exclaimed, "all the Northern States and all the power of the world can't beat the South; and why?—because the South has got cotton, and cotton is king."

The Central Illinois officer did not suggest the propriety of purchasing lots, but he did intimate I would be doing service if I informed the world at large, they could get excellent land, at sums varying from ten to twenty-five dollars an acre. In America a man's income is represented by capitalizing all that he is worth, and whereas in England we say a man has so much a year, the Americans, in representing his value, observe that he is worth so many dollars, by which they mean that all he has in the world would realise the amount.

It sounds very well to an Irish tenant farmer, an English cottier, or a cultivator in the Lothians, to hear that he can get land at the rate of from £2 to £5 per acre, to be his for ever, liable only to state taxes; but when he comes to see a parallelogram marked upon the map as "good soil, of unfathomable richness," and finds in effect that he must cut down trees, eradicate stumps, drain off water, build a house, struggle for high-priced labour, and contend with imperfect roads, the want of many things to which he has been accustomed in the old country, the land may not appear to him such a bargain. In the wooded districts he has, indeed, a sufficiency of fuel as long as trees and stumps last, but they are, of course, great impediments to tillage. If he goes to the prairie he finds that fuel is scarce and water by no means wholesome.

When we left this swamp and forest, and came out after a run of many miles on the clear lands which abut upon the prairie, large fields of corn lay around us, which bore a peculiarly blighted and harassed look. These fields were suffering from the ravages of an insect called the "army worm," almost as destructive to corn and crops as the locust-like hordes of North and South, which are vying with each other in laying waste the fields of Virginia. Night was falling as the train rattled out into the wild, flat sea of waving grass, dotted by patch-like Indian corn enclosures; but halts at such places as Jonesburgh and Cobden, enabled us to see that these settlements in Illinois were neither very flourishing nor very civilised.

There is a level modicum of comfort, which may be consistent with the greatest good of the greatest number, but which makes the standard of the highest in point of well-being very low indeed. I own, that to me, it would be more agreeable to see a flourishing community placed on a high level in all that relates to the comfort and social status of all its members than to recognise the old types of European civilisation, which place the castle on the hill, surround its outer walls with the mansion of doctor and lawyer, and drive the people into obscure hovels outside. But then one must confess that there are in the castle some elevating tendencies which cannot be found in the uniform level of citizen equality. There are traditions of nobility and noble deeds in the family; there are paintings on the walls; the library is stored with valuable knowledge, and from its precincts are derived the lessons not yet unlearned in Europe, that though man may be equal the condition of men must vary as the accidents of life or the effects of individual character, called fortune, may determine.

The towns of Jonesburgh and Cobden have their little teapot-looking churches and meeting-houses, their lager-bier saloons, their restaurants, their small libraries, institutes, and reading rooms, and no doubt they have also their political cliques, social distinctions and favouritisms; but it requires, nevertheless, little sagacity to perceive that the highest of the bourgeois who leads the mass at meeting and prayer, has but little to distinguish him from the very lowest member of the same body politic. Cobden, for example, has no less than four drinking saloons, all on the line of rail, and no doubt the highest citizen in the place frequents some one or other of them, and meets there the worst rowdy in the place. Even though they do carry a vote for each adult man, "locations" here would not appear very enviable in the eyes of the most miserable Dorsetshire small farmer ever ferreted out by "S. G. O."

A considerable number of towns, formed by accretions of small stores and drinking places, called magazines, round the original shed wherein live the station master and his assistants, mark the course of the railway. Some are important enough to possess a bank, which is generally represented by a wooden hut, with a large board nailed in front, bearing the names of the president and cashier, and announcing the success and liberality of the management. The stores are also decorated with large signs, recommending the names of the owners to the attention of the public, and over all of them is to be seen the significant announcement, "Cash for produce."

At Carbondale there was no coal at all to be found, but several miles farther to the north, at a place called Dugoine, a field of bituminous deposit crops out, which is sold at the pit's mouth for one dollar twenty-five cents, or about *5s. 2d.* a-ton. Darkness and night fell as I was noting such meagre particulars of the new district as could be learned out of the window of a railway carriage; and finally with a delicious sensation of cool night air creeping in through the windows, the first I had experienced for many a long day, we made ourselves up for repose, and were borne steadily, if not rapidly, through the great prairie, having halted for tea at the comfortable refreshment rooms of Centralia.

There were no physical signs to mark the transition from the land of the Secessionist to Union-loving soil. Until the troops were quartered there, Cairo was for Secession, and Southern Illinois is supposed to be deeply tainted with disaffection to Mr. Lincoln. Placards on which were printed the words, "Vote for Lincoln and Hamlin, for Union and Freedom," and the old battle-cry of the last election, still cling to the wooden walls of the groceries often accompanied by bitter words or offensive additions.

One of my friends argues that as slavery is at the base of Secession, it follows that States or portions of States will be disposed to join the Confederates or the Federalists just as the climate may be favourable or adverse to the growth of slave produce. Thus in the mountainous parts of the border States of Kentucky and Tennessee, in the north-western part of Virginia, vulgarly called the pan handle, and in the pine woods of North Carolina, where white men can work at the rosin and naval store manufactories, there is a decided feeling in favour of the Union; in fact, it becomes a matter of isothermal lines. It would be very wrong to judge of the condition of a people from the windows of a railway carriage, but the external aspect of the settlements along the line, far superior to that of slave hamlets, does not equal my expectations. We all know the aspect of a wood in a gentleman's park which is submitting to the axe, and has been partially cleared, how raw and bleak the stumps look, and how dreary is the naked land not yet turned into arable. Take such a patch and fancy four or five houses made of pine planks, sometimes not painted, lighted by windows in which there is, or has been, glass, each guarded by a paling around a piece of vegetable garden, a pig house, and poultry box; let one be a grocery, which means a whisky shop, another the post-office, and a third the store where "cash is given for produce." Multiply these groups if you desire a larger settlement, and place a wooden church with a Brobdignag spire and Lilliputian body out in a waste, to be approached only by a causeway of planks; before each grocery let there be a gathering of tall men in sombre clothing, of whom the majority have small newspapers and all of whom are chewing tobacco; near the stores let there be some light wheeled carts and ragged horses, around which are knots of unmistakeably German women; then see the deep tracks which lead off to similar settlements in the forest or prairie, and you have a notion, if your imagination is strong enough, of one of these civilising centres which the Americans assert to be the homes of the most cultivated and intelligent communities in the world.

Next morning, just at dawn, I woke up and got out on the platform of the carriage, which is the favourite resort of smokers and their antithetics, those who love pure fresh air, notwithstanding the printed caution "It is dangerous to stand on the platform;" and under the eye of early morn saw spread around a flat sea-like expanse not yet warmed into colour and life by the sun. The line was no longer guarded from daring Secessionists by soldiers' outposts, and small camps had disappeared. The train sped through the centre of the great verdant circle as a ship through the sea, leaving the rigid iron wake behind it tapering to a point at the horizon, and as the light spread over it the surface of the crisping corn waved in broad undulations beneath the breeze from east to west. This is the prairie indeed. Hereabouts it is covered with the finest crops, some already cut and stacked. Looking around one could see church spires rising in the distance from the white patches of houses, and by degrees the tracks across the fertile waste became apparent, and then carts and horses were seen toiling through the rich soil.

A large species of partridge or grouse appeared very abundant, and rose in flocks from the long grass at the side of the rail or from the rich carpet of flowers on the margin of the corn fields. They sat on the fence almost unmoved by the rushing engine, and literally swarmed along the line. These are called "prairie chickens" by the people, and afford excellent sport. Another bird about the size of a thrush, with a yellow breast and a harsh cry, I learned was "the sky-lark;" and *apropos* of the unmusical creature, I was very briskly attacked by a young lady patriot for finding fault with the sharp noise it made. "Oh, my! And you not to know that your Shelley loved it above all things! Didn't he write some verses—quite beautiful, too, they are—to the sky-lark." And so "the Britisher was dried up," as I read in a paper afterwards of a similar occurrence.

At the little stations which occur at every few miles—there are some forty of them, at each of which the train stops, in 365 miles between Cairo and Chicago—the Union flag floated in the air; but we had left all the circumstance of this inglorious war behind us, and the train rattled boldly over the bridges across rare streams, no longer in danger from Secession hatchets. The swamp had given place to the corn field. No black faces were turned up from the mowing, and free white labour was at work, and the type of the labourers was German and Irish.

The Yorkshireman expatiated on the fertility of the land, and on the advantages it held out to the emigrant. But I observed all the lots by the side of the rail, and apparently as far as the eye could reach, were occupied. "Some of the very best land lies beyond on each side," said he. "Out over there in the fat places is where we put our Englishmen." By digging deep enough good water is always to be had, and coal can be carried from the rail, where it costs only 7*s.* or 8*s.* a ton. Wood there is little or none in the prairies, and it was rarely indeed a clump of trees could be detected, or anything higher than some scrub brushwood. These little communities which we passed were but the growth of a few years, and as we approached the Northern portion of the line we could see, as it were, the village swelling into the town, and the town spreading out to the dimensions of the city. "I daresay, Major," says one of the passengers, "this gentleman never saw anything like these cities before. I'm told they've nothin' like them in Europe?" "Bless you," rejoined the Major, with a wink, "just leaving out London, Edinbro', Paris, and Manchester, there's nothing on earth to ekal them." My friend, who is a shrewd fellow, by way of explanation of his military title, says, "I was a major once, a major in the Queen's Bays, but they would put troop-sergeant before it them days." Like many Englishmen he complains that the jealousy of native-born Americans effectually bars the way to political position of any naturalised citizen, and all the places are kept by the natives.

The scene now began to change gradually as we approached Chicago, the prairie subsided into swampy land, and thick belts of trees fringed the horizon; on our right glimpses of the sea could be caught through openings in the wood—the inland sea on which stands the Queen of the Lakes. Michigan looks broad and blue as the Mediterranean. Large farmhouses stud the country, and houses which must be the retreat of merchants and citizens of means; and when the train, leaving the land altogether, dashes out on a pier and causeway built along the borders of the lake, we see lines of noble houses, a fine boulevard, a forest of masts, huge isolated piles of masonry, the famed grain elevators by which so many have been hoisted to fortune, churches and public edifices, and the apparatus of a great city; and just at nine o'clock the train gives its last steam shout and comes to a standstill in the spacious station of the Central Illinois Company, and in half-an-hour more I am in comfortable quarters at the Richmond House, where I find letters waiting for me, by which it appears that the necessity for my being in Washington in all haste, no longer exists. The wary General who commands the army is aware that the advance to Richmond, for which so many journals are clamouring, would be attended with serious risk at present, and the politicians must be content to wait a little longer

CHAPTER XLII.

Progress of events—Policy of Great Britain as regarded by the North—The American Press and its comments—Privacy a luxury—Chicago—Senator Douglas and his widow—American ingratitude—Apathy in volunteering—Colonel Turchin's camp.

I SHALL here briefly recapitulate what has occurred since the last mention of political events.

In the first place the South has been developing every day greater energy in widening the breach between it and the North, and preparing to fill it with dead; and the North, so far as I can judge, has been busy in raising up the Union as a nationality, and making out the crime of treason from the act of Secession. The South has been using conscription in Virginia, and is entering upon the conflict with unsurpassable determination. The North is availing itself of its greater resources and its foreign vagabondage and destitution to swell the ranks of its volunteers, and boasts of its enormous armies, as if it supposed conscripts well led do not fight better than volunteers badly officered. Virginia has been invaded on three points, one below and two above Washington, and passports are now issued on both sides.

The career open to the Southern privateers is effectually closed by the Duke of Newcastle's notification that the British Government will not permit the cruisers of either side to bring their prizes into or condemn them in English ports; but, strange to say, the Northerners feel indignant against Great Britain for an act which deprives their enemy of an enormous advantage, and which must reduce their privateering to the mere work of plunder and destruction on the high seas. In the same way the North affects to consider the declaration of neutrality, and the concession of limited belligerent rights to the seceding States, as deeply injurious and insulting; whereas our course has, in fact, removed the greatest difficulty from the path of the Washington Cabinet, and saved us from inconsistencies and serious risks in our course of action.

It is commonly said, "What would Great Britain have done if we had declared ourselves neutral during the Canadian rebellion, or had conceded limited belligerent rights to the Sepoys?" as if Canada and Hindostan have the same relation to the British Crown that the seceding States had to the Northern States. But if Canada, with its parliament, judges, courts of law, and its people, declared it was independent of Great Britain; and if the Government of Great Britain, months after that declaration was made and acted upon, permitted the new State to go free, whilst a large number of her Statesmen agreed that Canada was perfectly right, we could find little fault with the United States' Government for issuing a proclamation of neutrality the same as our own, when after a long interval of quiescence a war broke out between the two countries.

Secession was an accomplished fact months before Mr. Lincoln came into office, but we heard no talk of rebels and pirates till Sumter had fallen, and the North was perfectly quiescent—not only that—the people of wealth in New York were calmly considering the results of Secession as an accomplished fact, and seeking to make the best of it; nay, more, when I arrived in Washington some members of the Cabinet were perfectly ready to let the South go.

One of the first questions put to me by Mr. Chase in my first interview with him, was whether I thought a very injurious effect would be produced to the *prestige* of the Federal Government in Europe if the Northern States let the South have its own way, and told them to go in peace. "For my own part," said he, "I should not be averse to let them try it, for I believe they would soon find out their mistake." Mr. Chase may be finding out his mistake just now. When I left England the prevalent opinion, as far as I could judge, was, that a family quarrel, in which the South was in the wrong, had taken place, and that it would be better to stand by and let the Government put forth its strength to chastise rebellious children. But now we see the house is divided against itself, and that the family are determined to set up two separate establishments. These remarks occur to me with the more force because I see the New York papers are attacking me because I described a calm in a sea which was afterwards agitated by a storm. "What a false witness is this," they cry. "See how angry and how vexed is our Bermoothes, and yet the fellow says it was quite placid."

I have already seen so many statements respecting my sayings, my doings, and my opinions, in the American papers, that I have resolved to follow a general rule, with few exceptions indeed, which prescribes as the best course to pursue, not so much an indifference to these remarks as a fixed purpose to abstain from the hopeless task of correcting them. The "Quicklys" of the press are incorrigible. Commerce may well be proud of Chicago. I am not going to reiterate what every Crispinus from the old country has said again and again concerning this wonderful place—not one word of statistics, of corn elevators, of shipping, or of the piles of buildings raised from the foundation by ingenious applications of screws. Nor am I going to enlarge on the splendid future of that which has so much present prosperity, or on the benefits to mankind opened up by the Illinois Central Railway. It is enough to say that by the borders of this lake there has sprung up in thirty years a wonderful city of fine streets, luxurious hotels, handsome shops, magnificent stores, great warehouses, extensive quays, capacious docks; and that as long as corn holds its own, and the mouths of Europe are open, and her hands full, Chicago will acquire greater importance, size, and wealth with every year. The only drawback, perhaps, to the comfort of the money-making inhabitants, and of the stranger within the gates, is to be found in the clouds of dust and in the unpaved streets and thoroughfares, which give anguish to horse and man.

I spent three days here writing my letters and repairing the wear and tear of my Southern expedition; and although it was hot enough, the breeze from the lake carried health and vigour to the frame, enervated by the sun of Louisiana and Mississippi. No need now to wipe the large drops of moisture from the languid brow lest they blind the eyes, nor to sit in a state of semi-clothing, worn out and exhausted, and tracing with moist hand imperfect characters on the paper.

I could not satisfy myself whether there was, as I have been told, a peculiar state of feeling in Chicago, which induced many people to support the Government of Mr. Lincoln because they believed it necessary for their own interests to obtain decided advantages over the South in the field, whilst they were opposed *totis viribus* to the genius of emancipation and to the views of the black Republicans. But the genius and eloquence of the little giant have left their impress on the facile mould of democratic thought, and he who argued with such acuteness and ability last March in Washington, in his own study, against the possibility, or at least the constitutional legality, of using the national forces, and the militia and volunteers of the Northern States, to subjugate the Southern people, carried away by the great bore which rushed through the placid North when Sumter fell, or perceiving his inability to resist its force, sprung to the crest of the wave, and carried to excess the violence of the Union reaction.

Whilst I was in the South I had seen his name in Northern papers with sensation headings and descriptions of his magnificent crusade for the Union in the west. I had heard his name reviled by those who had once been his warm political allies, and his untimely death did not seem to satisfy their hatred. His old foes in the North admired and applauded the sudden apostasy of their eloquent opponent, and were loud in lamentations over his loss. Imagine, then, how I felt when visiting his grave at Chicago, seeing his bust in many houses, or his portrait in all the shop-windows, I was told that the enormously wealthy community of which he was the idol were permitting his widow to live in a state not far removed from penury.

"Senator Douglas, sir," observed one of his friends to me, "died of bad whisky. He killed himself with it while he was stumping for the Union all over the country." "Well," I said, "I suppose, sir, the abstraction called the Union, for which by your own account he killed himself, will give a pension to his widow." Virtue is its own reward, and so is patriotism, unless it takes the form of contracts.

As far as all considerations of wife, children, or family are concerned, let a man serve a decent despot, or even a constitutional country with an economising House of Commons, if he wants anything more substantial than lip-service. The history of the great men of America is full of instances of national ingratitude. They give more praise and less pence to their benefactors than any nation on the face of the earth. Washington got little, though the plundering scouts who captured André were well rewarded; and the men who fought during the War of Independence were long left in neglect and poverty, sitting in sack-cloth and ashes at the doorsteps of the temple of liberty, whilst the crowd rushed inside to worship Plutus.

If a native of the British isles, of the natural ignorance of his own imperfections which should characterise him, desires to be subjected to a series of moral shower-baths, douches, and shampooing with a rough glove, let him come to the United States. In Chicago he will be told that the English people are fed by the beneficence of the United States, and that all the trade and commerce of England are simply directed to the one end of obtaining gold enough to pay the western States for the breadstuffs exported for our population. We know what the South think of our dependence on cotton. The people of the east think they are striking a great blow at their enemy by the Morrill tariff, and I was told by a patriot in North Carolina, "Why, creation! if you let the Yankees shut up our ports, the whole of your darned ships will go to rot. Where will you get your naval stores from? Why, I guess in a year you could not scrape up enough of turpentine in the whole of your country for Queen Victoria to paint her nursery-door with."

Nearly one half of the various companies enrolled in this district are Germans, or are the descendants of German parents, and speak only the language of the old country; two-thirds of the remainder are Irish, or of immediate Irish descent; but it is said that a grand reserve of Americans born lies behind this *avante garde*, who will come into the battle should there ever be need for their services.

Indeed so long as the Northern people furnish the means of paying and equipping armies perfectly competent to do their work, and equal in numbers to any demands made for men, they may rest satisfied with the accomplishment of that duty, and with contributing from their ranks the great majority of the superior and even of the subaltern officers; but with the South it is far different. Their institutions have repelled immigration; the black slave has barred the door to the white free settler. Only on the seaboard and in the large cities are German and Irish to be found, and they to a man have come forward to fight for the South; but the proportion they bear to the native-born Americans who have rushed to arms in defence of their menaced borders, is of course far less than it is as yet to the number of Americans in the Northern States who have volunteered to fight for the Union.

I was invited before I left to visit the camp of a Colonel Turchin, who was described to me as a Russian officer of great ability and experience in European warfare, in command of a regiment consisting of Poles, Hungarians, and Germans, who were about to start for the seat of war; but I was only able to walk through his tents, where I was astonished at the amalgam of nations that constituted his battalion; though, on inspection, I am bound to say there proved to be an American element in the ranks which did not appear to have coalesced with the bulk of the rude and, I fear, predatory Cossacks of the Union. Many young men of good position have gone to the wars, although there was no complaint, as in Southern cities, that merchants' offices have been deserted, and great establishments left destitute of clerks and working hands In warlike operations, however, Chicago, with its communication open to the sea, its access to the head waters of the Mississippi, its intercourse with the marts of commerce and of manufacture, may be considered to possess greater belligerent power and strength than the great city of New Orleans; and there is much greater probability of Chicago sending its contingent to attack the Crescent City than there is of the latter being able to despatch a soldier within five hundred miles of its streets.

CHAPTER XLIII.

Niagara—Impression of the Falls—Battle scenes in the neighbourhood—A village of Indians—General Scott—Hostile movements on both sides—The Hudson—Military school at West Point—Return to New York—Altered appearance of the city—Misery and suffering—Altered state of public opinion, as to the Union and towards Great Britain.

At eight o'clock on the morning of the 27th I left Chicago for Niagara, which was so temptingly near that I resolved to make a detour by that route to New York. The line from the city which I took skirts the southern extremity of Lake Michigan for many miles, and leaving its borders at New Buffalo, traverses the southern portion of the state of Michigan by Albion and Jackson to the town of Detroit, or the outflow of Lake St. Clair into Lake Erie, a distance of 284 miles, which was accomplished in about twelve hours. The most enthusiastic patriot could not affirm the country was interesting. The names of the stations were certainly novel to a Britisher. Thus we had Kalumet, Pokagon, Dowagiac, Kalamazoo, Ypsilanti, among the more familiar titles of Chelsea, Marengo, Albion, and Parma.

It was dusk when we reached the steam ferry-boat at Detroit, which took us across to Windsor; but through the dusk I could perceive the Union Jack waving above the unimpressive little town which bears a name so respected by British ears. The customs' inspections seemed very mild; and I was not much impressed by the representative of the British crown, who, with a brass button on his coat and a very husky voice, exercised his powers on behalf of Her Majesty at the landing-place of Windsor. The officers of the railway company, who received me as if I had been an old friend, welcomed me as if I had just got out of a battle-field. "Well, I do wonder them Yankees have ever let you come out alive." "May I ask why?" "Oh, because you have not been praising them all round, sir. Why even the Northern chaps get angry with a Britisher, as they call us, if he attempts to say a word against those cursed niggers."

It did not appear the Americans are quite so thin-skinned, for whilst crossing in the steamer a passage of arms between the Captain, who was a genuine John Bull, and a Michigander, in the style which is called chaff or slang, diverted most of the auditors, although it was very much to the disadvantage of the Union champion. The Michigan man had threatened the Captain that Canada would be annexed as the consequence of our infamous conduct. "Why, I tell you," said the Captain, "we'd just draw up the negro chaps from our barbers' shops, and tell them we'd send them to Illinois if they did not lick you; and I believe every creature in Michigan, pigs and all, would run before them into Pennsylvania. We know what you are up to, you and them Maine chaps; but Lor' bless you, sooner than take such a lot, we'd give you ten dollars a head to make you stay in your own country; and we know you would go to the next worst place before your time for half the money. The very Bluenoses would secede if you were permitted to come under the old flag."

All night we travelled. A long day through a dreary, ill-settled, pine-wooded, half-cleared country, swarming with mosquitoes and biting flies, and famous for fevers. Just about daybreak the train stopped.

"Now, then," said an English voice; "now, then, who's for Clifton Hotel? All passengers leave cars for this side of the Falls." Consigning our baggage to the commissioner of the Clifton, my companion, Mr. Ward, and myself resolved to walk along the banks of the river to the hotel, which is some two miles and a half distant, and set out whilst it was still so obscure that the outline of the beautiful bridge which springs so lightly across the chasm, filled with furious hurrying waters, hundreds of feet below, was visible only as is the tracery of some cathedral arch through the dim light of the cloister.

The road follows the course of the stream, which whirls and gurgles in an Alpine torrent, many times magnified, in a deep gorge like that of the Tête Noire. As the rude bellow of the steam-engine and the rattle of the train proceeding on its journey were dying away, the echoes seemed to swell into a sustained, reverberating, hollow sound from the perpendicular banks of the St. Lawrence. We listened. "It is the noise of the Falls," said my companion; and as we walked on the sound became louder, filling the air with a strange quavering note, which played about a tremendous uniform bass note, and silencing every other. Trees closed in the road on the river side, but when we had walked a mile or so, the lovely light of morning spreading with our steps, suddenly through an opening in the branches there appeared, closing up the vista—white, flickering, indistinct, and shroud-like—the Falls, rushing into a grave of black waters, and uttering that tremendous cry which can never be forgotten.

I have heard many people say they were disappointed with the first impression of Niagara. Let those who desire to see the water-leap in all its grandeur, approach it as I did, and I cannot conceive what their expectations are if they do not confess the sight exceeded their highest ideal. I do not pretend to describe the sensations or to endeavour to give the effect produced on me by the scene or by the Falls, then or subsequently; but I must say words can do no more than confuse the writer's own ideas of the grandeur of the sight, and mislead altogether those who read them. It is of no avail to do laborious statistics, and tell us how many gallons rush over in that down-flung ocean every second, or how wide it is, how high it is, how deep the earth-piercing caverns beneath. For my own part, I always feel the distance of the sun to be insignificant, when I read it is so many hundreds of thousands of miles away, compared with the feeling of utter inaccessibility to anything human which is caused by it when its setting rays illuminate some purple ocean studded with golden islands in dreamland.

Niagara is rolling its waters over the barrier. Larger and louder it grows upon us.

"I hope the hotel is not full," quoth my friend. I confess, for the time, I forgot all about Niagara, and was perturbed concerning a breakfastless ramble and a hunt after lodgings by the borders of the great river.

But although Clifton Hotel was full enough, there was room for us, too; and for two days a strange, weird-kind of life I led, alternating between the roar of the cataract outside and the din of politics within; for, be it known, that at the Canadian side of the Falls many Americans of the Southern States, who would not pollute their footsteps by contact with the soil of Yankee-land, were sojourning, and that merchants and bankers of New York and other Northern cities had selected it as their summer retreat, and, indeed, with reason; for after excursions on both sides of the Falls, the comparative seclusion of the settlements on the left bank appears to me to render it infinitely preferable to the Rosherville gentism and semi-rowdyism of the large American hotels and settlements on the other side.

It was distressing to find that Niagara was surrounded by the paraphernalia of a fixed fair. I had looked forward to a certain degree of solitude. It appeared impossible that man could cockneyfy such a magnificent display of force and grandeur in nature. But, alas! it is haunted by what poor Albert Smith used to denominate "harpies." The hateful race of guides infest the precincts of the hotels, waylay you in the lanes, and prowl about the unguarded moments of reverie. There are miserable little peepshows and photographers, bird stuffers, shell polishers, collectors of crystals, and proprietors of natural curiosity shops.

There is, besides, a large village population. There is a watering-side air about the people who walk along the road worse than all their mills and factories working their water privileges at both sides of the stream. At the American side there is a lanky, pretentious town, with big hotels, shops of Indian curiosities, and all the meagre forms of the bazaar life reduced to a minimum of attractiveness which destroy the comfort of a traveller in Switzerland. I had scarcely been an hour in the hotel before I was asked to look at the Falls through a little piece of coloured glass. Next I was solicited to purchase a collection of muddy photographs, representing what I could look at with my own eyes for nothing. Not finally by any means, I was assailed by a gentleman who was particularly desirous of selling me an enormous pair of cow's-horns and a stuffed hawk. Small booths and peepshows corrupt the very margin of the bank, and close by the remnant of the "Table Rock," a Jew (who, by-the-bye, deserves infinite credit for the zeal and energy he has thrown into the collections for his museum), exhibits bottled rattle-snakes, stuffed monkeys, Egyptian mummies, series of coins, with a small living menagerie attached to the shop, in which articles of Indian manufacture are exposed for sale. It was too bad to be asked to admire such *lusus naturæ* as double-headed calves and dogs with three necks by the banks of Niagara.

As I said before, I am not going to essay the impossible or to describe the Falls. On the English side there are, independently of other attractions, some scenes of recent historic interest, for close to Niagara are Lundy's Lane and Chippewa. There are few persons in England aware of the exceedingly severe fighting which characterised the contests between the Americans and the English and Canadian troops during the campaign of 1814. At Chippewa, for example, Major-General Riall, who, with 2000 men, one howitzer, and two 24-pounders, attacked a force f Americans of a similar strength, was repulsed with a loss of 500 killed and wounded; and on he morning of the 25th of July the action of Lundy's Lane, between four brigades of Americans and seven field-pieces, and 3100 men of the British and seven field-pieces, took place in which the Americans were worsted, and retired with a loss of 854 men and two guns, whilst the British lost 878. On the 14th of August following Sir Gordon Drummond was repulsed with a loss of 905 men out of his small force in an attack on Fort Erie; and on the 17th of September an American sortie from the place was defeated with a loss of 510 killed and wounded, the British having lost 609. In effect the American campaign was unsuccessful: but their failures were redeemed by their successes on Lake Champlain, and in the affair of Plattsburgh.

There was more hard fighting than strategy in these battles, and their results were not, on the whole, creditable to the military skill of either party. They were sanguinary in proportion to the number of troops engaged, but they were very petty skirmishes considered in the light of contests between two great nations for the purpose of obtaining specific results. As England was engaged in a great war in Europe, was far removed from the scene of operations, was destitute of steampower, whilst America was fighting, as it were, on her own soil, close at hand, with a full opportunity of putting forth all her strength, the complete defeat of the American invasion of Canada was more honourable to our arms than the successes which the Americans achieved in resisting aggressive demonstrations.

In the great hotel of Clifton we had every day a little war of our own, for there were —— but why should I mention names? Has not government its bastiles? There were in effect men, and women too, who regarded the people of the Northern States and the government they had selected very much as the men of '98 looked upon the government and people of England; but withal these strong Southerners were not very favourable to a country which they regarded as the natural ally of the abolitionists, simply because it had resolved to be neutral.

On the Canadian side these rebels were secure. British authority was embodied in a respectable old Scottish gentleman, whose duty it was to prevent smuggling across the boiling waters of the St. Lawrence, and who performed it with zeal and diligence worthy of a higher post. There was indeed a withered triumphal arch which stood over the spot where the young Prince of our royal house had passed on his way to the Table Rock, but beyond these signs and tokens there was nothing to distinguish the American from the British side, except the greater size and activity of the settlements upon the right bank. There is no power in nature, according to great engineers, which cannot be forced to succumb to the influence of money. The American papers actually announce that "Niagara is to be sold;" the proprietors of the land upon their side of the water have resolved to sell their water privileges! A capitalist could render the islands the most beautifully attractive places in the world.

Life at Niagara is like that at most watering-places, though it is a desecration to apply such a term to the Falls, and there is no bathing there, except that which is confined to the precincts of the hotels and to the ingenious establishment on the American side, which permits one to enjoy the full rush of the current in covered rooms with sides pierced, to let it come through with undiminished force and with perfect security to the bather. There are drives and picnics, and mild excursions to obscure places in the neighbourhood, where only the roar of the Falls gives an idea of their presence. The rambles about the islands, and the views of the boiling rapids above them, are delightful, but I am glad to hear from one of the guides that the great excitement of seeing a man and boat carried over occurs but rarely. Every year, however, hapless creatures crossing from one shore to the other, by some error of judgment or miscalculation of strength, or malign influence, are swept away into the rapids, and then, notwithstanding the wonderful rescues effected by the American blacksmith and unwonted kindnesses of fortune, there is little chance of saving body corporate or incorporate from the headlong swoop to destruction.

Next to the purveyors of curiosities and hotel keepers, the Indians, who live in a village at some distance from Niagara, reap the largest profit from the crowds of visitors who repair annually to the Falls. They are a harmless and by no means elevated race of semi-civilised savages, whose energies are expended on whiskey, feather fans, bark canoes, ornamental mocassins, and carved pipe stems. I had arranged for an excursion to see them in their wigwams one morning, when the news was brought to me that General Scott had ordered, or been forced to order, the advance of the Federal troops encamped in front of Washington, under the command of McDowell, against the Confederates, commanded by Beauregard, who was described as occupying a most formidable position, covered with entrenchments and batteries in front of a ridge of hills, through which the railway passes to Richmond.

The New York papers represent the Federal army to be of some grand indefinite strength, varying from 60,000 to 120,000 men, full of fight, admirably equipped, well disciplined, and provided with an overwhelming force of artillery General Scott, I am very well assured, did not feel such confidence in the result of an invasion of Virginia, that he would hurry raw levies and a rabble of regiments to undertake a most arduous military operation.

The day I was introduced to the General he was seated at a table in the unpretending room which served as his boudoir in the still humbler house where he held his head-quarters. On the table before him were some plans and maps of the harbour defences of the Southern ports. I inferred he was about to organise a force for the occupation of positions along the coast. But when I mentioned my impression to one of his officers, he said, "Oh, no, the General advised that long ago; but he is now convinced we are too late. All he can hope, now, is to be allowed time to prepare a force for the field, but there are hopes that some compromise will yet take place."

The probabilities of this compromise have vanished: few entertain them now. They have been hanging Secessionists in Illinois, and the courthouse itself has been made the scene of Lynch law murder in Ogle county. Petitions, prepared by citizens of New York to the President, for a general convention to consider a compromise, have been seized. The Confederates have raised batteries along the Virginia shore of the Potomac. General Banks, at Baltimore, has deposed the police authorities "*proprio motu*," in spite of the protest of the board. Engagements have occurred between the Federal steamers and the Confederate batteries on the Potomac. On all points, wherever the Federal pickets have advanced in Virginia, they have encountered opposition and have been obliged to halt or to retire.

* * * * * *

As I stood on the verandah this morning, looking for the last time on the Falls, which were covered with a grey mist, that rose from the river and towered uuto the sky in columns which were lost in the clouds, a voice beside me said, "Mr. Russell, that is something like the present condition of our country, mists and darkness obscure it now, but we know the great waters are rushing behind, and will flow till eternity." The speaker was an earnest, thoughtful man, but the country of which he spoke was the land of the South. "And do you think," said I, "when the mists clear away the Falls will be as full and as grand as before?" "Well," he replied, "they are great as it is, though a rock divides them; we have merely thrown our rock into the waters, —they will meet all the same in the pool below." A coloured boy, who has waited on me at the hotel, hearing I was going away, entreated me to take him on any terms, which were, I found, an advance of nine dollars, and twenty dollars a month, and, as I heard a good account of him from the landlord, I installed the young man into my service. In the evening I left Niagara on my way to New York.

July 2nd.—At early dawn this morning, looking out of the sleeping car, I saw through the mist a broad, placid river on the right, and on the left high wooded banks running sharply into the stream, against the base of which the rails were laid. West Point, which is celebrated for its picturesque scenery, as much as for its military school, could not be seen through the fog, and I regretted time did not allow me to stop and pay a visit to the academy. I was obliged to content myself with the handiwork of some of the ex-pupils. The only camaraderie I have witnessed in America exists among the West Point men. It is to Americans what our great public schools are to young Englishmen. To take a high place at West Point is to be a first-class man, or wrangler. The academy turns out a kind of military aristocracy, and I have heard complaints that the Irish and Germans are almost completely excluded, because the nominations to West Point are obtained by political influence; and the foreign element, though powerful at the ballot box, has no enduring strength. The Murphies and Schmidts seldom succeed in shoving their sons into the American institution. North and South, I have observed, the old pupils refer everything military to West Point. "I was with Beauregard at West Point. He was three above me." Or, "M'Dowell and I were in the same class." An officer is measured by what he did there, and if professional jealousies date from the state of common pupilage, so do lasting friendships. I heard Beauregard, Lawton, Hardee, Bragg, and others, speak of M'Dowell, Lyon, M'Clellan, and other men of the academy, as their names turned up in the Northern papers, evidently judging of them by the old school standard. The number of men who have been educated there greatly exceeds the modest requirements of the army. But there is likelihood of their being all in full work very soon.

At about nine a.m., the train reached New York, and in driving to the house of Mr. Duncan, who accompanied me from Niagara, the first thing which struck me was the changed aspect of the streets. Instead of peaceful citizens, men in military uniforms thronged the pathways, and such multitudes of United States' flags floated from the windows and roofs of the houses as to convey the impression that it was a great holiday festival. The appearance of New York when I first saw it was very different. For one day, indeed, after my arrival, there were men in uniform to be seen in the streets, but they disappeared after St. Patrick had been duly honoured, and it was very rarely I ever saw a man in soldier's clothes during the rest of my stay. Now, fully a third of the people carried arms, and wore dressed in some kind of martial garb.

The walls are covered with placards from military companies offering inducements to recruits. An outburst of military tailors has taken place in the streets; shops are devoted to militia equipments; rifles, pistols, swords, plumes, long boots, saddle, bridle, camp beds, canteens, tents, knapsacks, have usurped the place of the ordinary articles of traffic. Pictures and engravings—bad, and very bad—of the "battles" of Big Bethel and Vienna, full of furious charges, smoke and dismembered bodies, have driven the French prints out of the windows. Innumerable "General Scotts" glower at you from every turn, making the General look wiser than he or any man ever was. Ellsworths in almost equal proportion, Grebles and Winthrops—the Union martyrs—and Tompkins, the temporary hero of Fairfax courthouse.

The "flag of our country" is represented in a coloured engraving, the original of which was not destitute of poetical feeling, as an angry blue sky through which meteors fly streaked by the winds, whilst between the red stripes the stars just shine out from the heavens, the flag-staff being typified by a forest tree bending to the force of the blast. The Americans like this idea—to my mind it is significant of bloodshed and disaster. And why not! What would become of all these pseudo-Zouaves who have come out like an eruption over the States, and are in no respect, not even in their baggy breeches, like their great originals, if this war were not to go on? I thought I had had enough of Zouaves in New Orleans, but *dis aliter visum.*

They are overrunning society, and the streets here, and the dress which becomes the broad-chested, stumpy, short-legged Celt, who seems specially intended for it, is singularly unbecoming to the tall and slightly-built American. Songs "On to glory," "Our country," new versions of "Hail, Columbia," which certainly cannot be considered by even American complacency a "happy land" when its inhabitants are preparing to cut each other's throats, of the "star-spangled banner," are displayed in booksellers' and music-shop windows, and patriotic sentences emblazoned on flags float from many houses. The ridiculous habit of dressing up children and young people up to ten and twelve years of age as Zouaves and vivandières has been caught up by the old people, and Mars would die with laughter if he saw some of the abdominous, be-spectacled light infantry men who are hobbling along the pavement.

There has been indeed a change in New York: externally it is most remarkable, but I cannot at all admit that the abuse with which I was assailed for describing the indifference which prevailed on my arrival was in the least degree justified. I was desirous of learning how far the tone of conversation "in the city" had altered, and soon after breakfast I went down Broadway to Pine Street and Wall Street. The street in all its length was almost draped with flags — the warlike character of the shops was intensified. In front of one shop window there was a large crowd gazing with interest at some object which I at last succeeded in feasting my eyes upon. A grey cap with a tinsel badge in front, and the cloth stained with blood, was displayed, with the words, "Cap of Secession officer killed in action." On my way I observed another crowd of women, some with children in their arms, standing in front of a large house and gazing up earnestly and angrily at the windows. I found they were wives, mothers, and sisters, and daughters of volunteers who had gone off and left them destitute.

The misery thus caused has been so great that the citizens of New York have raised a fund to provide food, clothes, and a little money—a poor relief, in fact, for them, and it was plain that they were much needed, though some of the applicants did not seem to belong to a class accustomed to seek aid from the public. This already! But Wall Street and Pine Street are bent on battle. And so this day, hot from the South and impressed with the firm resolve of the people, and finding that the North has been lashing itself into fury, I sit down and write to England, on my return to the city. "At present dismiss entirely the idea, no matter how it may originate, that there will be, or can be, peace, compromise, union, or secession, till war has determined the issue."

As long as there was a chance that the struggle might not take place, the merchants of New York were silent, fearful of offending their Southern friends and connections, but inflicting infinite damage on their own government and misleading both sides. Their sentiments, sympathies, and business bound them with the South; and, indeed, till "the glorious uprising," the South believed New York was with them, as might be credited from the tone of some organs in the press, and I remember hearing it said by Southerners in Washington, that it was very likely New York would go out of the Union! When the merchants, however, saw that the South was determined to quit the Union, they resolved to avert the permanent loss of the great profits derived from their connection with the South by some present sacrifices. They rushed to the platforms—the battle-cry was sounded from almost every pulpit—flag raisings took place in every square, like the planting of the tree of liberty in France in 1848, and the oath was taken to trample Secession under foot, and to quench the fire of the Southern heart for ever.

The change in manner, in tone, in argument, is most remarkable. I met men to-day who last March argued coolly and philosophically about the right of Secession. They are now furious at the idea of such wickedness—furious with England, because she does not deny their own famous doctrine of the sacred right of insurrection. "We must maintain our glorious Union, sir." "We must have a country." "We cannot allow two nations to grow up on this Continent, sir." "We must possess the entire control of the Mississippi." These "musts," and "can'ts," and "won'ts," are the angry utterances of a spirited people who have had their will so long that they at last believe it is omnipotent. Assuredly, they will not have it over the South without a tremendous and long-sustained contest, in which they must put forth every exertion, and use all the resources and superior means they so abundantly possess.

It is absurd to assert, as do the New York people, to give some semblance of reason to their sudden outburst, that it was caused by the insult to the flag at Sumter. Why, the flag had been fired on long before Sumter was attacked by the Charleston batteries! It had been torn down from United States' arsenals and forts all over the South; and but for the accident which placed Major Anderson in a position from which he could not retire, there would have been no bombardment of the fort, and it would, when evacuated, have shared the fate of all the other Federal works on the Southern coast. Some of the gentlemen who are now so patriotic and Unionistic, were last March prepared to maintain that if the President attempted to reinforce Sumter or Pickens, he would be responsible for the destruction of the Union. Many journals in New York and out of it held the same doctrine.

One word to these gentlemen. I am pretty well satisfied that if they had always spoken, written, and acted as they do now, the people of Charleston would not have attacked Sumter so readily. The abrupt outburst at the North and the demonstration at New York filled the South, first with astonishment, and then with something like fear, which was rapidly fanned into anger by the press and the politicians, as well as by the pride inherent in slaveholders.

I wonder what Mr. Seward will say when I get back to Washington. Before I left, he was of opinion—at all events, he stated—that all the States would come back, at the rate of one a month. The nature of the process was not stated; but we are told there are 250,000 Federal troops now under arms, prepared to try a new one.

Combined with the feeling of animosity to the rebels, there is, I perceive, a good deal of ill-feeling towards Great Britain. The Southern papers are so angry with us for the Order in Council closing British ports against privateers and their prizes, that they advise Mr. Rust and Mr. Yancey to leave Europe. We are in evil case between North and South. I met a reverend doctor, who is most bitter in his expressions towards us; and I dare say, Bishop and General Leonidas Polk, down South, would not be much better disposed. The clergy are active on both sides; and their flocks approve of their holy violence. One journal tells with much gusto of a blasphemous chaplain, a remarkably good rifle shot, who went into one of the skirmishes lately, and killed a number of rebels—the joke being in the fact, that each time he fired and brought down his man, he exclaimed, piously, "May Heaven have mercy on your soul!" One Father Mooney, who performed the novel act for a clergyman of "christening" a big gun at Washington the other day, wound up the speech he made on the occasion, by declaring "the echo of its voice would be *sweet music*, inviting the children of Columbia to share the comforts of his father's home." Can impiety, and folly, and bad taste, go further?

CHAPTER XLIV.

Departure for Washington—A "servant"—The American Press on the War—Military aspect of the States—Philadelphia—Baltimore—Washington—Lord Lyons—Mr. Sumner—Irritation against Great Britain—"Independence" day—Meeting of Congress—General state of affairs.

July 3rd.—Up early, breakfasted at five A. M., and left my hospitable host's roof, on my way to Washington. The ferry-boat, which is a long way off, starts for the train at seven o'clock; and so bad are the roads, I nearly missed it. On hurrying to secure my place in the train, I said to one of the railway officers, "If you see a coloured man in a cloth cap and dark coat with metal buttons, will you be good enough, sir, to tell him I'm in this carriage." "Why so, sir?" "He is my servant." "Servant," he repeated; "your servant! I presume you're a Britisher; and if he's your servant, I think you may as well let him find you." And so he walked away, delighted with his cleverness, his civility, and his rebuke of an aristocrat.

Nearly four months since I went by this road to Washington. The change which has since occurred is beyond belief. Men were then speaking of place under Government, of compromises between North and South, and of peace; now they only talk of war and battle. Ever since I came out of the South, and could see the newspapers, I have been struck by the easiness of the American people, by their excessive credulity. Whether they wish it or not, they are certainly deceived. Not a day has passed without the announcement that the Federal troops were moving, and that "a great battle was expected" by somebody unknown, at some place or other.

I could not help observing the arrogant tone with which writers of stupendous ignorance on military matters write of the operations which they think the Generals should undertake. They demand that an army, which has neither adequate transport, artillery, nor cavalry, shall be pushed forward to Richmond to crush out Secession, and at the same time their columns teem with accounts from the army, which prove that it is not only ill-disciplined, but that it is ill-provided. A general outcry has been raised against the war department and the contractors, and it is openly stated that Mr. Cameron, the Secretary, has not clean hands. One journalist denounces "the swindling and plunder" which prevailed under his eyes. A minister who is disposed to be corrupt can be so with facility under the system of the United States, because he has absolute control over the contracts, which are rising to an enormous magnitude, as the war preparations assume more formidable dimensions. The greater part of the military stores of the State are in the South—arms, ordnance, clothing, ammunition, ships, machinery, and all kinds of *matériel* must be prepared in a hurry.

The condition in which the States present themselves, particularly at sea, is a curious commentary on the offensive and warlike tone of their Statesmen in their dealings with the first maritime power of the world. They cannot blockade a single port effectually. The Confederate steamer Sumter has escaped to sea from New Orleans, and ships run in and out of Charleston almost as they please. Coming so recently from the South, I can see the great difference which exists between the two races, as they may be called, exemplified in the men I have seen, and those who are in the train going towards Washington. These volunteers have none of the swash-buckler bravado, gallant-swaggering air of the Southern men. They are staid, quiet men, and the Pennsylvanians, who are on their way to join their regiment in Baltimore, are very inferior in size and strength to the Tennesseans and Carolinians.

The train is full of men in uniform. When I last went over the line, I do not believe there was a sign of soldiering beyond perhaps the "conductor," who is always described in the papers as being "gentlemanly," with his badge. And, *à-propos* of badges, I see that civilians have taken to wearing shields of metal on their coats, enamelled with the stars and stripes, and that men who are not in the army try to make it seem they are soldiers by affecting military caps and cloaks.

The country between Washington and Philadelphia is destitute of natural beauties, but it affords abundant evidence that it is inhabited by a prosperous, comfortable, middle-class community. From every village church, and from many houses, the Union flag was displayed. Four months ago not one was to be seen. When we were crossing in the steam ferry-boat at Philadelphia, I saw some volunteers looking up and smiling at a hatchet which was over the cabin door, and it was not till I saw it had the words "States Rights' Fire Axe" painted along the handle I could account for the attraction. It would fare ill with any vessel in Southern waters which displayed an axe to the citizens inscribed with "Down with States Rights" on it. There is certainly less vehemence and bitterness among the Northerners; but it might be erroneous to suppose there was less determination.

Below Philadelphia, from Havre-de-Grâce all the way to Baltimore, and thence on to Washington, the stations on the rail were guarded by soldiers, as though an enemy were expected to destroy the bridges and to tear up the rails. Wooden bridges and causeways, carried over piles and embankments, are necessary, in consequence of the nature of the country; and at each of these a small camp was formed for the soldiers who have to guard the approaches. Sentinels are posted, pickets thrown out, and in the open field by the way-side troops are to be seen moving, as though a battle was close at hand. In one word, we are in the State of Maryland. By these means alone are communications maintained between the North and the capital. As we approach Baltimore the number of sentinels and camps increase, and earthworks have been thrown up on the high grounds commanding the city. The display of Federal flags from the public buildings and some shipping in the river was so limited as to contrast strongly with those symbols of Union sentiments in the Northern cities.

Since I last passed through this city the streets have been a scene of bloodshed. The conductor of the car on which we travelled from one terminus to the other, along the street railway, pointed out the marks of the bullets on the walls and in the window frames. "That's the way to deal with the Plug Uglies," exclaimed he; a name given popularly to the lower classes called Rowdies in New York. "Yes," said a fellow-passenger quietly to me, "these are the sentiments which are now uttered in the country which we call the land of freedom, and men like that desire nothing better than brute force. There is no city in Europe—Venice, Warsaw, or Rome—subject to such tyranny as Baltimore at this moment. In this Pratt Street there have been murders as foul as ever soldiery committed in the streets of Paris." Here was evidently the judicial blindness of a States Rights fanatic, who considers the despatch of Federal soldiers through the State of Maryland without the permission of the authorities an outrage so flagrant as to justify the people in shooting them down, whilst the soldiers become murderers if they resist. At the corners of the streets strong guards of soldiers were posted, and patrols moved up and down the thoroughfares. The inhabitants looked sullen and sad. A small war is waged by the police recently appointed by the Federal authorities against the women, who exhibit much ingenuity in expressing their animosity to the stars and stripes—dressing the children, and even dolls, in the Confederate colours, and wearing the same in ribbons and bows. The negro population alone seemed just the same as before.

The Secession newspapers of Baltimore have been suppressed, but the editors contrive nevertheless to show their sympathies in the selection of their extracts. In to-day's paper there is an account of a skirmish in the West, given by one of the Confederates who took part in it, in which it is stated that the officer commanding the party "scalped" twenty-three Federals. For the first time since I left the South I see those advertisements headed by the figure of a negro running with a bundle, and containing descriptions of the fugitive, and the reward offered for imprisoning him or her, so that the owner may receive his property. Among the insignia enumerated are scars on the back and over the loins. The whip is not only used by the masters and drivers, but by the police; and in every report of petty police cases sentences of so many lashes, and severe floggings of women of colour, are recorded.

It is about forty miles from Baltimore to Washington, and at every quarter of a mile for the whole distance a picket of soldiers guarded the rails. Camps appeared on both sides, larger and more closely packed together; and the rays of the setting sun fell on countless lines of tents as we approached the unfinished dome of the Capitol. On the Virginian side of the river, columns of smoke rising from the forest marked the site of Federal encampments across the stream. The fields around Washington resounded with the words of command and tramp of men, and flashed with wheeling arms. Parks of artillery studded the waste ground, and long trains of white-covered wagons filled up the open spaces in the suburbs of Washington.

To me all this was a wonderful sight. As I drove up Pennsylvania Avenue I could scarce credit that busy thoroughfare—all red, white, and blue with flags, filled with dust from galloping chargers and commissariat carts; the side-walks thronged with people, of whom a large proportion carried sword or bayonet; shops full of life and activity—was the same as that through which I had driven the first morning of my arrival. Washington now, indeed, is the capital of the United States; but it is no longer the scene of beneficent legislation and of peaceful government. It is the representative of armed force engaged in war—menaced whilst in the very act of raising its arm by the enemy it seeks to strike.

To avoid the tumult of Willard's, I requested a friend to hire apartments and drove to a house in Pennsylvania Avenue, close to the War Department, where he had succeeded in engaging a sitting-room about twelve feet square, and a bedroom to correspond, in a very small mansion, next door to a spirit merchant's. At the Legation I saw Lord Lyons, and gave him a brief account of what I had seen in the South. I was sorry to observe he looked rather careworn and pale.

The relations of the United States' Government with Great Britain have probably been considerably affected by Mr. Seward's failure in his prophecies. As the Southern Confederacy develops its power, the Foreign Secretary assumes higher ground, and becomes more exacting and defiant. In these hot summer days, Lord Lyons and the members of the Legation dine early, and enjoy the cool of the evening in the garden: so after a while I took my leave, and proceeded to Gautier's. On my way I met Mr. Sumner, who asked me for Southern news very anxiously, and in the course of conversation with him I was confirmed in my impressions that the feeling between the two countries was not as friendly as could be desired. Lord Lyons had better means of knowing what is going on in the South, by communications from the British Consuls; but even he seemed unaware of facts which had occurred whilst I was there, and Mr. Sumner appeared to be as ignorant of the whole condition of things below Mason and Dixon's line as he was of the politics of Timbuctoo.

The importance of maintaining a friendly feeling with England appeared to me very strongly impressed on the Senator's mind. Mr. Seward has been fretful, irritable, and acrimonious; and it is not too much to suppose Mr. Sumner has been useful in allaying irritation. A certain despatch was written last June, which amounted to little less than a declaration of war against Great Britain. Most fortunately the President was induced to exercise his power. The despatch was modified, though not without opposition, and was forwarded to the English Minister with its teeth drawn. Lord Lyons, who is one of the suavest and quietest of diplomatists, has found it difficult, I fear, to maintain personal relations with Mr. Seward at times. Two despatches have been prepared for Lord John Russell, which could have had no result but to lead to a breach of the peace, had not some friendly interpositor succeeded in averting the wrath of the Foreign Minister.

Mr. Sumner is more sanguine of immediate success than I am, from the military operations which are to commence when General Scott considers the army fit to take the field. At Gautier's I met a number of officers, who expressed a great diversity of views in reference to those operations. General M'Dowell is popular with them, but they admit the great deficiencies of the subaltern and company officers. General Scott is too infirm to take the field, and the burdens of administration press the veteran to the earth.

July 4th.—"Independence Day." Fortunate to escape this great national festival in the large cities of the Union where it is celebrated with many days before and after of surplus rejoicing, by fireworks and an incessant fusillade in the streets, I was, nevertheless, subjected to the small ebullition of the Washington juveniles, to bell-ringing and discharges of cannon and musketry. On this day Congress meets. Never before has any legislative body assembled under circumstances so grave. By their action they will decide whether the Union can ever be restored, and will determine whether the States of the North are to commence an invasion for the purpose of subjecting by force of arms, and depriving of their freedom, the States of the South.

Congress met to-day, merely for the purpose of forming itself into a regular body, and there was no debate or business of public importance introduced. Mr. Wilson gave me to understand, however, that some military movements of the utmost importance might be expected in a few days, and that General M'Dowell would positively attack the rebels in front of Washington. The Confederates occupy the whole of Northern Virginia, commencing from the peninsula above Fortress Monroe on the right or east, and extending along the Potomac, to the extreme verge of the State, by the Baltimore and Ohio Railway. This immense line, however, is broken by great intervals, and the army with which M'Dowell will have to deal may be considered as detached, covering the approaches to Richmond, whilst its left flank is protected by a corps of observation, stationed near Winchester, under General Jackson. A Federal corps is being prepared to watch the corps and engage it, whilst M'Dowell advances on the main body. To the right of this again, or further west, another body of Federals, under General M'Clellan, is operating in the valleys of the Shenandoah and in Western Virginia; but I did not hear any of these things from Mr. Wilson, who was, I am sure, in perfect ignorance of the plans, in a military sense, of the general. I sat at Mr. Sumner's desk, and wrote the final paragraphs of a letter describing my impressions of the South in a place but little disposed to give a favourable colour to them.

CHAPTER XLV.

Interview with Mr. Seward—My passport—Mr. Seward's views as to the war—Illumination at Washington—My "servant" absents himself—New York journalism—The Capitol—Interior of Congress—The President's Message—Speeches in Congress—Lord Lyons—General M'Dowell—Low standard in the army—Accident to the "Stars and Stripes"—A street row—Mr. Bigelow—Mr. N. P. Willis.

WHEN the Senate had adjourned, I drove to the State Department, and saw Mr. Seward, who looked much more worn and haggard than when I saw him last, three months ago. He congratulated me on my safe return from the South in time to witness some stirring events. "Well, Mr. Secretary, I am quite sure that, if all the South are of the same mind as those I met in my travels, there will be many battles before they submit to the Federal Government."

"It is not submission to the Government we want; it is to assent to the principles of the Constitution. When you left Washington we had a few hundred regulars and some hastily-levied militia to defend the national capital, and a battery and a half of artillery under the command of a traitor. The Navy-yard was in the hands of a disloyal officer. We were surrounded by treason. Now we are supported by the loyal States which have come forward in defence of the best Government on the face of the earth, and the unfortunate and desperate men who have commenced this struggle will have to yield, or experience the punishment due to their crimes."

"But, Mr. Seward, has not this great exhibition of strength been attended by some circumstances calculated to inspire apprehension that liberty in the free States may be impaired; for instance, I hear that I must procure a passport in order to travel through the States and go into the camps in front of Washington."

"Yes, sir; you must send your passport here from Lord Lyons, with his signature. It will be no good till I have signed it, and then it must be sent to General Scott, as Commander-in-Chief of the United States army, who will subscribe it, after which it will be available for all legitimate purposes. You are not in any way impaired in your liberty by the process."

"Neither is, one may say, the man who is under surveillance of the police in despotic countries in Europe; he has only to submit to a certain formality, and he is all right; in fact, it is said by some people, that the protection afforded by a passport is worth all the trouble connected with having it in order."

Mr. Seward seemed to think it was quite likely. There were corresponding measures taken in the Southern States by the rebels, and it was necessary to have some control over traitors and disloyal persons. "In this contest," said he, "the Government will not shrink from using all the means which they consider necessary to restore the Union." It was not my place to remark that such doctrines were exactly identical with all that despotic governments in Europe have advanced as the ground of action in cases of revolt, or with a view to the maintenance of their strong Governments. "The Executive," said he, "has declared in the inaugural that the rights of the Federal Government shall be fully vindicated. We are dealing with an insurrection within our own country, of our own people, and the Government of Great Britain have thought fit to recognise that insurrection before we were able to bring the strength of the Union to bear against it, by conceding to it the status of belligerent. Although we might justly complain of such an unfriendly act in a manner that might injure the friendly relations between the two countries, we do not desire to give any excuse for foreign interference; although we do not hesitate, in case of necessity, to resist it to the uttermost, we have less to fear from a foreign war than any country in the world. If any European Power provokes a war, we shall not shrink from it. A contest between Great Britain and the United States would wrap the world in fire, and at the end it would not be the United States which would have to lament the results of the conflict."

I could not but admire the confidence—may I say the coolness?—of the statesman who sat in his modest little room within the sound of the enemy's guns, in a capital menaced by their forces, who spoke so fearlessly of war with a Power which could have blotted out the paper blockade of the Southern forts and coast in a few hours, and, in conjunction with the Southern armies, have repeated the occupation and destruction of the capital.

The President sent for Mr. Seward whilst I was in the State Department, and I walked up Pennsylvania Avenue to my lodgings, through a crowd of men in uniform who were celebrating Independence Day in their own fashion—some by the large internal use of fire-water, others by an external display of fire-works.

Directly opposite my lodgings are the head-quarters of General Mansfield, commanding the district, which are marked by a guard at the door and a couple of six-pounder guns pointing down the street. I called upon the General, but he was busy examining certain inhabitants of Alexandria and of Washington itself, who had been brought before him on the charge of being Secessionists, and I left my card, and proceeded to General Scott's head-quarters, which I found packed with officers. The General received me in a small room, and expressed his gratification at my return, but I saw he was so busy with reports, despatches, and maps, that I did not trespass on his time. I dined with Lord Lyons, and afterwards went with some members of the Legation to visit the camps, situated in the public square.

All the population of Washington had turned out in their best to listen to the military bands, the music of which was rendered nearly inaudible by the constant discharge of fireworks. The camp of the 12th New York presented a very pretty and animated scene. The men liberated from duty were enjoying themselves out and inside their tents, and the sutlers' booths were driving a roaring trade. I was introduced to Colonel Butterfield, commanding the regiment, who was a merchant of New York; but notwithstanding the training of the counting-house, he looked very much like a soldier, and had got his regiment very fairly in hand. In compliance with a desire of Professor Henry, the Colonel had prepared a number of statistical tables in which the nationality, height, weight, breadth of chest, age, and other particulars respecting the men under his command were entered. I looked over the book, and as far as I could judge, but two out of twelve of the soldiers were native-born Americans, the rest being Irish, German, English, and European-born generally. According to the commanding officer they were in the highest state of discipline and obedience. He had given them leave to go out as they pleased for the day, but at tattoo only 14 men out of 1000 were absent, and some of those had been accounted for by reports that they were incapable of locomotion owing to the hospitality of the citizens.

When I returned to my lodgings, the coloured boy whom I had hired at Niagara was absent, and I was told he had not come in since the night before. "These free coloured boys," said my landlord, "are a bad set; now they are worse than ever; the officers of the army are taking them all away from us; it's just the life they like; they get little work, have good pay; but what they like most is robbing and plundering the farmers' houses over in Virginia; what with Germans, Irish, and free niggers, Lord help the poor Virginians, I say; but they'll give them a turn yet."

The sounds in Washington to-night might have led one to believe the city was carried by storm. Constant explosion of fire-arms, fireworks, shouting, and cries in the streets, which combined with the heat and the abominable odours of the undrained houses and mosquitoes, to drive sleep far away.

July 5th.—As the young gentleman of colour, to whom I had given egregious ransom as well as an advance of wages, did not appear this morning, I was, after an abortive attempt to boil water for coffee and to get a piece of toast, compelled to go in next door, and avail myself of the hospitality of Captain Cecil Johnson, who was installed in the drawing-room of Madame Jost. In the forenoon, Mr. John Bigelow, whose acquaintance I made, much to my gratification in time gone by, on the margin of the Lake of Thun, found me out, and proffered his services; which, as the whileom editor of the *Evening Post* and as a leading Republican, he was in a position to render valuable and most effective; but he could not make a Bucephalus to order, and I have been running through the stables of Washington in vain, hoping to find something up to my weight —such flankless, screwy, shoulderless, cat-like creatures were never seen—four of them would scarcely furnish ribs and legs enough to carry a man, but the owners thought that each of them was fit for Baron Rothschild; and then there was saddlery and equipments of all sorts to be got, which the influx of officers and the badness and dearness of the material put quite beyond one's reach. Mr. Bigelow was of opinion that the army would move at once; "but," said I, "where is the transport—where the cavalry and guns?" "Oh," replied he, "I suppose we have got everything that is required. I know nothing of these things, but I am told cavalry are no use in the wooded country towards Richmond." I have not yet been able to go through the camps, but I doubt very much whether the material or commissariat of the grand army of the North is at all adequate to a campaign.

The presumption and ignorance of the New York journals would be ridiculous were they not so mischievous. They describe "this horde of battalion companies—unofficered, clad in all kinds of different uniform, diversely equipped, perfectly ignorant of the principles of military obedience and concerted action,"—for so I hear it described by United States officers themselves —as being "the greatest army the world ever saw; perfect in officers and discipline; unsurpassed in devotion and courage; furnished with every requisite; and destined on its first march to sweep into Richmond, and to obliterate from the Potomac to New Orleans every trace of rebellion."

The Congress met to-day to hear the President's Message read. Somehow or other there is not such anxiety and eagerness to hear what Mr. Lincoln has to say as one could expect on such a momentous occasion. It would seem as if the forthcoming appeal to arms had overshadowed every other sentiment in the minds of the people. They are waiting for deeds, and care not for words. The confidence of the New York papers, and of the citizens, soldiers, and public speakers, contrast with the dubious and gloomy views of the military men; but of this Message itself there are some incidents independent of the occasion to render it curious, if not interesting. The President has, it is said, written much of it in his own fashion, which has been revised and altered by his Ministers; but he has written it again and repeated himself, and after many struggles a good deal of pure Lincolnism goes down to Congress.

At a little after half-past eleven I went down to the Capitol. Pennsylvania Avenue was thronged as before, but on approaching Capitol Hill, the crowd rather thinned away, as though they shunned, or had no curiosity to hear, the President's Message. One would have thought that, where every one who could get in was at liberty to attend the galleries in both Houses, there would have been an immense pressure from the inhabitants and strangers in the city, as well as from the citizen soldiers, of which such multitudes were in the street; but when I looked up from the floor of the Senate, I was astonished to see that the galleries were not more than three parts filled. There is always a ruinous look about an unfinished building when it is occupied and devoted to business. The Capitol is situated on a hill, one face of which is scarped by the road, and has the appearance of being formed of heaps of rubbish. Towards Pennsylvania Avenue the long frontage abuts on a lawn shaded by trees, through which walks and avenues lead to the many entrances under the porticoes and colonnades; the face which corresponds on the other side looks out on heaps of brick and mortar, cut stone, and a waste of marble blocks lying half buried in the earth and cumbering the ground, which, in the magnificent ideas of the founders and planners of the city, was to be occupied by stately streets. The cleverness of certain speculators in land prevented the execution of the original idea, which was to radiate all the main avenues of the city from the Capitol as a centre, the intermediate streets being formed by circles drawn at regularly-increasing intervals from the Capitol, and intersected by the radii. The speculators purchased up the land on the side between the Navy-yard and the site of the Capitol; the result—the land is unoccupied, except by paltry houses, and the capitalists are ruined.

The Capitol would be best described by a series of photographs. Like the Great Republic itself, it is unfinished. It resembles it in another respect: it looks best at a distance; and, again, it is incongruous in its parts. The passages are so dark that artificial light is often required to enable one to find his way. The offices and bureaux of the committees are better than the chambers of the Senate and the House of Representatives. All the encaustics and the white marble and stone staircases suffer from tobacco juice, though there is a liberal display of spittoons at every corner. The official messengers, doorkeepers, and porters wear no distinctive badge or dress. No policemen are on duty, as in our Houses of Parliament; no soldiery, gendarmerie, or sergens-de-ville in the precincts; the crowd wanders about the passages as it pleases, and shows the utmost propriety, never going where it ought not to intrude. There is a special gallery set apart for women; the reporters are commodiously placed in an ample gallery, above the Speaker's chair; the diplomatic circle have their gallery facing the reporters, and they are placed so low down in the somewhat depressed Chamber, that every word can be heard from speakers in the remotest parts of the house very distinctly.

The seats of the members are disposed in a manner somewhat like those in the French Chambers. Instead of being in parallel rows to the walls, and at right angles to the Chairman's seat, the separate chairs and desks of the Senators are arranged in semicircular rows. The space between the walls and the outer semicircle is called the floor of the house, and it is a high compliment to a stranger to introduce him within this privileged place. There are leather cushioned seats and lounges put for the accommodation of those who may be introduced by Senators, or to whom, as distinguished members of Congress in former days, the permission is given to take their seats. Senators Sumner and Wilson introduced me to a chair, and made me acquainted with a number of Senators before the business of the day began.

Mr. Sumner, as the Chairman of the Committee on Foreign Relations, is supposed to be viewed with some jealousy by Mr. Seward, on account of the disposition attributed to him to interfere in diplomatic questions; but if he does so, we shall have no reason to complain, as the Senator is most desirous of keeping the peace between the two countries, and of mollifying any little acerbities and irritations which may at present exist between them. Senator Wilson is a man who has risen from what would be considered in any country but a republic the lowest ranks of the people. He apprenticed himself to a poor shoemaker when he was twenty-two years of age, and when he was twenty-four years old he began to go to school, and devoted all his earnings to the improvement of education. He got on by degrees, till he set up as a master shoemaker and manufacturer, became a "major-general" of State militia; finally was made Senator of the United States, and is now "Chairman of the Committee of the Senate on Military Affairs." He is a bluff man, of about fifty years of age, with a peculiar eye and complexion, and seems honest and vigorous. But is he not going ultra crepidam in such a post? At present he is much perplexed by the drunkenness which prevails among the troops, or rather by the desire of the men for spirits, as he has a New England mania on that point. One of the most remarkable-looking men in the House is Mr. Sumner. Mr. Breckinridge and he would probably be the first persons to excite the curiosity of a stranger, so far as to induce him to ask for their names. Save in height—and both are a good deal over six feet—there is no resemblance between the champion of States Rights and the orator of the Black Republicans. The massive head, the great chin and jaw, and the penetrating eyes of Mr. Breckinridge convey the idea of a man of immense determination, courage, and sagacity. Mr. Sumner's features are indicative of a philosophical and poetical turn of thought, and one might easily conceive that he would be a great advocate, but an indifferent leader of a party.

It was a hot day; but there was no excuse for the slop coats and light-coloured clothing and felt wide-awakes worn by so many Senators in such a place. They gave the meeting the aspect of a gathering of bakers or millers: nor did the constant use of the spittoons beside their desks, their reading of newspapers and writing letters during the dispatch of business, or the hurrying to and fro of the pages of the House between the seats, do anything but derogate from the dignity of the assemblage, and, according to European notions, violate the respect due to a Senate Chamber. The pages alluded to are smart boys, from twelve to fifteen years of age, who stand below the President's table, and are employed to go on errands and carry official messages by the members. They wear no particular uniform, and are dressed as the taste or means of their parents dictate.

The House of Representatives exaggerates all the peculiarities I have observed in the Senate, but the debates are not regarded with so much interest as those of the Upper House; indeed, they are of far less importance. Strong-minded statesmen and officers—Presidents or Ministers—do not care much for the House of Representatives, so long as they are sure of the Senate; and, for the matter of that, a President like Jackson does not care much for Senate and House together. There are privileges attached to a seat in either branch of the Legislature, independent of the great fact that they receive mileage and are paid for their services, which may add some incentive to ambition. Thus the members can order whole tons of stationery for their use, not only when they are in session, but during the recess. Their frank covers parcels by mail, and it is said that Senators without a conscience have sent sewing-machines to their wives and pianos to their daughters as little parcels by post. I had almost forgotten that much the same abuses were in vogue in England some century ago.

The galleries were by no means full, and in that reserved for the diplomatic body the most notable person was M. Mercier, the Minister of France, who, fixing his intelligent and eager face between both hands, watched with keen scrutiny the attitude and conduct of the Senate. None of the members of the English Legation were present. After the lapse of an hour, Mr. Hay, the President's Secretary, made his appearance on the floor, and sent in the Message to the Clerk of the Senate, Mr. Forney, who proceeded to read it to the House. It was listened to in silence, scarcely broken except when some Senator murmured "Good, that is so;" but in fact the general purport of it was already known to the supporters of the Ministry, and not a sound came from the galleries. Soon after Mr. Forney had finished, the galleries were cleared, and I returned up Pennsylvania Avenue, in which the crowds of soldiers around bar-rooms, oyster shops, and restaurants, the groups of men in officers' uniform, and the clattering of disorderly mounted cavaliers in the dust, increased my apprehension that discipline was very little regarded, and that the army over the Potomac had not a very strong hand to keep it within bounds.

As I was walking over with Captain Johnson to dine with Lord Lyons, I met General Scott leaving his office and walking with great difficulty between two aides-de-camp. He was dressed in a blue frock with gold lace shoulder straps, fastened round the waist by a yellow sash, and with large yellow lapels turned back over the chest in the old style, and moved with great difficulty along the pavement. "You see I am trying to hobble along, but it is hard for me to overcome my many infirmities. I regret I could not have the pleasure of granting you an interview to-day, but I shall cause it to be intimated to you when I may have the pleasure of seeing you; meantime I shall provide you with a pass and the necessary introductions to afford you all facilities with the army."

After dinner I made a round of visits, and heard the diplomatists speaking of the Message; few, if any of them, in its favour. With the exception perhaps of Baron Gerolt, the Prussian Minister, there is not one member of the Legations who justifies the attempt of the Northern States to assert the supremacy of the Federal Government by the force of arms. Lord Lyons, indeed, in maintaining a judicious reticence whenever he does speak, gives utterance to sentiments becoming the representative of Great Britain at the court of a friendly Power, and the Minister of a people who have been protagonists to slavery for many a long year.

July 6th.—I breakfasted with Mr. Bigelow this morning, to meet Gen. McDowell, who commands the army of the Potomac, now so soon to move. He came in without an aide-de-camp, and on foot, from his quarters in the city. He is a man about forty years of age, square and powerfully built, but with rather a stout and clumsy figure and limbs, a good head covered with close-cut thick dark hair, small light-blue eyes, short nose, large cheeks and jaws, relieved by an iron-grey tuft somewhat of the French type, and affecting in dress the style of our gallant allies. His manner is frank, simple, and agreeable, and he did not hesitate to speak with great openness of the difficulties he had to contend with, and the imperfection of all the arrangements of the army.

As an officer of the regular army he has a thorough contempt for what he calls "political generals"—the men who use their influence with President and Congress to obtain military rank, which in time of war places them before the public in the front of events, and gives them an appearance of leading in the greatest of all political movements. Nor is General McDowell enamoured of volunteers, for he served in Mexico, and has from what he saw there formed rather an un favourable opinion of their capabilities in the field. He is inclined, however, to hold the Southern troops in too little respect; and he told me that the volunteers from the slave states, who entered the field full of exultation and boastings, did not make good their words, and that they suffered especially from sickness and disease, in consequence of their disorderly habits and dissipation. His regard for old associations was evinced in many questions he asked me about Beauregard, with whom he had been a student at West Point, where the Confederate commander was noted for his studious and reserved habits, and his excellence in feats of strength and athletic exercises.

As proof of the low standard established in his army, he mentioned that some officers of considerable rank were more than suspected of selling rations, and of illicit connections with sutlers for purposes of pecuniary advantage. The General walked back with me as far as my lodgings, and I observed that not one of the many soldiers he passed in the streets saluted him, though his rank was indicated by his velvet collar and cuffs, and a gold star on the shoulder strap.

Having written some letters, I walked out with Captain Johnson and one of the attachés of the British Legation, to the lawn at the back of the White House, and listened to the excellent band of the United States Marines, playing on a kind of dais under the large flag recently hoisted by the President himself, in the garden. The occasion was marked by rather an ominous event. As the President pulled the halyards and the flag floated aloft, a branch of a tree caught the bunting and tore it, so that a number of the stars and stripes were detached and hung dangling beneath the rest of the flag, half detached from the staff.

I dined at Captain Johnson's lodgings next door to mine. Beneath us was a wine and spirit store, and crowds of officers and men flocked indiscriminately to make their purchases, with a good deal of tumult, which increased as the night came on. Later still, there was a great disturbance in the city. A body of New York Zouaves wrecked some houses of bad repute, in one of which a private of the regiment was murdered early this morning. The cavalry patrols were called out and charged the rioters, who were dispersed with difficulty after resistance in which men on both sides were wounded. There is no police, no provost guard. Soldiers wander about the streets, and beg in the fashion of the mendicant in "Gil Blas" for money to get whiskey. My coloured gentleman has been led away by the Saturnalia and has taken to gambling in the camps, which are surrounded by hordes of rascally followers and sutlers' servants, and I find myself on the eve of a campaign, without servant, horse, equipment, or means of transport.

July 7th.—Mr. Bigelow invited me to breakfast, to meet Mr. Senator King, Mr. Olmsted, Mr. Thurlow Weed, a Senator from Missouri, a West Point professor, and others. It was indicative of the serious difficulties which embarrass the action of the Government to hear Mr. Wilson, the Chairman of the Military Committee of the Senate, inveigh against the officers of the regular army, and attack West Point itself. Whilst the New York papers were lauding Gen. Scott and his plans to the skies, the Washington politicians were speaking of him as obstructive, obstinate, and prejudiced—unfit for the times and the occasion.

General Scott refused to accept cavalry and artillery at the beginning of the levy, and said that they were not required; now he was calling for both arms most urgently. The officers of the regular army had followed suit. Although they were urgently pressed by the politicians to occupy Harper's Ferry and Manassas, they refused to do either, and the result is that the enemy have obtained invaluable supplies from the first place, and are now assembled in force in a most formidable position at the second. Everything as yet accomplished has been done by political generals —not by the officers of the regular army. Butler and Banks saved Baltimore in spite of General Scott. There was an attempt made to cry up Lyon in Missouri; but in fact it was Frank Blair, the brother of the Postmaster-General, who had been the soul and body of all the actions in that State. The first step taken by McClellan in Western Virginia was atrocious—he talked of slaves in a public document as property. Butler, at Monroe, had dealt with them in a very different spirit, and had used them for State purposes under the name of contraband. One man alone displayed powers of administrative ability, and that was Quartermaster Meigs; and unquestionably from all I heard, the praise was well bestowed. It is plain enough that the political leaders fear the consequences of delay, and that they are urging the military authorities to action, which the latter have too much professional knowledge to take with their present means. These Northern men know nothing of the South, and with them it is *omne ignotum pro minimo.* The West Point professor listened to them with a quiet smile, and exchanged glances with me now and then, as much as to say, "Did you ever hear such fools in your life?"

But the conviction of ultimate success is not less strong here than it is in the South. The difference between these gentlemen and the Southerners is, that in the South the leaders of the people, soldiers and civilians, are all actually under arms, and are ready to make good their words by exposing their bodies in battle.

I walked home with Mr. N. P. Willis, who is at Washington for the purpose of writing sketches to the little family journal of which he is editor, and giving war "anecdotes;" and with Mr. Olmsted, who is acting as a member of the New York Sanitary Commission, here authorised by the Government to take measures against the reign of dirt and disease in the Federal camp. The Republicans are very much afraid that there is, even at the present moment, a conspiracy against the Union in Washington—nay, in Congress itself; and regard Mr. Breckenridge, Mr. Bayard, Mr. Vallandigham, and others as most dangerous enemies, who should not be permitted to remain in the capital. I attended the Episcopal church and heard a very excellent discourse, free from any political allusion. The service differs little from our own, except that certain euphemisms are introduced in the Litany and elsewhere, and the prayers for Queen and Parliament are offered up *nomine mutato* for President and Congress.

CHAPTER XLVI.

Arlington Heights and the Potomac—Washington—The Federal camp—General M'Dowell—Flying rumours—Newspaper correspondents—General Fremont—Silencing the Press and Telegraph—A Loan Bill—Interview with Mr. Cameron—Newspaper criticism on Lord Lyons—Rumours about M'Clellan—The Northern army as reported and as it is—General M'Clellan.

July 8th.—I hired a horse at a livery stable, and rode out to Arlington Heights, at the other side of the Potomac, where the Federal army is encamped, if not on the sacred soil of Virginia, certainly on the soil of the district of Columbia, ceded by that State to Congress for the purposes of the Federal Government. The Long Bridge which spans the river, here more than a mile broad, is an ancient wooden and brick structure, partly of causeway, and partly of platform, laid on piles and uprights, with drawbridges for vessels to pass. The Potomac, which in peaceful times is covered with small craft, now glides in a gentle current over the shallows unbroken by a solitary sail. The "rebels" have established batteries below Mount Vernon, which partially command the river, and place the city in a state of blockade.

As a consequence of the magnificent conceptions which were entertained by the founders regarding the future dimensions of their future city, Washington is all suburb and no city. The only difference between the denser streets and the remoter village-like environs, is that the houses are better and more frequent, and the roads not quite so bad in the former. The road to the Long Bridge passes by a four-sided shaft of blocks of white marble, contributed, with appropriate mottoes, by the various States, as a fitting monument to Washington. It is not yet completed, and the materials lie in the field around, just as the Capitol and the Treasury are surrounded by the materials for their future and final development. Further on, is the red, and rather fantastic, pile of the Smithsonian Institute, and then the road makes a dip to the bridge, past some squalid little cottages, and the eye reposes on the shore of Virginia, rising in successive folds, and richly wooded, up to a moderate height from the water. Through the green forest leaves gleams the white canvas of the tents, and on the highest ridge westward rises an imposing structure, with a portico and colonnade in front, facing the river, which is called Arlington House, and belongs by descent, through Mr. Custis, from the wife of George Washington, to General Lee, Commander-in-Chief of the Confederate army. It is now occupied by General M'Dowell as his head-quarters, and a large United States flag floats from the roof, which shames even the ample proportions of the many stars and stripes rising up from the camps in the trees.

At the bridge there was a post of volunteer soldiers. The sentry on duty was sitting on a stump, with his firelock across his knees, reading a newspaper. He held out his hand for my pass, which was in the form of a letter, written by General Scott, and ordering all officers and soldiers of the army of the Potomac to permit me to pass freely without let or hindrance, and recommending me to the attention of Brigadier-General M'Dowell and all officers under his orders. "That'll do, you may go," said the sentry. "What pass is that, Abe?" inquired a non-commissioned officer. "It's from General Scott, and says he's to go wherever he likes." "I hope you'll go right away to Richmond, then, and get Jeff Davis's scalp for us," said the patriotic sergeant.

At the other end of the bridge a weak *tête de pont*, commanded by a road-work further on, covered the approach, and turning to the right I passed through a maze of camps, in front of which the various regiments, much better than I had expected to find them, broken up into small detachments, were learning elementary drill. A considerable number of the men were Germans, and the officers were for the most part in a state of profound ignorance of company drill, as might be seen by their confusion and inability to take their places when the companies faced about, or moved from one flank to the other. They were by no means equal in size or age, and, with some splendid exceptions, were inferior to the Southern soldiers. The camps were dirty, no latrines—the tents of various patterns—but on the whole they were well castrametated.

The road to Arlington House passed through some of the finest woods I have yet seen in America, but the axe was already busy amongst them, and the trunks of giant oaks were prostrate on the ground. The tents of the General and his small staff were pitched on the little plateau in which stood the house, and from it a very striking and picturesque view of the city, with the White House, the Treasury, the Post Office, Patent Office, and Capitol, was visible, and a wide spread of country, studded with tents also as far as the eye could reach, towards Maryland. There were only four small tents for the whole of the head-quarters of the grand army of the Potomac, and in front of one we found General M'Dowell, seated in a chair, examining some plans and maps. His personal staff, as far as I could judge, consisted of Mr. Clarence Brown, who came over with me, and three other officers, but there were a few connected with the departments at work in the rooms of Arlington House. I made some remark on the subject to the General, who replied that there was great jealousy on the part of the civilians respecting the least appearance of display, and that as he was only a brigadier, though he was in command of such a large army, he was obliged to be content with a brigadier's staff. Two untidy-looking orderlies, with ill-groomed horses, near the house, were poor substitutes for the force of troopers one would see in attendance on a general in Europe, but the use of the telegraph obviates the necessity of employing couriers. I went over some of the camps with the General. The artillery is the most efficient-looking arm of the service, but the horses are too light, and the number of the different calibres quite destructive to continuous efficiency in action. Altogether I was not favourably impressed with what I saw, for I had been led by reiterated statements to believe to some extent the extravagant stories of the papers, and expected to find upwards of 100,000 men in the highest state of efficiency, whereas there were not more than a third of the number, and those in a very incomplete, ill-disciplined state. Some of these regiments were called out under the President's proclamation for three months only, and will soon have served their full time, and as it is very likely they will go home, now the bubbles of national enthusiasm have all escaped, General Scott is urged not to lose their services, but to get into Richmond before they are disbanded.

It would scarcely be credited, were I not told it by General M'Dowell, that there is no such thing procurable as a decent map of Virginia. He knows little or nothing of the country before him, more than the general direction of the main roads, which are bad at the best; and he can obtain no information, inasmuch as the enemy are in full force all along his front, and he has not a cavalry officer capable of conducting a reconnaissance, which would be difficult enough in the best hands, owing to the dense woods which rise up in front of his lines, screening the enemy completely. The Confederates have thrown up very heavy batteries at Manassas, about thirty miles away, where the railway from the West crosses the line to Richmond, and I do not think General M'Dowell much likes the look of them, but the cry for action is so strong the President cannot resist it.

On my way back I rode through the woods of Arlington, and came out on a quadrangular earthwork, called Fort Corcoran, which is garrisoned by the 69th Irish, and commands the road leading to an aqueduct and horse-bridge over the Potomac. The regiment is encamped inside the fort, which would be a slaughter-pen if exposed to shell-fire. The streets were neat, the tents protected from the sun by shades of evergreens and pine boughs. One little door, like that of an icehouse, half buried in the ground, was opened by one of the soldiers, who was showing it to a friend, when my attention was more particularly attracted by a sergeant who ran forward in great dudgeon, exclaiming "Dempsey! Is that you going into the 'magazine' wid yer pipe lighted?" I rode away with alacrity.

In the course of my ride I heard occasional dropping shots in the camp. To my looks of inquiry, an engineer officer said quietly, "They are volunteers shooting themselves." The number of accidents from the carelessness of the men is astonishing; in every day's paper there is an account of deaths and wounds caused by the discharge of firearms in the tents.

Whilst I was at Arlington House, walking through the camp attached to head-quarters, I observed a tall red-bearded officer seated on a chair in front of one of the tents, who bowed as I passed him, and as I turned to salute him, my eye was caught by the apparition of a row of Palmetto buttons down his coat. One of the officers standing by said, "Let me introduce you to Captain Taylor, from the other side." It appears that he came in with a flag of truce, bearing a despatch from Jefferson Davis to President Lincoln, countersigned by General Beauregard at Manassas. Just as I left Arlington, a telegraph was sent from General Scott to send Captain Taylor, who rejoices in the name of Tom, over to his quarters.

The most absurd rumours were flying about the staff, one of whom declared very positively that there was going to be a compromise, and that Jeff. Davis had made an overture for peace. The papers are filled with accounts of an action in Missouri, at a place called Carthage, between the Federals commanded by Colonel Sigel, consisting for the most part of Germans, and the Confederates under General Parsons, in which the former were obliged to retreat, although it is admitted the State troops were miserably armed, and had most ineffective artillery, whilst their opponents had every advantage in both respects, and were commanded by officers of European experience. Captain Taylor alluded to the news in a jocular way to me, and said, "I hope you will tell the people in England we intend to whip the Lincolnites in the same fashion wherever we meet them," a remark which did not lead me to believe there was any intention on the part of the Confederates to surrender so easily.

July 9th.—Late last night the President told General Scott to send Captain Taylor back to the Confederate lines, and he was accordingly escorted to Arlington in a carriage, and thence returned without any answer to Mr. Davis's letter, the nature of which has not transpired.

A swarm of newspaper correspondents has settled down upon Washington, and great are the glorifications of the high-toned paymasters, gallant doctors, and subalterns accomplished in the art of war, who furnish minute items to my American brethren, and provide the yeast which overflows in many columns; but the Government experience the inconvenience of the smallest movements being chronicled for the use of the enemy, who, by putting one thing and another together, are no doubt enabled to collect much valuable information. Every preparation is being made to put the army on a war footing, to provide them with shoes, ammunition waggons, and horses.

I had the honour of dining with General Scott, who has moved to new quarters, near the War Department, and met General Fremont, who is designated, according to rumour, to take command of an important district in the West, and to clear the right bank of the Mississippi and the course of the Missouri. "The pathfinder" is a strong Republican and Abolitionist, whom the Germans delight to honour—a man with a dreamy, deep blue eye, a gentlemanly address, pleasant features, and an active frame, but without the smallest external indication of extraordinary vigour, intelligence, or ability; if he has military genius, it must come by intuition, for assuredly he has no professional acquirements or experience. Two or three members of Congress, and the General's staff, and Mr. Bigelow, completed the company. The General has become visibly weaker since I first saw him. He walks down to his office, close at hand, with difficulty; returns a short time before dinner, and reposes; and when he has dismissed his guests at an early hour, or even before he does so, stretches himself on his bed, and then before midnight rouses himself to look at despatches or to transact any necessary business. In case of an action it is his intention to proceed to the field in a light carriage, which is always ready for the purpose, with horses and driver; nor is he unprepared with precedents of great military commanders who have successfully conducted engagements under similar circumstances.

Although the discussion of military questions and of politics was eschewed, incidental allusions were made to matters going on around us, and I thought I could perceive that the General regarded the situation with much more apprehension than the politicians, and that his influence extended itself to the views of his staff. General Fremont's tone was much more confident. Nothing has become known respecting the nature of Mr. Davis's communication to President Lincoln, but the fact of his sending it at all is looked upon as a piece of monstrous impertinence. The General is annoyed and distressed by the plundering propensities of the Federal troops, who have been committing terrible depredations on the people of Virginia. It is not to be supposed, however, that the Germans, who have entered upon this campaign as mercenaries, will desist from so profitable and interesting a pursuit as the detection of Secesh sentiments, chickens, watches, horses, and dollars. I mentioned that I had seen some farm-houses completely sacked close to the aqueduct. The General merely said, "It is deplorable!" and raised up his hands as if in disgust. General Fremont, however, said, "I suppose you are familiar with similar scenes in Europe. I hear the allies were not very particular with respect to private property in Russia"—a remark which unfortunately could not be gainsaid. As I was leaving the General's quarters, Mr. Blair, accompanied by the President, who was looking more anxious than I had yet seen him, drove up, and passed through a crowd of soldiers, who had evidently been enjoying themselves. One of them called out, "Three cheers for General Scott!" and I am not quite sure the President did not join him.

July 10*th*.—To-day was spent in a lengthy excursion along the front of the camp in Virginia, round by the chain bridge which crosses the Potomac about four miles from Washington.

The Government have been coerced, as they say, by the safety of the Republic, to destroy the liberty of the press, which is guaranteed by the Constitution, and this is not the first instance in which the Constitution of the United States will be made *nominis umbra*. The telegraph, according to General Scott's order, confirmed by the Minister of War, Simon Cameron, is to convey no despatches respecting military movements not permitted by the General; and to-day the newspaper correspondents have agreed to yield obedience to the order, reserving to themselves a certain freedom of detail in writing their despatches, and relying on the Government to publish the official accounts of all battles very speedily. They will break this agreement if they can, and the Government will not observe their part of the bargain. The freedom of the press, as I take it, does not include the right to publish news hostile to the cause of the country in which it is published; neither can it involve any obligation on the part of Government to publish any despatches which may be injurious to the party they represent. There is a wide distinction between the publication of news which is known to the enemy as soon as to the friends of the transmitters, and the utmost freedom of expression concerning the acts of the Government or the conduct of past events; but it will be difficult to establish any rule to limit or extend the boundaries to which discussion can go without mischief, and in effect the only solution of the difficulty in a free country seems to be to grant the press free licence, in consideration of the enormous aid it affords in warning the people of their danger, in animating them with the news of their successes, and in sustaining the Government in their efforts to conduct the war.

The most important event to-day is the passage of the Loan Bill, which authorises Mr. Chase to borrow, in the next year, a sum of £50,000,000, on coupons, with interest at 7 per cent. and irredeemable for twenty years—the interest being guaranteed on a pledge of the Customs duties. I just got into the House in time to hear Mr. Vallandigham, who is an ultra-democrat, and very nearly a secessionist, conclude a well-delivered argumentative address. He is a tall, slight man, of a bilious temperament, with light flashing eyes, dark hair and complexion, and considerable oratorical power. "Deem me of I wouldn't just ride that Vallandiggaim on a reay-al," quoth a citizen to his friend, as the speaker sat down, amid a few feeble expressions of assent. Mr. Chase has also obtained the consent of the Lower House to his bill for closing the Southern ports by the decree of the President, but I hear some more substantial measures are in contemplation for that purpose. Whilst the House is finding the money the Government are preparing to spend it, and they have obtained the approval of the Senate to the enrolment of half a million of men, and the expenditure of one hundred millions of dollars to carry on the war.

I called on Mr. Cameron, the Secretary of War. The small brick house of two stories, with long passages, in which the American Mars prepares his bolts, was, no doubt, large enough for the 20,000 men who constituted the armed force on land of the great Republic, but it is not sufficient to contain a tithe of the contractors who haunt its precincts, fill all the lobbies and crowd into every room. With some risk to coat-tails, I squeezed through iron-masters, gun-makers, clothiers, shoemakers, inventors, bakers, and all that genus which fattens on the desolation caused by an army in the field, and was introduced to Mr. Cameron's room, where he was seated at a desk surrounded by people, who were also grouped round two gentlemen as clerks in the small room. "I tell you, General Cameron, that the way in which the loyal men of Missouri have been treated is a disgrace to this Government," shouted out a big, black, burly man—"I tell you so, sir." "Well, General," responded Mr. Cameron, quietly, "so you have several times. Will you, once for all, condescend to particulars?" "Yes, sir; you and the Government have disregarded our appeals. You have left us to fight our own battles. You have not sent us a cent——" "There, General, I interrupt you. You say we have sent you no money," said Mr. Cameron, very quietly. "Mr. Jones will be good enough to ask Mr. Smith to step in here." Before Mr. Smith came in, however, the General, possibly thinking some member of the press was present, rolled his eyes in a Nicotian frenzy, and perorated: "The people of the State of Missouri, sir, will power-out every drop of the blood which only flows to warm patriotic hearts in defence of the great Union, which offers freedom to the enslaved of mankind, and a home to persecuted progress, and a few-ture to civil-zation. We demand, General Cameron, in the neame of the great Western State——" Here Mr. Smith came in, and Mr. Cameron said, "I want you to tell me what disbursements, if any, have been sent by this department to the State of Missouri." Mr. Smith was quick at figures, and up in his accounts, for he drew out a little memorandum book, and replied (of course, I can't tell the exact sum), "General, there has been sent, as by vouchers, to Missouri since the beginning of the levies, six hundred and seventy thousand dollars and twenty-three cents." The General looked crest-fallen, but he was equal to the occasion. "These sums may have been sent, sir, but they have not been received. I declare in the face of——" "Mr. Smith will show you the vouchers, General, and you can then take any steps needful against the parties who have misappropriated them."

"That is only a small specimen of what we have to go through with our people," said the Minister, as the General went off with a lofty toss of his head, and then gave me a pleasant sketch of the nature of the applications and interviews which take up the time and clog the movements of an American statesman. "These State organisations give us a great deal of trouble." I could fully understand that they did so. The immediate business that I had with Mr. Cameron—he is rarely called General now that he is Minister of War—was to ask him to give me authority to draw rations at cost price, in case the army took the field before I could make arrangements, and he seemed very well disposed to accede; "but I must think about it, for I shall have all our papers down upon me if I grant you any facility which they do not get themselves." After I left the War Department, I took a walk to Mr. Seward's, who was out. In passing by President's Square, I saw a respectably-dressed man up in one of the trees, cutting off pieces of the bark, which his friends beneath caught up eagerly. I could not help stopping to ask what was the object of the proceeding. "Why, sir, this is the tree Dan Sickles shot Mr. —— under. I think it's quite a remarkable spot."

July 11th.—The diplomatic circle is so *totus teres atque rotundus*, that few particles of dirt stick on its periphery from the road over which it travels. The radii are worked from different centres, often far apart, and the tires and naves often fly out in wide divergence; but for all social purposes it is a circle, and a very pleasant one. When one sees M. de Stoeckel speaking to M. Mercier, or joining in with Baron Gerolt and M. de Lisboa, it is safer to infer that a little social re-union is at hand for a pleasant civilised discussion of ordinary topics, some music, a rubber, and a dinner, than to resolve with the *New York Correspondent*, "that there is reason to believe that a diplomatic movement of no ordinary significance is on foot, and that the ministers of Russia, France, and Prussia have concerted a plan of action with the representative of Brazil, which must lead to extraordinary complications, in view of the temporary embarrassments which distract our beloved country. The Minister of England has held aloof from these reunions for a sinister purpose no doubt, and we have not failed to discover that the emissary of Austria, and the representative of Guatemala, have abstained from taking part in these significant demonstrations. We tell the haughty nobleman who represents Queen Victoria, on whose son we so lately lavished the most liberal manifestations of our good will, to beware. The motives of the Court of Vienna, and of the republic of Guatemala, in ordering their representatives not to join in the reunion which we observed at three o'clock to-day, at the corner of Seventeenth Street and One, are perfectly transparent; but we call on Mr. Seward instantly to demand of Lord Lyons a full and ample explanation of his conduct on the occasion, or the transmission of his papers. There is no harm in adding, that we have every reason to think our good ally of Russia, and the minister of the astute monarch, who is only watching an opportunity of leading a Franco-American army to the Tower of London and Dublin Castle, have already moved their respective Governments to act in the premises."

That paragraph, with a good heading, would sell several thousands of the "New York Stabber" to-morrow.

July 12th.—There are rumours that the Federals, under Brigadier M'Clellan, who have advanced into Western Virginia, have gained some successes; but so far it seems to have no larger dimensions than the onward raid of one clan against another in the Highlands. And whence do rumours come? From Government departments, which, like so many Danaes in the clerks' rooms, receive the visits of the auriferous Jupiters of the press, who condense themselves into purveyors of smashes, slings, baskets of champagne, and dinners. M'Clellan is, however, considered a very steady and respectable professional soldier. A friend of his told me to-day one of the most serious complaints the Central Illinois Company had against him was that, during the Italian war, he seemed to forget their business; and that he was busied with maps stretched out on the floor, whereupon he, superincumbent, penned out the points of battle and strategy when he ought to have been attending to passenger trains and traffic. That which was flat blasphemy in a railway office may be amazingly approved in the field.

July 13th.—I have had a long day's ride through the camps of the various regiments across the Potomac, and at this side of it, which the weather did not render very agreeable to myself or the poor hack that I had hired for the day, till my American Quatermaine gets me a decent mount. I wished to see with my own eyes what is the real condition of the army which the North have sent down to the Potomac, to undertake such a vast task as the conquest of the South. The Northern papers describe it as a magnificent force, complete in all respects, well-disciplined, well-clad, provided with fine artillery, and with every requirement to make it effective for all military operations in the field.

In one word, then, they are grossly and utterly ignorant of what an army is or should be. In the first place, there are not, I should think, 30,000 men of all sorts available for the campaign. The papers estimate it at any number from 50,000 to 100,000, giving the preference to 75,000. In the next place, their artillery is miserably deficient; they have not, I should think, more than five complete batteries, or six batteries, including scratch guns, and these are of different calibres, badly horsed, miserably equipped, and provided with the worst set of gunners and drivers which I, who have seen the Turkish field-guns, ever beheld. They have no cavalry, only a few scarecrow men, who would dissolve partnership with their steeds at the first serious combined movement, mounted in high saddles, on wretched mouthless screws, and some few regulars from the frontiers, who may be good for Indians, but who would go over like ninepins at a charge from Punjaubee irregulars. Their transport is tolerably good, but inadequate; they have no carriage for reserve ammunition; the commissariat drivers are civilians, under little or no control; the officers are unsoldierly-looking men; the camps are dirty to excess; the men are dressed in all sorts of uniforms; and from what I hear, I doubt if any of these regiments have ever performed a brigade evolution together, or if any of the officers know what it is to deploy a brigade from column into line. They are mostly three months' men, whose time is nearly up. They were rejoicing to-day over the fact that it was so, and that they had kept the enemy from Washington "without a fight." And it is with this rabblement that the North propose not only to subdue the South, but according to some of their papers, to humiliate Great Britain, and conquer Canada afterwards.

I am opposed to national boasting, but I do firmly believe that 10,000 British regulars, or 12,000 French, with a proper establishment of artillery and cavalry, would not only entirely repulse this army with the greatest ease, under competent commanders, but that they could attack them and march into Washington over them or with them whenever they pleased. Not that Frenchman or Englishman is perfection, but that the American of this army knows nothing of discipline, and what is more, cares less for it.

Major-General M'Clellan — I beg his pardon for styling him Brigadier—has really been successful. By a very well-conducted and rather rapid march, he was enabled to bring superior forces to bear on some raw levies under General Garnett (who came over with me in the steamer), which fled after a few shots, and were utterly routed, when their gallant commander fell, in an abortive attempt to rally them by the banks of Cheat river. In this "great battle" M'Clellan's loss is less than 30 killed and wounded, and the Confederates loss is less than 100. But the dispersion of such guerilla bands has the most useful effect among the people of the district; and M'Clellan has done good service, especially as his little victory will lead to the discomfiture of all Secessionists in the valley of the Kenawha, and in the valley of Western Virginia. I left Washington this afternoon, with the Sanitary Commissioners, for Baltimore, in order to visit the Federal camps at Fortress Monroe, to which we proceeded down the Chesapeake the same night.

CHAPTER XLVII.

Fortress Monroe—General Butler—Hospital accommodation—Wounded soldiers—Aristocratic pedigrees—A great gun—Newport News—Fraudulent contractors—General Butler—Artillery practice—Contraband negroes—Confederate lines—Tombs of American loyalists—Troops and contractors—Duryea's New York Zouaves—Military calculations—A voyage by steamer to Annapolis.

July 14th.—At six o'clock this morning the steamer arrived at the wharf under the walls of Fortress Monroe, which presented a very different appearance from the quiet of its aspect when first I saw it, some months ago. Camps spread around it, the parapets lined with sentries, guns looking out towards the land, lighters and steamers alongside the wharf, a strong guar dat the end of the pier, passes to be scrutinised and permits to be given. I landed with the members of the Sanitary Commission, and repaired to a very large pile of buildings, called "The Hygeia Hotel," for once on a time Fortress Monroe was looked upon as the resort of the sickly, who required bracing air and an abundance of oysters; it is now occupied by the wounded in the several actions and skirmishes which have taken place, particularly at Bethel; and it is so densely crowded that we had difficulty in procuring the use of some small dirty rooms to dress in. As the business of the Commission was principally directed to ascertain the state of the hospitals, they considered it necessary in the first instance to visit General Butler, the commander of the post, who has been recommending himself to the Federal Government by his activity ever since he came down to Baltimore, and the whole body marched to the fort, crossing the drawbridge after some parley with the guard, and received permission, on the production of passes, to enter the court.

The interior of the work covers a space of about seven or eight acres, as far as I could judge, and is laid out with some degree of taste; rows of fine trees border the walks through the grass plots; the officers' quarters, neat and snug, are surrounded with little patches of flowers, and covered with creepers. All order and neatness, however, were fast disappearing beneath the tramp of mailed feet, for at least 1200 men had pitched their tents inside the place. We sent in our names to the General, who lives in a detached house close to the sea face of the fort, and sat down on a bench under the shade of some trees to avoid the excessive heat of the sun until th commander of the place could receive the Commissioners. He was evidently in no great hurry to do so. In about half an hour an aide-de-camp came out to say that the General was getting up, and that he would see us after breakfast. Some of the Commissioners, from purely sanitary considerations, would have been much better pleased to have seen him at breakfast, as they had only partaken of a very light meal on board the steamer at five o'clock in the morning; but we were interested meantime by the morning parade of a portion of the garrison, consisting of 300 regulars, a Massachusetts' volunteer battalion, and the 2nd New York Regiment.

It was quite refreshing to the eye to see the cleanliness of the regulars—their white gloves and belts, and polished buttons, contrasted with the slovenly aspect of the volunteers; but, as far as the material went, the volunteers had by far the best of the comparison. The civilians who were with me did not pay much attention to the regulars, and evidently preferred the volunteers, although they could not be insensible to the magnificent drum-major who led the band of the regulars. Presently General Butler came out of his quarters, and walked down the lines, followed by a few officers. He is a stout, middle-aged man, strongly built, with coarse limbs, his features indicative of great shrewdness and craft, his forehead high, the elevation being in some degree due perhaps to the want of hair; with a strong obliquity of vision, which may perhaps have been caused by an injury, as the eyelid hangs with a peculiar droop over the organ.

The General, whose manner is quick, decided and abrupt, but not at all rude or unpleasant, at once acceded to the wishes of the Sanitary Commissioners, and expressed his desire to make my stay at the fort as agreeable and useful as he could. "You can first visit the hospitals in company with these gentlemen, and then come over with me to our camp, where I will show you everything that is to be seen. I have ordered a steamer to be in readiness to take you to Newport News." He speaks rapidly, and either affects or possesses great decision. The Commissioners accordingly proceeded to make the most of their time in visiting the Hygeia Hotel, being accompanied by the medical officers of the garrison.

The rooms, but a short time ago occupied by the fair ladies of Virginia, when they came down to enjoy the sea breezes, were now crowded with Federal soldiers, many of them suffering from the loss of limb or serious wounds, others from the worst form of camp disease. I enjoyed a small national triumph over Dr. Bellows, the chief of the Commissioners, who is of the "sangre azul" of Yankeeism, by which I mean that he is a believer, not in the perfectibility, but in the absolute perfection, of New England nature, which is the only human nature that is not utterly lost and abandoned—Old England nature, perhaps, being the worst of all. We had been speaking to the wounded men in several rooms, and found most of them either in the listless condition consequent upon exhaustion, or with that anxious air which is often observable on the faces of the wounded when strangers approach. At last we came into a room in which two soldiers were sitting up, the first we had seen, reading the newspapers. Dr. Bellows asked where they came from; one was from Concord, the other from Newhaven. "You see, Mr. Russell," said Dr. Bellows, "how our Yankee soldiers spend their time. I knew at once they were Americans when I saw them reading newspapers." One of them had his hand shattered by a bullet, the other was suffering from a gun-shot wound through the body. "Where were you hit?" I inquired of the first. "Well," he said, "I guess my rifle went off when I was cleaning it in camp." "Were you wounded at Bethel?" I asked of the second. "No, sir," he replied; "I got this wound from a comrade, who discharged his piece by accident in one of the tents as I was standing outside." "So," said I, to Dr. Bellows, "whilst the Britishers and Germans are engaged with the enemy, you Americans employ your time shooting each other!"

These men were true mercenaries, for they were fighting for money—I mean the strangers. One poor fellow from Devonshire said, as he pointed to his stump, "I wish I had lost it for the sake of the old island, sir," paraphrasing Sarsfield's exclamation as he lay dying on the field. The Americans were fighting for the combined excellences and strength of the States of New England, and of the rest of the Federal power over the Confederates, for they could not in their heart of hearts believe the Old Union could be restored by force of arms. Lovers may quarrel and may reunite, but if a blow is struck there is no *redintegratio amoris* possible again. The newspapers and illustrated periodicals which they read were the pabulum that fed the flames of patriotism incessantly. Such capacity for enormous lying, both in creation and absorption, the world never heard. Sufficient for the hour is the falsehood.

There were lady nurses in attendance on the patients; who followed—let us believe, as I do, out of some higher motive than the mere desire of human praise—the example of Miss Nightingale. I loitered behind in the rooms, asking many questions respecting the nationality of the men, in which the members of the Sanitary Commission took no interest, and I was just turning into one near the corner of the passage when I was stopped by a loud smack. A young Scotchman was dividing his attention between a basin of soup and a demure young lady from Philadelphia, who was feeding him with a spoon, his only arm being engaged in holding her round the waist, in order to prevent her being tired, I presume. Miss Rachel, or Deborah, had a pair of very pretty blue eyes, but they flashed very angrily from under her trim little cap at the unwitting intruder, and then she said, in severest tones, "Will you take your medicine, or not?" Sandy smiled, and pretended to be very penitent.

When we returned with the doctors from our inspection we walked round the parapets of the fortress, why so called I know not, because it is merely a fort. The guns and mortars are old-fashioned and heavy, with the exception of some new-fashioned and very heavy Columbiads, which are cast-iron 8-, 10-, and 12-inch guns, in which I have no faith whatever. The armament is not sufficiently powerful to prevent its interior being searched out by the long range fire of ships with rifle guns, or mortar boats; but it would require closer and harder work to breach the masses of brick and masonry which constitute the parapets and casemates. The guns, carriages, rammers, shot, were dirty, rusty, and neglected; but General Butler told me he was busy polishing up things about the fortress as fast as he could.

Whilst we were parading these hot walls in the sunshine, my companions were discussing the question of ancestry. It appears your New Englander is very proud of his English descent from good blood, and it is one of their isms in the Yankee States that they are the salt of the British people and the true aristocracy of blood and family, whereas we in the isles retain but a paltry share of the blue blood defiled by incessant infiltrations of the muddy fluid of the outer world. This may be new to us Britishers, but is a Q. E. D. If a gentleman left Europe 200 years ago, and settled with his kin and kith, intermarrying his children with their equals, and thus perpetuating an ancient family, it is evident he may be regarded as the founder of a much more honourable dynasty than the relative who remained behind him, and lost the old family place, and sunk into obscurity. A singular illustration of the tendency to make much of themselves may be found in the fact, that New England swarms with genealogical societies and bodies of antiquaries, who delight in reading papers about each other's ancestors, and tracing their descent from Norman or Saxon barons and earls. The Virginians opposite, who are flouting us with their Confederate flag from Sewall's Point, are equally given to the "genus et proavos."

At the end of our promenade round the ramparts, Lieutenant Butler, the General's nephew and aide-de-camp, came to tell us the boat was ready, and we met His Excellency in the court-yard, whence we walked down to the wharf. On our way, General Butler called my attention to an enormous heap of hollow iron lying on the sand, which was the Union gun that is intended to throw a shot of some 350 lbs. weight or more, to astonish the Confederates at Sewall's Point opposite, when it is mounted. This gun, if I mistake not, was made after the designs of Captain Rodman, of the United States artillery, who in a series of remarkable papers, the publication of which has cost the country a large sum of money, has given us the results of long-continued investigations and experiments on the best method of cooling masses of iron for ordnance purposes, and of making powder for heavy shot. The piece must weigh about 20 tons, but a similar gun, mounted on an artificial island called the Rip Raps, in the Channel opposite the fortress, is said to be worked with facility. The Confederates have raised some of the vessels sunk by the United States officers when the Navy Yard at Gosport was destroyed, and as some of these are to be converted into rams, the Federals are preparing their heaviest ordnance, to try the effect of crushing weights at low velocities against their sides, should they attempt to play any pranks among the transport vessels. The General said: "It is not by these great masses of iron this contest is to be decided: we must bring sharp points of steel, directed by superior intelligence." Hitherto General Butler's attempts at Big Bethel have not been crowned with success in employing such means, but it must be admitted that, according to his own statement, his lieutenants were guilty of carelessness and neglect of ordinary military precautions in the conduct of the expedition he ordered. The march of different columns of troops by night concentrating on a given point is always liable to serious interruptions, and frequently gives rise to hostile encounters between friends, in more disciplined armies than the raw levies of United States volunteers.

When the General, Commissioners, and Staff had embarked, the steamer moved across the broad estuary to Newport News. Among our passengers were several medical officers in attendance on the Sanitary Commissioners, some belonging to the army, others who had volunteered from civil life. Their discussion of professional questions and of relative rank assumed such a personal character, that General Butler had to interfere to quiet the disputants, but the exertion of his authority was not altogether successful, and one of the angry gentlemen said in my hearing, "I'm d—d if I submit to such treatment if all the lawyers in Massachusetts with stars on their collars were to order me to-morrow."

On arriving at the low shore of Newport News we landed at a wooden jetty, and proceeded to visit the camp of the Federals, which was surrounded by a strong entrenchment, mounted with guns on the water face; and on the angles inland, a broad tract of cultivated country, bounded by a belt of trees, extended from the river away from the encampment; but the Confederates are so close at hand that frequent skirmishes have occurred between the foraging parties of the garrison and the enemy, who have on more than one occasion pursued the Federals to the very verge of the woods.

Whilst the Sanitary Commissioners were groaning over the heaps of filth which abound in all camps where discipline is not most strictly observed, I walked round amongst the tents, which, taken altogether, were in good order. The day was excessively hot, and many of the soldiers were lying down in the shade of arbours formed of branches from the neighbouring pine wood, but most of them got up when they heard the General was coming round. A sentry walked up and down at the end of the street, and as the General came up to him he called out "Halt. The man stood still. "I just want to show you, sir, what scoundrels our Government has to deal with. This man belongs to a regiment which has had new clothing recently served out to it. Look what it is made of." So saying the General stuck his fore-finger into the breast of the man's coat, and with a rapid scratch of his nail tore open the cloth as if it was of blotting paper. "Shoddy, sir. Nothing but shoddy. I wish I had these contractors in the trenches here, and if hard work would not make honest men of them, they'd have enough of it to be examples for the rest of their fellows."

A vivacious, prying man, this Butler, full of bustling life, self-esteem, revelling in the exercise of power. In the course of our rounds we were joined by Colonel Phelps, who was formerly in the United States army, and saw service in Mexico, but retired because he did not approve of the manner in which promotions were made, and who only took command of a Massachusetts regiment because he believed he might be instrumental in striking a shrewd blow or two in this great battle of Armageddon—a tall, saturnine, gloomy, angry-eyed, sallow man, soldier-like too, and one who places old John Brown on a level with the great martyrs of the Christian world. Indeed one, not so fierce as he, is blasphemous enough to place images of our Saviour and the hero of Harper's Ferry on the mantel-piece, as the two greatest beings the world has ever seen. "Yes, I know them well. I've seen them in the field. I've sat with them at meals. I've travelled through their country. These Southern slave-holders are a false, licentious, godless people. Either we who obey the laws and fear God, or they who know no God except their own will and pleasure, and know no law except their passions, must, rule on this continent, and I believe that Heaven will help its own in the conflict they have provoked. I grant you they are brave enough, and desperate too, but surely justice, truth, and religion, will strengthen a man's arm to strike down those who have only brute force and a bad cause to support them." But Colonel Phelps was not quite indifferent to material aid, and he made a pressing appeal to General Butler to send him some more guns and harness for the field-pieces he had in position, because, said he, "in case of attack, please God I'll follow them up sharp, and cover these fields with their bones." The General had a difficulty about the harness, which made Colonel Phelps very grim, but General Butler had reason in saying he could not make harness, and so the Colonel must be content with the results of a good rattling fire of round, shell, grape, and canister, if the Confederates are foolish enough to attack his batteries.

There was nothing to complain of in the camp, except the swarms of flies, the very bad smells, and perhaps the shabby clothing of the men. The tents were good enough. The rations were ample, but nevertheless there was a want of order, discipline, and quiet in the lines which did not augur well for the internal economy of the regiments. When we returned to the river face, General Butler ordered some practice to be made with a Sawyer rifle gun, which appeared to be an ordinary cast-iron piece, bored with grooves, on the shunt principle, the shot being covered with a composition of a metallic amalgam like zinc and tin, and provided with flanges of the same material to fit the grooves. The practice was irregular and unsatisfactory. At an elevation of 24 degrees, the first shot struck the water at a point about 2000 yards distant. The piece was then further elevated, and the shot struck quite out of land, close to the opposite bank, a distance of nearly three miles. The third shot rushed with a peculiar hurtling noise out of the piece, and flew up in the air, falling with a splash into the water about 1500 yards away. The next shot may have gone half across the continent, for assuredly it never struck the water, and most probably ploughed its way into the soft ground at the other side of the river. The shell practice was still worse, and on the whole I wish our enemies may always fight us with Sawyer guns, particularly as the shells cost between £6 and £7 a-piece.

From the fort the General proceeded to the house of one of the officers, near the jetty, formerly the residence of a Virginian farmer, who has now gone to Secessia, where we were most hospitably treated at an excellent lunch, served by the slaves of the former proprietor. Although we boast with some reason of the easy level of our mess-rooms, the Americans certainly excel us in the art of annihilating all military distinctions on such occasions as these; and I am not sure the General would not have liked to place a young Doctor in close arrest, who suddenly made a dash at the liver wing of a fowl on which the General was bent with eye and fork, and carried it off to his plate. But on the whole there was a good deal of friendly feeling amongst all ranks of the volunteers, the regulars being a little stiff and adherent to etiquette.

In the afternoon the boat returned to Fortress Monroe, and the General invited me to dinner, where I had the pleasure of meeting Mrs. Butler, his staff, and a couple of regimental officers from the neighbouring camp. As it was still early, General Butler proposed a ride to visit the interesting village of Hampton, which lies some six or seven miles outside the fort, and forms his advance post. A powerful charger, with a tremendous Mexican saddle, fine housings, blue and gold embroidered saddle-cloth, was brought to the door for your humble servant, and the General mounted another, which did equal credit to his taste in horseflesh; but I own I felt rather uneasy on seeing that he wore a pair of large brass spurs, strapped over white jean brodequins. He took with him his aide-camp and a couple of orderlies. In the precincts of the fort outside, a population of contraband negroes has been collected, whom the General employs in various works about the place, military and civil; but I failed to ascertain that the original scheme of a debit and credit account between the value of their labour and the cost of their maintenance had been successfully carried out. The General was proud of them, and they seemed proud of themselves, saluting him with a ludicrous mixture of awe and familiarity as he rode past. "How do, Massa Butler? How do, General?" accompanied by absurd bows and scrapes. "Just to think," said the General, "that every one of these fellows represents some 1000 dollars at least out of the pockets of the chivalry yonder." "Nasty, idle, dirty beasts," says one of the staff, *sotto voce;* "I wish to Heaven they were all at the bottom of the Chesapeake. The General insists on it that they do work, but they are far more trouble than they are worth."

The road towards Hampton traverses a sandy spit, which, however, is more fertile than would be supposed from the soil under the horses' hoofs, though it is not in the least degree interesting. A broad creek or river interposed between us and the town, the bridge over which had been destroyed. Workmen were busy repairing it, but all the planks had not yet been laid down or nailed, and in some places the open space, between the upright rafters allowed us to see the dark waters flowing beneath. The Aide said, "I don't think, General, it is safe to cross;" but his chief did not mind him until his horse very nearly crashed through a plank, and only regained its footing with unbroken legs by marvellous dexterity; whereupon we dismounted, and, leaving the horses to be carried over in the ferry boat, completed the rest of the transit, not without difficulty. At the other end of the bridge a street lined with comfortable houses, and bordered with trees, led us into the pleasant town or village of Hampton—pleasant once, but now deserted by all the inhabitants except some pauperised whites and a colony of negroes. It was in full occupation of the Federal soldiers, and I observed that most of the men were Germans, the garrison at Newport News being principally composed of Americans. The old red brick houses, with cornices of white stone; the narrow windows and high gables, gave an aspect of antiquity and European comfort to the place, the like of which I have not yet seen in the States. Most of the shops were closed; in some the shutters were still down, and the goods remained displayed in the windows. "I have allowed no plundering," said the General; "and if I find a fellow trying to do it, I will hang him as sure as my name is Butler. See here," and as he spoke he walked into a large woollen-draper's shop, where bales of cloth were still lying on the shelves, and many articles such as are found in a large general store in a country town were disposed on the floor or counters; "they shall not accuse the men under my command of being robbers." The boast, however, was not so well justified in a visit to another house occupied by some soldiers. "Well," said the General, with a smile, "I daresay you know enough of camps to have found out that chairs and tables are irresistible; the men will take them off to their tents, though they may have to leave them next morning."

The principal object of our visit was the fortified trench which has been raised outside the town towards the Confederate lines. The path lay through a churchyard filled with most interesting monuments. The sacred edifice of red brick, with a square clock tower rent by lightning, is rendered interesting by the fact that it is almost the first church built by the English colonists of Virginia. On the tombstones are recorded the names of many subjects of his Majesty George III., and familiar names of persons born in the early part of last century in English villages, who passed to their rest before the great rebellion of the Colonies had disturbed their notions of loyalty and respect to the Crown. Many a British subject, too, lies there, whose latter days must have been troubled by the strange scenes of the war of independence. With what doubt and distrust must that one at whose tomb I stand have heard that George Washington was making head against the troops of His Majesty King George III.! How the hearts of the old men who had passed the best years of their existence, as these stones tell us, fighting for His Majesty against the French, must have beaten when once more they heard the roar of the Frenchman's ordnance uniting with the voices of the rebellious guns of the colonists from the plains of Yorktown against the entrenchments in which Cornwallis and his deserted band stood at hopeless bay! But could these old eyes open again, and see General Butler standing on the eastern rampart which bounds their resting-place, and pointing to the spot whence the rebel cavalry of Virginia issue night and day to charge the loyal pickets of His Majesty The Union, they might take some comfort in the fulfilment of the vaticinations which no doubt they uttered, "It cannot, and it will not, come to good."

Having inspected the works—as far as I could judge, too extended, and badly traced—which I say with all deference to the able young engineer who accompanied us to point out the various objects of interest—the General returned to the bridge, where we remounted, and made a tour of the camps of the force intended to defend Hampton, falling back on Fortress Monroe in case of necessity. Whilst he was riding *ventre à terre*, which seems to be his favourite pace, his horse stumbled in the dusty road, and in his effort to keep his seat the General broke his stirrup leather, and the ponderous brass stirrup fell to the ground; but, albeit a lawyer, he neither lost his seat nor his *sang froid*, and calling out to his orderly "to pick up his toe plate," the jean slippers were closely pressed, spurs and all, to the sides of his steed, and away we went once more through dust and heat so great I was by no means sorry when he pulled up outside a pretty villa, standing in a garden, which was occupied by Colonel Max Weber, of the German Turner Regiment, once the property of General Tyler. The camp of the Turners, who are members of various gymnastic societies, was situated close at hand; but I had no opportunity of seeing them at work, as the Colonel insisted on our partaking of the hospitalities of his little mess, and produced some bottles of sparkling hock and a block of ice, by no means unwelcome after our fatiguing ride. His Major, whose name I have unfortunately forgotten, and who spoke English better than his chief, had served in some capacity or other in the Crimea, and made many inquiries after the officers of the Guards whom he had known there. I took an opportunity of asking him in what state the troops were. "The whole thing is a robbery," he exclaimed; "this war is for the contractors; the men do not get a third of what the Government pay for them; as for discipline, my God! it exists not. We Germans are well enough, of course; we know our affair; but as for the Americans, what would you? They make colonels out of doctors and lawyers, and captains out of fellows who are not fit to brush a soldier's shoe." "But the men get their pay?" "Yes; that is so. At the end of two months, they get it, and by that time it is due to sutlers, who charge them 100 per cent."

It is easy to believe these old soldiers do not put much confidence in General Butler, though they admit his energy. "Look you; one good officer with 5000 steady troops, such as we have in Europe, shall come down any night and walk over us all into Fortress Monroe whenever he pleased, if he knew how these troops were placed."

On leaving the German Turners, the General visited the camp of Duryea's New York Zouaves, who were turned out at evening parade, or more properly speaking, drill. But for the ridiculous effect of their costume the regiment would have looked well enough; but riding down on the rear of the ranks the discoloured napkins tied round their heads, without any fez cap beneath, so that the hair sometimes stuck up through the folds, the ill-made jackets, the loose bags of red calico hanging from their loins, the long gaiters of white cotton—instead of the real Zouave yellow and black greave, and smart white gaiter—made them appear such military scarecrows, I could scarcely refrain from laughing outright. Nevertheless the men were respectably drilled, marched steadily in columns of company, wheeled into line, and went past at quarter distance at the double much better than could be expected from the short time they had been in the field, and I could with all sincerity say to Col. Duryea, a smart and not unpretentious gentleman, who asked my opinion so pointedly that I could not refuse to give it, that I considered the appearance of the regiment very creditable. The shades of evening were now falling, and as I had been up before 5 o'clock in the morning, I was not sorry when General Butler said, "Now we will go home to tea, or you will detain the steamer." He had arranged before I started that the vessel, which in ordinary course would have returned to Baltimore at 8 o'clock, should remain till he sent down word to the captain to go.

We scampered back to the fort, and judging from the challenges and vigilance of the sentries, and inlying pickets, I am not quite so satisfied as the Major that the enemy could have surprised the place. At the tea-table there were no additions to the General's family; he therefore spoke without any reserve. Going over the map, he explained his views in reference to future operations, and showed cause, with more military acumen than I could have expected from a gentleman of the long robe, why he believed Fortress Monroe was the true base of operations against Richmond.

I have been convinced for some time, that if a sufficient force could be left to cover Washington, the Federals should move against Richmond from the Peninsula, where they could form their depôts at leisure, and advance, protected by their gunboats, on a very short line which offers far greater facilities and advantages than the inland route from Alexandria to Richmond, which, difficult in itself from the nature of the country, is exposed to the action of a hostile population, and, above all, to the danger of constant attacks by the enemies' cavalry, tending more or less to destroy all communication with the base of the Federal operations.

The threat of seizing Washington led to a concentration of the Union troops in front of it, which caused in turn the collection of the Confederates on the lines below to defend Richmond. It is plain that if the Federals can cover Washington, and at the same time assemble a force at Monroe strong enough to march on Richmond, as they desire, the Confederates will be placed in an exceedingly hazardous position, scarcely possible to escape from; and there is no reason why the North, with their overwhelming preponderance, should not do so, unless they be carried away by the fatal spirit of brag and bluster which comes from their press to overrate their own strength and to despise their enemy's. The occupation of Suffolk will be seen, by any one who studies the map, to afford a most powerful leverage to the Federal forces from Monroe in their attempts to turn the enemy out of their camps of communication, and to enable them to menace Richmond as well as the Southern States most seriously.

But whilst the General and I are engaged over our maps and mint juleps, time flies, and at last I perceive by the clock that it is time to go. An aide is sent to stop the boat, but he returns ere I leave with the news that "She is gone." Whereupon the General sends for the Quartermaster Talmadge, who is out in the camps, and only arrives in time to receive a severe "wigging." It so happened that I had important papers to send off by the next mail from New York, and the only chance of being able to do so depended on my being in Baltimore next day. General Butler acted with kindness and promptitude in the matter. "I promised you should go by the steamer, but the captain has gone off without orders to leave, for which he shall answer when I see him. Meantime it is my business to keep my promise. Captain Talmadge, you will at once go down and give orders to the most suitable transport steamer or chartered vessel available, to get up steam at once and come up to the wharf for Mr. Russell."

Whilst I was sitting in the parlor which served as the General's office, there came in a pale, bright-eyed, slim young man in a subaltern's uniform, who sought a private audience, and unfolded a plan he had formed, on certain data gained by nocturnal expeditions, to surprise a body of the enemy's cavalry which was in the habit of coming down every night and disturbing the pickets at Hampton. His manner was so eager, his information so precise, that the General could not refuse his sanction, but he gave it in a characteristic manner. "Well, sir, I understand your proposition. You intend to go out as a volunteer to effect this service. You ask my permission to get men for it. I cannot grant you an order to any of the officers in command of regiments to provide you with these; but if the Colonel of your regiment wishes to give leave to his men to volunteer, and they like to go with you, I give you leave to take them. I wash my hands of all responsibility in the affair." The officer bowed and retired, saying, "That is quite enough, General."*

At 10 o'clock the Quartermaster came back to say that a screw steamer called the Elizabeth was getting up steam for my reception, and I bade good-by to the General, and walked down with his aide and nephew, Lieutenant Butler, to the Hygeia Hotel to get my light knapsack. It was a lovely moonlight night, and as I was passing down an avenue of trees an officer stopped me, and exclaimed, "General Butler, I hear you have given leave to Lieutenant Blank to take a party of my regiment and go off scouting to-night after the enemy. It is too hard that—" What more he was going to say I know not, for I corrected the mistake, and the officer walked hastily on towards the General's quarters. On reaching the Hygeia Hotel I was met by the correspondent of a New York paper, who as commissary-general, or, as they are styled in the States, officer of subsistence, had been charged to get the boat ready, and who explained to me it would be at least an hour before the steam was up; and whilst I was waiting in the porch I heard many Virginian, and old world stories as well, the general upshot of which was that all the rest of the world could be "done" at cards, in love, in drink, in horseflesh, and in fighting, by the true-born American. Gen. Butler came down after a time, and joined our little society, nor was he by any means the least shrewd and humorous *raconteur* of the party. At 11 o'clock the Elizabeth uttered some piercing cries, which indicated she had her steam up; and so I walked down to the jetty, accompanied by my host and his friends, and wishing them good bye, stepped on board the little vessel, and with the aid of the negro cook, steward, butler, boots, and servant, roused out the captain from a small wooden trench which he claimed as his berth, turned into it, and fell asleep just as the first difficult convulsions of the screw aroused the steamer from her coma, and forced her languidly against the tide in the direction of Baltimore.

July 15th.—I need not speak much of the events of last night, which were not unimportant, perhaps, to some of the insects which played a leading part in them. The heat was literally overpowering; for in addition to the hot night there was the full power of most irritable boilers close at hand to aggravate the natural *désagrémens* of the situation. About an hour after dawn, when I turned out on deck, there was nothing visible but a warm grey mist; but a knotty old pilot on deck told me we were only going six knots an hour against tide and wind, and that we were likely to make less way as the day wore on. In fact, instead of being near Baltimore, we were much nearer Fortress Monroe. Need I repeat the horrors of this day! Stewed, boiled, baked, and grilled on board this miserable Elizabeth, I wished M. Montalembert could have experienced with m what such an impassive nature could inflict in misery on those around it. The captain was a shy, silent man, much given to short naps in my temporary berth, and the mate was so wild, he might have swam off with perfect propriety to the woods on either side of us, and taken to

* It may be stated here, that this expedition met with a disastrous result. If I mistake not, the officer, and with him the correspondent of a paper who accompanied him, were killed by the cavalry whom he meant to surprise, and several of the volunteers were also killed or wounded.

a tree as an aborigen or chimpanzee. Two men of most retiring habits, the negro, a black boy, and a very fat negress who officiated as cook, filled up the "balance" of the crew.

I could not write, for the vibration of the deck of the little craft gave a St. Vitus dance to pen and pencil; reading was out of the question from the heat and flies; and below stairs the fat cook banished repose by vapours from her dreadful caldrons, where, Medea-like, she was boiling some death broth. Our breakfast was of the simplest and—may I add?—the least enticing; and if the dinner could have been worse it was so; though it was rendered attractive by hunger, and by the kindness of the sailors who shared it with me. The old pilot had a most wholesome hatred of the Britishers, and not having the least idea till late in the day that I belonged to the old country, favoured me with some very remarkable views respecting their general mischievousness and inutility. As soon as he found out my secret he became more reserved, and explained to me that he had some reason for not liking us, because all he had in the world, as pretty a schooner as ever floated and a fine cargo, had been taken and burnt by the English when they sailed up the Potomac to Washington. He served against us at Bladensburg. I did not ask him how fast he ran; but he had a good rejoinder ready if I had done so, inasmuch as he was up West under Commodore Perry on the lakes when we suffered our most serious reverses. Six knots an hour! hour after hour! And nothing to do but to listen to the pilot.

On both sides a line of forest just visible above the low shores. Small coasting craft, schooners, pungys, boats laden with wood creeping along in the shallow water, or plying down empty before wind and tide.

"I doubt if we'll be able to catch up them forts afore night," said the skipper. The pilot grunted, "I rather think yu'll not." "H—— and thunder! Then we'll have to lie off till daylight?" "They may let you pass, Captain Squires, as you've this Europe-an on board, but anyhow we can't fetch Baltimore till late at night or early in the morning."

I heard the dialogue, and decided very quickly that as Annapolis lay somewhere ahead on our left, and was much nearer than Baltimore, it would be best to run for it while there was daylight. The captain demurred. He had been ordered to take his vessel to Baltimore, and General Butler might come down on him for not doing so; but I proposed to sign a letter stating he had gone to Annapolis at my request, and the steamer was put a point or two to westward, much to the pleasure of the Palinurus, whose "old woman" lived in the town. I had an affection for this weather-beaten, watery-eyed, honest old fellow, who hated us as cordially as Jack detested his Frenchman in the old days before *ententes cordiales* were known to the world. He was thoroughly English in his belief that he belonged to the only sailor race in the world, and that they could beat all mankind in seamanship; and he spoke in the most unaffected way of the Britishers as a survivor of the old war might do of Johnny Crapaud—"They were brave enough no doubt, but, Lord bless you, see them in a gale of wind! or look at them sending down top-gallant masts, or anything sailor-like in a breeze. *You'd* soon see the differ. And, besides, they *never can* stand again us at close quarters." By-and-by the houses of a considerable town, crowned by steeples, and a large Corinthian-looking building, came in view. "That's the State House. That's where George Washington—first in peace, first in war, and first in the hearts of his countrymen—laid down his victorious sword without any one asking him, and retired amid the applause of the civilized world." This flight I am sure was the old man's treasured relic of school-boy days, and I'm not sure he did not give it to me three times over. Annapolis looks very well from the river side. The approach is guarded by some very poor earthworks and one small fort. A dismantled sloop of war lay off a sea wall, banking up a green lawn covered with trees, in front of an old-fashioned pile of buildings, which formerly, I think, and very recently indeed, was occupied by the cadets of the United States Naval School. "There was a lot of them seceders. Lord bless you! these young ones is all took by these States Rights' doctrines—just as the ladies is caught by a new fashion."

About seven o'clock the steamer hove alongside a wooden pier which was quite deserted. Only some ten or twelve sailing boats, yachts, and schooners lay at anchor in the placid waters of the port which was once the capital of Maryland, and for which the early Republicans prophesied a great future. But Baltimore has eclipsed Annapolis into utter obscurity. I walked to the only hotel in the place, and found that the train for the junction with Washington had started, and that the next train left at some impossible hour in the morning. It is an odd Rip Van Winkle sort of a place. Quaint-looking boarders came down to the tea-table and talked Secession, and when I was detected, as must ever soon be the case, owing to the hotel book, I was treated to some ill-favoured glances, as my recent letters have been denounced in the strongest way for their supposed hostility to States Rights and the Domestic Institution. The spirit of the people has, however, been broken by the Federal occupation, and by the decision with which Butler acted when he came down here with the troops to open communications with Washington after the Baltimoreans had attacked the soldiery on their way through the city from the north.

CHAPTER XLVIII.

The "State House" at Annapolis—Washington—General Scott's quarters—Want of a staff—Rival camps—Demand for horses—Popular excitement—Lord Lyons—General M'Dowell's movements—Retreat from Fairfax Court House—General Scott's quarters—General Mansfield—Battle of Bull's Run.

July 16th.—I baffled many curious and civil citizens by breakfasting in my room, where I remained writing till late in the day. In the afternoon I walked to the State House. The hall door was open, but the rooms were closed and I remained in the hall, which is graced by two indifferent huge statues of Law and Justice holding gas lamps, and by an old rusty cannon, dug out of the river, and supposed to have belonged to the original British colonists, whilst an officer whom I met in the portico went to look for the porter and the keys. Whether he succeeded I cannot say, for after waiting some half hour I was warned by my watch that it was time to get ready for the train, which started at 4.15 P.M. The country through which the single line of rail passes is very hilly, much wooded, little cultivated, cut up by water-courses and ravines. At the junction with the Washington line from Baltimore there is a strong guard thrown out from the camp near at hand. The officers, who had a mess in a little wayside inn on the line, invited me to rest till the train came up, and from them I heard that an advance had been actually ordered, and that if the "rebels" stood there would soon be a tall fight close to Washington. They were very cheery, hospitable fellows, and enjoyed their new mode of life amazingly. The men of the regiment to which they belonged were Germans, almost to a man. When the train came in I found it was full of soldiers, and I learned that three more heavy trains were to follow, in addition to four which had already passed laden with troops.

On arriving at the Washington platform, the first person I saw was General M'Dowell alone, looking anxiously into the carriages. He asked where I came from, and when he heard from Annapolis, inquired eagerly if I had seen two batteries of artillery—Barry's and another—which he had ordered up, and was waiting for, but which had "gone astray." I was surprised to find the General engaged on such duty, and took leave to say so. "Well, it is quite true, Mr. Russell; but I am obliged to look after them myself, as I have so small a staff, and they are all engaged out with my head-quarters. You are aware I have advanced? No! Well, you have just come in time, and I shall be happy, indeed, to take you with me. I have made arrangements for the correspondents of our papers to take the field under certain regulations, and I have suggested to them they should wear a white uniform, to indicate the purity of their character." The General could hear nothing of his guns; his carriage was waiting, and I accepted his offer of a seat to my lodgings. Although he spoke confidently, he did not seem in good spirits. There was the greatest difficulty in finding out anything about the enemy. Beauregard was said to have advanced to Fairfax Court House, but he could not get any certain knowledge of the fact. "Can you not order a reconnaissance?" "Wait till you see the country. But even if it were as flat as Flanders, I have not an officer on whom I could depend for the work. They would fall into some trap, or bring on a general engagement when I did not seek it or desire it. I have no cavalry such as you work with in Europe." I think he was not so much disposed to undervalue the Confederates as before, for he said they had selected a very strong position, and had made a regular *levée en masse* of the people of Virginia, as a proof of the energy and determination with which they were entering on the campaign.

As we parted the General gave me his photograph, and told me he expected to see me in a few days at his quarters, but that I would have plenty of time to get horses and servants, and such light equipage as I wanted, as there would be no engagement for several days. On arriving at my lodgings I sent to the livery stables to inquire after horses. None fit for the saddle to be had at any price. The sutlers, the cavalry, the mounted officers, had been purchasing up all the droves of horses which came to the markets. M'Dowell had barely extra mounts for his own use. And yet horses must be had; and, even provided with them, I must take the field without tent or servant, canteen or food —a waif to fortune.

July 17th.—I went up to General Scott's quarters, and saw some of his staff—young men, some of whom knew nothing of soldiers, not even the enforcing of drill—and found them reflecting, doubtless, the shades which cross the mind of the old chief, who was now seeking repose. M'Dowell is to advance to-morrow from Fairfax Court House, and will march some eight or ten miles to Centreville, directly in front of which, at a place called Manassas, stands the army of the Southern enemy. I look around me for a staff, and look in vain. There are a few plodding old pedants, with map and rules and compasses, who sit in small rooms and write memoranda; and there are some ignorant and not very active young men, who loiter about the head-quarters' halls, and strut up the street with brass spurs on their heels and kepis raked over their eyes as though they were soldiers, but I see no system, no order, no knowledge, no dash!

The worst-served English general has always a young fellow or two about him who can fly across country, draw a rough sketch map, ride like a foxhunter, and find something out about the enemy and their position, understand and convey orders, and obey them. I look about for the types of these in vain. M'Dowell can find out nothing about the enemy; he has not a trustworthy map of the country; no knowledge of their position, force, or numbers. All the people, he says, are against the Government. Fairfax Court House was abandoned as he approached, the enemy in their retreat being followed by the inhabitants. "Where were the Confederate entrenchments?" "Only in the imagination of those New York newspapers; when they want to fill up a column they write a full account of the enemy's fortifications. No one can contradict them at the time, and it's a good joke when it's found out to be a lie." Colonel Cullum went over the maps with me at General Scott's, and spoke with some greater confidence of M'Dowell's prospects of success. There is a considerable force of Confederates at a place called Winchester, which is connected with Manassas by rail, and this force could be thrown on the right of the Federals as they advanced, but that another corps, under Patterson, is in observation, with orders to engage them if they attempt to move eastwards.

The batteries for which General M'Dowell was looking last night have arrived, and were sent on this morning. One is under Barry, of the United States regular artillery, whom I met at Fort Pickens. The other is a volunteer battery. The onward movement of the army has been productive of a great improvement in the streets of Washington, which are no longer crowded with turbulent and disorderly volunteers, or by soldiers disgracing the name, who accost you in the by-ways for money. There are comparatively few to-day; small shoals, which have escaped the meshes of the net, are endeavouring to make the most of their time before they cross the river to face the enemy.

Still horse-hunting, but in vain—Gregson, Wroe—*et hoc genus omne*. Nothing to sell except at unheard-of rates; tripeds, and the like, much the worse for wear, and yet possessed of some occult virtues, in right of which the owners demanded egregious sums. Everywhere I am offered a gig or a vehicle of some kind or another, as if the example of General Scott had rendered such a mode of campaigning the correct thing. I saw many officers driving over the Long Bridge with large stores of provisions, either unable to procure horses or satisfied that a waggon was the chariot of Mars. It is not fair to ridicule either officers or men of this army, and if they were not so inflated by a pestilent vanity, no one would dream of doing so; but the excessive bragging and boasting in which the volunteers and the press indulge really provoke criticism and tax patience and forbearance overmuch. Even the regular officers, who have some idea of military efficiency, rather derived from education and foreign travels than from actual experience, bristle up and talk proudly of the patriotism of the army, and challenge the world to show such another, although in their hearts, and more, with their lips, they own they do not depend on them. The white heat of patriotism has cooled down to a dull black; and I am told that the gallant volunteers, who are to conquer the world when they "have got through with their present little job," are counting up the days to the end of their service, and openly declare they will not stay a day longer. This is pleasant, inasmuch as the end of the term of many of M'Dowell's, and most of Patterson's, three months' men, is near at hand. They have been faring luxuriously at the expense of the Government—they have had nothing to do—they have had enormous pay—they knew nothing, and were worthless as to soldiering when they were enrolled. Now, having gained all these advantages, and being likely to be of use for the first time, they very quietly declare they are going to sit under their fig-trees, crowned with civic laurels and myrtles, and all that sort of thing. But who dare say they are not splendid fellows—full-blooded heroes, patriots, and warriors—men before whose majestic presence all Europe pales and faints away?

In the evening I received a message to say that the advance of the army would take place to-morrow as soon as General M'Dowell had satisfied himself by a reconnaissance that he could carry out his plan of turning the right of the enemy by passing Occaguna Creek. Along Pennsylvania Avenue, along the various shops, hotels, and drinking-bars, groups of people were collected, listening to the most exaggerated accounts of desperate fighting and of the utter demoralisation of the rebels. I was rather amused by hearing the florid accounts which were given on the hall of Willard's by various inebriated officers, who were drawing upon their imagination for their facts, knowing, as I did, that the entrenchments at Fairfax had been abandoned without a shot on the advance of the Federal troops. The New York papers came in with glowing descriptions of the magnificent march of the grand army of the Potomac, which was stated to consist of upwards of 70,000 men; whereas I knew not half that number were actually on the field. Multitudes of people believe General Winfield Scott, who was now fast asleep in his modest bed in Pennsylvania Avenue, is about to take the field in person. The horse-dealers are still utterly impracticable. A citizen who owned a dark bay, spavined and ringboned, asked me one thousand dollars for the right of possession. I ventured to suggest that it was not worth the money. "Well," said he, "take it or leave it. If you want to see this fight a thousand dollars is cheap. I guess there were chaps paid more than that to see Jenny Lind on her first night; and this battle is not going to be repeated, I can tell you. The price of horses will rise when the chaps out there have had themselves pretty well used up with bowie-knives and six-shooters."

July 18th.—After breakfast. Leaving headquarters, I went across to General Mansfield's, and was going upstairs, when the General* himself, a white-headed, grey-bearded, and rather soldierly-looking man, dashed out of his room in some excitement, and exclaimed, "Mr. Russell, I fear there is bad news from the front." "Are they fighting, General?" "Yes, sir. That fellow Tyler has been engaged, and we are whipped." Again I went off to the horse-dealer; but this time the price of the steed had been raised to £220; "for," says he, "I don't want my animals to be ripped up by them cannon and them musketry, and those who wish to be guilty of such cruelty must pay for it." At the War Office, at the Department of State, at the Senate, and at the White House, messengers and orderlies running in and out, military aides, and civilians with anxious faces, betokened the activity and perturbation which reigned within. I met Senator Sumner radiant with joy. "We have obtained a great success; the rebels are falling back in all directions. General Scott says we ought to be in Richmond by Saturday night." Soon afterwards a United States officer, who had visited me in company with General Meigs, riding rapidly past, called out, "You have heard we are whipped; these confounded volunteers have run away." I drove to the Capitol, where people said one could actually see the smoke of the cannon; but on arriving there it was evident that the fire from some burning houses, and from wood cut down for cooking purposes, had been mistaken for tokens of the fight.

It was strange to stand outside the walls of the Senate whilst legislators were debating inside respecting the best means of punishing the rebels and traitors, and to think that amidst the dim horizon of woods which bounded the west towards the plains of Manassas, the army of the United States was then contending, at least with doubtful fortune, against the forces

* Since killed in action

of the desperate and hopeless outlaws whose fate these United States senators pretended to hold in the hollow of their hands. Nor was it unworthy of note that many of the tradespeople along Pennsylvania Avenue, and the ladies whom one saw sauntering in the streets, were exchanging significant nods and smiles, and rubbing their hands with satisfaction. I entered one shop, where the proprietor and his wife ran forward to meet me. "Have you heard the news? Beauregard has knocked them into a cocked hat." "Believe me," said the good lady, "it is the finger of the Almighty is in it. Didn't he curse the niggers, and why should he take their part now with these Yankee Abolitionists, against true white men?" "But how do you know this?" said I. "Why, it's all true enough, depend upon it, no matter how we know it. We've got our underground railway as well as the Abolitionists."

On my way to dinner at the Legation I met the President crossing Pennsylvania Avenue, striding like a crane in a bulrush swamp among the great blocks of marble, dressed in an oddly cut suit of grey, with a felt hat on the back of his head, wiping his face with a red-pocket-handkerchief. He was evidently in a hurry, on his way to the White House, where I believe a telegraph has been established in communication with M'Dowell's head-quarters. I may mention, by-the-bye, in illustration of the extreme ignorance and arrogance which characterise the low Yankee, that a man in the uniform of a Colonel said to me to-day, as I was leaving the War Department, "They have just got a telegraph from M'Dowell. Would it not astonish you Britishers to hear that, as our General moves on towards the enemy, he trails a telegraph wire behind him just to let them know in Washington which foot he is putting first?" I was imprudent enough to say, "I assure you the use of the telegraph is not such a novelty in Europe or even in India. When Lord Clyde made his campaign the telegraph was laid in his track as fast as he advanced." "Oh, well, come now," quoth the Colonel, "that's pretty good, that is; I believe you'll say next, your General Clyde and our Benjamin Franklin discovered lightning simultaneously."

The calm of a Legation contrasts wonderfully in troubled times with the excitement and storm of the world outside. M. Mercier perhaps is moved to a vivacious interest in events. M. Stoeckl becomes more animated as the time approaches when he sees the fulfilment of his prophecies at hand. M. Tassara cannot be indifferent to occurrences which bear so directly on the future of Spain in Western seas; but all these diplomatists can discuss the most engrossing and portentous incidents of political and military life, with a sense of calm and indifference which was felt by the gentleman who resented being called out of his sleep to get up out of a burning house because he was only a lodger.

There is no Minister of the European Powers in Washington who watches with so much interest the march of events as Lord Lyons, or who feels as much sympathy perhaps in the Federal Government as the constituted Executive of the country to which he is accredited; but in virtue of his position he knows little or nothing officially of what passes around him and may be regarded as a medium for the communication of despatches to Mr. Seward, and for the discharge of a great deal of most causeless and unmeaning vituperation from the conductors of the New York press against England.

On my return to Captain Johnson's lodgings I received a note from the head-quarters of the Federals, stating that the serious action between the two armies would probably be postponed for some days. M'Dowell's original idea was to avoid forcing the enemy's position directly in front, which was defended by movable batteries commanding the fords over a stream called "Bull's Run." He therefore proposed to make a demonstration on some point near the centre of their line, and at the same time throw the mass of his force below their extreme right, so as to turn it and get possession of the Manassas Railway in their rear: a movement which would separate him, by-the-bye, from his own communications, and enable any general worth his salt to make a magnificent counter by marching on Washington, only 27 miles away, which he could take with the greatest ease, and leave the enemy in the rear to march 120 miles to Richmond, if they dared, or to make a hasty retreat upon the higher Potomac, and to cross into the hostile country of Maryland.

M'Dowell, however, has found the country on his left densely wooded and difficult. It is as new to him as it was to Braddock, when he cut his weary way through forest and swamp in this very district to reach, hundreds of miles away, the scene of his fatal repulse at Fort Du Quesne. And so, having moved his whole army, M'Dowell finds himself obliged to form a new plan of attack, and, prudently fearful of pushing his under-done and over-praised levies into a river in face of an enemy, is endeavouring to ascertain with what chance of success he can attack and turn their left.

Whilst he was engaged in a reconnaissance to-day, General Tyler did one of those things which must be expected from ambitious officers, without any fear of punishment, in countries where military discipline is scarcely known. Ordered to reconnoitre the position of the enemy on the left front, when the army moved from Fairfax to Centreville this morning, General Tyler thrust forward some 3000 or 4000 men of his division down to the very banks of "Bull's Run," which was said to be thickly wooded, and there brought up his men under a heavy fire of artillery and musketry, from which they retired in confusion.

The papers from New York to-night are more than usually impudent and amusing. The retreat of the Confederate outposts from Fairfax Court House is represented as a most extraordinary success; at best it was an affair of outposts; but one would really think that it was a victory of no small magnitude. I learn that the Federal troops behaved in a most ruffianly and lawless manner at Fairfax Court House. It is but a bad beginning of a campaign for the restoration of the Union, to rob, burn, and destroy the property and houses of the people in the State of Virginia. The enemy are described as running in all directions, but it is evident they did not intend to defend the advanced works, which were merely constructed to prevent surprise or cavalry inroads.

I went to Willard's, where the news of the battle, as it was called, was eagerly discussed. One little man in front of the cigar-stand declared it was all an affair of cavalry. "But how could that be among the piney woods and with a river in front, major?" "Our boys, sir, left their horses, crossed the water at a run, and went right away through them with their swords and six-shooters." "I tell you what it is, Mr. Russell," said a man who followed me out of the crowd and placed his hand on my shoulder, "they were whipped like curs, and they ran like curs, and I know it." "How?" "Well, I'd rather be excused telling you."

July 19th.—I rose early this morning in order to prepare for contingencies and to see off Captain Johnson, who was about to start with despatches for New York, containing, no doubt, the intelligence that the Federal troops had advanced against the enemy. Yesterday was so hot that officers and men on the field suffered from something like sun-stroke. To unaccustomed frames to-day the heat felt unsupportable. A troop of regular cavalry, riding through the street at an early hour, were so exhausted, horse and man, that a runaway cab could have bowled them over like ninepins

I hastened to General Scott's quarters, which were besieged by civilians outside and full of orderlies and officers within. Mr. Cobden would be delighted with the republican simplicity of the Commander-in-Chief's establishment, though it did not strike me as being very cheap at the money on such an occasion. It consists, in fact, of a small three-storied brick house, the parlours on the ground floor being occupied by subordinates, the small front room on the first floor being appropriated to General Scott himself, the smaller back room being devoted to his staff, and two rooms up-stairs most probably being in possession of waste papers and the guardians of the mansion. The walls are covered with maps of the coarsest description and with rough plans and drawings, which afford information and amusement to the orderlies and the stray aide-de-camps. "Did you ever hear anything so disgraceful in your life as the stories which are going about of the affair yesterday?" said Colonel Cullum. "I assure you it was the smallest affair possible, although the story goes that we have lost thousands of men. Our total loss is under ninety—killed, wounded, and missing; and I regret to say nearly one-third of the whole are under the latter head." "However that may be, Colonel," said I, "it will be difficult to believe your statement after the columns of type which appear in the papers here." "Oh! Who minds what they say?" "You will admit, at any rate, that the retreat of these undisciplined troops from an encounter with the enemy will have a bad effect?" "Well, I suppose that's likely enough, but it will soon be swept away in the excitement of a general advance. General Scott, having determined to attack the enemy, will not halt now, and I am going over to Brigadier M'Dowell to examine the ground and see what is best to be done."

On leaving the room two officers came out of General Scott's apartment; one of them said, "Why, Colonel, he's not half the man I thought him. Well, any way he'll be better there than M'Dowell. If old Scott had legs he's good for a big thing yet."

For hours I went horse-hunting; but Rothschild himself, even the hunting Baron, could not have got a steed. In Pennsylvania Avenue the people were standing in the shade under the ailantus trees, speculating on the news brought by dusty orderlies, or on the ideas of passing Congress men. A party of captured Confederates, on their march to General Mansfield's quarters, created intense interest, and I followed them to the house, and went up to see the General, whilst the prisoners sat down on the pavement and steps outside. Notwithstanding his affectation of calm and self-possession, General Mansfield, who was charged with the defence of the town, was visibly perturbed. "These things, sir," said he, "happen in Europe too. If the capital should fall into the hands of the rebels the United States will be no more destroyed than they were when you burned it." From an expression he let fall, I inferred he did not very well know what to do with his prisoners. "Rebels taken in arms in Europe are generally hung or blown away from guns, I believe; but we are more merciful." General Mansfield evidently wished to be spared the embarrassment of dealing with prisoners.

I dined at a restaurant kept by one Boulanger, a Frenchman, who utilised the swarms of flies infesting his premises by combining masses of them with his soup and made dishes. At an adjoining table were a lanky boy in a lieutenant's uniform, a private soldier, and a man in plain clothes; and for the edification of the two latter the warrior youth was detailing the most remarkable stories, in the Munchausen style, ear ever heard. "Well, sir, I tell you, when his head fell off on the ground, his eyes shut and opened twice, and his tongue came out with an expression as if he wanted to say something." "There were seven balls through my coat, and it was all so spiled with blood and powder, I took it off and threw it in the road. When the boys were burying the dead, I saw this coat on a chap who had been just smothered by the weight of the killed and wounded on the top of him, and I says, 'Boys, give me that coat; it will just do for me with the same rank; and there is no use in putting good cloth on a dead body.'" "And how many do you suppose was killed, Lieutenant?" "Well, sir! it's my honest belief, I tell you, there was not less than 5000 of our boys, and it may be twice as many of the enemy, or more; they were all shot down just like pigeons; you might walk for five rods by the side of the Run, and not be able to put your foot on the ground." "The dead was that thick?" "No, but the dead and the wounded together." No incredulity in the hearers—all swallowed: possibly disgorged into the notebook of a Washington contributor.

After dinner I walked over with Lieutenant H. Wise, inspected a model of Stevens' ram, which appears to me an utter impossibility in face of the iron-clad embrasured fleet now coming up to view, though it is spoken of highly by some naval officers and by many politicians. For years their papers have been indulging in mysterious volcanic puffs from the great centre of nothingness as to this secret and tremendous war-engine, which was surrounded by walls of all kinds, and only to be let out on the world when the Great Republic in its might had resolved to sweep everything off the seas. And lo! it is an abortive ram! Los Gringos went home, and I paid a visit to a family whose daughters—bright-eyed, pretty and clever—were seated out on the door-steps amid the lightning flashes, one of them, at least, dreaming with open eyes of a young artillery officer then sleeping among his guns, probably, in front of Fairfax Court House.

CHAPTER XLIX.

Skirmish at Bull's Run—The Crisis in Congress—Dearth of Horses—War Prices at Washington—Estimate of the effects of Bull's Run—Password and Countersign—Transatlantic View of "The Times"—Difficulties of a Newspaper Correspondent in the Field.

July 20th.—The great battle which is to arrest rebellion, or to make it a power in the land, is no longer distant or doubtful. M'Dowell has completed his reconnaissance of the country in front of the enemy, and General Scott anticipates that he will be in possession of Manassas to-morrow night. All the statements of officers concur in describing the Confederates as strongly entrenched along the line of Bull's Run covering the railroad. The New York papers, indeed, audaciously declare that the enemy have fallen back in disorder. In the main thoroughfares of the city there is still a scattered army of idle soldiers moving through the civil crowd, though how they come here no one knows. The officers clustering round the hotels, and running in and out of the bar-rooms and eating-houses, are still more numerous. When I inquired at the head-quarters who these were, the answer was that the majority were skulkers, but that there was no power at such a moment to send them back to their regiments or punish them. In fact, deducting the reserves, the rear-guards, and the scanty garrisons at the earthworks, M'Dowell will not have 25,000 men to undertake his seven day's march through a hostile country to the Confederate capital, and yet, strange to say, in the pride and passion of the politicians, no doubt is permitted to rise for a moment respecting his complete success.

I was desirous of seeing what impression was produced upon the Congress of the United States by the crisis which was approaching, and drove down to the Senate at noon. There was no appearance of popular enthusiasm, excitement, or emotion, among the people in the passages. They drank their iced water, ate cakes or lozenges, chewed and chatted, or dashed at their acquaintances amongst the members, as though nothing more important than a railway bill or a postal concession was being debated inside. I entered the Senate, and found the House engaged in not listening to Mr. Latham, the Senator for California, who was delivering an elaborate lecture on the aspect of political affairs from a Republican point of view. The Senators were, as usual, engaged in reading newspapers, writing letters, or in whispered conversation, whilst the Senator received his applause from the people in the galleries, who were scarcely restrained from stamping their feet at the most highly-flown passages. Whilst I was listening to what is by courtesy called the debate, a messenger from Centreville sent in a letter to me, stating that General M'Dowel would advance early in the morning, and expected to engage the enemy before noon. At the same moment a Senator who had received a despatch left his seat and read it to a brother legislator, and the news it contained was speedily diffused from one seat to another, and groups formed on the edge of the floor eagerly discussing the welcome intelligence.

The President's hammer again and again called them to order; and from out of this knot, Senator Sumner, his face lighted with pleasure, came to tell me the good news. "M'Dowell has carried Bull's Run without firing a shot. Seven regiments attacked it at the point of the bayonet, and the enemy immediately fled. General Scott only gives M'Dowell till mid-day to-morrow to be in possession of Manassas." Soon afterwards, Mr. Hay, the President's secretary, appeared on the floor to communicate a message to the Senate. I asked him if the news was true. "All I can tell you," said he, "is that the President has heard nothing at all about it, and that General Scott, from whom we have just received a communication, is equally ignorant of the reported success."

Some Senators and many Congress-men have already gone to join M'Dowell's army, or to follow in its wake, in the hope of seeing the Lord deliver the Philistines into his hands. As I was leaving the Chamber with Mr. Sumner, a dust-stained, toil-worn man, caught the Senator by the arm, and said, "Senator, I am one of your constituents. I come from ——town, in Massachusetts, and here are letters from people you know, to certify who I am. My poor brother was killed yesterday, and I want to go out and get his body to send back to the old people; but they won't let me pass without an order." And so Mr. Sumner wrote a note to General Scott and another to General Mansfield, recommending that poor Gordon Frazer should be permitted to go through the Federal lines on his labour of love; and the honest Scotchman seemed as grateful as if he had already found his brother's body.

Every carriage, gig, waggon, and hack has been engaged by people going out to see the fight. The price is enhanced by mysterious communications respecting the horrible slaughter in the skirmishes at Bull's Run. The French cooks and hotel-keepers, by some occult process of reasoning, have arrived at the conclusion that they must treble the prices of their wines and of the hampers of provisions which the Washington people are ordering to comfort themselves at their bloody Derby. "There was not less than 18,000 men, sir, killed and destroyed. I don't care what General Scott says to the contrary, he was not there. I saw a reliable gentleman, ten minutes ago, as cum straight from the place, and he swore there was a string of waggons three miles long with the wounded. While these Yankees lie so, I should not be surprised to hear they did not lose 1000 men in that big fight the day before yesterday."

When the newspapers came in from New York I read flaming accounts of the ill-conducted reconnaissance against orders, which was terminated by a most dastardly and ignominious retreat, "due," say the New York papers, "to the inefficiency and cowardice of some of the officers." Far different was the behaviour of the modest chroniclers of these scenes, who, as they tell us, "stood their ground as well as any of them, in spite of the shot, shell, and rifle-balls that whizzed past them for many hours." General Tyler alone, perhaps, did more, for "he was exposed to the enemy's fire for nearly four hours;" and when we consider that this fire came from masked batteries, and that the wind of round shot is unusually destructive (in America), we can better appreciate the danger to which he was so gallantly indifferent. It is obvious that in this first encounter the Federal troops gained no advantage; and as they were the assailants, their repulse, which cannot be kept secret from the rest of the army, will have a very damaging effect on their *morale*.

General Johnston, who has been for some days with a considerable force in an entrenched position at Winchester, in the valley of the Shenandoah, had occupied General Scott's attention, in consequence of the facility which he possessed to move into Maryland by Harper's Ferry, or to fall on the Federals by the Manassas Gap Railway, which was available by a long march from the town he occupied. General Patterson, with a Federal corps of equal strength, had accordingly been despatched to attack him, or, at all events, to prevent his leaving Winchester without an action; but the news to-night is that Patterson, who was an officer of some reputation, has allowed Johnston to evacuate Winchester, and has not pursued him; so that it is impossible to predict where the latter will appear.

Having failed utterly in my attempts to get a horse, I was obliged to negotiate with a livery-stable keeper, who had a hooded gig, or tilbury, left on his hands, to which he proposed to add a splinter-bar and pole, so as to make it available for two horses, on condition that I paid him the assessed value of the vehicle and horses, in case they were destroyed by the enemy. Of what particular value my executors might have regarded the guarantee in question, the worthy man did not inquire, nor did he stipulate for any value to be put upon the driver; but it struck me that, if these were in any way seriously damaged, the occupants of the vehicle were not likely to escape. The driver, indeed, seemed by no means willing to undertake the job; and again and again it was proposed to me that I should drive, but I persistently refused.

On completing my bargain with the stable-keeper, in which it was arranged with Mr. Wroe that I was to start on the following morning early, and return at night before twelve o'clock, or pay a double day, I went over to the Legation, and found Lord Lyons in the garden. I went to request that he would permit Mr. Warre, one of the *attachés*, to accompany me, as he had expressed a desire to that effect. His Lordship hesitated at first, thinking perhaps that the American papers would turn the circumstance to some base uses, if they were made aware of it; but finally he consented, on the distinct assurance that I was to be back the following night, and would not, under any event, proceed onwards with General M'Dowell's army till after I had returned to Washington. On talking over the matter with Mr. Warre, I resolved that the best plan would be to start that night if possible, and proceed over the long bridge, so as to overtake the army before it advanced in the early morning.

It was a lovely moonlight night. As we walked through the street to General Scott's quarters, for the purpose of procuring a pass, there was scarcely a soul abroad; and the silence which reigned contrasted strongly with the tumult prevailing in the day-time. A light glimmered in the General's parlour; his aides were seated in the verandah outside smoking in silence, and one of them handed us the passes which he had promised to procure; but when I told them that we intended to cross the long bridge that night, an unforeseen obstacle arose. The guards had been specially ordered to permit no person to cross between tattoo and daybreak who was not provided with the countersign; and without the express order of the General, no subordinate officer can communicate that countersign to a stranger. "Can you not ask the General?" "He is lying down asleep, and I dare not venture to disturb him."

As I had all along intended to start before daybreak, this *contretemps* promised to be very embarrassing, and I ventured to suggest that General Scott would authorise the countersign to be given when he awoke. But the *aide-de-camp* shook his head, and I began to suspect from his manner and from that of his comrades that my visit to the army was not regarded with much favour—a view which was confirmed by one of them, who, by the way, was a civilian, for in a few minutes he said, "In fact, I would not advise Warre and you to go out there at all; they are a lot of volunteers and recruits, and we can't say how they will behave. They may probably have to retreat. If I were you I would not be near them." Of the five or six officers who sat in the verandah, not one spoke confidently or with the briskness which is usual when there is a chance of a brush with an enemy.

As it was impossible to force the point, we had to retire, and I went once more to the horse dealer's, where I inspected the vehicle and the quadrupeds destined to draw it. I had spied in the stall a likely-looking Kentuckian nag, nearly black, light, but strong, and full of fire, with an undertaker's tail and something of a mane to match, which the groom assured me I could not even look at, as it was bespoke by an officer; but after a little strategy I prevailed on the proprietor to hire it to me for the day, as well as a boy, who was to ride it after the gig till we came to Centreville. My little experience in such scenes decided me to secure a saddle-horse. I knew it would be impossible to see anything of the action from a gig; that the roads would be blocked up by commissariat waggons, ammunition reserves, and that in case of anything serious taking place, I should be deprived of the chance of participating after the manner of my vocation in the engagement, and of witnessing its incidents. As it was not incumbent on my companion to approach so closely to the scene of action, he could proceed in the vehicle to the most convenient point, and then walk as far as he liked, and return when he pleased; but from the injuries I received in the Indian campaign, I could not walk very far. It was finally settled that the gig, with two horses and the saddle-horse ridden by a negro boy, should be at my door as soon after daybreak as we could pass the Long Bridge.

I returned to my lodgings, laid out an old pair of Indian boots, cords, a Himalayan suit, an old felt hat, a flask, revolver, and belt. It was very late when I got in, and I relied on my German landlady to procure some commissariat stores; but she declared the whole extent of her means would only furnish some slices of bread, with intercostal layers of stale ham and mouldy Bologna sausage. I was forced to be content, and got to bed after midnight, and slept, having first arranged that in case of my being very late next night a trustworthy Englishman should be sent for, who would carry my letters from Washington to Boston in time for the mail which leaves on Wednesday. My mind had been so much occupied with the coming event that I slept uneasily, and once or twice I started up, fancying I was called. The moon shone in through the musquito curtains of my bed, and just ere daybreak I was aroused by some noise in the adjoining room, and looking out, in a half dreamy state, imagined I saw General M'Dowell standing at the table, on which a candle was burning low, so distinctly that I woke up with the words, "General, is that you?" Nor did I convince myself it was a dream till I had walked into the room.

July 21st.—The calmness and silence of the streets of Washington this lovely morning suggested thoughts of the very different scenes which, in all probability, were taking place at a few miles' distance. One could fancy the hum and stir round the Federal bivouacs, as the troops woke up and were formed into column of march towards the enemy. I much regretted that I was not enabled to take the field with General M'Dowell's army, but my position was surrounded with such difficulties that I could not pursue the course open to the correspondents of the American newspapers. On my arrival in Washington I addressed an application to Mr. Cameron, Secretary at War, requesting him to sanction the issue of rations and forage from the Commissariat to myself, a servant, and a couple of horses, at the contract prices, or on whatever other terms he might think fit, and I had several interviews with Mr. Leslie, the obliging and indefatigable chief clerk of the War Department, in reference to the matter; but as there was a want of precedents for such a course, which was not at all to be wondered at, seeing that no representative of an English newspaper had ever been sent to chronicle the progress of an American army in the field, no satisfactory result could be arrived at, though I had many fair words and promises.

A great outcry had arisen in the North against the course and policy of England, and the journal I represented was assailed on all sides as a Secession organ, favourable to the rebels and exceedingly hostile to the Federal government and the cause of the Union. Public men in America are alive to the inconveniences of attacks by their own press; and as it was quite impossible to grant to the swarms of correspondents from all parts of the Union the permission to draw supplies from the public stores, it would have afforded a handle to turn the screw upon the War Department, already roundly abused in the most influential papers, if Mr. Cameron acceded to me, not merely a foreigner, but the correspondent of a foreign journal which was considered the most powerful enemy of the policy of his government, privileges which he denied to American citizens, representing newspapers which were enthusiastically supporting the cause for which the armies of the North were now in the field.

To these gentlemen indeed, I must here remark, such privileges were of little consequence. In every camp they had friends who were willing to receive them in their quarters, and who earned a word of praise in the local papers for the gratification of either their vanity or their laudable ambition in their own neighbourhood, by the ready service which they afforded to the correspondents. They rode Government horses, had the use of Government waggons, and through fear, favour, or affection, enjoyed facilities to which I had no access. I could not expect persons with whom I was unacquainted to be equally generous, least of all when by doing so they would have incurred popular obloquy and censure; though many officers in the army had expressed in very civil terms the pleasure it would give them to see me at their quarters in the field. Some days ago I had an interview with Mr. Cameron himself, who was profuse enough in promising that he would do all in his power to further my wishes; but he had, nevertheless, neglected sending me the authorisation for which I had applied. I could scarcely stand a baggage train and commissariat upon my own account, nor could I well participate in the system of plunder and appropriation which has marked the course of the Federal army so far, devastating and laying waste all the country behind it.

Hence, all I could do was to make a journey to see the army on the field, and to return to Washington to write my report of its first operation, knowing there would be plenty of time to overtake it before it could reach Richmond, when, as I hoped, Mr. Cameron would be prepared to accede to my request, or some plan had been devised by myself to obviate the difficulties which lay in my path. There was no *entente cordiale* exhibited towards me by the members of the American press; nor did they, any more than the generals, evince any disposition to help the alien correspondent of the *Times*, and my only connection with one of their body, the young designer, had not, indeed, inspired me with any great desire to extend my acquaintance. General M'Dowell, on giving me the most hospitable invitation to his quarters, refrained from offering the assistance which, perhaps, it was not in his power to afford; and I confess, looking at the matter calmly, I could scarcely expect that he would, particularly as he said, half in jest, half seriously, "I declare I am not quite easy at the idea of having your eye on me, for you have seen so much of European armies, you will, very naturally, think little of us, generals and all."

CHAPTER L.

To the scene of action—The Confederate camp—Centreville—Action at Bull Run—Defeat of the Federals—Disorderly retreat to Centreville—My ride back to Washington.

Punctual to time our carriage appeared at the door, with a spare horse, followed by the black quadruped on which the negro boy sat with difficulty, in consequence of its high spirits and excessively hard mouth. I swallowed a cup of tea and a morsel of bread, put the remainder of the tea into a bottle, got a flask of light Bordeaux, a bottle of water, a paper of sandwiches, and having replenished my small flask with brandy, stowed them all away in the bottom of the gig; but my friend, who is not accustomed to rise very early in the morning, did not make his appearance, and I was obliged to send several times to the legation to quicken his movements. Each time I was assured he would be over presently; but it was not till two hours had elapsed, and when I had just resolved to leave him behind, that he appeared in person, quite unprovided with *viaticum*, so that my slender store had now to meet the demands of two instead of one. We are off at last. The amicus and self find contracted space behind the driver. The negro boy, grinning half with pain and "the balance" with pleasure, as the Americans say, held on his rampant charger, which made continual efforts to leap into the gig, and thus through the deserted city we proceeded towards the Long Bridge, where a sentry examined our papers, and said with a grin, "You'll find plenty of Congressmen on before you." And then our driver whipped his horses through the embankment of Fort Runyon, and dashed off along a country road, much cut up with gun and cart wheels, towards the main turnpike.

The promise of a lovely day, given by the early dawn, was likely to be realised to the fullest, and the placid beauty of the scenery as we drove through the woods below Arlington, and beheld the white buildings shining in the early sunlight, and the Potomac, like a broad silver riband dividing the picture, breathed of peace. The silence close to the city was unbroken. From the time we passed the guard beyond the Long Bridge, for several miles we did not meet a human being, except a few soldiers in the neighbourhood of the deserted camps, and when we passed beyond the range of tents we drove for nearly two hours through a densely-wooded, undulating country; the houses, close to the roadside, shut up and deserted, window-high in the crops of Indian corn, fast ripening for the sickle; alternate field and forest, the latter generally still holding possession of the hollows, and, except when the road, deep and filled with loose stones, passed over the summit of the ridges, the eye caught on either side little but fir-trees and maize, and the deserted wooden houses, standing amidst the slave quarters.

The residences close to the lines gave signs and tokens that the Federals had recently visited them. But at the best of times the inhabitants could not be very well off. Some of the farms were small, the houses tumbling to decay, with unpainted roofs and side walls, and windows where the want of glass was supplemented by panes of wood. As we got further into the country the traces of the debateable land between the two armies vanished, and negroes looked out from their quarters, or sickly-looking women and children were summoned forth by the rattle of the wheels to see who was hurrying to the war. Now and then a white man looked out, with an ugly scowl on his face, but the country seemed drained of the adult male population, and such of the inhabitants as we saw were neither as comfortably dressed nor as healthy looking as the shambling slaves who shuffled about the plantations. The road was so cut up by gun-wheels, ammunition and commissariat waggons, that our horses made but slow way against the continual draft upon the collar; but at last the driver, who had known the country in happier times, announced that we had entered the high road for Fairfax Court-house. Unfortunately my watch had gone down, but I guessed it was then a little before nine o'clock. In a few minutes afterwards I thought I heard, through the eternal clatter and jingle of the old gig, a sound which made me call the driver to stop. He pulled up, and we listened. In a minute or so, the well-known boom of a gun, followed by two or three in rapid succession, but at a considerable distance, reached my ear. "Did you hear that?" The driver heard nothing, nor did my companion, but the black boy on the led horse, with eyes starting out of his head, cried, "I hear them, massa; I hear them, sure enough, like de gun in de navy yard;" and as he spoke the thudding noise, like taps with a gentle hand upon a muffled drum, were repeated, which were heard both by Mr. Warre and the driver. "They are at it! We shall be late! Drive on as fast as you can!" We rattled on still faster, and presently came up to a farm-house, where a man and woman, with some negroes beside them, were standing out by the hedge-row above us, looking up the road in the direction of a cloud of dust, which we could see rising above the tops of the trees. We halted for a moment. "How long have the guns been going, sir?" "Well, ever since early this morning," said he; "they've been having a fight. And I do really believe some of our poor Union chaps have had enough of it already. For here's some of them darned Secessionists marching down to go to Alexandry." The driver did not seem altogether content with this explanation of the dust in front of us, and presently, when a turn of the road brought to view a body of armed men, stretching to an interminable distance, with bayonets glittering in the sunlight through the clouds of dust, seemed inclined to halt or turn back again. A nearer approach satisfied me they were friends, and as soon as we came up with the head of the column I saw that they could not be engaged in the performance of any military duty. The men were marching without any resemblance of order, in twos and threes or larger troops. Some without arms, carrying great bundles on their backs; others with their coats hung from their firelocks; many foot sore. They were all talking and in haste; many plodding along laughing, so I concluded that they could not belong to a defeated army, and imagined M'Dowell was effecting some flank movement. "Where are you going to, may I ask?"

"If this is the road to Alexandria, we are going there."

"There is an action going on in front, is there not?"

"Well, so we believe, but we have not been fighting."

Although they were in such good spirits, they were not communicative, and we resumed our journey, impeded by the straggling troops and by the country cars containing their baggage and chairs, and tables and domestic furniture, which had never belonged to a regiment in the field. Still they came pouring on. I ordered the driver to stop at a rivulet, where a number of men were seated in the shade, drinking the water and bathing their hands and feet. On getting out I asked an officer, "May I beg to know, sir, where your regiment is going to?" "Well, I reckon, sir, we are going home to Pennsylvania." "This is the 4th Pennsylvania Regiment, is it not, sir?" "It is so, sir; that's the fact." "I should think there is severe fighting going on behind you, judging from the firing (for every moment the sound of the cannon had been growing more distinct and more heavy)?" "Well, I reckon, sir, there is." I paused for a moment, not knowing what to say, and yet anxious for an explanation; and the epauletted gentleman, after a few second's awkward hesitation, added, "We are going home because, as you see, the men's time's up, sir. We have had three months of this sort of work, and that's quite enough of it." The men who were listening to the conversation expressed their assent to the noble and patriotic utterances of the centurion, and, making him a low bow, we resumed our journey.

It was fully three and a half miles before the last of the regiment passed, and then the road presented a more animated scene, for white-covered commissariat waggons were visible, wending towards the front, and one or two hack carriages, laden with civilians, were hastening in the same direction. Before thq doors of the wooden farm-houses the coloured people were assembled, listening with outstretched necks to the repeated reports of the guns. At one time, as we were descending the wooded road, a huge blue dome, agitated by some internal convulsion, appeared to bar our progress, and it was only after infinite persuasion of rein and whip that the horses approached the terrific object, which was an inflated balloon, attached to a waggon, and defying the efforts of the men in charge to jockey it safely through the trees.

It must have been about eleven o'clock when we came to the first traces of the Confederate camp, in front of Fairfax Court-house, where they had cut a few trenches and levelled the trees across the road, so as to form a rude abattis; but the works were of a most superficial character, and would scarcely have given cover either to the guns, for which embrasures were left at the flanks to sweep the road, or to the infantry intended to defend them.

The Confederate force stationed here must have consisted, to a considerable extent, of cavalry. The bowers of branches, which they had made to shelter their tents, camp tables, empty boxes, and packing-cases, in the *débris* one usually sees around an encampment, showed they had not been destitute of creature comforts.

Some time before noon the driver, urged continually by adjurations to get on, whipped his horses into Fairfax Court-honse, a village which derives its name from a large brick building, in which the sessions of the county are held. Some thirty or forty houses, for the most part detached, with gardens or small strips of land about them, form the main street. The inhabitants who remained had by no means an agreeable expression of countenance, and did not seem on very good terms with the Federal soldiers, who were lounging up and down the streets, or standing in the shade of the trees and doorways. I asked the sergeant of a picket in the street how long the firing had been going on. He replied that it had commenced at half-past seven or eight, and had been increasing ever since. "Some of them will lose their eyes and back teeth," he said, "before it is over." The driver, pulling up at a roadside inn in the town, here made the startling announcement that both he and his horses must have something to eat, and although we would have been happy to join him, seeing that we had no breakfast, we could not afford the time, and were nôt displeased when a thin-faced, shrewish woman, in black, came out into the verandah, and said she could not let us have anything unless we liked to wait till the regular dinner hour of the house, which was at one o'clock. The horses got a bucket of water, which they needed in that broiling sun; and the cannonade, which by this time had increased into a respectable tumult that gave evidence of a well-sustained action, added vigour to the driver's arm, and in a mile or two more we dashed into a village of burnt houses, the charred brick chimney stacks standing amidst the blackened embers being all that remained of what was once German Town. The firing of this village was severely censured by General M'Dowell, who probably does not appreciate the value of such agencies employed "by our glorious Union army to develope loyal sentiments among the people of Virginia."

The driver, passing through the town, drove straight on, but after some time I fancied the sound of the guns seemed dying away towards our left. A big negro came shambling along the roadside—the driver stopped and asked him, "Is this the road to Centreville?" "Yes, sir; right on, sir: good road to Centreville, massa," and so we proceeded, till I became satisfied from the appearance of the road that we had altogether left the track of the army. At the first cottage we halted, and inquired of a Virginian, who came out to look at us, whether the road led to Centreville. "You're going to Centreville, are you?" "Yes, by the shortest road we can." "Well, then—you're going wrong—right away! Some people say there's a bend of road leading through the wood a mile further on, but those who have tried it lately have come back to German Town, and don't think it leads to Centreville at all." This was very provoking, as the horses were much fatigued and we had driven several miles out of our way. The driver, who was an Englishman, said, "I think it would be best for us to go on and try the road anyhow. There's not likely to be any Seceshers about there, are there, sir?"

"What did you say, sir?" inquired the Virginian, with a vacant stare upon his face.

"I merely asked whether you think we are likely to meet with any Secessionists if we go along that road?"

"Secessionists!" repeated the Virginian, slowly pronouncing each syllable as if pondering on the meaning of the word—"Secessionists! Oh no, *sir;* I don't believe there's such a thing as a Secessionist in the whole of this country."

The boldness of this assertion, in the very hearing of Beauregard's cannon, completely shook the faith of our Jehu in any information from that source, and we retraced our steps to German Town, and were directed into the proper road by some negroes, who were engaged exchanging Confederate money at very low rates for Federal copper with a few straggling soldiers. The faithful Muley Moloch, who had been capering in our rear so long, now complained that he was very much burned, but on further inquiry it was ascertained he was merely suffering from the abrading of his skin against an English saddle.

In an hour more we had gained the high road to Centreville, on which were many buggies, commissariat carts, and waggons full of civilians, and a brisk canter brought us in sight of a rising ground, over which the road led directly through a few houses on each side, and dipped out of sight, the slopes of the hill being covered with men, carts, and horses, and the summit crested with spectators, with their backs turned towards us, and gazing on the valley beyond. "There's Centreville," says the driver, and on our poor panting horses were forced, passing directly through the Confederate bivouacs, commissariat parks, folds of oxen, and two German regiments, with a battery of artillery, halting on the rising ground by the roadside. The heat was intense. Our driver complained of hunger and thirst, to which neither I nor my companion were insensible; and so pulling up on the top of the hill, I sent the boy down to the village which we had passed, to see if he could find shelter for the horses, and a morsel for our breakfastless selves.

It was a strange scene before us. From the hill a densely wooded country, dotted at intervals with green fields and cleared lands, spread five or six miles in front, bounded by a line of blue and purple ridges, terminating abruptly in escarpments towards the left front, and swelling gradually towards the right into the lower spines of an offshoot from the Blue Ridge Mountains. On our left the view was circumscribed by a forest which clothed the side of the ridge on which we stood, and covered its shoulder far down into the plain. A gap in the nearest chain of the hills in our front was pointed out by the bystanders as the Pass of Manassas, by which the railway from the West is carried into the plain, and still nearer at hand, before us, is the junction of that rail with the line from Alexandria, and with the railway leading southwards to Richmond. The intervening space was not a dead level; undulating lines of forest marked the course of the streams which intersected it, and gave, by their variety of colour and shading, an additional charm to the landscape which, enclosed in a framework of blue and purple hills, softened into violet in the extreme distance, presented one of the most agreeable displays of simple pastoral woodland scenery that could be conceived.

But the sounds which came upon the breeze, and the sights which met our eyes, were in terrible variance with the tranquil character of the landscape. The woods far and near echoed to the roar of cannon, and thin frayed lines of blue smoke marked the spots whence came the muttering sound of rolling musketry; the white puffs of smoke burst high above the tree-tops, and the gunners' rings from shell and howitzer marked the fire of the artillery.

Clouds of dust shifted and moved through the forest; and through the wavering mists of light blue smoke, and the thicker masses which rose commingling from the feet of men and the mouths of cannon, I could see the gleam of arms and the twinkling of bayonets.

On the hill beside me there was a crowd of civilians on horseback, and in all sorts of vehicles, with a few of the fairer, if not gentler sex. A few officers and some soldiers, who had straggled from the regiments in reserve, moved about among the spectators, and pretended to explain the movements of the troops below, of which they were profoundly ignorant.

The cannonade and musketry had been exaggerated by the distance and by the rolling echoes of the hills; and sweeping the position narrowly with my glass from point to point, I failed to discover any traces of close encounter or very severe fighting. The spectators were all excited, and a lady with an opera-glass who was near me was quite beside herself when an unusually heavy discharge roused the current of her blood—"That is splendid. Oh, my! Is not that first-rate? I guess we will be in Richmond this time to-morrow." These, mingled with coarser exclamations, burst from the politicians who had come out to see the triumph of the Union arms. I was particularly irritated by the constant applications for the loan of my glass. One broken-down looking soldier observing my flask, asked me for a drink, and took a startling pull, which left but little between the bottom and utter vacuity.

"Stranger, that's good stuff, and no mistake. I have not had such a drink since I come South. I feel now as if I'd like to whip ten Seceshers."

From the line of the smoke it appeared to me that the action was in an oblique line from our left, extending farther outwards towards the right, bisected by a road from Centreville, which descended the hill close at hand and ran right across the undulating plain, its course being marked by the white covers of the baggage and commissariat waggons as far as a turn of the road, where the trees closed in upon them. Beyond the right of the curling smoke clouds of dust appeared from time to time in the distance, as if bodies of cavalry were moving over a sandy plain.

Notwithstanding all the exultations and boastings of the people at Centreville, I was well convinced no advance of any importance or any great success had been achieved, because the ammunition and baggage waggons had never moved, nor had the reserves received any orders to follow in the line of the army.

The clouds of dust on the right were quite inexplicable. As we were looking, my philosophic companion asked me in perfect seriousness, "Are we really seeing a battle now? Are they supposed to be fighting where all that smoke is going on? This is rather interesting, you know."

Up came our black boy. "Not find a bit to eat, sir, in all the place." We had, however, my little paper of sandwiches, and descended the hill to a bye lane off the village, where, seated in the shade of the gig, Mr. Warre and myself, dividing our provision with the driver, wound up a very scanty, but much relished, repast with a bottle of tea and half the bottle of Bordeaux and water, the remainder being prudently reserved at my request for contingent remainders. Leaving orders for the saddle-horse, which was eating his first meal, to be brought up the moment he was ready, I went with Mr. Warre to the hill once more, and observed that the line had not sensibly altered whilst we were away.

An English gentleman, who came up flushed and heated from the plain, told us that the Federals had been advancing steadily in spite of a stubborn resistance, and had behaved most gallantly.

Loud cheers suddenly burst from the spectators as a man dressed in the uniform of an officer, whom I had seen riding violently across the plain in an open space below, galloped along the front, waving his cap and shouting at the top of his voice. He was brought up by the press of people round his horse close to where I stood. "We've whipped them on all points," he cried. "We have taken all their batteries. They are retreating as fast as they can, and we are after them." Such cheers as rent the welkin! The Congress-men shook hands with each other, and cried out, "Bully for us! Bravo! didn't I tell you so?" The Germans uttered their martial cheers, and the Irish hurrahed wildly. At this moment my horse was brought up the hill, and I mounted and turned towards the road to the front, whilst Mr. Warre and his companion proceeded straight down the hill.

By the time I reached the lane, already mentioned, which was in a few minutes, the string of commissariat waggons was moving onwards pretty briskly, and I was detained until my friends appeared at the roadside. I told Mr. Warre I was going forward to the front as fast as I could, but that I would come back, under any circumstances, about an hour before dusk, and would go straight to the spot where we had put up the gig by the roadside, in order to return to Washington. Then getting into the fields, I pressed my horse, which was quite recovered from his twenty-seven miles' ride and full of spirit and mettle, as fast as I could, making detours here and there to get through the ox fences, and by the small streams which cut up the country. The firing did not increase, but rather diminished in volume, though it now sounded close at hand.

I had ridden between three and a half and four miles, as well as I could judge, when I was obliged to turn for the third and fourth time into the road by a considerable stream, which was spanned by a bridge, towards which I was threading my way, when my attention was attracted by loud shouts in advance, and I perceived several waggons coming from the direction of the battlefield, the drivers of which were endeavouring to force their horses past the ammunition carts going in the contrary direction near the bridge; a thick cloud of dust rose behind them, and running by the side of the waggons were a number of men in uniform, whom I supposed to be the guard. My first impression was that the waggons were returning for fresh supplies of ammunition. But every moment the crowd increased; drivers and men cried out with the most vehement gestures, "Turn back! Turn back! We are whipped." They seized the heads of the horses and swore at the opposing drivers. Emerging from the crowd, a breathless man, in the uniform of an officer, with an empty scabbard dangling by his side, was cut off by getting between my horse and a cart for a moment. "What is the matter, sir? What is all this about?" "Why it means we are pretty badly whipped, that's the truth," he gasped, and continued.

By this time the confusion had been communicating itself through the line of waggons towards the rear, and the drivers endeavoured to turn round their vehicles in the narrow road, which caused the usual amount of imprecations from the men and plunging and kicking from the horses.

The crowd from the front continually increased, the heat, the uproar, and the dust were beyond description, and these were augmented when some cavalry soldiers, flourishing their sabres and preceded by an officer, who cried out, "Make way there—make way there for the General," attempted to force a covered waggon, in which was seated a man with a bloody handkerchief round his head, through the press.

I had succeeded in getting across the bridge with great difficulty before the waggon came up, and I saw the crowd on the road was still gathering thicker and thicker. Again I asked an officer, who was on foot, with his sword under his arm, "What is all this for?" "We are whipped, sir. We are all in retreat. You are all to go back." "Can you tell me where I can find General M'Dowell?" "No! nor can any one else."

A few shells could be heard bursting not very far off, but there was nothing to account for such an extraordinary scene. A third officer, however, confirmed the report that the whole army was in retreat, and that the Federals were beaten on all points, but there was nothing in this disorder to indicate a general rout. All these things took place in a few seconds. I got up out of the road into a corn-field, through which men were hastily walking or running, their faces streaming with perspiration, and generally without arms, and worked my way for about half a mile or so, as well as I could judge, against an increasing stream of fugitives, the ground being strewed with coats, blankets, firelocks, cooking tins, caps, belts, bayonets — asking in vain where General M'Dowell was.

Again I was compelled by the condition of the fields to come into the road; and having passed a piece of wood and a regiment which seemed to be moving back in column of march in tolerably good order, I turned once more into an opening close to a white house, not far from the lane, beyond which there was a belt of forest. Two field-pieces unlimbered near the house, with panting horses in the rear, were pointed towards the front, and along the road beside them there swept a tolerably steady column of men mingled with field ambulances and light baggage carts, back to Centreville. I had just stretched out my hand to get a cigar-light from a German gunner, when the dropping shots which had been sounding through the woods in front of us, suddenly swelled into an animated fire. In a few seconds a crowd of men rushed out of the wood down towards the guns, and the artillerymen near me seized the trail of a piece, and were wheeling it round to fire, when an officer or sergeant called out, "Stop! stop! They are our own men;" and in two or three minutes the whole battalion came sweeping past the guns at the double, and in the utmost disorder. Some of the artillerymen dragged the horses out of the tumbrils; and for a moment the confusion was so great I could not understand what had taken place; but a soldier whom I stopped, said, "We are pursued by their cavalry; they have cut us all to pieces."

Murat himself would not have dared to move a squadron on such ground. However, it could not be doubted that something serious was taking place; and at that moment a shell burst in front of the house, scattering the soldiers near it, which was followed by another that bounded along the road; and in a few minutes more out came another regiment from the wood, almost as broken as the first. The scene on the road had now assumed an aspect which has not a parallel in any description I have ever read. Infantry soldiers on mules and draught horses, with the harness clinging to their heels, as much frightened as their riders; negro servants on their masters' chargers; ambulances crowded with unwounded soldiers; waggons swarming with men who threw out the contents in the road to make room, grinding through a shouting, screaming mass of men on foot, who were literally yelling with rage at every halt, and shrieking out, "Here are the cavalry! Will you get on?" This portion of the force was evidently in discord.

There was nothing left for it but to go with the current one could not stem. I turned round my horse from the deserted guns, and endeavoured to find out what had occurred as I rode quietly back on the skirts of the crowd. I talked with those on all sides of me. Some uttered prodigious nonsense, describing batteries tier over tier, and ambuscades, and blood running knee deep. Others described how their boys carried whole lines of intrenchments, but were beaten back for want of reinforcements. The names of many regiments were mentioned as being utterly destroyed. Cavalry and bayonet charges and masked batteries played prominent parts in all the narrations. Some of the officers seemed to feel the disgrace of defeat; but the strangest thing was the general indifference with which the event seemed to be regarded by those who collected their senses as soon as they got out of fire, and who said they were just going as far as Centreville, and would have a big fight to-morrow.

By this time I was unwillingly approaching Centreville in the midst of heat, dust, confusion, imprecations inconceivable. On arriving at the place where a small rivulet crossed the road, the throng increased still more. The ground over which I had passed going out was now covered with arms, clothing of all kinds, accoutrements thrown off and left to be trampled in the dust under the hoofs of men and horses. The runaways ran alongside the waggons, striving to force themselves in among the occupants, who resisted tooth and nail. The drivers spurred, and whipped, and urged the horses to the utmost of their bent. I felt an inclination to laugh, which was overcome by disgust, and by that vague sense of something extraordinary taking place which is experienced when a man sees a number of people acting as if driven by some unknown terror. As I rode in the crowd, with men clinging to the stirrup-leathers, or holding on by anything they could lay hands on, so that I had some apprehension of being pulled off, I spoke to the men, and asked them over and over again not to be in such a hurry. "There's no enemy to pursue you. All the cavalry in the world could not get at you." But I might as well have talked to the stones.

For my own part, I wanted to get out of the ruck as fast as I could, for the heat and dust were very distressing, particularly to a half-starved man. Many of the fugitives were in the last stages of exhaustion, and some actually sank down by the fences, at the risk of being trampled to death. Above the roar of the fight, which was like the rush of a great river, the guns burst forth from time to time.

The road at last became somewhat clearer; for I had got ahead of some of the ammunition train and waggons, and the others were dashing up the hill towards Centreville. The men's great-coats and blankets had been stowed in the trains; but the fugitives had apparently thrown them out on the road, to make room for themselves. Just beyond the stream I saw a heap of clothing tumble out of a large covered cart, and cried out after the driver, "Stop! stop! All the things are tumbling out of the cart." But my zeal was checked by a scoundrel putting his head out, and shouting with a curse, "If you try to stop the team, I'll blow your —— brains out." My brains advised me to adopt the principle of non-intervention.

It never occurred to me that this was a grand débâcle. All along I believed the mass of the army was not broken, and that all I saw around was the result of confusion created in a crude organisation by a forced retreat; and knowing the reserves were at Centreville and beyond, I said to myself, "Let us see how this will be when we get to the hill." I indulged in a quiet chuckle, too, at the idea of my philosophical friend and his stout companion finding themselves suddenly enveloped in the crowd of fugitives, but knew they could easily have regained their original position on the hill. Trotting along briskly through the fields, I arrived at the foot of the slope on which Centreville stands, and met a German regiment just deploying into line very well and steadily—the men in the rear companies laughing, smoking, singing, and jesting with the fugitives, who were filing past; but no thought of stopping the waggons, as the orders repeated from mouth to mouth were that they were to fall back beyond Centreville.

The air of the men was good. The officers were cheerful, and one big German with a great pipe in his bearded mouth, with spectacles on nose, amused himself by pricking the horses with his sabre point, as he passed, to the sore discomfiture of the riders. Behind the regiment came a battery of brass field-pieces, and another regiment in column of march was following the guns. They were going to form line at the end of the slope, and no fairer position could well be offered for a defensive attitude, although it might be turned. But it was getting too late for the enemy, wherever they were, to attempt such an extensive operation. Several times I had been asked by officers and men, "Where do you think we will halt? Where are the rest of the army?" I always replied "Centreville," and I had heard hundreds of the fugitives say they were going to Centreville.

I rode up the road, turned into the little street which carries the road on the right-hand side to Fairfax Court-house and the hill, and went straight to the place where I had left the buggy in a lane on the left of the road beside a small house and shed, expecting to find Mr. Warre ready for a start, as I had faithfully promised Lord Lyons he should be back that night in Washington. The buggy was not there. I pulled open the door of the shed in which the horses had been sheltered out of the sun. They were gone. "Oh," said I, to myself, "of course! What a stupid fellow I am! Warre has had the horses put in, and taken the gig to the top of the hill, in order to see the last of it before we go." And so I rode over to the ridge; but arriving there, could see no sign of our vehicle far or near. There were two carriages of some kind or other still remaining on the hill, and a few spectators, civilians and military, gazing on the scene below, which was softened in the golden rays of the declining sun. The smoke wreaths had ceased to curl over the green sheets of billowy forest as sea foam crisping in a gentle breeze breaks the lines of the ocean. But far and near yellow and dun-coloured piles of dust seamed the landscape, leaving behind them long trailing clouds of lighter vapours which were dotted now and then by white puff-balls from the bursting of shell. On the right these clouds were very heavy and seemed to approach rapidly, and it occurred to me they might be caused by an advance of the much-spoken-of and little seen cavalry; and remembering the cross-road from German Town, it seemed a very fine and very feasible operation for the Confederates to cut right in on the line of retreat and communication, in which case the fate of the army and of Washington could not be dubious. There were now few civilians on the hill, and these were thinning away. Some were gesticulating and explaining to one another the causes of the retreat, looking very hot and red. The confusion among the last portion of the carriages and fugitives on the road, which I had outstripped, had been renewed again, and the crowd there presented a remarkable and ludicrous aspect through the glass; but there were two strong battalions in good order near the foot of the hill, a battery on the slope, another on the top, and a portion of a regiment in and about the houses of the village.

A farewell look at the scene presented no new features. Still the clouds of dust moved onwards denser and higher; flashes of arms lighted them up at times; the fields were dotted by fugitives, among whom many mounted men were marked by their greater speed, and the little flocks of dust rising from the horses' feet.

I put up my glass, and turning from the hill, with difficulty forced my way through the crowd of vehicles which were making their way towards the main road in the direction of the lane, hoping that by some lucky accident I might find the gig in waiting for me. But I sought in vain; a sick soldier, who was on a stretcher in front of the house, near the corner of the lane, leaning on his elbow, and looking at the stream of men and carriages, asked me if I could tell him what they were in such a hurry for, and I said they were merely getting back to their bivouacs. A man dressed in civilian's clothes grinned as I spoke. "I think they'll go farther than that," said he; and then added, "If you're looking for the waggon you came in, it's pretty well back to Washington by this time. I think I saw you down theere with a nigger and two men. Yes. They're all off, gone more than an hour and a half ago, I think, and a stout man—I thought was you at first—along with them."

Nothing was left for it but to brace up the girths for a ride to the Capitol, for which, hungry and fagged as I was, I felt very little inclination. I was trotting quietly down the hill road beyond Centreville, when suddenly the guns on the other side, or from a battery very near, opened fire, and a fresh outburst of artillery sounded through the woods. In an instant the mass of vehicles and retreating soldiers, teamsters, and civilians, as if agonised by an electric shock, quivered throughout the tortuous line. With dreadful shouts and cursings, the drivers lashed their maddened horses, and leaping from the carts, left them to their fate, and ran on foot. Artillerymen and foot soldiers, and negroes mounted on gun horses, with the chain traces and loose trappings trailing in the dust, spurred and flogged their steeds down the road or by the side paths. The firing continued and seemed to approach the hill, and at every report the agitated body of horsemen and waggons was seized, as it were, with a fresh convulsion.

Once more the dreaded cry, "The cavalry! cavalry are coming!" rang through the crowd, and looking back to Centreville, I perceived coming down the hill, between me and the sky, a number of mounted men, who might, at a hasty glance, be taken for horsemen in the act of sabreing the fugitives. In reality, they were soldiers and civilians, with, I regret to say, some officers among them, who were whipping and striking their horses with sticks or whatever else they could lay hands on. I called out to the men who were frantic with terror beside me, "They are not cavalry at all; they're your own men" —but they did not heed me. A fellow who was shouting out, "Run! run!" as loud as he could, beside me, seemed to take delight in creating alarm; and as he was perfectly collected as far as I could judge, I said, "What on earth are you running for? What are you afraid of?" He was in the roadside below me, and at once turning on me, and exclaiming, "I'm not afraid of you," presented his piece and pulled the trigger so instantaneously, that, had it gone off, I could not have swerved from the ball. As the scoundrel deliberately drew up to examine the nipple, I judged it best not to give him another chance, and spurred on through the crowd, where any man could have shot as many as he pleased without interruption. The only conclusion I came to was, that he was mad or drunken. When I was passing by the line of the bivouacs a battalion of men came tumbling down the bank from the field into the road, with fixed bayonets, and as some fell in the road and others tumbled on top of them, there must have been a few ingloriously wounded.

I galloped on for a short distance to head the ruck, for I could not tell whether this body of infantry intended moving back towards Centreville or were coming down the road; but the mounted men galloping furiously past me, with a cry of "Cavalry! cavalry!" on their lips, swept on faster than I did, augmenting the alarm and excitement. I came up with two officers who were riding more leisurely; and touching my hat, said, "I venture to suggest that these men should be stopped, sir. If not, they will alarm the whole of the post and pickets on to Washington. They will fly next, and the consequences will be most disastrous." One of the two, looking at me for a moment, nodded his head without saying a word, spurred his horse to full speed, and dashed on in front along the road. Following more leisurely, I observed the fugitives in front were suddenly checked in their speed; and as I turned my horse into the wood by the roadside to get on so as to prevent the chance of another blockup, I passed several private vehicles, in one of which Mr. Raymond, of the *New York Times*, was seated with some friends, looking by no means happy. He says in his report to his paper, "About a mile this side of Centreville a stampede took place amongst the teamsters and others, which threw everything into the utmost confusion, and inflicted very serious injuries. Mr. Eaton, of Michigan, in trying to arrest the flight of some of these men, was shot by one of them, the ball taking effect in his hand." He asked me, in some anxiety, what I thought would happen. I replied, "No doubt M'Dowell will stand fast at Centreville to-night. These are mere runaways, and unless the enemy's cavalry succeed in getting through at this road, there is nothing to apprehend."

And I continued through the wood till I got a clear space in front on the road, along which a regiment of infantry was advancing towards me. They halted ere I came up, and with levelled firelocks arrested the men on horses and the carts and waggons galloping towards them, and blocked up the road to stop their progress. As I tried to edge by on the right of the column by the left of the road, a soldier presented his firelock at my head from the higher ground on which he stood, for the road had a deep trench cut on the side by which I was endeavouring to pass, and sung out, "Halt! Stop—or I fire!" The officers in front were waving their swords and shouting out, "Don't let a soul pass! Keep back! keep back!" Bowing to the officer who was near me, I said, "I beg to assure you, sir, I am not running away. I am a civilian and a British subject. I have done my best as I came along to stop this disgraceful rout. I am in no hurry; I merely want to get back to Washington to-night. I have been telling them all along there are no cavalry near us." The officer to whom I was speaking, young and somewhat excited, kept repeating, "Keep back, sir! keep back! you must keep back." Again I said to him, "I assure you I am not with this crowd; my pulse is as cool as your own." But as he paid no attention to what I said, I suddenly bethought me of General Scott's letter, and addressing another officer, said, "I am a civilian going to Washington; will you be kind enough to look at this pass, specially given to me by General Scott?" The officer looked at it, and handed it to a mounted man, either adjutant or colonel, who, having examined it, returned it to me, saying, "Oh, yes! certainly. Pass that man!" And with a cry of "Pass that man!" along the line, I rode down the trench very leisurely, and got out on the road, which was now clear, though some fugitives had stolen through the woods on the flanks of the column and were in front of me.

A little further on there was a cart on the right-hand side of the road, surrounded by a group of soldiers. I was trotting past, when a respectable-looking man in a semi-military garb, coming out from the group, said, in a tone of much doubt and distress, "Can you tell me, sir, for God's sake, where the 69th New York are? These men tell me they are all cut to pieces." "And so they are," exclaimed one of the fellows, who had the number of the regiment on his cap.

"You hear what they say, sir?" exclaimed the man.

"I do, but I really cannot tell you where the 69th are."

"I'm in charge of these mails, and I'll deliver them if I die for it; but is it safe for me to go on? You are a gentleman, and I can depend on your word."

His assistant and himself were in the greatest perplexity of mind, but all I could say was, "I really can't tell you; I believe the army will halt at Centreville to-night, and I think you may go on there with the greatest safety, if you can get through the crowd." "Faith, then, he can't," exclaimed one of the soldiers.

"Why not?" "Sure, arn't we cut to pieces? Didn't I hear the kurnel himsilf saying we was all of us to cut and run, every man on his own hook, as well as he could? Stop at Cinthreville, indeed!"

I bade the mail agent* good evening and rode on, but even in this short colloquy stragglers on foot and on horseback, who had turned the flanks of the regiment by side paths or through the woods, came pouring along the road once more.

---

* I have since met the person referred to, an Englishman living in Washington, and well known at the Legation and elsewhere. Mr. Dawson came to tell me that he had seen a letter in an American journal, which was copied extensively all over the Union, in which the writer stated he accompanied me on my return to Fairfax Courthouse, and that the incident I related in my account of Bull Run did not occur, but that he was the individual referred to, and could swear with his assistant that every word I wrote was true. I did not need any such corroboration for the satisfaction of any who know me; and I was quite well aware that if one came from the dead to bear testimony in my favour before the American journals and public, the evidence would not countervail the slander of any characterless scribe who sought to gain a moment's notoriety by a flat contradiction of my narrative. I may add, that Dawson begged of me not to bring him before the public, "because I am now sutler to the ——th, over in Virginia, and they would dismiss me." "What! for certifying to the truth?" "You know, sir, it might do me harm." Whilst on this subject, let me remark that some time afterwards I was in Mr. Brady's photographic studio in Pennsylvania Avenue, Washington, when the very intelligent and obliging manager introduced himself to me, and said that he wished to have an opportunity of repeating to me personally what he had frequently told persons in the place, that he could bear the fullest testimony to the complete accuracy of my account of the panic from Centreville down the road at the time I left, and that he and his assistants, who were on the spot trying to get away their photographic van and apparatus, could certify that my description fell far short of the disgraceful spectacle and of the excesses of the flight.

Somewhere about this I was accosted by a stout, elderly man, with the air and appearance of a respectable mechanic, or small tavern-keeper, who introduced himself as having met me at Cairo. He poured out a flood of woes on me, how he had lost his friend and companion, nearly lost his seat several times, was unaccustomed to riding, was suffering much pain from the unusual position and exercise, did not know the road, feared he would never be able to get on, dreaded he might be captured and ill-treated if he was known, and such topics as a selfish man in a good deal of pain or fear is likely to indulge in. I calmed his apprehensions as well as I could, by saying, "I had no doubt M'Dowell would halt and show fight at Centreville, and be able to advance from it in a day or two to renew the fight again; that he couldn't miss the road; whiskey and tallow were good for abrasions;" and as I was riding very slowly, he jogged along, for he was a burr, and would stick, with many "Oh dears! Oh! dear me!" for most part of the way, joining me at intervals, till I reached Fairfax Court-house. A body of infantry were under arms in a grove near the Court-house, on the right-hand side of the road. The door and windows of the houses presented crowds of faces black and white; and men and women stood out upon the porch, who asked me as I passed, "Have you been at the fight?" "What are they all running for?" "Are the rest of them coming on?" to which I gave the same replies as before.

Arrived at the little inn where I had halted in the morning, I perceived the sharp-faced woman in black standing in the verandah with an elderly man, a taller and younger one dressed in black, a little girl, and a woman who stood in the passage of the door. I asked if I could get any thing to eat. "Not a morsel; there's not a bit left in the house, but you can get something, perhaps, if you like to stay till supper-time." "Would you oblige me by telling me where I can get some water for my horse?" "Oh, certainly," said the elder man, and calling to a negro, he directed him to bring a bucket from the well or pump, into which the thirsty brute buried its head to the eyes. Whilst the horse was drinking, the taller or younger man, leaning over the verandah, asked me quietly, "What are all the people coming back for?—what's set them a running towards Alexandria?"

"Oh, it's only a fright the drivers of the commissariat waggons have had; they are afraid of the enemy's cavalry."

"Ah!" said the man, and looking at me narrowly, he inquired, after a pause, "Are you an American?"

"No, I am not, thank God; I'm an Englishman."

"Well, then," said he, nodding his head and speaking slowly through his teeth, "there *will* be cavalry after them soon enough; there is 20,000 of the best horsemen in the world in old Virginny."

Having received full directions from the people at the inn for the road to the Long Bridge, which I was most anxious to reach instead of going to Alexandria or to Georgetown, I bade the Virginian good evening; and seeing that my stout friend, who had also watered his horse by my advice at the inn, was still clinging alongside, I excused myself by saying I must press on to Washington, and galloped on for a mile, until I got into the cover of a wood, where I dismounted to examine the horse's hoofs and shift the saddle for a moment, wipe the sweat off his back, and make him and myself as comfortable as could be for our ride into Washington, which was still seventeen or eighteen miles before me. I passed groups of men, some on horseback, others on foot, going at a more leisurely rate towards the capital; and as I was smoking my last cigar by the side of the wood, I observed the number had rather increased, and that among the retreating stragglers were some men who appeared to be wounded.

The sun had set, but the rising moon was adding every moment to the lightness of the road as I mounted once more and set out at a long trot for the capital. Presently I was overtaken by a waggon with a small escort of cavalry and an officer riding in front. I had seen the same vehicle once or twice along the road, and observed an officer seated in it with his head bound up with a handkerchief, looking very pale and ghastly. The mounted officer leading the escort asked me if I was going into Washington and knew the road. I told him I had never been on it before, but thought I could find my way; "at any rate, we'll find plenty to tell us." "That's Colonel Hunter inside the carriage: he's shot through the throat and jaw, and I want to get him to the doctor's in Washington as soon as I can. Have you been to the fight?"

"No, sir."

"A member of Congress, I suppose, sir?"

"No, sir, I'm an Englishman."

"Oh indeed, sir, then I'm glad you did not see it; so mean a fight, sir, I never saw; we whipped the cusses and drove them before us, and took their batteries and spiked their guns, and got right up in among all their dirt-works and great batteries and forts, driving them before us like sheep, when up more of them would get, as if out of the ground; then our boys would drive them again till we were fairly worn out; they had nothing to eat since last night and nothing to drink. I myself have not tasted a morsel since two o'clock last night. Well, there we were, waiting for reinforcements and expecting M'Dowell and the rest of the army, when whish! they threw open a whole lot of masked batteries on us, and then came down such swarms of horsemen on black horses, all black as you never saw, and slashed our boys over finely. The colonel was hit, and I thought it best to get him off as well as I could, before it was too late. And, my God! when they did take to running they did it first-rate, I can tell you," and so the officer, who had evidently taken enough to affect his empty stomach and head, chattering about the fight, we trotted on in the moonlight: dipping down into the valleys on the road, which seemed like inky lakes in the shadows of the black trees, then mounting up again along the white road, which shone like a river in the moonlight—the country silent as death, though once, as we crossed a small water-course and the noise of the carriage wheels ceased, I called the attention of my companions to a distant sound, as of a great multitude of people mingled with a faint report of cannon. "Do you hear that?" "No, I don't. But it's our chaps, no doubt. They're coming along fine, I can promise you." At last some miles further on we came to a picket, or main guard, on the roadside, who ran forward, crying out, "What's the news? anything fresh? are we whipped? is it a fact?" "Well, gentlemen," exclaimed the Major, reining up for a moment, "we are knocked into a cocked hat—licked to h——l." "Oh, pray don't say that," I exclaimed; "it's not quite so bad; it's only a drawn battle, and the troops will occupy Centreville to-night, and the posts they started from this morning."

A little further on we met a line of commissariat carts, and my excited and rather injudicious military friend appeared to take the greatest pleasure in replying to their anxious queries for news, "We are whipped! Whipped like h——."

At the cross-roads now and then we were perplexed, for no one knew the bearings of Washington, though the stars were bright enough; but good fortune favoured us and kept us straight, and at a deserted little village, with a solitary church on the roadside, I increased my pace, bade good-night and good speed to the officer, and having kept company with two men in a gig for some time, got at length on the guarded road leading towards the capital, and was stopped by the pickets, patrols, and grand rounds, making repeated demands for the last accounts from the field. The houses by the roadside were all closed up and in darkness. I knocked in vain at several for a drink of water, but was answered only by the angry barkings of the watch-dogs from the slave quarters. It was a peculiarity of the road that the people, and soldiers I met, at points several miles apart, always insisted that I was twelve miles from Washington. Up hills, down valleys, with the silent, grim woods for ever by my side, the white roads and the black shadows of men, still I was twelve miles from the Long Bridge, but suddenly I came upon a grand guard under arms, who had quite different ideas, and who said I was only about four miles from the river: they crowded round me. "Well, man, and how is the fight going?" I repeated my tale. "What does he say?" "Oh, begorra, he says we're not bet at all; it's all lies they have been telling us; we're only going back to the ould lines for the greater convaniency of fighting to-morrow again; that's illigant, hooro!"

All by the sides of the old camps the men were standing, lining the road, and I was obliged to evade many a grasp at my bridle by shouting out, "Don't stop me; I've important news; it's all well!" and still the good horse, refreshed by the cool night air, went clattering on, till from the top of the road beyond Arlington I caught a sight of the lights of Washington and the white buildings of the Capitol, and of the Executive Mansion, glittering like snow in the moonlight. At the entrance to the Long Bridge the sentry challenged, and asked for the countersign. "I have not got it, but I've a pass from General Scott." An officer advanced from the guard, and on reading the pass permitted me to go on without difficulty. He said, "I have been obliged to let a good many go over to-night before you, Congress-men and others. I suppose you did not expect to be coming back so soon. I fear it's a bad business." "Oh, not so bad, after all; I expected to have been back to-night before nine o'clock, and crossed over this morning without the countersign." "Well, I guess," said he, "we don't do such quick fighting as that in this country."

As I crossed the Long Bridge there was scarce a sound to dispute the possession of its echoes with my horse's hoofs. The poor beast had carried me nobly and well, and I made up my mind to buy him, as I had no doubt he would answer perfectly to carry me back in a day or two to M'Dowell's army by the time he had organised it for a new attack upon the enemy's position. Little did I conceive the greatness of the defeat, the magnitude of the disasters which it had entailed upon the United States, or the interval that would elapse before another army set out from the banks of the Potomac onward to Richmond. Had I sat down that night to write my letter, quite ignorant at the time of the great calamity which had befallen his army, in all probability I would have stated that M'Dowell had received a severe repulse, and had fallen back upon Centreville; that a disgraceful panic and confusion had attended the retreat of a portion of his army, but that the appearance of the reserves would probably prevent the enemy taking any advantage of the disorder; and as I would have merely been able to describe such incidents as fell under my own observation, and would have left the American journals to narrate the actual details, and the dispatches of the American Generals the strategical events of the day, I should have led the world at home to believe, as, in fact, I believed myself, that M'Dowell's retrograde movement would be arrested at some point between Centreville and Fairfax Court-house.

The letter that I was to write occupied my mind whilst I was crossing the Long Bridge, gazing at the lights reflected in the Potomac from the city. The night had become overcast, and heavy clouds rising up rapidly obscured the moon, forming a most phantastic mass of shapes in the sky.

At the Washington end of the bridge I was challenged again by the men of a whole regiment, who, with piled arms, were halted on the chaussée, smoking, laughing, and singing. "Stranger, have you been to the fight?" "I have been only a little beyond Centreville." But that was quite enough. Soldiers, civilians, and women, who seemed to be out unusually late, crowded round the horse, and again I told my stereotyped story of the unsuccessful attempt to carry the Confederate position, and the retreat to Centreville to await better luck next time. The soldiers alongside me cheered, and those next them took it up, till it ran through the whole line, and must have awoke the night-owls.

As I passed Willard's hotel a little further on, a clock—I think the only public clock which strikes the hours in Washington—tolled out the hour; and I supposed, from what the sentry told me, though I did not count the strokes, that it was eleven o'clock. All the rooms in the hotel were a blaze of light. The pavement before the door was crowded, and some mounted men and the clattering of sabres on the pavement led me to infer that the escort of the wounded officer had arrived before me. I passed on to the livery-stables, where every one was alive and stirring.

"I'm sure," said the man, "I thought I'd never see you nor the horse back again. The gig and the other gentleman has been back a long time. How did he carry you?"

"Oh, pretty well; what's his price?"

"Well, now that I look at him, and to you, it will be 100 dollars less than I said. I'm in good heart to-night."

"Why so? A number of your horses and carriages have not come back yet, you tell me."

"Oh, well, I'll get paid for them some time or another. Oh, such news! such news!" said he, rubbing his hands. "Twenty thousand of them killed and wounded! May-be they're not having fits in the White House to-night!"

I walked to my lodgings, and just as I turned the key in the door a flash of light made me pause for a moment, in expectation of the report of a gun; for I could not help thinking it quite possible that, somehow or another, the Confederate cavalry would try to beat up the lines, but no sound followed. It must have been lightning. I walked up-stairs, and saw a most welcome supper ready on the table—an enormous piece of cheese, a sausage of unknown components, a knuckle-bone of ham, and a bottle of a very light wine of France; but I would not have exchanged that repast and have waited half an hour for any banquet that Soyer or Careme could have prepared at their best. Then, having pulled off my boots, bathed my head, trimmed candles, and lighted a pipe, I sat down to write. I made some feeble sentences, but the pen went flying about the paper as if the spirits were playing tricks with it. When I screwed up my utmost resolution, the "y's" would still run into long streaks, and the letters combine most curiously, and my eyes closed, and my pen slipped, and just as I was aroused from a nap, and settled into a stern determination to hold my pen straight, I was interrupted by a messenger from Lord Lyons, to inquire whether I had returned, and if so, to ask me to go up to the Legation, and get something to eat. I explained, with my thanks, that I was quite safe, and had eaten supper, and learned from the servant that Mr. Warre and his companion had arrived about two hours previously. I resumed my seat once more, haunted by the memory of the Boston mail, which would be closed in a few hours, and I had much to tell, although I had not seen the battle. Again and again I woke up, but at last the greatest conqueror but death overcame me, and, with my head on the blotted paper, I fell fast asleep.

CHAPTER LI.

A runaway crowd at Washington—The army of the Potomac in retreat—Mail-day—Want of order and authority—Newspaper lies—Alarm at Washington—Confederate prisoners—General M'Clellan—M. Mercier—Effects of the defeat on Mr. Seward and the President—M'Dowell—General Patterson.

July 22nd.—I awoke from a deep sleep this morning, about six o'clock. The rain was falling in torrents, and beat with a dull, thudding sound on the leads outside my window; but, louder than all, came a strange sound, as if of the tread of men, a confused tramp and splashing, and a murmuring of voices. I got up and ran to the front room, the windows of which looked on the street, and there, to my intense surprise, I saw a steady stream of men covered with mud, soaked through with rain, who were pouring irregularly, without any semblance of order, up Pennsylvania Avenue towards the Capitol. A dense stream of vapour rose from the multitude; but looking closely at the men, I perceived they belonged to different regiments, New Yorkers, Michiganders, Rhode Islanders, Massachusetters, Minnesotians, mingled pellmell together. Many of them were without knapsacks, crossbelts, and firelocks. Some had neither greatcoats nor shoes, others were covered with blankets. Hastily putting on my clothes, I ran down stairs and asked an "officer," who was passing by, a pale young man, who looked exhausted to death, and who had lost his sword, for the empty sheath dangled at his side, where the men were coming from. "Where from? Well, sir, I guess we're all coming out of Verginny as far as we can, and pretty well whipped too." "What! the whole army, sir?" "That's more than I know. They may stay that like. I know I'm going home. I've had enough of fighting to last my lifetime."

The news seemed incredible. But there, before my eyes, were the jaded, dispirited, broken remnants of regiments passing onwards, where and for what I knew not, and it was evident enough that the mass of the grand army of the Potomac was placing that river between it and the enemy as rapidly as possible. "Is there any pursuit?" I asked of several men. Some were too surly to reply; others said, "They're coming as fast as they can after us." Others, "I guess they've stopped it now—the rain is too much for them." A few said they did not know, and looked as if they did not care. And here came one of these small crises in which a special correspondent would give a good deal for the least portion of duality in mind or body. A few sheets of blotted paper and writing materials lying on the table beside the burnt-out candles reminded me that the imperious post-day was running on. "The mail for Europe, *viâ* Boston, closes at one o'clock, Monday, July 22nd," stuck up in large characters, warned me I had not a moment to lose. I knew the event would be of the utmost interest in England, and that it would be important to tell the truth as far as I knew it, leaving the American papers to state their own case, that the public might form their own conclusions.

But then, I felt, how interesting it would be to ride out and watch the evacuation of the sacred soil of Virginia, to see what the enemy were doing, to examine the situation of affairs, to hear what the men said, and, above all, find out the cause of this retreat and headlong confusion, investigate the extent of the Federal losses and the condition of the wounded—in fact, to find materials for a dozen of letters. I would fain, too, have seen General Scott, and heard his opinions, and have visited the leading senators, to get a notion of the way in which they looked on this catastrophe. — "I do perceive here a divided duty."—But the more I reflected on the matter the more strongly I became convinced that it would not be advisable to postpone the letter, and that the events of the 21st ought to have precedence of those of the 22nd, and so I stuck up my usual notice on the door outside of "Mr. Russell is out," and resumed my letter.

Whilst the rain fell, the tramp of feet went

steadily on. As I lifted my eyes now and then from the paper, I saw the beaten, foot-sore, spongy-looking soldiers, officers, and all the debris of the army filing through mud and rain, and forming in crowds in front of the spirit-stores. Underneath my room is the magazine of Jost, negociant en vins, and he drives a roaring trade this morning, interrupted occasionally by loud disputes as to the score. When the lad came in with my breakfast he seemed a degree or two lighter in colour than usual. "What's the matter with you?" "I 'spects, massa, the Secesh-ers soon be in here. I'm a free nigger; I must go, sar, afore de come cotch me." It is rather pleasant to be neutral under such circumstances.

I speedily satisfied myself I could not finish my letter in time for post, and I therefore sent for my respectable Englishman to go direct to Boston by the train which leaves this at four o'clock to-morrow morning, so as to catch the mail steamer on Wednesday, and telegraphed to the agents there to inform them of my intention of doing so. Visitors came knocking at the door, and insisted on getting in—military friends who wanted to give me their versions of the battle—the *attachés* of legations and others, who desired to hear the news and have a little gossip; but I turned a deaf ear doorwards, and they went off into the outer rain again.

More draggled, more muddy, and down-hearted, and foot-weary and vapid, the great army of the Potomac still straggled by. Towards evening I seized my hat and made off to the stable to inquire how the poor horse was. There he stood, nearly as fresh as ever, a little tucked up in the ribs, but eating heartily, and perfectly sound. A change had come over Mr. Wroe's dream of horseflesh. "They'll be going cheap now," thought he, and so he said aloud, "If you'd like to buy that horse, I'd let you have him a little under what I said. Dear! dear! it must a' been a sight sure-ly to see them Yankees running; you can scarce get through the Avenue with them."

And what Mr. W. says is quite true. The rain has abated a little, and the pavements are densely packed with men in uniform, some with, others without, arms, on whom the shopkeepers are looking with evident alarm. They seem to be in possession of all the spirit-houses. Now and then shots are heard down the street or in the distance, and cries and shouting, as if a scuffle or a difficulty were occurring. Willard's is turned into a barrack for officers, and presents such a scene in the hall as could only be witnessed in a city occupied by a demoralised army. There is no provost guard, no patrol, no authority visible in the streets. General Scott is quite overwhelmed by the affair, and is unable to stir. General M'Dowell has not yet arrived. The Secretary of War knows not what to do, Mr. Lincoln is equally helpless, and Mr. Seward, who retains some calmness, is, notwithstanding his military rank and militia experience, without resource or expedient. There are a good many troops hanging on about the camps and forts on the other side of the river, it is said; but they are thoroughly disorganised, and will run away if the enemy comes in sight without a shot, and then the capital must fall at once. Why Beauregard does not come I know not, nor can I well guess. I have been expecting every hour since noon to hear his cannon. Here is a golden opportunity. If the Confederates do not grasp that which will never come again on such terms, it stamps them with mediocrity.

The morning papers are quite ignorant of the defeat, or affect to be unaware of it, and declare yesterday's battle to have been in favour of the Federals generally, the least arrogant stating that M'Dowell will resume his march from Centreville immediately. The evening papers, however, seem to be more sensible of the real nature of the crisis: it is scarcely within the reach of any amount of impertinence or audacious assertion to deny what is passing before their very eyes. The grand army of the Potomac is in the streets of Washington, instead of being on its way to Richmond. One paper contains a statement which would make me uneasy about myself if I had any confidence in these stories, for it is asserted "that Mr. Russell was last seen in the thick of the fight, and has not yet returned. Fears are entertained for his safety."

Towards dark the rain moderated and the noise in the streets waxed louder; all kinds of rumours respecting the advance of the enemy, the annihilation of Federal regiments, the tremendous losses on both sides, charges of cavalry, stormings of great intrenchments and stupendous masked batteries, and elaborate reports of unparalleled feats of personal valour, were circulated under the genial influence of excitement, and by the quantities of alcohol necessary to keep out the influence of the external moisture. I did not hear one expression of confidence, or see one cheerful face in all that vast crowd which but a few days before constituted an army, and was now nothing better than a semi-armed mob. I could see no cannon returning, and to my inquiries after them, I got generally the answer, "I suppose the Seceshers have got hold of them."

Whilst I was at table, several gentlemen who have *entrée* called on me, who confirmed my impressions respecting the magnitude of the disaster that is so rapidly developing its proportions. They agree in describing the army as disorganised. Washington is rendered almost untenable, in consequence of the conduct of the army, which was not only to have defended it, but to have captured the rival capital. Some of my visitors declared it was dangerous to move abroad in the streets. Many think the contest is now over; but the gentlemen of Washington have Southern sympathies, and I, on the contrary, am persuaded this prick in the great Northern balloon will let out a quantity of poisonous gas, and rouse the people to a sense of the nature of the conflict on which they have entered. The inmates of the White House are in a state of the utmost trepidation, and Mr. Lincoln, who sat in the telegraph operator's room with General Scott and Mr. Seward, listening to the dispatches as they arrived from the scene of action, left it in despair when the fatal words tripped from the needle, and the defeat was clearly revealed to him.

Having finally cleared my room of visitors and locked the door, I sat down once more to my desk, and continued my narrative. The night wore on, and the tumult still reigned in the city. Once, indeed, if not twice, my attention was aroused by sounds like distant cannon and outbursts of musketry, but on reflection I was satisfied the Confederate general would never be rash enough to attack the place by night, and that, after all the rain which had fallen, he in all probability would give horses and men a day's rest, marching them through the night, so as to appear before the city in the course of to-morrow. Again and again I was interrupted by soldiers clamouring for drink and for money, attracted by the light in my windows; one or two irrepressible and irresistible friends actually succeeded in making their way into my room—just as on the night when I was engaged in writing an account of the last attack on the Redan, my hut was stormed by visitors, and much of my letter was penned under the apprehension of a sharp pair of spurs fixed in the heels of a jolly little adjutant, who, overcome by fatigue and rum-and-water, fell asleep in my chair, with his legs cocked up on my writing-table; but I saw the last of them about midnight, and so continued writing till the morning light began to steal through the casement. Then came the trusty messenger, and, at 3 A.M., when I had handed him the parcel and looked round to see all my things were in readiness, lest a rapid toilet might be necessary in the morning, with a sigh of relief I plunged into bed, and slept.

July 23rd.—The morning was far advanced when I awoke, and hearing the roll of waggons in the street, I at first imagined the Federals were actually about to abandon Washington itself; but on going to the window, I perceived it arose from an irregular train of commissariat carts, country waggons, ambulances, and sutlers' vans, in the centre of the street, the paths being crowded as before with soldiers, or rather with men in uniform, many of whom seemed as if they had been rolling in the mud. Poor General Mansfield was running back and forwards between his quarters and the War Department, and in the afternoon some efforts were made to restore order, by appointing rendezvous to which the fragment of regiments should repair, and by organising mounted patrols to clear the streets. In the middle of the day I went out through the streets, and walked down to the long bridge with the intention of crossing, but it was literally blocked up from end to end with a mass of waggons and ambulances full of wounded men, whose cries of pain echoed above the shouts of the drivers, so that I abandoned the attempt to get across, which, indeed, would not have been easy with any comfort, owing to the depth of mud in the roads. To-day the aspect of Washington is more unseemly and disgraceful, if that were possible, than yesterday afternoon.

As I returned towards my lodgings a scene of greater disorder and violence than usual attracted my attention. A body of Confederate prisoners, marching two and two, were with difficulty saved by their guard from the murderous assaults of a hooting rabble, composed of civilians and men dressed like soldiers, who hurled all kinds of missiles they could lay their hands upon over the heads of the guard at their victims, spattering them with mud and filthy language. It was very gratifying to see the way in which the dastardly mob dispersed at the appearance of a squad of mounted men, who charged them boldly, and escorted the prisoners to General Mansfield. They consisted of a picket or grand guard, which, unaware of the retreat of their regiment from Fairfax, marched into the Federal lines before the battle. Their just indignation was audible enough. One of them, afterwards, told General M'Dowell, who hurried over as soon as he was made aware of the disgraceful outrages to which they had been exposed, "I would have died a hundred deaths before I fell into these wretches' hands, if I had known this. Set me free for five minutes, and let any two, or four, of them insult me when my hands are loose."

Soon afterwards a report flew about that a crowd of soldiers were hanging a Secessionist. A senator rushed to General M'Dowell, and told him that he had seen the man swinging with his own eyes. Off went the General, *ventre à terre*, and was considerably relieved by finding that they were hanging merely a dummy or effigy of Jeff. Davis, not having succeeded in getting at the original yesterday.

Poor M'Dowell has been swiftly punished for his defeat, or rather for the unhappy termination to his advance. As soon as the disaster was ascertained beyond doubt, the President telegraphed to General M'Clellan to come and take command of his army. It is a commentary full of instruction on the military system of the Americans, that they have not a soldier who has ever handled a brigade in the field fit for service in the North.

The new commander-in-chief is a brevet-major who has been in civil employ on a railway for several years. He went once, with two other West Point officers, commissioned by Mr. Jefferson Davis, then Secretary of War, to examine and report on the operations in the Crimea, who were judiciously despatched when the war was over, and I used to see him and his companions poking about the ruins of the deserted trenches and batteries, mounted on horses furnished by the courtesy of British officers, just as they lived in English quarters, when they were snubbed and refused an audience by the Duke of Malakhoff in the French camp. Major M'Clellan forgot the affront, did not even mention it, and showed his Christian spirit by praising the allies, and damning John Bull with very faint applause, seasoned with lofty censure. He was very young, however, at the time, and is so well spoken of that his appointment will be popular; but all that he has done to gain such reputation, and to earn the confidence of the government, is to have had some skirmishes with bands of Confederates in Western Virginia, in which the leader, Garnett, was killed, his "forces" routed, and finally, to the number of a thousand, obliged to surrender as prisoners of war. That success, however, at such a time, is quite enough to elevate any man to the highest command. M'Clellan is about thirty-six years of age, was educated at West Point, where he was junior to M'Dowell, and a class-fellow of Beauregard.

I dined with M. Mercier, the French minister, who has a prettily situated house on the heights of Georgetown, about a mile and a half from the city. Lord Lyons, Mr. Monson, his private secretary, M. Baroche, son of the French minister, who has been exploiting the Southern states, were the only additions to the family circle. The minister is a man in the prime of life, of more than moderate ability, with a rapid manner and quickness of apprehension. Ever since I first met M. Mercier he has expressed his conviction that the North never can succeed in conquering the South, or even restoring the Union, and that an attempt to do either by armed force must end in disaster. He is the more confirmed in his opinions by the result of Sunday's battle, but the inactivity of the Confederates gives rise to the belief that they suffered seriously in the affair. M. Baroche has arrived at the conviction, without reference to the fate of the Federals in their march to Richmond, that the Union is utterly gone—as dead as the Achaian league.

Whilst Madame Mercier and her friends are conversing on much more agreeable subjects, the men hold a tobacco council under the shade of the magnificent trees, and France, Russia, and minor powers talk politics, Lord Lyons alone not joining in the nicotian controversy. Beneath us flowed the Potomac, and on the wooded heights at the other side, the Federal flag rose over Fort Corcoran and Arlington House, from which the grand army had set forth a few days ago to crush rebellion and destroy its chiefs. There, sad, anxious, and despairing, Mr. Lincoln and Mr. Seward were at that very moment passing through the wreck of the army, which, silent as ruin itself, took no notice of their presence.

It had been rumoured that the Confederates were advancing, and the President and the Foreign Minister set out in a carriage to see with their own eyes the state of the troops. What they beheld filled them with despair. The plateau was covered with the men of different regiments, driven by the patrols out of the city, or arrested in their flight at the bridges. In Fort Corcoran the men were in utter disorder, threatening to murder the officer of regulars who was essaying to get them into some state of efficiency to meet the advancing enemy. He had menaced one of the officers of the 69th with death for flat disobedience to orders; the men had taken the part of their captain; and the President drove into the work just in time to witness the confusion. The soldiers with loud cries demanded that the officer should be punished, and the President asked him why he had used such violent language towards his subordinate. "I told him, Mr. President, that if he refused to obey my orders I would shoot him on the spot; and I here repeat it, sir, that if I remain in command here, and he or any other man refuses to obey my orders, I'll shoot him on the spot."

The firmness of Sherman's language and demeanour in presence of the chief of the State overawed the mutineers, and they proceeded to put the work in some kind of order to resist the enemy.

Mr. Seward was deeply impressed by the scene, and retired with the President to consult as to the best course to pursue, in some dejection, but they were rather comforted by the telegrams from all parts of the North, which proved that, though disappointed and surprised, the people were not disheartened or ready to relinquish the contest.

The accounts of the battle in the principal journals are curiously inaccurate and absurd. The writers have now recovered themselves. At first they yielded to the pressure of facts and to the accounts of their correspondents. They admitted the repulse, the losses, the disastrous retreat, the loss of guns, in strange contrast to their prophecies and wondrous hyperboles about the hyperbolic grand army. Now they set themselves to stem the current they have made. Let any one read the New York journals for the last week, if he wishes to frame an indictment against such journalism as the people delight to honour in America.

July 24th.—I rode out before breakfast in company with Mr. Monson across the Long Bridge over to Arlington House. General M'Dowell was seated at a table under a tree in front of his tent, and got out his plans and maps to explain the scheme of battle.

Cast down from his high estate, placed as a subordinate to his junior, covered with obloquy and abuse, the American General displayed a calm self-possession and perfect amiability which could only proceed from a philosophic temperament and a consciousness that he would outlive the calumnies of his countrymen. He accused nobody; but it was not difficult to perceive he had been sacrificed to the vanity, self-seeking, and disobedience of some of his officers, and to radical vices in the composition of his army.

When M'Dowell found he could not turn the enemy's right as he intended, because the country by the Occoquan was unfit for the movements of artillery, or even infantry, he reconnoitred the ground towards their left, and formed the project of turning it by a movement which would bring the weight of his columns on their extreme left, and at the same time overlap it, whilst a strong demonstration was made on the ford at Bull's Run, where General Tyler brought on the serious skirmish of the 18th. In order to carry out this plan, he had to debouch his columns from a narrow point at Centreville, and march them round by various roads to points on the upper part of the Run, where it was fordable in all directions, intending to turn the enemy's batteries on the lower roads and bridges. But although he started them at an early hour, the troops moved so slowly the Confederates became aware of their design, and were enabled to concentrate considerable masses of troops on their left.

The Federals were not only slow, but disorderly. The regiments in advance stopped at streams to drink and fill their canteens, delaying the regiments in the rear. They wasted their provisions, so that many of them were without food at noon, when they were exhausted by the heat of the sun and by the stifling vapours of their own dense columns. When they at last came into action, some divisions were not in their places, so that the line of battle was broken; and those which were in their proper position were exposed, without support, to the enemy's fire. A delusion of masked batteries pressed on their brain. To this was soon added a hallucination about cavalry, which might have been cured had the Federals possessed a few steady squadrons to manœuvre on their flanks and in the intervals of their line. Nevertheless, they advanced and encountered the enemy's fire with some spirit; but the Confederates were enabled to move up fresh battalions, and to a certain extent to establish an equality between the numbers of their own troops and the assailants, whilst they had the advantages of better cover and ground. An apparition of a disorderly crowd of horsemen in front of the much-boasting Fire Zouaves of New York threw them into confusion and flight, and a battery which they ought to have protected was taken. Another battery was captured by the mistake of an officer, who allowed a Confederate regiment to approach the guns, thinking they were Federal troops, till their first volley destroyed both horses and gunners. At the critical moment, General Johnston, who had escaped from the feeble observation and untenacious grip of General Patterson and his time-expired volunteers, and had been hurrying down his troops from Winchester by train, threw his fresh battalions on the flank and rear of the Federal right. When the General ordered a retreat, rendered necessary by the failure of the attack —disorder spread, which increased—the retreat became a flight, which degenerated—if a flight can degenerate—into a panic, the moment the Confederates pressed them with a few cavalry and horse artillery. The efforts of the Generals to restore order and confidence were futile. Fortunately a weak reserve was posted at Centreville, and these were formed in line on the slope of the hill, whilst M'Dowell and his officers exerted themselves with indifferent success to arrest the mass of the army, and make them draw up behind the reserve, telling the men a bold front was their sole chance of safety. At midnight it became evident the *morale* of the army was destroyed, and nothing was left but a speedy retrograde movement, with the few regiments and guns which were in a condition approaching to efficiency, upon the defensive works of Washington.

Notwithstanding the reverse of fortune, M'Dowell did not appear willing to admit his estimate of the Southern troops was erroneous, or to say, "Change armies, and I'll fight the battle over again." He still held Mississippians, Alabamians, Louisianians, very cheap, and did not see, or would not confess, the full extent of the calumny which had fallen so heavily on him personally. The fact of the evening's inactivity was conclusive in his mind that they had a dearly-bought success, and he looked forward, though in a subordinate capacity, to a speedy and glorious revenge.

July 25th.—The unfortunate General Patterson, who could not keep Johnston from getting away from Winchester, is to be dismissed the service—honourably, of course—that is, he is to be punished because his men would insist on going home in face of the enemy, as soon as their three months were up, and that time happened to arrive just as it would be desirable to operate against the Confederates. The latter have lost their chance. The Senate, the House of Representatives, the Cabinet, the President, are all at their ease once more, and feel secure in Washington. Up to this moment the Confederates could have taken it with very little trouble. Maryland could have been roused to arms, and Baltimore would have declared for them. The triumph of the non-aggressionists, at the head of which is Mr. Davis, in resisting the demands of the party which urges an actual invasion of the North as the best way of obtaining peace, may prove to be very disastrous. Final material results must have justified the occupation of Washington.

I dined at the Legation, where were Mr. Sumner and some English visitors desirous of going South. Lord Lyons gives no encouragement to these adventurous persons.

July 26th.—Whether it is from curiosity to hear what I have to say or not, the number of my visitors is augmenting. Among them was a man in soldier's uniform, who sauntered into my room to borrow "five or ten dollars," on the ground that he was a waiter at the Clarendon Hotel when I was stopping there, and wanted to go North, as his time was up. His anecdotes were stupendous. General Meigs and Captain Macomb, of the United States Engineers, paid me a visit, and talked of the disaster very sensibly. The former is an able officer, and an accomplished man; the latter, son, I believe, of the American general of that name, distinguished in the war with Great Britain. I had a long conversation with General M'Dowell, who bears his supercession with admirable fortitude, and complains of nothing except the failure of his officers to obey orders, and the hard fate which condemned him to lead an army of volunteers—Captain Wright, aide de camp to General Scott, Lieutenant Wise, of the Navy, and many others. The communications received from the Northern States have restored the spirits of all Union men, and not a few declare they are glad of the reverse, as the North will now be obliged to put forth all its strength.

CHAPTER LII.

Attack of Illness—General M'Clellan—Reception at the White House—Drunkenness among the Volunteers—Visit from Mr. Olmsted—Georgetown—Intense Heat—M'Clellan and the Newspapers—Reception at Mr. Seward's—Alexandria—A Storm—Sudden Death of an English Officer—The Maryland Club—A Prayer and Fast Day—Financial Difficulties.

July 27th.—So ill to-day from heat, bad smells in the house, and fatigue, that I sent for Dr. Miller, a great, fine Virginian practitioner, who ordered me powders to be taken in "mint juleps." Now mint juleps are made of whisky, sugar, ice, very little water, and sprigs of fresh mint, to be sucked up after the manner of sherry cobblers, if so it be pleased, with a straw.

"A powder every two hours, with a mint julep. Why, that's six a day, Doctor. Won't that be —eh?—won't that be rather intoxicating?"

"Well, sir, that depends on the constitution. You'll find they will do you no harm, even if the worst takes place."

Day after day, till the month was over and August had come, I passed in a state of powder and julep, which the Virginian doctor declared saved my life. The first time I stirred out the change which had taken place in the streets was at once apparent: no drunken rabblement of armed men, no begging soldiers; instead of these were patrols in the streets, guards at the corners, and a rigid system of passes. The North begin to perceive their magnificent armies are mythical, but knowing they have the elements of making one, they are setting about the manufacture. Numbers of tapsters and serving-men, and *canaille* from the cities, who now disgrace swords and shoulder-straps, are to be dismissed. Round the corner, with a kind of staff at his heels and an escort, comes Major General George B. M'Clellan, the young Napoleon (of Western Virginia), the conqueror of Garnett, the captor of Peagrim, the commander-in-chief, under the President, of the army of the United States. He is a very squarely-built, thick-throated, broad-chested man, under the middle height, with slightly-bowed legs, a tendency to *embonpoint*. His head, covered with a closely-cut crop of dark auburn hair, is well set on his shoulders. His features are regular and prepossessing—the brow small, contracted, and furrowed; the eyes deep and anxious-looking. A short, thick, reddish moustache conceals his mouth; the rest of his face is clean shaven. He has made his father-in-law, Major Marcy, chief of his staff, and is a good deal influenced by his opinions, which are entitled to some weight, as Major Marcy is a soldier, and has seen frontier wars, and is a great traveller. The task of licking this army into shape is of Herculean magnitude. Every one, however, is willing to do as he bids: the President confides in him, and "Georges" him; the press fawn upon him, the people trust him; he is "the little corporal" of unfought fields—*omnis ignotus pro mirifico*, here. He looks like a stout little captain of dragoons, but for his American seat and saddle. The latter is adapted to a man who cannot ride: if a squadron so mounted were to attempt a fence or ditch, half of them would be ruptured or spilled. The seat is a marvel to any European. But M'Clellan is nevertheless "the man on horseback" just now, and the Americans must ride in his saddle, or in anything he likes.

In the evening of my first day's release from juleps the President held a reception or levée, and I went to the White House about nine o'clock, when the rooms were at their fullest. The company were arriving on foot, or crammed in hackney coaches, and did not affect any neatness of attire or evening dress. The doors were open: any one could walk in who chose. Private soldiers, in hodden grey and hob-nailed shoes, stood timorously chewing on the threshold of the state apartments, alarmed at the lights and gilding, or, haply, by the marabout feathers and finery of a few ladies who were in ball costume, till, assured by fellow-citizens there was nothing to fear, they plunged into the dreadful revelry. Faces familiar to me in the magazines of the town were visible in the crowd which filled the reception-rooms and the ball-room, in a small room off which a military band was stationed.

The President, in a suit of black, stood near the door of one of the rooms near the hall, and shook hands with every one of the crowd, who was then "passed" on by his secretary, if the President didn't wish to speak to him. Mr. Lincoln has recovered his spirits, and seemed in good humour. Mrs. Lincoln, who did the honours in another room, surrounded by a few ladies, did not appear to be quite so contented. All the ministers are present except Mr. Seward, who has gone to his own state to ascertain the frame of mind of the people, and to judge for himself of the sentiments they entertain respecting the war. After walking up and down the hot and crowded rooms for an hour, and seeing and speaking to all the celebrities, I withdrew. Colonel Richardson, in his official report, states Colonel Miles lost the battle of Bull Run by being drunk and disorderly at a critical moment. Colonel Miles, who commanded a division of three brigades, writes to say he was not in any such state, and has demanded a court of inquiry. In a Philadelphia paper it is stated M'Dowell was helplessly drunk during the action, and sat up all the night before drinking, smoking, and playing cards. M'Dowell never drinks, and never has drunk, wine, spirits, malt, tea, or coffee, or smoked or used tobacco in any form, nor does he play cards; and that remark does not apply to many other Federal officers.

Drunkenness is only too common among the American volunteers, and General Butler has put it officially in orders, that "the use of intoxicating liquors prevails to an alarming extent among the officers of his command," and has ordered the seizure of their grog, which will only be allowed on medical certificate. He announces, too, that he will not use wine or spirits, or give any to his friends, or allow any in his own quarters in future—a quaint, vigorous creature, this Massachusetts lawyer.

The outcry against Patterson has not yet subsided, though he states that, out of twenty-three regiments composing his force, nineteen refused to stay an hour over their time, which would have been up in a week, so that he would have been left in an enemy's country with four regiments. He wisely led his patriot band back, and let them disband themselves in their own borders. Verily, these are not the men to conquer the South.

Fresh volunteers are pouring in by tens of thousands to take their places from all parts of the Union, and in three days after the battle, 80,000 men were accepted. Strange people! The regiments which have returned to New York after disgraceful conduct at Bull Run, with the stigmata of cowardice impressed by their commanding officers on the colours and souls of their corps, are actually welcomed with the utmost enthusiasm, and receive popular ovations! It becomes obvious every day that M'Clellan does not intend to advance till he has got some semblance of an army: that will be a long time to come; but he can get a good deal of fighting out of them in a few months. Meantime the whole of the Northern states are waiting anxiously for the advance which is to take place at once, according to promises from New York. As Washington is the principal scene of interest, the South being tabooed to me, I have resolved to stay here till the army is fit to move, making little excursions to points of interest. The details in my diary are not very interesting, and I shall make but brief extracts.

August 2nd.—Mr. Olmsted visited me in company with a young gentleman named Ritchie, son-in-law of James Wadsworth, who has been serving as honorary aide-de-camp on M'Dowell's staff, but is now called to higher functions. They dined at my lodgings, and we talked over Bull Run again. Mr. Ritchie did not leave Centreville till late in the evening, and slept at Fairfax Court-house, where he remained till 8.30 A.M. on the morning of July 22nd, Wadsworth not stirring for two hours later. He said the panic was "horrible, disgusting, sickening," and spoke in the harshest terms of the officers, to whom he applied a variety of epithets. Prince Napoleon has arrived.

August 3rd.—M'Clellan orders regular parades and drills in every regiment, and insists on all orders being given by bugle note. I had a long ride through the camps, and saw some improvement in the look of the men. Coming home by Georgetown, met the Prince driving with M.

Mercier, to pay a visit to the President. I am sure that the politicians are not quite well pleased with this arrival, because they do not understand it, and cannot imagine a man would come so far without a purpose. The drunken soldiers now resort to quiet lanes and courts in the suburbs. Georgetown was full of them. It is a much more respectable and old-world looking place than its vulgar, empty, overgrown, mushroom neighbour, Washington. An officer who had fallen in his men to go on duty was walking down the line this evening, when his eye rested on the neck of a bottle sticking out of a man's coat. "Thunder," quoth he, "James, what have you got there?" "Well, I guess, captain, it's a drop of real good Bourbon." "Then let us have a drink," said the captain; and thereupon proceeded to take a long pull and a strong pull, till the man cried out, "That is not fair, Captain. You won't leave me a drop"—a remonstrance which had a proper effect, and the captain marched down his company to the bridge.

It was extremely hot when I returned, late in the evening. I asked the boy for a glass of iced water. "Dere is no ice, massa," he said. "No ice? What's the reason of that?" "De Seceshers, massa, block up de river, and touch off deir guns at de ice-boats." The Confederates on the right bank of the Potomac have now established a close blockade of the river. Lieutenant Wise, of the Navy Department, admitted the fact, but said that the United States gunboats would soon sweep the rebels from the shore.

August 4th.—I had no idea that the sun could be powerful in Washington; even in India the heat is not much more oppressive than it was here to-day. There is this extenuating circumstance, however, that after some hours of such very high temperature, thunder-storms and tornadoes cool the air. I received a message from General M'Clellan that he was about to ride along the lines of the army across the river, and would be happy if I accompanied him; but as I had many letters to write for the next mail, I was unwillingly obliged to abandon the chance of seeing the army under such favourable circumstances. There are daily arrivals at Washington of military adventurers from all parts of the world, some of them with many extraordinary certificates and qualifications; but, as Mr. Seward says, "It is best to detain them with the hope of employment on the Northern side, lest some really good man should get among the rebels." Garibaldians, Hungarians, Poles, officers of Turkish and other contingents, the executory devises and remainders of European revolutions and wars, surround the State department, and infest unsuspecting politicians with illegible testimonials in unknown tongues.

August 5th.—The roads from the station are crowded with troops, coming from the North as fast as the railway can carry them. It is evident, as the war fever spreads, that such politicians as Mr. Crittenden, who resist the extreme violence of the Republican party, will be stricken down. The Confiscation Bill, for the emancipation of slaves and the absorption of property belonging to rebels, has, indeed, been boldly resisted in the House of Representatives; but it passed with some trifling amendments. The journals are still busy with the affair of Bull Run, and each seems anxious to eclipse the other in the absurdity of its statements. A Philadelphia journal, for instance, states to-day that the real cause of the disaster was not a desire to retreat, but a mania to advance. In its own words, "the only drawback was the impetuous feeling to go ahead and fight." Because one officer is accused of drunkenness, a great movement is on foot to prevent the army getting any drink at all.

General M'Clellan invited the newspaper correspondents in Washington to meet him to-day, and with their assent drew up a treaty of peace and amity, which is a curiosity in its way. In the first place, the editors are to abstain from printing anything which can give aid or comfort to the enemy, and their correspondents are to observe equal caution; in return for which complaisance, Government is to be asked to give the press opportunities for obtaining and transmitting intelligence suitable for publication, particularly touching engagements with the enemy. The Confederate privateer Sumter has forced the blockade at New Orleans, and has already been heard of destroying a number of Union vessels.

August 6th.—Prince Napoleon, anxious to visit the battle-field at Bull Run, has, to Mr. Seward's discomfiture, applied for passes, and arrangements are being made to escort him as far as the Confederate lines. This is a recognition of the Confederates, as a belligerent power, which is by no means agreeable to the authorities. I drove down to the Senate, where the proceedings were very uninteresting, although Congress was on the eve of adjournment, and returning, visited Mr. Seward, Mr. Bates, Mr. Cameron, Mr. Blair, and left cards for Mr. Breckinridge. The old woman who opened the door at the house where the latter lodged said, "Massa Breckinridge pack up all his boxes; I s'pose he not cum back here again."

August 7th.—In the evening I went to Mr. Seward's, who gave a reception in honour of Prince Napoleon. The Minister's rooms were crowded and intensely hot. Lord Lyons and most of the diplomatic circle were present. The Prince wore his Order of the Bath, and bore the onslaughts of politicians, male and female, with much good humour. The contrast between the uniforms of the officers of the United States army and navy and those of the French in the Prince's suit by no means redounded to the credit of the military tailoring of the Americans. The Prince, to whom I was presented by Mr. Seward, asked me particularly about the roads from Alexandria to Fairfax Court-house, and from there to Centreville and Manassas. I told him I had not got quite so far as the latter place, at which he laughed. He inquired with much interest about General Beauregard, whether he spoke good French, if he seemed a man of capacity, or was the creation of an accident and of circumstances. He has been to Mount Vernon, and is struck with the air of neglect around the place. Two of his horses dropped dead from the heat on the journey, and the Prince, who was perspiring profusely in the crowded room, asked me whether the climate was not as bad as midsummer in India. His manner was perfectly easy, but he gave no encouragement to bores, nor did he court popularity by unusual affability, and he moved off long before the guests were tired of looking at him. On returning to my rooms, a German gentleman named Bing—who went out with the Federal army from Washington, was taken prisoner at Bull's Run, and carried to Richmond—came to visit me, but his account of what he saw in the dark and mysterious South was not lucid or interesting.

August 8th.—I had arranged to go with Mr. Olmsted and Mr. Ritchie to visit the hospitals, but the heat was so intolerable, we abandoned the idea till the afternoon, when we drove across the Long Bridge and proceeded to Alexandria. The town, which is now fully occupied by military, and is abandoned by the respectable inhabitants, has an air, owing to the absence of women and children, which tells the tale of a hostile occupation. In a large building, which had once been a school, the wounded of Bull Run were lying, not uncomfortably packed, nor unskilfully cared for, and the arrangements were, taken altogether, creditable to the skill and humanity of the surgeons. Close at hand was the church in which George Washington was wont in latter days to pray, when he drove over from Mount Vernon — further on, Marshall House, where Ellsworth was shot by the Virginian landlord, and was so speedily avenged. A strange train of thought was suggested by the rapid grouping of incongruous ideas, arising out of the proximity of these scenes. As one of my friends said, "I wonder what Washington would do if he were here now—and how he would act if he were summoned from that church to Marshall House, or to this hospital?" The man who uttered these words was not either of my companions, but wore the shoulder-straps of a Union officer. "Stranger still," said I, "would it be to speculate on the thoughts and actions of Napoleon in this crisis, if he were to wake up and see a Prince of his blood escorted by Federal soldiers to the spot where the troops of the Southern States had inflicted on them a signal defeat, in a land where the nephew who now sits on the throne of France has been an exile." It is not quite certain that many Americans understand who Prince Napoleon is, for one of the troopers belonging to the escort who took him out from Alexandria declared positively he had ridden with the Emperor. The excursion is swallowed, but not well digested. In Washington the only news to-night is, that a small privateer from Charleston, mistaking the St. Lawrence for a merchant-vessel, fired into her, and was at once sent to Mr. Davy Jones by a rattling broadside. Congress having adjourned, there is but little to render Washington less uninteresting than it must be in its normal state.

The truculent and overbearing spirit which arises from the uncontroverted action of democratic majorities developes itself in the North, where they have taken to burning newspaper offices, and destroying all the property belonging to the proprietors and editors. These actions are a strange commentary on Mr. Seward's declaration "that no volunteers are to be refused because they do not speak English, inasmuch as the contest for the Union is a battle of the free men of the world for the institutions of self-government."

August 11th.—On the old Indian principle, I rode out this morning very early, and was rewarded by a breath of cold, fresh air, and by the sight of some very disorderly regiments just turning out to parade in the camps; but I was not particularly gratified by being mistaken for Prince Napoleon by some Irish recruits, who shouted out, "Bonaparte for ever!" and gradually subsided into requests for "something to drink your Royal Highness's health with." As I returned, I saw on the steps of General Mansfield's quarters a tall, soldierly-looking young man, whose breast was covered with Crimean ribbons and medals, and I recognised him as one who had called upon me a few days before, renewing our slight acquaintance before Sebastopol, where his courage was conspicuous, to ask me for information respecting the mode of obtaining a commission in the Federal army.

Towards mid-day an ebony sheet of clouds swept over the city. I went out, regardless of the threatening storm, to avail myself of the coolness to make a few visits; but soon a violent wind arose, bearing clouds like those of an Indian dust-storm down the streets. The black sheet overhead became agitated like the sea, and tossed about grey clouds, which careered against each other and burst into lightning; then suddenly, without other warning, down came the rain—a perfect tornado; sheets of water flooding the streets in a moment, turning the bed into water-courses and the channels into deep rivers. I waded up the centre of Pennsylvania Avenue, past the President's house, in a current which would have made a respectable trout-stream; and on getting opposite my own door, made a rush for the porch, but, forgetting the deep channel at the side, stepped into a rivulet which was literally above my hips, and I was carried off my legs, till I succeeded in catching the kerbstone, and escaped into the hall as if I had just swum across the Potomac.

On returning from my ride next morning, I took up the Baltimore paper, and saw a paragraph announcing the death of an English officer at the station; it was the poor fellow whom I saw sitting at General Mansfield's steps yesterday. The consul was absent on a short tour, rendered necessary by the failure of his health consequent on the discharge of his duties. Finding the Legation were anxious to see due care taken of the poor fellow's remains, I left for Baltimore at a quarter to three o'clock, and proceeded to inquire into the circumstances connected with his death. He had been struck down at the station by some cerebral attack, brought on by the heat and excitement; had been carried to the police station and placed upon a bench, from which he had fallen with his head downwards, and was found in that position, with life quite extinct, by a casual visitor. My astonishment may be conceived when I learned that not only had the Coroner's inquest sat and returned its verdict, but that the man had absolutely been buried the same morning, and so my mission was over, and I could only report what had occurred at Washington. Little value indeed has human life in this new world, to which the old gives vital power so lavishly, that it is regarded as almost worthless. I have seen more "fuss" made over an old woman killed by a cab in London than there is over half a dozen deaths, with suspicion of murder attached, in New Orleans or New York.

I remained in Baltimore a few days, and had

an opportunity of knowing the feelings of some of the leading men in the place. It may be described in one word—intense hatred of New England and black republicans, which has been increased to mania by the stringent measures of the military dictator of the American Warsaw, the searches of private houses, domiciliary visits, arbitrary arrests, the suppression of adverse journals, the overthrow of the corporate body—all the acts, in fact, which constitute the machinery and the grievances of a tyranny. When I spoke of the brutal indifference of the police to the poor officer previously mentioned, the Baltimoreans told me the constables appointed by the Federal general were scoundrels who led the Plug Uglies in former days—the worst characters in a city not sweet or savoury in repute—but that the old police were men of very different description. The Maryland Club, where I had spent some pleasant hours, was now like a secret tribunal or the haunt of conspirators. The police entered it a few days ago, searched every room, took up the flooring, and even turned up the coals in the kitchen and the wine in the cellar. Such indignities fired the blood of the members, who are, with one exception, opposed to the attempt to coerce the South by the sword. Not one of them but could tell of some outrage perpetrated on himself or on some members of his family by the police and Federal authority. Many a *delator amici* was suspected but not convicted. Men sat moodily reading the papers with knitted brows, or whispering in corners, taking each other apart, and glancing suspiciously at their fellows.

There is a peculiar stamp about the Baltimore men which distinguishes them from most Americans—a style of dress, frankness of manner, and a general appearance assimmilating them closely to the upper classes of Englishmen. They are fond of sport and travel, exclusive and high-spirited, and the iron rule of the Yankee is the more intolerable because they dare not resent it, and are unable to shake it off.

I returned to Washington on 15th August. Nothing changed; skirmishes along the front; M'Clellan reviewing. The loss of General Lyon, who was killed in an action with the Confederates under Ben McCullough, at Wilson's Creek, Springfield, Missouri, in which the Unionists were with difficulty extricated by General Sigel from a very dangerous position, after the death of their leader, is severely felt. He was one of the very few officers who combined military skill and personal bravery with political sagacity and moral firmness. The President has issued his proclamation for a day of fast and prayer, which, say the Baltimoreans, is a sign that the Yankees are in a bad way, as they would never think of praying or fasting if their cause was prospering. The stories which have been so sedulously spread, and which never will be quite discredited, of the barbarity and cruelty of the Confederates to all the wounded, ought to be set at rest by the printed statement of the eleven Union surgeons just released, who have come back from Richmond, where they were sent after their capture on the field of Bull Run, with the most distinct testimony that the Confederates treated their prisoners with humanity. Who are the miscreants who tried to make the evil feeling, quite strong enough as it is, perfectly fiendish, by asserting the rebels burned the wounded in hospitals, and bayoneted them as they lay helpless on the field?

The pecuniary difficulties of the Government have been alleviated by the bankers of New York, Philadelphia, and Boston, who have agreed to lend them fifty millions of dollars, on condition that they receive the Treasury notes which Mr. Chase is about to issue. As we read the papers and hear the news, it is difficult to believe that the foundations of society are not melting away in the heat of this conflict. Thus, a Federal judge, named Garrison, who has issued his writ of habeas corpus for certain prisoners in Fort Lafayette, being quietly snuffed out by the commandant, Colonel Burke, desires to lead an army against the fort and have a little civil war of his own in New York. He applies to the commander of the county militia, who informs Garrison he can't get into the fort, as there was no artillery strong enough to breach the walls, and that it would require 10,000 men to invest it, whereas only 1400 militiamen were available. What a farceur Judge Garrison must be! In addition to the gutting and burning of newspaper offices, and the exercitation of the editors on rails, the republican grand juries have taken to indicting the democratic journals, and Fremont's provost marshal in St. Louis has, *proprio motu*, suppressed those which he considers disaffected. A mutiny which broke out in the Scotch Regiment 79th N. Y. has been followed by another in the 2nd Maine Regiment, and a display of cannon and of cavalry was required to induce them to allow the ringleaders to be arrested. The President was greatly alarmed, but M'Clellan acted with some vigour, and the refractory volunteers are to be sent off to a pleasant station called the "Dry Tortugas" to work on the fortifications.

Mr. Seward, with whom I dined and spent the evening on 16th August, has been much reassured and comforted by the demonstrations of readiness on the part of the people to continue the contest, and of confidence in the cause among the moneyed men of the great cities. "All we want is time to develope our strength. We have been blamed for not making greater use of our navy and extending it at once. It was our first duty to provide for the safety of our capital. Besides, a man will generally pay little attention to agencies he does not understand. None of us knew anything about a navy. I doubt if the President ever saw anything more formidable than a river steamboat, and I don't think Mr. Welles, the Secretary of the Navy, knew the stem from the stern of a ship. Of the whole Cabinet, I am the only member who ever was *fairly* at sea or crossed the Atlantic. Some of us never even saw it. No wonder we did not understand the necessity for creating a navy at once. Soon, however, our Government will be able to dispose of a respectable marine, and when our army is ready to move, co-operating with the fleet, the days of the rebellion are numbered."

"When will that be, Mr. Secretary?"

"Soon; very soon, I hope. We can, however, bear delays. The rebels will be ruined by it."

CHAPTER LIII.

Return to Baltimore — Colonel Carroll — A Priest's view of the Abolition of Slavery — Slavery in Maryland —

Harper's Ferry—John Brown—Back by train to Washington—Further accounts of Bull Run—American vanity—My own unpopularity for speaking the truth—Killing a "Nigger" no murder—Navy Department.

On the 17th August I returned to Baltimore on my way to Drohoregan Manor, the seat of Colonel Carroll, in Maryland, where I had been invited to spend a few days by his son-in-law, an English gentleman of my acquaintance. Leaving Baltimore at 5.40 P.M., in company with Mr. Tucker Carroll, I proceeded by train to Ellicott's Mills, a station fourteen miles on the Ohio and Baltimore railroad, from which our host's residence is distant more than an hour's drive. The country through which the line passes is picturesque and undulating, with hills and valleys and brawling streams, spreading in woodland and glade, ravine, and high uplands on either side, haunted by cotton factories, poisoning air and water; but it has been a formidable district for the engineers to get through, and the line abounds in those triumphs of engineering which are generally the ruin of shareholders.

All these lines are now in the hands of the military. At the Washington terminus there is a guard placed to see that no unauthorised person or unwilling volunteer is going north; the line is watched by patrols and sentries; troops are encamped along its course. The factory chimneys are smokeless; half the pleasant villas which cover the hills or dot the openings in the forest have a deserted look and closed windows. And so these great works, the Carrolton viaduct, the Thomas viaduct, and the high embankments and great cuttings in the ravine by the river side, over which the line passes, have almost a depressing effect, as if the people for whose use they were intended had all become extinct. At Ellicott's Mills, which is a considerable manufacturing town, more soldiers and Union flags. The people are Unionists, but the neighbouring gentry and country people are Seceshers.

This is the case wherever there is a manufacturing population in Maryland, because the workmen are generally foreigners, or have come from the Northern States, and feel little sympathy with States rights' doctrines, and the tendencies of the landed gentry to a Conservative action on the slave question. There was no good will in the eyes of the mechanicals as they stared at our vehicle; for the political bias of Colonel Carroll was well known, as well as the general sentiments of his family. It was dark when we reached the manor, which is approached by an avenue of fine trees. The house is old-fashioned, and has received additions from time to time. But for the black faces of the domestics, one might easily fancy he was in some old country house in Ireland. The family have adhered to their ancient faith. The founder of the Carrolls in Maryland came over with the Catholic colonists led by Lord Baltimore, or by his brother, Leonard Calvert, and the colonel possesses some interesting deeds of grant and conveyance of the vast estates, which have been diminished by large sales year after year, but still spread over a considerable part of several counties in the State.

Colonel Carroll is an immediate descendant of one of the leaders in the revolution of 1776, and he pointed out to me the room in which Carroll, of Carrolton, and George Washington, were wont to meet when they were concocting their splendid treason. One of his connections married the late Marquis Wellesley, and the colonel takes pleasure in setting forth how the daughter of the Irish recusant, who fled from his native country all but an outlaw, sat on the throne of the Queen of Ireland, or, in other words, held court in Dublin Castle as wife of the Viceroy. Drohoregan is supposed to mean "Hall of the Kings," and called after an old place belonging, some time or other, to the family, the early history of which, as set forth in the Celtic authorities and Irish antiquarian works, possesses great attractions for the kindly, genial old man—kindly and genial to all but the Abolitionists and black republicans; nor is he indifferent to the reputation of the State in the Revolutionary War, where the "Maryland line" seems to have differed from many of the contingents of the other States in not running away so often at critical moments in the serious actions. Colonel Carroll has sound arguments to prove the sovereign independence and right of every State in the Union, derived from family teaching and the lessons of those who founded the Constitution itself.

On the day after my arrival the rain fell in torrents. The weather is as uncertain as that of our own isle. The torrid heats at Washington, the other day, were succeeded by bitter cold days; now there is a dense mist, chilly and cheerless, seeming as a sort of strainer for the even down pour that falls through it continuously. The family, after breakfast, slipped round to the little chapel which forms the extremity of one wing of the house. The coloured people on the estate were already trooping across the lawn and up the avenue from the slave quarters, decently dressed for the most part, having due allowance for the extraordinary choice of colours in their gowns, bonnets, and ribbons, and for the unhappy imitations, on the part of the men, of the attire of their masters. They walked demurely and quietly past the house, and presently the priest, dressed like a French curé, trotted up, and service began. The negro' houses were of a much better and more substantial character than those one sees in the South, though not remarkable for cleanliness and good order. Truth to say, they were palaces compared to the huts of Irish labourers, such as might be found, perhaps, on the estates of the colonel's kinsmen at home. The negroes are far more independent than they are in the South. They are less civil, less obliging, and, although they do not come cringing to shake hands as the field-hands on a Louisiana plantation, less servile. They inhabit a small village of brick and wood houses, across the road, at the end of the avenue, and in sight of the house. The usual swarms of little children, poultry, pigs, enlivened by goats, embarrassed the steps of the visitor, and the old people, or those who were not finely dressed enough for mass, peered out at the strangers from the glassless windows.

When chapel was over, the boys and girls came up for catechism, and passed in review before the ladies of the house, with whom they were on very good terms. The priest joined us in the verandah when his labours were over, and talked with intelligence of the terrible war which has burst over the land. He has just returned from a tour in the Northern States, and it is his belief the native Americans there will not enlist, but that they will get foreigners to fight their battles. He admitted that slavery was in itself an evil, nay, more, that it was not profitable in Maryland. But what are the landed proprietors to do? The slaves have been bequeathed to them as property by their fathers, with certain obligations to be respected, and duties to be fulfilled. It is impossible to free them, because, at the moment of emancipation, nothing short of the confiscation of all the labour and property of the whites would be required to maintain the negroes, who would certainly refuse to work unless they had their masters' land as their own. Where is white labour to be found? Its introduction must be the work of years, and meantime many thousands of slaves, who have a right to protection, would canker the land.

In Maryland they do not breed slaves for the purpose of selling them as they do in Virginia, and yet Colonel Carroll and other gentlemen, who regarded the slaves they inherited almost as members of their families, have been stigmatised by abolition orators as slave-breeders and slave-dealers. It was these insults which stung the gentlemen of Maryland and of the other Slave States to the quick, and made them resolve never to yield to the domination of a party which had never ceased to wage war against their institutions and their reputation and honour.

A little knot of friends and relations joined Colonel Carroll at dinner. There are few families in this part of Maryland which have not representatives in the other army across the Potomac; and if Beauregard could but make his appearance, the women alone would give him welcome such as no conqueror ever received in liberated city.

Next day the rain fell incessantly. The mail was brought in by a little negro boy on horseback, and I was warned by my letters that an immediate advance of M'Clellan's troops was probable. This is an old story. "Battle expected to-morrow" has been a heading in the papers for the last fortnight. In the afternoon I was driven over a part of the estate in a close carriage, through the windows of which, however, I caught glimpses of a beautiful country, wooded gloriously, and soft, sylvan, and well-cultivated as the best parts of Hampshire and Gloucestershire, the rolling lands of which latter country, indeed, it much resembled in its large fields, heavy with crops of tobacco and corn. The weather was too unfavourable to admit of a close inspection of the fields; but I visited one or two tobacco houses, where the fragrant Maryland was lying in masses on the ground, or hanging from the rafters, or filled the heavy hogsheads with compressed smoke.

Next day I took the train at Ellicott's Mills, and went to Harper's Ferry. There is no one spot, in the history of this extraordinary war, which can be well more conspicuous. Had it nothing more to recommend it than the scenery, it might well command a visit from the tourist; but as the scene of old John Brown's raid upon the Federal arsenal, of that first passage of arms between the abolitionists and the slave conservatives, which has developed this great contest; above all, as the spot where important military demonstrations have been made on both sides, and will necessarily occur hereafter, this place, which probably derives its name from some wretched old boatman, will be renowned for ever in the annals of the civil war of 1861. The Patapsco, by the bank of which the rail is carried for some miles, has all the character of a mountain torrent, rushing through gorges or carving out its way at the base of granite hills, or boldly cutting a path for itself through the softer slate. Bridges, viaducts, remarkable archways, and great spans of timber trestle-work leaping from hill to hill, enable the rail to creep onwards and upwards by the mountain side to the Potomac at Point of Rocks, whence it winds its way over undulating ground, by stations with eccentric names to the river's bank once more. We were carried on to the station next to Harper's Ferry on a ledge of the precipitous mountain range which almost overhangs the stream. But few civilians were in the train. The greater number of passengers consisted of soldiers and sutlers, proceeding to their encampments along the river. A strict watch was kept over the passengers, whose passes were examined by officers at the various stations. At one place an officer who really looked like a soldier entered the train, and on seeing my pass told me in broken English that he had served in the Crimea, and was acquainted with me and many of my friends. The gentleman who accompanied me observed, "I do not know whether he was in the Crimea or not, but I do know that till very lately your friend the Major was a dancing-master in New York." A person of a very different type made his offers of service, Colonel Gordon, of the 2nd Massachusetts Regiment, who caused the train to run on as far as Harper's Ferry, in order to give me a sight of the place, although in consequence of the evil habit of firing on the carriages in which the Confederates across the river have been indulging, the locomotive generally halts at some distance below the bend of the river.

Harper's Ferry lies in a gorge formed by a rush of the Potomac through the mountain ridges, which it cuts at right angles to its course at its junction with the river Shenandoah. So trenchant and abrupt is the division that little land is on the divided ridge to build upon. The precipitous hills on both sides are covered with forest, which has been cleared in patches here and there on the Maryland shore, to permit of the erection of batteries. On the Virginian side there lies a mass of blackened and ruined buildings, from which a street lined with good houses stretches up the hill. Just above the junction of the Shenandoah with the Potomac, an elevated bridge or viaduct 300 yards long leaps from hill-side to hill-side. The arches had been broken—the rails which ran along the top torn up, and there is now a deep gulf fixed between the shores of Maryland and Virginia. The rail to Winchester from this point has been destroyed, and the line along the Potomac has also been ruined.

But for the batteries which cover the shoal water at the junction of the two rivers below the bridge, there would be no difficulty in crossing to the Maryland shore, and from that side the whole of the ground around Harper's Ferry is completely commanded. The gorge is almost as deep as the pass of Killiecrankie, which it resembles in most respects except in breadth and the size of the river between, and if ever a railroad finds its way to Blair Athol, the passengers will find something to look at very like the scenery on the route to Harper's Ferry. The vigilance required to guard the pass of the river above and below this point is incessant, but the Federals possess the advantage on their side of a deep canal parallel to the railway and running above the level of the river, which would be a more formidable obstacle than the Potomac to infantry or guns. There is reason to believe that the Secessionists in Maryland cross backwards and forwards whenever they please, and the Virginians, coming down at their leisure to the opposite shore, inflict serious annoyance on the Federal troops by constant rifle practice.

Looking up and down the river the scenery is picturesque, though it is by no means entitled to the extraordinary praises which American tourists lavish upon it. Probably old John Brown cared little for the wild magic of streamlet or rill, or for the blended charm of vale and woodland. When he made his attack on the arsenal now in ruins, he probably thought a valley was as high as a hill, and that there was no necessity for water running downwards—assuredly he saw as little of the actual heights and depths around him when he ran across the Potomac to revolutionize Virginia. He has left behind him millions either as clear-sighted or as blind as himself. In New England parlours a statuette of John Brown may be found as a pendant to the likeness of our Saviour. In Virginia his name is the synonym of all that is base, bloody, and cruel.

Harper's Ferry at present, for all practical purposes, may be considered as Confederate property. The few Union inhabitants remain in their houses, but many of the Government workmen and most of the inhabitants have gone off South. For strategical purposes its possession would be most important to a force desiring to operate on Maryland from Virginia. The Blue Ridge range running up to the Shenandoah divides the country so as to permit a force debouching from Harper's Ferry to advance down the valley of the Shenandoah on the right, or to move to the left between the Blue Ridge and the Katoctin mountains towards the Manassas railway at its discretion. After a false alarm that some Secesh cavalry were coming down to renew the skirmishing of the day before, I returned, and, travelling to Relay House, just saved the train to Washington, where I arrived after sunset. A large number of Federal troops are employed along these lines, which they occupy as if they were in a hostile country. An imperfectly formed regiment broken up into these detachments, and placed in isolated posts, under ignorant officers, may be regarded as almost worthless for military operations. Hence the constant night alarms—the mistakes—the skirmishes and instances of misbehaviour which arise along these extended lines.

On the journey from Harper's Ferry, the concentration of masses of troops along the road, and the march of heavy artillery trains, caused me to think a renewal of the offensive movement against Richmond was immediate, but at Washington I heard that all M'Clellan wanted or hoped for at present was to make Maryland safe and to gain time for the formation of his army. The Confederates appear to be moving towards their left, and M'Clellan is very uneasy lest they should make a vigorous attack before he is prepared to receive them.

In the evening the New York papers came in with the extracts from the London papers containing my account of the battle of Bull's Run. Utterly forgetting their own versions of the engagement, the New York editors now find it convenient to divert attention from the bitter truth that was in them to the letter of the foreign newspaper correspondent, who, because he is a British subject, will prove not only useful as a conductor to carry off the popular wrath from the American journalists themselves, but as a means by induction of charging the vials afresh against the British people, inasmuch as they have not condoled with the North on the defeat of armies which they were assured would, if successful, be immediately led to effect the disruption of the British empire. At the outset I had foreseen this would be the case, and deliberately accepted the issue; but when I found the Northern journals far exceeding in severity anything I could have said, and indulging in general invective against whole classes of American soldiery, officers, and statesmen, I was foolish enough to expect a little justice, not to say a word of the smallest generosity.

August 21*st*.—The echoes of Bull Run are coming back with a vengeance. This day month the miserable fragments of a beaten, washed out, demoralised army were flooding in disorder and dismay the streets of the capital from which they had issued forth to repel the tide of invasion. This day month, and all the editors and journalists in the States, weeping, wailing, and gnashing their teeth, infused extra gall into their ink, and poured out invective, abuse, and obloquy on their defeated general and their broken hosts. The President and his ministers, stunned by the tremendous calamity, sat listening in fear and trembling for the sound of the enemy's cannon. The veteran soldier, on whom the boasted hopes of the nation rested, heartsick and beaten down, had neither counsel to give nor action to offer. At any moment the Confederate columns might be expected in Pennsylvania Avenue to receive the welcome of their friends and the submission of their helpless and disheartened enemies.

All this is forgotten—and much more, which need not now be repeated. Saved from a great peril, even the bitterness of death, they forget the danger that has passed, deny that they uttered cries of distress and appeals for help, and swagger in all the insolence of recovered strength. Not only that, but they turn and rend those whose writing has been dug up after thirty days, and comes back as a rebuke to their pride.

Conscious that they have insulted and irritated their own army, that they have earned the bitter hostility of men in power, and have for once inflicted a wound on the vanity to which they have given such offensive dimensions, if not life itself, they now seek to run a drag scent between the public nose and their own unpopularity, and to create such an amount of indignation and to cast so much odium upon one who has had greater facilities to know, and is more willing to tell the truth, than any of their organs, that he will be unable henceforth to perform his duties in a country where unpopularity means simply a political and moral atrophy or death. In the telegraphic summary some days ago a few phrases were picked out of my letters, which were but very faint paraphrases of some of the sentences which might be culled from Northern newspapers; but the storm has been gathering ever since, and I am no doubt to experience the truth of De Tocqueville's remark, "that a stranger who injures American vanity, no matter how justly, may make up his mind to be a martyr."

August 22nd.—

> "The little dogs and all,
> Tray, Blanche, and Sweetheart,
> See they bark at me."

The North have recovered their wind, and their pipers are blowing with might and main. The time given them to breathe after Bull Run has certainly been accompanied with a greater development of lung and power of blowing than could have been expected. The volunteer army which dispersed and returned home to receive the *Io Pæans* of the North, has been replaced by better and more numerous levies, which have the strong finger and thumb of General M'Clellan on their windpipe, and find it is not quite so easy as it was to do as they pleased. The North, besides, has received supplies of money, and is using its great resources, by land and sea, to some purpose, and as they wax fat they kick.

A general officer said to me, "Of course you will never remain when once all the press are down upon you. I would not take a million dollars and be in your place." "But is what I've written untrue?" "God bless you! do you know, in this country, if you can get enough of people to start a lie about any man, he would be ruined, if the Evangelists came forward to swear the story was false There are thousands of people who this moment believe that M'Dowell, who never tasted anything stronger than a watermelon in all his life, was helplessly drunk at Bull's Run. Mind what I say; they'll run you into a mud-hole as sure as you live." I was not much impressed with the danger of my position further than that I knew there would be a certain amount of risk from the rowdyism and vanity of what even the Americans admit to be the lower orders, for which I had been prepared from the moment I had despatched my letter; but I confess I was not by any means disposed to think that the leaders of public opinion would seek the small gratification of revenge, and the petty popularity of pandering to the passions of the mob, by creating a popular cry against me. I am not aware that any foreigner ever visited the United States who was injudicious enough to write one single word derogatory to their claims to be the first of created beings, who was not assailed with the most viperous malignity and rancour. The man who says he has detected a single spot on the face of their sun should prepare his winding-sheet.

The *New York Times*, I find, states "that the terrible epistle has been read with quite as much avidity as an average President's message. We scarcely exaggerate the fact when we say, the first and foremost thought on the minds of a very large portion of our people after the repulse at Bull's Run was, what will Russell say?" and then they repeat some of the absurd sayings attributed to me, who declared openly from the very first that I had not seen the battle at all, to the effect "that I had never seen such fighting in all my life, and that nothing at Alma or Inkerman was equal to it." An analysis of the letter follows, in which it is admitted that "with perfect candour I purported to give an account of what I saw, and not of the action which I did not see;" and the writer, who is, if I mistake not, the Hon. Mr. Raymond, of the *New York Times*, like myself a witness of the facts I describe, quotes a passage in which I say, "There was no flight of troops, no retreat of an army, no reason for all this precipitation," and then declares "that my letter gives a very spirited and perfectly just description of the panic which impelled and accompanied the troops from Centreville to Washington. He does not, for he cannot, in the least exaggerate its horrible disorder, or the disgraceful behaviour of the incompetent officers by whom it was aided, instead of being checked. He saw nothing whatever of the fighting, and therefore says nothing whatever of its quality. He gives a clear, fair, perfectly just and accurate, as it is a spirited and graphic account of the extraordinary scenes which passed under his observation. Discreditable as those scenes were to our army, we have nothing in connection with them whereof to accuse the reporter; he has done justice alike to himself, his subject, and the country."

Ne nobis blandiar, I may add, that at least I desired to do so, and I can prove from Northern papers that if their accounts were true, I certainly much "extenuated and naught set down in malice"—nevertheless, Philip drunk is very different from Philip sober, frightened, and running away, and the man who attempts to justify his version to the inebriated polycephalous monarch is sure to meet such treatment as inebriated despots generally award to their censors.

August 23rd.—The torrent is swollen to-day by anonymous letters threatening me with bowie-knife and revolver, or simply abusive, frantic with hate, and full of obscure warnings. Some bear the Washington post-mark; others came from New York; the greater number—for I have had nine—are from Philadelphia. Perhaps they may come from the members of that "gallant" 4th Pennsylvania Regiment.

August 24th.—My servant came in this morning to announce a trifling accident—he was exercising my horse, and at the corner of one of those charming street-crossings, the animal fell and broke its leg. A "vet" was sent for. I was sure that such a portent had never been born in those Daunian woods. A man about twenty-seven or twenty-eight stone weight, middle-aged and active, with a fine professional feeling for distressed horse-flesh; and I was right in my conjectures that he was a Briton, though the vet had become Americanised, and was full of enthusiasm about "our war for the Union," which was yielding him a fine harvest. He complained there was a good many bad characters about Washington. The matter is proved beyond doubt by what we see, hear, and read. To-day there is an account in the papers of a brute shooting a negro boy dead, because he asked him for a chew of tobacco. Will he be hanged? Not the smallest chance of it. The idea of hanging a white man for killing a nigger! It is more preposterous here than it is in India, where our authorities have actually executed whites for the murder of natives.

Before dinner I walked down to the Washington navy yard. Captain Dahlgren was sorely perplexed with an intoxicated Senator, whose name it is not necessary to mention, and who seemed to think he paid me a great compliment by expressing his repeated desire "to have a good look at" me. "I guess you're quite notorious now. You'll excuse me because I've dined, now—and so you are the Mr. &c., &c., &c." The Senator informed me that he was "none of your d——d blackfaced republicans. He didn't care a d—— about niggers—his business was to do good to his fellow white men, to hold our glorious Union together, and let the niggers take care of themselves."

I was glad when a diversion was effected by the arrival of Mr. Fox, Assistant-Secretary of the Navy, and Mr. Blair, Postmaster-General, to consult with the Captain, who is greatly looked up to by all the members of the Cabinet—in fact he is rather inconvenienced by the perpetual visits of the President, who is animated by a most extraordinary curiosity about naval matters and machinery, and is attracted by the novelty of the whole department, so that he is continually running down "to have a talk with Dahlgren" when he is not engaged in "a chat with George." The Senator opened such a smart fire on the Minister that the latter retired, and I mounted and rode back to town. In the evening Major Clarence Brown, Lieutenant Wise, a lively, pleasant, and amusing little sailor, well-known in the States as the author of "Los Gringos," who is now employed in the Navy Department, and a few of the gentlemen connected with the Foreign Legations, came in, and we had a great international reunion and discussion till a late hour. There is a good deal of agreeable banter reserved for myself, as to the exact form of death which I am most likely to meet. I was seriously advised by a friend not to stir out unarmed. The great use of a revolver is that it will prevent the indignity of tarring and feathering, now pretty rife, by provoking greater violence. I also received a letter from London, advising me to apply to Lord Lyons for protection, but that could only be extended to me within the walls of the Legation.

August 25th.—I visited the Navy Department, which is a small red-brick building two stories high, very plain and even humble. The subordinate departments are conducted in rooms below stairs. The executive are lodged in the rooms which line both sides of the corridor above. The walls of the passage are lined with paintings in oil and water colours, engravings and paintings in the worst style of art. To the latter considerable interest attaches, as they are authentic likenesses of naval officers who gained celebrity in the wars with Great Britain—men like Perry, M'Donough, Decatur, and Hull, who, as the Americans boast, was "the first man who compelled a British frigate of greater force than his own to strike her colours in fair fight." Paul Jones was not to be seen, but a drawing is proudly pointed to of the attack of the American fleet on Algiers as a proof of hatred to piracy, and of the prominent part taken by the young States in putting an end to it in Europe. In one room are several swords, surrendered by English officers in the single frigate engagements, and the duplicates of medals, in gold and silver, voted by Congress to the victors. In Lieutenant Wise's room there are models of the projectiles, and a series of shot and shell used in the navy, or deposited by inventors. Among other relics was the flag of Captain Ward's boat, just brought in, which was completely riddled by the bullet-marks received in the ambuscade in which that officer was killed, with nearly all of his boat's crew, as they incautiously approached the shore of the Potomac, to take off a small craft placed there to decoy them by the Confederates. My business was to pave the way for a passage on board a steamer, in case of any naval expedition starting before the army was ready to move, but all difficulties were at once removed by the promptitude and courtesy of Mr. Fox, the Assistant-Secretary, who promised to give me an order for a passage whenever I required it. The extreme civility and readiness to oblige of all American officials, high and low, from the gate-keepers and door-porters up to the heads of departments, cannot be too highly praised, and it is ungenerous to accept the explanation offered by an English officer to whom I remarked the circumstance, that it is due to the fact that each man is liable to be turned out at the end of four years, and therefore makes all the friends he can.

In the afternoon I rode out with Captain Johnson, through some charming woodland scenery on the outskirts of Washington, by a brawling stream, in a shady little ravine, that put me in mind of the Dargle. Our ride led us into the camps, formed on the west of Georgetown, to cover the city from the attacks of an enemy advancing along the left bank of the Potomac, and in support of several strong forts and earthworks placed on the heights. One regiment consists altogether of Frenchmen—another is of Germans—in a third I saw an officer with a Crimean and Indian medal on his breast, and several privates with similar decorations. Some of the regiments were on parade, and crowds of civilians from Washington were enjoying the novel scene, and partaking of the hospitality of their friends. One old lady, whom I have always seen about the camps, and who is a sort of ancient heroine of Saragossa, had an opportunity of being useful. The 15th Massachusetts, a fine-looking body of men, had broken up camp, and were marching off to the sound of their own voices chanting "Old John Brown," when one of the enormous trains of baggage waggons attached to them was carried off by the frightened mules, which probably had belonged to Virginian farmers, and one of the soldiers, in trying to stop it, was dashed to the ground and severely injured. The old lady was by his side in a moment, and out came her flask of strong waters, bandages, and medical comforts and apparatus. "It's well I'm here for this poor Union soldier; I'm sure I always have something to do in these camps." On my return late, there was a letter on my table requesting me to visit General [illegible] was then too far advanced to avail myself of the invitation, which was only delivered after I left my lodgings.

CHAPTER LIV.

A tour of inspection round the camp—A troublesome horse—M'Dowell and the President—My description of Bull's Run endorsed by American officers—Influence of the Press—Newspaper correspondents—Dr. Bray—My letters—Captain Meagher—Military adventurers—

Probable duration of the war—Lord A. Vane Tempest—The American journalist—Threats of assassination.

August 26th.—General Van Vliet called from General M'Clellan to say that the Commander-in-Chief would be happy to go round the camps with me when he next made an inspection, and would send round an orderly and charger in time to get ready before he started. These little excursions are not the most agreeable affairs in the world; for M'Clellan delights in working down staff and escort, dashing from the Chain Bridge to Alexandria, and visiting all the posts, riding as hard as he can, and not returning till past midnight, so that if one has a regard for his cuticle, or his mail-days, he will not rashly venture on such excursions. To-day he is to inspect M'Dowell's division.

I set out accordingly with Captain Johnson over the Long Bridge, which is now very strictly guarded. On exhibiting my pass to the sentry at the entrance, he called across to the sergeant and spoke to him aside, showing him the pass at the same time. "Are you Russell, of the London *Times?*" said the sergeant. I replied, "If you look at the pass, you will see who I am." He turned it over, examined it most narrowly, and at last, with an expression of infinite dissatisfaction and anger upon his face, handed it back, saying to the sentry, "I suppose you must let him go."

Meantime Captain Johnson was witching the world with feats of noble horsemanship, for I had lent him my celebrated horse Walker, so called because no earthly equestrian can induce him to do anything but trot violently, gallop at full speed, or stand on his hind legs. Captain Johnson laid the whole fault of the animal's conduct to my mismanagement, affirming that all it required was a light hand and gentleness, and so, as he could display both, I promised to let him have a trial to-day. Walker, on starting, however, insisted on having a dance to himself, which my friend attributed to the excitement produced by the presence of the other horse, and I rode quietly along whilst the captain proceeded to establish an acquaintance with his steed in some quiet bye-street. As I was crossing the Long Bridge, the forbidden clatter of a horse's hoofs on the planks caused me to look round, and on, in a cloud of dust, through the midst of shouting sentries, came my friend of the gentle hand and unruffled temper, with his hat thumped down on the back of his head, his eyes gleaming, his teeth clenched, his fine features slightly flushed, to say the least of it, sawing violently at Walker's head, and exclaiming, "You brute! I'll teach you to walk!" till he brought up by the barrier midway on the bridge. The guard, *en masse*, called the captain's attention to the order, "All horses to walk over the bridge." "Why, that's what I want him to do. I'll give any man among you one hundred dollars who can make him walk along this bridge or anywhere else." The redoubtable steed, being permitted to proceed upon its way, dashed swiftly through the *tête de pont*, or stood on his hind legs when imperatively arrested by a barrier or *abattis;* and on these occasions my excellent friend, as he displayed his pass in one hand and restrained Bucephalus with the other, reminded me of nothing so much as the statue of Peter the Great, in the square on the banks of the Neva, or the noble equestrian monument of General Jackson which decorates the city of Washington. The troops of M'Dowell's division were already drawn up on a rugged plain, close to the river's margin, in happier days the scene of the city races. A pestilential odour rose from the slaughter-houses close at hand, but, regardless of odour or marsh, Walker continued his violent exercise, evidently under the idea that he was assisting at a retreat of the grand army as before.

Presently General M'Dowell and one of his aides cantered over, and whilst waiting for General M'Clellan, he talked of the fierce outburst directed against me in the press. "I must confess," he said, laughingly, "I am much rejoiced to find you are as much abused as I have been. I hope you mind it as little as I did. Bull's Run was an unfortunate affair for both of us, for had I won it, you would have had to describe the pursuit of the flying enemy, and then you would have been the most popular writer in America, and I would have been lauded as the greatest of generals. See what measure has been meted to us now. I'm accused of drunkenness and gambling; and you, Mr. Russell—well! I really do hope you are not so black as you are painted." Presently a cloud of dust on the road announced the arrival of the President, who came upon the ground in an open carriage, with Mr. Seward by his side, accompanied by General M'Clellan and his staff in undress uniform, and an escort of the very dirtiest and most unsoldierly dragoons, with filthy accoutrements and ungroomed horses, I ever saw. The troops dressed into line and presented arms, whilst the band struck up the "Star-spangled Banner," as the Americans have got no tune which corresponds with our National Anthem, or is in any way complimentary to the quadrennial despot who fills the President's chair.

General M'Dowell seems on most excellent terms with the present Commander-in-Chief, as he is with the President. Immediately after Bull's Run, when the President first saw M'Dowell, he said to him, "I have not lost a particle of confidence in you," to which the General replied, "I don't see why you should, Mr. President." But there was a curious commentary, either on the sincerity of Mr. Lincoln, or in his utter subserviency to mob opinion, in the fact that he who can overrule Congress and act pretty much as he pleases in time of war, had, without opportunity for explanation or demand for it, at once displaced the man in whom he still retained the fullest confidence, degraded him to command of a division of the army of which he had been General-in-Chief, and placed a junior officer over his head.

After some ordinary movements, the march past took place, which satisfied me that the new levies were very superior to the three months' men, though far, indeed, from being soldiers. Finer material could not be found in physique. With the exception of an assemblage of miserable scarecrows in rags and tatters, swept up in New York and commanded by a Mr. Kerrigan, no division of the ordinary line, in any army, could show a greater number of tall, robust men in the prime of life. A soldier standing near me, pointing out Kerrigan's corps, said, "The boy who commands that pretty lot recruited them first for the Secesshes in New York, but, finding he could not get them away, he handed them over to Uncle Sam." The men were silent as they marched past, and did not cheer for President or Union.

I returned from the field to Arlington House, having been invited with my friend to share the general's camp dinner. On our way along the road, I asked Major Brown why he rode over to us before the review commenced. "Well," said he, "my attention was called to you by one of our staff saying 'there are two Englishmen,' and the general sent me over to invite them, and followed when he saw who it was." "But how could you tell we were English?" "I don't know," said he; "there were other civilians about, but there was something about the look of you two which marked you immediately as John Bull."

At the general's tent we found General Sherman, General Keyes, Wadsworth, and some others. Dinner was spread on a table covered by the flap of the tent, and consisted of good plain fare, and a dessert of prodigious watermelons. I was exceedingly gratified to hear every officer present declare in the presence of the general who had commanded the army, and who himself said no words could exaggerate the disorder of the route, that my narrative of Bull's Run was not only true, but moderate.

General Sherman, whom I met for the first time, said, "Mr. Russell, I can endorse every word that you wrote; your statements about the battle, which you say you did not witness, are equally correct. All the stories about charging batteries and attacks with the bayonet are simply falsehoods, so far as my command is concerned, though some of the troops did fight well. As to cavalry charges, I wish we had had a few cavalry to have tried one; those Black Horse fellows seemed as if their horses ran away with them." General Keyes said, "I don't think you made it half bad enough. I could not get the men to stand after they had received the first severe check. The enemy swept the open with a tremendous musketry fire. Some of our men and portions of regiments behaved admirably: we drove them easily at first; the cavalry did very little indeed; but when they did come on I could not get the infantry to stand, and after a harmless volley they broke." These officers were brigadiers of Tyler's division.

The conversation turned upon the influence of the press in America, and I observed that every soldier at table spoke with the utmost dislike and antipathy of the New York journals, to which they gave a metropolitan position, although each man had some favourite paper of his own which he excepted from the charge made against the whole body. The principal accusations made against the press were that the conductors are not gentlemen, that they are calumnious and corrupt, regardless of truth, honour, anything but circulation and advertisements. "It is the first time we have had a chance of dealing with these fellows, and we shall not lose it."

I returned to Washington at dusk over the aqueduct bridge. A gentleman who introduced himself to me as correspondent of one of the cheap London papers, sent out specially on account of his great experience to write from the States, under the auspices of the leaders of the advanced liberal party, came to ask if I had seen an article in the *Chicago Tribune*, purporting to be written by a gentleman who says he was in my company during the retreat, contradicting what I report. I was advised by several officers—whose opinion I took—that it would be derogatory to me if I noticed the writer. I read it over carefully, and must say I am surprised—if anything could surprise me in American journalism—at the impudence and mendacity of the man. Having first stated that he rode along with me from point to point at a certain portion of the road, he states that he did not hear or see certain things which I say that I saw and heard, or deliberately falsifies what passed, for the sake of a little ephemeral applause, quotations in the papers, increased importance to himself, and some more abuse of the English correspondent.

This statement made me recall the circumstance alluded to more particularly. I remembered well the flurried, plethoric, elderly man, mounted on a broken-down horse, who rode up to me in great trepidation, with sweat streaming over his face, and asked me if I was going into Washington. "You may not recollect me, sir; I was introduced to you at Cay-roe, in the hall of the hotel. I'm Dr. Bray, of the *Chicago Tribune*." I certainly did not remember him, but I did recollect that a dispatch from Cairo appeared in the paper, announcing my arrival from the South, and stating I complained on landing that my letters had been opened in the States, which was quite untrue and which I felt called on to deny, and supposing Dr. Bray to be the author, I was not at all inclined to cement our acquaintance, and continued my course with a bow.

But the Doctor whipped his steed up alongside mine, and went on to tell me that he was in the most terrible bodily pain and mental anxiety. The first on account of desuetude of equestrian exercise; the other on account of the defeat of the Federals and the probable pursuit of the Confederates. "Oh! it's dreadful to think of! They know me well, and would show me no mercy. Every step the horse takes I'm in agony. I'll never get to Washington. Could you stay with me, sir? as you know the road." I was moved to internal chuckling, at any rate, by the very prostrate condition—for he bent well over the saddle—of poor Dr. Bray, and so I said to him, "Don't be uneasy, sir. There is no fear of your being taken. The army is not defeated, in spite of what you see; for there will be always runaways and skulkers when a retreat is ordered. I have not the least doubt M'Dowell will stand fast at Centreville, and rally his troops tonight on the reserve, so as to be in a good position to resist the enemy to-morrow. I'll have to push on to Washington, as I must write my letters, and I fear they will stop me on the bridge without the countersign, particularly if these runaways should outstrip us. As to your skin, pour a little whiskey on some melted tallow and rub it well in, and you'll be all right to-morrow or next day, as far as that is concerned."

I actually, out of compassion to his sufferings—for he uttered cries now and then as though Lucina were in request—reined up, and walked my horse, though most anxious to get out of the dust and confusion of the runaways, and comforted him about a friend whom he missed, and for whose fate he was as uneasy as the concern he felt for his own woes permitted him to be; suggested various modes to him of easing the jolt and of quickening the pace of his steed, and at last, really bored excessively by an uninteresting and self-absorbed companion, who was besides detaining me needlessly on the road, I turned on some pretence into a wood by the side, and continued my way as well as I could, till I got off the track, and, being guided to the road by the dust and shouting, I came out on it somewhere near Fairfax Court, and there, to my surprise, dropped on the Doctor, who, animated by some agency more powerful than the pangs of an abraded cuticle, and taking advantage of the road, had got thus far ahead. We entered the place together, halted at the same inn to water our horses, and then seeing that it was getting on towards dusk, and that the wave of the retreat was rolling onward in increased volume, I pushed on and saw no more of him. Ungrateful Bray! Perfidious Bray! Some day, when I have time, I must tell the people of Chicago how Bray got into Washington, and how he left his horse, and what he did with it, and how Bray behaved on the road. I dare say they who know him can guess.

The most significant article I have seen for some time as a test of the taste, tone, and temper of the New York public, judging by their most widely-read journal, is contained in it to-night. It appears that a gentleman named Muir, who is described as a relative of Mr. Mure, the consul at New Orleans, was seized on the point of starting for Europe, and that among his papers, many of which were of a "disloyal character," which is not astonishing, seeing that he came from Charleston, was a letter written by a foreign resident in that city, in which he stated he had seen a letter from me to Mr. Bunch describing the flight at Bull's Run, and adding that Lord Lyons remarked, when he heard of it, he would ask Mr. Seward whether he would not now admit the Confederates were a belligerent power, whereupon Maudit calls on Mr. Seward to demand explanations from Lord Lyons, and to turn me out of the country, because in my letter to the "Times" I made the remark that the United States would probably now admit the South were a belligerent power.

Such an original observation could never have occurred to two people—genius concerting with genius could alone have hammered it out. But Maudit is not satisfied with the humiliation of Lord Lyons and the expulsion of myself—he absolutely insists upon a miracle, and his moral vision being as perverted as his physical, he declares that I must have sent to the British Consul at Charleston a duplicate copy of the letter which I furnished with so much labour and difficulty just in time to catch the mail by special messenger from Boston. "These be thy Gods, O Israel!"

My attention was also directed to a letter from certain officers of the disbanded 69th Regiment, who had permitted their Colonel to be dragged away a prisoner from the field of Bull's Run. Without having read my letter, these gentlemen assumed that I had stigmatised Captain T. F. Meagher as one who had misconducted himself during the battle, whereas all I had said on the evidence of eye-witnesses was "that in the rout he appeared at Centreville, running across country, and uttering exclamations in the hearing of my informant, which indicated that he, at least, was perfectly satisfied that the Confederates had established their claims to be considered a belligerent power." These officers state that Captain Meagher behaved extremely well up to a certain point in the engagement, when they lost sight of him, and from which period they could say nothing about him. It was subsequent to that very time he appeared at Centreville; and long before my letter returned to America giving credit to Captain Meagher for natural gallantry in the field, I remarked that he would no doubt feel as much pained as any of his friends at the ridicule cast upon him by the statement that he, the Captain of a company, "went into action mounted on a magnificent charger, and waving a green silk flag, embroidered with a golden harp, in the face of the enemy."

A young man, wearing the Indian war medal with two clasps, who said his name was Mac Ivor Hilstock, came in to inquire after some unknown friend of his. He told me he had been in Tomb's troop of Artillery during the Indian mutiny, and had afterwards served with the French volunteers during the siege of Caprera. The news of the Civil War has produced such an immigration of military adventurers from Europe that the streets of Washington are quite filled with medals and ribands. The regular officers of the American Army regard them with considerable dislike, the greater inasmuch as Mr. Seward and the politicians encourage them. In alluding to the circumstance to General M'Dowell, who came in to see me at a late dinner, I said, "A great many Garibaldians are in Washington just now." "Oh," said he, in his quiet way, "it will be quite enough for a man to prove that he once saw Garibaldi to satisfy us in Washington that he is quite fit for the command of a regiment. I have recommended a man because he sailed in the ship which Garibaldi came in over here, and I'm sure it will be attended to."

August 27th.—Fever and ague, which General M'Dowell attributes to watermelons, of which he, however, had eaten three times as much as I had. Swallowed many grains of quinine, and lay panting in the heat in-doors. Two English visitors, Mr. Lamy and a Captain of the 17th, called on me; and, afterwards, I had a conversation with M. Mercier and M. Stoeckl on the aspect of affairs. They are inclined to look forward to a more speedy solution than I think the North is weak enough to accept. I believe that peace is possible in two years or so, but only by the concession to the South of a qualified independence. The naval operations of the Federals will test the Southern mettle to the utmost. Having a sincere regard and liking for many of the Southerners whom I have met, I cannot say their cause, or its origin, or its aim, recommends itself to my sympathies; and yet I am accused of aiding it by every means in my power, because I do not re-echo the arrogant and empty boasting and insolent outbursts of the people in the North, who threaten, as the first-fruits of their success, to invade the territories subject to the British crown, and to outrage and humiliate our flag.

It is melancholy enough to see this great republic tumbling to pieces; one would regret it all the more but for the fact that it re-echoed the voices of the obscene and filthy creatures which have been driven before the lash of the lictor from all the cities of Europe. Assuredly it was a great work, but all its greatness and the idea of its life was of man, not of God. The principle of veneration, of obedience, of subordination, and self-control did not exist within. Washington-worship could not save it. The elements of destruction lay equally sized, smooth, and black at its foundations, and a spark suffices to blow the structure into the air.

August 28*th*.—Raining. Sundry officers turned in to inquire of me, who was quietly in bed at Washington, concerning certain skirmishes reported to have taken place last night. Sold one horse and bought another; that is, I paid ready money in the latter transaction, and in the former received an order from an officer on the paymaster of his regiment, on a certain day not yet arrived.

To-day Lord A. V. Tempest is added to the number of English arrivals; he amused me by narrating his reception at Willard's on the night of his arrival. When he came in with the usual ruck of passengers, he took his turn at the book, and wrote down Lord Adolphus Vane Tempest, with possibly M.P. after it. The clerk, who was busily engaged in showing that he was perfectly indifferent to the claims of the crowd who were waiting at the counter for their rooms, when the book was finished, commenced looking over the names of the various persons, such as Leonidas Buggs, Rome, N.Y.; Doctor Onesiphorous Bowells, D.D., Syracuse; Olynthus Craggs, Palmyra, Mo.; Washington Whilkes, Indianapolis, writing down the numbers of the rooms, and handing over the keys to the waiters at the same time. When he came to the name of the English nobleman, he said, "Vane Tempest, No. 125." "But stop," cried Lord Adolphus. "Lycurgus Siccles," continued the clerk, "No. 23." "I insist upon it, sir," broke in Lord Adolphus —"you really must hear me. I protest against being put in 125. I can't go up so high." "Why," said the clerk, with infinite contempt, "I can put you at twice as high—I'll give you No. 250 if I like." This was rather too much, and Lord Adolphus put his things into a cab, and drove about Washington until he got to earth in the two-pair back of a dentist's, for which, no doubt, *tout vu*, he paid as much as for an apartment at the Hotel Bristol.

A gathering of American officers and others, amongst whom was Mr. Olmsted, enabled him to form some idea of the young men's society of Washington, which is a strange mixture of politics and fighting, gossip, gaiety, and a certain apprehension of a wrath to come for their dear republic. Here is Olmsted prepared to lay down his life for free speech over a united republic, in one part of which his freedom of speech would lead to irretrievable confusion and ruin; whilst Wise, on the other hand, seeks only to establish a union which shall have a large fleet, be powerful at sea, and be able to smash up abolitionists, newspaper people, and political agitators at home.

August 29*th*.—It is hard to bear such a fate as befalls an unpopular man in the United States, because in no other country, as De Tocqueville* remarks, is the press so powerful when it is unanimous. And yet he says, too, "The journalist of the United States is usually placed in a very humble position, with a scanty education and a vulgar turn of mind. His characteristics consist of an open and coarse appeal to the passions of the populace, and he habitually abandons the principles of political science to assail the characters of individuals, to track them into private life, and disclose all their weaknesses and errors. The individuals who are already in possession of a high station in the esteem of their fellow-citizens are afraid to write in the newspapers, and they are thus deprived of the most powerful instrument which they can use to excite the passions of the multitude to their advantage. The personal opinions of the editors have no kind of weight in the eyes of the public. The only use of a journal is, that it imparts the knowledge of certain facts; and it is only by altering and distorting those facts that a journalist can contribute to the support of his own views." When the whole of the press, without any exception in so far as I am aware, sets deliberately to work, in order to calumniate, vilify, insult, and abuse a man who is at once a stranger, a rival, and an Englishman, he may expect but one result, according to De Tocqueville.

* P. 200, Spencer's American edition, New York, 1858.

The teeming anonymous letters I receive are filled with threats of assassination, tarring, feathering, and the like; and one of the most conspicuous of literary shirri is in perfect rapture at the notion of a new "sensation" heading, for which he is working as hard as he can. I have no intention to add to the number of his castigations.

In the afternoon I drove to the waste grounds beyond the Capitol, in company with Mr. Olmsted and Captain Haworth, to see the 18th Massachusetts Regiment, who had just marched in, and were pitching their tents very probably for the first time. They arrived from their state with camp equipments, waggons, horses, harness, commissariat stores complete, and were clad in the blue uniform of the United States; for the volunteer fancies in greys and greens are dying out. The men were uncommonly stout young fellows, with an odd, slouching, lounging air about some of them, however, which I could not quite understand till I heard one sing out, "Hallo, sergeant, where am I to sling my hammock in this tent?" Many of them, in fact, are fishermen and sailors from Cape Cod, New Haven, and similar maritime places.

CHAPTER LV.

Personal unpopularity—American naval officers—A gun levelled at me in fun—Increase of odium against me—Success of the Hatteras expedition—General Scott and M'Clellan—M'Clellan on his camp-bed—General Scott's pass refused—Prospect of an attack on Washington—Skirmishing—Anonymous letters—General Halleck—General M'Clellan and the Sabbath—Rumoured death of Jefferson Davis—Spread of my unpopularity—An offer for my horse—Dinner at the Legation—Discussion on Slavery.

August 31*st*.—A month, during which I have been exposed to more calumny, falsehood, not to speak of danger, than I ever passed through, has been brought to a close. I have all the pains and penalties attached to the *digito monstrari et dicier hic est*, in the most hostile sense. On going into Willard's the other day, I said to the clerk behind the bar, "Why I heard, Mr. So-and-so, you were gone?" "Well, sir, I'm not. If I was, you would have lost the last man who is ready to say a word for you in this house, I can tell you." Scowling faces on every side—women turning up their pretty little noses—people turning round in the streets, or stopping to stare in front of me—the proprietors of the shops where I am known pointing me out to others; the words uttered, in various tones, "So, that's Bull-Run Russell!"—for, oddly enough, the Americans seem to think that a disgrace to their arms becomes diminished by fixing the name of the scene as a *sobriquet* on one who described it —these, with caricatures, endless falsehoods, rumours of duels, and the like, form some of the little *désagrémens* of one who was so unfortunate as to assist at the retreat, the first he had ever seen, of an army which it would in all respects have suited him much better to have seen victorious.

I dined with Lieutenant Wise, and met Captain Dahlgren, Captain Davis, U.S.N., Captain Foote, U.S.N., and Colonel Fletcher Webster,* son of the great American statesman, now commanding a regiment of volunteers. The latter has a fine head and face; a full, deep eye; is quaint and dry in his conversation, and a poet, I should think, in heart and soul, if outward and visible signs may be relied on. The naval captains were excellent specimens of the accomplished and able men who belong to the United States Navy. Foote, who is designated to the command of the flotilla which is to clear the Mississippi downwards, will, I am certain, do good service—a calm, energetic, skilful officer. Dahlgren, who, like all men with a system, very properly watches everything which bears upon it, took occasion to call for Captain Foote's testimony to the fact that he battered down a six-foot granite wall in China with Dahlgren shells. It will run hard against the Confederates when they get such men at work on the rivers and coasts, for they seem to understand their business thoroughly, and all they are not quite sure of is the readiness of the land forces to co-operate with their expeditionary movements. Incidentally I learned from the conversation—and it is a curious illustration of the power of the President—that it was he who ordered the attack on Charleston harbour, or, to speak with more accuracy, the movement of the armed squadron to relieve Sumter by force, if necessary; and that he came to the conclusion it was feasible principally from reading the account of the attack on Kinburn by the allied fleets. There was certainly an immense disproportion between the relative means of attack and defence in the two cases; but, at all events, the action of the Confederates prevented the attempt.

September 1st.—Took a ride early this morning over the Long Bridge. As I was passing out of the earthwork called a fort on the hill, a dirty German soldier called out from the parapet, "Pull-Run Russell! you shall never write Pull's Runs again," and at the same time cocked his piece, and levelled it at me. I immediately rode round into the fort, the fellow still presenting his firelock, and asked him what he meant, at the same time calling for the sergeant of the guard, who came at once, and, at my request, arrested the man, who recovered arms, and said, "It was a choake—I vant to freeken Pull-Run Russell." However, as his rifle was capped and loaded, and on full cock, with his finger on the trigger, I did not quite see the fun of it, and I accordingly had the man marched to the tent of the officer, who promised to investigate the case, and make a formal report of it to the brigadier, on my return to lay the circumstances before him. On reflection I resolved that it was best to let the matter drop; the joke might spread, and it was quite unpleasant enough as it was to bear the insolent looks and scowling faces of the guards at the posts, to whom I was obliged to exhibit my pass whenever I went out to ride.

On my return I heard of the complete success of the Hatteras expedition, which shelled out and destroyed some sand batteries guarding the entrance to the great inland sea and navigation called Pamlico Sound, in North Carolina, furnishing access to coasters for many miles into the Confederate States, and most useful to them in forwarding supplies and keeping up communications throughout. The force was commanded by General Butler, who has come to Washington with the news, and has already made his speech to the mob outside Willard's. I called down to see him, but he had gone over to call on the President. The people were jubilant, and one might have supposed Hatteras was the key to Richmond or Charleston, from the way they spoke of this unparalleled exploit.

There is a little French gentleman here against whom the fates bear heavily. I have given him employment as an amanuensis and secretary for some time back, and he tells me many things concerning the talk in the city which I do not hear myself, from which it would seem that there is an increase of ill feeling towards me every day, and that I am a convenient channel for concentrating all the abuse and hatred so long cherished against England. I was a little tickled by an account he gave me of a distinguished lady, who sent for him to give French lessons, in order that she might become equal to her high position in mastering the difficulties of the courtly tongue. I may mention the fact, as it was radiated by the press through all the land, that Mrs. M. N., having once on a time "been proficient in the language, has forgotten it in the lapse of years, but has resolved to renew her studies, that she may better discharge the duties of her elevated station." The master went to the house and stated his terms to a lady whom he saw there; but as she marchandéd a good deal over small matters of cents, he never supposed he was dealing with the great lady, and therefore made a small reduction in his terms, which encouraged the enemy to renew the assault till he stood firmly on three shillings a lesson, at which point the lady left him, with the intimation that she would consider the matter and let him know. And now, the licentiate tells me, it has become known he is my private secretary, he is not considered eligible to do *avoir* and *etre* for the satisfaction of the good lady, who really is far better than her friends describe her to be.

September 2nd.—It would seem as if the North were perfectly destitute of common sense. Here they are as rampant because they have succeeded with an overwhelming fleet in shelling out the defenders of some poor unfinished earthworks, on a spit of sand on the coast of North Carolina, as if they had already crushed the

* Since killed in action.

Southern rebellion. They affect to consider this achievement a counterpoise to Bull Run.

Surely the press cannot represent the feelings of the staid and thinking masses of the Northern States! The success is unquestionably useful to the Federalists, but it no more adds to their chances of crushing the Confederacy, than shooting off the end of an elephant's tail contributes to the hunter's capture of the animal.

An officious little person, who was buzzing about here as correspondent of a London newspaper, made himself agreeable by coming with a caricature of my humble self at the battle of Bull Run, in a laborious and most unsuccessful imitation of *Punch*, in which I am represented with rather a flattering face and figure, seated before a huge telescope, surrounded by bottles of London stout, and looking at the fight. This is supposed to be very humorous and amusing, and my good-natured friend was rather astonished when I cut it out and inserted it carefully in a scrap-book, opposite a sketch from fancy of the N. Y. Fire Zouaves charging a battery and routing a regiment of cavalry, which appeared last week in a much more imaginative and amusing periodical, which aspires to describe with pen and pencil the actual current events of the war.

Going out for my usual ride to-day, I saw General Scott, between two aides-de-camp, slowly pacing homewards from the War Office. He is still Commander-in-Chief of the army, and affects to direct movements and to control the disposition of the troops, but a power greater than his increases steadily at General M'Clellan's head-quarters. For my own part, I confess that General M'Clellan does not appear to me a man of action, or, at least, a man who intends to act as speedily as the crisis demands. He should be out with his army across the Potomac, living among his generals, studying the composition of his army, investigating its defects, and, above all, showing himself to the men as soon afterwards as possible, if he cannot be with them at the time, in the small affairs which constantly occur along the front, and never permitting them to receive a blow without taking care that they give at least two in return. General Scott, *jam fracta membra labore*, would do all the work of departments and superintendence admirably well; but, as Montesquieu taught long ago, faction and intrigue are the cancers which peculiarly eat into the body politic of republics, and M'Clellan fears, no doubt, that his absence from the capital, even though he went but across the river, would animate his enemies to undermine and supplant him.

I have heard several people say lately, "I wish old Scott would go away," by which they mean that they would be happy to strike him down when his back was turned, but feared his personal influence with the President and his Cabinet. Two months ago, and his was the most honoured name in the States; one was sickened by the constant repetition of elaborate plans, in which the General was represented playing the part of an Indian juggler, and holding an enormous boa constrictor of a Federal army in his hands, which he was preparing to let go as soon as he had coiled it completely round the frightened Secessionist rabbit; "now none so poor to do him reverence." Hard is the fate of those who serve republics. The officers who met the old man in the street to-day passed him by without a salute or mark of recognition, although he wore his uniform coat, with yellow lapels and yellow sash; and one of a group which came out of a *restaurant* close to the General's house, exclaimed, almost in his hearing, "Old fuss and feathers don't look first-rate to-day."

In the evening I went with a Scotch gentleman, who was formerly acquainted with General M'Clellan when he was superintendent of the Central Illinois Railway, to his head-quarters, which are in the house of Captain Wilkes, at the corner of President Square, near Mr. Seward's, and not far from the spot where General Sickles shot down the unhappy man who had temporarily disturbed the peace of his domestic relations. The parlours were full of officers smoking, reading the papers, and writing, and after a short conversation with General Marcy, Chief of the Staff, Van Vliet, aide-de-camp of the Commander-in-Chief, led the way up-stairs to the top of the house, where we found General M'Clellan, just returned from a long ride, and seated in his shirt sleeves on the side of his camp-bed. He looked better than I have yet seen him, for his dress showed to advantage the powerful, compact formation of his figure, massive throat, well-set head, and muscular energy of his frame. Nothing could be more agreeable or easy than his manner. In his clear, dark-blue eye was no trace of uneasiness or hidden purpose; but his mouth, covered by a short, thick moustache, rarely joins in the smile that overspreads his face when he is animated by telling or hearing some matter of interest. Telegraph wires ran all about the house, and as we sat round the General's table, despatches were repeatedly brought in from the Generals in the front. Sometimes M'Clellan laid down his cigar and went off to study a large map of the position, which was fixed to the wall close to the head of his bed; but more frequently the contents of the despatches caused him to smile or to utter some exclamation, which gave one an idea that he did not attach much importance to the news, and had not great faith in the reports received from his subordinate officers, who are always under the impression that the enemy are coming on in force.

It is plain the General has got no high opinion of volunteer officers and soldiers. In addition to unsteadiness in action, which arises from want of confidence in the officers as much as from any other cause, the men labour under the great defect of exceeding rashness, a contempt for the most ordinary precautions, and a liability to unaccountable alarms and credulousness of false report; but, admitting all these circumstances, M'Clellan has a soldier's faith in *gros bataillons*, and sees no doubt of ultimate success in a military point of view, provided the politicians keep quiet, and, charming men as they are, cease to meddle with things they don't understand. Although some very good officers have deserted the United States army and are now with the Confederates, a very considerable majority of West Point officers have adhered to the Federals. I am satisfied, by an actual inspection of the lists, that the Northerners retain the same preponderance in officers who have received a military education, as they possess in wealth and other means, and resources for carrying on the war.

The General consumes tobacco largely, and not only smokes cigars, but indulges in the more naked beauties of a quid. From tobacco we wandered to the Crimea, and thence went half round the world, till we halted before the Virginian watch-fires, which these good volunteers will insist on lighting under the very noses of the enemy's pickets; nor was it till late we retired, leaving the General to his well-earned repose.

General M'Clellan took the situation of affairs in a very easy and philosophical spirit. According to his own map and showing, the enemy not only overlapped his lines from the batteries by which they blockaded the Potomac on the right, to their extreme left on the river above Washington, but have established themselves in a kind of salient angle on his front, at a place called Munson's Hill, where their flag waved from entrenchments within sight of the Capitol. However, from an observation he made, I imagined that the General would make an effort to recover his lost ground; at any rate, beat up the enemy's quarters, in order to see what they were doing; and he promised to send an orderly round and let me know; so, before I retired, I gave orders to my groom to have "Walker" in readiness.

September 3rd.—Notwithstanding the extreme heat, I went out early this morning to the Chain Bridge, from which the reconnoissance hinted at last night would necessarily start. This bridge is about four and a half or five miles above Washington, and crosses the river at a picturesque spot almost deserving the name of a gorge, with high banks on both sides. It is a light aërial structure, and spans the river by broad arches, from which the view reminds one of Highland or Tyrolean scenery. The road from the city passes through a squalid settlement of European squatters, who in habitation, dress, appearance, and possibly civilisation, are quite as bad as any negroes on any Southern plantation I have visited. The camps of a division lie just beyond, and a gawky sentry from New England, with whom I had some conversation, amused me by saying that the Colonel "was a darned deal more affeerd of the Irish squatters taking off his poultry at night than he was of the Secessioners; anyways, he puts out more sentries to guard them than he has to look after the others."

From the Chain Bridge I went some distance towards Falls Church, until I was stopped by a picket, the officer of which refused to recognise General Scott's pass. "I guess the General's a dead man, sir." "Is he not Commander-in-Chief of the United States army?" "Well, I believe that's a fact, sir; but you had better argue that point with M'Clellan. He is our boy, and I do believe he'd like to let the London *Times* know how we Green Mountain boys can fight, if they don't know already. But all passes are stopped anyhow, and I had to turn back a Congress-man this very morning, and lucky for him it was, because the Seceshers are just half a mile in front of us." On my way back by the upper road I passed a farmer's house, which was occupied by some Federal officers, and there, seated in the verandah, with his legs cocked over the railings, was Mr. Lincoln, in a felt hat, and a loose grey shooting coat and long vest, "letting off," as the papers say, one of his jokes, to judge by his attitude and the laughter of the officers around him, utterly indifferent to the Confederate flag floating from Munson's Hill.

Just before midnight a considerable movement of troops took place through the streets, and I was about starting off to ascertain the cause, when I received the information that General M'Clellan was only sending off two brigades and four batteries to the Chain Bridge to strengthen his right, which was menaced by the enemy. I retired to bed, in order to be ready for any battle which might take place to-morrow, but was roused up by voices beneath my window, and going out on the verandah, could not help chuckling at the appearance of three foreign ministers and a banker, in the street below, who had come round to inquire, in some perturbation, the cause of the nocturnal movement of men and guns, and seemed little inclined to credit my assurances that nothing more serious than a reconnaissance was contemplated. The ministers were in high spirits at the prospect of an attack on Washington. Such agreeable people are the governing party of the United States at present, that there is only one representative of a foreign power here who would not like to see them flying before Southern bayonets. The banker, perhaps, would have liked a little time to set his affairs in order. "When will the sacking begin?" cried the ministers. "We must hoist our flags." "The Confederates respect private property, I suppose?" As to flags, be it remarked that Lord Lyons has none to display, having lent his to Mr. Seward, who required it for some festive demonstration.

September 4th.—I rode over to the Chain Bridge again with Captain Haworth this morning at seven o'clock, on the chance of there being a big fight, as the Americans say; but there was only some slight skirmishing going on; dropping shots now and then. Walker, excited by the reminiscences of Bull Run noises, performed most remarkable feats, one of the most frequent of which was turning right round when at full trot or canter, and then kicking violently. He also gallopped in a most lively way down a road which in winter is the bed of a torrent, and jumped along among the boulders and stones in an agile, cat-like manner, to the great delectation of my companion.

The morning was intensely hot, so I was by no means indisposed to get back to cover again. Nothing would persuade people there was not serious fighting somewhere or other. I went down to the Long Bridge, and was stopped by the sentry, so I produced General Scott's pass, which I kept always as a *dernier ressort*, but the officer on duty here also refused it, as passes were suspended. I returned and referred the matter to Colonel Cullum, who consulted Generrl Scott, and informed me that the pass must be considered as perfectly valid, not having been revoked by the General, who, as Lieutenant-General commanding the United States army, was senior to every other officer, and could only have his pass revoked by the President himself. Now it was quite plain that it would do me no good to have an altercation with the sentries at every post in order to have the satisfaction of reporting the matter to General Scott. I therefore procured a letter from Colonel Cullum, stating, in writing, what he said in words, and with that and the pass went to General M'Clellan's head-quarters, where I was told by his aides the General was engaged in a kind of council of war. I sent up my papers, and Major Hudson, of his staff, came down after a short time, and said that "General M'Clellan thought it would be much better if General Scott had given me a new special pass; but as General Scott had thought fit to take the present course on his own responsibility, General M'Clellan could not interfere in the matter;" whence it may be inferred there is no very pleasant feeling between head-quarters of the army of the Potomac and head-quarters of the army of the United States.

I went on to the Navy yard, where a look-out man, who can command the whole of the country to Munson's Hill, is stationed, and I heard from Captain Dahlgren that there was no fighting whatever. There were columns of smoke visible from Capitol Hill, which the excited spectators declared were caused by artillery and musketry, but my glass resolved them into emanations from a vast extent of hanging wood and brush which the Federals were burning in order to clear their front. However, people were so positive as to hearing cannonades and volleys of musketry, that we went out to the reservoir hill at Georgetown, and, gazing over the debateable land of Virginia—which, by the way, is very beautiful these summer sunsets—became thoroughly satisfied of the delusion. Met Van Vliet as I was returning, who had just seen the reports at head-quarters, and averred there was no fighting whatever. My landlord had a very different story. His friend, an hospital steward, "had seen ninety wounded men carried into one ward from over the river, and believed the Federals had lost 1000 killed and wounded and twenty-five guns."

Sept. 5th.—Raining all day. M'Clellan abandoned his intention of inspecting the lines, and I remained in, writing. The anonymous letters still continue. Received one from an unmistakeable Thug to-day, with the death's-head, cross-bones, and coffin, in the most orthodox style of national-school drawing.

The event of the day was the appearance of the President in the Avenue in a suit of black, and a parcel in his hand, walking umbrella-less in the rain. Mrs. Lincoln has returned, and the worthy "Executive" will no longer be obliged to go "browsing round," as he says, among his friends at dinner-time. He is working away at money matters with energy, but has been much disturbed in his course of studies by General Fremont's sudden outburst in the West, which proclaims emancipation, and draws out the arrow which the President intended to discharge from his own bow.

Sept. 6th. — At 3.30 P.M. General M'Clellan sent over an orderly to say he was going across the river, and would be glad of my company; but I was just finishing my letters for England, and had to excuse myself for the moment; and when I was ready, the General and staff had gone *ventre à terre* into Virginia. After post, paid my respects to General Scott, who is about to retire from the command on his full-pay of about £3500 per annum, which is awarded to him on account of his long services.

A new Major-General — Halleck — has been picked up in California, and is highly praised by General Scott and by Colonel Cullum, with whom I had a long talk about the officers on both sides. Halleck is a West Point officer, and has published some works on military science which are highly esteemed in the States. Before California became a State, he was secretary to the governor or officer commanding the territory, and eventually left the service and became a lawyer in the district, where he has amassed a large fortune. He is a man of great ability, very calm, practical, earnest, and cold, devoted to the Union—a soldier, and something more. Lee is considered the ablest man on the Federal side, but he is slow and timid. "Joe" Johnson is their best strategist. Beauregard is nobody and nothing—so think they at head-quarters. All of them together are not equal to Halleck, who is to be employed in the West.

I dined at the Legation, where were the Russian Minister, the Secretary of the French Legation, the representative of New Granada, and others. As I was anxious to explain to General M'Clellan the reason of my inability to go out with him, I called at his quarters about eleven o'clock, and found he had just returned from his ride. He received me in his shirt, in his bedroom at the top of the house; introduced me to General Burnside—a soldierly, intelligent-looking man, with a very lofty forehead, and uncommonly bright dark eyes; and we had some conversation about matters of ordinary interest for some time, till General M'Clellan called me into an ante-chamber, where an officer was writing a despatch, which he handed to the General. "I wish to ask your opinion as to the wording of this order. It is a matter of importance. I see that the men of this army, Mr. Russell, disregard the Sabbath, and neglect the worship of God; and I am resolved to put an end to such neglect, as far as I can. I have, therefore, directed the following order to be drawn up, which will be promulgated to-morrow." The General spoke with much earnestness, and with an air which satisfied me of his sincerity. The officer in waiting read the order, in which, at the General's request, I suggested a few alterations. The General told me he had received "sure information that Beauregard has packed up all his baggage, struck his tents, and is evidently preparing for a movement, so you may be wanted at a moment's notice." General Burnside returned to my rooms, in company with Mr. Lamy, and we sat up, discoursing of Bull's Run, in which his brigade was the first engaged in front. He spoke like a man of sense and a soldier of the action, and stood up for the conduct of some regiments, though he could not palliate the final disorder. The papers circulate rumours of "Jeff. Davis's death;" nay, accounts of his burial. The public does not believe, but buys all the same.

Sept. 7th.—Yes; "Jeff. Davis must be dead." There are some touching lamentations in the obituary notices over his fate in the other world. Meanwhile, however, his spirit seems quite alive; for there is an absolute certainty that the Confederates are coming to attack the Capitol. Lieut. A. Wise and Lord A. Vane Tempest argued the question whether the assault would be made by a flank movement above or direct in front; and Wise maintained the latter thesis with vigour not disproportioned to the energy with which his opponent demonstrated that the Confederates could not be such madmen as to march up to the Federal batteries. There is actually "a battle" raging (in the front of the Philadelphia newspaper offices) this instant—*Populus vult decipi—decipiatur.*

Sept. 8th.—Rode over to Arlington House. Went round by Aqueduct Bridge, Georgetown, and out across Chain Bridge to Brigadier Smith's head-quarters, which are established in a comfortable house belonging to a Secessionist farmer. The General belongs to the regular army, and, if one can judge from externals, is a good officer. A libation of Bourbon and water was poured out to friendship, and we rode out with Captain Poe, of the Topographical Engineers, a hard-working, eager fellow, to examine the trench which the men were engaged in throwing up to defend the position they have just occupied on some high knolls, now cleared of wood, and overlooking ravines which stretch towards Falls Church and Vienna. Everything about the camp looked like fighting: Napoleon guns planted on the road; Griffin's battery in a field near at hand; mountain howitzers unlimbered; strong pickets and main guards; the five thousand men all kept close to their camps, and two regiments, in spite of M'Clellan's order, engaged on the trenches, which were already mounted with field-guns. General Smith, like most officers, is a Democrat and strong anti-Abolitionist, and it is not too much to suppose he would fight any rather than Virginians. As we were riding about, it got out among the men that I was present, and I was regarded with no small curiosity, staring, and some angry looks. The men do not know what to make of it when they see their officers in the company of one whom they are reading about in the papers as the most &c. &c. the world ever saw. And, indeed, I know well enough, so great is their passion and so easily are they misled, that without such safeguard the men would in all probability carry out the suggestions of one of their particular guides, who has undergone so many cuffings that he rather likes them. Am I not the cause of the disaster at Bull's Run?

Going home, I met Mr. and Mrs. Lincoln in their new open carriage. The President was not so good-humoured, nor Mrs. Lincoln so affable, in their return to my salutation as usual. My unpopularity is certainly spreading upwards and downwards at the same time, and all because I could not turn the battle of Bull's Run into a Federal victory, because I would not pander to the vanity of the people, and, least of all, because I will not bow my knee to the degraded creatures who have made the very name of a free press odious to honourable men. Many of the most foul-mouthed and rabid of the men who revile me because I have said the Union as it was never can be restored, are as fully satisfied of the truth of that statement as I am. They have written far severer things of their army than I have ever done. They have slandered their soldiers and their officers as I have never done. They have fed the worst passions of a morbid democracy till it can neither see nor hear; but they shall never have the satisfaction of either driving me from my post, or inducing me to deviate a hair's-breadth from the course I have resolved to pursue, as I have done before in other cases—greater and graver, as far as I was concerned, than this.

Sept. 9th.—This morning, as I was making the most of my toilet after a ride, a gentleman in the uniform of a United States officer came up-stairs and marched into my sitting-room, saying he wished to see me on business. I thought it was one of my numerous friends coming with a message from some one who was going to avenge Bull's Run on me. So, going out as speedily as I could, I bowed to the officer, and asked his business. "I've come here because I'd like to trade with you about that chestnut horse of yours." I replied that I could only state what price I had given for him, and say that I would take the same, and no less. "What may you have given for him?" I discovered that my friend had been already to the stable and ascertained the price from the groom, who considered himself bound in duty to name a few dollars beyond the actual sum I had given, for when I mentioned the price the countenance of the man of war relaxed into a grim smile. "Well, I reckon that help of yours is a pretty smart chap, though he does come from your side of the world." When the preliminaries had been arranged, the officer announced that he had come on behalf of another officer to offer me an order on his paymaster, payable at some future date, for the animal, which he desired, however, to take away upon the spot. The transaction was rather amusing, but I consented to let the animal go, much to the indignation and uneasiness of the Scotch servant, who regarded it as contrary to all the principles of morality in horse-flesh.

Lord A. V. Tempest and another British subject who applied to Mr. Seward to-day for leave to go South, were curtly refused. The Foreign Secretary is not very well pleased with us just now, and there has been some little uneasiness between him and Lord Lyons, in consequence of representations respecting an improper excess in the United States marine on the lakes, contrary to treaty. The real cause, perhaps, of Mr. Seward's annoyance is to be found in the exaggerated statements of the American papers respecting British reinforcements for Canada, which, in truth, are the ordinary reliefs. These small questions in the present condition of affairs cause irritation; but if the United States were not distracted by civil war, they would be seized eagerly as pretexts to excite the popular mind against Great Britain.

The great difficulty of all, which must be settled some day, relates to San Juan; and every American I have met is persuaded Great Britain is in the wrong, and must consent to a compromise or incur the risk of war. The few English in Washington, I think, were all present at dinner at the Legation to-day.

September 10th.—A party of American officers passed the evening where I dined—all, of course, Federals, but holding very different views. A Massachusetts Colonel, named Gordon, asserted that slavery was at the root of every evil which afflicted the Republic; that it was not necessary in the South or anywhere else, and that the South maintained the institution for political as well as private ends. A Virginian Captain, on the contrary, declared that slavery was in itself good; that it could not be dangerous, as it was essentially conservative, and desired nothing better than to be left alone; but that the Northern fanatics, jealous of the superior political influence and ability of Southern statesmen, and sordid Protectionists who wished to bind the South to take their goods exclusively, perpetrated all the mischief. An officer of the District of Columbia assigned all the misfortunes of the country to universal suffrage, to foreign immigration, and to these alone. Mob-law revolts well-educated men, and people who pride themselves because their fathers lived in the country before them will not be content to see a foreigner who has been but a short time on the soil exercising as great influence over the fate of the country as himself. A contest will, therefore, always be going on between those representing the oligarchical principle and the pollarchy; and the result must be disruption, sooner or later, because there is no power in a republic to restrain the struggling factions which the weight of the crown compresses in monarchical countries.

I dined with a namesake—a major in the United States Marines—with whom I had become accidentally acquainted, in consequence of our letters frequently changing hands, and spent an agreeable evening in company with naval and military officers; not the less so because our host had some marvellous Madeira, dating back from the Conquest—I mean of Washington. Several of the officers spoke in the highest terms of General Banks, whom they call a most remarkable man; but so jealous are the politicians that he will never be permitted, they think, to get a fair chance of distinguishing himself.

CHAPTER LVI.

A Crimean acquaintance—Personal abuse of myself—Close firing—A reconnaissance—Major-General Bell—The Prince de Joinville and his nephews—American estimate of Louis Napoleon—Arrest of members of the Maryland Legislature—Life at Washington—War cries—News from the Far West—Journey to the Western States—Along the Susquehannah and Juniata—Chicago—Sport in the prairie—Arrested for shooting on Sunday—The town of Dwight—Return to Washington—Mr. Seward and myself.

September 11*th*.—A soft-voiced, round-faced, rather good-looking young man, with downy moustache, came to my room, and introduced himself this morning as Mr. H. H. Scott, formerly of Her Majesty's 57th Regiment. "Don't you remember me? I often met you at Cathcart's Hill. I had a big dog, if you remember, which used to be about the store belonging to our camp." And so he rattled on, talking of old Street and young Jones with immense volubility, and telling me how he had gone out to India with his regiment, had married, lost his wife, and was now travelling for the benefit of his health and to see the country. All the time I was trying to remember his face, but in vain. At last came the purport of his visit. He had been taken ill at Baltimore, and was obliged to stop at an hotel, which had cost him more than he had anticipated; he had just received a letter from his father, which required his immediate return, and he had telegraphed to New York to secure his place in the next steamer. Meantime, he was out of money, and required a small loan to enable him to go back and prepare for his journey, and of course he would send me the money the moment he arrived in New York. I wrote a cheque for the amount he named, with which Lieutenant or Captain Scott departed; and my suspicions were rather aroused by seeing him beckon a remarkably ill-favoured person at the other side of the way, who crossed over and inspected the little slip of paper held out for his approbation, and then, taking his friend under the arm, walked off rapidly towards the bank.

The papers still continue to abuse me *faute de mieux;* there are essays written about me; I am threatened with several farces; I have been lectured upon at Willard's by a professor of rhetoric; and I am a stock subject with the leaden penny funny journals, for articles and caricatures. Yesterday I was abused on the ground that I spoke badly of those who treated me hospitably. The man who wrote the words knew they were false, because I have been most careful in my correspondence to avoid anything of the kind. A favourite accusation, indeed, which Americans make against foreigners is, "that they have abused our hospitality," which oftentimes consists in permitting them to live in the country at all at their own expense, paying their way at hotels and elsewhere, without the smallest suspicion that they were receiving any hospitality whatever.

To-day, for instance, there comes a lively corporal of artillery, John Robinson, who quotes Sismondi, Guizot, and others, to prove that I am the worst man in the world; but his fiercest invectives are directed against me on the ground that I speak well of those people who give me dinners; the fact being, since I came to America, that I have given at least as many dinners to Americans as I have received from them.

Just as I was sitting down to my desk for the remainder of the day, a sound caught my ear which, repeated again and again, could not be mistaken by accustomed organs, and placing my face close to the windows, I perceived the glass vibrate to the distant discharge of cannon, which, evidently, did not proceed from a review or a salute. Unhappy man that I am! here is Walker lame, and my other horse carried off by the West-country captain. However, the sounds were so close that in a few moments I was driving off towards the Chain Bridge, taking the upper road, as that by the canal has become a sea of mud filled with deep holes.

In the windows, on the house-tops, even to the ridges partially overlooking Virginia, people were standing in high excitement, watching the faint puffs of smoke which rose at intervals above the tree-tops, and at every report a murmur—exclamations of "There, do you hear that?"—ran through the crowd. The driver, as excited as any one else, urged his horses at full speed, and we arrived at the Chain Bridge just as General M'Call—a white haired, rather military-looking old man—appeared at the head of his column, hurrying down to the Chain Bridge from the Maryland side, to reinforce Smith, who was said to be heavily engaged with the enemy. But by this time the firing had ceased, and just as the artillery of the General's column commenced defiling through the mud, into which the guns sank to the naves of the wheels, the head of another column appeared, entering the bridge from the Virginia side with loud cheers, which were taken up again and again. The carriage was halted to allow the 2nd Wisconsin to pass; and a more broken-down, white-faced, sick, and weakly set of poor wretches I never beheld. The heavy rains had washed the very life out of them; their clothing was in rags, their shoes were broken, and multitudes were foot-sore. They cheered, nevertheless, or whooped, and there was a tremendous clatter of tongues in the ranks concerning their victory; but, as the men's faces and hands were not blackened by powder, they could have seen little of the engagement. Captain Poe came along with dispatches for General M'Clellan, and gave me a correct account of the affair.

All this noise and firing and excitement, I found, simply arose out of a reconnaissance made towards Lewinsville, by Smith and a part of his brigade, to beat up the enemy's position, and enable the topographical engineers to procure some information respecting the country. The Confederates worked down upon their left flank with artillery, which they got into position at an easy range without being observed, intending, no doubt, to cut off their retreat and capture or destroy the whole force; but, fortunately for the reconnoitring party, the impatience of their enemies led them to open fire too soon. The Federals got their guns into position also, and covered their retreat, whilst reinforcements poured out of camp to their assistance, "and I doubt not," said Poe, "but that they will have an account of a tremendous scalping match in all the papers to-morrow, although we have only six or seven men killed, and twelve wounded." As we approached Washington the citizens, as they are called, were waving Federal banners out of the windows and rejoicing in a great victory; at least, the inhabitants of the inferior sort of houses. Respectability in Washington means Secession.

Mr. Monson told me that my distressed young British subject, Captain Scott, had called on him at the Legation early this morning for the little pecuniary help which had been, I fear, wisely refused there, and which was granted by me. The States have become, indeed, more than ever the *cloacina gentium*, and Great Britain contributes its full quota to the stream.

Thus time passes away in expectation of some onward movement, or desperate attack, or important strategical movements; and night comes to assemble a few friends, Americans and English, at my rooms or elsewhere, to talk over the disappointed hopes of the day, to speculate on the future, to chide each dull delay, and to part with a hope that to-morrow would be more lively than to-day. Major-General Bell, who commanded the Royals in the Crimea, and who has passed some half century in active service, turned up in Washington, and has been courteously received by the American authorities. He joined to-night one of our small reunions, and was infinitely puzzled to detect the lines which separated one man's country and opinions from those of the other.

September 11*th.*— Captain Johnson, Queen's messenger, started with despatches for England from the Legation to-day, to the regret of our little party. I observe by the papers certain wiseacres in Philadelphia have got up a petition against me to Mr. Seward, on the ground that I have been guilty of treasonable practices and misrepresentations in my letter dated August 10th. There is also to be a lecture on the 17th at Willard's, by the Professor of Rhetoric, to a volunteer regiment, which the President is invited to attend—the subject being myself.

There is an absolute nullity of events, out of which the New York papers endeavour, in vain, to extract a *caput mortuum* of sensation headings. The Prince of Joinville and his two nephews, the Count of Paris and the Duke of Chartres, have been here for some days, and have been received with marked attention by the President, Cabinet, politicians, and military. The Prince has come with the intention of placing his son at the United States Naval Academy, and his nephews with the head-quarters of the Federal army. The *impressement* exhibited at the White House towards the French princes is attributed by ill-natured rumours and persons to a little pique on the part of Mrs. Lincoln, because the Princess Clothilde did not receive her at New York, but considerable doubts are entertained of the Emperor's "loyalty" towards the Union. Under the wild extravagance of professions of attachment to France are hidden suspicious that Louis Napoleon may be capable of treasonable practices and misrepresentations, which, in time, may lead the Philadelphians to get up a petition against M. Mercier.

The news that twenty-two members of the Maryland Legislature have been seized by the Federal authorities has not produced the smallest effect here: so easily do men in the midst of political troubles bend to arbitrary power, and so rapidly do all guarantees disappear in a revolution. I was speaking to one of General M'Clellan's aides de camp this evening respecting these things, when he said—"If I thought he would use his power a day longer than was necessary, I would resign this moment. I believe him incapable of any selfish or unconstitutional views, or unlawful ambition, and you will see that he will not disappoint our expectations."

It is now quite plain M'Clellan has no intention of making a general offensive movement against Richmond. He is aware his army is not equal to the task — commissariat deficient, artillery wanting, no cavalry; above all, ill-officered, incoherent battalions. He hopes, no doubt, by constant reviewing and inspection, and by weeding out the preposterous fellows who render epaulettes ridiculous, to create an infantry which shall be able for a short campaign in the fine autumn weather; but I am quite satisfied he does not intend to move now, and possibly will not do so till next year. I have arranged therefore to pay a short visit to the West, penetrating as far as I can, without leaving telegraphs and railways behind, so that if an advance takes place, I shall be back in time at Washington to assist at the earliest battle. These Federal armies do not move like the corps of the French republic, or Crawford's Light Division.

In truth, Washington life is becoming exceedingly monotonous and uninteresting. The pleasant little evening parties or tertulias which once relieved the dulness of this dullest of capitals, take place no longer. Very wrong indeed would it be that rejoicings and festivities should occur in the capital of a country menaced with destruction, where many anxious hearts are grieving over the lost, or tortured with fears for the living.

But for the hospitality of Lord Lyons to the English residents, the place would be nearly insufferable, for at his house one met other friendly ministers who extended the circle of invitations, and two or three American families completed the list which one could reckon on his fingers. Then at night, there were assemblages of the same men, who uttered the same opinions, told the same stories, sang the same songs, varied seldom by strange faces or novel accomplishments, but always friendly and social enough—not conducive perhaps to very early rising, but innocent of gambling, or other excess. A flask of Bordeaux, a wicker-covered demijohn of Bourbon, a jug of iced-water, and a bundle of cigars, with the latest arrival of newspapers, furnished the *matériel* of these small symposiums, in which Americans and Englishmen and a few of the members of foreign Legations, mingled in a friendly cosmopolitan manner. Now and then a star of greater magnitude came down upon us: a senator or an "earnest man," or a "live man," or a constitutional lawyer, or a remarkable statesman, coruscated, and rushing off into the outer world left us befogged, with our glimmering lights half extinguished with tobacco smoke.

Out of doors excessive heat alternating with thunder-storms and tropical showers—dust beaten into mud, or mud sublimated into dust—eternal reviews, each like the other—visits to camp, where we saw the same men and heard the same stories of perpetual abortive skirmishes—rides confined to the same roads and paths by lines of sentries, offered no greater attraction than the city, where one's bones were racked with fever and ague, and where every evening the pestilential vapours of the Potomac rose higher and spread further. No wonder that I was glad to get away to the Far West, particularly as I entertained hopes of witnessing some of the operations down the Mississippi, before I was summoned back to Washington, by the news that the grand army had actually broken up camp, and was about once more to march against Richmond.

September 12th.—The day passed quietly, in spite of rumours of another battle; the band played in the President's garden, and citizens and citizenesses strolled about the grounds as if Secession had been annihilated. The President made a fitful appearance, in a grey shooting suit, with a number of despatches in his hand, and walked off towards the State Department quite unnoticed by the crowd. I am sure not half a dozen persons saluted him—not one of the men I saw even touched his hat. General Bell went round the works with M'Clellan, and expressed his opinion that it would be impossible to fight a great battle in the country which lay between the two armies—in fact, as he said, "a general could no more handle his troops among the woods, than he could regulate the movements of rabbits in a cover. You ought just to make a proposition to Beauregard to come out on some plain and fight the battle fairly out where you can see each other."

September 16th.—It is most agreeable to be removed from all the circumstance without any of the pomp and glory of war. Although there is a tendency in the North, and, for aught I know, in the South, to consider the contest in the same light as one with a foreign enemy, the very battle-cries on both sides indicate a civil war. "The Union for ever"—"States rights"—and "Down with the Abolitionists," cannot be considered national. M'Clellan takes no note of time even by its loss, which is all the more strange because he sets great store upon it in his report on the conduct of the war in the Crimea. However, he knows an army cannot be made in two months, and that the larger it is, the more time there is required to harmonize its components. The news from the Far West indicated a probability of some important operations taking place, although my first love—the army of the Potomac—must be returned to. Any way there was the great Western Prairie to be seen, and the people who have been pouring from their plains so many thousands upon the Southern States to assert the liberties of those coloured races whom they will not permit to cross their borders as freemen. Mr. Lincoln, Mr. Blair, and other Abolitionists, are actuated by similar sentiments, and seek to emancipate the slave, and remove from him the protection of his master, in order that they may drive him from the continent altogether, or force him to seek refuge in emigration.

On the 18th of September, I left Baltimore in company with Major-General Bell, C.B., and Mr. Lamy, who was well acquainted with the Western States: stopping one night at Altoona, in order that we might cross by daylight the fine passes of the Alleganies, which are traversed by bold gradients, and remarkable cuttings, second only in difficulty and extent to those of the railroad across the Sömmering.

So far as my observation extends, no route in the United States can give a stranger a better notion of the variety of scenery and of resources, the vast extent of territory, the difference in races, the prosperity of the present, and the probable greatness of the future, than the line from Baltimore by Harrisburg and Pittsburg to Chicago, traversing the great States of Pennsylvania, Ohio, and Indiana. Plain and mountain, hill and valley, river and meadow, forest and rock, wild tracts through which the Indian roamed but a few years ago, lands covered with the richest crops; rugged passes, which Salvator would have peopled with shadowy groups of bandits; gentle sylvan glades, such as Gainsborough would have covered with waving corn; the hum of mills, the silence of the desert and waste, sea-like lakes whitened by innumerable sails, mighty rivers carving their way through continents, sparkling rivulets that lose their lives amongst giant wheels: seams and lodes of coal, iron, and mineral wealth, cropping out of desolate mountain sides; busy, restless manufacturers and traders alternating with stolid rustics, hedges clustering with grapes, mountains whitening with snow; and beyond, the great Prairie stretching away to the backbone of inhospitable rock, which, rising from the foundations of the world, bars the access of the white man and civilization to the bleak inhospitable regions beyond, which both are fain as yet to leave to the savage and wild beast.

Travelling along the banks of the Susquehannah, the visitor, however, is neither permitted to admire the works of nature in silence, nor to express his admiration of the energy of man in his own way. The tyranny of public opinion is upon him. He must admit that he never saw anything so wonderful in his life; that there is nothing so beautiful anywhere else; no fields so green, no rivers so wide and deep, no bridges so lofty and long; and at last he is inclined to shut himself up, either in absolute grumpy negation, or to indulge in hopeless controversy. An American gentleman is as little likely as any other well-bred man to force the opinions or interrupt the reveries of a stranger; but if third-class Esquimaux are allowed to travel in first-class carriages, the hospitable creatures will be quite likely to insist on your swallowing train oil, eating blubber, or admiring snow-drifts, as the finest things in the world. It is infinitely to the credit of the American people that actual offence is so seldom given and is still more rarely intended—always save and except in the one particular, of chewing tobacco. Having seen most things that can irritate one's stomach, and being in company with an old soldier, I little expected that any excess of the sort could produce disagreeable effects; but on returning from this excursion, Mr. Lamy and myself were fairly driven out of a carriage, on the Pittsburg line, in utter loathing and disgust, by the condition of the floor. The conductor, passing through, said, "You must not stand out there, it is against the rules; you can go in and smoke," pointing to the carriage. "In there!" exclaimed my friend, "why, it is too filthy to put a wild beast into." The conductor looked in for a moment, nodded his head, and said, "Well, I concede it is right bad; the citizens *are* going it pretty strong," and so left us.

The scenery along the Juniata is still more picturesque than that of the valley of the Susquehannah. The borders of the route across the Alleganies have been described by many a writer; but notwithstanding the good fortune which favoured us, and swept away the dense veil of vapours on the lower ranges of the hills, the landscape scarcely produced the effect of scenery on a less extended scale, just as the scenery of the Himalayas is not so striking as that of the Alps, because it is on too vast a scale to be readily grasped.

Pittsburg, where we halted next night, on the Ohio, is certainly, with the exception of Birmingham, the most intensely sooty, busy, squalid, foul-housed, and vile-suburbed city I have ever seen. Under its perpetual canopy of smoke, pierced by a forest of blackened chimneys, the ill-paved streets, swarm with a streaky population whose white faces are smutched with soot-streaks—the noise of vans and drays which shake the houses as they pass, the turbulent life in the thoroughfares, the wretched brick tenements,—built in waste places on squalid mounds, surrounded by heaps of slag and broken brick—all these give the stranger the idea of some vast manufacturing city of the Inferno; and yet a few miles beyond, the country is studded with beautiful villas, and the great river, bearing innumerable barges and steamers on its broad bosom, rolls its turbid waters between banks rich with cultivated crops.

The policeman at Pittsburg station—a burly Englishman—told me that the war had been of the greatest service to the city. He spoke not only from a policeman's point of view, when he said that all the rowdies, Irish, Germans, and others had gone off to the war, but from the manufacturing stand-point, as he added that wages were high, and that the orders from contractors were keeping all the manufacturers going. "It is wonderful," said he, "what a number of citizens come back from the South by rail, in these new metallic coffins."

A long, long day, traversing the State of Indiana by the Fort Wayne route, followed by a longer night, just sufficed to carry us to Chicago. The railway passes through a most uninteresting country, which in part is scarcely rescued from a state of nature by the hand of man; but it is wonderful to see so much done, when one hears that the Miami Indians and other tribes were driven out, or, as the phrase is, "removed," only twenty years ago—"conveyed, the wise call it"—to the reserves.

From Chicago, where we descended at a hotel which fairly deserves to be styled magnificent, for comfort and completeness, Mr. Lamy and myself proceeded to Racine, on the shores of Lake Michigan, and thence took the rail for Freeport, where I remained for some days, going out in the surrounding prairie to shoot in the morning, and returning at nightfall. The prairie chickens were rather wild. The delight of these days, notwithstanding bad sport, cannot be described, nor was it the least ingredient in it to mix with the fresh and vigorous race who are raising up cities on these fertile wastes. Fortunately for the patience of my readers, perhaps, I did not fill my diary with the records of each day's events, or of the contents of our bags; and the note-book in which I jotted down some little matters which struck me to be of interest has been mislaid; but in my letters to England I gave a description of the general aspect of the country, and of the feelings of the people, and arrived at the conclusion that the tax-gatherer will have little chance of returning with full note-books from his tour in these districts. The dogs which were lent to us were generally abominable; but every evening we returned in company with great leather-greaved and jerkined men, hung round with belts and hooks, from which were suspended strings of defunct prairie chickens. The farmers were hospitable, but were suffering from a morbid longing for a failure of crops in Europe, in order to give some value to their corn and wheat, which literally cumbered the earth.

Freeport! Who ever heard of it? And yet it has its newspapers, more than I dare mention, and its big hotel lighted with gas, its billiard rooms and saloons, magazines, railway stations, and all the proper paraphernalia of local self-government, with all their fierce intrigues and giddy factions.

From Freeport our party returned to Chicago, taking leave of our excellent friend and companion Mr. George Thompson of Racine. The authorities of the Central Illinois Railway, to whose courtesy and consideration I was infinitely indebted, placed at our disposal a magnificent sleeping carriage; and on the morning after our arrival, having laid in a good stock of supplies, and engaged an excellent sporting guide and dogs, we started, attached to the regular train from Chicago, until the train stopped at a shunting place near the station of Dwight, in the very centre of the prairie. We reached our halting-place, were detached, and were shot up a siding in the solitude, with no habitation in view, except the wood shanty, in which lived the family of the Irish overseer of this portion of the road—a man happy in the possession of a piece of gold which he received from the Prince of Wales, and for which he declared, he would not take the amount of the National Debt.

The sleeping carriage proved most comfortable quarters. After breakfast in the morning, Mr.

Lamy, Col. Foster, Mr. ——, of the Central Illinois rail, the keeper, and myself, descending the steps of our movable house, walked in a few strides to the shooting grounds, which abounded with quail, but were not so well peopled by the chickens. The quail were weak on the wing, owing to the lateness of the season, and my companions grumbled at their hard luck, though I was well content with fresh air, my small share of birds, and a few American hares. Night and morning the train rushed by, and when darkness settled down upon the prairie, our lamps were lighted, dinner was served in the carriage, set forth with inimitable potatoes cooked by the old Irishwoman. From the dinner-table it was but a step to go to bed. When storm or rain rushed over the sea-like plain, I remained in the carriage writing, and after a long spell of work, it was inexpressibly pleasant to take a ramble through the flowering grass and the sweet-scented broom, and to go beating through the stunted under-cover, careless of rattle-snakes, whose tiny prattling music I heard often enough without a sight of the tails that made it.

One rainy morning, the 29th September, I think, as the sun began to break through drifting rain clouds, I saw my companions preparing their guns, the sporting chaperon Walker filling the shot flasks, and making all the usual arrangements for a day's shooting. "You don't mean to say you are going out shooting on a Sunday!" I said. "What, on the prairies!" exclaimed Colonel Foster. "Why, of course we are; there's nothing wrong in it here. What nobler temple can we find to worship in than lies around us? It is the custom of the people hereabout to shoot on Sundays, and it is a work of necessity with us, for our larder is very low."

And so, after breakfast, we set out, but the rain came down so densely that we were driven to the house of a farmer, and finally we returned to our sleeping carriage for the day. I never fired a shot nor put a gun to my shoulder, nor am I sure that any of my companions killed a bird.

The rain fell with violence all day, and at night the gusts of wind shook the carriage like a ship at sea. We were sitting at table after dinner, when the door at the end of the carriage opened, and a man, in a mackintosh dripping wet, advanced with unsteady steps along the centre of the carriage, between the beds, and taking off his hat, in the top of which he searched diligently, stood staring with lack-lustre eyes from one to the other of the party, till Colonel Foster exclaimed, "Well, sir, what do you want?"

"What do I want?" he replied, with a slight thickness of speech, "which of you is the Honourable Lord William Russell, correspondent of the London *Times?* That's what I want."

I certified to my identity; whereupon, drawing a piece of paper out of his hat, he continued, "Then I arrest you, Honourable Lord William Russell, in the name of the people of the Commonwealth of Illinois," and thereupon handed me a document declaring that one Morgan, of Dwight, having come before him that day and sworn that I, with a company of men and dogs, had unlawfully assembled, and by firing shots, and by barking and noise, had disturbed the peace of the State of Illinois, he, the subscriber or justice of the peace, as named and described, commanded the constable Pedgers, or whatever his name was, to bring my body before him to answer to the charge.

Now this town of Dwight was a good many miles away, the road was declared by those who knew it to be very bad, the night was pitch dark, the rain falling in torrents, and as the constable, drawing out of his hat paper after paper with the names of impossible persons upon them, served subpœnas on all the rest of the party to appear next morning, the anger of Colonel Foster could scarcely be restrained, by kicks under the table and nods and becks and wreathed smiles from the rest of the party. "This is infamous! It is a political persecution!" he exclaimed, whilst the keeper joined in chorus, declaring he never heard of such a proceeding before in all his long experience of the prairie, and never knew there was such an act in existence. The Irishmen in the hut added that the informer himself generally went out shooting every Sunday. However, I could not but regret I had given the fellow an opportunity of striking at me, and though I was the only one of the party who raised an objection to our going out at all, I was deservedly suffering for the impropriety—to call it here by no harsher name.

The constable, a man of a liquid eye and a cheerful countenance, paid particular attention meantime to a large bottle upon the table, and as I professed my readiness to go the moment he had some refreshment that very wet night, the stern severity becoming a minister of justice, which marked his first utterances, was sensibly mollified; and when Mr. —— proposed that he should drive back with him and see the prosecutor, he was good enough to accept my written acknowledgment of the service of the writ, and promise to appear the following morning, as an adequate discharge of his duty—combined with the absorption of some Bourbon whisky—and so retired.

Mr. —— returned late at night, and very angry. It appears that the prosecutor—who is not a man of very good reputation, and whom his neighbours were as much astonished to find the champion of religious observances as they would have been if he was to come forward to insist on the respect due to the seventh commandment—with the insatiable passion for notoriety, which is one of the worst results of American institutions, thought he would gain himself some little reputation by causing annoyance to a man so unpopular as myself. He and a companion having come from Dwight for the purpose, and hiding in the neighbourhood, had, therefore, devoted their day to lying in wait and watching our party; and as they were aware in the railway carriage I was with Colonel Foster, they had no difficulty in finding out the names of the rest of the party. The magistrate being his relative, granted the warrant at once; and the prosecutor, who was in waiting for the constable, was exceedingly disappointed when he found that I had not been dragged through the rain.

Next morning, a special engine which had been ordered up by telegraph appeared alongside the car; and a short run through a beautiful country brought us to the prairie town of Dwight. The citizens were astir—it was a great day—and as I walked with Colonel Foster, all the good people seemed to be enjoying an unexampled treat in gazing at the stupendous criminal. The court-house, or magistrate's office, was suitable to the republican simplicity of the people of Dwight; for the chamber of justice was on the first floor of a house over a store, and access was obtained to it by a ladder from the street to a platform, at the top of which I was ushered into the presence of the court—a plain whitewashed room. I am not sure there was even an engraving of George Washington on the walls. The magistrate in a full suit of black, with his hat on, was seated at a small table, behind him a few books, on plain deal shelves, provided his fund of legal learning. The constable, with a severer visage than that of last night, stood upon the right hand; three sides of the room were surrounded by a wall of stout honest Dwightians, among whom I produced a profound sensation, by the simple ceremony of taking off my hat, which they no doubt considered a token of the degraded nature of the Britisher, but which moved the magistrate to take off his head-covering; whereupon some of the nearest removed theirs, some putting them on again, and some remaining uncovered; and then the informations were read, and on being asked what I had to say, I merely bowed, and said I had no remarks to offer. But my friend, Colonel Foster, who had been churning up his wrath and forensic lore for some time, putting one hand under his coat tail, and elevating the other in the air, with modulated cadences, poured out a fine oratorical flow which completely astonished me, and whipped the audience morally off their legs completely. In touching terms he described the mission of an illustrious stranger, who had wandered over thousands of miles of land and sea to gaze upon the beauties of those prairies which the Great Maker of the Universe had expanded as the banqueting tables for the famishing millions of pauperised and despotic Europe. As the representative of an influence which the people of the great State of Illinois should wish to see developed, instead of contracted, honoured instead of being insulted, he had come among them to admire the grandeur of nature, and to behold with wonder the magnificent progress of human happiness and free institutions. (Some thumping of sticks, and cries of "Bravo, that's so," which warmed the Colonel into still higher flights.) I began to feel if he was as great in invective as he was in eulogy, it was well he had not lived to throw a smooth pebble from his sling at Warren Hastings. As great indeed! Why, when the Colonel had drawn a beautiful picture of me examining coal deposits—investigating strata—breathing autumnal airs, and culling flowers in unsuspecting innocence, and then suddenly denounced the serpent who had dogged my steps, in order to strike me down with a justice's warrant, I protest it is doubtful, if he did not reach to the most elevated stage of vituperative oratory, the progression of which was marked by increasing thumps of sticks, and louder murmurs of applause, to the discomfiture of the wretched prosecutor. But the magistrate was not a man of imagination; he felt he was but elective after all; and so, with his eye fixed upon his book, he pronounced his decision, which was that I be amerced in something more than half the maximum fine fixed by the statute, some five-and-twenty shillings or so, the greater part to be spent in the education of the people, by transfer to the school fund of the State.

As I was handing the notes to the magistrate, several respectable men coming forward, exclaimed, "Pray oblige us, Mr. Russell, by letting us pay the amount for you; this is a shameful proceeding." But thanking them heartily for their proffered kindness, I completed the little pecuniary transaction and wished the magistrate good morning, with the remark that I hoped the people of the State of Illinois would always find such worthy defenders of the statutes as the prosecutor, and never have offenders against their peace and morals more culpable than myself. Having undergone a severe scolding from an old woman at the top of the ladder, I walked to the train, followed by a number of the audience, who repeatedly expressed their extreme regret at the little persecution to which I had been subjected. The prosecutor had already made arrangements to send the news over the whole breadth of the Union, which was his only reward: as I must do the American papers the justice to say that, with a few natural exceptions, those which noticed the occurrence unequivocally condemned his conduct.

That evening, as we were planning an extension of our sporting tour, the mail rattling by deposited our letters and papers, and we saw at the top of many columns the startling words, "Grand Advance of the Union Army." "M'Clellan Marching on Richmond." "Capture of Munson's Hill." "Retreat of the Enemy—30,000 Men Seize Their Fortifications." Not a moment was to be lost; if I was too late, I never would forgive myself. Our carriage was hooked on to the return train, and at 8 o'clock P.M. I started on my return to Washington, by way of Cleveland.

At half-past 3 on the 1st October the train reached Pittsburg, just too late to catch the train for Baltimore; but I continued my journey at night, arriving at Baltimore after noon, and reaching Washington at 6 P.M. on the 2nd of October.

October 3rd.—In Washington once more—all the world laughing at the pump and the wooden guns at Munson's Hill, but angry withal because M'Clellan should be so befooled as they considered it, by the Confederates. The fact is M'Clellan was not prepared to move, and therefore not disposed to hazard a general engagement, which he might have brought on had the enemy been in force; perhaps he knew they were not, but found it convenient nevertheless to act as though he believed they had established themselves strongly in his front, as half the world will give him credit for knowing more than the civilian strategists who have already got into disgrace for urging M'Dowell on to Richmond. The Federal armies are not handled easily. They are luxurious in the matter of baggage, and canteens, and private stores; and this is just the sort of war in which the general who moves lightly and rapidly, striking blows unexpectedly and deranging communications, will obtain great results.

Although Beauregard's name is constantly mentioned, I fancy that, crafty and reticent as he is, the operations in front of us have been directed by an officer of larger capacity. As yet M'Clellan has certainly done nothing in the field to show he is like Napoleon. The value of his labours in camp has yet to be tested. I dined at the Legation, and afterwards there was a meeting at my rooms, where I heard of all that had passed during my absence.

October 4th.—The new expedition, of which I have been hearing for some time past, is about to sail to Port Royal, under the command of General Burnside, in order to reduce the works erected at the entrance of the Sound, to secure a base of operations against Charleston, and to cut in upon the communication between that place and Savannah. Alas, for poor Trescot! his plantations, his secluded home! What will the good lady think of the Yankee invasion, which surely must succeed, as the naval force will be overwhelming? I visited the division of General Egbert Viele, encamped near the Navy-yard, which is bound to Annapolis, as a part of General Burnside's expedition. When first I saw him, the general was an emeritus captain, attached to the 7th New York Militia; now he is a Brigadier-General, if not something more, commanding a corps of nearly 5000 men, with pay and allowances to match. His good lady wife, who accompanied him in the Mexican campaign,—whereof came a book, lively and light, as a lady's should be,—was about to accompany her husband in his assault on the Carolinians, and prepared for action, by opening a small broadside on my unhappy self, whom she regarded as an enemy of our glorious Union; and therefore an ally of the Evil Powers on both sides of the grave. The women, North and South, are equally pitiless to their enemies; and it was but the other day, a man with whom I am on very good terms in Washington, made an apology for not asking me to his house, because his wife was a strong Union woman.

A gentleman who had been dining with Mr. Seward to-night told me the Minister had complained that I had not been near him for nearly two months; the fact was, however, that I had called twice immediately after the appearance in America of my letter dated July 22nd, and had met Mr. Seward afterwards, when his manner was, or appeared to me to be, cold and distant, and I had therefore abstained from intruding myself upon his notice; nor did his answer to the Philadelphia petition—in which Mr. Seward appeared to admit the allegations made against me were true, and to consider I had violated the hospitality accorded me—induce me to think that he did not entertain the opinion which these journals which set themselves up to be his organs had so repeatedly expressed.

CHAPTER LVII.

Another Crimean acquaintance—Summary dismissal of a newspaper correspondent—Dinner at Lord Lyons'—Review of artillery—"Habeas Corpus"—The President's duties—M'Clellan's policy—The Union Army—Soldiers and the patrol—Public men in America—Mr. Seward and Lord Lyons—A Judge placed under arrest—Death and funeral of Senator Baker—Disorderly troops and officers—Official fibs—Duck-shooting at Baltimore.

October 5th.—A day of heat extreme. Tumbled in upon me an old familiar face and voice, once Forster of a hospitable Crimean hut behind Mother Seacole's, commanding a battalion of Land Transport Corps, to which he had descended or sublimated from his position as ex-Austrian dragoon and *beau sabreur* under old Radetzsky in Italian wars; now a colonel of distant volunteers, and a member of the Parliament of British Columbia. He was on his way home to Europe, and had travelled thus far out of his way to see his friend.

After him came in a gentleman, heated, wild-eyed, and excited, who had been in the South, where he was acting as correspondent to a London newspaper, and on his return to Washington had obtained a pass from General Scott. According to his own story, he had been indulging in a habit which free-born Englishmen may occasionally find to be inconvenient in foreign countries in times of high excitement, and had been expressing his opinion pretty freely in favour of the Southern cause in the bar-rooms of Pennsylvania Avenue. Imagine a Frenchman going about the taverns of Dublin during an Irish rebellion, expressing his sympathy with the rebels, and you may suppose he would meet with treatment at least as peremptory as that which the Federal authorities gave Mr. D——. In fine, that morning early, he had been waited upon by an officer, who requested his attendance at the Provost Marshal's office; arrived there, a functionary, after a few queries, asked him to give up General Scott's pass, and when Mr. D—— refused to do so, proceeded to execute a terrible sort of process verbal on a large sheet of foolscap, the initiatory flourishes and prolegomena of which so intimidated Mr. D——, that he gave up his pass and was permitted to depart, in order that he might start for England by the next steamer.

A wonderful Frenchman, who lives up a back street, prepared a curious banquet, at which Mr. Irvine, Mr. Warre, Mr. Anderson, Mr. Lamy, and Colonel Forster assisted; and in the evening Mr. Lincoln's private secretary, a witty, shrewd, and pleasant young fellow, who looks a little more than eighteen years of age, came in with a friend, whose name I forget; and by degrees the circle expanded, till the walls seemed to have become elastic, so great was the concourse of guests.

October 6th.—A day of wandering around, and visiting, and listening to rumours all unfounded. I have applied for permission to accompany the Burnside expedition, but I am advised not to leave Washington, as M'Clellan will certainly advance as soon as the diversion has been made down South.

October 7th.—The heat to-day was literally intolerable, and wound up at last in a tremendous thunder-storm with violent gusts of rain. At the Legation, where Lord Lyons entertained the English visitors at dinner, the rooms were shaken by thunder claps, and the blinding lightning seemed at times to turn the well-illuminated rooms into caves of darkness.

October 8th.—A review of the artillery at this side of the river took place to-day, which has been described in very inflated language by the American papers, the writers on which—never having seen a decently-equipped force of the kind—pronounce the sight to have been of unequalled splendour; whereas the appearance of horses and men was very far from respectable in all matters relating to grooming, cleanliness, and neatness. General Barry has done wonders in simplifying the force and reducing the number of calibres, which varied according to the fancy of each State, or men of each officer who raised a battery; but there are still field-guns of three inches and of three inches and a half, Napoleon guns, rifled 10 lb. Parrots, ordinary 9-pounders, a variety of howitzers, 20 lb. Parrot rifled guns, and a variety of different projectiles in the caissons. As the men rode past, the eye was distressed by discrepancies in dress. Many wore red or white worsted comforters round their necks, few had straps to their trousers; some had new coats, others old; some wore boots, others shoes; not one had clean spurs, bits, curb-chains, or buttons. The officers cannot get the men to do what the latter regard as works of supererogation.

There were 72 guns in all; and if the horses were not so light, there would be quite enough to do for the Confederates to reduce their fire, as the pieces are easily handled, and the men like artillery and take to it naturally, being in that respect something like the natives of India.

While I was standing in the crowd, I heard a woman say, "I doubt if that Russell is riding about here. I should just like to see him to give him a piece of my mind. They say he's honest, but I call him a poor pre-jewdiced Britisher. This sight 'll give him fits." I was quite delighted at my incognito. If the caricatures were at all like me, I should have what the Americans call a bad time of it.

On the return of the batteries a shell exploded in a caisson just in front of the President's house, and, miraculous to state, did not fire the other projectiles. Had it done so, the destruction of life in the crowded street—blocked up with artillery, men, and horses, and crowds of men, women, and children—would have been truly frightful. Such accidents are not uncommon—a waggon blew up the other day "out West," and killed and wounded several people; and though the accidents in camp from firearms are not so numerous as they were, there are still enough to present a heavy casualty list.

Whilst the artillery were delighting the citizens, a much more important matter was taking place in an obscure little court-house—much more destructive to their freedom, happiness, and greatness than all the Confederate guns which can ever be ranged against them. A brave, upright, and honest judge, as in duty bound, issued a writ of *habeas corpus*, sued out by the friends of a minor, who, contrary to the laws of the United States, had been enlisted by an American general, and was detained by him in the ranks of his regiment. The officer refused to obey the writ, whereupon the judge issued an attachment against him, and the Federal brigadier came into court and pleaded that he took that course by order of the President. The court adjourned, to consider the steps it should take.

I have just seen a paragraph in the local paper, copied from a west country journal, headed "Good for Russell," which may explain the unusually favourable impression expressed by the women this morning. It is an account of the interview I had with the officer who came "to trade" for my horse, written by the latter to a Green Bay newspaper, in which, having duly censured my "John Bullism" in not receiving with the utmost courtesy a stranger, who walked into his room before breakfast on business unknown, he relates as a proof of honesty (in such a rare field as trading in horseflesh) that, though my groom had sought to put ten dollars in my pocket by a mild exaggeration of the amount paid for the animal, which was the price I said I would take, I would not have it.

October 9th.—A cold, gloomy day. I am laid up with the fever and ague, which visit the banks of the Potomac in autumn. It annoyed me the more because General M'Clellan is making a reconnaissance to-day towards Lewinsville, with 10,000 men. A gentleman from the War Department visited me to-day, and gave me scanty hopes of procuring any assistance from the authorities in taking the field. Civility costs nothing, and certainly if it did United States officials would require high salaries, but they often content themselves with fair words.

There are some things about our neighbours which we may never hope to understand. To-day, for instance, a respectable person, high in office, having been good enough to invite me to his house, added, "You shall see Mrs. A., sir. She is a very pretty and agreeable young lady, and will prove nice society for you," meaning his wife.

Mr. N. P. Willis was good enough to call on me, and in the course of conversation said, "I hear M'Clellan tells you everything. When you went away West I was very near going after you, as I suspected you heard something." Mr. Willis could have had no grounds for this remark, for very certainly it has no foundation in fact. Truth to tell, General M'Clellan seemed, the last time I saw him, a little alarmed by a paragraph in a New York paper, from the Washington correspondent, in which it was invidiously stated, "General M'Clellan, attended by Mr. Russell, correspondent of the London *Times*, visited the camps to-day. All passes to civilians and others were revoked." There was not the smallest ground for the statement on the day in question, but I am resolved not to contradict anything which is said about me, but the General could not well do so; and one of the favourite devices of the Washington correspondent to fill up his columns, is to write something about me, to state I have been refused passes, or have got them, or whatever else he likes to say.

Calling on the General the other night at his usual time of return, I was told by the orderly, who was closing the door, "The General's gone to bed tired, and can see no one. He sent the same message to the President, who came inquiring after him ten minutes ago."

This poor President! He is to be pitied; surrounded by such scenes, and trying with all his might to understand strategy, naval warfare, big guns, the movements of troops, military maps, reconnaissances, occupations, interior and exterior lines, and all the technical details of the art of slaying. He runs from one house to another, armed with plans, papers, reports, recommendations, sometimes good-humoured, never angry, occasionally dejected, and always a little fussy. The other night, as I was sitting in the parlour at headquarters, with an English friend who had come to see his old acquaintance the General, walked in a tall man with a navvy's cap, and an ill-made shooting suit, from the pockets of which protruded paper and bundles. "Well," said he to Brigadier Van Vliet, who rose to receive him, "is George in?"

"Yes, sir. He's come back, but is lying down, very much fatigued. I'll send up, sir, and inform him you wish to see him."

"Oh, no; I can wait. I think I'll take supper with him. Well, and what are you now,—I forget your name—are you a major, or a colonel, or a general?"

"Whatever you like to make me, sir."

Seeing that General M'Clellan would be occupied, I walked out with my friend, who asked me when I got into the street why I stood up when that tall fellow came into the room. "Because it was the President." "The President of what?" "Of the United States." "Oh! come, now you're humbugging me. Let me have another look at him." He came back more incredulous than ever, but when I assured him I was quite serious, he exclaimed, "I give up the United States after this."

But for all that, there have been many more courtly presidents who, in a similar crisis, would have displayed less capacity, honesty, and plain dealing than Abraham Lincoln.

October 10*th*.—I got hold of M'Clellan's report on the Crimean war, and made a few candid remarks on the performance, which does not evince any capacity beyond the reports of our itinerant artillery officers who are sent from Woolwich abroad for their country's good. I like the man, but I do not think he is equal to his occasion or his place. There is one little piece of policy which shows he is looking ahead—either to gain the good will of the army, or for some larger object. All his present purpose is to make himself known to the men personally, to familiarize them with his appearance, to gain the acquaintance of the officers; and with this object he spends nearly every day in the camps, riding out at nine o'clock, and not returning till long after nightfall, examining the various regiments as he goes along, and having incessant inspections and reviews. He is the first Republican general who could attempt to do all this without incurring censure and suspicion. Unfortunate M'Dowell could not inspect his small army without receiving a hint that he must not assume such airs, as they were more becoming a military despot than a simple lieutenant of the great democracy.

October 11*th*.—Mr. Mure, who has arrived here in wretched health from New Orleans, after a protracted and very unpleasant journey through country swarming with troops mixed with guerillas, tells me that I am more detested in New Orleans than I am in New York. This is ever the fate of the neutral, if the belligerents can get him between them. The Girondins and men of the *juste milieu* are ever fated to be ground to powder. The charges against me were disposed of by Mr. Mure, who says that what I wrote of in New Orleans was true, and has shown it to be so in his correspondence with the Governor, but, over and beyond that, I am disliked, because I do not praise the peculiar institution. He amused me by adding that the mayor of Jackson, with whom I sojourned, had published "a card," denying point-blank that he had ever breathed a word to indicate that the good citizens around him were not famous for the love of law, order, and life, and a scrupulous regard to personal liberty. I can easily fancy Jackson is not a place where a mayor suspected by the citizens would be exempted from difficulties now and then; and if this disclaimer does my friend any good, he is very heartily welcome to it and more. I have received several letters lately from the parents of minors, asking me to assist them in getting back their sons, who have enlisted illegally in the Federal army. My writ does not run any further than a Federal judge's.

October 12*th*.—The good people of New York and of the other Northern cities, excited by constant reports in the papers of magnificent reviews and unsurpassed military spectacles, begin to flock towards Washington in hundreds where formerly they came in tens. The woman-kind are particularly anxious to feast their eyes on our glorious Union army. It is natural enough that Americans should feel pride and take pleasure in the spectacle; but the love of economy, the hatred of military despotism, and the frugal virtues of republican government, long since placed aside by the exigencies of the Administration, promise to vanish for ever.

The feeling is well expressed in the remark of a gentleman to whom I was lamenting the civil war: "Well, for my part, I am glad of it. Why should you in Europe have all the fighting to yourselves? Why should we not have our bloody battles, and our big generals, and all the rest of it? This will stir up the spirits of our people, do us all a power of good, and end by proving to all of you in Europe, that we are just as good and first-rate in fighting as we are in ships, manufactures, and commerce."

But the wealthy classes are beginning to feel rather anxious about the disposal of their money: they are paying a large insurance on the Union, and they do not see that anything has been done to stop the leak or to prevent it foundering. Mr. Duncan has arrived; to-day I drove with him to Alexandria, and I think he has been made happy by what he saw, and has no doubt "the Union is all right." Nothing looks so irresistible as your bayonet till another is seen opposed to it.

October 13*th*.—Mr. Duncan, attended by myself and other Britishers, made an extensive excursion through the camps on horseback, and I led him from Arlington to Upton's House, up by Munson's Hill, to General Wadsworth's quarters, where we lunched on camp fare, and, from the observatory erected at the rear of the house in which he lives, had a fine view, this bright, cold, clear autumn day, of the wonderful expanse of undulating forest lands, streaked with rows of tents, which at last concentrated into vast white patches in the distance, towards Alexandria. The country is desolate, but the camps are flourishing, and that is enough to satisfy most patriots bent upon the subjugation of their enemies.

October 14*th*.—I was somewhat distraught, like a small Hercules twixt Vice and Virtue, or Garrick between Comedy and Tragedy, by my desire to tell Duncan the truth, and at the same time respect the feelings of a friend. There was a rabbledom of drunken men in uniforms under our window, who resisted the patrol clearing the streets, and one fellow drew his bayonet, and, with the support of some of the citizens, said that he would not allow any regular to put a finger on him. D— said he had witnessed scenes just as bad, and talked of lanes in garrison towns in England, and street rows between soldiers and civilians; and I did not venture to tell him the scene we witnessed was the sign of a radical vice in the system of the American army, which is, I believe, incurable in these large masses. Few soldiers would venture to draw their bayonets on a patrol. If they did, their punishment would be tolerably sure and swift, but for all I knew this man would be permitted to go on his way rejoicing. There is news of two Federal reverses to-day. A descent was made on Santa Rosa Island, and Mr. Billy Wilson's Zouaves were driven under the guns of Pickens, losing in the scurry of the night attack—as prisoner only I am glad to say —poor Major Vogdes, of inquiring memory. Rosecrans, who utterly ignores the advantages of Shaksperian spelling, has been defeated in the West; but D— is quite happy, and goes off to New York contented.

October 15th.—Sir James Ferguson and Mr. R. Bourke, who have been travelling in the South and have seen something of the Confederate government and armies, visited us this evening after dinner. They do not seem at all desirous of testing by comparison the relative efficiency of the two armies, which Sir James, at all events, is competent to do. They are impressed by the energy and animosity of the South, which no doubt will have their effect on England also; but it will be difficult to popularize a Slave Republic as a new allied power in England. Two of General M'Clellan's aides dropped in, and the meeting abstained from general politics.

October 16th.—Day follows day and resembles its predecessor. M'Clellan is still reviewing, and the North are still waiting for victories and paying money, and the orators are still wrangling over the best way of cooking the hares which they have not yet caught. I visited General M'Dowell to-day in his tent at Arlington, and found him in a state of divine calm with his wife and *parvus Iulus.* A public man in the United States is very much like a great firework—he commences with some small scintillations which attract the eye of the public, and then he blazes up and flares out in blue, purple, and orange fires, to the intense admiration of the multitude, and dying out suddenly is thought of no more, his place being taken by a fresh roman candle or catherine wheel which is thought to be far finer than those which have just dazzled the eyes of the fickle spectators. Human nature is thus severely taxed. The Cabinet of State is like the museum of some cruel naturalist, who seizes his specimens whilst they are alive, bottles them up, forbids them to make as much as a contortion, labelling them "My last President," "My latest Commander-in-chief," or "My defeated General," regarding the smallest signs of life very much as did the French *petit maitre* who rebuked the contortions and screams of the poor wretch who was broken on the wheel, as contrary to *bienséance.* I am glad that Sir James Ferguson and Mr. Bourke did not leave without making a tour of inspection through the Federal camp, which they did to-day.

October 17th.—Dies non.

October 18th.—To-day Lord Lyons drove out with Mr. Seward to inspect the Federal camps, which are now in such order as to be worthy of a visit. It is reported in all the papers that I am going to England, but I have not the smallest intention of giving my enemies here such a treat at present. As Monsieur de Beaumont of the French Legation said, "I presume you are going to remain in Washington for the rest of your life, because I see it stated in the New York journals that you are leaving us in a day or two."

October 19th.—Lord Lyons and Mr. Seward were driving and dining together yesterday *en ami.* To-day Mr. Seward is engaged demolishing Lord Lyons, or at all events the British Government, in a despatch, wherein he vindicates the proceedings of the United States Government in certain arrests of British subjects which had been complained of, and repudiates the doctrine that the United States Government can be bound by the opinion of the law officers of the Crown respecting the spirit and letter of the American constitution. This is published as a set-off to Mr. Seward's circular on the seacoast defences which created so much depression and alarm in the Northern States, where it was at the time considered as a warning that a foreign war was imminent, and which has since been generally condemned as feeble and injudicious.

October 20th.—I saw General M'Clellan to-day, who gave me to understand that some small movement might take place on the right. I rode up to the Chain Bridge and across it for some miles into Virginia, but all was quiet. The sergeant at the post on the south side of the bridge had some doubts of the genuineness of my pass, or rather of its bearer.

"I heard you were gone back to London, where I am coming to see you some fine day with the boys here."

"No, sergeant, I am not gone yet, but when will your visit take place?"

"Oh, as soon as we have finished with the gentlemen across there."

"Have you any notion when that will be?"

"Just as soon as they tell us to go on and prevent the blackguard Germans running away."

"But the Germans did not run away at Bull Run?"

"Faith, because they did not get a chance—sure they put them in the rear, away out of the fighting."

"And why do you not go on now?"

"Well, that's the question we are asking every day."

"And can any-one answer it?"

"Not one of us can tell; but my belief is if we had one of the old 50th among us at the head of affairs we would soon be at them. I belonged to the old regiment once, but I got off and took up with shoe-making again, and faith if I sted in it I might have been sergeant-major by this time, only they hated the poor Roman Catholics."

"And do you think, sergeant, you would get many of your countrymen who had served in the old army to fight the old familiar red jackets?"

"Well, sir, I tell you I hope my arm would rot before I would pull a trigger against the old 50th; but we would wear the red jacket too—we have as good a right to it as the others, and then it would be man against man, you know; but if I saw any of them cursed Germans interfering I'd soon let daylight into them." The hazy dreams of this poor man's mind would form an excellent article for a New York newspaper, which on matters relating to England are rarely so lucid and logical. Next day was devoted to writing and heavy rain, through both of which, notwithstanding, I was assailed by many visitors and some scurrilous letters, and in the evening there was a Washington gathering of Englishry, Irishry, Scotchry, Yankees, and Canadians.

October 22nd.—Rain falling in torrents. As I write, in come reports of a battle last night, some forty miles up the river, which by signs and tokens I am led to believe was unfavourable to the Federals. They crossed the river intending to move upon Leesburg—were attacked by overwhelming forces and repulsed, but maintained themselves on the right bank till General Banks reinforced them and enabled them to hold their own. M'Clellan has gone or is going at once to the scene of action. It was three o'clock before I heard the news, the road and country were alike unknown, nor had I friend or acquaintance in the army of the Upper Potomac. My horse was brought round, however, and in company with Mr. Anderson, I rode out of Washington along the river till the falling evening warned us to retrace our steps, and we returned in pelting rain as we set out, and in pitchy darkness, without meeting any messenger or person with news from the battle-field. Late at night the White House was placed in deep grief by the intelligence that in addition to other losses, Brigadier and Senator Baker of California was killed. The President was inconsolable, and walked up and down his room for hours lamenting the loss of his friend. Mrs. Lincoln's grief was equally poignant. Before bedtime I told the German landlord to tell my servant I wanted my horse round at seven o'clock.

October 23rd.—Up at six, waiting for my horse and man. At eight walked down to stables. No one there. At nine became very angry—sent messengers in all directions. At ten was nearly furious, when, at the last stroke of the clock, James, with his inexpressive countenance, perfectly calm nevertheless, and betraying no symptom of solicitude, appeared at the door leading my charger. "And may I ask you where you have been till this time?" "Wasn't I dressing the horse, taking him out to water, and exercising him." "Good heavens! did I not tell you to be here at seven o'clock?" "No, sir; Carl told me you wanted me at ten o'clock, and here I am." "Carl, did I not tell you to ask James to be round here at seven o'clock?" "Not zeven clock, sere, but zehn clock. I tell him, you come at zehn clock." Thus at one blow was I stricken down by Gaul and Teuton, each of whom retired with the air of a man who had baffled an intended indignity, and had achieved a triumph over a wrong-doer.

The roads were in a frightful state outside Washington—literally nothing but canals, in which earth and water were mixed together for depths varying from six inches to three feet above the surface; but late as it was I pushed on, and had got as far as the turn of the road to Rockville, near the great falls, some twelve miles beyond Washington, when I met an officer with a couple of orderlies, hurrying back from General Banks's head-quarters, who told me the whole affair was over, and that I could not possibly get to the scene of action on one horse till next morning, even supposing that I pressed on all through the night, the roads being utterly villanous, and the country at night as black as ink; and so I returned to Washington, and was stopped by citizens, who seeing the streaming horse and splashed rider, imagined he was reeking from the fray. "As you were not there," says one, "I'll tell you what I know to be the case. Stone and Baker are killed; Banks and all the other generals are prisoners; the Rhode Island and two other batteries are taken, and 5000 Yankees have been sent to H— to help old John Brown to roast niggers."

October 24th.—The heaviest blow which has yet been inflicted on the administration of justice in the United States, and that is saying a good deal at present, has been given to it in Washington. The judge of whom I wrote a few days ago in the *habeas corpus* case, has been placed under military arrest and surveillance by the Provost-Marshal of the city, a very fit man for such work, one Colonel Andrew Porter. The Provost-Marshal imprisoned the attorney who served the writ, and then sent a guard to Mr. Merrick's house, who thereupon sent a minute to his brother judges the day before yesterday stating the circumstances, in order to show why he did not appear in his place on the bench. The Chief Judge Dunlop and Judge Morsell thereupon issued their writ to Andrew Porter greeting, to show cause why an attachment for contempt should not be issued against him for his treatment of Judge Merrick. As the sharp tongues of women are very troublesome, the United States officers have quite little harems of captives, and Mrs. Merrick has just been added to the number. She is a Wickliffe of Kentucky, and has a right to martyrdom. The inconsistencies of the Northern people multiply *ad infinitum* as they go on. Thus at Hatteras they enter into terms of capitulation with officers signing themselves of the Confederate States Army and Confederate States Navy; elsewhere they exchange prisoners; at New York they are going through the farce of trying the crew of a C. S. privateer, as pirates engaged in robbing on the high seas, on "the authority of a pretended letter of marque from one Jefferson Davis." One Jeff Davis is certainly quite enough for them at present.

Colonel and Senator Baker was honoured by a ceremonial which was intended to be a public funeral, rather out of compliment to Mr. Lincoln's feelings, perhaps, than to any great attachment for the man himself, who fell gallantly fighting near Leesburg. There is need for a republic to contain some elements of an aristocracy if it would make that display of pomp and ceremony which a public funeral should have to produce effect. At all events there should be some principle of reverence in the heads and hearts of the people, to make up for other deficiencies in it as a show or a ceremony. The procession down Pennsylvania Avenue was a tawdry, shabby string of hack carriages, men in light coats and white hats following the hearse, and three regiments of foot soldiers, of which one was simply an uncleanly, unwholesome-looking rabble. The President, in his carriage, and many of the ministers and senators, attended also, and passed through unsympathetic lines of people on the kerbstones, not one of whom raised his hat to the bier as it passed, or to the President, except a couple of Englishmen and myself who stood in the crowd, and that proceeding on our part gave rise to a variety of remarks among the bystanders. But as the band turned into Pennsylvania Avenue, playing something like the *minuet de la cour* in Don Giovanni, two officers in uniform came riding up in the contrary direction; they were smoking cigars; one of them let his fall on the ground, the other smoked lustily as the hearse passed, and reining up his horse, continued to puff his weed under the nose of President, ministers, and senators, with the air of a man who was doing a very soldierly correct sort of thing.

Whether the President is angry as well as grieved at the loss of his favourite or not, I cannot affirm, but he is assuredly doing that terrible thing which is called putting his foot down on the judges; and he has instructed Andrew Porter not to mind the writ issued yesterday, and has further instructed the United States Marshal, who has the writ in his hands to serve on the said Andrew, to return it to the court with the information that Abraham Lincoln has suspended the writ of *habeas corpus* in cases relating to the military.

October 26th.—More reviews. To-day rather a pretty sight—12 regiments, 16 guns, and a few squads of men with swords and pistols on horseback, called cavalry, comprising Fitz-John Porter's division. M'Clellan seemed to my eyes crestfallen and moody to-day. Bright eyes looked on him; he is getting up something like a staff, among which are the young French princes, under the tutelage of their uncle, the Prince of Joinville. Whilst M'Clellan is reviewing, our Romans in Washington are shivering; for the blockade of the Potomac by the Confederate batteries stops the fuel boats. Little care these enthusiastic young American patriots in crinoline, who have come to see M'Clellan and the soldiers, what a cord of wood costs. The lower orders are very angry about it, however. The nuisance and disorder arising from soldiers, drunk and sober, riding full gallop down the streets, and as fast as they can round the corners, has been stopped, by placing mounted sentries at the principal points in all the thoroughfares. The "officers" were worse than the men; the papers this week contain the account of two accidents, in one of which a colonel, in another a major, was killed by falls from horseback, in furious riding in the city.

Forgetting all about this fact, and spurring home pretty fast along an unfrequented road, leading from the ferry at Georgetown into the city, I was nearly spitted by a "dragoon," who rode at me from under cover of a house, and shouted "stop" just as his sabre was within a foot of my head. Fortunately his horse, being aware that if it ran against mine it might be injured, shied, and over went dragoon, sabre and all, and off went his horse, but as the trooper was able to run after it, I presume he was not the worse; and I went on my way rejoicing.

M'Clellan has fallen very much in my opinion since the Leesburg disaster. He went to the spot, and with a little—nay, the least—promptitude and ability could have turned the check into a successful advance, in the blaze of which the earlier repulse would have been forgotten. It is whispered that General Stone, who ordered the movement, is guilty of treason—a common crime of unlucky generals—at all events he is to be displaced, and will be put under surveillance. The orders he gave are certainly very strange.

The official right to fib, I presume, is very much the same all over the world, but still there is more dash about it in the States, I think, than elsewhere. "Blockade of the Potomac!" exclaims an official of the Navy Department. "What are you talking of? The Department has just heard that a few Confederates have been practising with a few light field-pieces from the banks, and has issued orders to prevent it in the future." "Defeat at Leesburg!" cries little K——, of M'Clellan's staff, "nothing of the kind. We drove the Confederates at all points, retained our position on the right bank, and only left it when we pleased, having whipped the enemy so severely they never showed since." "Any news, Mr. Cash, in the Treasury to-day?" "Nothing, sir, except that Mr. Chase is highly pleased with everything; he's only afraid of having too much money, and being troubled with his balances." "The State Department all right, Mr. Protocol?" "My dear sir! delightful! with everybody, best terms. Mr. Seward and the Count are managing delightfully; most friendly assurances; Guatemala particularly; yes, and France too. Yes, I may say France too; not the smallest difficulty at Honduras; altogether, with the assurances of support we are getting, the Minister thinks the whole affair will be settled in thirty days; no joking, I assure you; thirty days this time positively. Say for exactness on or about December 5th." The canvas-backs are coming in, and I am off for a day or two to escape reviews and abuse, and to see something of the famous wild-fowl shooting on the Chesapeake.

October 27th.—After church, I took a long walk round by the commissariat waggons, where there is, I think, as much dirt, bad language, cruelty to animals, and waste of public money, as can be conceived. Let me at once declare my opinion that the Americans, generally, are exceedingly kind to their cattle; but there is a hybrid race of ruffianly waggoners here, subject to no law or discipline, and the barbarous treatment inflicted on the transport animals is too bad even for the most unruly of mules. I mentioned the circumstance to General M'Dowell, who told me that by the laws of the United States there was no power to enlist a man for commissariat or transport duty.

October 28th.—Telegraphed to my friend at Baltimore that I was ready for the ducks. The Legation going to Mr. Kortwright's marriage at Philadelphia. Started with Lamy at 6 o'clock for Baltimore; to Gilmore House; thence to club. Every person present said that in my letter on Maryland I had understated the question, as far as Southern sentiments were concerned. In the club, for example, there are not six Union men at the outside. General Dix has fortified Federal Hill very efficiently, and the heights over Fort McHenry are bristling with cannons, and display formidable earthworks; it seems to be admitted that, but for the action of the Washington Government, the Legislature would pass an ordinance of Secession. Gilmore House—old-fashioned, good bed-rooms. Scarcely had I arrived in the passage, than a man ran off with a paragraph to the papers that Dr. Russell had come for the purpose of duck-shooting; and, hearing that I was going with Taylor, put in that I was going to Taylor's Ducking Shore. It appears that there are considerable numbers of these duck clubs in the neighbourhood of Baltimore. The canvas-back ducks have come in, but they will not be in perfection until the 10th of November; their peculiar flavour is derived from a water-plant called wild celery. This lies at the depth of several feet, sometimes nine or ten, and the birds dive for it.

October 29th.—At ten started for the shooting ground, Carroll's Island; my companion, Mr. Pennington, drove me in a light trap, and Mr.

Taylor and Lamy came with Mr. Tucker Carroll,* along with guns, &c. Passed out towards the sea, a long height commanding a fine view of the river; near this was fought the battle with the English, at which the "Baltimore defenders" admit they ran away. Mr. Pennington's father says he can answer for the speed of himself and his companions, but still the battle was thought to be glorious. Along the posting road to Philadelphia, passed the Blue Ball Tavern; on all sides except the left, great wooded lagoons visible, swarming with ducks; boats are forbidden to fire upon the birds, which are allured by wooden decoys. Crossed the Philadelphia Railway three times; land poor, covered with undergrowths and small trees, given up to Dutch and Irish and free niggers. Reached the duck-club-house in two hours and a half; substantial farmhouse, with out-offices, on a strip of land surrounded by water; Gunpowder River, Saltpetre River, facing Chesapeake; on either side lakes and tidal water; the owner, Slater, an Irishman, reputed very rich, self-made. Dinner at one o'clock; any number of canvas-back ducks, plentiful joints; drink whisky; company, Swan, Howard, Duval, Morris, and others, also extraordinary specimen named Smith, believed never to wash except in rain or by accidental sousing in the river. Went out for afternoon shooting; birds wide and high; killed seventeen; back to supper at dusk. M'Donald and a guitar came over; had a negro dance; and so to bed about twelve. Lamy got single bed; I turned in with Taylor, as single beds are not permitted when the house is full.

October 30*th*.—A light, a grim man, and a voice in the room at 4 a.m. awaken me; I am up first; breakfast; more duck, eggs, meat, mighty cakes, milk; to the gun-house, already hung with ducks, and then tramp to the "blinds" with Smith, who talked of the Ingines and wild sports in far Minnesota. As morning breaks, very red and lovely, dark visions and long streaky clouds appear, skimming along from bay or river. The men in the blinds, which are square enclosures of reeds about 4½ feet high, call out "Bay," "River," according to the direction from which the ducks are coming. Down we go in blinds; they come; puffs of smoke, a bang, a volley; one bird falls with flop; another by degrees drops, and at last smites the sea; there are five down; in go the dogs. "Who shot that?" "I did." "Who killed this?" "That's Tucker's!" "A good shot." "I don't know how I missed mine." Same thing again. The ducks fly prodigious heights—out of all range one would think. It is exciting when the cloud does rise at first. Day voted very bad. Thence I move homeward; talk with Mr. Slater till the trap is ready; and at twelve or so, drive over to Mr. M'Donald; find Lamy and Swan there; miserable shed of two-roomed shanty in a marsh; rough deal presses; white-washed walls; fiddler in attendance; dinner of ducks and steak; whisky, and thence proceed to a blind or marsh, amid wooden decoys; but there is no use; no birds; high tide flooding everything; examined M'Donald's stud; knocked to pieces trotting on hard ground. Rowed back to house with Mr. Pennington, and returned to the mansion; all the party had but poor sport; but every one had killed something. Drew lots for bed, and won this time; Lamy, however, would not sleep double, and reposed on a hard sofa in the parlour; indications favourable for ducks. It was curious, in the early morning, to hear the incessant booming of duck-guns, along all the creeks and coves of the indented bays and salt-water marshes; and one could tell when they were fired at decoys, or were directed against birds in the air; heard a salute fired at Baltimore very distinctly. Lamy and Mr. M'Donald met in their voyage up the Nile, to kill *ennui* and spend money.

October 31*st*.—No, no, Mr. Smith; it ain't of no use. At four a.m. we were invited, as usual, to rise, but Taylor and I reasoned from under our respective quilts, that it would be quite as good shooting if we got up at six, and I acted in accordance with that view. Breakfasted as the sun was shining above the tree-tops, and to my blind —found there was no shooting at all—got one shot only, and killed a splendid canvas-back—on returning to home, found nearly all the party on the move—140 ducks hanging round the house, the reward of our toils, and of these I received egregious share. Drove back with Pennington, very sleepy, followed by Mr. Taylor and Lamy. I would have stayed longer if sport were better. Birds don't fly when the wind is in certain points, but lie out in great "ricks," as they are called, blackening the waters, drifting in the wind, or with wings covering their heads—poor defenceless things! The red-head waits alongside the canvas-back till he comes up from the depths with mouth or bill full of parsley and wild celery, when he makes at him and forces him to disgorge. At Baltimore at 1.30—dined—Lamy resolved to stay—bade good-bye to Swan and Morris. The man at first would not take my ducks and boots to register or check them—twenty-five cents did it. I arrived at Washington late, because of detention of train by enormous transport; labelled and sent out game to the houses till James's fingers ached again. Nothing doing, except that General Scott has at last sent in resignation. M'Clellan is now indeed master of the situation. And so to bed, rather tired.

CHAPTER LVIII.

General Scott's resignation—Mrs. A. Lincoln—Unofficial mission to Europe—Uneasy feeling with regard to France—Ball given by the United States cavalry—The United States army—Success at Beaufort—Arrests—Dinner at Mr. Seward's—News of Captain Wilkes and the Trent—Messrs. Mason and Slidell—Discussion as to Wilkes—Prince de Joinville—The American Press on the Trent affair—Absence of thieves in Washington—"Thanksgiving Day"—Success thus far in favour of the North.

November 1*st*.—Again stagnation; not the smallest intention of moving; General Scott's resignation, of which I was aware long ago, is publicly known, and he is about to go to Europe, and end his days probably in France. M'Clellan takes his place, minus the large salary. Riding back from camp, where I had some trouble with a drunken soldier, my horse came down in a dark hole, and threw me heavily, so that my hat was crushed in on my head, and my right thumb sprained, but I managed to get up and ride home;

* Since killed in action fighting for the South at Antietam.

for the brute had fallen right on his own head, cut a piece out of his forehead between the eyes, and was stunned too much to run away. I found letters waiting from Mr. Seward and others, thanking me for the game, if canvas-backs come under the title.

November 2nd.—A tremendous gale of wind and rain blew all day, and caused much uneasiness, at the Navy Department and elsewhere, for the safety of the Burnside expedition. The Secessionists are delighted, and those who can, say "Afflavit Deus et hostes dissipantur." There is a project to send secret non-official commissioners to Europe, to counteract the machinations of the Confederates. Mr. Everett, Mr. R. Kennedy, Bishop Hughes, and Bishop M'Ilwaine are designated for the office; much is expected from the expedition, not only at home but abroad.

November 3rd.—For some reason or another, a certain set of papers have lately taken to flatter Mrs. Lincoln in the most noisome manner, whilst others deal in dark insinuations against her loyalty, Union principles, and honesty. The poor lady is loyal as steel to her family and to Lincoln the first; but she is accessible to the influence of flattery, and has permitted her society to be infested by men who would not be received in any respectable private house in New York. The gentleman who furnishes fashionable paragraphs for the Washington paper has some charming little pieces of gossip about "the first Lady in the Land" this week; he is doubtless the same who, some weeks back, chronicled the details of a raid on the pigs in the streets by the police, and who concluded thus: "We cannot but congratulate Officer Smith on the very gentlemanly manner in which he performed his disagreeable but arduous duties; nor did it escape our notice, that Officer Washington Jones was likewise active and energetic in the discharge of his functions."

The ladies in Washington delight to hear or to invent small scandals connected with the White House; thus it is reported that the Scotch gardener left by Mr. Buchanan has been made a lieutenant in the United States Army, and has been specially detached to do duty at the White House, where he superintends the cooking. Another person connected with the establishment was made Commissioner of Public Buildings, but was dismissed because he would not put down the expense of a certain state dinner to the public account, and charge it under the head of "Improvement to the Grounds." But many more better tales than these go round, and it is not surprising if a woman is now and then put under close arrest, or sent off to Fort M'Henry for too much *esprit* and inventiveness.

November 4th.—General Fremont will certainly be recalled. There is not the smallest incident to note.

November 5th.—Small banquets, very simple and tolerably social, are the order of the day as winter closes around us; the country has become too deep in mud for pleasant excursions, and at times the weather is raw and cold. General M'Dowell, who dined with us to-day, maintains there will be no difficulty in advancing during bad weather, because the men are so expert in felling trees, they can make corduroy roads wherever they like. I own the arguments surprised but did not convince me, and I think the General will find out his mistake when the time comes. Mr. Everett, whom I had expected, was summoned away by the unexpected intelligence of his son's death, so I missed the opportunity of seeing one whom I much desired to have met, as the great Apostle of Washington worship, in addition to his claims to higher distinction. He has admitted that the only bond which can hold the Union together is the common belief in the greatness of the departed general.

November 6th.—Instead of Mr. Everett and Mr. Johnson, Mr. Thurlow Weed and Bishop Hughes will pay a visit to Europe in the Federal interests. Notwithstanding the adulation of everything French, from the Emperor down to a Zouave's gaiter, in the New York press there is an uneasy feeling respecting the intentions of France, founded on the notion that the Emperor is not very friendly to the Federalists, and would be little disposed to expose his subjects to privation and suffering from the scarcity of cotton and tobacco if, by intervention, he could avert such misfortunes. The inactivity of M'Clellan, which is not understood by the people, has created an under-current of unpopularity, to which his enemies are giving every possible strength, and some people are beginning to think the youthful Napoleon is only a Brummagem Bonaparte.

November 7th.—After such bad weather, the Indian summer, *l'été de St. Martin*, is coming gradually, lighting up the ruins of the autumn's foliage still clinging to the trees, giving us pure, bright, warm days, and sunsets of extraordinary loveliness. Drove out to Bladensburgh with Captain Haworth, and discovered that my waggon was intended to go on to Richmond and never to turn back or round, for no roads in this part of the country are wide enough for the purpose. Dined at the Legation, and in the evening went to a grand ball, given by the 6th United States Cavalry in the Poor House near their camp, about two miles outside the city.

The ball took place in a series of small whitewashed rooms off long passages and corridors; many supper tables were spread; whisky, champagne, hot terrapin soup, and many luxuries graced the board; and although but two or three couple could dance in each room at a time, by judicious arrangement of the music several rooms were served at once. The Duke of Chartres, in the uniform of a United States Captain of Staff, was among the guests, and had to share the ordeal to which strangers were exposed by the hospitable entertainers, of drinking with them all. Some called him "Chatters"—others, "Captain Chatters;" but these were of the outside polloi, who cannot be kept out on such occasions, and who shake hands and are familiar with everybody.

The Duke took it all exceedingly well, and laughed with the loudest in the company. Altogether the ball was a great success—somewhat marred indeed in my own case by the bad taste of one of the officers of the regiment which had invited me, in adopting an offensive manner when about to be introduced to me by one of his brother officers. Colonel Emory, the officer in command of the regiment, interfered, and, finding that Captain A—— was not sober, ordered him to retire. Another small *contretemps* was caused by the master of the Work House, who had been indulging at least as freely as the captain, and at last began to fancy that the paupers had broken loose and were dancing about after hours below stairs. In vain he was led away and incarcerated in one room after another; his intimate knowledge of the architectural difficulties of the building enabled him to set all precautions at defiance, and he might be seen at intervals flying along the passages towards the music pursued by the officers, until he was finally secured in a dungeon without a window, and with a bolted and locked door between him and the ball-rooms.

November 8th.—Colonel Emory made us laugh this morning by an account of our Amphytrion of the night before, who came to him with a very red eye and curious expression of face to congratulate the regiment on the success of the ball. "The most beautiful thing of all was," said he,—"Colonel, I did not see one gentleman or lady who had taken too much liquor; there was not a drunken man in the whole company." I consulted my friends at the Legation with respect to our inebriated officer, on whose behalf Colonel Emory rendered his own apologies; but they were of opinion I had done all that was right and becoming in the matter, and that I must take no more notice of it.

November 9th.—Colonel Wilmot, R. A., who has come down from Canada to see the army, spent the day with Captain Dahlgren at the Navy Yard, and returned with impressions favourable to the system. He agrees with Dahlgren, who is dead against breech-loading, but admits Armstrong has done the most that can be effected with the system. Colonel Wilmot avers the English press are responsible for the Armstrong guns. He has been much struck by the excellence of the great iron-works he has visited in the States, particularly that of Mr. Sellers, in Philadelphia.

November 10th.—Visiting Mr. Mure the other day, who was still an invalid at Washington, I met a gentleman named Maury, who had come to Washington to see after a portmanteau which had been taken from him on the Canadian frontier by the police. He was told to go to the State Department and claim his property, and on arriving there was arrested and confined with a number of prisoners, my horse-dealing friend, Sammy Wroe, among them. We walked down to inquire how he was; the soldier who was on duty gave a flourishing account of him—he had plenty of whiskey and food, and, said the man, "I quite feel for Maury, because he does business in my State." These State influences must be overcome, or no Union will ever hold together.

Sir James Ferguson and Mr. Bourke were rather shocked when Mr. Seward opened the letters from persons in the South to friends in Europe, of which they had taken charge, and cut some passages out with a scissors; but a Minister who combines the functions of Chief-of-Police with those of Secretary of State must do such things now and then.

November 11th.—The United States have now, according to the returns, 600,000 infantry, 600 pieces of artillery, 61,000 cavalry in the field, and yet they are not only unable to crush the Confederates, but they cannot conquer the Secession ladies in their capital. The Southern people here trust in a break-down in the North before the screw can be turned to the utmost; and assert that the South does not want corn, wheat, leather, or food. Georgia makes cloth enough for all—the only deficiency will be in metal and *materiel* of war. When the North comes to discuss the question whether the war is to be against slavery or for the Union, leaving slavery to take care of itself, they think a split will be inevitable. Then the pressure of taxes will force on a solution, for the State taxes already amount to 2 to 3 per cent., and the people will not bear the addition. The North has set out with the principle of paying for everything, the South with the principle of paying for nothing; but this will be reversed in time. All the diplomatists, with one exception, are of opinion the Union is broken for ever, and the independence of the South virtually established.

November 12th.—An irruption of dirty little boys in the streets shouting out, "Glorious Union victory! Charleston taken!" The story is that Burnside has landed and reduced the forts defending Port Royal. I met Mr. Fox, Assistant-Secretary to the Navy, and Mr. Hay, Secretary to Mr. Lincoln, in the Avenue. The former showed me Burnside's despatches from Beaufort, announcing reduction of the Confederate batteries by the ships and the establishment of the Federals on the skirts of Port Royal. Dined at Lord Lyons', where were Mr. Chase, Major Palmer, U.S.E., and his wife, Colonel and Mrs. Emory, Professor Henry and his daughter, Mr. Kennedy and his daughter, Colonel Wilmot and the Englishry of Washington. I had a long conversation with Mr. Chase, who is still sanguine that the war must speedily terminate. The success at Beaufort has made him radiant, and he told me that the Federal General Nelson *—who is no other than the enormous blustering, boasting lieutenant in the navy whom I met at Washington on my first arrival—has gained an immense victory in Kentucky, killing and capturing a whole army and its generals.

A strong Government will be the end of the struggle, but before they come to it there must be a complete change of administration and internal economy. Indeed, the Secretary of the Treasury candidly admitted that the expenses of the war were enormous, and could not go on at the present rate very long. The men are paid too highly; every one is paid too much. The scale is adapted to a small army not very popular, in a country where labour is very well paid, and competition is necessary to obtain recruits at all. He has never disguised his belief the South might have been left to go at first, with a certainty of their return to the Union.

November 13th.—Mr. Charles Green, who was my host at Savannah, and Mr. Low, of the same city, have been arrested and sent to Fort Warren. Dining with Mr. Seward, I heard accidentally that Mrs. Low had also been arrested, but was now liberated. The sentiment of dislike towards England is increasing, because English subjects have assisted the South by smuggling and running the blockade. "It is strange," said Mr. Seward the other day, "that this great free and civilized Union should be supported by Germans, coming here semi-civilized or half-savage, who plunder and destroy as if they were living in the days of Agricola, whilst the English are the great smugglers who support our enemies in

* Since shot dead by the Federal General Jeff. C. Davis in a quarrel at Nashville.

their rebellion." I reminded him that the United States flag had covered the smugglers who carried guns and *matériel* of war to Russia, although they were at peace with France and England. "Yes, but then," said he, "that was a legitimate contest between great established powers, and I admit, though I lament the fact, that the public sympathy in this country ran with Russia during that war." The British public have a right to their sympathies too, and the Government can scarcely help it if private individuals aid the South on their own responsibility. In future, British subjects will be indicted instead of being sent to Fort La Fayette. Mr. Seward feels keenly the attacks in the *New York Tribune* on him for arbitrary arrests, and representations have been made to Mr. Greeley privately on the subject; nor is he indifferent to similar English criticisms.

General M'Dowell asserts there is no nation in the world whose censure or praise the people of the United States care about except England, and with respect to her there is a morbid sensitiveness which can neither be explained nor justified.

It is admitted, indeed, by Americans whose opinions are valuable, that the popular feeling was in favour of Russia during the Crimean war. Mr. Raymond attributes the circumstance to the influence of the large Irish element; but I am inclined to believe it is partly due at least to the feeling of rivalry and dislike to Great Britain, in which the mass of the American people are trained by their early education, and also in some measure to the notion that Russia was unequally matched in the contest.

November 14th.—Rode to cavalry camp, and sat in front of Colonel Emory's tent with General Stoneman, who is chief of the cavalry, and Captain Pleasanton; heard interesting anecdotes of the wild life on the frontiers, and of bushranging in California, of lassoing bulls and wild horses and buffaloes, and encounters with grizly bears—interrupted by a one-armed man, who came to the Colonel for "leave to take away George." He spoke of his brother who had died in camp, and for whose body he had come, metallic coffin and all, to carry it back to his parents in Pennsylvania.

I dined with Mr. Seward—Mr. Raymond, of New York, and two or three gentlemen, being the only guests. Mr. Lincoln came in whilst we were playing a rubber, and told some excellent West-country stories. "Here, Mr. President, we have got the two *Times*—of New York and of London—if they would only do what is right and what we want, all will go well." "Yes," said Mr. Lincoln, "if the bad Times would go where we want them, good Times would be sure to follow." Talking over Bull's Run, Mr. Seward remarked "that civilians sometimes displayed more courage than soldiers, but perhaps the courage was unprofessional. When we were cut off from Baltimore, and the United States troops at Annapolis were separated by a country swarming with malcontents, not a soldier could be found to undertake the journey and communicate with them. At last a civilian"—(I think he mentioned the name of Mr. Cassius Clay)—"volunteered, and executed the business. So, after Bull's Run, there was only one officer, General Sherman, who was doing anything to get the troops into order when the President and myself drove over to see what we could do on that terrible Tuesday evening." Mr. Teakle Wallis and others, after the Baltimore business, told him the people would carry his head on their pikes; and so he went to Auburn to see how matters stood, and a few words from his old friends there made him feel his head was quite right on his shoulders.

November 15th.—Horse-dealers are the same all the world over. To-day comes one with a beast for which he asked £50. "There was a Government agent looking after this horse for one of them French princes, I believe, just as I was talking to the Kentuck chap that had him. 'John,' says he, 'that's the best-looking horse I've seen in Washington this many a day.' 'Yes,' says I, 'and you need not look at him any more.' 'Why?' says he. 'Because,' says I, 'it's one that I want for Lord John Russell, of the London *Times*,' says I, 'and if ever there was a man suited for a horse, or a horse that was suited for a man, they're the pair, and I'll give every cent I can raise to buy my friend, Lord Russell, that horse.'" I could not do less than purchase, at a small reduction, a very good animal thus recommended.

November 16th.—A cold, raw day. As I was writing, a small friend of mine, who appears like a stormy petrel in moments of great storm, fluttered into my room, and having chirped out something about a "Jolly row"—"Seizure of Mason and Slidell"—"British flag insulted," and the like, vanished. Somewhat later, going down 17th Street, I met the French Minister, M. Mercier, wrapped in his cloak, coming from the British Legation. "Vous avez entendu quelqu' chose de nouveau?" "Mais non, excellence." And, then, indeed, I learned there was no doubt about the fact that Captain Wilkes, of the U. S. steamer San Jacinto, had forcibly boarded the Trent, British mail steamer, off the Bahamas, and had taken Messrs. Mason, Slidell, Eustis, and M'Clernand from on board by armed force, in défiance of the protests of the captain and naval officer in charge of the mails. This was indeed grave intelligence, and the French Minister considered the act a flagrant outrage, which could not for a moment be justified.

I went to the Legation, and found the young diplomatists in the "Chancellerie" as demure and innocent as if nothing had happened, though perhaps they were a trifle more lively than usual. An hour later, and the whole affair was published in full in the evening papers. Extraordinary exultation prevailed in the hotels and bar-rooms. The State Department has made of course no communication respecting the matter. All the English are satisfied that Mason and his friends must be put on board an English mail packet from the San Jacinto under a salute.

An officer of the United States navy—whose name I shall not mention here—came in to see the buccaneers, as the knot of English bachelors of Washington are termed, and talk over the matter. "Of course," he said, "we shall apologize and give up poor Wilkes to vengeance by dismissing him, but under no circumstance shall we ever give up Mason and Slidell. No, sir; not a man dare propose such a humiliation to our flag." He says that Wilkes acted on his own responsibility, and that the San Jacinto was coming home from the African station when she encountered the Trent. Wilkes knew the rebel emissaries were on board, and thought he would cut a dash and get up a little sensation, being a bold and daring sort of a fellow with a quarrelsome disposition and a great love of notoriety, but an excellent officer.

November 17th.—For my sins I went to see a dress parade of the 6th Regular Cavalry early this morning, and underwent a small purgatory from the cold, on a bare plain, whilst the men and officers, with red cheeks and blue noses, mounted on horses with staring coats, marched, trotted, and cantered past. The papers contain joyous articles on the Trent affair, and some have got up an immense amount of learning at a short notice; but I am glad to say we had no discussion in camp. There is scarcely more than one opinion among thinking people in Washington respecting the legality of the act, and the course Great Britain must pursue. All the Foreign Ministers, without exception, have called on Lord Lyons—Russia, France, Italy, Prussia, Denmark. All are of accord. I am not sure whether the important diplomatist who represents the mighty interests of the Hanse Towns has not condescended to admit England has right on her side.

November 18th.—There is a storm of exultation sweeping over the land. Wilkes is the hero of the hour. I saw Mr. F. Seward at the State Department at ten o'clock; but as at the British Legation the orders are not to speak of the transaction, so at the State Department a judicious reticence is equally observed. The lawyers are busy furnishing arguments to the newspapers. The officers who held their tongues at first, astonished at the audacity of the act, are delighted to find any arguments in its favour.

I called at General M'Clellan's new head-quarters to get a pass, and on my way met the Duke of Chartres, who shook his young head very gravely, and regarded the occurrence with sorrow and apprehension. M'Clellan, I understand, advised the immediate surrender of the prisoners; but the authorities, supported by the sudden outburst of public approval, refused to take that step. I saw Lord Lyons, who appeared very much impressed by the magnitude of the crisis. Thence I visited the Navy Department, where Captain Dahlgren and Lieutenant Wise discussed the affair. The former, usually so calm, has too much sense not to perceive the course England must take, and as an American officer naturally feels regret at what appears to be the humiliation of his flag; but he speaks with passion, and vows that if England avails herself of the temporary weakness of the United States to get back the rebel commissioners by threats of force, every American should make his sons swear eternal hostility to Great Britain. Having done wrong, stick to it! Thus men's anger blinds them, and thus come wars.

It is obvious that no Power could permit political offenders sailing as passengers in a mail-boat under its flag, from one neutral port to another, to be taken by a belligerent, though the recognition of such a right would be, perhaps, more advantageous to England than to any other Power. But, notwithstanding these discussions, our naval friends dined and spent the evening with us, in company with some other officers.

I paid my respects to the Prince of Joinville, with whom I had a long and interesting conversation, in the course of which he gave me to understand he thought the seizure an untoward and unhappy event, which could not be justified on any grounds whatever, and that he had so expressed himself in the highest quarters. There are, comparatively, many English here at present; Mr. Chaplin, Sir F. Johnstone, Mr. Weldon, Mr. Browne, and others, and it may be readily imagined this affair creates deep feeling and much discussion.

November 19th.—I rarely sat down to write under a sense of greater responsibility, for it is just possible my letter may contain the first account of the seizure of the Southern Commissioners which will reach England; and, having heard all opinions and looked at authorities, as far as I could, it appears to me that the conduct of the American officer, now sustained by his Government, is without excuse. I dined at Mr. Corcoran's, where the Ministers of Prussia, Brazil, and Chili, and the Secretary of the French Legation, were present; and, although we did not talk politics, enough was said to show there was no dissent from the opinion expressed by intelligent and uninterested foreigners.

November 20th.—To-day a grand review, the most remarkable feature of which was the able disposition made by General M'Dowell to march seventy infantry regiments, seventeen batteries, and seven cavalry regiments, into a very contracted space, from the adjoining camps. Of the display itself I wrote a long account, which is not worth repeating here. Among the 55,000 men present there were at least 20,000 Germans and 12,000 Irish.

November 22nd.—All the American papers have agreed that the Trent business is quite according to law, custom, and international comity, and that England can do nothing. They cry out so loudly in this one key there is reason to suspect they have some inward doubts. General M'Clellan invited all the world, including myself, to see a performance given by Hermann, the conjuror, at his quarters, which will be aggravating news to the bloody-minded, serious people in New England.

Day after day passes on, and finds our Micawbers in Washington waiting for something to turn up. The Trent affair, having been proved to be legal and right beyond yea or nay, has dropped out of the minds of all save those who are waiting for news from England; and on looking over my diary I can see nothing but memoranda relating to quiet rides, visits to camps, conversations with this one or the other, a fresh outburst of anonymous threatening letters, as if I had anything to do with the Trent affair, and notes of small social reunions at our own rooms and the Washington houses which were open to us.

November 25th.—I remarked the other evening that, with all the disorder in Washington, there are no thieves. Next night, as we were sitting in our little symposium, a thirsty soldier knocked at the door for a glass of water. He was brought in and civilly treated. Under the date of the 27th, accordingly, I find it duly entered that "the vagabond who came in for water must have had a confederate, who got into the hall whilst we were attending to his comrade, for yesterday there was a great lamentation over cloaks and great-coats missing from the hall, and as the day wore on the area of plunder was extended. Carl discovers he has been robbed of his best clothes, and Caroline has lost her watch and many petticoats."

Thanksgiving Day on the 28th was celebrated by enormous drunkenness in the army. The weather varied between days of delicious summer—soft, bright, balmy, and beautiful beyond expression—and days of wintry storm, with torrents of rain.

Some excitement was caused at the end of the month by the report I had received information from England that the law officers of the Crown had given it as their opinion that a United States man-of-war would be justified by Lord Stowell's decisions in taking Mason and Slidell even in the British Channel, if the Nashville transferred them to a British mail steamer. This opinion was called for in consequence of the Tuscarora appearing in Southampton Water; and, having heard of it, I repeated it in strict confidence to some one else, till at last Baron de Stoeckl came to ask me if it was true. Receiving passengers from the Nashville, however, would have been an act of direct intercourse with an enemy's ship. In the case of the Trent the persons seized had come on board as lawful passengers at a neutral port.

The tide of success runs strongly in favour of the North at present, although they generally get the worst of it in the small affairs in the front of Washington. The entrance to Savannah has been occupied, and by degrees the fleets are biting into the Confederate lines along the coast, and establishing positions which will afford bases of operations to the Federals hereafter. The President and Cabinet seem in better spirits, and the former indulges in quaint speculations, which he transfers even to State papers. He calculates, for instance, there are human beings now alive who may ere they die behold the United States peopled by 250 millions of souls. Talking of a high mound on the prairie, in Illinois, he remarked, "that if all the nations of the earth were assembled there, a man standing on its top would see them all, for that the whole human race would fit on a space twelve miles square, which was about the extent of the plain."

CHAPTER LIX.

A Captain under arrest—Opening of Congress—Colonel D'Utassy—An ex-pugilist turned Senator—Mr. Cameron—Ball in the officers' huts—Presentation of standards at Arlington—Dinner at Lord Lyons'—Paper currency—A polyglot dinner—Visit to Washington's Tomb—Mr. Chase's Report—Colonel Seaton—Unanimity of the South—The Potomac blockade—A Dutch-American Crimean acquaintance—The American Lawyers on the Trent affair—Mr. Sumner—M'Clellan's Army—Impressions produced in America by the English Press on the affair of the Trent—Mr. Sumner on the crisis—Mutual feelings of the two nations—Rumours of war with Great Britain.

December 1*st*.—A mixed party of American officers and English went to-day to the post at Great Falls, about sixteen or seventeen miles up the Potomac, and were well repaid by the charming scenery, and by a visit to an American military station in a state of nature. The captain in command told us over a drink that he was under arrest, because he had refused to do duty as lieutenant of the guard, he being a captain. "But I have written to M'Clellan about it," said he, "and I'm d—d if I stay under arrest more than three days longer." He was not aware that the General's brother, who is a captain on his staff, was sitting beside him at the time. This worthy centurion further informed us he had shot a man dead a short time before for disobeying his orders. "That he did," said his sympathising and enthusiastic orderly, "and there's the weapon that done it." The captain was a boot and shoe maker by trade, and had travelled across the isthmus before the railway was made to get orders for his boots. A hard, determined, fierce "sutor," as near a savage as might be.

"And what will you do, captain," asked I, "if they keep you in arrest?"

"Fight for it, sir. I'll go straight away into Pennsylvania with my company, and we'll whip any two companies they can send to stop us."

Mr. Sumner paid me a visit on my return from our excursion, and seems to think everything is in the best possible state.

December 2*nd*.—Congress opened to-day. The Senate did nothing. In the House of Representatives some Buncombe resolutions were passed about Captain Wilkes, who has become a hero—"a great interpreter of international law," and also recommending that Messrs. Mason and Slidell be confined in felons' cells, in retaliation for Colonel Corcoran's treatment by the Confederates. M. Blondel, the Belgian minister, who was at the court of Greece during the Russian war, told me that when the French and English fleets lay in the Piræus, a United States vessel, commanded, he thinks, by Captain Stringham, publicly received M. Persani, the Russian ambassador, on board, hoisted and saluted the Russian flag in the harbour, whereupon the French Admiral, Barbier de Tinan, proposed to the English Admiral to go on board the United States vessel and seize the ambassador, which the British officer refused to do.

December 3*rd*.—Drove down to the Capitol, and was introduced to the floor of the Senate by Senator Wilson, and arrived just as Mr. Forney commenced reading the President's message, which was listened to with considerable interest. At dinner, Colonel D'Utassy, of the Garibaldi legion, who gives a curious account of his career. A Hungarian by birth, he went over from the Austrian service, and served under Bem; was wounded and taken prisoner at Temesvar, and escaped from Spielberg, through the kindness of Count Bennigsen, making his way to Semlin, in the disguise of a servant, where M. Fonblanque, the British consul, protected him. Thence he went to Kossuth at Shumla, finally proceeded to Constantinople, where he was engaged to instruct the Turkish cavalry; turned up in the Ionian Islands, where he was engaged by the late Si. H. Ward, as a sort of Secretary and Interpreter, in which capacity he also served Sir G. Le Mar chant. In the United States he was earning hi livelihood as a fencing, dancing, and languag master; and when the war broke out he exerte himself to raise a regiment, and succeeded in completing his number in seventeen days, being all the time obliged to support himself by his lessons. I tell his tale as he told it to me.

One of our friends, of a sporting turn, dropped

in to-night, followed by a gentleman dressed in immaculate black, and of staid deportment, whose name I did not exactly catch, but fancied it was that of a senator of some reputation. As the stranger sat next me, and was rubbing his knees nervously, I thought I would commence conversation.

"It appears, sir, that affairs in the south-west are not so promising. May I ask you what is your opinion of the present prospects of the Federals in Missouri?"

I was somewhat disconcerted by his reply, for rubbing his knees harder than ever, and imprecating his organs of vision in a very sanguinary manner, he said—

"Well, d—— if I know what to think of them. They're a b—— rum lot, and they're going on in a d—— rum way. That's what I think."

The supposed legislator, in fact, was distinguished in another arena, and was no other than a celebrated pugilist, who served his apprenticeship in the English ring, and has since graduated in honours in America.

I dined with Mr. Cameron, Secretary-of-War, where I met Mr. Forney, Secretary of the Senate; Mr. House, Mr. Wilkeson, and others, and was exceedingly interested by the shrewd conversation and candid manner of our host. He told me he once worked as a printer in the city of Washington, at ten dollars a week, and twenty cents an hour for extra work at the case on Sundays. Since that time he has worked onwards and upwards, and amassed a large fortune by contracts for railways and similar great undertakings. He says the press rules America, and that no one can face it and live; which is about the worst account of the chances of an honest longevity I can well conceive. His memory is exact, and his anecdotes, albeit he has never seen any but Americans, or stirred out of the States, very agreeable. Once there lived at Washington a publican's daughter, named Mary O'Neil, beautiful, bold, and witty. She captivated a Member of Congress, who failed to make her less than his wife; and by degrees Mrs. Eaton—who may now be seen in the streets of Washington, an old woman, still bright-eyed and alas! bright checked, retaining traces of her great beauty—became a leading personage in the State, and ruled the imperious, rugged, old Andrew Jackson so completely, that he broke up his Cabinet and dismissed his ministers on her account. In the days of her power she had done some trifling service to Mr. Cameron, and he has just repaid it by conferring some military appointment on her grandchild.

The dinner, which was preceded by deputations, was finished by one which came from the Far West, and was introduced by Mr. Hannibal Hamlin, the Vice-President; Mr. Owen Lovejoy, Mr. Bingham, and other ultra-Abolitionist members of Congress; and then speeches were made, and healths were drunk, and toasts were pledged, till it was time for me to drive to a ball given by the officers of the 5th United States Cavalry, which was exceedingly pretty, and admirably arranged in wooden huts, especially erected and decorated for the occasion. A huge bonfire in the centre of the camp, surrounded by soldiers, by the carriage drivers, and by negro servants, afforded the most striking play of colour and variety of light and shade I ever beheld.

December 4th.—To Arlington, where Senator Ira Harris presented flags—that is, standards—to a cavalry regiment called after his name; the President, Mrs. Lincoln, ministers, generals, and a large gathering present. Mr. Harris made a very long and a very fierce speech; it could not be said *Ira furor brevis est;* and Colonel Davies, in taking the standard, was earnest and lengthy in reply. Then a barrister presented colour No. 2, in a speech full of poetical quotations, to which Major Kilpatrick made an excellent answer. Though it was strange enough to hear a political disquisition on the causes of the rebellion from a soldier in full uniform, the proceedings were highly theatrical and very effective. "Take, then, this flag," &c.—"Defend it with your," &c. —"Yes, sir, we, will guard this sacred emblem with —," &c. The regiment then went through some evolutions, which were brought to an untimely end by a *feu de joie* from the infantry in the rear, which instantly broke up the squadrons, and sent them kicking, plunging, and falling over the field, to the great amusement of the crowd.

Dined with Lord Lyons, where was Mr. Galt, Financial Minister of Canada; Mr. Stewart, who has arrived to replace Mr. Irvine, and others. In our rooms, a grand financial discussion took place in honour of Mr. Galt, between Mr. Butler Duncan and others, the former maintaining that a general issue of national paper was inevitable. A very clever American maintained that the North will be split into two great parties by the result of the victory which they are certain to gain over the South—that the Democrats will offer the South concessions more liberal than they could ever dream of, and that both will unite agains the Abolitionists and Black Republicans.

December 6th.—Mr. Riggs says the paper currency scheme will produce money, and make every man richer. He is a banker, and ought to know; but to my ignorant eye it seems likely to prove most destructive, and I confess, that whatever be the result of this war, I have no desire for the ruin of so many happy communities as have sprung up in the United States. Had it been possible for human beings to employ popular institutions without intrigue and miserable self-seeking, and to be superior to faction and party passion, the condition of parts of the United States must cause regret that an exemption from the usual laws which regulate human nature was not made in America; but the strength of the United States—directed by violent passions, by party interest, and by selfish intrigues—was becoming dangerous to the peace of other nations, and therefore there is an utter want of sympathy with them in their time of trouble.

I dined with Mr. Galt, at Willard's, where we had a very pleasant party, in spite of financial dangers.

December 7th.—A visit to the Garibaldi Guard with some of the Englishry, and an excellent dinner at the mess, which presented a curious scene, and was graced by sketches from a wonderful polyglot chaplain. What a company!—the officers present were composed as follows:—Five Spaniards, six Poles and Hungarians, two Frenchmen—the most soldierly-looking men at table—one American, four Italians, and nine Teutons of various States in Germany.

December 8th.—A certain excellent Colonel who commands a French regiment visited us today. When he came to Washington, one of the

Foreign Ministers who had been well acquainted with him said, "My dear Colonel, what a pity we can be no longer friends." "Why so, Baron?" "Ah, we can never dine together again." "Why not? Do you forbid me your table?" "No, Colonel, but how can I invite a man who can command the services of at least 200 cooks in his own regiment?" "Well then, Baron, you can come and dine with me." "What! how do you think I could show myself in your camp—how could I get my hair dressed to sit at the table of a man who commands 300 coiffeurs?" I rode out to overtake a party who had started in carriages for Mount Vernon to visit Washington's tomb, but missed them in the wonderfully wooded country which borders the Potomac, and returned alone.

December 9th.—Spent the day over Mr. Chase's report, a copy of which he was good enough to send me with a kind note, and went out in the evening with my head in a state of wild financial confusion, and a general impression that the financial system of England is very unsound.

December 10th.—Paid a visit to Colonel Seaton, of the *National Intelligencer*, a man deservedly respected and esteemed for his private character, which has given its impress to the journal he has so long conducted. The New York papers ridicule the Washington organ, because it does not spread false reports daily in the form of telegraphic "sensation" news, and indeed one may be pretty sure that a fact is a fact when it is found in the *Intelligencer;* but the man, nevertheless, who is content with the information he gets from it, will have no reason to regret, in the accuracy of his knowledge or the soundness of his views, that he has not gone to its noisy and mendacious rivals. In the minds of all the very old men in the States, there is a feeling of great sadness and despondency respecting the present troubles, and though they cling to the idea of a restoration of the glorious Union of their youth, it is hoping against hope. "Our game is played out. It was the most wonderful and magnificent career of success the world ever saw, but rogues and gamblers took up the cards at last; they quarrelled, and are found out."

In the evening, supped at Mr. Forney's, where there was a very large gathering of gentlemen connected with the press; Mr. Cameron, Secretary of War; Colonel Mulligan, a tall young man, with dark hair falling on his shoulders, round a Celtic impulsive face, and a hazy enthusiastic-looking eye; and other celebrities. Terrapin soup and canvas-backs, speeches, orations, music, and song, carried the company onwards among the small hours.

December 11th.—The unanimity of the people in the South is forced on the conviction of the statesmen and people of the North, by the very success in their expeditions in Secession. They find the planters at Beaufort and elsewhere burning their cotton and crops, villages and towns deserted at their approach, hatred in every eye, and curses on women's tongues. They meet this by a corresponding change in their own programme. The war which was made to develop and maintain Union sentiment in the South, and to enable the people to rise against a desperate faction which had enthralled them, is now to be made a crusade against slaveholders, and a war of subjugation—if need be, of extermination—against the whole of the Southern States. The Democrats will, of course, resist this barbarous and hopeless policy. There is a deputation of Irish Democrats here now, to effect a general exchange of prisoners, which is an operation calculated to give a legitimate character to the war, and is *pro tanto* a recognition of the Confederacy as a belligerent power.

December 12th.—The navy are writhing under the disgrace of the Potomac blockade, and deny it exists. The price of articles in Washington which used to come by the river affords disagreeable proof to the contrary. And yet there is not a true Yankee in Pennsylvania Avenue who does not believe, what he reads every day, that his glorious navy could sweep the fleets of France and England off the seas to-morrow, though the Potomac be closed, and the Confederate batteries throw their shot and shell into the Federal camps on the other side. I dined with General Butterfield, whose camp is pitched in Virginia, on a knoll and ridge from which a splendid view can be had over the wooded vales and hills extending from Alexandria towards Manassas, whitened with Federal tents and huts. General Fitz-John Porter and General M'Dowell were among the officers present.

December 12th.—A big-bearded, spectacled, moustachioed, spurred, and booted officer threw himself on my bed this morning ere I was awake. "Russell, my dear friend, here you are at last; what ages have passed since we met!" I sat up and gazed at my friend. "Bohlen! don't you remember Bohlen, and our rides in Turkey, our visit to Shumla and Pravady, and all the rest of it?" Of course I did. I remembered an enthusiastic soldier, with a fine guttural voice, and splendid war saddle and saddle-cloth, and brass stirrups and holsters, worked with eagles all over and a uniform coat and cap with more eagles flying amidst laurel leaves and U. S's in gold, who came out to see the fighting in the East, and made up his mind that there would be none, when he arrived at Varna, and so started off incontinent up the Danube, and returned to the Crimea when it was too late; and a very good, kindly, warm-hearted fellow was the Dutch-American, who—once more in his war paint, this time acting Brigadier-General*—renewed the memories of some pleasant days far away; and our talk was of cavasses and khans, and tchibouques, and pashas, till his time was up to return to his fighting Germans of Blenker's division.

He was *not* the good-natured officer who said the other day, "The next day you come down, sir, if my regiment happens to be on picket duty, we'll have a little skirmish with the enemy, just to show you how our fellows are improved." "Perhaps you might bring on a general action, Colonel." "Well, sir, we're not afraid of that, either! Let 'em come on." It did so happen that some young friends of mine, of H.M.'s 30th, who had come down from Canada to see the army here, went out a day or two ago with an officer on General Smith's staff, formerly in our army, who yet suffers from a wound received at the Alma, to have a look at the enemy with a detachment of men. The enemy came to have a look at them, whereby it happened that shots were exchanged, and the bold Britons had to ride back

* Since killed in action in Pope's retreat from the north of Richmond.

as hard as they could, for their men skedaddled, and the Secession cavalry slipping after them, had a very pretty chase for some miles; so the 30th men saw more than they bargained for.

Dined at Baron Gerolt's, where I had the pleasure of meeting Judge Daly, who is perfectly satisfied the English lawyers have not a leg to stand upon in the Trent case. On the faith of old and very doubtful, and some purely supposititious, cases, the American lawyers have made up their minds that the seizure of the "rebel" ambassadors was perfectly legitimate and normal. The Judge expressed his belief that if there was a rebellion in Ireland, and that Messrs. Smith O'Brien and O'Gorman ran the blockade to France, and were going on their passage from Havre to New York in a United States steamer, they would be seized by the first British vessel that knew the fact. "Granted; and what would the United States do?" "I am afraid we should be obliged to demand that they be given up; and if you were strong enough at the time, I dare say you would fight sooner than do so." Mr. Sumner, with whom I had some conversation this afternoon, affects to consider the question eminently suitable for reference and arbitration.

In spite of drills and parades, M'Clellan has not got an army yet. A good officer, who served as brigade-major in our service, told me the men were little short of mutinous, with all their fine talk, though they could fight well. Sometimes they refuse to mount guard, or to go on duty not to their tastes; officers refuse to serve under others to whom they have a dislike; men offer similar personal objections to officers. M'Clellan is enforcing discipline, and really intends to execute a most villanous deserter this time.

December 15th.—The first echo of the San Jacinto's guns in England reverberated to the United States, and produced a profound sensation. The people had made up their minds John Bull would acquiesce in the seizure, and not say a word about it; or they affected to think so; and the cry of anger which has resounded through the land, and the unmistakable tone of the British press, at once surprise, and irritate, and disappoint them. The American journals, nevertheless, pretend to think it is a mere vulgar excitement, and that the press is "only indulging in its habitual bluster."

December 16th.—I met Mr. Seward at the ball and cotillon party, given by M. de Lisboa; and as he was in very good humour, and was inclined to talk, he pointed out to the Prince de Joinville, and all who were inclined to listen, and myself, how terrible the effects of a war would be if Great Britain forced it on the United States. "We will wrap the whole world in flames!" he exclaimed. "No power so remote that she will not feel the fire of our battle and be burned by our conflagration." It is inferred that Mr. Seward means to show fight. One of the guests, however, said to me, "That's all bugaboo talk. When Seward talks that way, he means to break down. He is most dangerous and obstinate when he pretends to agree a good deal with you." The young French Princes, and the young and pretty Brazilian and American ladies, danced and were happy, notwithstanding the storms without.

Next day I dined at Mr. Seward's, as the Minister had given *carte blanche* to a very lively and agreeable lady, who has to lament over an absent husband in this terrible war, to ask two gentlemen to dine with him, and she had been pleased to select myself and M. de Geoffroy, Secretary of the French Legation, as her thick and her thin *umbræ;* and the company went off in the evening to the White House, where there was a reception, whereat I imagined I might be *de trop*, and so home.

Mr. Seward was in the best spirits, and told one or two rather long, but very pleasant, stories. Now it is evident he must by this time know Great Britain has resolved on the course to be pursued, and his good-humour, contrasted with the irritation he displayed in May and June, is not intelligible.

The Russian Minister, at whose house I dined next day, is better able than any man to appreciate the use made of the Czar's professions of regret for the evils which distract the States by the Americans; but it is the fashion to approve of everything that France does, and to assume a violent affection for Russia. The Americans are irritated by war preparations on the part of England, in case the Government of Washington do not accede to their demands; and, at the same time, much annoyed that all European nations join in an outcry against the famous project of destroying the Southern harbours by the means of the stone fleet.

December 20th.—I went down to the Senate, as it was expected at the Legation and elsewhere the President would send a special message to the Senate on the Trent affair; but, instead, there was merely a long speech from a senator, to show the South did not like democratic institutions. Lord Lyons called on Mr. Seward yesterday to read Lord Russell's dispatch to him, and to give time for a reply; but Mr. Seward was out, and Mr. Sumner told me the Minister was down with the Committee of Foreign Relations, where there is a serious business in reference to the state of Mexico and certain European Powers under discussion, when the British Minister went to the State Department.

Next day Lord Lyons had two interviews with Mr. Seward, read the despatch, which simply asks for surrender of Mason and Slidell and reparation, without any specific act named, but he received no indication from Mr. Seward of the course he would pursue. Mr. Lincoln has "put down his foot" on no surrender. "Sir!" exclaimed the President, to an old Treasury official the other day, "I would sooner die than give them up." "Mr. President," was the reply, "your death would be a great loss, but the destruction of the United States would be a still more deplorable event."

Mr. Seward will, however, control the situation, as the Cabinet will very probably support his views; and Americans will comfort themselves, in case the captives are surrendered, with a promise of future revenge, and with the reflection that they have avoided a very disagreeable intervention between their march of conquest and the Southern Confederacy. The general belief of the diplomatists is, that the prisoners will not be given up, and in that case Lord Lyons and the Legation will retire from Washington for the time, probably to Halifax, leaving Mr. Monson to wind up affairs and clear out the archives. But it is understood that there is no ultimatum, and that Lord Lyons is not to indicate any course of action, should Mr. Seward inform him the United States Government refuses to comply with the demands of Great Britain.

Any humiliation which may be attached to concession will be caused by the language of the Americans themselves, who have given in their press, in public meetings, in the Lower House, in the Cabinet, and in the conduct of the President, a complete ratification of the act of Captain Wilkes, not to speak of the opinions of the lawyers, and the speeches of their orators, who declare "they will face any alternative, but that they will never surrender." The friendly relations which existed between ourselves and many excellent Americans are now rendered somewhat constrained by the prospect of a great national difference.

December (Sunday) *22nd.*—Lord Lyons saw Mr. Seward again, but it does not appear that any answer can be expected before Wednesday. All kinds of rumours circulate through the city, and are repeated in an authoritative manner in the New York papers.

December 23rd.—There was a tremendous storm, which drove over the city and shook the houses to the foundation. Constant interviews took place between the President and members of the Cabinet, and so certain are the people that war is inevitable, that an officer connected with the executive of the Navy Department came in to tell me General Scott was coming over from Europe to conduct the Canadian campaign, as he had thoroughly studied the geography of the country, and that in a very short time he would be in possession of every strategic position on the frontier, and chaw up our reinforcements. Late in the evening, Mr. Olmsted called to say he had been credibly informed Lord Lyons had quarrelled violently with Mr. Seward, had flown into a great passion with him, and so departed. The idea of Lord Lyons being quarrelsome, passionate, or violent, was preposterous enough to those who knew him; but the American papers, by repeated statements of the sort, have succeeded in persuading their public that the British Minister is a plethoric, red-faced, large-stomached man in top-boots, knee-breeches, yellow waistcoat, blue cut-away, brass buttons, and broad-brimmed white hat, who is continually walking to the State Department in company with a large bull-dog, hurling defiance at Mr. Seward at one moment, and the next rushing home to receive despatches from Mr. Jefferson Davis, or to give secret instructions to the British Consuls to run cargoes of quinine and gunpowder through the Federal blockade. I was enabled to assure Mr. Olmsted there was not the smallest foundation for the story; but he seemed impressed with a sense of some great calamity, and told me there was a general belief that England only wanted a pretext for a quarrel with the United States; nor could I comfort him by the assurance that there were good reasons for thinking General Scott would very soon annex Canada, in case of war.

CHAPTER LX.

News of the death of the Prince Consort—Mr. Sumner and the Trent Affair—Dispatch to Lord Russell—The Southern Commissioners given up—Effects on the friends of the South—My own unpopularity at New York—Attack of fever—My tour in Canada—My return to New York in February—Successes of the Western States—Mr. Stanton succeeds Mr. Cameron as Secretary of War—Reverse and retreat of M'Clellan—My free pass—The Merrimac and Monitor—My arrangement to accompany M'Clellan's head-quarters—Mr. Stanton refuses his sanction—National vanity wounded by my truthfulness—My retirement and return to Europe.

December 24th.—This evening came in a telegram from Europe with news which cast the deepest gloom over all our little English circle. Prince Albert dead! At first no one believed it; then it was remembered that private letters by the last mail had spoken despondingly of his state of health, and that the "little cold" of which we had heard was described in graver terms. Prince Albert dead!. "Oh, it may be Prince Alfred," said some; and sad as it would be for the Queen and the public to lose the Sailor Prince, the loss could not be so great as that which we all felt to be next to the greatest. The preparations which we had made for a little festivity to welcome in Christmas morning were chilled by the news, and the eve was not of the joyous character which Englishmen delight to give it, for the sorrow which fell on all hearts in England had spanned the Atlantic, and bade us mourn in common with the country at home.

December 25th.—Lord Lyons, who had invited the English in Washington to dinner, gave a small quiet entertainment, from which he retired early.

December 26th.—No answer yet. There can be but one. Press people, soldiers, sailors, ministers, senators, Congress-men, people in the street, the voices of the bar-room—all are agreed. "Give them up? Never! We'll die first!" Senator Sumner, M. de Beaumont, M. de Geoffroy, of the French Legation, dined with me, in company with General Van Vliet, Mr. Anderson, and Mr. Lamy, &c.; and in the evening Major Anson, M.P., Mr. Johnson, Captain Irwin, U.S.A., Lt. Wise, U.S.N., joined our party, and after much evasion of the subject, the English despatch and Mr. Seward's decision turned up and caused some discussion. Mr. Sumner, who is Chairman of the Committee on Foreign Relations of the Senate, and in that capacity is in intimate *rapport* with the President, either is, or affects to be incredulous respecting the nature of Lord Russell's despatch this evening, and argues that, at the very utmost, the Trent affair can only be a matter for mediation, and not for any peremptory demand, as the law of nations has no exact precedent to bear upon the case, and that there are so many instances in which Sir W. Scott's (Lord Stowell's) decisions in principle appear to justify Captain Wilkes. All along he has held this language, and has maintained that at the very worst there is plenty of time for protocols, despatches, and references, and more than once he has said to me, "I hope you will keep the peace; help us to do so,"—the peace having been already broken by Captain Wilkes and the Government.

December 27th.—This morning Mr. Seward sent in his reply to Lord Russell's despatch—"grandis et verbosa epistola." The result destroys my prophecies, for, after all, the Southern Commissioners or Ambassadors are to be given up. Yesterday, indeed, in an under-current of whispers among the desponding friends of the South, there went a rumour that the Government had resolved to yield. What a collapse! What a bitter mortification! I had scarcely finished the perusal of an article in a Washington paper,—which, let it be understood, is an organ of Mr. Lincoln,—stating that "Mason and Slidell would *not* be surrendered, and assuring the people they need entertain no apprehension of such a dishonourable concession," when I learned beyond all possibility of doubt, that Mr. Seward had handed in his despatch, placing the Commissioners at the disposal of the British Minister. A copy of the despatch will be published in the *National Intelligencer* to-morrow morning at an early hour, in time to go to Europe by the steamer which leaves New York.

After dinner, those who were in the secret were amused by hearing the arguments which were started between one or two Americans and some English in the company, in consequence of a positive statement from a gentleman who came in, that Mason and Slidell had been surrendered. I have resolved to go to Boston, being satisfied that a great popular excitement and uprising will, in all probability, take place on the discharge of the Commissioners from Fort Warren. What will my friend, the general, say, who told me yesterday "he would snap his sword, and throw the pieces into the White House, if they were given up."

December 28th.—The *National Intelligencer* of this morning contains the dispatches of Lord Russel, M. Thouvenel, and Mr. Seward. The bubble has burst. The rage of the friends of compromise, and of the South, who saw in a war with Great Britain the complete success of the Confederacy, is deep and burning, if not loud; but they all say they never expected anything better from the cowardly and braggart statesmen who now rule in Washington.

Lord Lyons has evinced the most moderate and conciliatory spirit, and has done everything in his power to break Mr. Seward's fall on the softest of eider down. Some time ago we were all prepared to hear nothing less would be accepted than Captain Wilkes taking Messrs. Mason and Slidell on board the San Jacinto, and transferring them to the Trent, under a salute to the flag, near the scene of the outrage; at all events, it was expected that a British man-of-war would have steamed into Boston, and received the prisoners under a salute from Fort Warren; but Mr. Seward, apprehensive that some outrage would be offered by the populace to the prisoners and the British Flag, has asked Lord Lyons that the Southern Commissioners may be placed, as it were, surreptitiously, in a United States boat, and carried to a small seaport in the State of Maine, where they are to be placed on board a British vessel as quietly as possible; and this exigent, imperious, tyrannical, insulting British Minister has cheerfully acceded to the request. Mr. Conway Seymour, the Queen's messenger, who brought Lord Russell's despatch, was sent back with instructions for the British Admiral, to send a vessel to Providence-town for the purpose; and as Mr. Johnson, who is nearly connected with Mr. Eustis, one of the prisoners, proposed going to Boston to see his brother-in-law, if possible, ere he started, and as there was not the smallest prospect of any military movement taking place, I resolved to go northwards with him; and we left Washington accordingly on the morning of the 31st of December, and arrived at the New York Hotel the same night.

To my great regret and surprise, however, I learned that it would be impracticable to get to Fort Warren and see the prisoners before their surrender. My unpopularity, which had lost somewhat of its intensity, was revived by the exasperation against everything English, occasioned by the firmness of Great Britain in demanding the Commissioners; and on New Year's Night, as I heard subsequently, Mr. Grinnell and other members of the New York Club were exposed to annoyance and insult, by some of their brother members, in consequence of inviting me to be their guest at the club.

The illness which had prostrated some of the strongest men in Washington, including General M'Clellan himself, developed itself as soon as I ceased to be sustained by the excitement, such as it was, of daily events at the capital, and by expectations of a move; and for some time an a tack of typhoid fever confined me to my room, and left me so weak that I was advised not to return to Washington till I had tried change of air. I remained in New York till the end of January, when I proceeded to make a tour in Canada, as it was quite impossible for any operation to take place on the Potomac, where deep mud, alternating with snow and frost, bound the contending armies in winter quarters.

On my return to New York, at the end of February, the North was cheered by some signal successes achieved in the West principally by gunboats, operating on the lines of the great rivers. The greatest results have been obtained in the capture of Fort Donaldson and Fort Henry, by Commodore Foote's flotilla co-operating with the land forces. The possession of an absolute naval supremacy, of course, gives the North United States powerful means of annoyance and inflicting injury and destruction on the enemy; it also secures for them the means of seizing upon bases of operations wherever they please, of breaking up the enemy's lines, and maintaining communications; but the example of Great Britain in the revolutionary war should prove to the United States that such advantages do not, by any means, enable a belligerent to subjugate a determined people resolved on resistance to the last. The long-threatened encounter between Bragg and Browne has taken place at Pensacola, without effect, and the attempts of the Federals to advance from Port Royal have been successfully resisted. Sporadic skirmishes have sprung up over every border State; but, on the whole, success has inclined to the Federals in Kentucky and Tennessee.

On the 1st March, I arrived in Washington once more, and found things very much as I had left them: the army recovering the effect of the winter's sickness and losses, animated by the victories of their comrades in Western fields, and by the hope that the ever-coming to-morrow would see them in the field at last. In place of Mr. Cameron, an Ohio lawyer named Stanton has been appointed Secretary of War. He came to Washington, a few years ago, to conduct some legal proceedings for Mr. Daniel Sickles, and by his energy, activity, and a rapid conversion from democratic to republican principles, as well as by his Union sentiments, recommended himself to the President and his Cabinet.

The month of March passed over without any remarkable event in the field. When the army started at last to attack the enemy—a movement which was precipitated by hearing that they were moving away—they went out only to find the Confederates had fallen back by interior lines towards Richmond, and General M'Clellan was obliged to transport his army from Alexandria to the peninsula of York Town, where his reverses, his sufferings, and his disastrous retreat, are so well known and so recent, that I need only mention them as among the most remarkable events which have yet occurred in this war.

I had looked forward for many weary months to participating in the movement and describing its results. Immediately on my arrival in Washington, I was introduced to Mr. Stanton by Mr. Ashman, formerly member of Congress and Secretary to Mr. Daniel Webster, and the Secretary, without making any positive pledge, used words, in Mr. Ashman's presence, which led me to believe he would give me permission to draw rations, and undoubtedly promised to afford me every facility in his power. Subsequently he sent me a private pass to the War Department to enable me to get through the crowd of contractors and jobbers; but on going there to keep my appointment, the Assistant-Secretary of War told me Mr. Stanton had been summoned to a Cabinet Council by the President.

We had some conversation respecting the subject matter of my application, which the Assistant-Secretary seemed to think would be attended with many difficulties, in consequence of the number of correspondents to the American papers who might demand the same privileges, and he intimated to me that Mr. Stanton was little disposed to encourage them in any way whatever. Now this is undoubtedly honest on Mr. Stanton's part, for he knows he might render himself popular by granting what they ask; but he is excessively vain, and aspires to be considered a rude, rough, vigorous Oliver Cromwell sort of man, mistaking some of the disagreeable attributes and the accidents of the external husk of the Great Protector for the brain and head of a statesman and a soldier.

The American officers with whom I was intimate gave me to understand that I could accompany them, in case I received permission from the Government; but they were obviously unwilling to encounter the abuse and calumny which would be heaped upon their heads by American papers, unless they could show the authorities did not disapprove of my presence in their camp. Several invitations sent to me were accompanied by the phrase, "You will of course get a written permission from the War Department, and then there will be no difficulty." On the evening of the private theatricals by which Lord Lyons enlivened the ineffable dulness of Washington, I saw Mr. Stanton at the Legation, and he conversed with me for some time. I mentioned the difficulty connected with passes. He asked me what I wanted. I said, "An order to go with the army to Manassas." At his request I procured a sheet of paper, and he wrote me a pass, took a copy of it, which he put in his pocket, and then handed the other to me. On looking at it, I perceived that it was a permission for me to go to Manassas and back, and that all officers, soldiers, and others, in the United States service, were to give me every assistance and show me every courtesy; but the hasty return of the army to Alexandria rendered it useless.

The Merrimac and Monitor encounter produced the profoundest impression in Washington, and unusual strictness was observed respecting passes to Fortress Monroe.

March 19th.—I applied at the Navy Department for a passage down to Fortress Monroe, as it was expected the Merrimac was coming out again, but I could not obtain leave to go in any of the vessels. Captain Hardman showed me a curious sketch of what he called the Turtle Thor, an iron-cased machine with a huge claw or grapnel, with which to secure the enemy whilst a steam hammer or a high iron fist, worked by the engine, cracks and smashes her iron armour. "For," says he, "the days of gunpowder are over."

As soon as General M'Clellan commenced his movement, he sent a message to me by one of the French princes, that he would have great pleasure in allowing me to accompany his head-quarters in the field. I find the following, under the head of March 22nd:—

"Received a letter from General Marcy, chief of the staff, asking me to call at his office. He told me General M'Clellan directed him to say he had no objection whatever to my accompanying the army, 'but,' continued General Marcy, 'you know we are a sensitive people, and that our press is exceedingly jealous. General M'Clellan has many enemies who seek to pull him down, and scruple at no means of doing so. He and I would be glad to do anything in our power to help you, if you come with us, but we must not expose ourselves needlessly to attack. The army is to move to the York and James Rivers at once.' "

All my arrangements were made that day with General Van Vliet, the quartermaster-general of headquarters. I was quite satisfied, from Mr. Stanton's promise and General Marcy's conversation, that I should have no further difficulty. Our party was made up, consisting of Colonel Neville; Lieutenant-Colonel Fletcher, Scotch Fusilier Guards; Mr. Lamy, and myself; and our passage was to be provided in the quartermaster-general's boat. On the 26th of March, I went to Baltimore in company with Colonel Rowan, of the Royal Artillery, who had come down for a few days to visit Washington, intending to go on by the steamer to Fortress Monroe, as he was desirous of seeing his friends on board the Rinaldo, and I wished to describe the great flotilla assembled there and to see Captain Hewett once more.

On arriving at Baltimore, we learned it would be necessary to get a special pass from General Dix, and on going to the General's head-quarters his aide-de-camp informed us that he had received special instructions recently from the War Department to grant no passes to Fortress Monroe unless to officers and soldiers going on duty, or to persons in the service of the United States. The aide-de-camp advised me to telegraph to Mr. Stanton for permission, which I did, but no answer was received, and Colonel Rowan and I returned to Washington, thinking there would be a better chance of securing the necessary order there.

Next day we went to the Department of War, and were shown into Mr. Stanton's room—his secretary informing us that he was engaged in the next room with the President and other Ministers in a council of war, but that he would no doubt receive a letter from me and send me out a reply. I accordingly addressed a note to Mr. Stanton, requesting he would be good enough to give an order to Colonel Rowan, of the British army, and myself, to go by the mail boat from Baltimore to Monroe. In a short time Mr. Stanton sent out a note in the following words:—"Mr. Stanton informs Mr. Russell no passes to Fortress Monroe can be given at present, unless to officers in the United States service." We tried the Navy Department, but no vessels were going down, they said; and one of the officers suggested that we should ask for passes to go down and visit H. M. S. Rinaldo exclusively, which could not well be refused, he thought, to British subjects, and promised to take charge of the letter for Mr. Stanton and to telegraph the permission down to Baltimore. There we returned by the afternoon train and waited, but neither reply nor pass came for us.

Next day we were disappointed also, and an officer of the Rinaldo, who had come up on duty from the ship, was refused permission to take us down on his return. I regretted these obstructions principally on Colonel Rowan's account, because he would have no opportunity of seeing the flotilla. He returned next day to New York, whilst I completed my preparations for the expedition and went back to Washington, where I received my pass, signed by General M'Clellan's chief of the staff, authorising me to accompany the head-quarters of the army under his command. So far as I know, Mr. Stanton sent no reply to my last letter, and calling with General Van Vliet at his house on his reception night, the door was opened by his brother-in-law, who said, "The Secretary was attending a sick child and could not see any person that evening," so I never met Mr. Stanton again.

Stories had long been current concerning his exceeding animosity to General M'Clellan, founded perhaps on his expressed want of confidence in the General's abilities, as much as on the dislike he felt towards a man who persisted in disregarding his opinions on matters connected with military operations. His infirmities of health and tendency to cerebral excitement had been increased by the pressure of business, by the novelty of power, and by the angry passions to which individual antipathies and personal rancour give rise. No one who ever saw Mr. Stanton would expect from him courtesy of manner or delicacy of feeling; but his affectation of bluntness and straightforwardness of purpose might have led one to suppose he was honest and direct in purpose, as the qualities I have mentioned are not always put forward by hypocrites to cloak finesse and sinister action.

The rest of the story may be told in a few words. It was perfectly well known in Washington that I was going with the army, and I presume Mr. Stanton, if he had any curiosity about such a trifling matter, must have heard it also. I am told he was informed of it at the last moment, and then flew out into a coarse passion against General M'Clellan because he had dared to invite or to take anyone without his permission. What did a Republican General want with foreign princes on his staff, or with foreign newspaper correspondents to puff him up abroad?

Judging from the stealthy, secret way in which Mr. Stanton struck at General M'Clellan the instant he had turned his back upon Washington, and crippled him in the field by suddenly withdrawing his best division without a word of notice, I am inclined to fear he gratified whatever small passion dictated his course on this occasion also, by waiting till he knew I was fairly on board the steamer with my friends and baggage, just ready to move off, before he sent down a despatch to Van Vliet and summoned him at once to the War Office. When Van Vliet returned in a couple of hours, he made the communication to me that Mr. Stanton had given him written orders to prevent my passage, though even here he acted with all the cunning and indirection of the village attorney, not with the straightforwardness of Oliver Cromwell, whom it is laughable to name in the same breath with his imitator. He did not write, "Mr. Russell is not to go," or "The *Times* correspondent is forbidden a passage," but he composed two orders, with all the official formula of the War Office, drawn up by the Quartermaster General of the army, by the direction and order of the Secretary of War. No. 1 ordered "that no person should be permitted to embark on board any vessel in the United States service without an order from the War Department." No. 2 ordered "that Colonel Neville, Colonel Fletcher, and Captain Lamy, of the British army, having been invited by General M'Clellan to accompany the expedition, were authorized to embark on board the vessel."

General Van Vliet assured me that he and General M'Dowell had urged every argument they could think of in my favour, particularly the fact that I was the specially invited guest of General M'Clellan, and that I was actually provided with a pass by his order from the chief of his staff.

With these orders before me, I had no alternative.

General M'Clellan was far away. Mr. Stanton had waited again until he was gone. General Marcy was away. I laid the statement of what had occurred before the President, who at first gave me hopes, from the wording of his letter, that he would overrule Mr. Stanton's order, but who next day informed me he could not take it upon himself to do so.

It was plain I had now but one course left. My mission in the United States was to describe military events and operations, or, in defect of them, to deal with such subjects as might be interesting to people at home. In the discharge of my duty, I had visited the South, remaining there until the approach of actual operations and the establishment of the blockade, which cut off all communication from the Southern States except by routes which would deprive my correspondence of any value, compelled me to return to the North, where I could keep up regular communication with Europe. Soon after my return, as unfortunately for myself as the United States, the Federal troops were repulsed in an attempt to march upon Richmond, and terminated a disorderly retreat by a disgraceful panic. The whole incidents of what

I saw were fairly stated by an impartial witness, who, if anything, was inclined to favour a nation endeavouring to suppress a rebellion, and who was by no means impressed, as the results of his recent tour, with the admiration and respect for the people of the Confederate States which their enormous sacrifices, extraordinary gallantry, and almost unparallelled devotion, have long since extorted from him in common with all the world. The letter in which that account was given came back to America after the first bitterness and humiliation of defeat had passed away, and disappointment and alarm had been succeeded by such a formidable outburst of popular resolve, that the North forgot everything in the instant anticipations of a glorious and triumphant revenge.

Every feeling of the American was hurt—above all, his vanity and his pride, by the manner in which the account of the reverse had been received in Europe; and men whom I scorned too deeply to reply to, dexterously took occasion to direct on my head the full storm of popular indignation. Not, indeed, that I had escaped before. Ere a line from my pen reached America at all—ere my first letter had crossed the Atlantic to England—the jealousy and hatred felt for all things British—for press or principle, or representative of either—had found expression in Northern journals; but that I was prepared for. I knew well no foreigner had ever penned a line—least of all, no Englishman—concerning the United States of North America, their people, manners, and institutions, who had not been treated to the abuse which is supposed by their journalists to mean criticism, no matter what the justness or moderation of the views expressed, the sincerity of purpose, and the truthfulness of the writer. In the South, the press threatened me with tar and feathers, because I did not see the beauties of their domestic institutions, and wrote of it in my letters to England exactly as I spoke of it to every one who conversed with me on the subject when I was amongst them; and now the Northern papers recommended expulsion, ducking, riding rails, and other cognate modes of insuring a moral conviction of error: endeavoured to intimidate me by threats of duels or personal castigations; gratified their malignity by ludicrous stories of imaginary affronts or annoyances to which I never was exposed; and sought to prevent the authorities extending any protection towards me, and to intimidate officers from showing me any civilities.

In pursuance of my firm resolution I allowed the slanders and misrepresentations which poured from their facile sources for months to pass by unheeded, and trusted to the calmer sense of the people, and to the discrimination of those who thought over the sentiments expressed in my letters, to do me justice.

I need not enlarge on the dangers to which I was exposed. Those who are acquainted with America, and know the life of the great cities, will best appreciate the position of a man who went forth daily in the camps and streets holding his life in his hand. This expression of egotism is all I shall ask indulgence for. Nothing could have induced me to abandon my post or to recoil before my assailants; but at last a power I could not resist struck me down. When to the press and populace of the United States, the President and the Government of Washington added their power, resistance would be unwise and impracticable. In no camp could I have been received—in no place useful. I went to America to witness and describe the operations of the great army before Washington in the field, and when I was forbidden by the proper authorities to do so, my mission terminated at once.

On the evening of April 4th, as soon as I was in receipt of the President's last communication, I telegraphed to New York to engage a passage by the steamer which left on the following Wednesday. Next day was devoted to packing up and to taking leave of my friends—English and American—whose kindnesses I shall remember in my heart of hearts, and the following Monday I left Washington, of which, after all, I shall retain many pleasant memories and keep souvenirs green for ever. I arrived in New York late on Tuesday evening, and next day I saw the shores receding into a dim grey fog, and ere the night fell was tossing about once more on the stormy Atlantic, with the head of our good ship pointing, thank Heaven, towards Europe.

THE END.

CONTENTS.

www.ingramcontent.com/pod-product-compliance
Lightning Source LLC
Chambersburg PA
CBHW030125030726
47498CB00007B/2548

* 9 7 8 3 7 4 4 6 6 0 8 7 7 *